For George Grosse. I love you Granddad. Rest in peace.

For my dad, Nicholas Sr., the greatest exterminator of all time.

For my son Benjamin. Dream big little man.

© 2018 Nicholas C. Ritter, Jr.

Chapter 1

There's something about Ciroc Red Berry. Is it the smell? That sweet, tantalizing smell. Or is it the taste? Straight or with juice, it's hands down the best-flavored Vodka around. Tracy Yellen pondered these questions as people do when they are three sheets to the wind. She stared fixedly at the clear bottle in her hand. Finally, she decided it didn't matter and drained the last shot into her mouth. It slid down her throat followed by the inevitable burn that felt so incredibly good.

Tracy lived in Havre de Grace. Well, she *existed* in Havre de Grace. Tracy hadn't *lived* in a very long time. The single mother of two was the purest definition of a deadbeat parent. She spent her life subsisting off the government and drowning her supposed sorrows in bottles of liquor.

Men floated in and out of Tracy's life like phantoms in a nightmare. She was still decent looking. Not great. Not Angelina Jolie or Jennifer Aniston but having two kids and drinking herself to death hadn't affected her five feet, one-hundred-and-ten-pound body. It was her face that showed her age. She was thirty-three, but her face looked closer to forty-five. The wrinkles and the dark circles, a direct consequence of her habitual drinking and chain smoking, highlighted her once beautiful features.

The two-story townhouse Section 8 rented for her was in desperate need of repair. The brick was dirty and bestrewed with ivy. The front porch was covered in bags of rotting garbage, and the backyard looked like the jungle in Jumanji. If the outside of the house was a dump, then the inside could adequately be described as a putrid version of hell. Piles of dirty laundry, dishes, trash and cigarette butts decorated every room. The one and only bathroom looked like it hadn't been cleaned in a millennium. The toilet bowl, stained a deep dark yellow, wouldn't even be acceptable at the worst truck stop. All in all, it was total squalor, not a place where two children, both under the age of ten, should grow up.

Tracy sat in the backyard, her rear end glued to the only chair left that hadn't been swallowed by the jungle. Finished with the Vodka, she chucked the empty bottle into the weeds. She listened for the sound of shattering glass, but it didn't come. Shrugging she lit a cigarette. Deep inhales pulled smoke from the Marlboro Red into her lungs. It felt good and mixed perfectly with the alcohol already in her system. Her mind was at ease.

The moon shone brightly in the sky. It was a full moon. A bright circle of white light. It reminded her of her childhood. The perilous journey, growing up in a trailer park not far from her house now. Her father, an abusive alcoholic and her mother, an intravenous drug user, had only lived into their forties. They hadn't even left enough money for their little girl to bury them. No big deal. Good riddance, as far as Tracy was concerned. The circle of life really did come all the way around. Her parents provided her with the same terrible existence that she was providing for her kids.

Tracy flicked her cigarette into the jungle almost on the same trajectory as the Vodka bottle. Her daily exploitation of her body was over. Time to pass out, wake up tomorrow and do it all over again, like a tennis ball bouncing off a brick wall eventually coming to rest in a pool of sewage at the bottom of a gutter.

Tracy stumbled inside, pulling open the tattered screen door and letting it slam behind her. She didn't bother locking it; there was nothing in her home to steal. If a prowler did get in and decided to rape her, it wouldn't be much different than the three or four men who traipsed over a few times a week to do the same. She walked past a pile of hair that had, up until a few days ago, been their pitbull Princess. Tracy hadn't even noticed the dead dog until her little girl screamed bloody murder one morning And of course, Tracy being that horrible excuse for a mother that she was, slapped the girl for screaming and left the unconscious pet on its makeshift bed, insisting that the dog was sleeping. The carcass didn't stink yet, so there was no need to dispose of it.

The TV blared in the living room. The sound made Tracy's head whirl. She thought about turning it off but decided the effort it would take to cross the small room was too much to bear. She ignored the loud sound and proceeded up the stairs. Her bed was calling her name. The master bedroom had maroon wall-to-wall carpet. It was stained with spots of vomit, urine and burn holes. Her mattress lay on the floor. There was no bedframe present, nor a box spring. No need for it. After all, by the time Tracy hit the sack, she was so intoxicated that comfort was the furthest thing from her mind.

A thump sounded throughout the second floor as Tracy thudded onto her bed. She rolled over and laid motionless on her back. The alcohol took her entirely as if it were a ship on the seven seas. The snores of a drunk echoed off the walls drowning out the sound of the TV downstairs.

And that was when the first one decided to make its appearance. She had been hiding all day. It was time. She smelled the drunk's breath. It made her hungry. She was starving. Her little legs carried her up from the carpet onto the mattress. She looked around briefly, then wiggled her way under the body of the drunk woman. She preferred to wedge herself between her prey and the sheets. Nice and cozy. She was so tiny that she couldn't be felt, not that Tracy could feel her anyway.

More joined the first one, crawling quickly up onto the mattress. They were so hungry. So famished. Dog could sustain them but humans… humans were what they really craved. They all wedged themselves under the drunk woman, their little bodies worming their way against the woman's bare skin. Then they struck in unison, sinking their sharp little fangs into flesh.

Tracy winced. She felt several pinches under her back. *That's strange.* She rolled back and forth then fell back to sleep.

They felt her roll. They shuddered with fear, but nothing happened. No squishing this time. Before, some of them would have died but not now. Now they were strong, their exoskeletons being able to withstand the weight of a human body. They began to feed again, sinking their fangs deep and sucking blood. The precious blood tasted so good. It was warm and salty. Their bodies became swollen. One after another, they drank their fill, returning to the floor under the mattress, being replaced by their hungry brethren that had patiently waited their turn.

Tracy's heart raced. Her eyes flitted open. *What's happening?* She felt weak. Her heart thumped uncontrollably as if it were attempting to escape her ribcage. *Thump, thump, thump.* She tried to sit up, but she couldn't. Her strength drained. *God help me! Thump, thump, thump. What the hell was happening?* Her eyes went out of focus. *Was it the booze? Have I finally reached my limit? Thump, thump, thump.* Her heartbeat was accelerating faster. *Thump, thump, thump, thump.* Her eyes lost focus again. Her vision faded in and out. *Thump, thump, thump, thump.* Her eyes faded one last time; her heart gave one last beat, *thump!* Tracy was no more.

Chapter 2

Pop! The loud sound was met with cheers as the bubbles flowed down the sides of the bottle of Dom Perignon. It was a celebration. A party for the twenty-three scientists present in the lab. They had done it. The approved application for patent number 3450892004 sat on display in the middle of the white table. Seven years of stress and over twenty thousand hours of work had gone into this document. This beautiful, remarkable pile of paper.

The entire room was white. The walls, the ceiling, the tables, the floor tiles and the lab coats. When the LED lights lit up, the room was blinding to work in, like the sun shining on newly fallen snow.

Smiles and high fives were exchanged as if this were a high school graduation. It was a celebration of the safest and most ecologically friendly pesticide ever created. Since the archaic days of DDT, chemists had been trying in vain to develop a pesticide that was safe for humans, animals, and plants. Finally, Sentrix's chemical division had done it. Dio Insecticide would remake the world.

Dio Insecticide was the perfect name. It consisted of two natural plant-based chemicals, mixed in the right proportions that proved to be extremely lethal to insects. Dio Insecticide had no smell and could be applied anywhere. The applicator had no need for protective equipment at all. No mask. No gloves. No need to worry about inhaling Dio Insecticide or accidentally getting it on your skin. Dio Insecticide was harmless to endoskeleton animals. It was specifically designed to kill creatures with exoskeletons. So, yes it would harm crabs, shrimp, and other crustaceans. But there was no need for concern because Dio Insecticide was also water soluble. Water, the Earth's most abundant resource, rendered Dio Insecticide completely harmless. Runoff was no longer a problem. *Need to treat a house next to a river?* Go for it. *Need to treat a property with a well?* Go for it. Dio Insecticide was a modern-day miracle.

Dr. Paul Rudd, the lead scientist on the team, had envisioned Dio Insecticide when he was touring the Amazon rainforest. The local aboriginal tribes used an oil made from tree sap to keep insects away from their camps. Dr. Rudd, who had been plagued by mosquitos ever since he had arrived, was in desperate need of a bug repellant. He had emptied his two cans of *Off* within three days of his arrival in the hot, humid, mosquito-ridden climate. In fact, he was so desperate, his skin itched so bad, that he picked up a handful of the sap oil and rubbed it on from head to toe. The natives found this to be very amusing, jibber jabbering in their foreign tongue and laughing profusely. Laughter was a universal language, understood by any culture from sea to shining sea but Dr. Rudd didn't care. Shockingly, the sap oil worked. He reapplied it after each shower, which in the Amazon was a luxury one partook once every two weeks. Throughout the remainder of his trip, mosquitos avoided Rudd like cats avoided water. In fact, the sap oil worked so well, that Rudd packed large vials of it in his suitcase and lugged them back to the States for further testing.

Rudd underwent several health examinations once he was stateside. A normal routine after returning from a 3rd world tropical climate. The most interesting test was a liver enzyme count, which came back normal. *Normal?*

That was strange. The pours of the skin are the fastest way to absorb chemicals into the bloodstream. Rudd had been expecting his liver to be malfunctioning at an alarming rate after being subjected to the sap oil for several months. The oil had had no ill effects on his liver. Very positive results in Rudd's mind. Next, he underwent an MRI with contrast. Again, the test came back normal. All his internal organs were functioning perfectly.

Sentrix, a world leader in the pest control industry, hired Rudd after learning of his trek through the Amazon and his discovery of the new revolutionary pesticide. The resources of his new employer allowed Rudd to expand his horizons. He and his team ran countless tests on the sap oil and for the first time since returning to the states, Dr. Rudd questioned the outlook of his miracle cure. The sap oil proved to be a great repellant, but it was not lethal to insects. The team of scientists dabbed the oil on cockroaches, ants, spiders, bees, beetles and of course, bed bugs. The results were disheartening. Zero fatalities. It repelled the bugs, which squirmed and twitched, rubbing themselves on any available surface in the tank trying to remove the oil from their bodies. If the team, placed oil around the insects' food source, the bugs would starve themselves to death. Death by starvation was pure suffering. Curiously though, the bugs would rather suffer this horrible fate than go near the oil.

They had to find another component, something just as safe but with the lethality factor. The answer happened to be planted nonchalantly in Dr. Rudd's garden. Standing like sentinels, guarding his prize-winning tomato plants were marigolds. The golden yellow annuals had been used for thousands of years to protect field crops from the invasion of pests. The African marigold, surprisingly native to Mexico despite its name, had been gathered by the Aztecs for medicinal and decorative purposes. Ironically, the flower of the Marigold is called "the flower of the dead" which is exactly what Dr. Rudd would use it for.

The team isolated the toxic compound, IU785, as it came to be called, released by the roots of the Marigold, which eliminated harmful worms in the soil. Next, they applied IU785 to lab rodents and determined it had zero harmful effects. This, however, was not conclusive enough for Dr. Rudd. The wily scientist with nerves of steel reverted to his Amazonian days and secretly rubbed IU785 all over his body. He did this harrowing task for several weeks. Then he underwent another liver test and an MRI. The results were normal.

Finally, the lethality of IU785 had to be tested. It was a tense moment. The scientists proceeded; anxiety was turning their stomachs into mush; their hands were gripping the table until their knuckles turned white. The team sprayed the toxic chemical on a variety of bugs, which to their cheers and hosannas, died instantly. They had found component number two and Dio Insecticide had been born.

That had been four years ago. Those first few years would become known as the *fun years* because what followed could be defined as mundane torture. The last four years had been gut-wrenching. The back and forth, tug of war with the US patent office and the EPA, brought the team to the breaking point. Government bureaucracy tended to do that. It was unbelievable. Here they were trying to create a dream chemical, a pesticide whose safety and ecology was unmatched in the industry and the government wanted to hang them for it. Every week the

EPA had a new problem with their filings. The classification was changed more times than the sex of Bruce Jenner. The patent office found more problems with their application than a health inspection of a Chinese food carryout. But it was all worth it.

After seven years, twenty thousand hours and fifteen million dollars, Dio Insecticide was officially born, and so, the team celebrated. They opened three more bottles of Dom Perignon and feasted on a smorgasbord of seafood, meats, and delicacies. Great times were ahead. They all looked forward to being hailed as heroes, the team that changed the industry.

Chapter 3

Timmy Austin was about to lose his virginity. At 18, with over forty dates under his belt, it was about damn time. The Ford F150 with the oversized cab was perfect for it. His truck was pulled over on a back road off I-95 in Harford County, Maryland. The windows were steamed up like a Russian bathhouse. The temperature in the cab felt well over three thousand degrees. Timmy could barely contain his enthusiasm or the hard-on in his pants.

Amanda Meltzer was a tease. The two of them had been on at least forty dates, although Timmy had eventually lost count. He was pretty sure it was forty. *Well, who cared.* This date was all that mattered. Amanda's pants were off, and her small four-feet-nine-inch frame was tantalizing to look at. She was wearing a sexy black bra, which shined in the light of the cab and the thinnest G-string panties Timmy had ever seen. *They barely cover anything!* He thought, as he rubbed his hands and squeezed her bottom passionately.

The trip had been a long one. Timmy was on his way from his home in Boston to visit his elderly grandmother in Virginia. At first, he didn't want to go. Driving ten hours by himself seemed like a terrible idea, but after his girlfriend, Amanda, had agreed to go with him, the trip became one of positivity. Living in a Catholic household, Timmy found it difficult, damn near impossible, to sneak a kiss, let alone a quickie. It was even more difficult at Amanda's house, where her father, a burly man who spent his life behind a shovel, watched over them like a guard at a North Korean prison camp. Timmy would probably rather be caught by the North Koreans than by Amanda's father. The harsh punishment meted out by a Communist regime seemed pleasant in comparison. So, this trip was his best shot at finally achieving the most important goal of his young life.

They kissed, their tongues twirling in each other's mouths like earthworms after a heavy rain. Amanda climbed on top of Timmy and began to dry hump him, rubbing herself on his crotch with the ferocity of a wild animal. It was so close now. Timmy reached down to unzip his fly, but her hand stopped him. *Damn that hand!*

"Not here." She said in a sweet sexy voice while she pecked his lips.

"Come on. No one's around." He pleaded. He was so close. *Please don't stop now.*

"It's my first time too. I want it to be special."

Special! You got to be kidding me. Timmy thought. *What could be more special then right here on the side of the road in the cab of my truck?* Then he had an idea. *Bingo!*

"I saw a motel back about a mile or so." Timmy said and waited for the axe to drop, but it didn't. Instead, she said the most romantic words he had ever heard.

"I'm ready. Let's go."

He felt a twitch in his genitals.

She dressed while Timmy drove, speeding towards the small motel like Juan Manuel Fangio in '57 at Nürburgring. Arriving in the parking lot, Timmy hopped out and ran into the office of the Goodnight Sleep Motel. *Funny name.* If it were up to Timmy, he would not be sleeping at all.

"I'd like to rent a room for the night." Timmy exclaimed.

The old, wrinkled, heavy-set woman turned slowly from her edition of Intouch magazine to peer down at him through her glasses perched at the end of her nose. "How old are you?" She barked at the young man.

Timmy was eighteen, but his round face and soft features made him appear much younger. "Eighteen. I'm eighteen." The words leapt from his mouth.

"Slow down boy." The old woman commanded. "I'll need to see some ID."

Timmy thrust his hand into the back of his pants and grabbed his wallet. He fumbled with it for a second before producing his driver's license and handing it over. The woman stared at it for what seemed like an eternity.

"It's real." Timmy said before he could stop himself.

"Yes, I can see that." She sat the ID in front of her and began copying down the information.

Timmy looked through the glass window at his truck where Amanda was sitting impatiently. She gave him a *"what's going on?"* look which Timmy answered with a shrug of his shoulders. Finally, the woman handed the ID back to him.

"How many adults in the room?" She asked, her eyes boring holes into Timmy's face.

"None…" He began than quickly caught himself. "I mean two. I just turned eighteen." He said sheepishly.

She raised an eyebrow. "One night?"

"Yes ma'am."

"Forty-two dollars." The woman said, holding out her hand.

Timmy counted out several crisp bills and placed them into the woman's outstretched palm. Almost done, Timmy signed his name on the room registry. The woman handed him a key and Timmy exited the office like Superman from a phone booth.

The kissing commenced again as soon as the door to the room shut. Room number 16 was disgusting, but the two young lovers could have cared less. Their minds were so focused on each other's bodies that the moldy carpet and the old peeling wallpaper were the least of their concerns. They made their way to the bed amidst a tornado of discarded clothing. By the time they hit the sheets, Timmy was completely naked, and Amanda was only wearing the tiny G-string.

He tried doing it fast at first but failed with flying colors. No matter how many adult films one sees, watching porn does not count as training for the real thing. Amanda, knowing her body, guided him with her hands. It was the shortest, most amazing feeling of his life. Amanda, on the other hand, had merely been mildly pleased. It kind of hurt and the orgasm her friends bragged about, hadn't happened. However, seeing Timmy so happy made her happy too. They laid there together, their naked bodies locked in a tight embrace. Timmy fell asleep, snoring loudly.

That's when she felt it. It was weird, like tiny blades of grass touching her leg. She didn't realize that it was tiny legs crawling up her lush thighs, making their way under her body. Timmy stirred. *Was he feeling the same thing?* He rolled on his back. Amanda opened her eyes. She felt a sensation on her feet, like a feather caressing them. It was giving her the creeps. She kicked under the sheets. She could feel Timmy's heartbeat. It was fast. Well, after what they had just done -it should be. There it was again. That feeling on her leg then... *ouch!* She felt several pinches on her back. She rolled. *Was it the sheets?* The pinches came back. They hurt. She tried to sit up, but she couldn't. *Oh my God, I'm paralyzed!*

"Timmy!" She gasped. "Timmy!"

He didn't answer.

"Timmy!" She began to cry. She couldn't move. She was scared. She looked over at Timmy, the love of her life and realized that she could no longer feel his heart beat. To her horror, his eyes were staring at her, open and lifeless. She could not scream anymore. She was getting weak, and her heartbeat was getting fast. She could feel it thumping loudly in her chest. Faster and faster, thumping, like the tail of an excited dog. *What was happening?* That was her last thought. The last thing that went through her brain before her heart stopped beating.

Chapter 4

$2.25 billion. That was the revenue last year of
Sentrix Pest Management Company. It was a startling
number, ten figures that smelled like victory. They had
won. The fight was over, and like the Union Army after
Gettysburg, victory was just around the corner.

Sentrix was a powerhouse. They had two hundred
and eleven field offices throughout the world with over
twenty-five thousand technicians and ten thousand sales
personnel. Additionally, the company had two private jets,
a skyscraper in New York and over thirty thousand
vehicles. Their motto said it all -*We Service the Globe.*

They truly did service the globe, for over a hundred
years. Two brothers in 1903 started Sentrix. Raymond and
Phillip Johnson decided they would take on New York
City's burgeoning rodent problem and they succeeded.
Their success in doing battle with the prolifically large rats
in the five boroughs garnished them nationwide prestige.
Pictures on the wall in the company's headquarters showed
Ray and Phil -as they would come to be known- holding up
the carcasses of two dead rats. They called the company
Johnson's Rat Raiders. For the first few decades, the
company grew steadily at seven percent a year up until the
deaths of its founders. Johnson's Rat Raiders then went to
the kids, who like most spoiled rich kids, sold their
inheritance for a pittance to a large pest control company in
New Jersey, Sinclaire's Pest and Wildlife Service Inc. The
newly merged goliath was renamed Sentrix. That was in
1937. The company never went public. A single family, the
Reynolds, owned it. The company passed through
generations of the family, who appointed executives to run
the day to day operations of the firm which grew to heights

never imagined by the Johnson brothers. Over the years, the Reynolds relied more and more on their handpicked and carefully cultivated managers. And that's how Carter Ritler came to be President and CEO of the largest pest control company on the planet.

Carter grew up poor, dirt poor. So poor that he could not remember one time in his childhood where he received a birthday or Christmas present. His parents couldn't afford it. He never blamed them for it and loved the happy childhood they gave him regardless. His father worked on the docks of Manhattan in terrible conditions. His father's already meager paychecks were trimmed even leaner thanks to the friendly neighborhood mob boss, who siphoned off a portion of pay for the privilege of working on his pier. Carter's mother, a compassionate, giving woman, gave birth to three children: Carter, Beth, and George. Carter was the oldest, and as the oldest, he had been the lab rat. His parents often practiced rearing skills on him before dispensing the justice out to his younger siblings. Essentially, Carter's rear end was a whole hell of a lot redder.

No way was he ever going to join his father working on the docks. He had watched his father slave away for tyrannical foremen and egregiously corrupt mafia connected union organizers for decades. His father's experience drove Carter to study hard and pursue business. He was always a good businessman. He had his own paper route when he was eleven, and by thirteen he ran a business employing an army of his fellow schoolmates selling cigarettes, gum and soda door to door. This paid for his college education at Harvard and thanks to his grades -the ivy league school accepted him in a flash. Four years later,

Carter was out with a bachelor's degree in business administration. He joined several firms, slowly building his impressive resume before he landed the job of a lifetime - President and CEO of Sentrix.

Sentrix offered Carter a $10 million a year salary plus unprecedented -and completely ridiculous- benefits. Sweet as honeysuckle benefits, like unlimited use of one of the company's private jets and a chauffeured Maybach to and from work. His life was so different from where it had begun. He owned a $7 million condo in Manhattan, a gigantic mansion in ritzy Palm Beach and a fleet of luxury autos including a Lamborghini Aventador and a Ferrari California T. *Man what my parents would think of me now. Too bad they didn't live long enough to see it.*

Beth and George had though, to Carter's dismay. His two younger siblings matured into the biggest leeches known to science. They should have been in an aquarium in a lab, where they could be studied to observe their ravenous sucking behavior up close and personal. George -a degenerate gambler who never saw a crap table he didn't like- frequently hit up his rich older brother for loans, which he never repaid. Beth reminded Carter of Connie in the Godfather Part 2. She attempted to achieve the same success as Carter by courting rich older men. This backfired because -although the men enjoyed her between their sheets- most of them were already married and would never leave their wives for a woman of Beth's ilk. So, Carter cared for them. It was the least he could do to repay his parents' sacrifices.

Today, Carter was very pleased. His new project was almost complete. One of the most necessary parts had been deemed ready months ago and now Dio Insecticide -

the chemical he had received so much flak for from the board- had been approved by the EPA and the USPTO. He decided he would buy himself something nice as *congratulations, a pat on the back, a job well done chap.*

He went watch shopping. He had always desired a Patek Philippe and today was the day. Carter was not married and had no kids -well if you didn't count Beth and George- so spending $250,000 on a watch was not ridiculous at all. Plus, shocking though it was, the man with everything had an image problem. Carter seldom viewed himself as *the boss*. He always saw himself as a little man, which translated into being constantly angry at the world. The houses, cars, watches, women, jets strived to, but could not, fill the void in his life. The giant hole in his chest left there by the impoverished environment of his youth.

Carter entered the famous Tiffany and Co. A ruckus broke out between the three sales reps as they vied for the chance to serve this suave man who reeked of green. A pretty woman in her mid-thirties won the wrestling match and scrambled over to greet him. Carter was accustomed to such patronage. After all, he was handsome, classy and wealthy.

"Good evening Mr. Ritler. Can I help you find something?" She said, a little too pleasantly. She knew his name. That was no surprise. He had been in Tiffany's at least a thousand times and had always spent quite a considerable amount of money. He was a sales rep's wet dream. They probably had a picture of him on the wall in their breakroom with the words *RICH CHUMP* written below it.

"I wanted to see your line of Patek Philippe watches."

"Certainly. Right this way sir." She smiled, Patek Philippe would contribute a handsome commission bonus to her monthly salary and right before the holidays. It would be a good Christmas this year.

She led him over to a display case. She slid the lock open and laid out several watches for him to try on. Carter was instantly mesmerized. This is what it was all about. The arduous work, the long hours, the constant aggravation, all boiled down to this moment -trying on the most expensive watches in the world. Screw the booze and drugs; this was the real high. If the addicts of the world only realized it, then maybe instead of slinking down to the street corner, they'd go to school, get a degree and land a plum job. It was during this high that Carter's phone began to vibrate in his pocket. He pulled it out and stared at the number before answering.

"Yeah." Carter barked.

"Sir, we have a problem."

Chapter 5

The smell of butter frying in the pan wafted throughout the house. It made its way up the stairs like a swarm of bees on a summer breeze, landing on the hairs in the nostril of Detective Bill Patterson as he snored in his bed. His nose twitched, unconsciously sniffing the air. His eyes sprung open and he sat bolt upright. His feet hit the floor and the morning stretch commenced.

Works every time, Cindi Patterson thought, smiling, as she heard her husband's loud footfalls across the bedroom floor. She cracked three eggs into the pan, frying them over medium, then placing them onto a freshly toasted everything bagel. She called it the triple decker, and because of her husband's recently discovered high cholesterol, she only made it for him once a week. She would have to find something else to arouse his senses. He was a tough man to get out of bed in the morning.

Footsteps descended the stairs. A minute later, Detective Patterson rounded the corner, kissed his wife good morning and sat down. Cindi placed the egg sandwich in front of him with a cup of coffee and a glass of orange juice. Her breakfast -consumed earlier- consisted of half a grapefruit and a whole apple, which is why the fifty-year-old woman had a body no older than thirty and a cholesterol level lower than a politician's morality. Despite already eating, she sat down and drank her coffee across from her husband. The daily routine in the Patterson house had begun.

Loud howls pierced the air as two beagles burst through the doggy door and into the kitchen. Yelps and the sound of claws on hardwood composed the symphony of the morning. The tricolored dogs were rescued from a shelter in Delaware a year ago. Detective Paterson regularly accused the dogs stealing every minute of every day away from the, now, child-free home. They were not his favorite subject.

"Tom moves out and you decide to get dogs." Bill growled.

Cindi was trying to decide which was worse: the barking of the dogs or the whining of her husband. Definitely her husband. She loved the dogs. They were her life. It was hard for mothers -especially mothers who had only raised one child- to adapt themselves to the fact that their baby was grown up and on his own. That was the case with Tom who had recently taken a job with Microsoft and moved to Washington state. She missed Tom. The young man was the equalizer of the home. And now he was gone. He had leapt out of the nest and by God had learned to fly.

"Awe. They love their Daddy." Cindi said. The two beagles, their giant ears flapping in the air as if they were preparing for takeoff, jumped on Bill, nearly knocking his egg sandwich onto the floor. Their long, slobbery tongues licked Bill's face from forehead to chin.

"Damn dogs!" He yelled, pushing the dogs away like a celebrity facing the paparazzi. He saw the hurt look on his wife's face. He loved his Cindi, loved her from the moment they had locked eyes, so many years ago in a galaxy that was light years away. He took several deep calming breaths before he spoke. "At least let's get them trained." He said. The dogs were now wrestling with each other, biting ears and rolling jovially across the kitchen floor.

"I called a trainer. He's coming next week." Cindi's calm was remarkable. No wonder her blood pressure was an amazing 110 over 70. She was so calm in fact that Bill couldn't figure out what she was thinking. She had only two emotions -happy and sad. That was it. Those two basic emotions. Cindi never got angry. Never raised her voice. Never popped the wall a good one. Never slammed a phone. She would either smile or cry. And her sad, would cause the clouds to open up and rain to fall on earth for a thousand years.

"Good." Bill finished the last bite of his sandwich. He placed the plate into the empty sink, downed the last gulp of orange juice and kissed his wife goodbye.

"Go catch the bad guys." She said.

"I wish." And he really did.

Bill Patterson was the only detective on Havre de Grace's small police force. It was a nice, safe job. Just the kind of job police officers like Bill despise. Cops love action. The more, the merrier. The action is the reason most of them take the job in the first place. Carry a gun in the wild west and all that jazz. The problem was, in this town, there was no action. Sure, you have your drugs, your occasional assault-and-batteries and on the very rare occasion, like the blue moon crashes to earth and causes a giant tsunami kind of occasion -a murder, usually a result of domestic violence, *husband kills wife, wife kills husband* kind of thing. And that was all fine and dandy. The problem Bill had was that these crimes are self-solvable. No real police work needed. No detecting. No collecting prints. No following a deadly killer into a dark alley. No approaching a lunatic and announcing in a theatrical voice -

I'm your huckleberry!- It stunk. There was a serial killer in town about ten years ago, who deposited some bodies by the railroad track but sadly, he was only passing through.

Bill's job was an oxymoron in the purest definition of the word. He was a homicide detective in a town where they weren't any homicides. Still, that was what was on his business card. *Detective William Patterson, Homicide.* Despite his specific title, Bill got every criminal case the town had to offer. He was the washing machine at the local laundromat. Drugs -call Bill. Guns -call Bill. Stolen cars - call Bill. After all, what was Chief John -Havre de Grace's longest-serving police chief- supposed to do; he had to justify Bill's salary somehow.

But today was different. Minutes after leaving his house, Bill received a call that changed his life forever. The call came as he pulled into the local Royal Farms for a pack of cigars. His radio squawked, and he snatched the receiver up like a grenade in a foxhole.

"Go ahead."

"Multiple 10-54s at 1215 Morrison." Sargeant O'Hara, Havre de Grace's dispatcher since the civil freaking war, said. 10-54 was a dead body. Multiple 10-54s were, well… This vastly peaked Bill's interest, although he thought it might be a prank. Not many 10-54s in this town.

"10-4." Bill replied, replacing the small receiver. He slammed the Ford Crown Vic into drive, turned on his blue and reds and peeled wheels out of the lot.

Three dead bodies, not one, three, plus a dog. The first was a woman in her thirties. Bill knew her. Her name was Tracy. He had responded many times to this house for domestic violence calls and disorderly conduct complaints. The two other bodies were Tracy's two kids: Adam, age eight and Sarah, age five. All three were found in their beds. No sign of forced entry and no sign of foul play. The dog had been dead much longer than the three people upstairs. That was obvious. It was the smell that enabled the detective and every other cop that entered the house, to make that foregone conclusion. The carcass of the dog reeked like raw chicken sitting in the hot sun.

The house looked like a pig sty and smelled like the rectum of an elephant on an all bean diet. The odor of rotting garbage mixed with the odor of decomposing dog like two opposing NFL teams. No matter where you went, you were going to get plowed.

Detective Patterson, walked calmly amongst the trash, puffing on one of his signature cigars. *What a disgusting lifestyle. And kids lived here. Kids.* He thought as he looked around. Two uniformed officers stood next to him, and they too looked like they were thinking along the same lines. Patterson walked upstairs, his shoes kicking empty soda cans and dirty toys the whole way. When he reached the bedrooms, it took all his power not to vomit. The kids lay amongst the disgust, on a single mattress on the floor. Only one small, thin sheet covered both children. Their skin was white, ghostly white, which was not uncommon in dead bodies. The scene made Bill violently ill. The contents of his stomach churned like an active volcano. Next, he went into Tracy's room. The sight of the woman's pale body didn't register the same revulsion. *Any mother who would allow drugs and alcohol to rule her life and let her kids live in squalor deserves this.* Patterson thought but didn't say out loud. He peered down onto her corpse, loathing infesting his soul.

The medical examiner arrived. She was a tall, skinny woman with the athletic build of a track runner. One of many coroners in Harford County, she primarily worked the northeast corridor. Her name was Patty Kilgore.

Patty took out a pair of rubber gloves and began poking and prodding the body of the woman. She had decided to start here. Even as a coroner the sight of two dead children made her skin crawl.

"Who found them?" Patty asked.

"The Plumber. He was supposed to fix her toilet." Patterson answered, frowning like *glad I don't have that freaking job.*

"No sign of foul play. If I might venture a guess, I'd say carbon monoxide. Was the furnace on?"

"I doubt it. It's been seventy some degrees lately. My furnace isn't on." Bill inferred.

"True but she does have kids."

Bill gave her a look like *really, you think this piece of shit cared about her children.* "The door was open."

"Open?" Patty asked, looking up at the detective.

"Yep. That's what the plumber said."

"Plenty of ventilation. That's strange." Patty said, more to herself. "I've never seen a body look so pale before. Well…" She thought for several seconds. "I have. Usually blood loss." Patty mumbled. She had a tendency of verbalizing her thoughts. She lifted the body up on one side and peered underneath. "No livor mortis."

"English."

"Livor mortis described the blood pooling in the lowest part of the body. She's laying on her back. So, her back should have a dark bruise. But it doesn't."

A uniformed police officer came up the stairs a second later, and Bill was happy for the interruption. Coroners always gave him the creeps. *How can someone work with the dead all day, every day?*

"Detective, the oven was on with the door open." The uniform cop said.

"There you go. A poor man's furnace." Patty said. "I feel terrible about the children."

"So, do I." Patterson said. "I hate to see this." He waved his hand around the house indicating the conditions. Patterson turned to the cop. "Any leads on the father?"

The uniform cop shook his head. "No sir. No one knows. We talked to the old lady next door, Mrs. Phelps, she's lived here for decades, says she never met the children's father."

"Check their birth certificates. Knowing this woman, the kids probably have different fathers." Patterson replied.

"Yeah. Tracy was a wild one." The uniform cop reminisced.

"I take it you were here a few times." Patty asked, rejoining the conversation.

"Too many. The forgotten." The uniform cop said before he descended the stairs.

"What did he mean by that?" Patty asked looking up again.

"The Forgotten. That's what we call people like this. The ones society has left behind."

Chapter 6

"You're out of your damn mind!" Harry Roseland exclaimed, slamming his fist on his desk. "No way I'm putting this out there."

James sighed in frustration. "It's real. It's coming." He said, staring across the desk into the eyes of his boss.

"Do you see the weather out there?" Roseland lifted his hand and gestured to the window. "Seventy degrees. Do you know what people are going to say?"

"I am very confident sir. It is December."

Harry Roseland rose from his chair and rubbed his temples. "James, people already think we are a bunch of crooks. They think we're wrong all the time. Listen to me." He said waving off James' attempted interruption. "Now, you want me to tell them that in a week there is going to be an ice storm?"

"It's not just an ice storm sir. It's…"

"Yeah, yeah, I know, the biggest ice storm to hit this area in sixty years. James, it's seventy degrees outside!" He started to pace. That wasn't a good sign.

Harry Roseland resembled the stereotypical newspaper boss -white with a shiny bald head, a fat gut held up by suspenders and a beet-red face. He looked like he stepped right out of a comic book like Harry was the editor of the fictitious Daily Planet. This thought made James smile inwardly. A little bit of levity in the current situation.

"What if I'm right?" James asked.

The question stopped Harry Roseland in his tracks. "You're brilliant. I'll give you that. If you're right, then we're fucked." Roseland sat back down behind his desk. "I am going to release it." He conceded. "CYA. Cover your ass. I'm betting you're right. But…"

"If I'm wrong, you can have my walking papers."

"Fuck that. If you're wrong, I'll fire your ass so fast you won't have time to hand me your papers."

"Thanks Dad." James said and stood. He left the office before his father could say another word.

The newsroom of Channel Nine buzzed with activity. Reporters ran from desk to printer to copy machine and to each other, in a mad dash. Computers went from white word document screens too bright, colorful screen savers in the blink of an eye. Cups of coffee were either in hand or sitting unoccupied on piles of research. James loved it all. The twenty-eight-year-old had spent the better part of his life, enjoying the smells, sights, and atmosphere of this place. It was home to him.

James was a meteorologist -a newly graduated meteorologist. His predictions of changing weather systems were not always accepted with appreciation, evident in his latest meeting with his father. No, for the most part, they were blasted like the proclamations of a local preacher giving unfavorable sermons of sin from the pulpit. But no one could say James' predictions were wrong. In fact, he was right almost a hundred percent of the time. He became famous a year ago when he predicted Hurricane Andrea which churned its way up the Chesapeake Bay slamming into Channel Nine's home turf -the little port town of Havre de Grace. Thanks to James, the townsfolk were ready.

Windows were boarded up, sandbags piled high and boats properly moored. The storm was the worst act of God in a century, a category five, with winds up to 165 mph but Havre de Grace survived. Which was astonishing considering the town was below sea level, situated at the mouth of the Susquehanna River in Harford County, Maryland.

If James' predictions were again validated, this storm, packing ice thicker than bulletproof glass, would be far more devastating than anything mother nature had ever thrown at them. It would make Hurricane Andrea look like a thunderstorm after a sizzling summer day. Snow was bad but ice -*was really bad.* Snow could be plowed, and roads could be made passible. Ice was different. Ice would transform the largest and most modern city in the US into a 3rd world country. James could not even imagine what it would do to his small town.

The conditions were perfect. A cold front was moving in from the south which would drop temperatures to twenty-eight degrees. The next ingredient to this deadly cocktail was the storm system building off the coast of Africa. That system would slowly churn its way across the Atlantic, picking up moisture from the ocean before making landfall in the northeast United States. The storm would drop rain at an alarming rate of a ¼ inch per hour for two days. The rain droplets would be super-cooled by the air, turning into ice. X plus Y plus Z equals -*they were shit out of luck.*

James walked into the bathroom. A meeting with his father, ever since he was a child, always made him have to pee. He unzipped, performed the task, zipped up and washed his hands. He considered himself in the mirror, admiring his black skin and handsome features. James prayed the storm wouldn't happen. He prayed he would be fired instead. His job wasn't worth the injuries and the deaths this storm would inflict. It could bring the whole state of Maryland to a standstill. Emergency responders and paramedics would never reach people in time. The damage to homes and businesses would be catastrophic, but that would be minuscule in comparison to the number of lives that would be lost. Damage to property can be repaired, but lives could never be reclaimed. *God help us if this storm comes.* He silently prayed on his way through the bathroom door.

His desk was covered in a collage of documents. There is a method to the madness, and that was certainly the case here. James could, if asked, produce any chart or map from the pile in the blink of an eye. He sat down. A tornado twisted on his computer screen. The mouse clicked once, and the tornado vanished. The mouse clicked several more times and various graphs of data appeared.

"Guess who?" A woman's voice said as hands grabbed James' shoulders.

He didn't turn. "It only works if you skip a day or two."

Kelly Halle sat her cute butt down right on his desk. "How's dad today?" She asked, inclining her head to Harry's door.

"Depends. If you've got pictures of Spiderman, then pretty good." James smiled.

"What about Batman?"

"He's in one of his moods. I kind of blew up his morning."

"Ice storm?" She asked, crooking an eyebrow fixed above one of her amazing blue eyes.

"It's coming." James said defensively, getting very serious. He never joked about his work.

Kelly picked up a file from his desk and slapped him playfully across the face. "Lighten up, would you."

"What are you working on?" James had a serious crush on Kelly. Her blond hair, blue eyes, and curvy body made his head whirl. He never told her, not that she needed telling. James didn't possess a great poker face, or even a decent one, not even one that would win a hand against a bunch of 1st graders.

"Three dead bodies. A woman and two kids."

"In this town?"

"Got a call from my buddy in blue."

James knew she had heard about it while lying in bed with her cop boyfriend. Envy swelled in his innards.

"Good luck with that." He managed to say, after a long and awkward pause.

"Gotta get permission from the man before I head over there. He's got me doing some crazy piece on graffiti. You want to tag along?"

James acted like he was thinking about it. "Nah. I got a lot of work here. Let me know how it goes." *No way. I am not putting myself through another awkward meeting with your tool of a boyfriend, who undoubtedly, would be on the scene with every other cop in this small town. Maybe I should go up there and set-up a donut stand. I'd make a killing at the killing.* He frowned inwardly. *A little too dark even for my sense of humor.*

Kelly patted him on the back before disappearing into Harry's office. James sat back in his chair and daydreamed. *Man, what I would give to wake up next to her.*

Chapter 7

Commotion is common at crime scenes. Usually from distraught family members, wailing over the loss of the deceased, or disgruntled photographers, wailing over the loss of a million-dollar shot. *This was a new one.* Detective Patterson thought, staring blankly at the man being restrained by the uniformed officers.

"You're an exterminator?" Patterson asked puzzled.

"Yes sir. I was supposed to do a follow-up here." George Martin replied.

"I can't let you in. There are three dead bodies in that house." A thought crossed the Detective's mind. "You didn't spray anything in there recently, did you?"

George scowled at him with dark eyes. "I used bait in there two weeks ago."

"Bait?"

George pulled a gun from his belt which turned out to be a bad move. Firearms exited holsters around him like it was the OK Corral. George, not startled at all by the five-gun barrels aimed at his head, stared back at them.

"It's a bait gun." He said dully, not backing down. The blue plastic bait dispenser looked like something out of Star Trek. *Beam me up Scotty and away from these nincompoops.*

"Cool it boys!" Patterson commanded. The cops lowered their weapons. Patterson tried to smooth over the incident. "Small town. Most of these boys haven't had an opportunity to pull their pieces. They're a bit jumpy." He smiled at George who returned it halfheartedly. "Why do you want to get in there so bad?"

"House was loaded with roaches. I tried a new bait. Just wanted to see how it worked." George answered honestly.

"You take your job very seriously." Patterson said.

George nodded.

"You got anything for mice?" One of the uniform officers asked. He was a squirrelly man, so skinny he could probably hula-hoop with a fruit loop.

"Get your ass back over there Jackson." Patterson barked. He turned back to George. "Not something I deal with often. Very unusual."

"I can come back." George said.

"No. No. Five minutes. Just in the kitchen." Patterson lifted the yellow crime scene tape to let George through.

"Thanks a lot." George replied.

The kitchen was exactly as George remembered it. Dirty dishes that hadn't been cleaned in forever piled so high they teetered on the edge of disaster. Grease covered the walls, the ceiling, the cabinets, and the refrigerator, in a thick, yellowish haze. In fact, everything a sickening shade of yellow. The smell of course was far worse, thanks to the addition of the decaying dog. He was used to that smell; he had smelled it his entire life. Dead mice, dead rats, dead squirrels, he had smelled them all. It came with the territory. Dead things, the life of an exterminator and George had lived that life for thirty years, ever since the ripe age of sixteen. He loved it -killing bugs, catching mice and most importantly solving problems. George *loved* to solve problems. If he could leave a customer with a smile on their face, then he was a happy man.

What the hell? He thought when he opened the kitchen cabinets. The roaches he had expected to see were all dead. That was impossible. Even with a new bait, there should at least be a few running around, especially since the house had one of the worst infestations he had ever seen. But they were all dead. Either this was the most effective bait he had ever used, or something else had happened here. He checked the refrigerator last. When he had first pulled it out two weeks ago, thousands, literally thousands of German cockroaches were calling it home. Surely, there would be some alive here, but there wasn't. Now the back of the refrigerator contained thousands of dead roaches, their carcasses piled high on the floor and in the motor.

George had never seen anything like it before in his entire career. He scooped up a handful of carcasses and placed them in a container which he placed in his pocket. This was incredible. The new bait must be a miracle. Cheap and extremely effective.

"Find what you were looking for?" Patterson asked when George reappeared outside.

"I think so." George replied, still perplexed.

The Detective attempted to make small talk as he walked George back to his truck. "You work around here often?"

"Two days a week. The other three, sometimes four, I'm in Baltimore. What happened to the people in there?"

"Carbon monoxide. That's my guess."

George stored that away in his mind. *Could the poisonous gas have killed the roaches too?* He would have to check when he got back to his shop. He would send some of the samples down to the university.

"That's a shame. That stuff always scares me. I got a few detectors around my house." George said.

"Same here brother."

"Thanks for letting me in."

"No problem. You got a card? You know just in case we find out you're the murderer?" Patterson chuckled.

George didn't take too kindly to his words. "Sure thing." He handed the Detective a card, hopped in his truck and drove off.

Chapter 8

Bugs, bugs, bugs. That's what Carter saw when he entered the lab. Glass aquariums full of every species of creepy crawlers one could imagine. Cockroaches, spiders, bed bugs, and countless others. All were crawling up the sides of their enclosures in a vain attempt at escape. It gave Carter the creeps. He hated this place and tried his hardest to stay away as much as possible.

Men and women in lab coats milled about, checking charts, looking into microscopes, depositing food or water into tanks or just plain standing there conversing with one another. *Nerds.* Carter thought as he walked over to the king of the nerds.

Dr. Richard Sangmore probably got stuffed in a multitude of lockers in his day. He looked no more than four feet tall, was rail thin and sported a pair of thick glasses that made the microscope lenses he was peering into look thin. Dr. Sangmore sprang to attention when Carter approached his desk.

"Good morning Richard." Carter said, refusing to call the man doctor. Doctors to him had an MD next to their name, not a Ph.D. Plus Dr. Sangmore worked for him and he was not about to give someone who worked for him one iota of dignity. "What did you mean we have a problem?"

Dr. Sangmore looked nervous, shaking slightly. He said in a high-pitched voice that fit the bill perfectly. "We received feedback from the first test site that was alarming." He stood up and hurried across the room to pick up a manila folder on the table. "I think we should step outside."

Carter followed Sangmore through the door. The two stood alone in the hallway. Sangmore looked around as if he was reenacting a scene from a bad spy novel. Finally, he peered up at the surveillance camera winking at him from the ceiling. *No possibility of avoiding them, they're everywhere. Gordon Reynolds' eyes and ears.*

"I'm very busy Richard." Carter said, lifting his hand to glance at his Breitling wristwatch that should have been a new Patek Philippe.

"Yes sir." Sangmore stuttered. "Our team on site reported that the test subjects are deceased."

"Deceased?!" Carter exclaimed, his eyes wide. "What do you mean? I thought you designed them to be stronger. Their exoskeletons harder. You're telling me…"

"No, no. You misunderstand." Sangmore interrupted. "The subjects in the house are deceased. The human subjects."

Carter looked shocked. "The human subjects?"

"Yes sir. It appears they died during feeding. It is strange…"

Carter raised a hand to silence the man. He had to think. He turned and looked out the window at the blue skyline of Manhattan. The view calmed him, calmed his mind.

"It happened before. The mice. The mice in the lab were killed. We thought it was because of their weight, but it appears as if that is not the case."

"How many people know about this?"

Sangmore thought about the question, his glasses appearing opaque in the fluorescent light of the hallway. "The team in Havre de Grace and you and I." Sangmore said.

"Keep it that way." Carter commanded pointing a finger in the nerdy scientist's face.

"Yes sir." Sangmore said.

"We are days away from the IPO and if news leaks out…" Carter let the rest trail off.

Carter left the man standing in the hallway. He walked quickly to the elevator, riding it up to the top floor of the eighty-floor building. The top of the building was the top of the world, literally, regarding pest management. The eightieth floor housed the administrative offices. His office was there, with its polished mahogany wood paneling and plush green carpet. However, his office wasn't where he was heading. Instead, he went to the opposite end of the hall. There he knocked upon the last of the large oak doors.

"Come." A voice boomed from within the room.

Carter opened the door and walked inside. There at an oversized desk, intricately carved out of a single piece of wood, sat one of the wealthiest men in the world, Gordon Reynolds. He was an old man with gray hair slicked back and a face that resembled the desk he occupied -wooden and polished. He did not look up but continued to read a document laid out before him.

"They killed them." Carter announced.

"Who?" Gordon replied, still not looking up.

"The human subjects. Our new species killed them."

Gordon slowly folded the piece of paper in front of him and placed it to one side. Only then did he flash his dangerous eyes at the man who was currently running his company.

"Is that a problem?" Gordon asked is his cold voice.

"Yes. That was never the plan." Carter said. "Stronger. Breed faster. Fewer blood meals. Immune to known chemicals. Not lethal. That was not our intention."

"Then you have a problem Mr. Carter." Gordon stated.

No shit there's a problem! Carter considered the eyes of the older man. He couldn't stand this ancient prick. *Family businesses. What a laugh. Men getting their positions in life, based entirely on nepotism. Not skill. Not experience.*

"If you remember, I was against releasing them. If the board would have listened to me, this…"

Gordon abruptly cut him off. "The board has spent $100 million on this little project of yours!" He exclaimed. "We want results. Not empty promises. Plus, I don't see what all the fuss is about. The bugs kill. So, what? This creates an even better scenario than originally anticipated. More pandemonium. More panic. More profit."

"A woman and her two kids are dead!" Carter hurled. "What happens if word ever gets out?"

Gordon stood up from his desk. For an eighty-year-old, the man was spry. "Then I suggest you make sure word never gets out, Mr. Ritler."

"There are more out there. Three more test sites."

"Send more people there. Try the new product. If it's effective, then problem solved."

"And if not?" Carter allowed the question to dangle in midair.

"Then I suggest you double your security detail Carter."

Plain and simple. Carter thought when he had returned to his office. He poured himself a glass of scotch from the bottle of Johnny Walker Black he kept for just these occasions. He preferred the blended whiskey as opposed to being a single malt snob. The first sip calmed him. *Plain and simple.* He thought again. If the information of what they were doing ever leaked out, Carter would be the one to fall. The board would see to that. After all, he was the man running the company.

Chapter 10

No blood in the bodies. According to a careful autopsy conducted by the Harford County medical examiner's office, there was no blood found in the bodies of Tracy and her two children. No sign of any puncture wounds either. Which was just insane, impossible, *unbelievable!*

Detective Patterson read the report to himself repeatedly. At first glance, he thought it was a joke. No blood in the bodies. No blood found at the scene. No sign of any puncture wounds. He was starting to believe in vampires. Transylvania, Salem's Lot. Victims in bed, no sign of forced entry, well, the screen door *was* open. No sign of foul play. No carbon monoxide poison. And no blood in either of the three victims. Was this a joke? A prank? One of those shows where some asshole with hair sticking up to the ceiling jumps out and screams. *We got you! Ha ha ha ha! There's the camera! Right there! You see it?* Patterson's brain attempted to mull the possibilities when Kelly Halle walked into his office. *Who the hell let her in?* He wondered to himself as the reporter took the liberty, and the chair, across from him. *Pretty women -they can get away with murder.*

"I was wondering if I can have a minute Detective?" Kelly asked, batting her big eyes.

He put out his hand palm up like *looks like you already took one.*

"Sorry for the intrusion. I tried to talk to you at the crime scene yesterday, but I must have just missed you." She said.

"What a shame." Patterson said sarcastically, wishing he could light a cigar but department rules, were department rules, as stupid and ridiculous as they may be. "What can I do for you?"

"I was wondering what the police thought about the fact that the bodies recovered yesterday contained zero blood with no visible puncture wounds?"

Patterson stared down at the report in front of him. *Did the coroner leak it to the media before sending it to us?* Then he remembered that Kelly was in a relationship with one of his officers. *The dopey one. What was his name again? Martin, Tony, Mike, it was Mike.* Patterson would have to put a stop to that. *Leaking evidence to reporters, what was wrong with that idiot!?*

"Ms. Halle." Patterson spoke as if he were reading from a paper. "We are working around the clock, trying to find out exactly what happened to the victims in question. We'll have a press conference as soon as any new leads develop."

She pounced on his words. "You don't have any new leads?"

"I am not saying that." He said quickly holding up his hand. He continued. "All I am saying is that the department is working very hard to sort out all the evidence and get to the bottom of this."

Patterson liked her. Not in a sexual way, even though she was easy on the eyes. He liked her in a way an Uncle would like a niece. She was sophisticated and very witty.

"I'm baffled. Blood loss and no puncture wounds. How does that happen?" She continued, persistent as hell.

"I don't know. Strictly off the record." Patterson answered. He really didn't know. He had never, in his career of thirty years, seen anything like this before. In fact, he had never even heard of anything like this.

"Care to venture a guess?"

Patterson shook his head. "No."

Kelly rose, thanked the detective and exited the office. Her recent squeeze Mike wasn't in the station, which was good. Things hadn't been going so well between the two of them. The sex was great, as far as sex was concerned but Kelly wasn't really into sex, not like Mike, who barely left her alone. It wasn't the sex. It was Mike. He had transformed like one of those robots in that movie with Megan Fox. But instead of a Camaro transforming into a cool robot, Mike had just transformed into an asshole. He was mean to her, all the time. Nothing pleased him, not even the sex. He practically demanded it from her. He had left the foreplay on the doormat and was apt to barge right in. She had been pondering breaking up with him. Pondering things that she had never thought about before. Things like her handsome co-worker who obviously -pretty damn obviously- couldn't keep his eyes off of her. She liked that. It made her feel special. It was romantic. And James had had a crush on her for -years? Yeah. Years. He was shy. She kind of liked that too. Shy was good. Maybe she had had enough of those pompous, narcissistic pricks she was so used to dating.

She left the station. The other cops on duty watched her like ravenous dogs. One of them drooled out of the side of his mouth. The officer standing next to the salivating man playfully punched him in the arm.

"Sorry." The man stammered, wiping his chin. "But have you ever…"

The other cop shook his head. "Mike's one lucky son of a bitch."

Chapter 11

The safest way to travel -that was a laugh. Every time he told someone he would rather take the train, the inevitable response was *-planes are the safest*. Not in his mind. It was the law of averages. The fact is more people take planes. The accidents don't look quite as bad when you add up how many flights land safely. The problem, at least for Hank, is that no one survives plane crashes. You go down in a plane; you're going to die, period. No chance. No last rites. Just dead. At least in a train, or a car, if you crash you have a really good chance of surviving. So, Hank drove and took the train.

He was a traveling salesman, which was like being a Bald Eagle. He was definitely on the endangered species list. Don't see many Bald Eagles and you most certainly don't see many traveling salesmen. But like the last few Bald Eagles, Hank still had a fighting chance. He was in a select field -paper. That's right, Hank sold paper. Not the typical 8 ½ by 11 sheets that you load into your printer tray. He sold paper products: toilet paper, paper towels, paper napkins, paper plates. If it came from a tree, then Hank sold it.

He loved Havre de Grace. It reminded him of towns in Maine. The little rinky-dink lakeside towns where big corporations couldn't find enough profit to drive out the ma and pas and everyone knew your name. Havre de Grace was a favorite stop for him. It was ten minutes from the Amtrak station in Aberdeen, and it sure beats Baltimore city. Yeah, you can find a fancier place to stay in Baltimore, not that Hank could afford a fancier place, but you also have a better chance of getting robbed, shot or murdered. In fact, your chances of meeting a grisly end in

Baltimore were better than catching a disease in a whorehouse in Thailand.

Hank didn't have a home. He wasn't necessarily homeless, he was just three years past a divorce and the little apartment he rented in New York, he saw less than his ex-wife. The road was his home. Hotel rooms, cheap diners, and train cars. He never stayed in one place for more than a day and never missed it when he left.

Havre de Grace was different. It was the smell of water. The breeze off the Susquehanna. The sunsets staring at the lighthouse. It was as close to home as he would ever get. He finished his juicy half-pound burger sitting at his favorite table by the water and drowned the last bite with a cold swig from his Budweiser. He loved it here.

The waitress walked over. She was young, probably just out of high school and already showing the signs of a premarital pregnancy. *Kids having kids, what's the world coming to?*

"How was everything?" She asked pleasantly.

"Excellent." He replied, and he meant every word of it. *Even the food tastes better here.*

"Can I get you anything else?"

"Just the check."

A minute later and the check arrived. It totaled fifteen dollars. Hank laid two twenties on the table before standing. *What can I say?* He felt sorry for her. She looked like a good girl. Probably an -*I can't believe you didn't wear a condom*- kind of situation. He had been there before with his first wife. And he had done the right thing.

Married his eighteen-year-old sweetheart, had a miscarriage and got divorced three years later. And that was thirty years ago. *Holy shit am I really fifty?* He walked over to the river and looked down. *Yep, I'm fifty alright.* Gray hair and all. He finished his beer, placed the empty bottle on the table and walked to his rental car.

The yellow bulbs of the street lights looked warm and inviting. It was only five. *Why not go out and have some fun?* He did. Fun for Hank was not indulging in frivolity at the local watering hole; fun was walking down the promenade on the last warm night of the year.

He began to stroll. He passed new parents pushing their kids in strollers, old couples pushing their spouses in wheelchairs and young lovers pushing their virginities to the limit. It was a scene that made him both happy and sad. *Maybe I could've had this life?* Maybe if he would have settled down, taken that job at his father in law's bakery he could have lived happily ever after. That's exactly what his second wife had said. It wasn't Hank that made her leave; it was Hank's mistress -his traveling sales job. He spent more time with *her* than he did with his wife. And the sad part was -his ex was right.

Hank had never been a homebody, preferring to travel. He liked the freedom. It was a freedom the likes of which hadn't been experienced since the days of the wild west when the cowboys would saddle up their steeds and head out into the wilderness. Hank was like Bilbo Baggins. He was never content sitting inside his hobbit hole while there were elves, dwarves, and dragons just a little way down the road.

The boards of the wooden walk-way creaked under his feet. He could see the water down below, dark and uninviting. Small insects floated around the lights lining the path, providing sustenance to the spiders. Spiders are remarkable creatures. Spinning masterpieces, drawing in their living prey with promises of warmth and comfort in the glow of light. Then pouncing, tying their prey up and sucking them dry. Sounds like some women he knew.

He kept walking, his goal in site. The lighthouse rose white and cylindrical on the horizon. It was romantic. A perfect place for a first kiss, a first anniversary, a drop to one knee and pop the question. He reached it. The long walk didn't wind him. He kept himself in decent shape. Plenty of workouts at the free hotel gyms to thank for that.

The lighthouse was beautiful. A sign of hope. A miracle in stormy seas. Like the thousands of sailors before, it bestowed on Hank calm and fortitude. *Land ho.* He looked at the rotating light and made up his mind. Five years from now, Hank the man with no home, afloat at sea, would find his land, retire and buy his first house, here in this small town. Maybe he'd find a nice woman around his age and finally settle down, grow old with her and push each other in their wheelchairs down the promenade. The thought made him smile.

TVs never work, at least not in hotel rooms. False advertising. *TV with cable and free movie channels.* All bullshit. There was no free HBO, Cinemax or Showtime and half the cable TV channels were out. And this wasn't a cheap, run-down motel either. It was the nicest hotel in Havre de Grace, the Best Eastern, a $150 a night kind of joint. No small chump change. He pondered calling the front desk but decided against it. They would probably send some maintenance man, stomach bulging out, hands covered in fried chicken grease with a perpetual snarl who would fumble with the TV and more times than not, would bend over and display the top half of his ass crack as a clandestine way of getting Hank to accept the faulty equipment.

At least AMC was working. He laughed as Abbott and Costello chased a ghost adorned in a white sheet throughout an old mansion. *Old movies were great.* He thought. No cursing, no sex, just amusement. He laid back in his bed, the black and white movie singing him a lullaby and putting him soundly to sleep.

He awoke suddenly and sat bolt upright. The tingling sensation on his feet made his nerves twitch. *What the hell was that?* He looked at the sheet covering his feet. Nothing. Well, he had to pee anyway. Funny thing about getting old, you're required to visit the facilities a hell of a lot more. He didn't like it one bit. *Somebody please find the fountain of youth, at least for my bladder's sake.* He thought.

The bathroom nightlight penetrated the room through the small crack at the base of the door. Hank's feet searched the floor for his slippers. Damn he really had to pee. To hell with the slippers.

His bare feet touched down on funky hotel carpet. He didn't even want to think of the excessive amounts of bodily fluids a UV light would find on this floor. *Disgusting.* The bathroom was only a few strides away when he stepped on something that moved. Something small and hard. *Am I imagining it or am I dreaming?* The object under his foot moved again. Not his imagination.

Damn! It had just bit him. It hurt. Maybe it was glass. He turned around and walked to the lamp next to the bed. Better turn the lights on. There might be more glass. *Damn!* Another piece of glass. *Son of a bitch!* He reached the light and flicked it on.

What he saw made him sick. Thousands of tiny brown bugs covered the carpet. He must be dreaming. This had to be a nightmare. The bugs began moving towards him. He felt fear swallow him whole. *Wake up! Wake up!* They were crawling up his legs. He swatted at them. *Wake up! Get off!* There were too many of them and they were biting. They reached his abdomen. *Wake up, damn it!* Their sharp teeth hurt. He felt woozy. Dizzy. His vision was fading. Weakness overtook his body. His heart was pounding. *Wake up!* Hank realized much too late… he was already awake.

Chapter 12

What was the worst case I've ever worked? She didn't have to think hard for the answer. She knew right away. The teenage bimbo who had locked her two kids in the car. That was it. The very worst. She would never forget it. The teenage mom -*that self-centered cunt*- decided it was way too much trouble to bring her one and two-year-old daughters inside. *What was that bitch's name? Cathy!*

Cathy wanted to have fun. She went over a friend's house, scored smack, got high then had sex. The whole escapade took fifteen hours. Not the sex, even porn stars can't last that long. Meanwhile, this *wonder mother* had left her children inside the car, in ninety-degree weather. They were dead by the time they got home.

It was Patty's task as the coroner to exam the babies' bodies. She vomited for weeks. Cried herself to sleep for months and prayed that that young slut would receive one of the hottest suites in hell. Cathy -*wonder mom*- got twenty years for child endangerment. *Child endangerment! How about murder!* She murdered those kids. *Twenty years in prison!* That was absurd. They should have beaten her to death with a baseball bat and broadcasted it live on television. Patty would have volunteered for the role of Babe Ruth. *Batters up slut!*

Patty always thought about this case every time she worked on something difficult. It plagued her mind. A mind that should be one hundred percent focused on the task at hand. Wasn't that the secret of success? Focus? Ask any successful person on earth; what was the one thing that helped them rise to the top? The answer will always be the same -focus. The ability to concentrate. It was the one thing Patty had problems with.

Death, the commonality of life. The event that made every person, no matter how rich or how poor, how strong or how weak, how powerful or how ineffective, totally equal. Death, or more precisely the dead, had interested Patty since she was a small girl. It happened when her pet rabbit died. Her parents had told her it was just *life*. Rabbits die. Nothing you can do about it. Patty was eight and she was curious. She forced her mother to drive her up to the local library where -to the librarian's dismay- Patty checked out books on the causes of death. She never did find out what killed Pete the rabbit, but the subject of death, fascinated her ever since.

She had been a Harford county coroner for over twenty years. She worked all kinds of cases: drug overdoses, suicides, murders, you name the cause and Patty had dissected it. This case, however, was one of a kind and was the reason why she was sitting in her office at 11 p.m. with a cup of coffee, staring at her computer screen. A cup of black coffee. Patty was a real gal. No cream or sugar for her. Just black and very strong.

Anemia had to be the cause. It had to be a blood disorder. Nothing else could explain total blood loss. Problem is, to detect anemia you must examine blood, which was the one thing the three dead bodies were without. Blood loss also ruled out poisoning. No poison could remove blood from the body, at least none of which that she was aware. Carbon monoxide was out. That had been her first guess. It was a good guess. Impoverished, appalling surroundings, heat generated by the oven instead of the furnace and the victims discovered sound asleep in their beds. But it hadn't been the hellish, odorless gas. Carbon monoxide wouldn't cause blood loss.

No puncture wounds were present during the autopsy. She had double and triple checked. There were none. It was all very strange. *Give it up and go home!* Her mind screamed. *Get some sleep, return refreshed in the morning and crack the case.* She shut down her computer thinking -*Well, at least the computer will catch some Zs.*

The temperature was dropping rapidly. It was crazy. Seventy degrees today and yesterday. Now, it felt like snow. She missed her home state. Florida stayed steady. Always warm. Grass perpetually green and flowers in constant bloom. If she ever retired and if she could ever convince Ted…

Her Audi was parked nearby, it's black glossy paint shining in the street lights. She loved that car. It was fast and agile. Perfect for the winding back roads that comprised her daily commute. The technology of the damn thing never ceased to amaze her. That thought crossed her mind every time her automatic headlights moved with the steering wheel. *Who would have thought? Automatic headlights? What will they think of next?* The twenty-minute drive gave her clarity. The tiredness wore off and it seemed like she was destined for another white night. That was depressing. Sleep always evaded her when she was riveted by a tough case. The Audi engine roared its throaty exhaust as she took another curve at breakneck speed.

The right-side garage door opened, and she pulled the Audi in. She always parked on the right, near the door to her house. Chivalry was not dead, at least not in her house. Her husband Ted parked to the left so his wife had a much shorter trek to the door. *Sweet Ted.* He was a great guy. He was a keeper. She fell madly in love with him from the moment they met twenty years ago. Like a good wife, she supported him as he attempted several business ventures before he finally hit the jackpot. His BMW M5 was already in the garage. He would still be up in his customary recliner watching the History channel. Ted loved history and she adored him for it. She never got tired of the never-ending tours of the various battlefields throughout the area. She had probably spent more time in Gettysburg than the Union army had. *Well, hell, hadn't they only fought for three days?* Maybe she *was* tired after all.

She stepped into the dark hallway leading into her kitchen from the garage. She took off her coat at the door. *Damn!* She had forgotten to take off the blue windbreaker with the words Coroner painted in yellow on the back. It was the coat she wore to crime scenes and in the many years of working them, she had very rarely brought it home. It was one of her ritualistic pet peeves. The grime, the blood, the disgust -she could almost taste it thanks to the damn coat. Patty battled germaphobia on a daily basis. Her cracked, over washed hands could attest to it. She looked at the blue windbreaker with scorn. That's how much this case bothered her. Her mind was elsewhere. Well, she would just have to bring it back in the morning and she would remember next time to leave the *sick* coat at the morgue. She washed her hands in the kitchen sink like a surgeon preparing for a procedure on a patient with a very weak immune system. Then she walked up the stairs to kiss her man.

The first bug climbed out of the blue windbreaker. It was small and resembled a tick; brown with six legs. The bug peered around, checking for danger. Making sure the coast was clear. Then the bug moved down onto the floor. When it reached the tile it peered around again, rotating its entire body. Nothing. No predators, stomping feet or vile chemicals. Eventually several others joined it on the floor. They could smell the woman. The carbon dioxide she exhaled enabled the bugs to track her movements throughout the vast home. It was the sweetest smell in the world like flowers in a spring breeze. They sniffed the air and moved, hunting their prey. They we *so* hungry. They needed to eat. Their bodies were famished. Some of the females in the group were pregnant -bursting with new instars, unable to give birth until a meal was consumed. That meal had just walked up the stairs a moment ago. And they could smell something else. Something even more tantalizing than one human being -they could smell two.

Chapter 13

Cockroaches are the world's most effective survivalists. The myth that gets bantered around the industry is that cockroaches would be able to withstand a nuclear blast. George doubted it, but it was still fun to tell people. George didn't have any nuclear weapons in his arsenal -just a B&G spray tank and a bait gun. So, he hoped the myth was just a myth.

The offices of Chesapeake Pest Management were in an old building that had once been a bank and it looked like a bank, sporting two large pane glass windows in the front and a green awning. The teller booths were long gone but the vault remained. When George and his brothers purchased the building on Philadelphia Road in Baltimore, they inquired about removing the old vault. The bids were so ridiculous that George's brother Chris, a notorious penny pincher from way back, almost had an aneurysm. Chris recommended doing it themselves. *How would you even get it out? A crane through the roof?* George remembered asking him. No way any dolly was going to handle the weight of that thing. So, the vault remained. Now, instead of stacks of greenbacks, it housed pesticides. The Maryland Department of Agriculture loved it. Every annual inspection warranted an appreciative comment about how secure it was to store dangerous chemicals inside a bank vault. No risk of accidents or natural disasters. *What could be safer?*

George's father, George Sr., started the business in 1955. He delivered bread and began killing roaches right out of the back of his delivery truck. No bullshit. *He actually stored his equipment on the back of a truck filled with bread!* Different times back then. If someone did that now, the EPA and the Department of Health would execute them. No trial, no jury, just here's the needle in the arm or the noose and a nearby elm.

Big George, as he was known throughout the industry, was very well liked. The father of nine kids lost his wife at the age of thirty-three. He had to put food on the table and as much as he loved hauling bread around, the business ironically didn't produce enough dough. So, Big George spotted an opportunity and started a pest control business. It was easy really. He already had contacts with the countless restaurants, thanks to the bread business. He had been in their kitchens, had seen their roaches, had talked to the owners and had heard their frustrations about their current pest control situations. Big George could solve their problems. That's what he told them, and he delivered. Big George had the gift. He didn't just control the pests, he eliminated them. Presto. Magic. The business took off.

George Sr. had four sons and five daughters but only the sons would join the business. Not that the tough gals couldn't handle the perils of the *bug life*, it was just the way Big George wanted it. In his archaic view of the world and the role of sexes in society, Big George felt women didn't belong killing bugs. Period, end of story. His sons were different. He started to bring them along in their early teens. Then when they became old enough and had families of their own to support, George made the same mistake every father does in a family business -he gave his sons shares. He split the business into five equal portions, giving twenty percent to each son and maintaining twenty for himself.

Big problems ensued, as they always do when nepotism rears its ugly head. The oldest son, Chris, the first company president after Big George retired, liked the whores. The trashier the better. He was married to a spinster of a woman, who probably didn't fulfill her marital duties in the bedroom or maybe Chris was just a sexual deviant. Either way, Chris' love of loose women eventually landed him in bed with the company secretary. She was married too. Not a good combination. Their secret lust affair almost brought the company to its knees. The two love-crazed birds decided there wasn't enough business to go around. Greedy and selfish, they started their own company and began siphoning off contracts. The situation was bleak. At the last minute, Big George came out of retirement and saved the day. The only thing Chris and his lady friend left with was a gigantic lawsuit and the clothes on their backs.

Ronnie, the third brother, was next in the family saga. He was the black sheep -every family has at least one. Sex didn't seduce Ronnie; the powder took him. White powder. More cocaine went up Ronnie's nose than what went over the Mexican border. At first his habit was a joke. *Here comes Ronnie, sunglasses on, stoned off his ass.* But after a while, the habit began affecting the reputation of the company. Ronnie stopped showing up for work and still wanted his paychecks. He poisoned a dog, crashed the company truck and got busted trying to sell dope to an undercover cop. Ronnie's goose was cooked, and Big George was more than happy to light the fire. Two sons down, two to go.

The fourth and youngest brother Patrick was boring -like watching a rerun of the movie Safe, or better yet like watching water churn in a stagnant pool. Patrick stayed at the family business and worked. That was it. He worked.

Patrick wasn't a salesman nor was he a natural leader. He was a backbreaker. If work needed to be done, Patrick was there to do it. And that's about it. Patrick was as simple as one plus one equals two. He liked to hunt, fish and trek through the wilderness. He was good with money and if the family gossip columns were true -Patrick was the wealthiest of them all.

George Jr., the second brother, forged his own path. He joined the company when he was a teen. Secretly, George hated the pest control business. Hated working with his family. Hated the fighting, the drama, the family politics. Hated being treated like he was second rate by his brother Chris and by the elites of society that like to snub their noses at anyone who wears a blue collar. When he was eighteen, fed up with everything, he quit the business and joined the army. He served in the First Gulf War, excelled in Ranger school, was recruited by a special operations unit and then left out of the blue. He never gave a reason to anyone. It was private. George Sr., plagued with the scandals and recent departure of Chris and Ronnie, begged George Jr. to return to the family business. *What could he say? No dad, I'm not going to help you in your time of need?* So, he went back. After his ten-year hiatus, he settled down and proved to be everything Big George could have ever hoped for. Unlike Patrick, George Jr. was a natural in the bug business. Unlike Chris, George Jr. was loyal. And unlike Ronnie, very unlike Ronnie, George Jr. had never done a drug in his life, not one. George Jr. made the business. He had the gift of gab and was naturally charming -like Cary Grant with military swagger. He sold the big accounts: the hospitals, nursing homes and government buildings. He took the business to the next level. But still, in secret, he never really accepted it.

At least Dad lived long enough to see his business blossom. George Jr. thought, as he zoomed the microscope in and out. His father had passed away three years before, exactly fifty-five years after Chesapeake was founded. What a show that funeral was. Drama city -like filming a Jerry Springer show at a funeral home. The only one who didn't show up was Chris. Guess he didn't want to bring his whore. He was better off anyway. The sisters would have eaten him alive -like a deer getting a drink in a lake filled with crocodiles. Those chicks are ruthless.

The cockroach bodies were laid out on a white tray. They looked enormous in the lens of the microscope. It was like a horror movie and George loved it. Despite his personal misgivings about the family and his father's business, bugs were his life. The compound eyes of the roaches stared back at George. He examined their heads, thoraxes and abdomens. Shriveled -that was the best way to describe what he was seeing. They looked shriveled like raisins. During his career as a bug man, he had seen literally millions of dead insects and none of them had ever looked even remotely like this.

Expert advice -that was the answer. He grabbed an envelope off his desk and slipped the vile of dead roaches into it. He addressed the envelope by hand, computers were still a mystery to him, and printers were the bane of his existence. If he had to spend one more hour on the phone with customer support, he would shoot himself. Pen and paper, simplicity is bliss. He dropped the envelope into the mailbox and flipped up the flag. Two days and he would have his reply.

Chapter 14

Something strange was in the air, like coming home early from school and finding your Dad trying on your Mom's underwear. He swears up and down that he is *not* into that sort of thing, but you can never get that image of him wearing a pink bra and panties out of your head. That was the way Detective Paterson felt right now. Not that that situation had ever happened to him as a child. Hell, his father was such a tough guy, the bra and panties would have caught on fire when they touched the old man's skin. But as he stared down at the two dead bodies in front of him, he could imagine that feeling of pure unchartered weirdness.

There were two dead teenagers in a motel room…a bad motel room. Rent by the hour kind of deal. Place where the sign should read *drugs, hookers and fugitives, we do not discriminate.* The two corpses lay in bed, naked, under the filthy sheets. The boy's eyes were open in a grotesque stare. The girl's pretty face showed fear, more like total terror. The expression was locked there forever, never to be undone. It made Patterson sick. *It has got to be drugs.* Two overdoses. Two more young people snapped from existence, their souls drowning in a river of dope.

Cops filled the room with a sea of blue uniforms. They busily searched the bathroom, the dresser drawers and the pockets of the clothing on the floor. The heavyset, elderly woman from the motel office stood off to one side getting interviewed by one of the officers. Patterson looked over. Something about the scene triggered a memory. *Something... Mike!* The sight of that cocky, arrogant young man reminded Patterson that he owed the cop a good smack for leaking information to his reporter girlfriend. He would take care of that later. The old woman Mike was interviewing wasn't crying. She looked calm, annoyed even, as if this kind of tragedy happened every day and was more of a burden to her schedule than a terrible loss. After all, she ran a sleazy motel on route 40, a highway for discarded souls, a highway for the *forgotten*.

Patterson stepped out of the open door. He needed air. Cold air. Two uniforms were pulling apart several suitcases in front of an F150 in the parking lot. The uniforms wore heavy winter jackets. *What happened to the nice weather?* Days like today, he almost prayed for global warming.

"You find anything?" He asked, approaching the cops by the pick-up.

"Just clothes. No drugs, no alcohol." The cop answered, trying to fold up a large red sweater and stuff it back into one of the bags.

So, they were good kids, except for the late-night dalliance in a motel bed. No sin there, at least not in Patterson's book. They were from Boston, according to their IDs. Both were eighteen, probably from good families, who would be devastated when they received the phone call. *That dreaded phone call.* He hated it. He even reviled it. He would have to make it. It was his job. His least favorite job. He couldn't imagine getting that call. He had a son that was miles away from home, which worried him constantly. It would kill him. Bring him to the brink. He had nightmares about a detective in Washington state phoning to say that Patterson's son was… *Stop thinking that way! Get it together!*

Where was the damn coroner? She should have been here by now. He thought, glancing around the parking lot. No sign of the white van with black lettering. Patty *was* busy. Five dead bodies in two days. That was enough to make anyone late. He rubbed his arms for warmth then decided to go back inside.

"How you doing? I'm Detective Patterson, Havre de Grace police department." Patterson said, introducing himself. The detective shook the heavyset woman's hand and glared at Mike, who took the hint and walked briskly away. Patterson would deal with him later.

"Fine." She replied coldly. "Better if you hadn't brought the whole damn police force. Bad for business you know."

Yeah right. Patterson thought. *The entire army showing up here wouldn't hurt this place's reputation.* He smiled at his own joke. "Very sorry for the inconvenience. Not your run of the mill situation here." He said gesturing to the bodies. "What's your name?"

"Hazel Rhodes." Her breathe stunk like stale cigarettes. It was repulsive.

"Were they acting funny when they checked in Mrs. Rhodes?"

"Nope and just call me Hazel. Mrs. Rhodes makes me sound old." She snapped then paused for a minute to think. "The boy was a little jumpy. Probably wanted to get into bed with his girl. Not high or anything. I'da known that."

Patterson didn't question her knowledge on spotting intoxicated individuals. It would have been like questioning a master chef if he knew how to cook a chicken. Hazel had in her thirty years of running the Goodnight Sleep Motel, seen her fair share, hell most people's fair share, of drunk and drugged out riff-raff.

"You gonna get 'em outta here soon? Gotta get the room cleaned." She asked impatiently.

The detective looked around as if to say, *this place, really!* But he didn't. He just flashed her a polite smile. "The coroner should be here any minute. You'll have the room back in no time."

"Good. Got a big weekend coming up."

That really made him nauseated. She was planning on renting this room right after two people died in it. Just sick. Real gruesome. Twisted in every sense of the word.

"What about the two rooms next door? You rent them last night?" The Detective asked, jutting his chin towards the rooms in question.

"The one there…" She pointed to the right. "Is a permanent."

"Permanent?"

"They pay monthly. Stay as long as they keep paying. The other room is vacant. I've got a lot of work to do." The woman had had enough of his questions. She gave the Detective a dirty look and walked briskly away.

Patterson strolled over to the room next door. He pounded on the door which shook like the tectonic plates of the San Andreas Fault. No answer. He pounded again. Finally, a raspy voice boomed from within.

"Yeah! Who da fuck is it?"

"Police." Patterson yelled in response. Right away he knew the room's permanent resident was either a drug addict or an alcoholic. He heard scuffling inside. The sounds of paraphernalia being stuffed into drawers, shoved under beds and flushed down the commode. Just to make sure the junkies were completely off their rocker, Patterson pounded on the door again. He smiled to himself as he did so.

The door opened. The smell of cigarettes, sex and marijuana smoke hit him full-on in the face. A woman stood in the doorframe, puffing on a Marlboro that she obviously just lit as if to say -*nothing to see here officer, we're just smoking cigarettes.* He didn't buy it. The woman looked like an old tire with the tread worn down. Her face was sunken; her eyes dark, her hair dirty and matted to her scalp. *Burning the candle at both ends and the middle.* Patterson thought, as he stared at this creature of the night.

"What can I do for you officer?" She asked, a little too politely. She seemed as nervous as a hen staring down a hungry fox.

"Two people passed away in the room next door. You hear or see anything suspicious last night?"

The woman twitched; her eyes blinked; her chest moved up and down with each rattling breath. She needed a fix. "Dead?" She asked, starting to come out of her room but then thought better of it. If she moved out of the doorframe, the cop would be able to see inside. Bad idea.

"Yes. Anything suspicious?" Right away he realized he was asking the wrong person. This junkie didn't even notice the fifty cop cars parked outside her room. *The world of the forgotten. Has it become such a regular occurrence, dead bodies at this motel, that she doesn't notice the commotion anymore?*

"Nah." She said. "Nothing. Wait a minute. Rex!" She screamed into the small room as if she was yelling across a mountain range. "Rex!"

A man appeared from the shadows. His appearance was worse than woman's, if that was at all possible. His teeth were hit or miss, like the person who knocked them out either hit or missed. Large tattoos covered every inch of his skinny frame. He put his arm around the woman, claiming his prize as if he was worried the Detective might be there to snatch his lady. *Please. Not if she was the last woman on earth.* Patterson thought to himself. He would rather die a lonely, asexual man.

"Yeah?" The man said, already up in arms, ready for a fight, defiant in the face of the *pol-lease.*

"You see or hear anything suspicious last night?" Patterson asked for what seemed like the millionth time.

"I heard fucking." The man answered, letting out a series of chucks that sounded like an old lawn mower trying to start.

"You heard what?" The detective clarified.

"That's what I said. Sounds like they was both going at it real good. They dead?" The man said.

"Yes. They are."

"Was it from the sex?" The man flashed another toothless grin.

"No, it wasn't." The detective had had enough. He turned and began to walk away from the two junkies. "Thanks for your time." He called back. *Junkies.*

Patty the coroner was in the room when Patterson arrived. She was late, but better late than never. She examined the two bodies with utmost care. She glanced up from her task for the briefest of seconds, registering the presence of the detective.

"Six dead in two days." Patty mumbled. "What's going on in this town?"

"Six! Late and getting your statistics out of whack. Two strikes Pat."

She glowered at him like a cornered rattlesnake. No sleep for her lately. "The woman and her two kids, these two and the man at the Best Eastern."

Patterson stared at her perplexed. "What man?" He finally managed to ask.

Now it was her turn to look stunned. "They found a body at the Best Eastern Hotel. Man in his forties. Dead on the floor. No one told you?"

Nope, they hadn't told him. *What the hell?* He grabbed his cell phone out of his pocket and dialed a number. "You found a body over at the Best Eastern?" He barked into the phone. "Would have been nice to know." He paused listening to the response. "I've got a cell phone." Another pause. "I'm not always near my car. Next time call the cell!" He pressed the end button with as much force as he could muster. *Cell phones -no way to really slam them down.* It made him miss the old landlines. *You need a good slam from time to time. Helps get the anger out.* At least in his opinion.

Patterson lit a cigar and turned back to Patty. "What happened at the Best Eastern?"

She shrugged. "No clue. Looks like the guy just died. No livor mortis. Just like the woman and her kids and…" She lifted the dead teen girl on to her side. "these two. Very strange."

Patterson started to worry. Six dead bodies in two days. *Six!* That's more than this town has ever experienced even during the crack pandemic in the eighties. Patterson should know, he's a veteran. Just a beat cop at the time, he remembered the crack heads dropping like flies. Great crack jacked the junkies up to a fever pitch and their hearts would explode. Literally blow inside their rib cages. *Boom!* Lights out. They found bodies in alleyways, motel rooms, crack houses and even on top of a roof. Dude was up there getting high when his reservation was canceled. The height probably helped -shorter trip to heaven for his soul, well more like a longer trip to hell.

"I'm betting the three today have no blood just like the others. Something is draining it. You believe in vampires?"

"Very funny."

"I wasn't joking." Patty said.

"Seriously. Any opinion other than Bela Lugosi in a tuxedo?"

"Honestly I don't know. I can venture a guess. Might be some kind of new super virus. Attacks the body internally, somehow drains the blood supply. It's possible." Patty rambled.

Patterson looked horrified. He almost dropped the cigar right out of his lips. His face went pale. Paler even than the bodies in the bed. *New virus? That's just great! Wonder who will come down with it next? Probably the dumbasses, mulling about at each crime scene without proper bio equipment on, like me for instance.*

"A super bug?" The detective asked, his voice trembling.

Patty shrugged. "Maybe. Nothing else can explain all this. Six people dead. No blood. No puncture wounds." Patty looked up and noticed the loss of color on the Detective's face. She changed the subject. "Getting cold out there."

Patterson looked outside, still consumed by the nightmare of a new super bug in town. "Yeah it is." He answered feebly.

"Crazy weather we're having. Seventy degrees one day, twenty the next. And they give me this jacket to walk around in." She pointed at the blue windbreaker she was wearing with the words coroner, stitched in yellow across the back.

"It is December." Patterson replied.

Chapter 15

Havre de Grace is a town of fags. Fuckin' rainbow-colored bridges! That's what it is -a rainbow-colored fuckin' bridge. No doubt about it. Pinks, oranges, pale colors that look like a freakin' rainbow. I don't go for that fag shit. Not in my line of work. Someone finds out I'm smoking the bratwurst and I'm freakin' dead. They don't give you a medal for diversity; they give you a twenty-two to the head. Neat and clean. Dig the hole, get on your knees and boom! And you won't hear the boom. You don't have time. By the time the boom registers with your freakin' ears and the signal goes to your brain -there ain't no freakin' brain to receive it. It's just a hollowed-out pile of mush.

Carlos had his Mustang GT in fifth gear. He was flying down the big hill into town. Route 155. Havre de Grace's ticket in and out. He hated 155. Hated all the cops that obviously have nothing better to do than pull people over and stick 'em with a ticket. He hated the drab scenery. It was the most boring road he had ever seen. But he really, really, really, exponentially loathed that stupid fuckin' rainbow-colored bridge. It was stupidest freaking welcome mat Carlos had ever seen. Welcoming people to *his* town and it was *his* fucking town. He ran it. He was the king. The overlord. Maybe he could get them to paint over that fucking bridge. Or maybe just pay a bunch of skater punks to tag the hell out of it. At least then no one would see the damn thing.

The speed limit was thirty-five but the speedometer in his 2005 race car was pushing well over seventy. *Fuck da pol-lease!* He didn't give a shit about speed limits. He broke the law every day, so what's the big deal with pushing the needle over the limit. He sold drugs, guns, hookers, and everything else in between. Big crimes. Felonies. There were no misdemeanors on his record. Speed was the least of his worries.

He was an entrepreneur. A hustler. Jay-Z in his Marcy project days. Hard knock life baby. You wanted coke, rock or grass -Carlos was your man. But you'd never meet Carlos. Fuck no. He was big time now. He had guys for that small-time shit. Street pushers. Corner slingers. You bought from Carlos' crew. No smack though. It was the only drug he didn't sell. Heroin was out. Too many ODs. Too much bad PR and despite what everyone says - bad PR is still bad PR, especially when it concerns drugs.

What was I supposed to do? Go to college? Be a doctor? Hell muthafuckin' no! He loved the life. He loved the money, the cars, the bitches. But most of all, he loved the action. The thrill of the chase. Closing in on the money like he was rounding third and heading for home. He never forgot his first taste, like a heroin addict's first hit. The way your head snaps back and the rush takes over, climbs up your legs, up your spine and takes your brain to places it's never been. Pure ecstasy. That's what it was like counting his first score. He had been fifteen at the time. He had stumbled upon a kid from the country who grew weed. Good weed. Weed that sent you to the moon without a freakin' rocket. There was just one problem- the country bumpkin didn't know what do with his cash crop. Enter Carlos. He convinced the cannabis-growing hick to sell him the weed for half price. Only fair. The hick would have gotten what? Who knows and who fucking cares. Fact is Carlos was smart. He saw an angle. Something big. He turned around and quadrupled his money. Bases loaded, home run in the ninth inning. He flipped a thousand into four and never looked back, just heard the crack of the bat and the crowd going wild.

Havre de Grace was his. He owned it. Carlos grew up on these streets. He watched the boats coming in; the fishermen unloading the fresh wriggling catch; the train crossing over the old bridge. He loved this town. It was a nice place. Good people. And let's be honest, it was good territory. It wasn't as if Havre de Grace was immune. The town had a dark side since its inception. That dark side, that twisted, yearning for the temptations of the flesh were what the young, 26-year-old Puerto Rican thrived on. He had discovered early on. Every town has their own version of the poor rundown neighborhood; the section out-of-towners are warned to stay away from. This town was no different. Hell, Carlos was raised in that section. His parents were poor; father working hard; mother raising six kids. The house was always in need of repair; landlord was always calling for the rent; refrigerator was always a little to bare. But it was home. Cliché bullshit. Every drug dealer has to have a sad sack story. Funny thing is, Carlos -the youngest of his six siblings- was the only one who went bad. The others: a priest, a doctor, a lawyer, a pharmacist, and a plumber. All went straight. All were successful, and all were embarrassed by their little drug dealing punk of a brother.

His Mustang rounded the curb onto Juanita Street. He was on a high. Not a drug high. He never dipped into his own supply. He was on a life high. He was on his way to make this little cutie he had been messing with for a week. He had been trying desperately to get those cute pink panties she always wore down around her ankles. This one was tough though. Carlos had no trouble getting girls. He was a little on the short side, but with dark tanned skin and a muscular physique. He had what the girls wanted; tattoos of skulls and dragons, artfully decorating his arms. And he was money, like a stack of hundred-dollar bills walking down the street. Gold chains dripped from his neck and a solid gold Rolex, accentuated his wrist. Usually chicks were -easy, take them out to the bar, have his homeboys show him some Michael Corleone respect, drop a couple of hundred on top shelf booze and he would be at their houses, digging them out by midnight. Not Sabrina. She wasn't impressed by the money, or the gangster chic. She was a good Catholic girl. He would have dropped her at date number one if she wasn't so damn sexy. Short brown hair, big doe eyes, lips to die for and the body. Oh my God. The body had more curves than Lombard Street in San Francisco. And she was short. Shorter than him, which he loved. He hated tall girls. You can't screw tall girls in your car, their heads always hit the ceiling. He loved screwing in his Mustang. He had an apartment of course, but there was just something about taking a girl in the car and screwing her brains out. Nothing like the fear of getting caught, it reminded him of his younger days, those teenage summers, trying to find a place to take your girl, slipping away into the shadows, looking over your shoulder. *Man, they're the best orgasms of my life.*

Today was the day. Sabrina was into it. They had been sexting back and forth, her texts getting hornier and hornier as the day progressed and she had finally asked him to come over and pick her up. She promised to wear the pink thong he loved so much. He had seen it popping out of the back of her jeans on their first date and he had never forgotten it. Pink thongs drove him nuts. No clue why, just one of those things. He would probably screw a *dude* if he was wearing a pink thong. *Damn! What the fuck!* That's going a little too far. *Here I go down that gay path again. Damn rainbow-colored bridge!* He would have to deal with that soon.

He pulled up out front of the white manor house. Rich girls and their manor houses. Another thing about Sabrina that was too hot to hold -her daddy was rich. Big construction guy. Mansion in Havre de Grace; mansion in Bethany Beach; mansion in Florida. Carlos had hit the jackpot. *Powerball baby! Powerball!* Daddy probably wouldn't like the fact that his little girl, his only daughter, the star of his universe, was tapping some drug dealing punk. A Latino drug dealing punk at that. But Carlos didn't care. He'd treat Daddy's girl well, like the princess she was -in public that is. Inside the bedroom was a whole different story. Rich girls like *the hold the door, pull out the chair* kind of attitude but get them in the sack and they want to be treated like the whores that they really are. Grabbing hair, gritting teeth, breaking beds -rich girls love that sort of shit.

The sun shined down on her like an angel. It glistened off her hair, highlighting each strand. She looked beautiful. The sun seemed to follow her as if she were a model on the runway as she walked down the curving sidewalk. It was twenty freaking degrees outside and still she wore a skirt. *It must be freezing in that damn thing.* He thought. She was crazy, loco, but he loved the skirt. It was black and short, ending just barely below her gorgeous ass.

He turned off the Nas CD he was playing as she got closer. Not appropriate for this situation. Not at all. Maybe Frankie Vale, Dean Martin or Frank Sinatra. He might be un hermano from the hood, but he was un hermano with class. He knew the songs to play for the ladies. None of that hip-hop shit.

He jumped out, ran over to the passenger door, opened it and flashed her his most charming smile. She kissed him; just a peck; no Frenching in front of the manor, but it was great. The feel of her lips against his gave him an instant woody. She got in. Embarrassed, he shut the door and tried to limp back to his side of the car. *This freaking girl*. He thought, trying to hide his aroused manhood in his jeans. *Wait until I get you home chica.*

They drove around a bit, talking, smiling, laughing, puppy love at its finest. She was twenty-one, on winter break from Frostburg. He loved listening to her voice. It had a sing-song quality to it. It fit her personality perfectly. God doesn't make mistakes. Sure, as hell He hadn't with Sabrina. Must have had all the tools on the table and the manual read and understood to a T.

It was five. A little early for dinner. He'd never been to a restaurant at five. Carlos knew right away why. It was like the geriatrics hour. Old farts ordering the early bird special, giving the waitresses a hard time, sending back their soups twenty times and tipping badly. It was funny. Carlos and Sabrina cracked jokes out loud, not like the old timers could hear them anyway. They couldn't even hear the people sitting at their tables, let alone what the young couple was saying across the room.

"Dessert?" The waitress asked.

Carlos looked at Sabrina. The look was a tell-all, like *all I want for dessert baby is you.* She returned it, flashing those big doe eyes.

"Just the check." He said. The waitress looked a little hurt, as if the dessert might add a few extra bucks to her tip. Nothing to fret over, he'd tip her big anyway. *Everyone's got to score once in a while.* He didn't disappoint. He laid out a hundred and a fifty for an $80 check. Sabrina, of course, was not impressed. She never was. She never saw her daddy lay out a tip like that. *Well that's why the rich people have all the money and us dopes are hustling for every penny.* Carlos thought, a little ashamed by her silent rebuke.

When they got back to the car, Sabrina stopped him from opening the door. She wanted a kiss. They made out like high schoolers in a stairwell. He slid his hand up her skirt. She didn't protest. He felt her ass, her bare ass, with the tiny piece of fabric in between those perfect cheeks. He hoped it was pink.

"You want to go back to my place?" He asked, trembling. *What the fuck? Trembling?* He, Carlos, never trembled when it came to a booty call, but this wasn't a normal booty call.

"More than anything." She sung in his ear.

He would have jumped into the air, hooting like an idiot but he didn't. His hand shook as he opened the door for her to get in. *Oh yeah, I'm gonna get me some.* Carlos smiled to himself. He jumped in and they were off.

That was when he heard it -a police siren. *Damn!* Right behind him and he was so into this hot little number he didn't even notice the muthafuckin' pol-lease. Sabrina was bad for business. He should have been on his game, head on a swivel, looking out for shit like this. He didn't have anything on him. No guns -never guns, this was

Maryland for Christ sakes. No drugs either. He definitely didn't carry drugs. He had had a few drinks. Some red wine but he didn't feel it. Still, it made him nervous. He pulled over to the side of the road.

"No worries baby." He reassured Sabrina. She didn't look nervous. *Maybe daddy owned the cops too.*

The officer stepped out. *Jesus Christ!* It was that punk ass piece of shit Mike. Crooked cops are the worst. He had forgotten Mike's envelope. Careless, rookie-ass mistake. Mike had a shit-eaten grin plastered on his face as he approached the Mustang. He was a tall cop, handsome - *fucking rainbow bridge again-* but he looked like a dick and in Mike's case, looks definitely weren't deceiving.

"Big C." Mike said smirking. "What the fuck Big C? You forget about me? Six dead in two days Big C. Hope it wasn't because of your smack." Mike leaned on the window and looked in. To Carlos' horror, Mike noticed Sabrina. The big dickhead cop licked his lips. "What do we have here Big C? Hi, my name's Mike. What's a pretty little thing like you doing with this cholo?" Mike said, grabbing Carlos' head and rubbing it forcefully.

"Dude, seriously, get the fuck off!" Carlos pushed the cop's hand away. If looks could kill, Carlos' cold dark eyes would have just earned him a conviction for a cop killing.

"Shut the fuck up you little prick! I'm talking to your lady friend." Mike looked back over at Sabrina. "You know these beaners got small dicks?"

Sabrina's eyes narrowed, her look even colder than Carlos'. Her voice was no longer sing-song but ice maiden.

"What's with white cops going racial? Does it come with the job or do they teach you that on the pig farm?"

Mike stared at her for a second. The smile disappeared off his face. "You better teach your bitch some manners." He spat at Carlos.

"Don't call her a bitch." Carlos replied, anger rising in his bloodstream, like lava in a volcano. *Look out Pompeii!*

Mike smacked him hard. Carlos took it, his face barely moving.

"Racial slurs and police brutality. A daily double. Nice." Sabrina said. She reached into her Coach purse and pulled out her cell phone. She was about to go George Holliday on Officer Mike. Another Rodney King film on the way.

"Fuck no you don't *bitch*!" Mike yelled at her, accentuating the word bitch. He walked quickly around the car, grabbed the door handle, yanked it open and pulled Sabrina out. Her skirt rolled up her thighs. She tried to balance the purse with one hand and pull her skirt down with the other. Mike threw her up against the hood. He pulled the purse from her hands and tossed into the gutter. Its contents spilled in dramatic fashion. Carlos opened the door. *Time to go Armageddon on this cocksucker.*

"Get the fuck back in the car!" Mike commanded. Carlos hesitated. "You hear me? Get-the-fuck-back-in-the-car!"

Carlos listened. *What am I supposed to do? Go away for punching a cop?* He would do ten freaking years.

Mike pulled Sabrina's skirt all the way up exposing her bare bottom to the cold wind. The bright fluorescent glow from the street lights bounced off her pale naked skin.

"Get off of me!" She screamed. She looked pleadingly at Carlos, like *you're really going to let this guy do this?* Carlos just stared back -a frustrated, defeated look in his eyes.

Mike started fondling her. "You hiding anything *bitch*?" His hands massaged her breasts, ass cheeks, legs and finally his fingers found their way inside her. She jumped as his fingers entered her. "How about here? Anything here?" He teased as he wedged his fingers deeper.

She screamed. Mike cupped his giant hand on her mouth. He kept at it. *Why the fuck not?* No one was around to hear her, and her dumb punk boyfriend didn't have the stones to do something. Plus, he was enjoying this. *Hell yes!* This was awesome. Nice young slut. A decent power trip. Maybe he would bend her over right here. Maybe stick something else inside her. He looked down at his fly.

Carlos reached inside his pocket, removing the large bankroll he kept there. "Here! Take it!" He yelled thrusting the bills out the window. "Take it! Take it!"

Mike stopped what he was doing. His eyes found the bankroll. The hunger for money took over, like a Weight Watcher's customer looking at the display counter of a bakery. He walked over and grabbed the bills. Sabrina lay on the hood, sobbing uncontrollably.

"Next time, you beaner punk, make sure the envelope is on time." Mike grabbed Carlos' face playfully.

Carlos pulled away seething, his breath entering and leaving his nose like a rhinoceros ready to charge.

Mike got back into his patrol car and sped away. Carlos jumped out and approached Sabrina. She was wounded, physically and mentally. He grabbed her skirt and pulled it back down. At first, she pushed him away but finally she gave in, collapsing into his arms. *Why did I let this happen? I could have done something. But what? It was a cop. The motherfuckin' law. What would I have done? I'm a drug dealer. A street criminal at their mercy and they know it.* He held her, feeling her whimpers and sobs. Each one like a knife in his solar plexus. *Where the hell where all the people? No one was out to see this?* Carlos looked around and that was when he noticed a person in the shadows. Some guy standing there with a cell phone aimed in his direction. The guy had gotten it all. Filmed the whole damn thing. Carlos could barely make out the guy's features in the low light.

"Hey! Give me a hand!" Carlos shouted. The man looked at him and then slowly walked over. Carlos got a better look at him. He recognized him from somewhere...*TV! That's it!* The guy was the weather dude on Channel 9. Carlos had just watched him that morning. Holy shit! And he had a tape of Officer Mike shaking him down and sexually assaulting Sabrina. *Now that's one hell of a storm.*

Chapter 16

The news of the sixth body hit Carter like an artillery round -155 mm, 1,850 feet per second, straight to the gut. Six people dead. *Six!* He couldn't stop thinking about it. It haunted his thoughts day and night. By body number five, he had already finished his entire bottle of Johnny Walker and was halfway through the second. *How the hell had this happened?* That's the question he had asked Dr. Sangmore. The good doc had no answers. Something went wrong. Some minuscule aspect in the gene sequence had fucked up, royally, and now six people were dead. They had to shut it down. The four test sites. Sites number one, two and four were active and people had died. Site three had nothing to report. Good for site three -for now.

He called Gordon, that ancient grump. *Shut it down.* He had said. *Hell no!* Was Gordon's emphatic reply. *There's blood on our hands.* Gordon didn't care. *The bugs can kill, so what?* More panic equals more profits in Gordon's bible. Carter cared. He had worked too hard, lost too much sleep, wasted too many brain cells, drained too much blood. *There's a hundred million at stake.* Gordon had said. *Fuck your hundred million. People are dying. What's a hundred million to a guy that's worth billions?* Gordon had hung up after hearing that. Of course, he had. Easy for that old miser to sit up in his ivory tower why the rest of us -well, in all actuality, not including Carter- reap the whirlwind. Carter had left the *rest of us* behind decades ago, but it still sounded good.

Dio Insecticide was ready. The question remained. *Do we send in the troops? Announce that bed bugs are killing people and try to eradicate them, or do we sit back and let the chips fall where they may?* If they revealed to the world this new species they had created, the world would surely rise up against them. *Grab your pitchforks folks. Time to string up another one percenter.* Then again, if they just sat back, Havre de Grace would be wiped out. All five thousand residents sucked dry. That's a lot of funerals. Plus, the bugs would spread, as they had originally intended them to. They would breed quicker than rabbits on Viagra creating a nationwide pandemic. There might be no chance to stop them. Stop them now, like Hitler at Munich. Do not let mass death break out, cut off the head of the snake before it poisons the well.

And that was where Lenny came in. Lenny Schultz was what most people would call a true-blue royal pain in the ass. The thirty-three-year-old was handsome, with hair parted so perfectly he must have used super glue to hold it in place. Lenny rose through the ranks the hard way. Born on the lower east side of Manhattan, his family, like Carter's, were very poor. It didn't intimidate Lenny. Nothing intimidated Lenny. The scrawny youth ran with a pack of hard chargers in the neighborhood and could brawl with the best of them. They called themselves the 14th Street Boys. *Don't mess with the 14 Boys, or you'd end up in the East River.* The 14th Street Boys ran dice games and peddled marijuana. Lenny was the money man. He was great with numbers. He discovered that he could do complicated equations in his head. No calculator required. Smart as a dolphin with a master's degree. But Lenny was heading for a life of crime. The next Jewish godfather like Myer Lanksy. Then he got busted. *Boom!* The curtain fell, and the show was over.

The 14 Boys had killed a man. It was always a joke with most of them -that you'd end up in the East River. No one in the gang took it seriously. A couple of beatings were one thing. Selling weed, running gambling, that was child's play. Shooting Pierce Bratt was totally different. Three of the older boys shot the unfortunate Pierce at a bar called Lucky's. Freaking Lucky's, sounded like a bar that should have been in Hell's Kitchen, with the whiskey and potato Irish. Lenny hadn't been there. Thankfully -he still bows down to God till this day for that stroke of luck- he had been sitting in his room reading Treasure Island. Robert Stevenson had saved his life. Lenny did get busted with the rest of the gang, but he was quickly released after his mother, his six siblings, three neighbors, and even the Rabbi, vouched that young Lenny was home and not out committing homicides. Even though he didn't spend a single night in jail, the arrest changed him. He decided to go straight. *Sorry, Myer, you lived in a different age.*

Lenny went straight -all the way straight. He studied hard, aced his exams, procured scholarships to Ivy League schools, graduated at the top of his class and landed a plum accounting job at Sentrix. Today, he was dressed in a finely tailored suit with glistening black shoes, sitting in the chair opposite Carter Ritler. Lenny was Carter's bulldog, and with the discovery of the sixth body, Carter *needed* his bulldog.

"Sangmore has no idea what happened?" Lenny asked, his voice as polished as his shoes.

Carter shook his head. His eyes were busy following his fingers as they twirled a pencil. "Someone screwed up." He replied coldly. He glanced up briefly before returning to his pencil.

"These things are bound to happen when you play God. I don't understand why we did this to begin with."

"The ability to create a monopoly."

"It's impossible."

The pencil Carter was twirling snapped in his hand. "Tell that to Gordon!" He exclaimed, his eyes alight with rage. "That old bastard isn't satisfied until every single penny left in the world is in his pocket! Doesn't he realize this will affect the IPO? Is he that stupid?" He didn't expect an answer to his question. The IPO was the real issue and this mess was a major thorn in its ass. The initial public offering of Sentrix would make all of them rich beyond their wildest dreams. Sentrix had been a privately-owned business for almost a hundred years -until now. The company was currently in the process of going public; selling a large majority of their shares on the open market. The reason was simple, strong revenue and considerable assets would translate into market value. Money for expansion. Money for conquest. And money for Carter. His reward for steering the company through the insane and turbulent galaxy of Wall Street would be exuberant. The screw-up in that shitty little town, could jeopardize the whole damn thing.

Lenny looked at his boss impassively. He wasn't hurt by the outburst like most dogs are when their masters scold them. "Gordon is not God. You cannot create a new species, release it on the globe without proper evaluation, then expect it to perform to your specifications. Haven't you ever read Jurassic Park?" Lenny asked.

"It's fiction." Carter said, rubbing his temples, trying to relieve the pressure in his head.

"I am well aware it's fiction, but the lessons are the same. The lessons are very real. We humans cannot play God. It doesn't work out for us like it does for Him." Lenny looked around the room. *When am I ever going to get an office like this?* Floor to ceiling windows with views of downtown Manhattan; an ornately carved desk; bookshelves covering the walls and green carpeting. *Green! The color of money and power. Carter has style.*

Carter conceded the point with a nod. He stood up and walked over to the windows. The sky was an endless blue with small fat clouds bobbing about. *It could all end. The money, the achievements, everything. A hundred-million-dollar bet. Double or nothing. And nothing was bad. Nothing was losing everything plus jail time as a consolation prize. You think Gordon is going to go to jail? Hell no.* He would simply point the slew of alphabet soup down the hall to Carter's office. *There's the man who runs my company!* he'd say, and Carter would be sunk. After all, it was Carter's idea to begin with. He stared out of the window at the small people below. He was one of them once, a century ago. At least it felt like a century. Since then he had conquered the world, staring down at his subjects from his eighty-story castle.

"I want you to contact Tony." Carter told Lenny without moving his eyes from the street below.

"Tony? What the hell do you want with that Neanderthal?"

"Just send for him." Carter barked.

Now Lenny felt wounded. *Send for Tony?* Number one, no one sends for Tony. The man lives by his own rules. He's an animal. A lion roaming the plains of the

Serengeti. A rogue. A man with little past and a major *I'm bigger than you* attitude. *Carter could and should count on me, not Tony. Fuck Tony.*

"I'll make the call." Lenny conceded, with hurt in his voice.

Carter turned. He loved Lenny. The man was truly his only friend. "This thing needs to be settled. I want you to conduct an internal investigation." Carter said, and Lenny got his balls back. A smile stretched across Lenny's face. Carter continued. "Keep it quiet. Talk to Sangmore. Talk to Rudd. I want a plan in place immediately. Confidentiality agreements for all the scientists involved."

"Didn't they sign them already?"

"Get better ones!" Carter barked. "If we don't shut this thing down... If we don't destroy the evidence... this thing could blow up in our faces. Think of the lawsuits. Think of the IPO. Put this to bed Lenny. Gather the information so I can convince Gordon to close this thing down while we still can."

Lenny jumped out of his chair. "Absolutely." He walked swiftly to the door.

"Len."

Lenny stopped in his tracks and wheeled around.

"Send Tony to Havre de Grace. Tell him to meet up with the team already on the ground. He'll run it from that end. He reports directly to you."

Lenny looked even happier. Tony reporting to him, that was awesome and a little scary. It was as if the angel of death was now under his command and that wasn't far from the truth. "I won't fail you." He said. He turned and went through the door, shutting it behind him.

"I know." Carter muttered to the empty office.

Chapter 17

Jamaican blue mountain coffee. The best in the world. Liquid cocaine. *And it was at Royal freaking farms? Yeah right.* No way any gas station anywhere -except for in Jamaica- would serve $40 a pound coffee for $1.50 a cup. It was absurd, but whatever this was it still tasted good. He loved the smell of it when it was poured fresh into his cup. The way it sends hot steam up from the bottom. That steam is the best, it smells so pure, so intoxicating. The problem was: Patterson smelled it way too much. Coffee was like food to him. Something the body just couldn't go without. It came with the job. Long hours translate into way too much caffeine, which in turn translates into the good doctor giving him a nice lecture at the conclusion of every BP check. Cuff on the arm equals: quit smoking, cut back on the coffee and try not to get stressed out. *Try not to get stressed out!* He's a police detective. Stress is certain to come with the job. First question at the application interview -*Can you handle stress?* Sure, he could handle stress. The stress of long hours; running down drug dealers; car chases; and, although it was extremely rare, the occasional dead body. One dead body. Not six. He could imagine what his doctor would say to him now. The BP machine would probably explode. *1,000 over 500!* He should be dead, but he wasn't. Instead, he was drinking more coffee.

He liked his coffee black. It tasted better, especially paired with a cigar. He was not a cream and sugar kind of guy. *What was the point of it anyway?* If you're going to order a coffee-flavored milkshake than get the milkshake. He grabbed a lid and snapped it on…

"I WANT A SLURPEE!" The shout, which was punctuated with wails, emanated from a little boy who pawed at a tall blond woman's jeans not two feet away from where Patterson stood.

Motherfucker! Patterson cursed in his mind as the lid in his hand cracked, the coffee cup tipped and the dark liquid inside dumped onto the counter and the floor.

"A SLURPEE!" The kid continued to wail. Little bulbous tears etched his cheeks.

"I said no." The woman hissed. She looked anxious and embarrassed, her eyes roving around the store.

"I WANT A…"

Patterson had had enough. The coffee continued to drip off the counter. The napkin holder was bare. One of the store clerks -a punk with more earrings in his ears than on display at the local mall- looked over at the burly detective irritated like *I hope you're going to clean that up buddy.*

"If you can't control your kid then get him the hell out of here." Patterson said, enunciating every word with anger and frustration.

The woman stared at him in disbelief. "He's only four." She pleaded. Now she was really embarrassed. The little boy looked terrified. His eyes bulged as he looked up at the detective.

"He needs to learn some respect." Patterson said, glowering.

The woman grabbed the kid's arm and, with tears beginning in her eyes, hustled the young boy out of the store. *Good riddance.* Patterson thought. Thank God, his son was grown up. Then it hit him. Patterson was becoming his father. A mean, miserable old grouch that hated children. *Son of a bitch!* He had never forgotten how his father had treated his own son, Tom. Every time little Tom cried, Patterson's dad would throw up his hands in disgust and complain about the noise. He couldn't let himself stoop that low. He paid for the coffee and hustled outside hoping to find the blond woman and her son in the parking lot. He could calm the boy down. Let him play with the siren in his police car. He felt obligated. His way of relieving some of the guilt. He hadn't had the courage to stand up to his father. Had never told him how he really felt and that fact ate him up inside. No wonder his son Tom hadn't attended the old man's funeral.

"Detective Patterson?" A man's card appeared in Patterson's face. The card -to the Detective's dismay- had the letters CNN written in bold print. "I'm Josh Clark with CNN. Do you have a minute?"

Patterson just stared. At first, he struggled to find the words. "How'd you find me here?" He managed to say.

The man smiled. "Actually, I just got to town. Went to the police station, they said you were out at a crime scene. I came here for a cup of coffee and well…" The reporter looked a little embarrassed. "You kind of fit the bill. I took a shot in the dark and I guess I was right."

"Fit the bill?" The detective asked in the harshest voice he could muster.

"You look like a detective straight out of central casting. Overcoat, investigative glare, plus you've got a gold shield pinned to your lapel." The reporter said snidely.

Patterson's glare made him think twice. "I mean come on. I look like a reporter, don't I?"

Josh Clark did look like a reporter. Horn-rimmed glasses, nerdy, with the neatest beard Patterson had ever seen, like it had been drawn on his face with a permanent marker. CNN is a national news station. That couldn't be good. It was like getting a flat tire in the pouring rain. Muddy, soaked to the bone with no one around to lend a helping hand.

"What can I do for you?" Patterson asked, putting his game face on.

"Six dead bodies in two days. You think it's the heroin epidemic?" The heroin problem in the US had gotten worse in recent years. Everyone from kids to the elderly were dying from opioids and it had hit Maryland particularly hard. Havre de Grace had fared far better than the rest of the state, but the six deaths did beg the question.

"I cannot comment on ongoing investigations." Patterson tried the normal *get the hell out of my face* ploy he used with the local-yokals but this wasn't a local paper kind of reporter. This SOB was persistent. Patterson would have to throw him a bone. *Here Fido, go catch.*

"Off the record detective." Josh persisted.

Patterson stared into the reporter's eyes. This guy wasn't going to give up. "The victims were not intravenous drug users." *Well, maybe one of them.* Patterson thought, his mind's eye focusing on the body of Tracy. "Also, there were no toxins in their systems."

"How about the three found today?"

Patterson shrugged. "The coroner's probably just getting to work on them as we speak. I won't know until tomorrow at the earliest."

"Gut feeling. Do you think the three today may have been ODs?"

You wish they were. Patterson thought but didn't say. Much more interesting story if drugs played a part. National newsworthy story. He could picture the headlines. *SIX DEAD IN SMALL TOWN. DRUGS TO BLAME.* "I don't have the luxury of gut feelings." He answered. "Not with six dead people on gurneys at the morgue."

"What about the reports that there was no blood in the bodies? Any idea why that would be the case?"

Patterson looked around for the microphones. *Where were the cameras?* This guy had to be filming this. He was so good, suave, determined, playing to an audience. But it was just the two of them standing in front of Royal Farms.

"Look kid, I don't have a clue. We're still investigating. I don't want to venture a guess."

"Okay. I understand." Josh pushed the card again into Patterson's face. "I'm staying at the Blue House Bed and Breakfast in town. Anything comes up, give me a call."

Patterson took the card and put it in his pocket. No way he was going to call but best to be polite. A bad story on the national news might hasten his retirement. "Sure thing." He said and walked to his car, finally getting the chance to take the first sip of his coffee which was now cold. *Mutherf-*

CNN was only the beginning. The calm before the storm. The storm hit like a hurricane in the Bahamas when he arrived at police headquarters. The who's who of local power were seated around the long table inside the station's glass conference room. The mayor, the police chief, the fire chief and the town council. All of the town council. Little old ladies in brightly colored overcoats looking like extras for Queen Elizabeth. The mayor -all three hundred pounds of him- sat at the head of the conference table, shifting his large girth from side to side in the uncomfortable chair.

The chief of the fire department and chief of police could have been twins, both had ruddy complexions, thanks to the frigid wind outside. They both had gray hair in full retreat on their scalps. And they both tried to hide their oncoming baldness by combing what remained of their hair forward. They also dressed the same, sporting cardigan sweaters. The scene would have been comical -like the Breakfast Club reunion, fifty years later- if it wasn't so serious. The tension rose like steam from the occupants of the room and hung in the air like a specter, visible for all to see.

Police Chief John Anderson spotted Patterson and walked out of the glass room to meet him. The chief looked stressed out. *Thanksgiving with all the in-laws and you just burned the turkey.*

"Three more?" Anderson asked, in a voice just above a whisper.

"Yes. A middle-aged man in the Best Eastern and two teens in that run-down motel on forty."

The Chief's face drooped down even further if that was possible. Obviously, he had already been aware of the three additional DOAs but hearing Patterson confirm it, really hit home. Last nail in the coffin. Last shovel of dirt thrown into the grave.

"Jesus Christ." Was all the Chief managed to say.

"What the hell's going on in there? Looks like a tea and cake convention." Patterson observed.

Anderson didn't laugh. He didn't even smile. "The governor called. The mayor of Baltimore called. Even Senator Aimes called. Everyone wants to know what's going on."

"I don't have any answers, John. You know as much as I do. It's a mystery." The Detective said. He tried to sound reassuring in front of his old friend and boss but the truth hidden in his words, the dreaded unknown, increased the tension.

"You think its drugs? If its drugs Bill, I want the assholes who are selling this shit! I want them charged with murder!" He exclaimed in a loud whisper. The chief's eyes narrowed dangerously.

"I don't think it's drugs. The M.E. thinks it might be a new virus or something along those lines. The victims had no blood in their bodies."

The horror in Chief Anderson's face made the Detective wish he had chosen his words more carefully.

"A new virus!" He hissed. "What are you saying? She thinks it's a disease killing these people. That's just great! I can't imagine what the old bags in that room will do. They'll pass ordinances barring people from leaving their homes. It'll be a damn police state."

"It's a theory." Patterson said, holding up his hand. "Just a theory. Since when do victims die of blood loss without puncture wounds. I've never seen it. Have you?"

"Hell no!" The chief's voice carried into the conference room. The old ladies and the mayor looked up, alarmed. Chief Anderson changed his face, putting a fake smile on and waving like an idiot. Nothing to see here folks. "Find out what's going on. Give me something. You need men, they're yours. Work around the clock. Just give me answers or half the old bags in that room will die of heart failure."

Patterson looked through the glass panels at the collection of conservative, eighty-year-olds and thought to himself that losing a few of them might not be a bad thing after all. Change things up a bit in this town. Revitalize it. Breath of fresh air. Then he shook it off and walked over to his desk.

Chapter 18

Trash blew in the wind. Yellow McDonald's wrappers, old newspapers, and rattling tin cans made their way from one yard to the other. If you could call them yards. They were very small; some dotted with dilapidated fences; some with sparse grass; most with bare earth. The carcasses of gutted autos looked like lawn ornaments in a surreal setting. Dogs -mostly pit bulls- secured with large metal chains, barked and howled at the Crown Vic as it rumbled down the gravel path. The mobile homes -modular homes in today's lingo- were decrepit structures in need of major tender love and care. The mobile homes were filled with dashed hopes and discarded dreams. The forgotten lived here. Society's outcasts. The worker bees that filled the factories, powered the machines, pushed the shovels of progress.

Patterson glanced around as he drove. He was looking for something or better yet someone. One of the forgotten. A long-standing member of the fraternity. Possibly the longest. The village elder. The one with all the knowledge. The stories of a past long ago. He spotted it. The home was the nicest of them all. A gem in a sea of blackness. It still had a yard, green grass and a small picket fence that was not in disrepair. Patterson pulled the Crown Vic into the driveway. He got out and walked step by step on a makeshift flagstone path to the front door. He knocked. A minute later, the door opened.

The old lady stared at him; her face wrinkled like an old catcher's mitt in need of a good oiling; her hair frizzy and gray; her eyes ancient and wise as if they had seen everything. All of society's good and evil. The eyes of the ages. She spoke in a harsh, gravelly voice that mirrored the neighborhood around her.

"What do ya want?" She barked, joining the choir of pit bulls in their incessant chatter.

Patterson wanted a lot. He wanted a million dollars; a house on the beach; a yacht; more time with his son but what he was here for was something else -answers.

"My name is Detective Bill Patterson with the Havre de Grace police department."

"I knew youse was a cop. I asked what ya want."

"Do you remember this woman? She lived here thirty years ago." Patterson showed the old woman a picture of Tracy. The woman studied it before replying.

"Tracy. I remember her. What she done?" The old lady asked.

"She's dead." Patterson said. The old woman's leathery face remained impassive. Patterson continued. "She has two kids. We can't find any information about the father. Do you know who he was?"

"She was always in trouble. Real loose girl. My grandbaby chased 'er for a while. They used to have sex right there in that ol' pick-up truck." She said, pointing to the truck -or what had once been a truck- disabled across the street, looking like the skeletal remains of an ancient mammal. "Caught 'em in der a bunch times. Wasn't his fault, she was a real looker."

Yeah, he must have tripped and fell right into her. Patterson thought as he turned to look at the truck.

"She got out. Left here. Married some rich guy. He was a doctor or sometin." The old lady paused to think, which looked like it took a ton of effort. "She was lucky. Damn near killed my grandbaby. He thought he was in *love*. Stupid fool. I told him -you can't love no whore. But he ain't listen."

"Do you know where I can find this rich dude she married?"

"Nope. Young guy. Twenty-five or thirty. Never knew his name. Met 'er at the pool hall. He grew up round here. Not in dis neighborhood but in *HaveaGrace* someplace. Met Tracy and she must have put a spell on him. He used to come round with his little sports car and pick 'er up. Little tin can thing. Then they got married, had a couple of kids, before he left 'er."

"Why'd he leave her?"

The woman laughed. It was a sick cackle like the wicked witch from the west if the witch was ninety and a three pack a day chain smoker.

"She was drunk and a whore. Took after 'er ol' man. He was a drunk too. When she got to drinkin' all hell'd break loose. She beat him, beat the kids and screw anything with two legs and a cock. You can take the girl out of the trailer park but..."

"You can't take the trailer park out of the girl." Patterson finished. "You sure he was the father of the two kids?"

The old lady shrugged her shoulders. "I dunno. Never tell with Tracy. Hell, dem kids might have two maybe three fadas, the way she whored around." She started cackling again.

"Thanks a lot." Patterson said and turned to leave.

"What 'appen to da kids?"

Patterson turned back to her. "They're dead."

The old woman cackled some more. "Good riddance. Best not have anythin' left of 'er offspring. Rip out da vine before it chokes da flowers." She kept cackling and shut the door.

Patterson could hear her cackles echoing inside the trailer as he got back into his car and drove away.

Chapter 19

If you are going to stay in Havre de Grace, there is nothing more tranquil, more scenic, more luxurious than the Blue House. Built in 1814, a year after British Admiral George Cockburn invaded the city and burned it to the ground. The house, which is actually white in color, is situated on the banks of the Susquehanna River. Ironically, the name Blue House refers to the color of the water and not to the house itself. The name fits. Fits perfectly like a well-tailored suit. Water, truly, is the house's most valuable asset. The divine views of the Susquehanna can be seen from every window and attract visitors from every corner of the globe to stay in the historic manor.

The estate, and the Blue House is indeed an estate, boasts fifteen acres of colorful gardens and rustic stone walkways. Newly freed slaves once tended the land surrounding the house and designed the landscapes as they are still laid out to this day. The property is wrapped by a wall of rocks two feet high, pulled from the grounds themselves. The boundary wall took 150 years to create and is still an ongoing project.

Several owners have come and gone. Ferdinand Phillipe, the prince of France, built the house but never occupied it. He remained in France until his death in 1842. Ferdinand's estate sold the house to Union Army General John Banks, who would later become a hero in the Civil War. He died in the battle of Gettysburg on July 2, 1863. His widow and her three sons occupied the home until 1916 when the last son died in the master bedroom. The house changed families again in 1919 when it was purchased by business tycoon Morris Till of B&O Railroad fame. Till had nine children. They roamed the vast hallways and played ball games in the green pastures. Unfortunately, the Till family went bankrupt in 1929, thanks in part to Black Friday. Despite his financial ruin, Till never sold the home and occupied it until his death in 1964.

After 1964, abandonment swallowed the Blue House. Ivy covered the white walls. The once well-manicured lawns and gardens became a haven for weeds and out of control shrubbery. The pier sank slowly into the water, like a shipwreck half eaten by the sea. The stone paths were reclaimed by the earth from whence they came. All that remained of the manor was the rock wall, untouched, unworn, but forgotten.

Once in a while, teenagers passing by would sneak onto the property to try and catch a glimpse of the spirits rumored to haunt the house and the grounds. Boaters on the river would pull up alongside what was left of the pier and admire the remnants of the once great treasure of Havre de Grace. And young lovers would hurl stones embedded with their deepest desires hoping to break a window and grant a wish.

The house crumbled for four decades. It seemed all hope of restoring the old manor was lost. Then she came. A savior. A history buff with ample time and plenty of money. Eleanor Smith, a wealthy woman in her early fifties, purchased the property for a steal. A bargain better than when Peter Thiel invested in Facebook. Eleanor Smith and her husband, Judge Julius Smith, dedicated their lives to the house. They cleaned up the grounds; trimmed the ivy; uncovered the stone path; painted the plastered walls; polished the wooden floors and rebuilt the pier. Eleanor spared no expense and only had one universal rule - everything had to be original. They scoured the countryside visiting antique shops, buying the items that were historically accurate. They even cornered the market on eBay and dealt with many a scurvy character on Craigslist to find exactly what they were looking for. The only touch of modernization were the windows. Eleanor was a devote environmentalist. Conservation of energy outweighed the rigid adherence of originality. Not to mention, the old windows were just plain dangerous. Although the original wavy glass windows were appealing to gaze through and gave the home a time capsule feel, the glass could cause serious injury if broken.

After four years and more than $500,000, the house was complete. Upon completion, Judge Julius decided to give up his seat on the bench, take his pension and retire. He was ten years older than his wife and wanted to devote the last years of his existence to running a bed and breakfast. It was a dream the couple mutually shared since the day they realized they couldn't have children. The Judge cooked a mean gourmet breakfast and his wife, despite her wealth, kept a clean house. These ingredients once mixed with the serenity and beauty of their estate proved to be a recipe for a very successful B&B.

Now, the Blue House Bed and Breakfast was celebrating its five-year anniversary. It didn't feel like five years. It felt like a century to the Smiths. It's always said that time flies when you are having fun, but the truth is, time spent well is like a robust red wine, swirled around in a glass and savored to the last drop. And the Smiths knew how to savor every last drop. They thrived on the business. Loved learning about their guests -the histories, the romances and the scandals.

Famous guests popped in from time to time. After all, Havre de Grace was a popular town to shoot movies and television shows in. Stars like Kevin Tracy, Tony Condo and director Patrick Jackson lounged by the indoor pool and sipped espressos on the covered porch overlooking the river. The Hollywood types were cool, but the Smith's favorite guest was Ron Mannity. Both Smiths were avid Democrats and staunch liberals. Thus they totally and completely disagreed with Mannity's politics, but they grew to love his jovialness. Mannity's witty humor won over even Eleanor and the King of Talk Radio returned several times as an honored guest. Mrs. Eleanor commanded the staff to keep Mannity's yearly visits a state secret. If it got out, it could significantly damage her standing in the local progressive movement.

The judge could have cared less about the famous guests. What the judge loved about the house was the solitude. *An empty house was a good house.* He would say from time to time, usually after a long and grueling weekend when the house was packed to the gills with admiring patrons. Which was a condition inflicted upon the house more and more often over the last year. Judge Julius was reaching a chasm in his life. The breaking point. He liked running the B&B, but it was getting old and tiresome. What he really loved was cracking the binding of a good book, smelling the ink of the words on the pages and sitting on the deck digesting the prose. He liked the sound of the water lapping at the sides of the rocks on the shore. It soothed his mind. Even during the cold months of winter, the judge would often be found in his wicker chair out in the fresh, crisp, sea air.

And that was where the judge was, sitting on the deck with an opened book nestled on his lap. But he wasn't reading. Instead, he stared out at the water, his mind deep in thought. It was chilly, but it didn't faze him. They currently had one guest staying at the house. That was it, just one, but one was one too many. Five years of playing the hotel game had chipped away at the judge's stamina. Eroded his soul like one of the rocks on the shore. Constantly battered by the sea until the face appeared worn and tattered. *I've got to tell her.* He thought glumly to himself. Eleanor loved the business. *Would she give it up? Probably not.* He answered. *But maybe...* He felt an unease that wasn't coming from his train of thought. It was an unease he often felt when his wife needed him. He stood, shut the book, and walked inside.

"Enjoying your stay Mr. Clark?" Eleanor's sweet voice asked as the young CNN reporter walked purposefully up to her desk.

"I was. Until this." Josh Clark's tone was aggressive, accusative. He laid out a napkin in front of the gray-haired woman with a shawl draped around her neck. The napkin contained a small bug, no larger than a pencil eraser. It was light brown in color and appeared flat as if it had already been squashed.

She adjusted the reading glasses perched on the end of her nose to get a closer look. "What is that?" Alarm and revulsion in her voice.

Josh rolled his eyes, ever the ivy league asshole. "It's a bed bug." He said matter-of-factly. His stunningly neat beard outlined the smirk that creased his lips.

Just then Judge Julius rounded the corner of the living room and stood side-by-side next to his wife. Julius always appeared when Eleanor was in trouble, as if she had her own personal bat signal, but instead of a bat it was a large gavel that flashed in the troubled sky.

"What is it, sweetheart?" The judge said in his soft, gentle voice.

"Look, I'm not going to report this to anyone. I just want to make you aware. I found this in my bed." Josh said quickly. Nervousness had crept into his stoic demeanor. The judge had a tendency of doing that to people. Despite the judge's skinny, seventy-year-old body and soft voice, his eyes were like little pools of fire. Years of staring into the faces of evil -the murderers, the rapists, the child molesters. Now, he turned that same ferocious glower into the eyes of Josh Clark. And Clark was *feeling* the heat, quite literally.

Eleanor covered her mouth with her hand and shook her head. "We've never had this problem before." She managed to say.

"Well, you do now." Josh was stubborn. He wasn't going to let it go. Despite his fear of the judge, he had a plan and so far and in so many places, it had worked.

"We can offer you another room." The judge replied, although the task of cleaning the room and exterminating the pests, would eat up whatever potential profit from Josh Clark's stay. *No big deal. He was the last.* This unprecedented turn of events had done it. He would put his foot down. *No more. Time to enjoy. Time to relax. No more guests.* The B&B was closed. No vacancies.

"Another room?" Josh asked arrogantly.

The judge examined the young man deeply. His thoughts running a thousand light years a second. *He's a reporter. He could potentially do serious damage to our reputation. It would cost more in the long run. Better clench your fists. White knuckle it.* "Yes. We'll move you to another room and your stay is on us. We apologize for the inconvenience."

Both he and Eleanor had gone through the training offered by their exterminator to handle bed bug problems. How to spot the evidence. How to prep for treatment and most importantly: how to handle a guest who discovers the bugs in their room. Rule number one: never ever under any circumstance, give the room away for free. This is an acknowledgment of guilt and the fact of the matter is that bed bugs are people pests. They travel with people and nine times out of ten are brought into establishments by the very guests who are complaining about them. What the hell though? No matter how much training, nothing can prepare one for real life. The Blue House had never, up until today, had a bedbug sighting. Not even a whisper. This was new territory. Unchartered waters. And they had been blindsided.

"I appreciate that." Josh replied. "I'll throw this out." He folded the napkin back up and before either the judge or Eleanor could protest, walked up the stairs and reentered his tainted room. Sneering broadly, he placed the folded napkin in his suitcase. *Works every time.* He thought to himself. He had gotten the bug from an exterminator friend of his and the little deceased pest had paid for many a hotel stay over the past three months. It was scummy, sure, but who really cares. The price of $250 a night was way scummier in his book. Guilt wasn't an emotion that plagued his conscience. The Smiths can afford it. *Sweet Eleanor* -daughter of oil baron Timothy Kosner, heiress to a $100 million-dollar fortune, married to a well-compensated judge- could afford to put up an amateur reporter such as himself.

The new room that the dead bed bug rewarded Josh was the Blue House's version of a presidential suite. It was the house's master bedroom, which rented for $400 a night, and was decorated with elegant antique furniture. A large bed with a canopy sat in the center of the eight hundred square feet. Original paintings of the American Revolution and the War of 1812 hung on the walls and beautifully hand carved molding trimmed the doors, windows and ceiling. It was truly priceless what skullduggery could afford. Josh could get used to these surroundings. Now, all he needed was a sexy, local hussy to share his oversized bed for the next couple of nights. He would have to go bar crawling to find one. Not tonight though. Tomorrow, after he had worked on the story of the six overdoses. Tonight, he would sleep.

Josh fixed himself a brandy from the complimentary carafe in the downstairs sitting room. The drink was strong. It calmed his nerves, loosened life's tie and unbuttoned stress' shirt. He stood by the large windows in the room and looked out over the dark water. Lights of the boats and barges reflected off the blackness. Red, green, yellow and white. He gulped down the rest of the liquor and undressed. His body slipped beneath the comforter. The sheets were soft and cold; the comforter fluffy; the brandy warm in his belly. Time for sleep. The house was quiet. Still, like death in a deep grave.

The bugs finished with the old woman with half of their hoard still hungry. If the hungry ones could talk, they would have accused the others of gluttony. *How 'bout leaving some for us, you greedy sons of bitches?* They had to find blood. Their numbers were too big now to rely on two elderly people to survive. And survival was key. It was their entire reason for existence. They were survivors. The judge and Eleanor were merely a snack. They would have to find something else. Something larger. Something younger like the fisherman who had wandered too far onto the shore. Great find on their part. The fisherman was a fatted calf. A nice meal that had aided in their reproduction. But half of the females were pregnant again. No condoms in the bug world. The pregnant ones needed blood.

The smell of fresh meat met their nostrils. It was close. So very close. They crawled; their tiny legs carrying them over the polished hardwood. They reached the stairs. The smell was getting stronger. It came down the stairs in waves. Carbon dioxide. The exhalation of their prey. It was so sweet, so tantalizing and, if they weren't mistaken, it was young. Young blood was so much better. So much more satisfying. One of their number, the scout, climbed up onto the wall and, when he had advanced further, the pack of hundreds followed. They appeared as black spots on the white wall, lit only by the light of the moon. At the top, they scurried under the gigantic wooden door only to find another set of stairs. They felt dismayed. Their stomachs ached with hunger. They needed blood now. But the smell, yes, the smell, was so strong now. So incredible. They knew they were close. They scurried up the wall and in a moment were at the top. Their prey, their meal, their survival, lay in bed, snuggled like a babe in its mother's arms, just the way they liked it. They made quick work of him. He was skinny. Not much blood here but enough to satisfy them, enough to aid them in their reproduction, their survival.

Josh Clark never felt the bites. The brandy had sapped his nerves. He died there, alone, in his comfortable bed that his lies had begotten, a victim of his own selfishness and greed.

Chapter 20

Bullets whizzed over his worried brow, zinging like yellow jackets protecting their nest. The smell of fire, sulfur and rot permeated his nostrils. His mouth gulped air mixed with sand, trying desperately to find enough oxygen to survive. Salty sweat mingled with sticky blood, burning his eyes. His body lay face down, motionless, fear paralyzing his limbs. He felt the metal of the rifle in his hands; it was hot; scorching his palms but he dared not let it go.

Suddenly an explosion erupted close-by. The ground shook. He felt the heat of the blast on his face. The shrapnel joined the bullets flying through the air and the enormous wave of sand, kicked up by the blast, buried him. If this was the end, then *why* could he still hear? *Why* were his ears still working? *Why* was he hearing the shouts? They were distant, like hearing water dripping in a cave, but they were there. The shouts got louder, coming closer, until finally they were right on top of him.

"Get the fuck up! Get up!"

He lifted his head, brushing the bloody sand off his face. The man was standing feet away from him. Another earth-shattering explosion erupted. He buried his face again. The shouts were drowned out by the blast. He had to move. He had to get up and *move!* Get away from this area. Get to cover, continue the mission. The shouts were loud.

"Get up! Get up!"

His eyes opened. He looked into the face of the man shouting. It was the Captain. *What was his name?* He couldn't remember. Momentary lapse or had he been hit?

Hank! Captain Hank was shouting, over and over again, attempting to regain control of his team. They shouldn't have come here. It was stupid, a rookie mistake. They had waltzed right into a hornet's nest, behind enemy lines with zero chance of escape. *Why?* The war was over. They had won. Yet they were here. They were here getting the shit kicked out of them.

"Get up! Get…"

The bullet struck Hank in the forehead and he toppled into the sand. Hank's eyes stared into oblivion. There was nothing in those eyes. They were dark and unseeing. The blood pumped steadily from Hank's head wound onto the sand. It mixed, forming a sickening deep-red paste.

Another explosion erupted, and Hank's body was thrown like a rag doll. Footsteps sounded, coming closer. Shuffling in the sand. Boots grinding the granular. *Crunch, crunch, crunch.* A few more steps and they would be able to see him. He fingered the hot metal of the rifle. *Crunch, crunch, crunch.* It was time. Now or never. Do or die. He rose, pointed his weapon and pulled the trigger.

Then he woke up. George's body was covered in sweat. A pool of the salty liquid left an outline on his bed sheets. It looked like the chalked outline at a crime scene. His breathing came in gasps as his lungs tried to catch up. His heart was racing. He sat up and swung his feet over the side of the mattress. The nightmare came to him often. It wasn't a really a nightmare -it was a memory. A memory of horrors he would love to forget. Love to suck out of his conscience and replace with anything else. Even a blank slate, complete darkness would be better.

George rose, walked into his living room, picked up his phone and pressed play. Two Steps from Hell pounded through the house. He loved epic music. It always put him in a good mood to start his day. It made him feel like he was the star of his very own movie. An action film like the Avengers or Man of Steel. It made him forget the memories of the past. The Sonos sound system was top notch. It was wireless, and he had a speaker in almost every room. The house was empty. No wife and no kids. So, George could play his music as loud as his heart desired, which was one of the many benefits of living alone.

He walked into the kitchen, his mind elsewhere, his body moving on autopilot. He placed a handful of beans into the coffee grinder and listened to the metallic whirl of the blades. The smell of freshly ground coffee was exotic, like the smell of ocean on an island in the Caribbean. The newly ground beans went into the gold filter. Only gold, no paper here. He pushed the switch. *Shit! The water!* He flipped the switch off and poured the water into the machine. Cold, filtered water was the key ingredient to making great coffee. It was the only reason he had a Brita. Tap water was good enough to drink, but not good enough for coffee. Coffee deserved the best.

His morning bathroom routine was finished within five minutes and timed perfectly with the last drop of the automatic coffee maker. George stared at his reflection in the mirror. *Still got it. Still one hell of a sexy beast.* He thought. Handsome with gentle eyes and a boyish face with a touch of experienced refinement. Black hair, highlighted with gray, the classic salt and pepper look. He ended his morning reflection *-or narcissistic adulation?-* and stepped into his clothes.

Mug in hand he proceeded to walk out onto his deck. His deck was his greatest and most treasured possession; built by his own hands. He had literally, and figuratively, poured sweat and blood into this work of art. It was cedar, not composite. The boards were laid out in a diamond pattern, culminating in an intricate weave in the center. He stained it every year to maintain the quality and extend the life of his masterpiece. The deck was enormous and boasted enough seats to fit twenty people, although he had never filled more than one. Well, maybe two, there was a few times when his brother stopped by for a coffee and sat out on the deck with him. But two was the max. George had very few friends and, well, his family was *-how to put this nicely?- Insane?* Probably a strong term, but it does fit.

The sun had just caressed the tips of the dew-soaked grass. Breathtaking. Simply breathtaking. Nothing like sipping a great cup of coffee and watching the sunrise. Exactly what he needed to forget the nightmares. They had been coming more frequently as of late.

Breakfast consisted of a bowl of cantaloupe dotted with ripe red strawberries and bloated little blueberries. Freshly cut and purchased from Wegman's, which had the best fruit, all year long. He missed the summer. Missed the warm weather, the girls in their short shorts and miniskirts, but most of all, he missed the fishing. Five a.m. sharp, out on his cabin cruiser, taking in the bay in all of its glory. Catching Rockfish, Perch, and Flounder. A little butter, lemon and granulated garlic, grilled to perfection and enjoyed. He could still taste it. It made his mouth water. Only a few more months of the cold and he'd be back on the water.

The F150s engine was cold. Even in the newest model, it took several minutes to warm up. Those minutes on a twenty-degree December morning felt like an eternity. He hated winter. The cold, who needs it. In the summer, he'd be running right now. Jogging through the neighborhood, scoping the chicks, usually the milfs, out for a few minutes away from their screaming little ones and complaining husbands. They always looked up and checked George out as he jogged past. Even at fifty, he looked good. Kept his body in peak shape. He spent five days a week jogging and weight training. He had passed his twenties in the rear-view mirror but hell, he looked better than he did at twenty.

"Hey bug man." A voice called.

It was Don. Annoying next-door neighbors. They were like winter, who needs them.

"Hey Don." George said, his mouth curled in a genuine smile.

"What's bugging you?" The forty-year-old man with his bulging beer gut protruding from his bathrobe sniggered.

"Very funny Don. Never heard that one before. Better get some new material." George said.

"It's still funny." Don said, waving off George's comment.

George had heard the same remark every day for the last thirty years from literally everyone, especially Don.

"How's Maria?" George asked.

"Great. She's in Cancun. Fun in the sun and all that shit. She's away so I'm gonna play. Wanna join me?"

Maria was Don's extremely good-looking wife. Shocking how a man as obnoxious as Don, and with as many rolls as Don sported, would be able to land a woman like that. And despite his good fortune, Don was a ravenous philanderer with the ugliest women George had ever laid eyes on. Ironic. The guy marries a knockout but gets his rocks off screwing hogs.

"Thanks anyway Don. I'll be working."

"Maybe I should try that sometime." Don ribbed. Don had a plush federal government job with an unjustifiable salary and more time off than a person on disability. In fact, George had rarely seen the man go to work at all. That was the government for you. No wonder the US is trillions of dollars in debt or better yet no wonder the government takes ten years to fix a freaking toilet if they've got people like Don working for them.

George, the hard-working entrepreneur, who, through his excessive income taxes, provided his lazy-baby womanizing neighbor with his exaggerated salary and outrageous benefits package, waved goodbye without another word. He got into his cold truck, rubbed his hands together in a failed attempt to warm them and drove off.

Twenty minutes and several miles later, George pulled into the driveway of a cookie cutter mansion with a well-maintained lawn. There he waited for the kid. Ocean was the newest trainee. Who the hell names their kid Ocean? Yuppy freaking parents with two BMWs in the driveway. Ocean, what will they think of next? When the kid first came in and introduced himself, George was taken aback. Prep school education, straight A's and a lacrosse player's haircut -in that his hair wasn't cut at all. It was long, brown and curly, hanging over his ears as if it were trying to escape his scalp.

"You really want to be an exterminator?" George had asked skeptically.

"Yeah, I do." Ocean had answered him, with a little too much enthusiasm in his voice.

"You know what we do?" George fixed the young man with his most penetrating stare. "We crawl around in shit and kill what lives there."

But the kid didn't blink. He went to work the next day and has been with them ever since. He was a good kid. A little spoiled, a little arrogant, but a decent worker. The type of kid that is almost nonexistent, so rare it was like running into Elvis Presley and having him sign an autograph for you to prove he is still alive.

The front door of the mini-mansion opened, and Ocean ran out. His uniform looked nice and crisp. *Mom must have been up late last night, putting in long hours on the ironing board.* George thought. And as usual, the kid wasn't wearing a jacket.

"It's twenty degrees. You're gonna freeze." George said when the kid got into the passenger side.

"I'm cool and why the hell are you rhyming? Trying out for the DJ Jazzy Jeff competition?"

"Yeah, you're gonna be cool, that's for sure." George answered ignoring the quip but smiling all the same. *Smartass kid.*

The first stop was a Jewish deli on the Westside. New accounts have their challenges, mainly roaches, and disgruntled owners that feel like the increased price they are paying warrants a magic show. It was funny how most people seem to think exterminators are a bunch of Harry Potters. No magic wands here. No spells to perform. Just good old-fashioned knuckle grease with a pinch of luck and a shit load of experience.

Ocean got really excited when he pulled a refrigerator out and discovered fifty roaches, falling all over each other trying to escape. *Not this time fellas.* Death rained down on them, courtesy of Ocean's spray tank. *Goodbye roaches you creepy little bastards.*

"Did you see that?" Ocean exclaimed when they were back in the truck, still excited.

"Great job kid."

"Tell me about it. They didn't know what hit 'em. I bet that takes care of that place."

Probably not but no need to bust the young guy's bubble. George was just as cocky at his age. Comes with the territory. It's the best thing about the job -the ability to help people solve their problems. Restore their reputations. Most restaurants have roaches but now in the internet age, a customer has to see just one and the restaurant is finished. One negative review on google. One picture posted with a caption reading *look who decided to join me for lunch* and you can say adiós to revenue and hola to bankruptcy.

George's cell phone rang. It was an annoying ring. A series of high pitched pings, like a submarine's dive alarm.

"Dude, get a new ringtone." Ocean complained, covering his ears in annoyance.

George didn't recognize the number. Usually it was a customer. He answered. It wasn't a customer. It was Dr. Phil and not the Dr. Phil from TV. This Dr. Phil was a world-renowned entomologist with the University of Maryland. The phone call had come much faster than George would have guessed. Two days in the mail; a day, maybe two, maybe even three to examine. That's how long it would have taken him. Dr. Phil had taken hours. The vile must have arrived the day before, probably in the afternoon and Phil had looked at it right away. Guess Dr. Phil liked what he saw.

"Bed bugs." Dr. Phil said, in an adenoidal tone.

"No, roaches."

"There were also bed bugs in that vile." Phil sounded thrilled.

"Okay. Did the bait kill them too?" George asked tentatively, hoping, wishing, *praying* he had just discovered a new method in the never-ending battle against the bedtime bloodsuckers.

"No. The bait didn't even kill the roaches as it was designed to do. I'm sorry George, I wish I had better news."

The answer floored George and he almost slammed on the brakes. He had spent a lot of money on that new bait, ordering it in bulk from his supplier.

"It's strange. German cockroaches are a natural predator to bed bugs. Not that I am suggesting releasing a

hoard of roaches into a house with a bed bug infestation."
Actually, Dr. Phil would probably like nothing better than
to witness just that, judging by the barely suppressed
excitement in his voice. "But it was the opposite in this
instance. The roaches in the vile were killed and drained by
the bed bugs. Drained is a bad word. The bedbugs ate them.
Sucked them dry like spiders do to flies."

George didn't answer. He was floored. Stunned into
silence.

After a few seconds Dr. Phil continued. "I've never
seen anything like this before. These bed bugs are
different."

"How so?"

"When I magnified them, I noticed the rostrum tip
was bigger. Much bigger than normal."

"Rostrum tip?" George asked perplexed, picturing a
giant bed bug penis in his mind.

"The beak." Phil replied in an obvious *you should
have known that* manner. "The beak is much larger and
sharper. Not to mention their exoskeletons can withstand
extreme damage. The bed bugs in the vile had significant
injuries. Injuries that they should have died from. Injuries
inflicted by the roaches. But the bed bugs didn't die. I've
never in all of my thirty years…"

"The people in that house died under unusual
circumstances. They were found in bed with no blood in
their bodies." George said and there was silence on the
other end of the line.

"No blood?" Phil asked.

"None. A woman and her two kids." George paused. "It couldn't have been the bugs. Could it?"

Silence passed for minutes that seemed like hours. The only sound on the other end of the line was Dr. Phil's nasally breathing.

"Phil?"

"I'm here." He answered, his voice subdued. "I believe we are looking at a whole new species. Bed bugs that can feed on roaches…"

"Do you think they can kill people?" George interrupted.

"Impossible." The answer came to quick, fired from the hip, an instantaneous response. Rehearsed and automatic.

"Why? Because they need a blood meal to reproduce?"

"Yes, but more importantly, they wouldn't be able to drink enough blood to be lethal."

"If this is a new species, if they could…"

"If they can kill, then we're in deep shit." Phil answered.

"How can we find out?" George asked, gripping the phone so hard in his hand it was in danger of breaking.

"The sheets. Check the sheets for blood spots. Also have the coroner check the bodies for microscopic puncture wounds." Phil paused. "I'm running more tests on the samples. I still don't know what killed the bed bugs. I'll find out and I'll get back to you in a few days. If you discover anything worthwhile…"

"You'll be the first to know."

Chapter 21

The darkness inside the closet reminded him of a pitch-black tunnel. Soft yellow light penetrated through the void underneath the door. *The light at the end of the tunnel.* He thought. The camera was in position with the lens secretly protruding out of the air conditioning vent, aimed into the bedroom. Not a sound could be heard throughout the house, not even a… Complete silence, overwhelming silence like the silence before death. The way the world stops, and you can feel your heart beating in your chest. *Thump, thump. Thump, thump.*

The creak of the front door opening and the chime from the alarm system echoed throughout the vastness of the large interior. Footsteps and laughter alerted the man in the closet that two people were climbing the stairs. The mumbled voices entered the room. The jovial flirtatiousness of the conversation could be understood even if the words could not.

The masked man, dressed head to toe in black, stood motionless inside the closet. He was a big man with wide shoulders and muscles the size of boxcars. He had a very serious face with a shaved head and piercing dark eyes. Those piercing eyes were illuminated with terrorizing brilliance by the LED backlight of the small screen held in his hands. To make absolutely sure the screen wouldn't give alert the two people in the bedroom of the mask man's presence, he had turned down the brightness to the lowest setting. He wasn't nervous about being caught. Of course, if the man and woman opened the closet door, they would discover him, but this would only hasten his departure. It wouldn't stop him, just take things up a notch.

The woman was hot; brown hair cut to her shoulders and the body of a porn star with a big rack and a full voluptuous figure. Her male companion was young, probably fifteen years her junior. They struggled in a desperate fight with each other's clothing; playing a dangerous game. Her dress slipped down and landed silently at her feet. Then her hands worked the younger man's belt buckle, opening his pants and pulling his manhood out. She worked the shaft like an expert, getting on her knees and taking it between her lips. The young man moaned, grasping her head with his hands. After a few minutes, he lifted her chin and spoke softly to her. Getting the hint, the woman stood up, pulled down the thong from between her beautiful ass cheeks and slowly slid it to her ankles. She kicked it with an effortless motion. It landed on the floor by the closet door. She pushed the young man onto the bed and mounted him. They humped for several minutes, moaning in unison. Her hands gripped the sheets, the muscles in her legs tightened and she screamed.

Time to move. The masked man in the closet fingered the item in his hand. It was a revolver, stolen from the very house he was hiding in. It had to be just right. He positioned the gun in his hand and turned the knob. The voyeur stepped out into the semi-lit room. His feet moved softly and quickly on the carpet. Before the two love makers knew what was going on, the masked man shoved the revolver into the outstretched hand of the woman, pointed it at her young lover and pulled the trigger. The young man's face showed shock with the suddenness of his life ending. The hole in his chest above his heart showered the woman with blood. Her mind had yet to realize what was happening. The signal from her eyes hadn't yet reached her brain and even if it had, her brain couldn't comprehend the signal it was receiving. The man twisted the woman's arm up and fired a round into her temple. Blood and brains shot out onto the bed and the far wall, creating a sickening abstract collage. She fell sideways off her dead lover. The deed was done. A nice little murder-suicide, exactly what his client had ordered.

The masked man took off the pair of gloves he was wearing, making sure to turn them inside out, and replaced them with a fresh pair from inside his pocket. He grabbed the camera. He would send the tape to the woman's husband. That was what his billionaire client wanted. *Make a tape of the cunt fucking, then kill her.* The man turned the tape off before he committed the murders. The client had wanted the murders on tape as well, but the man wasn't stupid or greedy enough to make that mistake. "Gimme All Your Loving" by ZZ Top flooded into the room. The music shattered the silence. The man reached into his pocket and pulled out his phone. It was a throwaway and only his handler had the number.

"Go." The masked man answered, holding the phone up to his ear.

"Another job." Replied the caller.

"Where?"

"Maryland."

"When?"

"Tonight. I'll have the information for you at the normal place within the hour."

Tony hung up the phone. He stared down at the bodies of the two-naked people lying in front of him. Tony was an independent operator. The handler set up the jobs and had direct contact with the clients. Tony never met the handler. He didn't know what the man looked like and couldn't have picked him out of a crowd even if he were wearing a tee-shirt with Tony's name on it. The arrangement had lasted ten years. Ten very successful years. The handler received ten percent of Tony's contract work which in the last year alone had amounted to $500,000. Not a bad salary, even if it did include the occasional accessory to murder.

Tony picked up the package an hour after leaving the mansion. The manila envelope contained a fake driver's license, bank card, social security card and a single sheet of paper. Typed on the paper was an address and the name of his contact once he arrived on scene. There was a phone number listed under the name and Tony guessed, or at least hoped, it belonged to a throwaway. He went home briefly to pack, then boarded a train destined for Havre de Grace.

Chapter 22

Dingy was the only way to describe it- dark, cold and wet. The walls were painted some unknown shade of blue; the carpet -stained, torn and gray. The ceiling was stucco or better yet some attempt at stucco. The old HVAC produced a clangorous drone instead of heat. Two beds, both of which lacked any support whatsoever, stood parallel taking up the majority of the tiny space. The bed to the left tilted slightly backward as if the numerous clandestine affairs had bent the frame.

If the bedroom was loathsome, then the bathroom could be equated to how African Americans feel when the name Jim Crow is mentioned. The bathroom was small, cramped and had more one-celled organisms growing in it than a microbiology lab. Attempting to use the bathroom was a nightmare. A child couldn't fit on the toilet, let alone a grown man. Even urinating -usually a simple task for a man- was a strenuous activity in these quarters. If you had to go number two, *fuhgeddaboudit*! you'd have a better chance leading the Detroit Lions to a Super Bowl victory.

To his horror, Peter had to go number two. His cheeks were clenching spasmodically; his face was sweating; his eyes swelled; he sat on the edge of the filthy motel bed debating whether he had time to drive to the McDonald's down the street or take his chances in the motel bathroom. McDonald's would very likely have a lengthy line of starving hags out for their morning dose of grease but going in there -his eyes focused on the bathroom door like looking at the entrance to hell- would be, well - hell. The drive is what really scared him. He should have never eaten that last burrito the night before. Beans and very sour cream, were unleashing Hulk and Thor in his intestinal tract. *Can I hold it?* He pondered to himself. He looked back at the bathroom door, swallowed hard, then slowly, carefully, stood up and walked out of the room to his car.

"Where the hell are you going?" Eric shouted from the other bed; his fat body rolling over in the fluid-stained excuse of a bed sheet. The sun from the open door, pierced the darkness of the room.

"Dude, I gotta take a shit." Peter answered, his eyes looking longingly at his car.

"The guy's supposed to be here first thing. Take a shit in the bathroom." Eric rolled back over to face the wall.

"No way. No fucking way! Like you could fit your fat ass on that toilet." Peter didn't wait for a reply. He walked out of the room and shut the door behind him.

Why couldn't Sentrix pay for better lodging? Those cheap bastards. $45 a night! They couldn't afford more than $45 a night?! It's not as if this town has a Waldorf or a Plaza. It's Havre de Grace! The best hotels here rent for what? Hundred and twenty-five bucks! Not freaking five hundred! After all, they were doing an important job. They were introducing the new species on the ground. The toughest go first. That was Pater's way of looking at it. He and Eric were like Navy Seals. Not physically of course; Eric was pushing a belt size that was beyond manufacturing capabilities. But in spirit, Seals were the first ones in and so were he and Eric. Their job was important. The start of a new era.

The deaths scared him. The bugs weren't supposed to kill, just be invincible to every pesticide, except the newborn Dio Insecticide of course. That was the original intent but that had all changed when the bugs started killing people. He had seen it on the news and it had shattered his usual stoic demeanor. Someone had fucked up. Thankfully it was not fat Eric or himself. They were just delivery boys. UPS for insects. Their jobs had been executed perfectly. So, no worries on their end. Well, maybe a few. If the cops found out the bugs were created in a lab, then they would search for the company that had created them and that behemoth would never allow their top tier to be prosecuted. They would blame the little shits that worked for them, especially Eric and himself. *It was them! They were the two guys who spread the bugs around town! Don't look over here. Look at the two bozos in that shitty motel room.* And what could Peter say -*everything.* He would give the cops everything: how the company had chosen the targets like a General looking at Al Qaeda members through the sites of a predator drone; how the company had given himself and Eric specific instructions on how the bugs should be placed throughout the test sites; and most importantly, how the company had acquired fake credentials, making Eric and himself appear as if they were fire marshals. It had been the perfect excuse to sneak into the targeted properties. But it still hadn't been easy. The bed and breakfast and the townhouse proved easier than the motel and hotel, which were a grueling endeavor. They only planted the bugs in one room at each location, however they had to inspect the fire alarms in *every freaking room!* The hotel had seventy and the motel forty. Come on, how would it look if the fire marshals only checked one room? Not good. Not believable at all and certainly memorable to the staff.

Peter made it to his car. His insides burned. Sweat poured off his face. His hand had just gripped the door handle when the *specialist* stopped him. Sentrix had sent word that a *specialist* was on his way to help with the situation on the ground.

"Peter or Eric?" The man asked in a cold, monotone voice. He was a big man, over six feet with a shaved head and deadly eyes.

"Peter." Peter was pissed. He had to shit. Now he had no choice but to shit in the motel room. He reluctantly stuck out his hand to the *specialist*.

"Name's Tony. Where's Eric?" Tony said, looking around the parking lot. He didn't shake Peter's hand, which hung awkwardly in the air for several seconds.

"He's inside." Peter answered, trying with all his might to hold his load. *This guy was a real asshole. Who doesn't shake hands? Even Howey Mandell does a fist pump if he doesn't want to shake hands but don't leave a dude hanging, that's just fucked up.*

Tony walked towards the door of the room. He didn't open it but just stood to one side, waiting for Peter to open the door. Peter did and motioned with his hand, sarcastically ushering Tony inside. *After you, you pretentious prick. Having people open the door for you. What an asshole!* Peter thought.

Eric stirred under the sheets, his bare chest displaying more rolls than a bakery counter at the crack of dawn. Tony sat his small and only bag on the ground. He looked around, his eyes coming to rest on the gigantic form under the sheets.

"Dude! Get the fuck up! Tony's here!" Peter yelled at Eric. To make his point even more clear, he aimed a swift kick at the fat man's backside; regretting the move instantly, as the crap he was holding gave a roar like a lion trapped in a cage. Lion, hell, like T-rex trapped in a cage.

"Yeah. Yeah." Eric groaned, getting to his feet. He was naked except for a very small pair of whitey-tightys, which were wedged deep into the crack of his ass. The sight was truly horrifying, even worse than the small bathroom Peter was dreading. Eric stretched, scratched his fat belly, adjusted his wedgie, then stuck out his hand to Tony. Peter didn't blame Tony this time for failing to shake the Eric's fat hand.

"Where's the bathroom?" Tony asked the one question Peter didn't want to answer.

Peter looked longingly now at the disgusting bathroom, then pointed as if it was the hardest thing he had ever done in his life. Tony disappeared for -at least what ass clenched Peter thought- an eternity. He returned, zipping up his fly. He stood in the exact same spot he had just vacated, as if it had been marked in invisible ink, facing the underwear-clad Eric and the hobbling from foot to foot Peter.

"What's the game plan?" Peter asked, his face contorted with anguish as his stomach let out another rumble. *T-Rex was coming! Must talk faster! Must talk faster!*

Tony looked at the two men, pausing for a few seconds on each of the men's faces, then he said: "Kill both of you. Contain the situation on the ground. Thwart any attempts by law enforcement." His voice was barely audible in the quiet room.

Peter stared at Tony, then he laughed. Eric joined the laughter and eventually, Tony even cracked a sly smile. "Dude, you know, you're a real asshole!" Peter bellowed.

Suddenly, Tony pulled a suppressed .22 pistol from under his sports coat. He put two shots into each of the men's heads; so quickly and so precisely, that even if someone was watching, they would have never seen the gun go up or come back down. Eric fell, his body causing a mini earthquake as it landed on the shitty motel floor. Peter toppled backward onto the bed and finally, in death, his bowels got some relief.

Chapter 23

Throughout his life, he'd heard the statement a thousand times: *your parents are white, but you're black.* Yes, he knew he was black and yes, he knew his parents were white. For a society that supposedly had moved beyond race, beyond color, beyond creed, it continued to identify people based on all three. And the people who shouted from the mountaintop that they weren't racist, were the absolute worst. They always made the statement as if it shocked their elitist code to see a white couple with a black son.

The answer wasn't complicated. It wasn't a scientific marvel or a supernatural event, it was quite simple -James had been adopted. He never knew his real parents. He'd heard rumors but none of them could be substantiated and he really didn't care. The truth, the real truth and nothing but the truth, was that Harry Roseland *was* his dad and Beth Roseland *was* his mom and that was it. *I'll take Plain and Simple for three hundred, Alex. And the answer is...*

James' real mother abandoned him when he was an infant. Left him right on the doorstep of St. Anthony's church in Baltimore. The pastor of the church, Father Lewis, took the baby in and contacted the authorities. A state-run maternity ward was the only option but that wasn't an option Father Lewis was willing to accept. Instead he called a young couple in his congregation who had tried, unsuccessfully, at conceiving a child of their own. That couple, the Roselands, were more than thrilled at the chance of adopting the little baby boy. To the Roselands, James was their child, he was their miracle.

Harry Roseland spent the better part of his life as a journalist at a small TV news station, Channel 9, in Havre de Grace. He was an amazing father to young James. He attended all the games, coached the teams, went on the boy scout camping trips and paid the private school tuitions. The only thing Harry lacked was emotions. Well, he had the anger and frustration down pat. But for the nurturing, encouraging side of parenting, Beth, Harry's wife, was a champ. She provided the shoulder to cry on, the arms to hug and the congratulatory pat on the back. James held a special place in his heart for his mom. He was a true-blue momma's boy.

Together the Roselands steered their son to incredible heights. James had been a golf star in high school, which earned him a full ride to Duke. He received a bachelor's degree in Meteorology and certifications from both the American Meteorology Association and the National Weather Association. When he returned to Havre de Grace as an esteemed college graduate, he was hired post haste by Channel 9 news. The news station had, at the time, experienced a change in leadership and the toughest producer ever to run the station -James' father Harry- had reluctantly taken the job as chief executive. He also *reluctantly* hired his son. At least he acted reluctant. He had to, otherwise the other employees and new hires might accuse him of favoritism. Inwardly though, the old Harry was smiling ear to ear at the conclusion of his son's interview, after all he had done a very good job as a father. James was a genius and he would prove to be the most capable weatherman in the country, if not the world.

It had been six years since the start of his employment at Channel 9. And what a crazy six years it was: a hurricane, two blizzards, fierce thunderstorms, a small tornado and now an ice storm. The smorgasbord of weather systems covered almost the entire curriculum of his degree. And James had predicted all of them. Everyone was impressed by his abilities. He appeared several times as a guest on the Weather Channel and on national news stations like CNN, MSNBC and Fox and had even been offered a world-class position at ABC. He had always dreamed of working at a mega-channel with millions of viewers and commanding a multiple six-figure salary, but he turned the offer down cold. He loved Channel 9; loved working for his Dad; loved the local town *everyone knows everybody's name* feel of Havre de Grace and he especially loved Kelly Halle.

Kelly, Kelly, Kelly. He adored her. Her vivid blue eyes; her heavenly lips; her golden blond hair; her inquisitive intellect; coexisting together inside of a masterful portrait that Da Vinci himself couldn't have imagined. James had tripped all over himself, literally, the first day he had seen her. It was three years ago, and Kelly was walking out of Harry's office after getting the job. She had a grin on her face that would have turned the coldest place on earth into a Caribbean beach. James was making his way back to his desk from the coffee machine when he caught sight of her and he ran head first into the water fountain. The big, five-gallon container positioned upside down on the fountain, toppled over and dumped its contents all over James and the floor. The women in the office screamed; the men howled with laughter; and Harry shouted with fury; but the only thing James heard was the cute little giggle from the beautiful girl that had caused the whole mess in the first place. That little giggle made all the difference in the world. It was if they were all alone, staring into each other's faces. It was their moment. Their time in history that forever endeared them to each other.

Three years and three boyfriends went by in the blink of an eye and still, James didn't make a move. Kelly changed romantic attachments annually as if she were changing apartments. New year, new lease. Each new romance was torment for James. He was forced to listen to her very detailed accounts of each perfect night and each raucous fight. The fights he loved but the perfect nights made him want to gouge his eyes out. *And he brought me flowers. Flowers! On our second date. Do you know where he took me? You won't believe it...* Actually, he would believe it and *yes, if a guy wants to get those skin-tight pants off your sexy ass, he will bring you flowers on the second date!* Kelly never even noticed James when she was single for the brief hiatus between squeezes. James was just a friend. Nothing more.

Now, James found himself in a very uncomfortable and interesting position: he had something on Kelly's new squeeze. *You've got to meet him. Mike's great. He's such a gentleman. No, Kelly, Mike's a dick. And not a big dick, no, no, he's a small, tiny dick with two little mini balls.* Not just for the fact that he was dating the girl of his dreams. No, Mike was a dick because he was a dick. James had thought that from the moment he met the cop. His unfavorable views of the man took a very steep spiral downward, as he watched in horror as Officer Mike molested that young girl Sabrina. It was horrifying, disgusting, repulsive and somehow, although he hated himself for saying it, satisfying. Not sexually. Nothing like that. Satisfying in the sense that he finally could ride in on his white horse, cell phone video in hand and sweep Kelly off her feet. He was fantasying about it while standing inside Carlos' apartment.

"It won't make no fuckin' difference." Carlos said. "If she doesn't like you bro then she ain't goin' to like you even if you show her dat tape. Shoot the messenger and all dat shit."

Fuck the messenger -he was a knight. "Mike's crooked. He deserves to be arrested, tried and convicted. Send him to the shit hole he would send you to in the blink of an eye." James said. He looked around Carlos' apartment. It was nice. Big for an apartment and well decorated. The drug dealer had style. It was a typical bachelor's pad: large leather sofa, enormous flat screen TV and framed posters of scenes from gangster movies like Godfather and Goodfellas. No Scarface though, which struck James as odd. Not that James was a racist but wasn't Tony Montana a Latino drug dealing kingpin? Two of Carlos' gang sat playing Call of Duty on the big flat screen. It was like a scene right out of Training Day. The two guys were the spitting images of Raymond Cruz and Noel Gugliemi, when they were sitting in that shitty apartment getting ready to put a shotgun barrel to Ethan Hawke's face. James had a fleeting image of himself being dragged into the bathroom; Carlos and his two boys putting a round or two in him while he was lying in the tub. Not a pretty picture. He shook his head and dismissed it.

"Yeah, he's crooked but so am I. I'm a fucking drug dealer Jimmy!" Carlos' had just met James the day before but somehow the little punk felt he had the right to call him Jimmy. "What's my word against his? They'd lock me up and throw away the key hermano."

"How's Sabrina?" James had helped Carlos bring Sabrina home after the incident. She hadn't been doing so well which wasn't surprising judging by the fact that she had been violated by the very public entity that civilians are supposed to trust, to call on for help when they need it. The entity that was supposed to protect them from molesters, not do the molesting.

"She's fucked up." Carlos answered. "I went over there this morning. Her mom says she won't leave her room. She should have stayed in the car, kept her fucking mouth shut. I told her. Don't get out. Shut the fuck up. Don't talk shit to the fuckin' pol-lease."

Really? Was this asshole really blaming an innocent bystander for the actions of a crooked cop? This made James even more pissed off. He shouldn't have come but Carlos begged him, said he had to talk to him before James went public with the tape.

"Did she tell her parents what happened?" James asked.

"What the fuck? What do you think? They'd be all over the HDG police like flies on shit. Fuck no. She didn't say shit. I warned her. She ain't stupid. You don't fuck wit da pol-lease. You know what I mean?"

James did not know what Carlos meant. Officer Mike was wrong. Dead wrong, like a drunk driver plowing into a carload of kids. *You do not take money from scumbag drug dealers -no offense Carlos- and you do not fucking molest women. Is this what society has come to? People afraid to take on the cops? We're talking about a crooked cop here not St. Francis of Assisi. Give me a fucking break.*

Carlos continued. "Yeah they'd lock Mike up. But his buddies would never forget. They'd get us. Probably shoot my ass." James shook his head. "Fuckin' A they would. Do me like they did Mike Brown or Freddie Gray. They cap me in a second holmes. Cops always stick together. They're like, umm, corn on the cobb."

"What?" James replied, looking at the drug dealer awkwardly.

"You know, all the corn sticks on the cobb." Carlos replied, like *duh, everybody knows that.*

"No, I don't know. That's the stupidest fucking thing I've ever heard."

"I've got to agree with the homey bro." One of the game playing gang bangers chimed in. "Stick together like glue or sumpin like dat. Fuck corn on the cob." Both gangbangers slapped hands and burst into laughter.

"Shut the fuck up!" Carlos exploded on the two men, who continued to laugh despite their boss' displeasure. "Look hermano, forget corn on the cobb." James nodded even though that remark would be extremely hard to overlook. "Don't show anyone dat tape. Do yourself a favor. Fuck it, do me a favor. Do Sabrina a favor. Delete the fucking tape."

James wasn't afraid of this punk. Funny as it was, he was actually starting to like him. The drug dealer had an award-winning, grade A personality. He was a professional salesman, well, funny enough, he actually was a professional salesman; maybe not in the legal sense of the word. James looked at his watch, then began to walk towards the door.

"I'll think about it." James said. He pumped Carlos' fist, before exiting the man's apartment. He had to hurry. He was supposed to be on the air in thirty minutes.

He really *did* think about it. The whole way to the office he thought about it. All twelve blocks he ping-ponged it around in his mind. He could care less about Carlos. He liked him but not enough to give a rat's furry ass if the punk went to jail or not. Carlos *was* a drug dealer. A peddler of evil wares that had undoubtedly brought about the end to many lives. He *did* care about Sabrina but more importantly -he cared about justice. *Yeah right! Be honest with yourself. It's about Kelly. And justice. Keep telling yourself that. Sounds a lot more noble.*

Channel 9 looked like Grand Central Station before a holiday: people bustling hither and tither; printers and fax machines whirring; keyboards being punched; and paper flying through the air like airplanes in a middle school classroom. The news was hot. Six dead bodies in two days. That was colossal for this town. JFK assassination big. A little morbid, maybe, but hell the media feeds on morbid like a mortician does. It's their bread and butter. It's what sells. No one watches the news if everyday life is Leave it to fucking beaver. No way. People want American Psycho. Rich guy with chainsaw.

James navigated his way through the crowd like an icebreaker through a glacier, slowly, carefully, but plowing steadily ahead. He reached his desk and grabbed his stack of notes before continuing on to the green room. The green room -which wasn't green- was a dressing room. It was where the magic happens. The transformation from *good enough to walk around in public* to *good enough to be seen on TV.* Ethel had worked the green room since the days TV meant an enormous box like contraption with tubes in the back. Ethel had to be older than ninety, at least that was what James guessed. He never actually thought of asking her. No way he was going to take that chance. He was terrified of the old woman with her swept-back white hair, wrinkled face and reading glasses. She looked like a sweet librarian, but she wasn't. Rumor had it that her first husband *volunteered* to go fight the Japanese during WW2, rather than deal with her. Rumor also had it that her second and third husband ran from her like hippy's do when faced with a barber's sheers. Ethel terrified everyone that was unfortunate enough to cross her path.

The old woman forced James into a chair and applied the necessary make-up to his face. A little here, a lot over there and *voila* -picture perfect. Ethel finished with him and moved on to her next victim. A second later and James was in front of a green screen. Green rooms, green screens, that was show business. The green screen was where the digital map would be superimposed. Several cameras aimed in his direction and a teleprompter screen sat awaiting the script. Everything was ready. Time to scare the hell out of this small town. Time to end all the holiday cheer. His palms were sweaty; his hands shook; he was as nervous as whore facing the preacher or an actor facing Ethel. And it wasn't because he was on TV. He was nervous because of the report he was about to give. He could visualize the paranoia, the panic, the fear. The long lines and empty shelves at every grocery store, convenience store and gas station from here to the Mississippi.

James could hear the voice of Hank Turner, Channel Nine's heavy set, red-faced anchor, coming from the small bud stuck in his ear. Hank introduced James.

"And now we go to our wonder of meteorologist, our lord of the skies, our crystal ball -James Roseland." Hank said in his jovial manner.

"Three, two, one and we're live." A phantom voice said from behind the cameras.

"Thank you, Hank. Good morning ladies and gentlemen. We are looking at cold temperatures for the foreseeable future." A display of Fahrenheit readings popped up on the prompter, while a more detailed and prettier display was seen by the viewers at home on their TV screens. There was also an audible sigh of sadness, an annoying sound effect if there ever was one, that erupted from a speaker. "High of twenty-eight today with a low of eleven overnight." James clicked a remote control gripped in his hand. A storm warning advisory painted in big bold, red letters appeared on the screen. "And the bad news is: there's an ice storm brewing in the Atlantic. It's very likely that this storm will produce severe winter weather conditions. The storm is due to hit on Friday and will likely stay in the area until early Sunday morning. Please beware that this is a very dangerous storm. Prepare to be stuck inside for two to three days. The storm will drop six to twelve inches of ice making streets and sidewalks impassable." Several screenshots of streets, sidewalks, cars and houses covered in the mystical glow of ice appeared on the viewers' TV screens. "The good news is…" As if there were any after James' end of the world announcement. "Is that the storm will be gone, and temperatures will rise slightly in time for Christmas. Sorry to say but there will not be a white Christmas this year folks. We'll be watching this storm closely and we'll keep you up to date as it progresses. Stay with Channel 9 news and stay safe Havre de Grace. Back to you Hank." *After this storm passes no one will be dreaming of a white Christmas. We'll all wish we were in Florida.*

It was over. A week of research; days of anxiety; twenty minutes of make-up; and it was over like a match in a tornado. Sixty seconds. *Sixty freaking seconds* that would transform this sleepy little town into Times Square on New Year's Eve.

He walked out of the studio and almost ran right into Kelly Halle. She looked great: a smart business suit that was painted on and an even smarter expression on her face. She smiled.

"You did great." She said.

He stared at her for several seconds. He didn't feel great. His delivery was terrible. It felt rehearsed and robotic. He fumbled with the phone in his pocket. He thought about just pulling it out and showing her. *Here's your beloved, cock sucker of a boyfriend, sexually assaulting a woman.* But he didn't.

"Thanks." He managed to say.

"What's wrong with you? Worried about your performance?" She asked, and she really did have a concerned look on her face as if she could sense something was off.

He thought about it. The words wouldn't come. They were there all right; swimming in the pool of his mind but they wouldn't surface. *Damn those beautiful eyes.* He looked away and answered. "No. Just the storm."

"That bad?"

Umm, yeah, it's going to be that bad. Hurricane Andrea on steroids, which in a town surrounded by water, was saying an awful lot. "I think it is. Much worse than we've ever seen. How have you been? How's the investigation going?" James wanted to change the subject, talking about her investigation just might do the trick.

"Nothing to report. Six dead bodies in two days and the cops don't know shit. They keep beating around the bush. The autopsy showed the victims died of blood loss. Massive blood loss. Like *all* their blood. Yet there were no wounds." Kelly looked at the floor as if the tiles might hold the answer to her burgeoning questions.

"That's freaking weird. What are we looking at? Vampires? Count Dracula back from the crypt?" James said, trying to be funny. Kelly tried but failed to suppress the smile that creased her mouth. James continued. "I mean that's pretty messed up." *Messed up! That's the best you can do?* James scolded himself. She had a way of doing that to him. When she was around, his brain had a flatulence attack like contestants at a bean eating contest.

"Yeah it is. I'm still grinding away though. What are you doing later? Mike and I are going out for drinks at Pierce's. You want to join us?"

Join you? You and Mike? You and Officer Molestation? Yeah right. He thought but he said something totally different. Something that shocked him. Something he couldn't pull back like a bullet leaving a gun. "Yeah. What time?" James replied.

Meanwhile, across the small expanse of Havre de Grace, Carlos was deep in thought. He had just finished watching James on Channel 9. Carlos was thinking about his own backside. Saving his own skin. CYA, cover your ass. If Officer Mike got nailed -thanks to the tape- it would mean the end of Carlos. The treacherous cop would turn states evidence like a king fucking rat. No doubt about it. But what could Mike tell them? Everything. Mike had everything. The drugs, the money, and there was that other thing. The thing that could land Carlos inside for a hundred years. Life without parole and Mike knew all about it. Because Officer Mike was actually a good cop. Not good in the sense of moral fortitude, good in the sense of natural investigative talent. Officer Mike was a human fucking bloodhound. He had solved that little piece of work Carlos had performed a few years back and he had approached Carlos with the deal of a lifetime: $3,000 a month or Officer Mike would reveal all and send Carlos to the hole for an eternity. What choice did Carlos have? He had made the deal. *Howie, I will walk away with the hundred grand. No sense in staying for the million which I'm bound to lose.*

Now everything was about to explode. Stick of dynamite with the fuse lit. Boom! Officer Mike would definitely trade up and what better than a dirty cop who can pin a murder on a drug-dealing gang leader. *Give 'em life folks.* Thankfully there was no death penalty in Maryland. Mike would do a few years, if any, and Carlos, Carlos would be black Melvin's pin cushion for the next hundred. *No thank you.* Carlos did the only thing he could do, he picked up the phone and made the call. *Sorry James, there's no loyalty amongst thieves.*

Chapter 24

George couldn't stop thinking about what Dr. Phil had told him: *new species of bed bugs, potentially lethal.* It was crazy. Insane asylum run by the insane. Absolutely nuts. After talking to Phil, George had tried to call Detective Patterson. He didn't have the cop's cell number, but Havre de Grace was a small town with an even smaller police force. *What kind of business card doesn't have a cell number? Especially today.* He thought as he dialed the HDG police mainline. He got the Detective's voicemail at his desk and left him a message. The gruff Sergeant who transferred him assured George that the Detective checks his messages at least once a month, so he probably wouldn't be getting back to George anytime soon. Well, fine, he'd just drop by. His last stop was in town anyway.

He couldn't concentrate on the task at hand. He tried talking to Ocean about it, but the young man was more interested in the text messages flying between himself and his girlfriend-flavor of the week, to be any kind of assistance. It felt good talking out loud anyway. Cleared his mind like a spray of window cleaner on a muddy windshield. Squeaky clean and ready for more dead bugs, bird shit and a little road grime threw in for good measure.

"Sir, the tiles of the bathroom floor need to be re-grouted." George told the irate owner of Mickey's Bar and Grill in downtown Baltimore. The problem with commercial contracts was the free emergency calls. Some people -like this old red-faced bastard- just love taking advantage of that particular clause. Mickey, owner of Mickey's -big surprise there- took the free emergency calls to the next level. The guy called at least twice a week with the stupidest complaints George had ever heard. *Yes sir, one ant is too many. Yes sir, we can make sure spiders won't bug customers on the patio. Yes sir, flies are not normal around your disgusting dumpster.* But it wasn't just Mickey's dumpster that was disgusting, it was Mickey's in its entirety. The place was a dive: old wooden floor that had been soaking up beer, piss and blood for over a century; tiles that looked like they had been laid by George Washington himself; and a bathroom that could be in a museum -like here is a prime example of what bathrooms looked like before indoor plumbing was invented.

"They're bugs! Just kill the damn bugs! Spray something!" Mickey, red-faced as usual, yelled at George; spittle flying from his oversized grotesque mouth.

"Fruit flies breed in rotting organic matter. They-are-a-sanitation-issue." George reiterated, accentuating every word, speaking slowly as if he were trying to relay a message to an extraterrestrial who had just landed from planet shithole. "They're breeding in urine trapped under the tiles of the bathroom floor." That was the sick part. The flies -that were so numerous you couldn't open your mouth without one using it as a nest- bred in piss. A fact that made you want to hurl when one of the little shits landed on your face.

"They're bugs!" Mickey spluttered. "Kill the damn bugs!"

Clean your fucking place! George thought. "I can spray but it won't be effective. Please understand what I'm saying to you." *You fucking idiot!* "The floor needs to be cleaned thoroughly and re-grouted." Mickey dismissed George with a wave of his hand and stormed off. George sprayed, not that it would help. Fruit flies breed faster than jackrabbits on Viagra. The pesticide couldn't penetrate the two hundred years of urine trapped under the asshole's floor. He made sure to put that in the report, not in those exact words but close enough. Mickey signed the report and grudgingly allowed them to leave.

Ocean looked sick. One of the fruit flies had floated right into his gaping mouth. The young man had coughed and gagged before running out to the truck and chugging more Listerine than is recommended on an annual basis. The kid's face was still ghostly pale.

"You alright?" George asked when the two were back in the truck on their way to Havre de Grace.

"I guess." Ocean moaned. "Did you see that fly?"

"Yep." George answered. He didn't want to hear a recap of the story. He had been an eyewitness.

"Gross. Fucking gross."

"Now you know how a frog feels." George joked but instantly regretted the jibe as Ocean's face turned even whiter. "If you're going to puke, do it out the window."

"I'm okay." Ocean replied, trying to control his gag reflex.

They rode the rest of the trip in silence, George thinking of the words of Dr. Phil and Ocean trying not to think at all. The kid went back to his phone. *The way these kids can type.* George thought, looking over at Ocean's fingers flying effortlessly over the keyboard in a rhythmic dance better than any Broadway show. It took George, what, fifteen minutes to type a sentence. This kid was writing more words than the Lord of the Rings trilogy in the same amount of time. Technology is the bane of the old.

They arrived in old town Havre de Grace around two in the afternoon. The town was a madhouse. A zoo where the animals had just escaped. Godzilla meets Tokyo. The news of the storm had obviously reached every ear. George had heard the weather forecast. It didn't worry him in the slightest. In fact, it pissed him off. Ice storms would mean work would have to be canceled. No sense in sending the trucks out, have them crash and his technicians sue the company for endangering them. No trucks on the road equal no revenue. He still had to pay salaries though. Salaries, mortgages, insurances. They wouldn't stop because of ice. They wouldn't stop for anything. He just hoped the weathermen were dead wrong on this one. *Let it pass. By God, please, let it pass.*

The last job of the day proved to be the most difficult. Bed bugs had been the savior of the pest control industry over the last decade. After fifty years of near extinction in North America, their sudden reappearance boosted growth in the market to an unprecedented height. At first it was an almost impossible task to eliminate the blood suckers. Without the old warhorses like DDT in their arsenal, pest companies were at a serious disadvantage. They tried everything. Every chemical that was labeled for use indoors. Nothing seemed to work. Then along came Temprid. The ultimate bed bug killing solution. A one hit wonder. Spray a house once and the bed bugs were gone forever.

Ocean grabbed the bottle of Temprid from the back of the truck. They entered the house with their masks on, resembling Bane, the archrival of Batman. The house they were treating was a haphazard structure, created out of the left-over materials. *A little bit of this, a little bit of that and you've got a house.* Even the stilts the house sat on, looked like discarded scrap. The one and only asset that made the structure a desirable property was the water. You could have a tent on waterfront property in Havre de Grace and it would cost an arm and a leg and maybe at least one testicle, to purchase.

George -the boat owning, water-loving, fish of a man- loved the house, even with its flawed appearance. He looked out at the frigid water and pictured his boat moored to the long pier, beckoning him to come and sail away. Well, maybe one day. Retirement dream.

Ocean lifted one of the box springs off its frame and leaned it against the wall. There they were. Little bastards, hiding inconspicuously under the stapled folds of the fabric. Their tan, reddish tick shaped bodies scurried as the smell of death reached their nostrils. *No food here boys and girls, just MOAC.* That was their nickname for Temprid - MOAC, *mother of all chemicals* like the well-known MOAB, mother of all bombs.

The kid was good. George thought as he observed Ocean tear apart the room. He smiled like a proud dad. He had taught the kid everything. George had never had kids, not that he hadn't wanted them, just that running your own business is a twenty-four-hour job. No time to meet someone; court her; marry her; impregnate her; deal with nine months of doctors' visits; late-night runs to Taco Bell; and eventually the hours of sitting in a small hospital room; waiting for the head, the chest, the legs and congratulations you're a dad. Truth is: running his business was the excuse he told people when they asked the inevitable question:

Why haven't you settled down? The real reason was himself. Well, not himself -his old job. The world of special operations and the nightmares that went along with it. The PTSD. That was what scared him and prevented him from bringing a woman into his life, let alone a child. *What if he...* He tried not to think about it. He had dates. He had sex. Not often. Not every day or every week or even every month but he did have sex at least twice a year. But the women he met, didn't stick around long enough to find out what really made George tick. He didn't blame them for it. He was distant, cold and wooden. Came with the territory.

He had grown to love Ocean like a son. It was the closest George had ever gotten to having a kid of his own. He loved hearing Ocean's war stories, twenty-year-old gripes and curious questions. He gave the kid advice, mainly about money, specifically budgeting your money. Don't live for now. He would tell the youth almost every day. Put away twenty percent. Rainy day fund. Fact is, the advice he gave Ocean, he had never personally followed. He omitted that part of it. It was advice he wished he had followed. Maybe if he had followed his own advice he could have bought a house on the water to park his boat.

"Check it out!" The kid yelled through his mask. A group of terrified bed bugs were huddling around a seam in the chair rail molding. Ocean smiled with his eyes and blasted them with a well-aimed stream from his tank. The bugs ran for it, their little legs moving faster than their bodies, a stellar impersonation of the Road Runner. *Beep, beep.* Blood ran down the walls like a scene from the Exorcist. The real sick thing about bed bugs is that they feed on blood which means they poop blood in the cracks they call home, and when the poop gets wet -thanks to the copious amounts of insecticide sprayed on it- it tends to pour out. Thus the walls literally run red with blood.

"Good job kid." George said. Two bedrooms to go.

A couple of hours later, George and Ocean stood in the kitchen recounting their adventures down bed bug alley with the aghast homeowner, a stunning Italian brunette whose hungry oval eyes beamed at George like a lion staring at a gazelle.

"I would recommend taking all of your kid's stuff and putting it right into the dryer on high heat if he ever goes to another sleepover."

"Ever is the keyword." Carmella said, batting her eyes.

"He's a kid. Comes with the territory." George said, smiling.

Carmella finished writing the check and handed it to George. "I'm not a dirty person." She assured the two men, in her sexy, smoky voice.

George had heard the same thing a thousand times. For some reason, every time a person is inflicted with bed bugs, they automatically think it has something to do with sanitation or personal hygiene. And it doesn't. Period. People can get bed bugs from literally anywhere. Hotels, motels, school buses, jobs, and in Carmella's case -a sleepover. Her son Cameron had returned home from a night at a friend's house with the buggers in tow. No cleaning in the world would have prevented that. Which is what George told her but of course, she didn't believe him.

"I would have your husband throw out the box spring in your son's room." George said purposefully. He was trying to probe her relationship status. *Is there a Mr. so and so at home? No, that's a shame. A woman like you with that round face, curvy body and perky rack, must have someone.*

"No husband. He ran off with his hairdresser." Carmella said, waving a hand before George could offer his bullshit heartfelt condolences. "Good riddance as far as I'm concerned. He left me the house which was the least he could do. He doesn't even see his son much. That sucks but hey, we can't all meet Mr. Right."

"You gonna see her again?" Ocean asked when they were loading up the truck.

"I don't know. Why, you think she likes me?"

The kid looked back in astonishment. "Umm. Yeah. She freaking likes you. She was staring at your crotch the whole time. Didn't you notice?"

He did but he didn't want to confirm Ocean's suspicions.

"She's hot dude but I wouldn't want to date her." The kid stated, shutting the tailgate.

"Oh yeah. Why?"

"I don't think you'd be alone in her bed." Ocean said sarcastically.

George laughed. "Yeah, I might want to cover myself with some MOAC pre-coitus."

"Pre-what?"

"Never mind."

They found Detective Patterson at the police station. He was in a very bad mood.

"What can I do for you gentlemen?" Patterson groaned.

"I think I might know what's been killing all those people." George said. One hell of an opening line which instantly made Patterson sit up straight in his office chair.

"What?" Patterson answered. *Could it be? Could the bug man have cracked the case?* If he had, Patterson would kiss him. He prepared to pucker up, then George finished his statement.

"Bed bugs."

"What the hell? Who showed you in here?" Patterson looked around for a neck to wring.

"I'm serious." George said. He could see that the detective was on the verge of tossing them out.

"Serious? Do you have any idea what's going on here? I've got six dead bodies on my hands. I've got the chief, the mayor and the town council so far up my ass when I spit it smells like Old Spice. And you come in here with some bullshit about bed..."

George interrupted. "They killed the roaches in the townhouse."

"Roaches, not people. Look I'm very busy..."

"Bed bugs don't kill roaches!" George shouted and suddenly the bustling station went silent. Several police officers looked over in alarm. George lowered his voice. "Roaches usually kill bed bugs. Dr. Phil…"

"Who?" Patterson asked, rubbing his temples.

"Dr. Phil is the resident entomologist at the University of Maryland. Phil thinks the bed bugs are a new species. They are stronger and more aggressive…"

"How does he know how strong they are?" Patterson asked, unimpressed. "Does he watch 'em bench press? Hey, look at that one, he's pushing two hundred." He mocked.

"Stronger as in more resilient."

"Whatever. I need leads not jokes. I don't care if the bed bugs killed the roaches, the spiders and the mailman. And I really don't care what some bald, wannabe Oprah bozo on TV has to say about it…"

"He works at the university. He's a bug doctor."

"Look…"

"Just check out the townhouse with me. See if we find bed bugs." The Detective looked like he was about to protest. George held up a hand. "If we can't then I'll let you be. You'll never hear from me again."

The Detective thought about this for several minutes. His fingers tapped his chin, his eyes stared fixedly at the exterminator. "Yeah. All right." He answered finally. "But only because I don't have any other leads to follow. Not because I believe in a New York minute that bed bugs did anything to those people."

Chapter 25

Tracy's townhouse condition hadn't changed. It was still filthy. Still disgraceful as if it had been frozen in time. A snow globe straight from hell. Thankfully, at least the dead dog had been removed. Patty, the coroner, must have done that. She loved animals. The sight of the rotting pet must have really bothered her. A pet deserves a proper burial.

Ocean looked like he was going to vomit. Fruit flies in the mouth all over again. He stood in the corner of Tracy's bedroom, his face as white as Casper the ghost. He tried to avoid rubbing up against the walls, which were stained yellow with nicotine. He hobbled from foot to foot in a desperate attempt to touch as little of the floor as possible. The floor was covered in a torrent of food debris and bodily fluids. Ocean tried to think of something other than his current reality. Anything was better than this. Despite his best efforts, nothing popped into his head.

George and Patterson lifted the mattress off the floor and stood it against the wall. The detective, puffing on a cigar, stood back to watch. He had done enough. Let the bug men do their thing. Their job gave him the creeps. How can someone work with bugs? He hated every insect that crossed his path. If it had more than four legs, it was not a friend of his.

The carpet under the mattress was clean, probably the only clean thing in the whole house. The dirt had failed in its attempt to sneak underneath the caved in pillow top. George played his flashlight over the clean carpet and the underside of the mattress. He shook his head. No bugs. George pulled the mattress and let it flop down with a loud thump. The torn sheet on top puffed up like the skirt of a very sleazy hooker in a wind storm.

George scoured the rest of the room with his powerful, three-hundred-lumen flashlight. He checked the closet -no bugs; the corners of the carpet -no bugs. He even moved the trash piled on the floor -still no bugs. Striking out, he moved into the children's room. Ocean reluctantly trailed behind, still hobbling, jumping in between the trash.

It didn't take long to find the bugs in the children's bedroom. They hid under the mattress, their tiny, flat bodies tucked into the filthy folds. Patterson jumped back when George showed him. Now, the Detective looked like Ocean's twin, his face ghastly pale. The cigar clenched between Patterson's teeth had gone out with epic finality.

George stood up triumphantly. "What did I tell you?" He said; his lips curled into a smile.

"I've never seen a bed bug before." Patterson said, grimacing. "I still don't think they killed them. Come on. We're talking about bed bugs. They've been around forever and they've never…"

"These aren't normal bed bugs." George looked closer at the bugs. They looked different than the bed bugs he had seen at Carmella's house early that day. These bugs were larger and George thought -he had to be wrong- that he could actually see the Rostrum tip. Bed bugs used the tip to penetrate the skin of their victims and suck their blood. Normally the tip would be microscopic and only visible with the aid of a microscope. *But…unless my eyes are … there's no way but… I can see it!* He was sure of it.

George continued. "Not only did they kill Tracy and her two kids but I'll bet my bottom dollar that they also killed the dog. Can you get in touch with the coroner…" George stopped talking midsentence. He noticed that one of the bugs was running across the floor in his direction. *What the fu-!* His mind screamed. The bug wasn't afraid of him. Now that he thought about it, the bugs hadn't flinched at all when he had shone his flashlight in their faces. They had just sat there, motionless, unafraid as if they were staring at something that aroused their desires, something like… something like… food. George picked up his foot and slammed his shoe down hard. *Adios.* He lifted his shoe expecting to find a crushed corpse but instead the bug was still there. Maybe it had slipped safely into the tread. He stomped several more times, turning his foot in different directions. Still the bed bug was alive and moving. It came closer. George stepped back.

Patterson and Ocean were watching this exhibition in horror; their minds working in unison, unknown to one another. *No way. This wasn't happening.* The bug continued forward, still coming at George. George moved again. The bug followed. *What the hell?* He brought the heavy metal flashlight down onto the bug. It kept moving. *This is crazy.* The other bugs must have gotten the same message as the first one. They all began hurrying towards the humans like ants to a picnic basket. *Meats back on the menu boys!* Patterson and Ocean didn't wait to be told, they ran. George followed. The trio flew down the steps, kicking piles of trash as they went until they reached the back door, which didn't impede them in the slightest. They crashed through the door like a hoard of coupon-crazed shoppers on Black Friday.

Outside the three stood by George's truck. Patterson and Ocean gasped for air.

"What…the…hell…was…that?" Ocean asked through bated breath.

George didn't answer. He was the only one not breathing heavy. His lungs were like those of an Olympic athlete. He stared at the house. He was trying to comprehend the startling turn of events.

"What do we do now?" Patterson asked.

"Get in touch with the coroner. Tell her to reexamine the bodies. Look for microscopic puncture wounds. I'm going to spray those bastards back to the stone age."

"Now?" Patterson asked, he and Ocean exchanging shocked glances.

"Now." George stated, without blinking an eye. "I've got to kill those damn things. Can you do me a favor?"

The detective glanced up at him.

"I need to get into the other two crime scenes." George said.

"No problem. You want to call the guy who owns this house?" Patterson asked.

"Judge Julius? I've done work for him for twenty years. He'll take my word for it. Trust me."

"Fine by me. I'll get in touch with the medical examiner." Patterson said and got into his car.

George looked over at Ocean. The kid seemed to have found his balls again. Ocean had on the determined look that George had come to admire.

"MOAC?" Ocean asked.

"MOAC." George replied. *Mother of all chemicals.*

Chapter 26

The bed bugs had lost their nerve. They scurried like rats in a dark subway tunnel with the approach of an oncoming train. They moved extremely fast; much faster than George had ever seen bed bugs move; astonishingly quick. The metal tanks, containing the deadly concoction of Temprid, were pumped, sprayed and pumped again, in a ritualistic cycle. Every crack and crevice were hosed and then a fogger was dispersed to really get the bugs moving. This same pattern was repeated throughout the house, from the second-floor bedrooms and bathrooms, to the downstairs living room and then -for shits and giggles, although it was very unlikely the bugs would be there- to the basement. The plentitude of refuse and personal items made the chances of success for the first treatment almost non-existent. Too many places for the bugs to hide.

George noticed that every pest in the house had been slaughtered. Piles of dead insects lay in every corner of the filthy house, as if the house had already been sprayed -which it hadn't. George would have known. After all, he would have been the one doing the spraying. It was frightening. This new breed of bed bugs had consumed every living thing in the house: the dog, the people and even their fellow insects. It was unbelievable to comprehend. Too incredible for even a moment of irrational thought.

George had a very long working relationship with Judge Julius, a retired circuit court judge, who owned several properties in the area including the famed Blue House Bed and Breakfast. Judge Julius had hired George's company twenty years ago when George Sr. still ran the show. They handled all of Julius' properties which included Tracy's townhouse.

He placed a call to the judge. Just to give him a heads up. *By the way, not only are your tenants dead but, as remarkable as this sounds, they were killed, more like murdered, by bed bugs.* The phone rang and rang and rang and eventually went to voicemail. It was a generic voicemail, listing only the telephone number. George left a brief message, careful not to sound the alarm. He would rather tell the judge in person. Usually, it was customary to acquire permission before treating a property. However, in Julius' case, George knew full well that the judge would give him permission in a heartbeat, especially after George had described the situation on the ground. *Kill the bastards*, the judge would say. He was a tough guy. The judge didn't look tough, but he had some serious eyes. Those eyes had bored into George on several occasions, usually during a dispute over a bill. George was no wimp, in fact, he was far from it, it comes with both of his chosen professions. But still, the judge was able to make George cower in his presence, the judge just had that way of looking right through you into your soul.

It was the thought of those eyes when George handed the judge the bill for this job, that made him decide to pop in at the Blue House as soon as he was finished. Ocean wouldn't like it. *The kid would want to go home, get a shower -or at least hopefully get a shower- and then ride over for a night of fornication with the girl he has been texting all day. To be young again.* George thought as he remembered the scorn he had exhibited when his father kept him out for a long day. *Life is so simple when you're young. Small bills and big fun. No worries about tomorrow,*

*live for the moment, the second, the hour. If I could do it all
over again.*

Patterson was still outside when they finished. He
was still shaken by his recent adventure into a bug's life.
No blame there. Bed bugs don't usually chase the bug men,
the roles were reversed this time. The detective was sitting
in his car, puffing madly on a cigar, talking on his cell
phone like a degenerate gambler with a hot tip. He noticed
the two men approaching him and hung up.

"I called Patty." George raised an eyebrow. "The
coroner." George nodded. "She's going to recheck, but she
says she probably would have noticed insect bites."

"There wouldn't be bite marks. Bed bugs don't
have fangs like a spider, they insert a long tip like a
mosquito."

Patterson looked like he had just contracted HIV
from his cigar. The paleness returned with a vengeance.
"Thanks for the information." He grunted. "Now I'm not
going to be able to sleep for a week."

"Why not? I sleep just fine." Ocean chimed in.

"Good for you." Patterson snapped. He turned to
George. "Give me your number." He commanded. George
obliged, reading it off to Patterson, while the grumpy man
stored it in his cell phone. "I'll call you about the other
locations. Think their dead?" Patterson nodded towards the
house.

"Time will tell." George answered.

"How much time?" Patterson asked.

"I'll stop back tomorrow. Most of the adults will be on their backs by then." George answered.

Patterson nodded. "I guess for a bug that's a terrible thing." The detective smiled. "When it comes to a gal…" He shook George's hand. "Or a man…" He shot a grin at Ocean. "Whatever you're into."

Ocean looked up in horror.

Patterson laughed. "Not that there's anything wrong with that." He said, quoting the line from a famous Seinfeld episode. He drove off without another word.

"What a dick." Ocean said when the detective's brake lights disappeared into the distance.

"He's not so bad. How would you like to have his job?" *Really, I just said that.* George thought to himself. He had hated it when adults said that to him. But the lesson was true. It just takes thirty years to figure it out.

Ocean wasn't thrilled when George told him they wouldn't be getting off anytime soon. "It's already 6." The young man groaned. "Ashley's supposed to come over. She's got something important to talk to me about."

Ashley, that must be the flavor of ice cream Ocean was dipping his spoon into this week. Well, Ashley would have to wait. Something important to talk about? That couldn't be good. When a woman -correction: girl- wants to talk to you about something important it's either one of three things: I want to be single, I cheated on you or I'm pregnant. Ocean was a good-looking guy who had rich parents, so then, I want to be single is probably out of the question. It's either I cheated, or I'm knocked up. George kept his thoughts to himself. The kid would find out soon enough and whatever it was, Ocean would live.

"Call her. Tell her you'll be home around seven." George replied as he drove in the direction of the Blue House. "How long have you been seeing this girl?"

"Four months."

That surprised George. He assumed Ocean was more of a player. *Four months, so, it was I'm knocked up.* George silently placed a bet on choice number 3, double or nothing.

"Did you get any live ones?" Ocean asked.

George nodded, a broad smile on his face. "Oh yeah baby. I'm going to send them off first thing in the morning. Dr. Phil's going to love us."

The Blue House was dark. The only lights visible were the small solar LEDs that lined the flagstone path leading from the driveway. An eerie feeling came over George, an unsettling chill that crept up his spine. Probably just his training. *Always be on alert.* They had drilled that into him in Ranger school. *An ounce of prevention is worth a pound of cure.* The quote from Benjamin Franklin was read over and over again by his anal-retentive instructor. Read, hell, shouted is more like it. If he ever went nuts, it was this quote that he would write on the walls of his padded cell.

The sky was pitch black. The daylight of winter ended at five. It was cold, freezing cold. Their breath -long clouds of chilled steam- lit up in the beams of their flashlights. The walk to the house took forever. Everything takes an eternity when it's cold. They reached the expansive, hand planed, wooden porch. George's fist contacted the oak door and sent thunderous booms over the estate that sounded like cannon blasts as if they were reenacting an old battle from a forgotten war. No one answered. That was unsettling. The judge was always home. His car was there, as was his wife's, and there was also an unidentified vehicle with Washington DC plates in the driveway. That signaled the presence of a paying guest. George beat the door again until his hand felt like it was going to break upon the wood like glass on a tile floor. The booms echoed into the night. No answer. No lights. No judge at the door.

"Maybe he's not home." Ocean said shivering.

George took off his jacket and handed it to the kid. At first Ocean refused on young, tough guy principles but he gave in at George's insistence. His teeth chattered his appreciation.

"When its twenty degrees outside, wear a jacket." George said. "There's always someone here." He tried the handle. It was open. He turned the knob and pushed the giant wooden door inward. It creaked like wind in need of a good oiling. The flashlight beams danced around the room.

"Hello! Anyone here! It's George, the bug man!" George shouted, his voice echoing in the black expanse. His biggest fear was the judge, rounding the corner with a .44 mag in his hand, cocked, locked and ready to rock. Being a judge, the guy must have some serious enemies. More than some -a lot of serious enemies. The judge would have to be prepared. Go out shooting. Send his enemies to hell on a crowded 747.

George felt uneasy. That feeling again. That chill. Something was off. He felt like he was being watched. Maybe the rumors were true. Maybe the Blue House was haunted. He wanted to turn, to glance behind him but he was terrified about what might be lurking back there. What if he saw a ghost? A full-figured apparition silently gazing at him? What would he do? How would he react? He would run. That was it. He would run like the wind and leave a man-shaped hole in whatever tried to stop him. He was prepared for almost anything living, but the dead -the dead scared the living shit out of him. He had enough ghosts in his past to fill the whole town with them. He saw them all the time. He saw them in his dreams. He saw them when he was awake.

"Hello!" Ocean screamed.

There was no reply. George wished he had his gun. There was something amiss -a piece of the puzzle that fell off the board onto the floor and had been kicked under the sofa. They moved into the house, their flashlights acting like spotlights in a 1920s silent horror film. George started mentally cataloging evidence. *No sign of a struggle. No furniture knocked down. No pictures hanging crooked on the walls. No vases lying shattered on the floor. Also, no judge and no Eleanor.*

"Dude, where are the lights?" Ocean asked.

Ocean played his bright white beam over the walls until he answered his own question. He walked over and flipped the switch. The lights in the grand foyer came alive like a fire in the middle of a pitch-black forest. Eleanor had had them replaced with LEDs; LEDs that are made to look like they came out of the turn of the century, as if Edison himself had constructed them in his workshop. It was a nice touch, highlighting the room with a soft yellowish light. Now George and Ocean could see everything. The exquisite hand-carved antiques and the colorful ornate area rugs made for a delectable, historical scene.

"Wow." The kid said, which shocked George. He looked at Ocean like *really kid, you like this kind of stuff, your twenty!*

They repeated the same act as if they were in a choreographed show. First flashlights, then the switch, then illumination, then Ocean exclaiming *WOW!* as he glanced around, then moving on. Still no sign of the judge and they were almost out of rooms on the first floor. George was beginning to think that maybe the house was empty. It was possible that the judge, Eleanor and his guest had gone out for the evening. That would be a very reasonable explanation. Havre de Grace was a walkable town. Very walkable, like Boston or Manhattan. But then again it *was* twenty degrees outside and the Judge and Eleanor *were* in their seventies. George hoped that they had thrown caution to the wind and had left their elderly souls behind for a night on the town. His hopes were dashed when he entered the final room on the first floor; the inn keeper's quarters. He saw them as soon as it stepped over the threshold; their bodies in bed, under the covers, holding each other as they journeyed into the afterlife, meeting it together, forever in love, even in death.

"What the fuck!" Ocean exclaimed. "Are they…"

George lifted a hand to silence the kid. He walked over to the bed and felt the judge's neck. There was no pulse. He did the same to Eleanor with the same damn result. They were both dead. They looked cold, pale, and somehow -although this couldn't be true- shriveled, as if the fluid that had once pumped through their veins had been sucked out of them with incredible force.

"Call 911." George commanded. Ocean stared at him in disbelief. He had never dialed those three digits in his life. Finally, reluctantly, as if he were in a trance, the kid pulled out his phone.

"Yes, we're at..." The kid said after the operator had picked up.

"The Blue House." George interjected.

"The Blue House. There are two dead bodies." Ocean paused listening to the operator. "We felt for a pulse." Another pause. 911 operators love asking a slew of questions, that in the situations that warrant calling the emergency hotline, one could do without. Ocean looked at George. "Do you know the address?"

"No." *It's the Blue House! Everybody knows the Blue House! This is Havre de Grace for Christ sakes!* "Tell them to look it up. The Blue House Bed and Breakfast."

Ocean repeated what George said. The operator asked a few more questions before Ocean hung up. The kid looked relieved, as if the phone call was worse than finding the bodies.

"Dude, this is fucked up. How do you think they died?"

"Same MO. Dead in bed. No sign of foul play. No break-in." It killed him that he couldn't roll the bodies over and check for livor mortis. That would definitively prove his theory beyond a reasonable doubt. But that was the job of the police. It would already take some serious explaining to get himself and Ocean out of any rigmarole. After all, they had entered a property without the owner's permission. He hoped Detective Patterson would be on the scene. That would make his explanations a whole lot easier.

"I'm going upstairs." George said. "You stay here."

"Hell no! I am staying with you. No freaking way." The kid shook his head from side to side vigorously. *Stay here with two dead people? In a creepy old house? Hell no!* He thought staring down at the bodies.

They proceeded upstairs. The stairs creaked with each step. The old boards, attached by spikes, not nails, strained against their holds, under the weight of the two men. They reached the top and George flipped a switch on the wall. The hallway was empty. They checked each bedroom. All of them were pristine except for the last. The last of the four had been occupied recently. The sheets were wrinkled into a ball at the foot of the bed. Towels were strewn about the bathroom. A pack of coffee, for the instant coffee machine, lay torn open on the table. George walked over to it. He opened the small coffee maker and saw the grinds, wet, used and cold, inside the paper filter. No way Eleanor would leave a room in this condition.

"I think someone stayed here." Ocean said.

George just stared at him in disbelief. "Really?" He replied sarcastically. "What gave it away?"

Ocean flipped him the bird. "Maybe they left."

"No way. You don't know Eleanor." George answered. "This room would have been spick and span literally seconds after a checkout."

Ocean looked at him, his expression telepathically saying *dude she's dead.* "Are there any more rooms?"

George shrugged and walked out into the hall. He looked up and down. *Man, the cops take a long time in this little town. They could probably walk here faster.* Just then his vision focused in on a figure standing in front of a closed door. George stared in wide-eyed disbelief. The figure was translucent. The pale image of a little girl in a tunic. George shook his head, trying desperately to clear his mind. This wasn't happening. It wasn't real. The little girl's face was dirty, sandy. She looked at George with big, oval eyes. Eyes that pleaded with him. Eyes that were accusatory. She lifted one of her hands and beckoned him to come. George couldn't move. He was frozen like a statue, set in stone. She beckoned. *Come here. I won't hurt you.* The waving hand said. The girl looked out of place. She didn't belong here even as a ghost. George knew it. He knew it because he had seen her before. She wasn't a remnant of the age from which the spirits of this house had originated. She was from a different time, a different place, a different world, some would say. *Come here George. Come closer. I'm not mad.* Her hand continued to talk to him.

"What is it? What the hell's wrong with you?" Ocean asked. He noticed his boss had gone ghostly white. He saw the color drain from George's face like mercury from a broken thermometer. "What the hell are you looking at?" Ocean stepped into the hall and peered into the semi-lit darkness in the direction George's wide eyes were staring. Nothing was there. The hallway was empty.

Come here. Trust me, as I trusted you. The beckoning hand and the oval eyes said silently. George felt cold. He was scared, hell, he was terrified. The little girl turned and that's when the real horror revealed itself. The little girl was torn; the flesh of her back ripped open; her insides showing. The holes were ragged, expertly crafted by the tools of a terrible trade. *Jesus Christ!* George's mind screamed. *No, no, no, no, no!* The image of the girl, the projection, vanished through the closed door. THROUGH the closed door! George could feel his heart racing. He could feel the blood pulsing in his veins. He grabbed the door frame to steady himself. He was shaking.

Ocean was perplexed. He looked from George to the empty hallway over and over again as if in doing so he would reveal whatever George's eyes were seeing. George's eyes were fixed on a closed door. Ocean advanced towards the door. He glanced back at George who seemed to be rooted to the spot, feet nailed to the floor. Ocean gripped the doorknob and turned.

It was an attic. Stairs going up into darkness. Nice stairs for an attic. Painted, with a carpet running down the center. Ocean had the sickening feeling that this was another bedroom. *Great.* He drawled glumly to himself. He looked back at George.

"You alright man?"

George was still pale. He looked terrible. His eyes appeared blank as if they contained no knowledge at all, just a vast blackness.

"I'm heading upstairs. You know, upstairs, into a dark fucking room, in this ancient fucking house where there's already two dead bodies downstairs." Ocean said sarcastically. "You want to join me or what?"

George snapped out of it. He shook his head and rubbed his temples.

"What the hell was that about?" Ocean asked.

"I don't know." George answered. His voice distant, barely a whisper in the silence of the old home.

The stairs took a very long time to climb. *Who the hell would want to stay up here?* Ocean asked himself. The question was answered for him when he laid eyes on the largest, most beautiful suite in the entire house. The suite had floor to ceiling windows overlooking the Susquehanna that took, sucked the breath right out of your chest. Ocean looked for a light switch but failed to locate one. He couldn't see a thing. He played his flashlight around. The beam landed on George, who stood stark still, his face looking down at the unconscious form on the bed. *Yep, there was another body. Marvelous. Simply marvelous.* The body was that of a young man, maybe thirty, thirty-five, with a neatly trimmed beard. The young man's face was as white as the sheets on which he lay.

"Police! Anyone here?! Police!" The shouts penetrated the darkness, echoing through the interior, shattering the silence of death.

"Keep your hands up and walk slowly." George commanded. Both men raised their hands and started back down the stairs.

Two cops, their handguns drawn, their muscles twitching, stood breathless at the base of the first-floor landing. They aimed their weapons at George who descended the stairs first.

"We're the ones who called!" George shouted at the officers. The cops looked shaky. They kept their metal cannons raised and ready. George noticed that the cop on the right had a serious case of the nerves. The cop's hand trembled. It was a slight movement. Nothing extreme but to a trained eye -and George's pupils had been polished into professional gems- the movement was very apparent and extremely worrisome. Nervous cops with their fingers on hairpin triggers.

"Put your goddamn guns down!" Patterson screamed at the two beat cops. They listened immediately, lowering their guns so fast it was as if Patterson had used the Force. "It's the bug man." The detective finished, as if everyone should *know* the bug man.

"Glad to see you." Ocean said, with a broad smile on his face. The first time he had ever faced the barrel of a gun and he prayed it would be the last. It was a strange and unwanted feeling peering down the barrel of an instrument of imminent destruction.

"Yeah, well I'm not. Thanks a lot for finding two more…"

"Three more." George told the detective whose face dropped south of Antarctica.

"Three more." The detective said quietly, depressed beyond comprehension. "Where?"

George led the cops to the bedroom on the first floor. Patterson looked down and frowned at the sight of Judge Julius and Eleanor lying in bed, beyond medical help. Next, they all made the long climb to the third floor where the last body was, wrapped in silky Egyptian bed sheets.

"Great." Patterson said, his demeanor reaching a new low. "This guy's a reporter from CNN." He pulled a card out of his pocket and showed it to George. The guy's name was Josh Clark and he was indeed a reporter for CNN, straight out of the Washington DC field office. That fact made the detective puff on his signature cigar with vigor, so much vigor that the large room began to fill with smoke within seconds.

"I'll call the coroner." Patterson sighed. He exited the room, a thick plume of acrid smoke trailing behind him.

Chapter 27

Transgenesis. That was how they had done it. Transgenesis -the means of introducing genes from one species into another. The method had altered the new species, making them perfect and in the process making them lethal.

The specimens that were chosen had incredibly rare and unique characteristics and abilities. These insects were super bugs, so to speak. The top of their class, the cream of the crop. They had been chosen like Olympic athletes -only the best need apply. The individual genes responsible for their talents, were isolated and transferred to the new species -Specimen 0618. That was the name for their new breed and that name was significant. The name was bestowed upon it based on survivability. Most had died. In fact, every specimen starting at Specimen 0001 and all the way up to Specimen 0617 had perished, unable to accept their new genetic makeup, but 0618 had survived. Number 0618 was the winner, the one who lived. Their miracle baby.

Specimen 0618 had genes from several different Arthropods incorporated in their makeup. The exoskeleton of an Arthropod is extremely resilient. Made from Chitin, the shell is multilayered and tough, like insect tank armor. Specimen 0618 also had genes from the Onthphagus Taurus or Horned Dung beetle, which gave it the strength of Superman. *Look out Lex Luther.* The Horned Dung Beetle can carry 1,141 times its own body weight. That's like a human being lifting an adult Humped Back whale.

Genes from the Sahara Ant were also added for temperature resiliency. The Sahara Ant can endure temperatures of 158 degrees Fahrenheit or 70 degrees Celsius. This would make Specimen 0618 impervious to temperature fluctuations, which in turn would render them invincible to heat treatments, the most common and effective method used to eliminate bed bugs. Heat was the major issue; cold temperatures have never been a problem for bed bugs. They can naturally tolerate and survive chilling temperatures of 14 degrees Fahrenheit. Anything below that was deemed irrelevant and uncommon.

The key to everything, the code that unlocked the doors to the kingdom, the magic combination was viral vectoring. Viruses are mother nature's suitcases. Little duffel bags that can be stuffed with contraband -in this case genetic material- and smuggled into the body of a living organism. The problem was: how to find a virus that would be able to carry the new genetic material without killing the species slated for infection. In other words, it was like playing Russian roulette but instead of a revolver, they were playing with five empty vials and the sixth filled with the Ebola virus. It was this heinous game that had led to the six hundred and seventeen fatalities. And it hadn't been a groundbreaking discovery that had finally led to Specimen 0618. It had been a kick in the ass with a size twenty shoe that had done it. The kick came from Carter Ritler, who threatened to cut off funding if the project failed to show results. It was on the day of the meeting between Dr. Sangmore -the lab's leading scientist- and Carter Ritler -the president of Sentrix- that the team discovered their perfect viral suitcase and Specimen 0618 was born.

Dr. Sangmore recounted all of this to Lenny, who sat pompously in a chair appearing uninterested as he stared into the face of the nerdy scientist. Lenny wore a dark, double-breasted suit that was outdated regarding fashion but still conveyed an intimidating *John Gotti* type aura. *Look at me; I'm rich; I'm ruthless; I'm the boss' pit bull. I will tear your muthafuckin' head off!* The message was heard loud and clear.

"How many scientists work in your lab?" Lenny asked, his legs crossed, his hair pristine with every strand gelled neatly into a classy sculpture.

Dr. Sangmore shifted uncomfortably in his chair. He looked around the room at his team hard at work. *They'll lose their jobs. There is no way to spare them. Lenny is an asshole. He's an asshole for holding this meeting in the lab, within earshot of my team. He's an asshole for questioning me on methods Lenny could never even begin to understand even if he somehow got ahold of a crystal freaking ball. And he's an asshole because he's just an asshole. Period!* Sangmore thought to himself, before looking at the floor and answering the question.

"Fourteen." Fourteen stellar men and women. Fourteen employees with families, with screaming, hungry little ones. Fourteen employees with mortgages to pay, vacations to enjoy, colleges to finance.

"Fourteen." Lenny repeated, jotting the number down, as if he didn't know it already. "All fourteen are trustworthy?"

"No one created these bugs. It was an accident. A result of playing God. An evolution that we couldn't have predicted." Sangmore was mad -his weak, perpetually bullied demeanor unwilling to tolerate this affront.

"Did anyone else have access to your lab?"

Anyone else? Of course, there were others. Anyone who worked at Sentrix with a high enough clearance could have accessed my lab. Scan a key card, punch the entrance button, walk through the airlock door. Child's play. Hell, the janitor could have accessed my lab and did every time he wanted to empty the goddamn trash! Sangmore knew what was happening. It was scapegoating 101. Sentrix, i.e. Carter fucking Ritler and greedy Gordon Reynolds were - through their attack dog Mr. Egotistical Lenny Schultz- trying to pin this mishap on *someone,* or a team of *someones.*

"Yes. Numerous people had access to the lab during the trials. You don't understand." Sangmore said, his voice high, pleading with Lenny's conscience, if the man had any. "These bugs weren't created to kill. It was a mistake, an unintended consequence. There's no way we could have predicted an outcome like this."

"How did you make the bugs invincible to pesticides?" Lenny asked, ignoring Sangmore's plea.

"By spraying pregnant bed bug females prior to giving birth, their offspring would almost always become immune to whichever pesticide their mother had perished from."

"Almost always?"

"There was always the occasional error which is normal in science. It took Edison ten thousand tries to create the incandescent light bulb. In other words, he failed ten thousand times. Ten thousand mistakes."

"I see." Lenny jotted something down on his pad. "I am assuming Dio Insecticide is the only pesticide that you didn't immunize the bugs to?" Lenny asked and Sangmore nodded. "How do you feed the bugs?"

Sangmore sounded defeated. A man standing in front of the noose, who accepts his punishment, wraps the noose around his own neck, feels the burn of the frayed rope on his skin, even though he's innocent. "We use rabbits. We strap feeding chambers onto the backs of rabbits. The chambers are clear containers with fine mesh screens at the bottom. The mesh screens allow the bugs to feed but not to escape."

Lenny didn't flinch. He wanted to. Oh yes, he wanted to jump out of his chair and head for the showers. But he didn't. The whole thing was giving him the willies. He silently composed himself. "None of the rabbits died during feeding?"

Sangmore shook his head so vigorously, his glasses nearly fell off. "No. They did not." Sangmore gripped the sides of the chair till his fingers turned white. "The mice did." He held his breath waiting for the blow.

"The mice?"

Sangmore looked as if he had sat in a puddle. He began speaking rapidly like a child in the principal's office who'd just been caught in a lie. "We started feeding the bugs with mice, but the mice suffered extensive blood loss and died. Again, it was an unintended consequence. After all, this has never been attempted. Never even thought of."

Lenny's eyes popped open. "And this didn't indicate to you there was a problem?"

"No."

This answer floored Lenny, who sat back in his chair and looked at the scientist full in the face. "No?" He asked incredulously.

"No. Mice are mice. Humans weigh far more. There is no correlation between the two. Plus, the rabbits didn't die and they were subjected to the same feeding method."

"Did the rabbits ever squeal in pain while being fed?"

"No." Sangmore answered.

"Are the bugs kept in cages unless they are being fed?"

"Yes. We bring them out from time to time to run various tests." Sangmore welled up the last remaining ounce of his courage and tried to make his closing argument. "There have never been any mistakes made at any time in my lab." He said, letting out a chest full of air as he finished.

Lenny nodded. He placed his small, spiral notebook into his inner jacket pocket. Despite the advances in hand-held devices, Lenny liked his notebook. It had a certain feel. Pen on paper. Old school. Plus, it made people nervous. Taking notes on a smartphone gave most people the impression that you weren't taking them seriously. That you were texting, Facebooking or playing a game. Lenny never played games, *never!* Not even in his spare time. Lenny was all business, all the time. So, he used a notebook.

"I think I've got everything I came for. Thank you, Mr. Sangmore,…"

"Doctor." Sangmore interrupted. *Fuck this sawed-off prick.*

Lenny just smiled, arrogantly. "I'll be in touch."

Sangmore decided to voice one last plea. "Look, my team is good. They are great. The best. They don't deserve to take the fall for this. If anyone has to be handed to the wolves, let it be me. Hang me. Put my head on the chopping block. I was the one in charge. I was the man with the plan, so to speak." *Actually it wasn't me at all. It was the assholes on the eightieth floor, but we all where they'll be when the curtain rises.*

Lenny grinned again. The image was that of a very well-manicured asshole. Cheeks open wide, hairless, but definitely a round, puckered, reddish hole where shit slides out. Lenny stood and walked out of the lab without another word.

Sangmore stood up from the chair. It was late, and he was shaking. He hadn't eaten all day. He couldn't eat. Not a bite. The meeting with Lenny had done that to him. He had been telephoned earlier in the day that the walking, talking rectum would be in to see him. Sangmore had tried to eat lunch, but he just played with his food like a five-year-old sitting in front of a plate of Brussel sprouts. Dinner went the same way. Sangmore fingered his hamburger, mainly pulling chunks of the bun off and rolling them into balls, laying them on the plate in a neat pattern only he could understand. Coffee was the only sustenance he had had before his meeting. Coffee and nerves, a terrifying daily double.

The vending machine held what he was looking for -Drake's coffee cake. He punched in the number of his selection and watched with muted anxiousness as the packaged carbohydrate fell from its enclosure. He opened it, removed the cake and ate it with unabashed savagery. It was good. He grabbed another and repeated the gluttony. Three dollars short and three cakes in his belly, Sangmore returned to the lab where he was met with concerned eyes. He knew they all wanted to talk to him. To be assured that their jobs were safe, their futures intact. He had zero answers for them. *Sorry folks, shows over and don't bother turning in your tickets for a refund because there is.... none!*

Chapter 28

"Smoke this shit!" T-Bone held out the tightly rolled blunt to the tiny, tightly packed brunette sitting next to him. She listened to the command like a private at boot camp, taking a big inhale of the green dragon. And that's all it took. The five foot nothing girl was high as the sky. Good year blimp high. Never coming down, sitting on the freaking moon high. It was good shit. Best shit this side of the Mississippi -*where ever the hell that was.*

It's funny what weed does to loose women. Screw the booze, the ultimate aphrodisiac is weed. It gets the heart racing, the blood pumping and the belt buckle as loose as the girl. It did in Gina's case. Before she knew it, she was balls deep smoking T-Bone's blunt and not the blunt in his hand, but the blunt between his legs -his short, fat, brown blunt. They weren't alone either. The living room of Carlos' apartment was packed like a hearse after a Jim Jones picnic. Carlos -the boss, or so he liked to be called these days- was telling T-Bone and Gina in a profanity-laced tirade *to get a freaking room!* They did, moving their stoned lovefest to one of the bedrooms, but not Carlos' bedroom, he had made that crystal clear.

"I catch you screwing in my room and I'll feed ya freakin' balls to Mr. Smith. Got it, homes?" Mr. Smith was Carlos' Alligator Gar -one hell of a freaking fish that gobbled down minnows like a fat man in a donut factory.

The apartment was filled to the brim with multicolored Bandanas, sagging jean shorts, long white tee-shirts and tattooed sleeves. All of Carlos' crew was there: T-Bone and his girl Gina; Juan Green, who for obvious reasons had rolled the blunt; Ricardo Fish, the guy literally stunk like fish; Javier the Gringo, who was half white; and Roberto Beans, because if you fed him beans you better run for your life. A multitude of girls were also at the party, outnumbering the boys two to one, which is exactly how Carlos liked his women, two of them to his one.

The beer flowed, kegs of it, courtesy of the liquor store down the street who owed Carlos a favor or two or three. The weed, nuggets the size of fingers, sat on plates in the middle of the table, ready to be broken, rolled and smoked. Loud thumps from the Bose sound system rumbled and shook the paper-thin walls which drove Carlos' neighbors crazy. But they wouldn't dream of complaining. That would be a very stupid thing. Which is what T-Bone and Juan Green had expressed to them, in no uncertain terms, on more than one occasion. The rhythm of Tupac and his arch-rival the Notorious BIG, sounded so clear that it was very freaking possible to think the two dead rappers were right there, in the room, performing the show live.

Great night for a party. Cold outside, warm and toasty inside. Good night to get drunk, get high and cuddle up to a cutie pie. Carlos was halfway between *I'm starting to feel it* and *I'm wasted bro!* It was a good place to be. Eyes a little droopy, head bouncing to the beat, body swaying. A gorgeous black chick gyrated her shapely ass in his face. For some reason, even though they were definitely not exclusive by any means, Carlos felt like he was cheating on his girl. *Sabrina, Sabrina, Sabrina.* His mind played her name over and over again. What had that white girl done to him? The only thing missing from the night, from this incredible party was… Sabrina and Carlos felt it. The party just wasn't the same without her. Sure, he'd go to

bed with the black chick. *What was her name again?*
Amanda? No, it was Amber. He would screw Amber's
brains out. *And why the fuck not? I've got needs.* But he
missed Sabrina. Missed her like he had never missed a girl
before. He watched as Amber pulled the strings of her red
thong up above her pants, hooking them with her thumbs
and rubbing her ass on his crotch. Amber was hot. He
would give her that. *But damn that Sabrina!* He pushed
Amber gently away, excusing himself but reassuring her he
would be back. He needed a cigarette.

Outside he lit it up. Smoke all the weed you want in
his place but no cigs, not at all. Weed was one thing. The
smell is tolerable. Cigarettes just stink. You want a fug, you
go outside. He fingered the cancer stick and plumped down
on one of his patio chairs. The night was dark and cold, but
he didn't feel it. It's the booze. The cold doesn't affect the
body as much when you're halfway down the old, wayward
slope. He inhaled deeply. Nothing like a cigarette when
you're drunk. It was the only time he smoked. Drink a beer,
have a cigarette. That should be a bumper sticker.

He was alone. Alone to think. Lost in his brain.
Mind swirling with the image of Sabrina. Her beautiful
face, her gorgeous eyes, her lustful physique. God, he
missed her. He stood up from the chair and looked from the
darkness that surrounded him into his living room. He
watched the faces of his boys as they twisted with raucous
laughter at a joke was told. Was it about him? He didn't
care. He was done with it. This life. The parties, the booze,
the drugs. He had had enough. *To be free.* End the slavery,
the bondage, the prison that was his existence. The life of
crime. It was a prison, whether you're inside the joint or
outside -you are in prison. You are watching the normal

people from behind bars. Metal or mental, it didn't matter. It was the same damn thing. Although the mental was easier to escape from.

The tip of the suppressor stabbed into the back of his neck. Carlos never heard the man come up behind him. The guy was a pro. Carlos froze with the lit cigarette in his hand; the glowing cherry moving slowly towards the filter; the grey smoke snaking its way up into the night sky.

"You move, you make a sound, you die." The voice was quiet, not even a decibel above a whisper.

Carlos nodded. He was frozen like an ice sculpture. He continued to watch the people inside, silently pleading for their help. They ignored him, unable to see their boss in his time of need.

"Carlos?" The voice asked, and Carlos nodded. The man's left hand frisked him, feeling for a weapon. There was none. "Turn around. Slowly." The voice commanded. Carlos did so, ever so slowly, not wanting to give this man any reason to pop his head open like can of beer.

The man's face was covered in shadow. The only feature Carlos could make out was the man's eyes -dark, cold and sinister, like the environment outside.

"What the fuck?" Carlos' voice quivered with fear. He was a tough gang banger but like any tough gang banger, get them by themselves and stick a suppressed gun to their head and they melt like a stick of butter in a hot frying pan. Gang leaders are only tough when they've got their gang to back them up.

"I need a local. Someone who knows the cops in this town. And you're that someone." The man answered.

"First, who the fuck are you? And second, why the fuck would I do anythin' for you?" Carlos was beginning to get some of his nerve back, not all of it, but a little at a time.

"Big C, right? That's what they call you?" The man asked, and Carlos nodded. "Well, Big C, do you remember a guy named Eddie?"

Carlos' voice caught in his throat. Everything stopped. Time stood still. He hadn't heard that name in a long time, a very long time. *Eddie. Eddie. Freaking Eddie Barnes.* Carlos' first and only murder. Eddie was a drug dealer from Abingdon. He fronted a half kilo of cocaine from Carlos and got nailed. The half key got confiscated and Eddie didn't have the money to cover. He started running his mouth all over town. Telling anyone who's anybody that he would go to the cops unless Carlos forgave his debt. Not a smart move. No one likes a rat. Carlos had no choice. Let Eddie run to the cops or take Eddie for a ride. So, Eddie went for a ride. Carlos told Eddie he would let the debt slide. *No big deal. No one knows when the coppers are coming. Freaking pigs.* He told Eddie exactly what Eddie wanted to hear and Eddie believed him. Eddie trusted him. So much so that Eddie went to meet Carlos in the parking lot of K-Mart to go over the details of Eddie's case. After all, it was Carlos, Eddie's buddy, Eddie's homeboy. Carlos didn't hesitate when Eddie pulled up. He put six shots from a .357 magnum into Eddie's face and left him in the driver's seat of the rat bastard's S10 pick-up.

"Did you know Eddie was in the army?" The cold voice whispered into Carlos' ear.

Carlos shook his head. He really didn't know that.

"He was. So was I. I knew Eddie. I liked Eddie. When he died I went looking for his killer. Talked to folks around town. They told me Eddie had a beef with you. That you probably put him on ice. Can you believe that Big C? Can you believe that people would say that about you?" The whisper mocked.

Carlos couldn't speak. He couldn't even nod. He just stood there. *That was six years ago. Six years!* Carlos had thought that only Officer Mike had ever figured it out. It was their secret. The pact that held the two together. The reason Carlos paid Mike the three grand a month. Mike had the gun. The only thing tying Carlos to the crime. *No way this guy can make the case without the gun.*

"I found the gun Big C. Found it in the house of that prick cop you pay."

Carlos' heart stopped beating. He stared back into those scary, soulless eyes, totally sober and totally defeated. It was as if the guy could read his mind.

"It's got your prints all over it. Dumb mistake Big C. Big fucking mistake. Rookie mistake. Always wear gloves Big C." The man's hands had black gloves covering them. Translation, this guy, holding the suppressed pistol was a fucking pro. No amateurs here, well except the dumb Latino gangbanger who probably was in the process of pissing his sagging jean shorts.

"What do you want me to do?" Carlos blurted out. *What do you want me to do master? You say the word. I'm Darth Vader and you're the Emperor. I'll obey your every command.* He thought.

"I'll let you know Big C. Glad to hear that you're on the reservation."

The sliding door opened. T-Bone, fresh from his romp in the sheets, stumbled outside. Great, now there was definitely going to be a shootout. Which basically meant that T-Bone was about to get popped and Carlos would die too, because pros don't leave any freakin' witnesses. Carlos turned away from the man with the gun, watching his big friend try to navigate his girth through the sliding door. Carlos waited to hear the signature pop, pop from the suppressor. But it never came. He turned back, and the evil-eyed man had vanished into the shadows.

"What the fuck's wrong with you?" T-Bone asked, slurring his words.

"Nothin'." Carlos responded, a little too quickly before slumping back into the chair.

Chapter 29

She remembered the house. Remembered it like it was yesterday. The spacious suites; the colonial era antiques; the romantic atmosphere. She had sat on that very deck with her husband, Ted; taking in the sights, the sounds and the aroma of the sea. She remembered Ted reading the Wall Street Journal while sipping a cup of espresso from the complimentary machine. She could still smell that sensual mix of ink and coffee. That had been a great trip. A great adventure. A memory from a bygone era.

The house was different. Different in the sense that Patty was here on the job. A job she had recently grown to despise. A job she had once loved. She had craved the knowledge and rejoiced in solving the case. It was in the last four days that she had begun to hate it. She stopped enjoying her work, like a lover who realizes her special someone is really someone else's special someone and has been the entire time.

The innkeepers: Eleanor, her white hair permanently set in that elegant style; the judge, his cold eyes staring. They looked so innocent in death. A tear fell from Patty's eye and rolled slowly down her cheek, splattering on the bed sheets. She was losing it. Who wouldn't lose it? Nine dead in four days. Nine lives lost, taken from this planet by the grim reaper. The reaper, that callous bastard. That bloodthirsty, ravenous wolf, set upon mankind. A gift from our maker. A curse of our mortality. Patty silently cursed death personified. Nine deaths in this small town. Nine people who wouldn't be returning home for Christmas. *Merry freaking Christmas!* She had almost forgotten about it. If it hadn't been for the lights and the decorations strewn throughout the town, the holiday would have come and gone without her even realizing it. She used to love seeing the ancient buildings highlighted with twinkling red and green. She used to stop, used to look, to gaze at the wonder, tis the season and all that horse shit. *Tis wasn't the fucking season! Not in this godforsaken town.*

"Any luck with the puncture wounds?" Detective Patterson asked, his voice shockingly soft and soothing. He realized Patty was having trouble. He could see it in her expression. That defeated look people get when they are overworked, underpaid and undernourished. Patty had been working around the clock. Rumor had it that she had even slept in the office the night before. The rumor was true, and Patterson knew it.

"I found them." She said. Bit of good news. Gold at the end of the rainbow with no evil little leprechaun standing sentinel over it. She tried to smile at the detective, but her muscles just wouldn't do it. "I don't know how I missed them. When I got up close with a magnifying glass I saw them. There were thousands of them. The bodies were riddled." Her voice faded away.

"What do you think of George's theory about the bugs?" He inquired gently, figuratively trying to hold onto the back of Patty's shirt as she teetered on the edge of life's abyss.

"George?"

"The exterminator. The guy I was telling you about."

"Yeah. Sorry, my mind's kinda…" Patterson shook his head to stop her. "I think it's true." She continued. "Totally validated. The puncture marks are there. The bodies have no blood. No sign of trauma. I hate to tell you but his theory fits." She sighed, sucking in a large breath of air.

"Were they small?"

"Microscopic. I did some research. Bed bugs feed using a rostrum tip. It's like a needle and a straw combined. They stick it into the flesh and drink." Patterson shuddered. Patty waited for the man to calm his nerves. "Usually the skin gets irritated after they feed. Most people develop large bumps like mosquito bites. The deceased didn't. But I think that's because most bed bug victims don't die. The skin has time to react. Not in this case."

Patterson shook his head. "Bugs killing people. I can't believe it." He said. "I going to have to check my hotel rooms extra carefully from now on. Second thought, I'll probably never go away again. If my wife finds out..." His voice trailed off.

Patty smiled. In her mind she could visualize Patterson's wife Cindi, spraying the detective down with pesticide as he walked through the door. The mental image brought some much-needed levity to the dark situation.

"Can we kill them?" Patty asked. It was a well-known myth, bantered around by local gadflies and the dishonest media, that bed bugs are impervious to pesticides.

"Oh yeah. I'm sure." Patterson lied. Truth is, he believed the wise tales. "George treated Tracy's house earlier. He's going to find out tomorrow how well it worked. Keep your fingers crossed."

She looked at him in astonishment. *Keep your fingers crossed?* Patty had dealt with nine deaths because of these bugs. She saw what they could do. She was keeping her fingers, toes, eyes and legs crossed. *Let them be dead by tomorrow. Please. For the sake of all the people living here.*

The bodies of Eleanor, judge Julius and the reporter, Josh Clark, were packed away in the coroner's van. The small utility vehicle was capable of holding four bodies. She had never filled the van to max capacity but give these bugs a few more days and she just might. Patty drove the long journey -thirty minutes- carpooling with the deceased. She wondered if she could travel in the high occupancy lanes because she was undeniably not alone. There were three other people in the vehicle with her. Although they wouldn't be able to attest to their presence. That would be a very awkward traffic stop, she thought to herself laughing at her own dark humor.

The morgue was deathly quiet, no pun intended. Dim lights reflected off the dusty surfaces. Small, square tiles lined the floor and covered the walls. It was bland, and it that had been the intent. The morgue was a serious place, not a place of rest or relaxation, unless you happened to be one of the dead. She rolled the gurneys in, white sheets covering the bodies. This was the final journey for the elderly sophisticates. Memories flooded back to her again. The judge -his reading glasses with that long rope chain drooping from his ears- immersed in the writings of JRR Tolkien. Eleanor engaged in a wild melee with the talking heads of the cable news on her TV screen. The Blue House would never be the same. She didn't know if the two had anyone to will it to. They had no children and no close relatives. The house would probably face a sad fate, returning to the dilapidated condition it had been before its restoration; sinking back into the shadows. The spirits of the judge and Eleanor would join the army of ghosts haunting the grounds. The grounds they all loved, tended and nurtured throughout the house's long history.

Patty slid each of the three bodies inside separate slots of the large refrigerated walk-in. She would operate on them tomorrow. She couldn't bare it tonight. She knew what she would find. No blood and the same microscopic puncture wounds she had overlooked on the rest of the corpses. The fact she would be dissecting people she had known, respected and loved -gave her the creeps. It churned her insides into a concoction of bubbling bile, making her nauseated.

She missed her husband. Missed Ted's voice. That calm, cool, collected voice. He was her drug of choice. She didn't drink. She didn't abuse narcotics. She lived on her husband. His laughter. The way he stared into her eyes and made her feel young again, like the entire world was at the tips of their fingers. That their life together was just beginning. She picked up the phone and tried to call him. The home phone rang and rang. She heard the familiar message and hung up.

Patty had spent the last thirty-six hours at the morgue, sleeping for a few of them on the small cot in her office. There were two other coroners who worked Harford County. They had both inquired about her state of wellbeing. *Can we help? Get you something to eat? Drive you home?* She declined. No, she was a warrior. A Roman legionnaire in formation to face insurmountable odds. Ted was what she really needed. She would find all that in the loving embrace of her husband. She would eat the food he would whip up for her. Drink the cold filtered water he would sit next to her plate. And fall soundly asleep wrapped in his muscular arms. She made up her mind and decided to go home. It was 10 p.m. The dead would wait, could wait, until tomorrow.

The house was quiet when she arrived. Ted's M5 parked in the same spot. Various tools sat idle on the workbench. He had probably been tinkering around earlier and had gone in to pass out in his favorite recliner. She walked into the house. She had forgotten again to leave her jacket at the office or at least in the car. She thought about walking it out and putting it in her Audi but decided that the strenuous nature of such a simple task was too much for her to bare in her condition. She threw her OCD to the wind and hung the jacket by the door.

She could hear the familiar sounds of North by Northwest floating down the stairs. She guessed the scene. Cary Grant driving the car, intoxicated, down that steep, winding road. She ascended the stairs. She didn't call out. She would surprise her sleeping man. Sit on his lap. Kiss him full on the mouth. If he refused to wake, no matter, she would take the remote, lower the volume of the TV and crawl under the covers. Just Ted's sheer presence in the room with her would be enough. She walked quietly down the hallway, the sound of the TV getting louder with every step. The door to the bedroom was ajar, flashes from the TV screen escaping through the small crack. She opened the door, looked in and collapsed onto the floor.

The wails of a hurt, dying animal echoed throughout the vast expanse of her home. Ted was dead. No doubt about it. No reason to approach him to know that much. His eyes were open and unseeing. The bottom of his jaw hung down, his tongue lolling out. She screamed. Gut

wrenching, terrifying screams into the darkness. *Not Ted!*
No, please, not Ted! He can't be dead! He's got to be alive!
He's playing a joke, a game. He's going to get up, laugh
and hug me. Tell me he's sorry for playing such a
thoughtless prank. But he's not getting up. He's not
moving. His chest isn't heaving with the breath of life. No.
No. No!

Seconds felt like minutes, minutes felt like hours as
she lay crumpled in a heap. Tears streamed down her face,
a waterfall of warm salt puddling on the floor. She kept
looking at her husband -the love of her life- praying that
this was a nightmare. Finally, she got to her knees. She
crawled over to him, each shift of her body felt like a
sledgehammer slamming into her chest. Her hand reached
up, stroked his face, felt his neck for a pulse. Her hand fell,
laying limp on the floor, as if it had been severed. *Ted is*
dead. Ted is number 10. Ted is number 10. She repeated it
over and over again as she wailed. Her face inches from the
hardwood. *Ted was number 10.*

She saw it, sitting there, looking curiously at her. A
small bug with six legs tucked under its oval-shaped body.
It was tan, or more like reddish in color and it seemed to be
staring. Staring right into her soul. Patty couldn't see its
eyes, it was too small for that, but what she did see, what
she assumed were its eyes bore into her like a drill in balsa
wood. It was one of them, she was sure of it. She slammed
her fist down. *Fuck you! Fuck you!* She beat it, attempting
to drive it into the floor. She thought the floor might crack
under the continuous barrage. She didn't care. *Let it crack!*
Let it splinter! Let this damn piece of shit be embedded into
the floor for an eternity! Her mind hissed. She couldn't feel
the pain. Blood came from her hand. It dripped on to the

floor. The blood felt *good. Die you bastard! Drown in my blood! Die!*

She lifted her bloody hand. *It was alive! ALIVE!* She must have missed. She hit it again, this time she felt the pain, but it wasn't the pain of her hand hitting the floor, it was a different pain. A pinch like a tiny knife sticking into her flesh. *The bastard bit me!* Then she looked around. More of them were coming. Hundreds, thousands, ringing her like natives around a fire; like Mayans around a human sacrifice. They didn't wait. Their tiny bodies moved, surging forward with incredible momentum. They covered her legs like ants on melting ice cream. She screamed, not in agony but in terror. She felt their bites, sharp, painful. Her hands worked furiously, sweeping the bugs off her body. She stood. *Damn those little bastards!* She felt weak, her mind swirled, her body cramped, her heart raced. She tripped and fell. More jumped on her, biting, feeding, drinking her blood. She crawled on all fours towards the stairs. Her hands swept her jeans, trying, desperately trying, to sweep the bugs off. She tumbled down, falling, slamming into each stair with heart-stopping force. When she landed at the bottom, she didn't miss a beat. She didn't have time. Not a second to spare. She looked up as she ran and saw the swarm of bugs running on the walls, racing down the stairs towards her. She ran full throttle, legs moving like an Olympic athlete.

The bugs were right on her tail. She made it through the living, the dining room, the kitchen. They were almost there. Inches away from her heels. *Time to feed. Time to finish her.* A blood meal to reproduce, to survive. The woman was in survival mode. They closed in. One of the bugs made it onto her shoe. It crawled up her leg and hung on for dear life.

Patty reached the door to the garage. She yanked it open with her hand, went through and pulled it shut behind her. She hoped it would stop them. It didn't. They came under the door, under the weather strip, their bodies a creepy mass moving like the sea at night rushing up the shore. She made it to her car and jumped in. She punched the start button. It failed to start. She pressed the brake pedal as hard as she could, then punched the little red button. The engine roared to life. *Ouch! Damn it!* She reached down and plucked the one off her jeans, rolled down her window and flicked the bastard back into the advancing mass of the others. The garage door was halfway open when she pounded the gear shifter into reverse and slammed her foot on the gas.

Chapter 30

The aroma of caramelizing peppers and onions floated throughout the house. He sliced the green and red bells thin and the onions thick. There was no reason for it. No secret formula handed down by the gods. Just personal preference. It had all started with a little bit of butter, a little olive oil and a few too many tablespoons of minced garlic. He let that simmer for just a second. Not too long. Then the peppers and onions; the basil; the oregano; and finally, the secret ingredient and this had been handed down by the gods – a glass of white wine. The smell of the whole glorious concoction would tempt the devil himself. *Devil went down to Georgia, but he wanted what George was cooking, to hell with a soul to steal.*

Finally, George sliced browned Italian sausages down the middle, long ways and placed them open side down onto the simmering peppers and onions. This way the flavors would invade the meat like an army of mourners at a rich man's funeral. The pan was covered, the heat was turned down to low and the man of the hour, the chef, the master of the kitchen, retired to his living room with a bottle of Coors in his hand. He had ten minutes to wallow in the sounds emanating from his Sonos system before he would be able to eat. He sat on the black leather sofa and listened to the magic fingers of Duke Ellington. The beer was cold, crisp, and refreshing, like lemonade on a hot summer day. He sipped it, hands playing an imaginary piano, nose sniffing the succulent aroma from the kitchen. It was heaven. Then the bell rang.

George glanced at his phone. *Who the hell would be here at 11 p.m.?* He never had visitors and never, ever, had pop-ins. Maybe it was his brother. Maybe Chris got into another fight with his wife. But normally he would call first, give George a profanity-laced blow by blow of the argument, then ask if he could come by when he was already in George's driveway.

What really made him nervous was his past. He had done *things* -unspeakable, terrible *things* in his former career. *Things* he had been ordered to do and sworn to secrecy over. Maybe those *things* had finally caught up to him. Maybe it was a uniformed officer who would ask - command- him to get in the car and George would never be seen or heard from again. It had happened before, the Army Ranger who *forgot* to pull the string on his parachute. The CIA man who *forgot* he was allergic to peanuts. The Navy Seal who *forgot* how to swim and drowned in his three-foot swimming pool. No bullshit. Real situations. True unsolved mysteries.

So, George answered the door with his Colt .45 pistol resting out of sight behind his back, which was like having Superman hiding behind the door. It was Ocean. *Ocean at 11 p.m.? Shouldn't he be knocking into some broad? Kicking back with his homeboys? Wrecking a 7-11 at eleven?* The kid was a mess. Shirt tucked in -odd in it of itself- hair gelled back, shined shoes. *What the hell's going on? Did the President reveal Rosewell really happened? The Pope tell everyone he's a Mormon? The Communist Chinese declare Mao was an evil bastard?* None of the above. Ocean's girlfriend was pregnant.

"Six weeks." Ocean said in a dull monotone. He sounded depressed like Santa had come but forgot his big red sack full of goodies. *Sorry, left 'em in the sleigh. Sleigh's in the shop, see you next year. Ho. Ho. Ho.*

"She's pregnant, you're not having a colonoscopy." George said, pulling the kid inside and closing the door. "You hungry?" George tried to conceal the forty-five. Ocean saw it.

"What's with the gat?"

The gat? "Nothing. Been a few break-ins in the neighborhood lately." George said, sliding the gun into the cabinets above his stove. "You hungry?" George repeated the question, hoping to delete the *gat* from Ocean's mind.

Ocean's face changed. A slight smile creased his lips. Not surprising, George's sausages and peppers would have convinced people jumping off the Brooklyn Bridge that life was great. Full of hope. Full of tasty food. George ushered Ocean to the table and sat him down.

"Beer?"

"I can't drink. Another six months."

George smiled, chiding. "And that's stopped you before?" He grabbed the kid a cold Coors from the fridge. George placed two rolls on two separate plates and filled them with a sausage and a slew of oil-drenched peppers and onions. They ate like wolves in Siberia, not speaking, not looking around, not even thinking, just biting, ripping, tearing, chewing the succulent food. The taste of the garlic; the bite of the peppers; the nip of the onions; the feel of piercing the skin of the sausage; and the crisp bubbles of the beer chasing it all down. It was truly a remarkable experience. Something to write in a diary. Something that would never be forgotten.

No words passed their lips for some time. When the plates were finished, the second beers passed out and opened, they finally spoke. Not in the house but bundled like ice fishermen in Alaska outside on George's deck. Ocean chain-smoked one cigarette after another like an accountant pouring over ledger books in an old black and white film. The only thing missing was the green visor.

"So?" George asked, considering the night sky, swigging his beer.

"So, what?" Ocean replied.

"What are you going to do?"

"I'm going to keep it." Ocean answered without a thought in the other direction. "I'm scared. I mean, my life's pretty much over."

George reached over and slapped the kid behind the head.

"What the hell was that for!" Ocean exclaimed rubbing the back of his head.

"That was your wake-up call. It's called life. Your life is just beginning. Life requires responsibility. You screw, you take the chance of creating life. That's a fact. Kids are great. You're going to love it." George held up his hand at Ocean's attempted interruption. "Sure, sure there will be hard times, but you'll love it, the good, the bad and forgive the cliché, the fucking ugly." He downed the rest of his beer and uncapped a new one.

Ocean looked out through the railings into the dark backyard. "You never had kids." He blurted out, a child's attempt at trying to make sense of reality.

"That's different. I would've loved to have kids. If I could only go back. If I could meet the Doc and hop in that

DeLorean, I'd change a lot of things in my life." George said, and he too became lost in the icy blackness of the night, staring off into space, thinking of all the things he would amend, the differences he could have made and the lives he could have saved.

"Name one?" Ocean broke the silence.

"I would have never joined the army." George stated.

"What did you do in the army?" Ocean asked. George rarely, if ever, spoke of his service and when he did, he was extraordinarily equivocal.

The silence that followed Ocean's question mirrored the quiet of the night. No sound. No bugs chirping. No owls hooting. Nothing. Not a peep. Just silence. Dracula holding that candle and saying: *Creatures of the night, where the hell are you?* Ocean guzzled down his second beer. George handed him another.

"I joined when I was eighteen." George began after several minutes, his voice low. "Hated the way the family business was going. Hated to see what my brothers were doing to my father."

Ocean knew the story of George's brothers. Hell, everyone who had anything to do with the pest control world in Maryland knew the story of George's brothers. Their lives read like a raunchy novel and a daytime television show combined. Maury Povich the bug man. Greed, drugs and sex, ingredients that soothed the morbid soul. Ocean let George speak. He didn't interrupt. Didn't tell him how tired he was of hearing the stories for the ten thousandth freaking time. He just listened, sipping his beer and allowing the alcohol to take him.

"I loved the army."

"You just said you wouldn't have…"

"I know what I said. Let me explain. I fit in. I followed orders. Felt comfortable giving orders. That's the perfect recipe for success in the army. I climbed the ladder, quickly being promoted to 1st lieutenant. Then I went to Ranger school. I passed. It was tough, but I was tougher. I had been raised to be tough." George took another long sip of his beer. "Then that's when it all went to hell."

"Why? You went to war?"

"Oh yeah. But that's not why. I did a tour in the First Gulf War and that's what did it. That's all it took. And then *they* came for me."

"Who?" Ocean asked, sitting up in his chair, smoking what had to be his tenth cigarette in the last twenty minutes.

"The *unit*. That's what they called it in my day. They recruited me, and I went through their selection process." George paused again to sip his beer.

The intrigue was more than Ocean was willing to accept. "And?"

"I passed with flying colors."

"What's the *unit*?"

George stared out into the black night, his eyes fixed on something far away that Ocean couldn't see.

"The elite of the elite. They're more secretive and are involved in more covert operations than any other unit in the military."

"More than the Seals?"

"Way more." George answered, his eyes remaining fixed, staring straight ahead, as if he were looking into the past, into a portal, another realm. His eyes were open but blind to the present.

"Delta?" The question erupted from the young man like a model rocket leaving its launcher.

George knew the name. *Yes, I was in Delta. Delta, the unit, the team that changed my life forever.* "Never heard of 'em." George denied, at the same time nodding his head affirmatively.

Ocean sat back in his chair. His face awed, star-struck like meeting your favorite celebrity and learning he is more down to earth than you thought. Denzel Washington meets Harry Homeowner. The kid had completely forgotten his worries. His pregnant girlfriend; his life-changing; his abrupt turn into adulthood, fatherhood, trunk packed with more responsibilities than it could possibly hold. Everything left his mind except what George was saying.

"I spent the next six years in the *unit*. Traveled to countries all over the world. I loved my job. Who wouldn't? Running around the world with a bunch of great guys, shooting guns, meeting spies, killing bad guys. It was a blast. Until…" George stopped. His mind tried to work out the possibilities. *Can I tell the kid?* He had never told anyone before. Never. Not even his old man before he died.

Can I trust him? He wanted to relieve his conscience. Wanted to get the weight of the boulder off his chest. Maybe the nightmares would stop or at least slow down. Maybe for once, he wouldn't wake up in a pool of his sweat.

"Until what?" Ocean was thrilled, like watching your team on the verge of winning the Superbowl, hands gripping; legs shaking; ass at the edge of the recliner; eyes transfixed on the screen. The final few seconds; the ball suspended in midair; the receiver in the N-zone awaiting the catch; the crowd holding their collective breath.

"Can I trust you?" George asked.

Ocean nodded. A little too quickly. A little too eagerly.

"I mean it. Can I trust you?" George asked again.

"Yes." Ocean answered.

George's face transformed from the gentle father figure to a dark sinister person Ocean didn't recognize. The effect was petrifying. A chill shot from Ocean's legs, up his spine and into his brain. He shook it off or attempted to shake it off.

"The unit is the tip of the spear. The guys who keep this country safe. The last faces the worst human beings on the planet see. Our guns stop wars before they start. Our bullets prevent nuclear weapons from being launched. Our blood ensures the safety of millions."

"A little exulted."

"Well…" George shrugged like *what can I say?* "Anyway, We were in Iraq. And we weren't supposed to be. Which was fine because we were always in places we weren't supposed to be. It was right after the First Gulf War ended. I thought we were going in to cancel Sadam's reservation. After all, it would've been us, our unit, that would've been called to do it. And he deserved it. That piece of shit killed a shit load of his own people. Gassed 'em. Killed 'em like cattle in a slaughterhouse." George opened the fourth beer. Ocean, sporting eyes like little glassy pools, reached for another one, which he cracked with juvenile enthusiasm.

"Saddam was a big proponent of chemical warfare. He had this guy. This general who ran his chemical weapons division. I don't remember his real name but most of us on the team called him the Gas-master. Instead of taking out Sadam, we went into Iraq to rub out the Gas-master. I have to say, I was a little disappointed. Not that I thought the Gas-master didn't deserve it. I did. But it was kind of like cutting off the rattler of a rattlesnake. I'd have rather cut off the snake's head. The head is where the real fangs are. The rattle just makes a lot of noise. But I did my job without protest. It was supposed to be quick and clean. Helicopter in, do the deed, helicopter out. Easy, a piece of cake. But it wasn't. Like every other mission, something always went wrong and this one went south in a big way. When we landed in the middle of that shit hole town, our ride went out, kicked the bucket. The pilot, Mister new-guy-hot-shot, misjudged the landing and the helicopter's propeller clipped a nearby building. Flew right off and exploded into a million razor-sharp pieces, cutting into everything and everybody within a two-block radius. Our plan of surprise ended up being the biggest fuck-up in covert ops history. It was like putting up a billboard in the middle of town. *Come get the Americans!* We're here.

We're in your backyard. We still canceled the Gas-master's reservation. Shot him in the head while he was raping a kid."

Ocean looked at George with revulsion. "A kid?"

"She was probably ten or eleven. The Gas-master liked his rape victims young. Guess he figured they'd be less likely to fight back." George paused to take a sip. "The sending the general to hell part of the mission went off perfectly. It was the get the hell out of dodge part that was the problem. As soon as we got out outside, the pit of the serpent opened up, coming from everywhere all at once. Seven-six-twos ripped and roared from every corner, every alley and every window and there was nowhere to hide. We didn't have a fucking chopper. HQ was sending one, but it would take time. Hunker down, they said. Hunker down! Where?! It's a fucking town in the middle of the desert where the houses are made out of the fucking sand. You know what a bullet does to sand?"

Ocean shook his head as if George were actually asking him.

"Why'd you kill the Gas-guy if you didn't have a way to get out?" Ocean asked.

"You always finish the mission. General Rapist, the Gas-master, was Saddam's chemical weapons expert. He was the guy responsible for killing all those Kurds. He was a real sick fuck. Killing him wasn't the problem. The problem was going out on the mission with an untrained, untested pilot. That was a bad command decision on Cap's part. And he paid for his mistake with his life. Took a round right through the head then got blown to bits by a mortar. Happened right next to me."

Ocean was horrified. He never knew about George's combat experience. He was stunned that his boss, a guy he got along with; a guy he really looked up to; had seen men die. Grotesque images of exploded bodies and head wounds floated in and out of Ocean's intoxicated imagination. He felt like puking. Sending the partly digested Italian sausages and peppers into the cold black night. *Thank God for beer.* The alcohol numbed him.

George spoke, his voice muffled as it traveled through the wintry night air. "I remember being pinned down. Afraid to lift my head. Afraid to look around. I turned to see the other men on my team. They were laying there. They needed a leader, someone to stand up, someone to get them the hell out. They looked scared. And these were tough guys. Guys that had seen the ass crack of life and had given it the old boot. These weren't wimps. But I saw fear in them." George stopped talking. The horror of the scene at the forefront of his mind took him. After a moment of silence, he continued. "I remember thinking I should get up. Get up and do something. Then I heard it. Footsteps in the sand. The crunch of boots. I looked around again to make sure it wasn't my guys. They weren't moving. They were hunkered down trying not to get shot. Someone was coming. I figured it had to be the enemy. They probably thought we were on the verge. They were coming to give us one last round. A nice, close one to the back of the head. I had to do something. I stood and…"

He couldn't finish. Ocean stared at him, bewildered, his eyes begging for more. George couldn't tell him the rest. Couldn't say that he had fired his weapon, unloaded his magazine into the people approaching but they weren't the enemy. *They were… they were…*

"And?" Ocean asked, his face pleading.

George sat there. He considered Ocean's eyes but all he could see were the eyes of the people he had slaughtered that day. Their dead, questioning expressions on Ocean's face. "I don't want to talk about it." George stated in a colossal one-eighty... *No more. Not now, not ever. Sorry kid.* He thought.

Ocean realized he'd lost. He gave up. The alcohol took him to happy places away from death and destruction. *To hell with George and his war stories.*

"How about Marty leaving us home with his daughters?" Ocean said trying to change the subject.

"I still can't believe that." George replied smiling.

"Tells us he's got to head out. Says his daughters can sign the bill." Ocean starts to chuckle. "I go in expecting to see freaking monsters. I mean come on, look at Marty, it's not as if he's Don Juan." Both men laugh uncontrollably.

"More like fell out of the ugly tree and hit every branch on the way down!" George exclaimed, roaring with mirth at the expense of one of their biggest clients.

"And his daughters. Fucking beautiful! I mean those bodies. Both sitting in the hot tub, bikinis on, talking about sex right in front of me." He began to mimic the girls' voices. "Daddy always walks in when Tommy's got his pants down. He's always ruining it." His voice switches back. "The whole time they're staring right at me while they're saying this. It was like a porno. Far out!"

"Yeah and then you say…" George begins but Ocean waves his hand trying to stop George from finishing. "Have you all seen any nipples around!" George is laughing so hard he's actually turning red.

"I meant…to say…mice around." Ocean could barely get the words out he was laughing so hard.

The laughter felt good. George's war story and Ocean's girlfriend troubles were miles away, barely visible on the horizon.

"That is funny but the best… the best goes to Freddy." Ocean said. "Greatest story ever." Ocean grabbed the arms of his chair to stop him from falling out, he was laughing that hard.

"Who does that? Seriously. Who the hell does that?" George said through his tears of hilarity. "It ain't normal."

The story, which George goes on to tell for like the thousandth time, starts out pretty much like every other story in George's life -at Chesapeake Pest Management. Freddy Daniels has worked there for a century. At least it seems like a century. Freddy is in his fifties and likes food better than anything else -literally anything else. Not food in its entirety but sweets; baked goods to be exact. Freddy would probably sell his own kids on the black market for a whipped-cream-topped strawberry shortcake. Sweets were what got Fred into this mess. Freddy was in a nursing home; wonderful place; real clean; a rarity for sure in the realm of long-term care. He had just entered his last room of the day and was about to commence his inspection when a nurse busted through the door and informed Freddy, to his horror, that the resident whose room he was currently standing in had just died. *Just* being the keyword. Died fifty minutes ago. What had started as a horror, turned out to be a delight when Fred noticed the now deceased resident had left a full tray of food behind. Obviously, the old statement: *you can't take it with you*, also pertains to lunch. On the tray were three chocolate chip cookies. Big chocolate chip cookies, nearly falling apart due to the sheer volume of the Nestle chips. After making sure the coast was crystal clear, Fred proceeded to devour the delectable morsels in a frenzy similar to an act committed by the Cookie Monster on Sesame Street. *COOKIES! YUM! YUM! YUM!* No one would have ever known about the incident if Fred himself - probably feeling a little guilty over the post-mortem theft- hadn't opened his colossal trap of a mouth and told one of his fellow techs about it. The story made it around the office faster than a wildfire in California and became a legend that would far outlive the chunky tech with the feverish appetite for sugar.

Ocean and George told several more stories, trying to beat the chill of the winter night. Finally, the bite of Jack Frost was more than they could bare, and they went in. Ocean attempted to say his goodbyes and head for the door.

"Where the hell are you going?" George asked, stopping the young man in his tracks. "What are you, five-foot-seven, one hundred and fifty pounds? I'd say six beers for you is four past the legal limit. And you're not even legal yet. So, you're staying." George's decision was final and non-negotiable.

Ocean looked a little flummoxed. He could drive. He wasn't exactly sober, but he wasn't exactly drunk either. He was about to fight. About to say I'm fine, give me a break old man But then he got a good look into the old man's serious eyes and realized there wouldn't be an argument, at all. Ocean pointed quizzically to the couch.

"I've got a three-bedroom house. One bedroom is mine. The other I use for an office. The third I use for the extremely rare occasion when someone spends the night." George answered.

"Thanks man." Ocean said. That sounded a hell of a lot better than a cold leather couch on a night like this.

Chapter 31

The floor was a ligneous masterpiece milled from the forest nearly three centuries ago. The light, more a gaseous glow, than an electrical filament, cast shadows in the corners like wreaths in the moonlight. The walls, yellowed with age and the smoke of a billion cigarettes, held secrets of a forgotten age. Their ears heard the innumerable lame lines of seduction; the breathy lustful whispers; the plans of countless crimes; and the laughter from the thousands of brainy one-liners. The bar top, once a gleaming creation, now dulled and weathered by spills and the nightly purification of bucket and rag.

The food was mediocre, but no one really cared. One didn't come to Pierce's for the food, one came for the rivers of bubbling hops and glasses of golden fermentation. They came to kick back at the bar stools and immerse in the happiness, the sorrow and the agony of life. Pierce's was the dive of Havre de Grace. And that is literally what the locals call this hole -*The Dive*. It is a dive -a plunge straight down to the alleys of the forgotten. A jump off the highest springboard with no safety net nor string of safety. Just *the hang* in midair before the freefall to the inky blackness below. No self-respecting plutocrat would ever find their way into this bar, and if they did, they'd receive more scowls than a flatulent man on an elevator. That had been the case for a century or so until the dawn of the *yuppie*. The *yuppie* -that young beast of fashionable retro- transformed Pierce's from a *shit hole* to a *shit hole with style*. Now, *The Dive* was a fashionable spot for the literary enlightened -the poets, the artists, the amateur novelists, the graphic designers and the musicians. They all flocked to Pierce's for a taste of the *other side*. Inspiration for their work. Reason for their persistence. They tapped their leather soles on the aged wood of the floor and marveled at the nicotine stained architecture.

Pierce's had a remarkable past. It was the oldest bar in Maryland still in operation. It had survived the perilous days of countless battles including being nearly burned to a smoldering pile of ash by the British in 1812, but thanks in part to a roaring business even in those days and a plump British colonel who liked his booze better than his orders - Pierce's was spared.

James walked in around nine. The bar was full as usual with the two warring clans engaged in their never-ending struggle for the soul of *The Dive*. The happy, smiling faced youngsters, who crowded around tables conversing amiably, and the frowning, jaundice faced old heads, who were slumped over the bar, sipping their daily afflictions with gnarled hands. The Allies and the Axis. But the Allies would win, money always won, and the fact was that people James' age -the new progressive elite- had the money and spent the money, far more than the old timers' penchant checks could afford, which guaranteed their inevitable victory.

He ordered a Reds Hard Cider which earned him several evil eyes from the old drunks who had secured the high ground of the bar top for the night. He could almost hear their thoughts out loud: *look at this young black punk, in his suit and tie, ordering a fruity tutti drink. Well, old farts, keep thinking it. The young black men with their hard apple ciders and their fresh clothes are here to stay. Losing the battle pops. Get with the millennium.* He wondered if the same thing was said back in the Middle Ages. If the young men battled the old guard with the same intensity.

Hey, it's year 1,000 pops. Time to move on. James smiled at the thought.

Two men sat at the bar. James watched them with amusement. Both were old, rumpled barflies. The taller of the two complained about the inequities of life to a short, gray-haired woman who looked about as interested as one would be observing an earthworm slither across a sidewalk. The shorter of the two men, stood next to the tall one and repeated everything the tall man said. It was like an act. *Abbott and Costello meet the Gray-Haired Lady.* It couldn't be real.

"I work twelve hours a day for that bastard." The tall man groaned.

"Twelve hours a day." The short man repeated.

"And they can't throw me a bone." The tall man complained, throwing up his hands.

"Can't throw me a bone." The short man repeated.

The bar door swung open and in walked Kelley. James froze; his eyes locked. She was breathtaking. She wore a chic blue knit sweater with tight navy-blue jeans and carried a yellow-orange handbag. The outfit told you everything you needed to know about Kelley. She had a bod -evident no matter what she was wearing- but she didn't flaunt it because she was classy, stylish and professional. No high heels. Just flats. Her hair tousled, not in a bad way, in an *I just threw this together and it looks so damn good* way. The only part of Kelley's ensemble that didn't fit her was her macho, arrogant boyfriend Officer Mike.

Mike, slim and muscular, was wearing a leather jacket and freaking cowboy boots under his jeans. He took in the room like a wrestler takes in an opponent. He sported a cocky look plastered his face, the same cocky look all cops have when they are out of uniform. The *hey I'm dressed like a normal dude, but I still got my gun* look. James wanted to smack him. Walk right up, take that gun out of his holster and pistol whip the bastard. Seeing him again really made James think of Carlos and Sabrina. James fingered his phone deep in his pocket. The phone that contained the piece of evidence that would destroy Mike's life forever. One look at the video and any cop in any jurisdiction would disown and disavow that smug piece of shit.

Kelly spotted James, smiled broadly and walked over. "Hey stranger." She said, giving James a hug. He used the hug as an opportunity to take an enormous whiff of her perfume. It was tantalizing like a hit of the world's greatest drug.

"I thought you said nine." James said returning her smile and holding up his watch.

"You can blame mister mirror, mirror on the wall here." She said as Officer Mike approached.

Mike pulled his hand out of his jacket pocket and held it out. "I think we've met before." He said to James. His voice was cold and intimidating.

James shook the outstretched hand but before he could relinquish his grasp Mike tightened his grip. He was strong. James felt his knuckles shifting under the pressure. He stared into Mike's eyes. *What was this guy's problem?* James thought as he tried desperately not to display any sign of anguish. Finally, Mike released and put his hand back into his jacket. The arrogant prick smiled broadly, winning the first battle of the night.

"You guys want a drink?" James asked, nodding to the bartender.

"You buying?" Mike replied in a gruff voice. Kelly shot him a look and was about to speak up.

"Sure, why not." James answered. Kelly looked at James and he could hear her mind mouthing the words *I'm sorry*. James just smiled in reply. Maybe telepathy was real.

A straight whiskey and not a *cheap* straight whiskey, was Mike's order. Kelly wanted a martini. The bartender -a kid with more tattoos than skin, his face looking like an earring display in a shopping mall- poured the drinks. James paid in cash. He preferred cash; one of his rules. He hated cards. *No one can steal your identity from a twenty-dollar-bill.* He would tell that to anyone who asked him why he preferred the greenback as opposed to the credit currency of modern times. And he was right of course.

Drinks in hand, the three moved their pow wow to a table in the corner. Mike and Kelly sat opposite James, who still nursed his hard apple cider.

"Did you hear about the Blue House?" Kelly asked. She had the excited glint of a reporter in her eyes. Reporters will get excited about *anything* that is newsworthy. Some of the most devastating events in history would garner a smile from a jumpy reporter. *Did you hear about the mass shooting? How about the bombing of that shopping mall?* Only reporters could get away with acting like that. Most people forgave them. They figured that reporters weren't actually excited about the horrific event itself, but the chance to cover the horrific event; find the clues; solve the crime; and then report it. Plus, the public is an unashamed slut for bad news. Say what you want about reporters. The fact is: if the public didn't watch, then the reporters wouldn't waste their time reporting it.

"The bed and breakfast?" James asked. He glanced over at Mike who was completely disinterested in the topic and instead was mentally undressing a pretty brunette sitting at the bar. *Pig.* James thought. *If I were with Kelly, my eyes would never leave her.*

Kelly nodded. "Three more unexplained deaths. The judge, his wife... and a CNN reporter!"

"Holy shit." James uttered, genuinely stunned by the news. He had never met the judge. Never stayed in the Blue House but this was Havre de Grace, and everyone knew everyone's name. The judge and Eleanor were famous in this small town. Big fish in a small pond.

Officer Mike dove back into the conversation. His voice harsh like acid rain on a bronze statue. "I told you not to report any of that." He snapped.

"Don't worry about it. James is my friend. He's not going to tell anybody." She pleaded. She was scared, cowering under the big cop's angry gaze.

"This geek?" Officer Mike sneered, pointing his thumb at James. "He'd sell his soul for a good story."

"He's not a reporter Mike. He's a meteorologist." She stammered.

What the hell did he mean by that? Mike knows I'm a meteorologist. Hell, everyone in this town knows. Does he know about the tape? Did Carlos rat me out? Sell me down the river for a little bit of leniency? James thought about this for several seconds while Mike and Kelly argued. He decided that there was no way Carlos would do that. After all, Mike was extorting Carlos and it was Carlos' girlfriend that had been sexually molested by *Officer Prick.*

"I don't fucking care!" Mike exclaimed rudely. "When I tell you things, you need to keep your fucking mouth shut you stupid twat!"

James took one look at Kelly's hurt face and saw that it was full of fear. She was afraid of Mike. Terrified, as if the big cop had smacked her around on occasion. Not that James would be surprised by such a revelation. Anger welled up from somewhere deep inside him.

"Don't talk to her like that." James said in a quiet but stern demeanor.

Mike looked at him with an evil glow. "Was I talking to you geek?"

James stood up. He didn't want to, didn't mean to, but he did. He squared his shoulders. James' wasn't a big guy. He worked out, occasionally, but pound for pound he could never match Officer Mike. Plus, the crooked cop was carrying a gun, so even if James got the drop on him - which he wouldn't- Mike would only have to pull his piece and James would be another statistic. Another unarmed black man mowed down by a white cop. The best thing this little act of bravery would accomplish is a Black Lives Matter protest in the center of town.

"Hey geek, you need to learn some manners." Mike threatened.

The bar got eerily quiet which added to the tension. Everyone seemed to be transfixed on the fight about to break out across the room. All eyes on the two would be scrappers. Pay per view for free. Drinks and a show.

"Did your parents ever tell you to respect women?" James shot back. He was cool, not petrified, scared a little, but calmer than he would have expected.

"I think I should teach you some manners home-boy." Mike grabbed the front of James shirt in one hand. "You know how many of your kind I've slammed on the concrete?"

"Big racist cop. Not really a unique quality in law enforcement these days." James stated.

"Racist cop? What the fuck do you know about racism asshole?" Mike taunted. He wanted James to answer. Wanted this preppy young black punk to break the calm and start the melee.

"Stop it Mike! Let him go!" Kelly shouted at her boyfriend. She too was now standing, trying to pull Mike's arm down. Trying to break the big cop's iron grip on James' shirt. He flicked her away like a feather. She fell back onto the bench.

"Hey fellas, take it outside." The bartender said, approaching the men. "I called the cops, they're on their way."

Mike laughed. It was an evil laugh like Satan at a show. "I am the muthafuckin' cops, you piece of shit."

"You're not a cop. You're a corrupt piece of trash." James spat at him.

Mike tightened his hold on James' shirt. "What'd you say?" He said through gritted teeth.

"You heard me." James answered. He held his ground, staring right into the cop's eyes. No one in the bar flinched. Shit was about to hit the fan. *Here we go.*

"I want that tape." Mike snarled.

James nearly lost his balance when he heard that. *Carlos, that drug dealing piece of crap.* Carlos had ratted him out. *I guess loyalty amongst thieves is really loyalty amongst thieves -in that there really is none.*

"Leave now or that tape will be all over the news by tomorrow morning." James said.

Mike stared at him. "Give it to me." He commanded. His voice was dangerously low.

James looked down and saw Mike's right hand disappear under his jacket into shoulder holster territory. *Great, now I'm going to get fucking shot. Think. Think damn it!* James played a thousand scenarios in his mind. All of them ended with his life being cut abruptly short.

"I don't have it with me." He said. "I made copies. Many, many copies. You kill me, and that tape will be everywhere."

"You're lying."

"No, I'm not." James pronounced with baited breath.

Mike looked like he was about to shoot, then his hand reappeared and it was empty. He let go of James' shirt and smoothed his own jacket back down as if he really cared about his appearance at a time like this.

"Let's go." Mike said to Kelly.

She looked back at him trying to gauge his potential reaction. She looked terrified. Scared shitless. It was plain to see. She shook her head. "I'm staying." She said and grimaced, expecting to receive a smack for her disobedience, the way a dog tucks its tail between its legs after knocking over the trash can.

Mike glared down at her. "Fine you stupid cunt. Stay with the geek." He looked back up at James and stuck a fat finger into his face. "I want that tape by tomorrow. All the copies. If not, I'll fucking find you. You can count on it."

Mike looked around the bar, challenging anyone to stand up and say something. No one did. Then he punched his way through the old wooden door. The whole bar took a collective sigh of relief and then the party commenced again as if nothing had happened. The music started, and the conversation picked up exactly where it had left off.

James sat back down. Kelly took a few minutes to compose herself. He realized with a pang that she had been crying. "You okay?" He asked delicately.

She didn't reply for several seconds, then she spoke. "What tape?"

Chapter 32

"This is amazing." That was her first thought as she entered.

The house was really a giant log cabin. A single living room compromised the majority of the first floor with two bedrooms and one bathroom upstairs. The living room boasted a ceiling with a commanding height of twenty feet. Immense beams, hewn from single trees glistening with shellac, held up the roofing planks. What really impressed Kelly, well, what really impressed anyone that entered James' humble abode, was the floor to ceiling stone fireplace and the shelves upon shelves of literary works spanning the length of the entire structure. So many books that the house had the distinct odor of a library -a smell of musty cellulose decay and ink. For a cultured person, the house was paradise. A place to kick up your heels and read a classical title next to the glow of a warm fire.

Kelly had no idea James was such an erudite. She always imagined he was more of a computer geek - studying weather charts in front of a bank of monitors or punching the joystick of an X-box. She walked slowly around the shelves, perusing the titles, delicately feeling the spines with her fingertips. They were organized alphabetically by author. Starting with John Quincy Adams, Conrad Aiken, Horatio Alger, Jr., Amelia A. Barr and so on and so on and so on.

"Have you read all these?" She asked, never taking her eyes off the books, making her way down the wall.

James watched her with delight. "Yes, I have." He said modestly. "All of them once. Some of them two or three times."

"Which ones are your favorites?"

James was glad she had forgotten about the tape. Let her drown herself in the books. He'd much rather talk about that. The rest of the time at the bar, she had pleaded with him to show her the tape. *What was on it? Was it Mike? Was it her? Was it a sex tape?* He scoffed at that. No way he'd ever keep a sex tape of that asshole and the woman he loved going at it. *How'd he get it?* James refused to answer. She kept it up until they left the bar around two in the morning. The only good thing about her journalistic prodding was that she had completely forgotten about Officer Mike. James hadn't. He had checked, double checked and triple checked the street outside Pierce's before he walked to his car. A crooked cop with a vendetta -that's all James needed. No thank you. I'll take the check.

"Lord of the Rings, Plato's Republic, Treasure Island, Huck Finn and Four Past Midnight." He answered.

"Four Past what?"

"Midnight. It's a book by Stephen King. Four novellas in one. My favorite story by King is Secret Window, Secret Garden. It's the second novella in the book." James walked over to the fire. He placed a couple of logs from the basket over a fire starter, pulled out the box of matches from his desk and lit the paper of the starter. Within minutes it was a massive conflagration.

Kelly sat down on the leather couch to get closer to the fire. James retreated into his small kitchen, retrieved two glasses of wine and then joined her. They didn't sit together like lovers, more like friends -a foot or so apart.

"Is it true King wrote Shawshank Redemption?" She asked.

James nodded. "And the Green Mile."

"Do you have any other favorites?"

"Dracula, The Time Machine, The Invisible Man and last but not least, the Hardy Boys series."

"The Hardy Boys?" She asked, sipping her wine, her voluptuous eyes fixed on his while she touched her lips to the rim of the glass and let the red liquid slip into her mouth.

James stopped breathing for a second. He nearly bolted into the kitchen to rinse icy water on his face. *Is this really happening? This stunning woman that I have been in love with for so many years, sitting on my couch, talking about books, sipping wine by the fire? If this is what heaven is like, then someone please kill me now. Shoot me. Please shoot me.* He thought to himself as he stared into her eyes.

"The Hardy Boys aren't a series most literary snobs would include in their list of the greats. But I think they're great. They're juvenile mystery stories about two brothers who solve crimes. I read them when I was a kid and never really put them down. They're my comfort books. If I want to cool off, I read a Hardy Boys' mystery. Always puts me in a good mood." He was being honest with her. *Yes, I'm a nerd. A huge nerd. I don't care if you know. I've given up trying to be someone else in your mind. If you prefer the big, macho cop who smacks you around then there's the door and don't let it hit you where the good Lord split you.* He thought but didn't say.

She nodded and took a second glance around the room. There was something here, something hopelessly romantic. Something like old rustic charm with a touch of chivalry.

"How'd you find this place?" She inquired.

"Amazon." James said smiling. You can find anything on Amazon. "I built it. I found the land, bought the plans, tweaked them a bit, handpicked the lumber and then hired contractors to build it. It's a lot cheaper than might you think. Probably because it's not in town and therefore not by the water." In fact, it was far away from town, near the border of the Susquehanna state park. Which gave this property just the right amount of woodsy charm. The two-acre lot was home to trees of all sizes, shapes and species. After all, you can't have a log cabin anywhere else but in the woods. It just wouldn't be right. One rarely if ever sees a log cabin on a shoreline or in the middle of a raging city. A cabin belongs in the woods from whence it came.

"I always thought you lived in town." She said and scooched slightly, ever so slightly, closer to James, who felt a surge of ecstasy run up his legs, linger for a second in his groan and then proceed to his head.

She looked at him for a long second and suddenly, without warning, she kissed him. Leaned over and kissed him on the mouth. He felt her tongue. Felt it twirl around his in an erotic dance. He placed his hand behind her head, her long, wavy hair running through his fingers. It felt amazing. He could live in this moment forever. Quit his job and spend the rest of his existence on earth making out with this gorgeous woman. She smelled like lilacs, sweet with a hint of vanilla. They kissed for what seemed like a year then slowly, as if falling from a great height, they split apart. She started crying. Why was she crying? Of all the things he imagined her doing after they kissed for the first time, crying was hardly one of them. It was unmistakable though, tears, small, fast-moving tears, fell from her eyes and dribbled down her cheeks onto her sweater.

"I really wasn't expecting that." He said. "I guess I'm a pretty lousy kisser." He smiled.

She smiled. "I'm sorry." She said. "Truth is, I've been in love with you for years. And I spent those years chasing clowns."

This took James by surprise, like opening a door in a nondescript hallway, walking through and falling fifty feet. She'd been in love with me for years? What? He felt like looking around, trying to see the person she was really speaking to, because it couldn't be him. Could it?

"I knew the first time we met and you spilled that water all over, that you'd be the perfect man for me. I guess I just wasn't ready for it." She dried her tears on a napkin James handed her.

"Well, if there's any consolation, I have been in love with you from that day too. The first time I saw you, the first time I looked into your eyes." He rubbed the skin under her eye with his thumb. "The first time I heard your voice. I could never get it out of my head. I knew right there that I couldn't stop until I had you. I…"

She cut him off, jumping into his arms, kissing him hard, voraciously on the mouth, her body writhing against his. She wrapped her legs around him, pushed her hips into him, wanting him, willing him to take her. He did. He lifted her, her lips and legs still locked. At this moment, he was stronger than an ox. He hefted her and carried her into his bedroom. They flopped onto the bed. A furious struggle ensued as the two lovers undressed one another - unbuttoning, unfastening, unzipping the various pieces of clothing barring each other from one another's body. She looked even better naked, not that it was a surprise. She had full breasts with tiny, perfect nipples. Her ass felt firm in his grasp, her legs long and smooth. Their lips never parted the entire time remaining fixed as if they had been smeared with super glue. He entered her. She gasped slightly which made him feel a sense of pride. He was big in that department, obviously a lot bigger than Mike. He pushed himself inside her, going slow, taking his time, enjoying every minute, every second. She surprised him, arching her hips up and thrusting his manhood into her fast and hard. She liked it. Loved it. She climaxed quickly, grabbing his back, squeezing with all her might, pulling him deeper, deeper, deeper inside her with her legs. He exploded. He couldn't hold it any longer. His legs shook uncontrollably. They laid like that for several minutes, their chests heaving in unison, their bodies shivering with the after effects of orgasm. Finally, they fell apart.

"That …was…amazing." James gasped.

Kelly just nodded, still unable to muster coherent speech. She rolled to her side, pulling his arm as she did. They fell asleep spooning naked, together at last.

Chapter 33

Patterson held his coffee mug in his hand. He was worried, like really worried, like getting a CT scan and finding an unknown lump worried. Maybe cancer, maybe not. Not sure until you get a giant needle shoved into the spot that the doctor swears up and down has been numbed but it still hurts like a son of a bitch. Worried like every time the phone rings you expect it to be the same doctor telling you he needs in to come in ASAP because of that lump, well that lump Mr. Patterson is not ... well you better just come in. The reason for Patterson's current anxiety was curled in a fetal position on his couch. Patty the coroner had shown up last night, sobbing and silent -refusing to utter a word to Patterson or his wife. Patty had just wandered into the house, into the darkened living room and somehow, via some miracle, located the couch, where she passed out almost immediately.

The detective tried, as detectives do, to get the truth out of Patty. She wasn't buying it. Her eyes stared out into infinity. They were red, swollen and drowning in tears. She didn't answer any of Patterson's inquiries. *What happened? What's going on? Is there another body? Someone you know? Someone you love? Do you want something to drink? Eat?* Nothing. Not a word. Just sobs. Finally, the detective, after losing a hushed argument in the corner with his wife Cindi, gave up and shoved off. He went upstairs and passed out.

Now, it was seven in the morning, the detective realized as he stared at his watch. He'd have to leave soon. He took a giant sip from the mug, draining the rest of the coffee down his throat; where it would work its way slowly into his bloodstream; and jump-start his heart. He pondered whether to wake Patty. If he knew Patty and he did, or at least he thought he did; she'd probably be pissed if he didn't wake her; then again, depending on what had occurred the night before, she might be pissed if he did. Women are harder to understand than the Canterbury Tales. At least with the Tales, one could read the cliff notes and stumble through the old English dialogue.

"Still asleep?" Cindi, Patterson's wife, asked approaching her husband surreptitiously from behind. She peered in on the unconscious form of Patty.

Patterson nodded. "I can't figure out if I should wake her up or not."

"Leave her." Cindi answered; settling the matter, once and for all.

"What about her job?"

Cindi paused for a second. "I have a bad feeling about this. Let her sleep."

Again, Patterson nodded. The wife is always right, and they really do wear the pants in a marriage. Like no shit they wear the pants. They pick whether you live or die, what type of furniture you buy, what kind of appliances you use and what temperature the thermostat is set too. A little warm and it's too damn hot. A little cold and it's too damn cold. You're not going to get a word in edgewise and even if you do, if you're a smart man, you listen to what your wife has to say regardless. Patterson was a smart man.

Breakfast wasn't the usual. Eggs, being a major contributor to high cholesterol -which Patterson debates every time he sees his doctor- are a once or twice a week luxury. Somebody please find the fountain of youth.

Instead of eggs, Patterson suffered -literally suffered like being tortured in the pit of some Mongolian prison- through a bowl of oatmeal which he believed was merely shredded cardboard with hot water poured on top. The few blueberries and raisins his Cindi threw in, just made matters worse, not better, but he *was* pushing sixty, so he suffered in silence.

After he was finished with his morning torture session, he kissed Cindi, the whole time fending off the terrorist hounds that doubled as her bodyguards. He was almost through the door, feet on the other side, hand on the outside knob when he heard a low mumble from within. It stopped him dead in his tracks. It was Patty. She was sitting up, the oblivion-look back in her sunken eyes and she was calling for him. He stepped back into the house and hurried into the living room -detective's curiosity propelling him like a speedboat over calm water.

"He's dead." The words left Patty's cracked lips like a gunshot at the start of the Olympic races.

"Who? Who's dead?" Patterson asked, taking a seat next to her.

"Ted. Ted's dead." That came out in a whisper.

Cindi joined them, standing silently in the door frame, unable to move further into the room.

"Your husband?" Patterson's gruff voice asked.

Patty nodded, a fresh round of sobs overtaking her body. "Yes. Ted's dead. They killed him."

"Who killed him Patty?" Patterson asked; the detective in him winning the internal struggle between inquisitor and empathetic friend.

Her hands cupped her face as she sobbed. That seemed to motivate Cindi, who entered the room and went over to sit on the couch. Her motherly, comforting qualities, which make Cindi so great, take over. She rubbed Patty's back and in silence reassured her things will be alright while at the same time glaring at her husband, her fierce eyes commanding him to soften his tone.

"Who killed him Patty?" He asked, much calmer this time.

"Those goddamn bugs! Those bastards killed him!" Patty shrieked in agony.

"You saw them? In your house?" Patterson's voice was sharp, with a touch of fear sprinkled on top.

"Yes. They tried to kill me. I ran. They chased me." Tears filled her eyes. "They chased me! What kind of bugs chase people? They weren't afraid of me." She sobbed.

Patterson looked at her for a long time before answering. "They chased me too Pat."

Cindi looked terrified. She stared at her husband in abstract horror as if he was the personification of a giant cockroach. "What bugs?" Her anxious voice asked, not really wanting to hear the answer.

"We have to go back. We have to get Ted." Patty said.

"We will Pat. We will."

"Where'd they come from?" Patty asked. "Why are they here? Why Havre de Grace?"

Chapter 34

That was the exact question Patterson asked George the minute the exterminator arrived in town that morning. *Where had these goddamn bugs come from?* George had no idea. Literally no idea. Sorry sir, I don't know why the chicken crossed the road, but he is now on the other side and killing people. The fact is that bed bugs are *people bugs*; they feed on people and sometimes animals; but they prefer people, like you'd prefer a filet mignon instead of chuck roast. Because they feed on people, they're obviously spread by people. Bed bugs tend to stick with their food source.

The real burning question was where this new breed of bed bugs had originated? If they killed the people they fed on, then how had they spread? It would be like burning your ride at the first pit stop. And was this new species only present in Havre de Grace or were they elsewhere? Killing people in other cities and towns. Did they come up the great northern highway as their brethren did a decade ago? The *great northern highway* is the term George uses to describe to his customers where the resurgence of bed bugs originated from. The *highway* stretches from south of the border down Mexico way and travels up to the states. It has been a common misnomer that bed bugs came from Europe born on the backs, or better yet, in the luggage, of European immigrants but that was bullshit. Bedbugs followed the wave of illegal immigration from Central and South America over the southern border. The reason for George's deduction was simple. He had treated hundreds, if not thousands of homes in the last ten years and predominantly -like ninety-five freaking percent- of the homes were occupied by illegal immigrants. How had he known they were illegals? Illegals, or undocumented workers as the left-wing press preferred to call them, worked in the countless restaurants George serviced. The restaurant owners stack the illegals up in hovel houses, sometimes two to three families at a time. They live in squalor. Try to live with fifteen people in one house and see what the conditions are like. Only illegals would allow themselves to be treated in this manner. Legal immigrants, unafraid of law enforcement, demand higher pay, reasonable housing and better working conditions from their employers. But illegals will accept anything, just for the chance, just for the one in a million shot at living the American dream. The chance to succeed. The chance to be great. An opportunity their countries -specifically their countries' governments- won't afford them.

George hated to see it. Hated the abuse. He was a staunch advocate of legal immigration; letting more people come to the States legally; making it cheaper; making it easier; making it quicker. But the fact was that illegals serve a purpose; they're abused for a reason. The rightwing politicians abuse them for cheaper labor, bowing down to the corporate lobbying wing of their party. The leftwing politicians abuse them for votes, allowing them to take the place of African Americans on the great well-fare plantation; making sure they're forever poor; giving them fish instead of teaching them how to fish; ensuring the left will continue to win elections for decades to come. And that's it. Plain and simple. Cheap labor and votes and for the rest of us -the good, law-abiding, taxpaying population, we get never-ending public debt and bed bugs.

"So why are they in Havre de Grace?" Patterson asked after George finished his tirade on illegal immigration.

George shrugged his shoulders. "Bed bugs have always been in Havre de Grace. Hell, I did a house yesterday for them on Juanita Street. Obviously not the ones that are killing people."

"Any word for the university?"

"I sent them the samples from the townhouses. Probably late today or early tomorrow." George answered. Earlier that morning, like six a.m. early, which didn't sit well with the nauseated, hung over Ocean, George instructed Lee, one of his techs, to take the samples down to the University on his way to D.C. The University of Maryland's campus is in College Park, a suburb of the nation's capital.

"Have you checked with any other cities? They might be experiencing something similar if this is a nation-wide outbreak."

"I'll do that." Patterson said, chagrinned at the fact that he hadn't thought of that himself.

Ocean walked, really stumbled out of the Lazy Trout Deli. *Lazy Trout? Lazy freaking trout? Who the hell name's their place lazy trout? What the hell is a lazy trout?* Ocean pondered, looking up at the sign. The food was good though. Incredibly good, dripping grease and loaded with carbs, just what the doctor ordered on a morning like this. Obviously, there wasn't any lazy trout working the griddle. George with his bowls of fruit. Who on God's green earth eats a bowl of fruit with a hangover? After he had finished the slices of cantaloupe, blueberries and strawberries at the crack of five at George's house, he nearly regurgitated a smoothie into George's toilet bowl. His stomach was doing the Shawn Johnson but without the gold medals. The egg, cheese and bacon on a plain bagel he held in his hand felt like redemption after a lifetime of sin.

Ocean tried not to look up, tried not to peer directly into the bright morning sun beaming off every damn thing in the vicinity. The car windows, the shop windows and even the damn sidewalk, dirty as it was, reflected the sun with a vengeance. *Why did I drink so much?* He was no heavyweight. Not now, not ever. Four beers and he was feeling it. *Four freaking beers! What kind of damn beer was that? Must have been some of that malt liquor shit. Yeah, yeah, keep telling yourself that.* He thought. *You blew it on four beers. You pussy.*

Ocean got into the truck, ate his sandwich and watched Patterson as the detective talked to George and shot fleeting glances his way. He hoped the detective didn't find out he was hitting the bottle last night and underage to boot. But the old dude smiled -smiled and looked right at Ocean as if he was saying, *you stupid little bastard. Knocking chicks up and getting plastered. Knocking chicks up!* Ocean had forgotten about that. Boy, ol' boy. What will his parents say? He hadn't told them. Not yet. Last night, he had gone right from Ashley's to George's.

Ocean wanted to tell George first. It wasn't that he couldn't tell his parents, he just connected better with George, who was like the older brother he had never had. Ocean wasn't afraid to tell his mother. That'd be easy. It was his old man that would be the tougher nut to crack. Tough like competing in a triathlon, then flying to the moon by flapping your wings. In other words -impossible. Ocean was never close to his father. His father being one of the those, *I know books, my colleagues, my business, my golf game and my clients better than I know my own son.* His father wouldn't be mad. His father would be *disappointed*; shake his head, walk into his study and sit all night sipping on a scotch *disappointed*. Ocean wished his father would get mad like go all Joe Pesci in Goodfellas on him. *You stupid motherfucker! You knocked your girl up! You motherfucker! Next time, if there will be a next time, maybe, maybe, you should think about pulling that little tool of yours out!* That would be much better than the silent, scotch neat, low light in the study reaction.

It was a beautiful day. The calm before the storm and if the weathermen were right -the one in this town usual always was- would hit tomorrow around noon. Despite the sun, it was cold. Frigid is a better description. The weather was an oxymoron, bright sun and cold temperatures. Just the sort of day George loathed. The sun made you think of happier times, summer days, warm, willing, opportunities abound. The cold made you want to stay inside, wrapped up in a blanket with the heat turned all the way up. To hell with winter.

The storm would be serious. He had conducted an impromptu meeting that morning with the eleven guys working for him. The message was simple: *if it's bad we'll let you know.* His brother Chris, sitting pompously in the corner, had reiterated over and over again that if they could work, they'd work. Chris was so predictable. He'd be home, feet warming over the fireplace while the guys crashed and burned on the highway. Chris had no empathy whatsoever. It wasn't part of his make-up. It was the one thing that wasn't swimming in his gene pool. Thankfully, George was president and therefore the decision rested with him and not the *think of the money not of the men* Chris. If the storm came and streets became impassible, George would send the boys home. No sense in getting anyone killed, especially his boys, who all had families with young children.

"I'm going back to the townhouse this evening." George said. For some reason, his instincts were bothering him. He glanced around. Why was his gut alarm going off? The only people present other than himself, Patterson and the hung-over Ocean were three older gents walking out of the Lazy Trout, their stomachs full and their mouths moving amicably, conversing about the various things their wives did to annoy them. *Can you believe she...* George caught sight of another man sitting in a late model Mustang parked nearby. He was young, probably mid-twenties and looked like a gangbanger: tattooed sleeves and a shaved head with a *mind your own business pops* expression etched on his face. Despite the outward appearance, the kid was innocuous enough. He just sat in his cool sled, probably trying to find some alone time to pack a blunt or execute some other form of illicit activity. Still there was something about him. Something that drew George's eye and set his instinctual alarm bells ringing. George made a mental note of the punk's license plate.

"Let me know if it worked." Patterson said.

"How's Patty? That's her name right? The coroner."

Patterson nodded. "She's at work. Tough old broad. I'm heading over to her house as we speak. Told her to stay at the morgue. I sent for her assistant. He'll come and get her husband's body. No need to screw up Patty's head any more than it already is."

"From what you told me, she'll probably show up anyway."

"Yeah, you're probably right. It's her house. What can I say?"

"Nothing." George walked with the Detective over to the Crown Victoria.

Patterson got in and rolled the window down. "Maybe you and the kid should come with me." Patterson's big, puppy dog eyes pleaded with George. It's funny how they could change so rapidly. One minute they were tough, perilous, I'll throw you through a brick wall and all that jazz. The next he was kind, gentle, easy going.

"We'll follow you." George said, without hesitation. He could move his schedule back a bit. No restaurants with early opening times, just a few old folk's homes. The good thing about nursing homes is that they're always open.

Patterson's detective Vic and George's truck pulled out of the parking lot one after the other. It was a somber procession like a hearse in route to the cemetery. Slow driving and plenty of time to look at your surroundings. The Mustang waited several seconds before it too pulled out of the lot and took position several hundred feet behind George's pick-up. The gangbanger thought he was slick, driving nonchalantly, attempting to appear as if he just happened to be heading in the same direction. He obviously had never encountered anyone of George's ilk. Thanks to Fort Bragg and the countless hours, days, weeks, months and years of the same, redundant instructions drilled into his head, George had become quite adept at all things James Bond. He picked up on the tail right away, like as soon as the dumb punk left the lot and turned. *Amateur.* George thought as he watched the stang in his rearview mirror. Now he tried to deduce who the driver was. He could be a reporter, it wasn't likely, but who knew these days. Tattoos and bad haircuts were almost a prerequisite for anything having to with mass communications. Reporter was a definite possibility, but this punk wasn't a reporter. George just knew like you knew you had to turn off the water before changing a pipe, or the gas before hooking up a new stove. It was natural. A basic reflex. Should he tell Patterson? Alert the Detective to the tail or just keep the punk in view? If he alerted Patterson, he'd have to explain how he knew the guy was up to no good, which either would be taken as *George was nuts* or *George had a secret in his past most exterminators don't have.* Betting on Patterson's brutal, stony personality, he'd bet on the former: *George was a nut.* So, he decided not to tell Patterson.

The third and most important question boggling George's mind was: who was the driver of the Stang actually following? Was it the detective or was it George? If it was the detective, then George was willing to disregard his instincts and chalk this up to a young, overly excited reporter, trying to get the jump on the story of a lifetime. If it was George, then it could be anyone. Could be the agency. Could be the unit. Could be DIA. Whoever it was, if they were after George, then they were bad freaking news.

Chapter 35

Save the Rainforest. That's what the sign read. Save the rainforest. Lenny stared at it as he waited for the elusive Paul Rudd to make his appearance. First Sangmore, then Rudd. First the creator, then the destroyer.

Lenny wasn't accustomed to waiting. Not in the slightest. No one made Lenny wait. It was unprecedented. Who the hell did this eccentric rain forest trekking quack think he was? And Rudd was definitely a rain forest trekking quack. His office was loaded with preserved wood, cemented leaves and pinned insects. Jars, upon jar of specimens. It was like a biology lesson on steroids. Lenny peered at each display one by one to pass the time. His very valuable time. Time he could be spending on much more important things like the IPO, which was fast approaching. He was leading the team of accountants working with the investment banks cataloging the minutia of figures, assets, revenues, profits and expenses. It was monotonous work. Work that had to be done in a timely fashion. The investment banks needed the numbers to place an exact market capitalization on Sentrix.

Finally, the good doctor walked through the office door. He took one look at Lenny and sighed deeply before taking his seat behind his small metal desk. Dr. Rudd looked weathered and cracked like some of his fossilized leaves. His brown hair was streaked with grey. His body large and bulky, poorly hidden behind a tight lab coat. He peered at Lenny through sunken eyes, eyes that had seen the world, the good and the bad.

"My apologies for making you wait. I had a sedulous task in need of my immediate attention." The doctor said rather cordially, but his body language conveyed annoyance, as if the appearance of this suave asshole from administration was extremely irritating to say the least.

"I am a very busy man, Dr. Rudd." Lenny said, because he just couldn't help making this loser feel even more like a loser. *I'm important, you're not.* It didn't affect Rudd. The old doctor looked even more exasperated.

"What can I do for you?"

"You worked closely with Sangmore…"

"Dr. Sangmore." Rudd interjected.

Lenny smiled, irritated by the interruption. "Dr. Sangmore, in his development of species 0618?"

"Yes, I did."

"I take it you are aware that the species in question, once released into the test sites, killed several people."

It wasn't a question, it was a challenge, like I know this little tidbit of confidential information is making its rounds in the research and development department, even though its supposed to be… well… *SECRET!* Rudd just stared in response.

"Are you aware of this doctor?"

"I am aware that the species in question have killed nine people to date. Last, I checked nine is not synonymous with several. Several usually indicates three not nine."

"Nine people to date." Lenny replied. He had tricked the doctor into giving him the answer he wanted, confirming that indeed the confidential information was being passed around these departments like a football at a frat house. "How did you hear about it doctor?"

Again, Rudd just gazed at Lenny for a few seconds before answering. "Lenny…"

"Leonard."

Rudd looked furious. "Leonard." He pronounced with great drama. "If you are here to check out the latest news in the gossip column then I suggest you speak to my subordinates. As I understand you have a very serious problem, if you don't mind can we please get down to business."

This really made Lenny acrimonious. He was supposed to be the intemperate one. They sat in silence for a minute or so; engaged in a fierce staring contest to the death. Finally, Lenny embarked once again on his list of questions.

"Why do you think species 0618 is killing people?"

"It was a flawed project to begin with. Ill-conceived. Executed ahead of schedule by a bumptious administration without proper evaluation."

"Flawed how?"

"One must not play God Leonard. You cannot mutate an insect without consequences."

No question. Lenny absolutely hated this man, but he couldn't disagree with his logic. Lenny himself, had argued to Carter this same theory. The Jurassic Park theory. Playing God and all that crap.

"It seemed like a plausible idea. Create a species that only we have the means to eliminate."

"It's a pipe dream. I'll reiterate, you cannot play God. It never works out for us mortals. Mother nature creates insects for specific reasons. Altering those reasons, alters reality which in almost any case is a losing battle. Take rabbits on the island of New Zealand as a prime example. They were introduced in the 1800s as a means of nutrition for sailors. Now these furry rodents are wreaking havoc on farms throughout the country, putting New Zealand's entire agricultural system in jeopardy. Creating species 0618 is similar although vastly different."

"Different how?"

"Different in that species 0618 was created purely for profit. To make money. To corner the market in pest control. To create the largest exterminating business in world history. That's the difference. Money is the root of evil, Leonard."

Money is the root of evil. Lenny wished he had a dime for every time he heard that phrase come from the lips of someone who is born wealthy. *Money is the root of evil.* Lenny thought snidely. The very essence of the phrase made him physically ill. Rudd would never understand the almighty profit machine. The dream that propelled men and women to great heights. After all, Rudd was born rich. Silver spoon, silver rattle, gold-plated toothbrush. He never had to taste struggle. Never had to wonder where his next meal would come from. Why should he? Mommy and daddy were always there to write the checks. He had read Rudd's dossier. Parents owned an oil company in Texas. A billion-dollar oil company. The rainforest trekking scientist stood to inherit a fortune. No wonder he could venture out into the wilderness, literally, without care. Most people would never have that luxury.

"What is your answer to this dilemma?"

"This is not a dilemma Leonard. A dilemma would be the vending machine running out of Twix bars. This is a catastrophe." Rudd sat back in his chair and closed his eyes. "Dio Insecticide." He said without opening them.

"Dio Insecticide will be able to stop the spread?"

"No question about it. Dio Insecticide was designed specifically to kill species 0618. It performed flawlessly in clinicals. Rendering a kill rate of seventy percent within the first sixty seconds." Rudd still had his eyes closed as if he were sleeping or bored with the conversation. Not something one would expect from the man who created the wonder chemical -his life's work.

"It killed species 0618 in tests?" Lenny already knew this. He had read the briefs. Dio Insecticide not only killed species 0618, it slaughtered them like ants under a magnifying glass. They never stood a chance.

"You already know that Leonard." *Don't waste my time, you smug little bastard.* Rudd thought but didn't say. "Send out a team armed with Dio Insecticide. Stop these bugs before it's too late. If they spread, if they evolve, Dio Insecticide may not be able to..." He left the rest unsaid. The warning was clear.

"Rabbits in New Zealand?" Lenny asked sarcastically.

Rudd became extremely angry, his face reddening, his veins popping. He slammed his fist down on the desk. "God damn it! Do you have any idea what's going on?! Any clue?! People are dying! Send out the fucking team! Put an end to this now!" Rudd tried and succeeded to get control over his temper. He relaxed, sitting back in his chair. "Before it's too late." He finished.

"One last question." Lenny said, ignoring the older man's outburst as if it hadn't happened at all. "Did you have access to the lab where species 0618 was created?"

Rudd knew what Sentrix was doing. They weren't interested in stopping this. They wouldn't take the risk. If they did, it would mean either covertly sending in the troops armed with Dio Insecticide -which would be next to near impossible- or coming out publicly and acknowledging their faults -which would be suicide. No, they wouldn't do either. They were lining up the suckers. Lining up people on the edge of the cliff to take the fall, the plunge into the vastness of blame, scandal and conviction. Dr. Rudd wouldn't take the bait. He wouldn't give this little prick the satisfaction. Sentrix was guilty, but not as a whole. Not the little men out there crawling in filth bringing in the revenue. Not the salesmen out hunting down the leads. Not the secretaries taking the calls from the distressed clients. No. The people who caused this, who created this, who were one hundred percent to blame was the administration. The Carters. The Reynolds. The Leonards. They're the ten-thousand-pound elephant in the room.

Chapter 36

All the evidence Lenny had gathered so far wasn't much at all. In fact, it was a smidgen above nothing. Just a smidgen, like a crumb in a five-gallon bucket. Carter had already called. Typical Carter. In thirty-six hours, Lenny had conducted four interviews; learned the basics of genetic engineering; explored solutions with the rainforest geek; and sent Tony to meet with the two delivery boys in Havre de Grace. But that wasn't good enough for Carter. No sir. He wanted magic which is something Lenny couldn't deliver. Sorry Carter but I'm not a gray-haired wizard running around the world with my good friends Frodo and Sam.

Lenny attempted to sum it all up for Carter. What had he really discovered? Bumpkiss, jack shit, a big goose egg. Nothing at all. The interviews had gone, well, terribly. He felt Sangmore was a bumbling moron of a geneticist and Rudd, that arrogant ass, was exactly that -an arrogant ass. So, he put together what he could which was a little bit of horse shit, mixed with a whole lot of fluff and a pinch of just plain deceit and *viola!* Something had stood out in his mind. Something that didn't fit. A piece of the puzzle was missing.

It was Rudd. The old scientist was fishy. Fishy like fell into a pond and made love to a school of bass. It was something about his attitude. Something about the way he flipped his lid. The anger in him rising to a fever pitch. *Was it guilt? Anxiety? Stop them now before it's too late? Or maybe remorse? Or was he right?* If Sentrix sent in a team armed with Dio Insecticide, the only pesticide that could kill these bugs, then they would pretty much be giving up the goat. *Yes, we did it. We created these bugs. We murdered these people, but we can make it all better.* At the very least, they'd be opening themselves up to nine wrongful death lawsuits which would total millions of dollars in damages. The worse would be prison.

Rudd didn't seem enthusiastic about Dio Insecticide. Sure, he had suggested they use the product, but he wasn't passionate about his creation. Lenny had seen inventors who had succeeded at their tasks and developed their ideas into marketable goods. These inventors could talk about their product all day. Talk about it until you plug your ears with cement because you were so sick of hearing about the what's-it. Their products were their life. They loved them, cherished them and were the best salesmen for them. Not Rudd. When it came to Dio Insecticide Rudd seemed dismissive and dull. Maybe it was the wealthy background -the rich parents, the spoiled life, the BMW on the sixteenth birthday. Maybe all that had made Rudd complacent, stripping him of any and all interest. Or maybe Lenny was just paranoid. He hadn't liked Rudd from the moment he met the man or better yet, from the moment the cocky scientist had forced Lenny to wait in his office. Plus, he had screamed at Lenny, who wasn't accustomed to being spoken to in that manner. The other possibility was maybe, just maybe, Rudd was dirty. Was it possible that Rudd, a disgruntled scientist, hell-bent on sabotaging this project, had secretly snuck into the lab and altered the bugs genetic code? It was plausible but was it possible? Rudd had the access. Rudd had the means. Rudd had the intelligence. But did Rudd have the motive? That was the $50 million question. *Alex, I'll take Disgruntled Rich Scientists with No Morals for five hundred please.*

Lenny decided to revert to his basic instinct - forensic accounting. There was something soothing about columns of figures. The lines of numbers felt real, in stark contrast to human beings. Numbers were reality. Numbers never cheated; stole; had affairs; got drunk; got high; nor committed murders. Numbers just were. They existed like the sky, the trees, the soil, a part of nature, a part of life, a part of reality. Fair and balanced.

Lenny's office was nice. Not big, not like Reynold's or Ritler's, but nice and cozy. Pictures of successful business titans hung on his walls. Portraits of John D. Rockefeller, Andrew Carnegie and J.P. Morgan; their stern, serious gazes fixed on the young Jewish accountant seated before them. None of the three moguls were Jews but this didn't bother Lenny in the slightest. Men and women who obsessed about one's religious affiliations to the point of alienating themselves within a certain community are truly lost despite feeling like they're found.

Rockefeller held the most prominent place in the room, directly behind the desk and rightfully so. Rockefeller was an accountant. His first job in fact was tending a ledger book for $300 a year. He had built Standard Oil on the back of good ledger keeping and had turned the small refining business into the most powerful corporation on earth. Lenny adored Rockefeller and often talked to the man in the quiet of his office. Conversing in a dream-like state with the ghost of the oil tycoon.

Lenny began to read the Rudd dossier. Paul Rudd was born in Houston, Texas. His father Harold owned a cattle ranch where he discovered black gold when his son Paul was just two years old. It was like the Beverly Hillbillies. Redneck farmer turned oil millionaire. Harold founded Texas Bell Oil and thanks to his newly acquired wealth, began to buy up struggling oil companies throughout the state. Texas Bell became a powerhouse, generating $300 million a year in revenue with an operating overhead of around 175 million dollars.

Rudd excelled in the private schools his parents' wealth afforded him. He earned a scholarship to Yale, where he studied biology and chemistry, achieving a doctorate in the latter. Dr. Rudd was then headhunted by KS Oil and Gas, a competitor of his father's firm, which operated offshore drills on both coasts of the United States and Mexico. He spent the next ten years attempting to develop a new process for refining crude before resigning from KS Oil and Gas and taking his well-known expedition through the Amazon rainforest, which eventually landed him in a roundabout way on the doorsteps of Sentrix Pest Management.

The dossier seemed straightforward. Rudd had never been involved in any illegal activities, extremist groups or unethical practices. That was the problem. The Rudd file was squeaky clean. Too clean like a freshly bleached murder scene, where one could still smell the disinfectant after the body had been hauled away.

For shits and giggles, Lenny pulled out Sangmore's file. Dr. Richard Sangmore had a nearly identical file with Dr. Rudd, except one noticeable difference: Richard -and Lenny had to admire the man for this- didn't have rich parents and had worked years paying off his student loans. Those same loans, totaling nearly $100,000, paid for his tuition at Princeton, where Sangmore had earned a doctorate in genetics. Sangmore then joined Heartfield Inc., a billion-dollar pharmaceutical company. While employed at Heartfield, Sangmore conducted experiments attempting to clone human organs to cure disease -making transplants far more affordable for the average man. He spent fifteen years at Heartfield before accepting a job with Sentrix to lead a team experimenting with genetic modification of insects. Just like Rudd's, nothing in Sangmore's file looked even remotely suspicious.

Total investment by Sentrix in the project codenamed *Goodnight Sleep Tight* topped $100 million. That was a big number, freaking huge. *$100 million!* It boggled the mind. Lenny briefly daydreamed about all the things he could buy with that kind of cash. The cars, the houses, the yachts and of course, the women. He'd have a house on the shore in the Hamptons; a yacht with three decks to tour the Bahamas; a Ferrari *-no, not a Ferrari-* a Bugatti *-yeah that's much better-* he'd have a Bugatti Chiron; and he'd have a model chick, someone with a body that never quit; someone who would make every man - *every freakin' man, even freakin' monks-* gauge their eyes out with envy. *That would be the life.*

Lenny read the column of figures one by one. Rudd's department received a poultry $15 million allocated for the development of Dio Insecticide. Fifteen million sounded like a lot of money but compared with the $85 million Sangmore's department had received -fifteen sounded like a bargain. The expenses of each department's budget seemed precise. All were itemized. A million here, a million there. The one-line item that stood out was a $10 million payment to a company called HydroLine Ltd. The entry was listed under Sangmore's department. It wasn't the largest line item. The largest was labor, which totaled nearly $42 million, but $10 million to one company was just a bit strange.

Lenny researched HydroLine on his computer. It was a limited partnership which made it difficult. Limited Partnerships protected the identity of their true owners, usually they were hidden behind layers of front companies. HydroLine had a very generic website, that despite the graphics and numerous pages of indistinguishable text, didn't really tell you shit. The company produced hoses, which wasn't hard to figure out, considering its name. So, Sentrix had spent $10 million on hoses? Lenny was no expert on piping, but the figure seemed a little high -like he hoped the hoses could transform water into wine or to hell with wine, he hoped the damn things could turn water into liquid gold. $10 million for hoses? *Yeah freakin' right.*

The ownership of Hydro Line as Lenny had suspected was shrouded in mystery. The company was based out of Salt Lake City. Lenny punched in the street address on Google Maps and got an image of a nondescript townhouse. *Okay, so now we're buying $10-million-dollar hoses from someone in a townhouse.* He kept digging, cutting layers of red tape with the clicks of his mouse. Hydro Line was owned by Jordan Giphardt and NTZ Ltd., another limited partnership. Jordan Giphardt was a scientist who lived in Salt Lake City. A Google search in the name revealed that Jordan had passed away in an automobile accident ten years ago. *Okay, so now we're buying hoses from someone in a townhouse, whose partner is a goddamn ghost!*

NTZ Ltd. was owned by two companies, BPG Ltd. and Tres Chic Ltd. This was like peeling an onion, every layer produces an acrid smell that just gets stronger as you get closer to the center. BPG was based out of Chicago, Illinois. The physical address was one would describe as a tenement building, not a place where a multimillion dollar corporation would be headquartered. Tres Chic Ltd. was headquartered in Montreal, Canada. Tres Chic, the name alone sounded more like a high-class salon or whore house than a company producing $10 million hoses. Tres Chic's headquarters was a cookie cutter mansion in a suave neighborhood of Montreal. Better than the other two: a townhouse and a tenement apartment but still not believable.

On and on, the limited train went. BPG Ltd., Tres Chic Ltd., HG Ltd., CGR Ltd., YPE Ltd. and on and on. Each google earth image was the same: an apartment, a house, a hollowed-out factory, or as in YPE's case, a desolate corner of desert real estate on Route 66, which must have been someone's idea of a joke -a very good joke but Lenny wasn't laughing. He finally came up with a name that showed some promise, Красивых горизонты, a Russian company based out of the Grand Cayman Islands. In English, the name Красивых горизонты meant Beautiful Horizons, which sounded like a travel agency *and not a goddamn hose manufacturer!*

He dialed the number Beautiful Horizons listed on their webpage and got an automated answering machine with an elegant computer voice instructing callers to leave a message. Lenny hung up the phone. The search ended there. He would file a disclosure claim with the government of the Grand Cayman Islands, but he had zero hopes it would lead to anything. Grand Cayman had a tendency of losing such claims. Attempting to discover anything of relevance regarding corporate entities on those islands was like wading into a Louisiana swamp hunting for treasure, in other words it was murky, muddy, with the occasional dead body.

He called Sangmore. He needed to know exactly what the good doctor had purchased from Hydro Line. His secretary informed Lenny that Sangmore was out of the building. He tried Sangmore's cell and got the voicemail. He left a message.

Lenny was tired. He had been at it all night, literally all night like it was now eight o'clock in the morning and he had never left. Lenny didn't care. He worked all night quite a lot. He had no wife, no kids and very few friends, except the occasional hanger-on or resurfacing old-time acquittance. He had no girlfriend to speak of and was one of those rare breeds of men who just didn't care about sex. He wasn't gay and of course he got pleasure from the proverbial *once in a blue moon* romp, but it didn't possess him. At those times he always felt like he could be doing something better, something more important, like making money. Plus, he hated the awkward after sex glow, that period where someone like himself, who's out for their own self-gratification, feels the perfunctory escape plan welling up in their mind. *O-kay, I've had a wonderful time. Thanks for the orgasm. Maybe, probably not, we can do this again sometime, but I've got to got to roll.* Work was what drove him. He achieved a phenomenal orgasm, figuring out tough problems. That was just him, who he was and there was no getting away from it.

The office was still semi-empty. The early morning work crowd had arrived at six thirty but the *sleep in, just five more minutes* crowd was -like usual- absent. Lenny staggered over to the coffee machine. He looked around at his subordinates. He hated them. Hated that he used to be like them. He felt like he was on a cloud gazing at these people scurrying around below on the street like rats in a maze of cubicles. He cursed Carter for not giving him the corner office on the top floor. The executive floor. The floor where Lenny longed to be.

The coffee tasted like shit, like mud at the bottom of a pond. He drank it anyway, gulping it down, holding his nose like a five-year-old consuming an undesirable vegetable. It did the trick, the caffeine jolting his system back to life.

"Jack, it's Lenny." On a whim, Lenny had called Special Agent Jack Wolf, an acquaintance from college. Jack was Lenny's only faithful friend, even if Lenny didn't see it.

"Turning yourself in Len?" Jack answered. "Whose head is on the chopping block today?"

Lenny's cutthroat tactics were well known. Even in college, Lenny wasn't only out to be the best, the king of the hill -he was also making sure he was the only king on top of that hill. He'd undermine and undercut anyone who could potentially challenge him for the crown.

"Very funny Jack." Lenny said in a serious tone.

Jack just laughed. Jack was good-natured to the core. Even though he was an FBI Agent, he had the uncanny ability to spot the good in people.

"Jack, I need a favor. I need to find out everything about a company called Beautiful Horizons in the Grand Cayman."

"Why? Did they swindle the great Lenny?"

"Company matter Jack. If you can't help, I understand."

Lenny listened to the sound of Jack punching keys. Several minutes went by before Lenny -jittery with anticipation- piped up.

"Anything?"

"Patience is a virtue Len." Jack said in his smooth manner which irked Lenny even more. "Okay... Beautiful horizons... got it. Looks like you've picked a winner. They are a shell of a shell of a shell." Jack said, and Lenny could sense the man was smiling. "Looks like they own a number of corporations all over the world. Some of the big ones include... Harkwood Resorts in the Carolinas. That's a big golf and spa place. I think they held the PGA there a few years ago. They also own KS Oil and Gas."

"KS?" Lenny asked, not entirely sure he had heard it correctly.

"Yeah, why is that relevant?"

"Thanks a lot Jack." Lenny went to replace the receiver, but Jack's shouts brought his ear back to the phone.

"Hold on a minute Len!" Jack yelled into the phone. "Beautiful Horizons looks like they're mobbed up, as in Russian mob."

"How can you tell?"

"They've been flagged which means they're a subject of an open investigation. I checked on the investigation and it's being run out of the bureau's ROC division. That doesn't stand for rock Lenny, that's Russian organized crime. You had better tread lightly. Those Russian dudes are sick fucks."

"Thanks again Jack."

"No problem. Remember, you didn't hear it…" Jack's words were cut off as Lenny replaced the receiver.

So, Beautiful Horizons owns KS Oil, the company Rudd worked at before he came to Sentrix. Beautiful Horizons also owns Hydro Line who received $10 million of Sentrix money. The ten-mill sounded like a payoff.

The scale was tipping in Rudd's favor, except in this case it wasn't a new car or a big bonus waiting at the finish line. Rudd was dirty and maybe Sangmore too. Could the two scientists be together in this endeavor? It was Sangmore's department that had initiated the payoff to Hydro Line. Anything was possible but what was the motive? What would corporations like Beautiful Horizons, KS Oil and the Russian mob have to gain?

Lenny would have to work harder on figuring that out. Right now, he had to call Carter and give his report. Maybe this time the smug bastard on the eightieth floor would be happy and maybe even appreciative. But Lenny doubted it.

Chapter 37

Kelly woke up and looked around the room. She tried to gauge where she was. A log cabin, books everywhere, a warm imprint next to her on the sheets, her body naked as the day she was born, then it all flooded back to her. *James. Oh James.* She squeezed the pillow and nuzzled her face into it, smelling his aroma. Where was he? He wasn't in bed. He wasn't even in the room. She worried for a second that perhaps last night was better for her than it was for him. The thoughts plagued her mind, driving her to sit up. Not another rejection. Not another romantic trip that ended in a fiery crash. She just couldn't bear it.

Then James walked into the room, balancing a tray of toast, eggs and coffee in his outstretched hands and putting her nightmares to bed, literally. She flashed him a smile that would have thawed Antarctica. He returned the smile before sitting the tray in front of her.

"I thought you left." Kelly said, still smiling like a person who realizes that dreams really do come true.

"What?" He asked, a shocked look on his face. "Why in God's name would I leave?"

She shrugged before delving into her breakfast. The eggs were delicious: soft, fluffy, with a generous amount of cheese. She had never tasted anything so good in her life.

"These are amazing." She said, her mouth crammed with food. "What's your secret?"

"A good chef never shares his recipes." He said grinning. Then he winked and whispered as if sharing the location of a hidden trove of pirate's gold. "It's the cream. I add half and half. That's it. A little half and half goes a long way."

He watched her eat. He felt proud, not haughty, but genuinely proud that someone, especially Kelly, would enjoy a dish he had personally prepared. He loved to cook. It was his second favorite activity besides reading. He only wished he could do both at the same time. Now that would be awesome. To be a good chef, you must be attentive to the food, like watching a three-year-old at the beach. You don't just let the surf take them out, you must stand there and hold their little hands, helping them to jump over every wave, easing them into the water one step at a time.

"So, you can turn up the heat in both the kitchen and the bedroom." Kelly stated after she had finished the meal and was sipping her coffee. It was a corny joke but a good one.

James smiled shyly, always the hopeless romantic. "If you say so."

A loud buzzing sound, like an angry beehive, sounded in the room. It was coming from the floor. Kelly rolled her eyes like how dare it ruin this moment. James located the source of the disruption. He reached down and picked up Kelly's pants. He gestured quizzically at her and she responded with a look like if you must. He pulled out her Samsung, tossing it onto the bed without even glancing at the caller ID. It was her phone after all and even though they had just made love -he didn't feel right looking at who was calling. Internally though, he was hoping it wasn't Officer Mike attempting to make amends for his behavior the night before.

Kelly didn't recognize the number. It was an out of state area code. She answered.

"Hello."

"Is this Kelly Halle?" The male caller asked in a nervous voice.

"Yes. Who is this?"

"You're a reporter?"

"Yes. Who I am speaking with?"

"I have a lead." The caller paused. Kelly imagined the man was sitting in a phone booth and had just heard a noise outside that made him jump. "Do you know where the Half Moon Motel is?"

"The one on Route 40, near the McDonald's?"

"I don't know. I've never seen the place. Just go there. Room 167. Look in the AC vent." The caller hung up.

Kelly pulled the phone away from her ear and looked at it as if she expected something to happen.

"Who was that?" James asked. He normally would have minded his own business. However, this time he felt justified after listening to Kelly's end of the strange conversation.

"I don't know." Kelly replied, shaking her head. "Some guy. He sounded nervous. He said I should go to the Half Moon Motel on Route 40. You want to tag along?"

"Yeah." James said, sounding a bit reluctant. But he was her only mode of transportation.

Are there still taxi cabs? James wondered as he drove to the Half Moon. He didn't see them often, not like in the old days before Uber, when yellow taxi cabs could be spotted at the corner of every intersection. Now they were an endangered species like bookstores.

The Half Moon was a dump. It should be called the full moon because it was literally a pile of feces that had just dropped out of a big ass full moon. The concrete building stretched as far as the eye could see and was sectioned into small square rooms with dirty windows, torn curtains and dilapidated AC units. Even the sidewalk was dirty -stained a few shades below black with highlights of green moss growing in spots. Very nice accommodations - for a rat. Shit even a rat would give this place a negative star rating on google. *I might eat out of a dumpster but I sure as hell ain't staying at the Half Moon Motel.*

Kelly pounded on the door of Room 167. There was no answer and the door was locked. She went to the front desk and returned a moment later with the key. Pretty women can get anything they want in life. They could rob a bank and the teller would voluntarily hand them the money while asking for their number and inquiring whether or not they were single.

"How'd you get that?" He asked.

"You don't want to know." She answered.

Kelly inserted the key card into the electronic lock and the little red light changed from red to green. The door swung open. The room was dark, humid and smelled like a cave. There was also a hint of feces in the air, subtle at first but overwhelming the farther they proceeded. It was also quiet -deathly silent.

The two bodies lay where they had taken their final breaths. The large fat man, dressed only in his underwear, was sprawled on the bed. Two neat bullet holes, centimeters apart, were cut into fat man's forehead. The other guy, his body face down, had certainly defecated when he died. This wasn't just a prediction on James' part - it was solid fact, truly solid, judging by the ungodly smell and the brown stain on the back of the man's trousers.

Kelly gasped as she entered. Her hands moved to her mouth, then to her stomach, as she contained, with difficulty, the vomit moving up her esophagus. The scene was horrific -blood, shit and dead bodies. It was like a soup recipe for a voodoo ritual.

"Jesus Christ." Was the only thing James was able to utter as his eyes roved the room. He pulled his cell phone from his pocket and began to dial the familiar digits.

"Wait!" Kelly shouted.

James looked surprised. "Wait for what? We're fucked already. Murder scene and somehow, we managed to discover it before the police based on some unknown snitch's information. We'll most likely be spending the entire duration of the ice storm inside police headquarters explaining ourselves." That sent a shudder up James' spine as with a jolt he remembered his altercation in the bar with Officer Mike. The crooked cop still had a hard-on for James and once he found out James had given Kelly his hard-on, Mike would most likely push for the death penalty. Not the strap you in a chair throw the switch kind of death penalty, but the kneel you in front of a hole in the middle of a cornfield kind. The kind where James takes a ride in Officer Mike's patrol car and is never seen or heard from again.

"Just wait." She said. She walked around the room with determination; her eyes searching for something. "You look in the drawers, I'll look at the vents."

"Now you want to disturb a crime scene? Haven't we committed enough felonies for one day? Let the cops find it, whatever it is." James pleaded but Kelly just ignored him as she began to prod the large HVAC unit under the window.

It was an old, rickety machine that served as both heat in the winter and air conditioning in the summer. Kelly flipped the lid of the small compartment on top of the machine, exposing the control knobs. The temperature knob was broken off, other than that, which seemed like an important thing, nothing else was in the small compartment. She got down on her hands and knees, wincing with disgust as she knelt on the carpet. Nothing under the damn thing. The caller had said look in the AC vent. This was the AC, but nothing was in it. She banged the front of the machine with her fist. Nothing. She tried to pull the front face plate off. It lifted a little -enough for her to peer at the AC's guts. Again, nothing.

"What are you looking for?" James asked, his patience wearing thin.

"I don't know." Kelly said in a faraway voice.

James rolled his eyes. *She doesn't know. Great! So, we're screwing around inside a murder scene. Correction, double murder scene and she doesn't know why.* He watched her stand up again and scan the room.

"Kell, let's go."

"There!" She exclaimed and bolted across the small room. She hopped up onto the bed on the far wall, straddling the dead fat man between her legs, reaching up to touch a small vent.

James was losing it man. *What the fuck was wrong with her!?* She just stepped on the body! He was pissed. He could visualize his career waving bye-bye, flipping the bird in the rear-view mirror as it squealed wheels out of the parking lot. James was rounding the monopoly board on his way straight to the big house -don't pass go, don't collect $200 and there won't be a get out of jail free card.

The vent cover fell onto the bed. Kelly didn't pay attention to it. Her adrenaline was pulsing. Her heart rate jacked like a steroid freak pumping iron at the gym. She reached her entire arm into the small vent. It was difficult. She extended as far as she could; her muscles aching with the strain; her fingers touching something hard and square. She grunted. Finally, her hand gripped enough of the object to slide it out. It was a box.

"What the fu…" James started to say as Kelly reached down to grab the vent off the chest of the dead man. She brushed the vent with her sleeve before replacing it. Then she leapt off the bed; the fat man's body reverberating with the movement.

"Let's go." She said, her voice dripping with excitement.

"We're calling the police." James stated. He had had enough of this.

"They'll ask how I got the tip."

"So? Tell them the truth. I got a phone call from a guy. Here's his number. He told me about the bodies, etc., etc. You have nothing to hide. You didn't murder these people."

"What about the box?"

"I think you should tell them."

"Absolutely not. They wouldn't have found it anyway."

"Now you are an expert on crime scene investigation techniques?" He asked rhetorically, then he realized with a stupid expression on his face, that Kelly was indeed an expert on police investigations. After all, she had been covering them for years.

"I'll tell them about the anonymous caller, but I'm not giving up the box."

"Whatever." James conceded. He called 911, speaking briefly with the emergency operator. The police were on their way. James turned back to Kelly. She was standing in front of James' car, the box sitting open on the hood. He walked over. When he got there, he peered in. The contents chilled him to the bone.

The box contained several small clear containers with tiny holes lining the sides. It was obvious the containers were used to house insects. There were six containers in total. Four were empty. Two were not. Inside those two were very small bugs. They looked like flat ticks and there were hundreds of them. They were huddled in the corner of the containers. Their delicate little brown bodies began to move, to quiver as if they could sense the presence of the two humans. They tumbled over each trying to climb to the top. They swarmed towards Kelly's fingers. She flinched, almost dropping the container on the ground. But there was no need to fear them, for they were trapped in their transparent prison.

"What are they?" James asked, his eyes fixed on the movement of the bugs.

"No clue." Kelly answered, without looking up. After another minute, she said. "I think they're bed bugs."

"Bedbugs!" James exclaimed in disgust, jumping back.

Kelly quickly looked up bed bugs on her phone. Thank you google. A second later and an image popped up on her screen. She compared it to the bugs in the jar.

"Definitely bed bugs." She said.

"What are we going to do with them?" James asked looking around nervously. His hands moving up and down his neck in a spasm; his mind whirling with unpleasant thoughts of the little brown bugs crawling on his skin.

Kelly didn't know what to do. Why were there two dead bodies in a motel room with bed bugs hidden in an AC vent? Who the hell carries bed bugs in vials? And most importantly of all, why were four of the vials empty?

"My uncle works with bugs. I'm going to show these to him. Maybe he'll have some answers." She said, unsure of herself.

"Great." James said, pausing for a second before reluctantly continuing. "You'd better put them in my trunk before the cops get here."

Chapter 38

The Mustang stayed on their tail. The driver of the Stang was a dunce. Real amateur hour. The moron must have been texting because he didn't even notice when George and Patterson pulled into Patty's driveway. Instead of slowing down or better yet passing the house, the driver of the Stang slammed on his brakes, barely avoiding making love to the back of George's truck. The rookie mistake proclaimed to the whole world his true intent. Not very subtle. The tatted-up dumbass would have been better off putting up a billboard in the center of the road like those on the strip Vegas. Neon lights and all. He must have realized his egregious error because he hit the gas hard, burning rubber as he peeled off and parked a few hundred feet up the street.

"Know who drives that car?" George asked Patterson as the two men hopped out.

Patterson glanced down the street at the Mustang. "Yep. That's that little asshole Carlos. Drug dealin' piece of Mexican dogshit. Why?"

George was shocked. *Drug dealer!* Not a great resume booster when the cops know what trade you're in.

"He followed us all the way from the Lazy Trout."

"Really?" Patterson asked in disbelief. The detective pulled a cigar from his jacket and lit it. It wasn't a crime scene until the appearance of Patterson's cigar. That made it official. The cigar is lit ladies and gentlemen, we've got a murder. "Wonder why?" The detective shrugged, then proceeded to walk up onto the porch as if the fact that someone had been tailing them -especially a known drug dealer- wasn't worthy of any concern. George marveled at the difference years of training made. Patterson was a detective but a detective in a small town. His views on potential threats were nonchalant to say the least. Whereas George's views were an entirely different ball game. George saw threats everywhere.

George looked over at Ocean, who seemed much better. The combination of salt, grease and carbs seemed to have nullified Ocean's stomach. That was a blessing because George had a feeling he'd need his little buddy at one hundred percent capacity.

Patterson looked around and silently thanked the heavens that Patty was a no-show. No big white death wagon with etched letters sat in the driveway. There was no way Patty could handle carting away the body of her own husband. Patty was tough, but no one was that tough. Patterson couldn't imagine himself in Patty's shoes. He couldn't fathom responding to his own house and finding the body of his wife Cindi, sucked dry, shriveled like a deflated balloon. It would kill him. Whatever strength he thought he had would drain out and he'd be left a sobbing mess.

The house was very nice. A stately brick house towering three stories, with a gigantic front porch. The bricks of the porch floor were laid out in a circular pattern adding to the splendor. Well maintained gardens -obviously professionally landscaped- lined the perimeter of the home. Purple aster flowers and artfully trimmed evergreen bushes seemed to be the green thumb's drug of choice. There was even a wrought iron bench set in the middle of the garden, which looked like it had recently been painted shiny jet black.

"You got a key?" George inquired as the three stood poised outside the front door. A huge freaking door that looked like it had been hand carved. Coroners must do pretty well for themselves. Maybe that's what he should've done instead of getting involved in the bug business. Dead bugs, dead bodies, what's the difference.

"You ready for this?" Patterson asked through the cigar clenched in his teeth. George and Ocean nodded in reply; concern mingled with resolve etching their faces.

Patterson guided the key into the lock and pushed the door open. Stately also described the interior of the residence. It looked like a museum. The foyer had blue walls, shiny white wainscoting, pillars -*freaking pillars!*- and a marble tiled floor. A large grand piano sat idle in the corner, its virgin keys covered, never played and now forgotten. Large oils depicting scenic retreats hung from the walls. The house was obviously childless. The very presence of children would have rendered this white gloved interior into a depiction of the streets of Berlin in '45.

"Where is he?" George whispered. The house compelled him to lower his voice, as if someone with a red jacket would come over and ask him to leave if he talked in a timbre above a whisper.

The effect was lost on the burly detective who practically yelled his response. "Upstairs."

They proceeded up the stairs, taking them one by one, in a neat compact line until they reached the second-floor landing. Creeping down the hall they could hear the TV blabbering incoherently, beckoning them forward. They saw Ted through the open door. Ted's body was slumped back in his chair, his mouth gaped, his tongue lolling out, his eyes staring vacantly into the vast unknown. They approached, caution in every step they took, all three remembering the day prior when the bugs chased them through Tracy's townhouse. Not a pleasant memory.

Patterson leaned down and touched his fingers to Ted's neck as if the dead man's appearance might be a well-executed theatrical performance. Give this guy an Oscar. Hell, give this guy a lifetime achievement award, cause this son of a bitch looks like he is really dead. Patterson removed his hand and looked at his watch.

"Where's the coroner?" He grumbled to himself. He wanted to get out of here as soon as possible.

To answer his question the doorbell rang out louder than church bells on top of Notre Dame cathedral. Someone please shoot Quasimodo which is exactly what Patterson was thinking, as he glared down the hallway leading to the stairs.

"The damn door is open. What the hell is wrong with that son of a bitch?" Patterson grunted.

The coroner made his way up. He was a heavy-set man in his early forties with an *I Love Leia* tee shirt under his blue official windbreaker. His name was Ron and Ron was out of breath when he reached the room. His face was beet red. His nostrils moved in and out like a rhinoceros in the midst of a stampede. Ron worked fast. He took his initial notes and pics of the body. For a fat man, Ron could really move and in thirty minutes flat, he had Ted stacked and packed in the back of the white utility van.

"How's Patty?" Patterson asked.

"She's messed up. But she's in. You know Patty." Ron answered as he slammed the back of the van shut.

Patterson nodded. He did know Patty and she was one tough broad.

George and Ocean were engaged in a Where's Waldo super match trying to locate the murderous bed bugs. They inspected the room as if they were combing a crime scene, which they were, as crazy as that sounds. The bugs didn't behave like normal bed bugs which tend to stay relatively close to their food source. In this case, the source wasn't renewable. These bugs had devoured their host in one feeding and they had moved on, in search of new hosts. There was no telling where the bugs were hiding. They kept at it like bloodhounds in search of a missing child. It was Ocean that located them first. George looked over at his protégé like the old lady's friend who just yelled bingo at the hall -a little jealous but overall happy and full of pride.

"Great job kid." George said, walking over and shining his own flashlight into the crack. The bugs began scurrying around as if they knew their lives had reached their climax.

"You gonna spray them?" Patterson asked, joining the two men. He jolted as he watched the bugs scatter from the crack, his skin crawling and itching as if he had contracted a particularly nasty case of the poisonous weed. His work was done and he wanted nothing more than to bolt from this hell hole. He had diligently documented the crime scene -maybe it was a crimescene- more like a suspicious death. Crime scene usual indicates malicious activity perpetrated by a human being. This was different.

It wasn't as if he could slap the cuffs on a bunch of six-legged insects. But then again, he was sentencing them to the gas chamber. So, in a way he was the judge, jury and executioner.

"I'm going burn the bastards out. Switch it up. We still don't know what we're dealing with."

"I thought you said you don't like heat because it leaves no chemical residual." Ocean protested. *Screw heat treatments.* The prep alone would take hours, especially in this house. Hours of hard labor. Spraying was easier. He hated heat treatments.

"I want to try something different. I don't want to rely solely on MOAC until we hear back from Phil or go back to the townhouse and see the results."

Laborious is the best word to describe a heat treatment. The treatment itself is a piece of cake, it's the preparation that's such a freaking bitch. First and foremost, all the oil paintings must go, which in this case is basically every painting in Patty's enormous house. The paintings and frames must be thoroughly inspected and then placed in the garage. Next, all the aerosol cans, pressurized sodas, wax figurines, delicate artifacts, and any combustible materials must be inspected and then removed. Then comes the clothes. All the clothes must be pulled out of drawers, closets, storage bins, you name it, and placed in loose stacks around the room so the heat can penetrate the fabric. Finally, the windows and doors must be taped shut, locking the heat in and the cold out.

The prep took them two hours. Patterson, bored out of his mind, walked outside and sat in his car. In no time he had turned the crown vic into a cigar smokehouse.

Ocean lugged in the large industrial portable heater and the gigantic fans while George completed several last-minute checks. The heater would increase the temperature of the house. The fans, placed in strategic spots would circulate the stifling air, ensuring that a uniform temperature was reached in every room or the treatment wouldn't work. If the temperature was one-degree cooler in just one room, the bugs would find that room and use it as a refuge.

The heater lit up like hell on a hot summer day. The devil was in the kitchen cooking up some fiery chili. The six elements glowed red. The fans were switched on and the two bug men exited the dwelling. Their work, for now, was complete.

Patterson's mood had gone from frustrated and bored to angry and murderous in the last sixty minutes.

"I've got the Department of Health and the council of hags waiting for me back at the station. The good news is two more dead bodies were found in the Half Moon Motel." Patterson growled.

"That's good news?" George asked. His eyes roved the street, searching for the Mustang. It had been several hours since they had arrived. The car was nowhere in sight. Guess Carlos got tired with his stakeout or even more worrisome, he wised up to his mistakes and was hiding far better.

"Hell yes it's good news!" Patterson exclaimed. "These two were shot. Now that's something I can handle. I've got to run. I'll catch up with you boys later today." He handed George the key to Patty's house. "Lock up." Then

he was gone, the familiar brake lights of the Crown Vic
disappearing around the corner.

Chapter 39

Great! James thought as, low and behold, the first cop to arrive on the scene was Officer Mike. Fucking Officer Mike with a shit eating grin on his face like *look at what we have here.* Kelly seemed to be thinking the same thing. Her face was downcast as if she was on the beach, bright sunny day and it just started to downpour.

"Well, well, well. Look at what the cat dragged in." Literally was the first thing out of Mike's mouth. He was smiling ear to ear. "How did you two come across a double homicide? Looking for a room last night and found it occupied?" Mike jeered.

"We just…" James started.

"We just what? Why don't you keep your fucking mouth shut punk." Mike said, squaring off in James' face. He walked over to the room and peered in.

"Anonymous tip. Some guy…" Kelly began but again Mike, feeling extremely pompous, rudely interrupted her.

"Was someone talking to you slut?"

"Hey, let's keep it civil Mike." James cut it. No fear this time just pure adrenaline.

Mike looked at James. The cop stood stark still, his thumbs looped in his belt, still smiling as if he had won the lottery. He didn't even pause to breathe, with Jackie Chang speed he tossed James head first onto the roof of the car. James' hands landed perfectly in the assumed position. Mike frisked him, ignoring Kelly's frantic shouts. James thought back to the incident with Carlos' girlfriend,

Sabrina. He prayed Mike wouldn't do the same thing to him. At least he wasn't wearing a skirt.

"Stop it Mike! Stop it!" Kelly exclaimed as Mike slapped cuffs onto James' wrists and led him to the squad car. "You're an asshole!" She bellowed.

"Keep bitchin'." Mike pushed James inside then rounded on her. "Keep bitchin' girly. Did you have fun last night?" Mike's voice was dark, disturbed, full of loathing.

"What are you charging him with? He didn't do anything!" She was crying now. Tears streaming down her cheeks. Her voice was high and shrill.

"Screwing a nigger. Just when I thought your cunt couldn't go lower. Man oh man." Mike said. He grabbed her, twisted her wrists hard, cuffed her and pushed her into the back seat next to James. Mike leaned into the open door, his face inches from Kelly's. "I'm taking both of you in and charging you with murder one. See if you can get your oily black head around that, nigger." He said before slamming the door shut.

Chapter 40

Patty was at the motel when Patterson arrived. She looked like shit. Total shit. Her hair was frizzed out like a mad scientist. Her clothes were disheveled. Her makeup was smeared from the hourly exposure of her tears. But she was there. Patterson admired her for that. Admired her resolve. Her determination. A day after her husband of thirty years was killed and she was working. Well, he'd probably be working too, if the same thing had happened to Cindy. *Be honest pussy, you know you wouldn't. Yeah, I'd probably be on a bridge somewhere, an empty bottle of Belvedere in my hand, cigar in my mouth, staring down into a roaring river wondering if I'd feel the impact or if my lights would just go out like flicking a switch. Click.*

"I think I can figure out how these two bit the dust." Patterson joked pointing to the two corpses with neat bullet wounds in their foreheads. He tried with desperation to lighten Patty's inconsolable mood. It didn't work. She didn't laugh, didn't smile, didn't even look up from the bodies.

"Did you go to my house?" She asked through gritted teeth.

Patterson cleared his throat. "Yes. We took care of it. I am very sorry…"

She held up a hand. "I know you are." She said. "Two bullet holes each. Pro shots." She said. Back to business. That was Patty. No room for play nor mourning nor anything normal.

"Don't see many like this around here." Patterson looked at the corpses. Definitely a pro. Holes were millimeters apart. Whoever the murderer was, he knew how to shoot.

"No, you don't see this every day." Patty began to drift off again into that realm where no one else was present. Just Patty and her colleagues: the dead.

"Apparently, two reporters found them. Both from Channel Nine. Well, one reporter and the weatherman."

"James Roseland?"

Patterson nodded.

"I like him." Patty said. "Never misses a beat that man. Who was the reporter?"

"Kelly Halle."

"Never heard of her."

"Crime reporter. Pretty girl. Smart. A little pushy. Anyway, they found the bodies."

"That's weird." Patty replied without looking up.

"Kelly said she got a phone call. Anonymous caller, telling her to come to this motel and check out this particular room."

"Sounds fishy."

"Yeah it does. We took them in for questioning."

Patty didn't reply. She just kept at her work, steady as a rock, jotting down notes onto a legal pad and occasionally snapping some photographs with a digital camera. Crime scene technicians from the Maryland State Police dusted for prints, which was an exercise in futility.

The Half Moon was probably one of the busiest motels for transients, criminals and the *forever forgotten*. There were thousands of prints on the door handles and on the surfaces in the room. All of which would most likely have criminal records. Not to mention, judging by the kill shots, a person with this much skill, would never leave prints at a crime scene. Someone like this perp was just too damn talented for that.

"Detective!" A young cop called from the door.

Patterson turned and glared at him. "Yeah." He barked. He was always cruel to the uniforms, even though he too had once worn the blue suit. It wasn't a question of forgetting where you came from, it was tradition, like leaving Santa milk and cookies. You just did it. He had been treated like crap by the chief of detectives back in the day, so who was he to act any different.

"Call for you." The cop said before hurriedly scurrying back outside as if he had just thrown a piece of meat into a lion cage.

Patterson walked out, jumped into his crown vic and picked up the radio receiver. "Go ahead." The dispatcher's voice came through scratchy. *Damn these sets!* Patterson thought to himself. Why couldn't they have the new upgraded version like the cops in Baltimore or DC? The budget, that's why. Havre de Grace just didn't have the funding like the big city forces do.

"Sir, there's another 10-54 at the Amtrak Station." The radio squawked.

"Got it." Patterson said. *Another 10-54! Jesus!* He used to love hearing the numbers 10-54 but now, after hearing them repeatedly for the last two days, he'd rather respond to a disturbance of the peace, a domestic spat, or a freaking cat in a tree -*just please no more 10-54s!* Maybe it was time to throw in the towel. Time to pack it in, collect his pension and move to somewhere sunny with plenty of sand. He kept a picture hidden in the darkest voids of his mind, the place where no one was allowed to enter; his special place; his safe room. The picture was mentally snapped years ago when Patterson was in his doctor's waiting room. There had been a magazine on the table, something innocuous, like Field and Stream or Reader's Digest. Inside was an advertisement for a cruise. He could see the page as clear as day. A young couple, the man in a white button up with the top four buttons open; the woman in a bikini, nothing but a string; together on some deserted island, alone, forgotten but in a good way. He could almost feel the sun beating down on him, almost smell the scent of the ocean as it sprayed the beach in a salty mist. Was it time? Was this the final hour? The final pitch? The swing. The connection. Watching the ball sail into the blue. Leave on a high note. The sound of his siren brought him crashing back to reality.

The 10-54 was different this time and Patterson lifted his head to the heavens in thanks as he stood over top of a homeless man, deceased on a bench. It was morbid to say the least. Not the body. That of course was the definition of morbid. But his soul. Patterson's soul. Morbid that the detective was no longer bothered by the sight of death -just so long as it wasn't people in the midst of sleep, with that pale, anemic look. Morbid that he was actually thankful that it was a normal death. Even the two guys in the motel. They were normal deaths. The loud whoosh of high-speed passenger trains sounded every few minutes.

Several people milled about the station. The sounds of travel. Luggage being handled, children screaming, hushed conversations on cell phones. Most passersby didn't even notice the dead man on the park bench feet from where they stood. The bum was a member of *the forgotten*, a fraternity that no one wanted to belong to, but some just happened upon and could never leave -while the rest of the world, well... just *forgot*.

The bum looked like a kind, old soul. His clothes were torn and tattered. A black undershirt with a dirty jean jacket on top. Soiled hands and a soiled face. Weeks of stubble that couldn't decide whether it was a beard or not. A ragged book bag comprised the entirety of the man's earthly possessions. The top of a cheap bottle of lost dreams stuck out through the zipper. Newspapers used as blankets to stay warm in this interminable cold. Exposure. That had to be it. The bum died from exposure. Exposure to the elements, exposure to life, to the ceaseless countdown of the hands of time.

Patterson looked at the dead man. The condition of this human being sapped the strength from the hardened detective. He hated getting calls like this. Of course, in the present climate it was somewhat of a relief, being that it wasn't *death by bugs,* but to Patterson it was a tragedy. Patterson felt a personal attachment to men of this man's ilk. To *the forgotten.* He kept the reason for his attachment a closely guarded secret. His older brother Sal -whom Patterson loved, revered and looked up to- had given his life to drugs. He went to chasing dreams at the tip of a needle. Sal died like the man on the bench -alone, cold and *forgotten.*

It was in memory of Sal that Patterson laid his fingers on the dead man's face and closed the lids of his eyes, whilst saying a prayer for God not to *forget* this man. For God to welcome this sinner into his kingdom, into His arms and for this man, this *forgotten* soul, to finally be remembered.

Patterson stood. Patty would arrive soon to take the deceased away. She would do the tests. Determine if the bum had indeed died from exposure as Patterson assumed or if he, like so many others, had been claimed by the newest form of death to hit this mortal world -*death by bug*. But he didn't think so. Patterson had been doing this a long time and he was pretty sure he was right this time.

Patterson looked around. He stared at the travelers. He envied them. Their obliviousness to their surroundings. Their ability to go, to leave it all behind, even if it was just for a little while. They were young, some were children, and some were old. Two of them appeared to be lovers. They stood, arms locked around each other, looking longingly into passionate eyes. Patterson's mind began to turn like an old machine, lay dormant for years that had just been switched on, the gears, without grease, creaked noisily and slowly came to life. He knew those two. Their faces. He knew their faces but from where? A train approached, coming to a complete stop at the platform. The two lovers ended their embrace and picked up the luggage by their feet. Where had he seen them before? Those faces. A man and a woman. They looked different but different how? Then it hit him, and he took off.

The couple saw Patterson approaching. Their eyes widened with fear, with recognition. They also started running, first towards the open door of the train. The train was a dead end and they knew it. They took one glance at the train and then back at Patterson, before they took off in the opposite direction towards the parking lot.

"Freeze!" Patterson shouted. He was running full fledge, his legs moving faster than the rest of his body like a cartoon. But he didn't feel like a damn cartoon. *Hell no!* His chest heaved, his lungs desperately gnawing at his throat in their vain attempt to obtain more oxygen. *Damn those cigars! Damn them!* Patterson cursed in his head. His heart hammered inside his rib cage like Santa's elves on a wooden toy.

"Freeze-god-damn-it!" Patterson had had enough. The couple had reached their car. The doors were open, and they were getting in. Patterson was fifty feet away when he pulled his gun -a Glock 9mm- from its holster and aimed as he ran. "Freeze!" He shouted and to his relief the couple stopped moving.

Or did they? The man had his hand in his pocket, obviously fumbling for his keys while the woman -already seated- had her hand on the passenger door ready to slam it shut. Patterson made it to the car, his body shaking, his heart racing, his lungs convulsing. He sucked in air in deep gasps.

"Put-your-hands-where-I-can-see-them!" He commanded in between gasps.

The woman lifted her hands out of the car. Patterson got a good look at her. He was right. *They're the junkies!* His mind screamed at him as if trying to make him grasp the concept. And it was the motel junkies frozen before him. The same junkies who he had questioned when the bodies of Timmy and Amanda had been discovered. No mistake about it. Gone were the tattoos, the missing teeth, the gaunt shallow faces, the druggy demeanor. In its place were yuppies. Professionals. Two business people on route to their next corporate plunder. Their disguises were unbelievable. The best Halloween masks ever. Freaking far out dude. The junky, drugged-out special. If he hadn't been who he was… That was his gift, his specialty. He remembered faces or better yet, he remembered eyes. The shape, the color, the way they looked at you. It was a unique trait that most people couldn't hide. Paterson never forgot eyes.

"I said show me your hands!" Patterson yelled at the young man, whose left hand still resided in his pocket. "Don't make me shoot you! Show me your fucking hands!" The Glock felt heavy to Patterson. His finger felt unsure on the trigger. He had never fired the weapon in the line of duty. Sure, he had gotten lots of practice on the range, where he was known far and wide as a prize-winning pistol marksman, but range time was a hell of a lot different from real life. He didn't want to use his weapon. Didn't sign up for it. Despite the cliché, he had signed on for the puzzles; the solving of crimes; connecting the dots and putting the criminals away. Cleaning the streets. Making sure the little old ladies felt safe. *Please don't be a knucklehead.* Patterson pleaded to the heavens.

The guy's hand appeared from his pocket. The movement was fast, well-orchestrated, practiced. The hand held a gun. The gun was pointed at Patterson's head, the barrel aimed right at his temple. Another second and Patterson would die, sure as shit. The explosion was earsplitting. Another thing the range doesn't train you for. Two more explosions followed the first in quick succession. The young man slumped down in the car, the gun falling idly onto the street below.

Chapter 41

"What the hell Bill?" Chief of Police John Anderson bellowed.

"The guy pulled a gun." Patterson replied.

"This is just great! Fucking beautiful! Thirteen dead bodies in two days and now an officer-involved shooting. You know how much fucking bull shit this is going to cause me?" Chief John paced up and down. The Chief was in his customary black overcoat over a red cardigan sweater. His face, like his sweater, was ruby red, partly from the cold wind but mostly from the anger. "Ever hear of wounding a suspect?"

"I didn't have a fucking chance to think!" Patterson yelled into the chief's face. He had had enough of his shit. "I'm really sorry you'll have more paperwork to do." He said; his voice dripping with sarcasm. "You could have had a dead cop on your hands, but I guess in the present political climate, that's a hell of a lot better." Patterson walked away leaving the chief fuming in his wake. He got into his crown vic and torched the gas.

Patterson was sure they were the junkies from the motel. He'd probably have a time trying to prove it, but it really wouldn't matter. She was fucked anyway. She also had been carrying a loaded gun, nestled in her handbag. That alone was ten years. Unregistered firearm. Hell, this is the people's republic of Maryland. Gun laws are strict in this state. Hopefully, the threat of going to jail for ten years would force her to pry open her lips and cooperate. So far though, she hadn't uttered a peep.

Patterson drove. He drove fast. Shifting lanes, pushing the V8 of the crown vic as hard to its limit; hearing the engine roar; hearing the throaty exhaust as it left the pipes. *You almost died tonight. You almost died. You would have been gone. Adiós. Ciao. Au revoir.* He thought as he ignored his speedometer and just flew. It felt good. Felt like washing his soul. Tonight, had been the first time in his life he had used his gun. First perp he had ever killed. He could see the guy's eyes. See the terrified look in the guy's face when his bullets tore into his skull. Those eyes, burning with the realization that his life was ending. Patterson would never forget that look. It would haunt his nightmares forever. That look of death on its way like a deer peering into headlights. Transfixed, stunned, paralyzed. He pushed the gas pedal down further attempting to push it through the floor. The engine revved harder. The stores, the houses, the empty fields, the train tracks of Route 40 flew by in a blur of colors. Finished with the cleansing, he eased off the pedal. Time to come back to reality.

The station was quiet when Patterson arrived. It was eerie like the hallways of a funeral parlor. Eyes followed him as he walked. He smoked his customary cigar as he strolled; not giving two shits about the no smoking policy. He was a killer. Taking lives. Fuck the world. He entered the interrogation room, smoke billowing around his face like Satan on Christmas day. The cute young reporter sat at the table; her blond hair and blue eyes looked inviting but he wasn't on the list and could have cared less if he was. The weatherman sat next to her, looking scared. Both had their hands free. The empty cuffs were on the table, ready to restrain hands again if necessary. The room was white on white, completely colorless. It had no feelings, no bias. Innocent until proven guilty.

Patterson pulled the out chair opposite them and sat down. He flipped through the manilla envelope on the metal table in front of him without saying a word. The silence was disheartening and conveyed a level of seriousness that neither James nor Kelly had ever experienced in their short, pampered existences they called lives. Patterson was in no mood for shenanigans today.

"Let's start with your names." Patterson said, as he hadn't just read a summary of their entire life history. It was an old cop trick. Get the suspects to talk about anything: names, birth dates, current addresses, favorite sports teams. Once they start talking, they usually don't stop. The real smart ones just keep their mouths shut, no matter what question they were asked. The smart ones only had four words to say and that were the most dreaded words in the world of law enforcement -*I want a lawyer*. But these two weren't smart. At least not street smart. They weren't career criminals. Hell, they weren't criminals at all. Patterson didn't, for an instant, believe they were guilty of anything except stupidity. The double homicide at the Half Moon Motel was just too good. Too professional. Well beyond the league of these two, with their preppy clothes and stylish haircuts.

"You know me. Kelly Halle. Channel Nine News." Kelly replied. She put on a good front with those *come do me* eyes but Paterson could tell she was nervous. She had never been on this side of the law before.

"And you?" Patterson looked over at James.

"James Roseland. Also with Channel 9. I am not a reporter though. I'm…"

"The weather guy. I know." Patterson said, cutting James off. "So, what the hell were you two idiots doing at that motel?"

Kelly and James looked uncomfortable, both shifting in their chairs. It was the tell. Something Patterson had seen before, countless times. Here comes the big lie. A great big one. A whopper and not the one from Burger King. The fish story to top all fish stories.

"I got an anonymous tip." Kelly answered. It was the truth but not the whole truth. *Sorry your honor, I swear to tell half the truth but I cannot, under any circumstances, tell the whole truth.*

"Really?" The detective said dubiously, not believing a word. "An anonymous tip directed you to a motel room, where there happened to be two dead bodies. Why?"

"I don't know. I get tips all the time."

"Yes, I'm well aware. Tips like the coroner's reports and where the next raid will be at the local crack house, but that comes from that prick uniform you're shacking up with. I highly doubt you get tips about double homicides very often."

James looked down at the table. Now wasn't the time to contradict the detective who didn't appear to be in the mood. *No, she's not shacking up with the uniform anymore. She's with me.* But that would've sounded lame. What he wanted to say was: *tell him about the box! Tell him Kell. We're up shits creek and that's the only paddle we've got.* He looked over at her but she didn't return the glance. His silent mind willed her to tell the truth. *Come on*

Kelly, just tell the man. Tell him you found a box in the room. Tell him.

"And how did you end up in this shit storm?" The detective asked turning to James. He had watched the young black man turn his eyes on Kelly. The eyes have it. James was the weaker of the two. He was the deer and Patterson was the hunter with a gun the size of Elmer Fudd's. He moved in for the kill.

"I was with Kelly this morning when she got the call." James said in the most honest voice he could muster.

"What, did you meet up for coffee?" He was going to make James say it but James was a gentleman in the first order.

"Yes, we met up for coffee." James lied.

"Where?" Patterson asked, sensing the lie.

"Umm… Dunkin Donuts!" James blurted out.

Patterson sat back in his chair and crossed his arms. "Okay. Dunkin Donuts for coffee and she got the call there?"

Great. Just great. James thought. The cops had Kelly's phone. If they had the ability to triangulate the coordinates of the call then they were fucked. The cops would find out Kelly was at James' house when she got the call and they would be caught lying and that would lead to the other lie or better yet the untold truth. And then the paddle would be in shit creek and they'd watch it float away in the current of their tarnished lives.

"Yes. She got the call while we were sitting in my car." James despaired.

"I thought you were drinking coffee."

"In my car. We were drinking coffee in my car at Dunkin Donuts." James said. His nerves were shot. *Let's just give up the goat.* This was a double homicide. Not just some run of the mill crime. *Give it up Kell. Tell him about the box. You found a box in the room with bugs in it. That's it. It's a simple thing.* They really weren't guilty of anything. Well, except tampering with evidence. James wondered what the penalty was for that. Probably not as serious as committing a double homicide.

"Did you search the motel room after you discovered the bodies?"

"No." Kelly lied.

Patterson considered her eyes with intent. "You didn't search the room?"

"No." She said firmly, concreting her dishonesty like the foundation of a skyscraper built on mud. Leaning tower of lies.

Chapter 42

"Are you scared?" Ashley Johnson asked in her sweet voice over the phone.

Ocean thought about it for several seconds before answering. "No babe. I'm not." The truth was, he was scared. Petrified. It was the end of fun. The end of adolescence. Grow up, get a job, get married, get a house with a picket fence. All that grown-up shit, it terrified him. Scared him shitless. It was her fault really. Her fault for making every freaking time so damn hot. Always pulling him close, whispering those sweet sexy one-liners in his ear, squeezing her legs around his hips, preventing him from… He let the thought go.

"Are you sure?" She asked.

"It'll be alright." He said, lying to himself and the world at large. "Did you tell your parents yet?" That was the real question. Ocean was dreading Ashley's mother's reaction. Her father -*Mr. Softy*- was the least terrifying of the duo. Ashley's mother -*Oh man*- was a whole different ball game. She was tough -an old-school Italian woman who raised four rowdy boys and one promiscuous girl; cooked huge tomato-soaked meals; cleaned the house from top to bottom with a pail; and could probably ring wine with a solid block. Mrs. Johnson cut a terrifying figure in the neighborhood. Five-foot-nothing with eyes like Satan on the Sabbath. No wonder her husband was like warm, vanilla pudding on a hot summer day. Mushy, gushy, enough to make you want to hurl.

"No, I was hoping you could be there when I did." Ocean pulled the cell phone away from his ear and swallowed a brick. That's the exact thing he prayed she wouldn't say. *Oh Lord, I'm a dead man.* Ocean stood, his back hitting a wooden mop handle nearly sending it and all its cleaning brethren cascading onto to the floor. He was hiding in a tiny closet in a hallway of a nursing home. One of Chesapeake Pest's many healthcare accounts. George was somewhere. Probably talking to the administrator or checking on the resurging roach infestation in the kitchen. Ocean had his work. He had inspected ten resident rooms before stumbling upon his current hideout to kill time.

"Babe?" Ashley said as Ocean returned the phone to his ear. "Babe are you there?"

"Yeah. Sorry. Spotty service. I'll be there. No worries."

"Did you tell your mom and dad yet?" She asked tentatively.

"Yeah. They're cool." He lied. "Gotta run."

"I love you."

"Love you too." He pushed end on the touchscreen and placed the phone back into his pocket. *Love you?* He didn't even know what love was. Well, he loved his mom, he loved his dad, but did he love Ashley? He loved the sex. He loved her face, her tits, her ass, and he definitely loved that little pink... but did he love her? His head was spinning. What was love? Lust- He knew what that felt like. The driving passion that welled up in his groin every time he saw her, every time he slid his hand up her curvy thighs... that had been the exact reason he had landed himself in this ungodly predicament, to begin with. The burning desire. That *damn she looks so good in that mini skirt, with the I-can't-believe-they're-panties underneath.* But was love like lust? *AHHH!* His brain screamed.

Ocean slowly cracked the door to the mop room. He was glad to get out. The small room was stifling and stunk like dirty, rotten water with a hint of urine. Not a place one ventured into lightly and certainly not a place one spent an extended period of time shut up inside. A plump nurse in pink scrubs shot Ocean an inquisitive look like *where the hell had this white boy come from* as she passed. The annoying ringing of thousands of depressed alert buttons and the mindless shouts of Alzheimer's patients echoed throughout the gleaming hallway. The scene was utter chaos. Ocean looked around confused, disoriented, his mind a giant bowl of mush. His focus momentarily narrowed on the image of George walking down the hall towards him. He looked George up and down as if seeing the man for the first time.

"All finished?" George asked. At first, Ocean didn't reply, his adolescent mind still far out, trudging through the land of premarital pregnancy and primal fear.

"Yes sir." Ocean replied, snapping back to reality. He shoved a piece of paper into George's outstretched hand. The sanitation and maintenance report or SMR for short -the most annoying part of the monthly contract. It spelled out, in detail, any areas that needed a good mopping or a new bead of caulk or anything else that was amiss. For the most part, the SMR was redundant. *Room is clean. Please clean under the bed. Floor behind nightstand is dirty. Caulk around base of toilet.* The same shit every time and the staff really could care less. It wasn't as if the reports made a hill of beans of a difference. Ocean would write the exact same problems over and over again, month after month. He felt like snatching last month's report from the reams of forgotten paperwork sitting in the front office bin and making copies of it. It was as if nothing was getting done. Hell, the bozos that run the place probably wouldn't even notice.

"Anything crazy?" George said, scanning the page.

Ocean looked at an elderly man who was reading a book upside-down. He nudged George.

"Besides him." George replied, smiling.

"No."

They began to walk. "How was Ashley?" George asked.

Ocean blinked, blindsided. George knew everything. He was like the guy in a poker game that judged everyone else's moves and he was always right.

"I don't know what you're talking about." Ocean replied, trying to control his poker face.

"Sure. Next time, you might want to think of a better hiding place." George looked at Ocean giving him that all-knowing, all-seeing smile.

Ocean looked at his phone. It was four o'clock. "Are we finished?" He asked tentatively.

"One more stop." George said. "Tracy's townhouse."

Ocean sighed.

They arrived at the townhouse a few minutes later. It wasn't the last job of the day. George was lying. It was

Ocean's last. After they checked the townhouse, George had every intention of dropping Ocean off and then returning Havre de Grace to visit Patty's house alone. The heating equipment had been cooking for seven hours. Plenty of time for the bed bugs in the house to be rendered extra crispy. George wanted to make sure the heat had worked. If it hadn't, he planned on using MOAC, aka Temprid, to wipe the remaining bugs out. He would've told Ocean the truth, but he knew the kid would insist on joining him. George didn't want him to. Ocean had bigger fish to fry, huge fish, like Humpback Whale size. He had to deal with his pregnant girlfriend and the newly minted grandparents, currently ignorant of the little bun in their daughter's oven.

Flashlights in hand, the two men ascended the stairs. The townhouse was eerily quiet as it had been on the previous day. George looked around at the filth and wondered if it would ever be cleaned up. After all, Judge Julius who owned the house was dead. And Julius had no children. No heirs to his lavish throne. The house would probably stay in this decrepit, filth-ridden state for all of eternity, like a museum of humanity's ugliness. A museum of society's forgotten.

The kids' former bedroom was clear of anything walking on more than two legs. Not one living bed bug was present and no dead ones either, which was abnormal. Usually after treatment -this case was far from the norm-there would be hundreds of deceased blood suckers -their exoskeletons forming an elephant graveyard- piled at the base of the bed. It made George uneasy. Extremely uneasy, like a monster lurking around the corner that everyone in the audience sees except for the morons on screen, those morons being George and Ocean. George could almost feel the audience's collective gasp. He could sense their hands gripping the armrests, their knuckles turning ghostly white.

Tracy's bedroom was also bedbug-free. None alive and none dead. George checked, and triple checked every corner, every crack, and every crevice. Nothing. A cold breeze was blowing from a partially opened window. A storm was coming. A shiver crept up George's spine. He looked, expecting to see thousands of bed bugs huddled in the corners of the walls up near the ceiling, their tiny little eyes staring, their rostrum tips dripping blood.

"Nothing." George said.

"Where're all the dead ones?" Ocean asked, scanning the ceiling with his flashlight.

"I don't know." George replied, his voice quiet, a worried look in his eyes. A look that was unsettling for Ocean. George was usually a very tough guy, but the look in George's eyes projected fear.

"Do you think it worked?"

"I hope so." George said. "Let's check downstairs." They went back down and inspected the rest of the house, finding the same -absolutely nothing. When they were done, they congregated in the kitchen for a powwow.

"I'm worried." Ocean said.

"Don't be. You don't see any live ones, do you?"

"Not about this. I'm worried about being a dad."

"Well, don't be about that either. You're going to be a great dad. Trust me."

"I don't know. My dad's not a great dad. I don't want my kid to grow up with a dad like mine. What if I turn out like him? What if I become my dad?"

George turned out his flashlight, plunging the house into complete darkness. He flicked the switch on the wall and the kitchen was flooded with dim light.

"Did I ever tell you about my dad?" George asked.

Ocean looked puzzled. Of course, George had talked about his dad. Hell, Ocean knew more about George's family than he did about his own. But despite the redundancy, he shook his head.

"I know I've told you about him, but I've never really told anybody who he really was. My dad raised nine kids by himself. My mom died when we all were still young. My oldest sister was only fourteen at the time. While raising nine kids, my dad started this company. He already had a full-time job delivering bread. It was tough and consumed all of his time. He never had time for baseball games, football, playing in the yard or helping with homework. He just worked. He put food on the table and a roof over our heads. We weren't rich, in fact, we were dirt poor. My dad couldn't afford to buy us Christmas or birthday presents or even take us out for pizza. He yelled, he cussed like a sailor and he'd give you an ass whooping if you just touched the line. You didn't even have to cross over it. Just touch it and you wouldn't be able to sit down for a week. He didn't have time for each of us individually. Hell, he didn't even have time for himself. But you know what?"

Ocean looked at George. "No, what?"

"He was the best dad in the world and I miss him every day. He was my best friend, my closest confidant, my strongest ally. I'd give anything to have him back. If I had kids and I could be half the man my father was, then I'd be doing alright." George's voice shook with the last words.

The kitchen fell silent for several seconds.

"You're going to be a great dad. Just remember your kid comes first. Nothing else matters. Do right by your kids and they'll never forget."

Ocean thought about this. That was some *real* shit. Some *sit on a chair and talk to Winfrey* kind of shit. He, of course, had never experienced poverty. His dad had been at every game, sitting on the sidelines watching and cheering. His dad had provided a nice life for him. Yeah, okay his dad was quiet, not very affectionate but he certainly loved his son. Ocean made a mental note to thank his dad as soon as he got home. Thank him for everything.

"I'm a little worried about what we saw in there or better yet what we didn't see."

"You think they might've made it out?" Ocean asked as the two walked towards the truck.

"Starting to. MOAC is a nonrepellent but PI isn't. PI will run the shit out of them. We sprayed MOAC first, so the bugs should've fled from their hiding spots and died. That's usually the case, but I'm worried that maybe... maybe there's access between this house and the one next door." George said. Tracy's was an end unit townhouse which meant that there was only one other house attached to it.

"You want to go check with the neighbor? See if they see anything."

"Yeah I do. Do you have time?" George knew the kid would say yes, even if Ocean didn't. He really loved this kid. He was a diamond in the rough. A young rich kid who wasn't afraid to work hard, late and get his hands dirty.

"I got time." Ocean said. *Like hell yes, I have time. I'd rather knock on a hundred doors than face the wicked witch of the Italian mainland.* He thought. The hard, fierce eyes of Ashley's mother floated in his head like dark clouds before an intense storm.

Ocean followed George up the stairs of the adjoining townhouse. The house was the identical twin of Tracy's minus the ungodly filth and endless clutter. The porch was nice, neat and extraordinarily clean like Mr. Clean *clean* -hell like Mr. Clean on steroids. Tiny nick knacks sat in neat rows on a shelf by the front door. The painted faces of gnomes and Mother Mary's stared up at the visitors. George deduced instantly that an old woman occupied the dwelling. Who else would display a collection nick knacks by the front door? It comes with the territory. He wondered if there was some kind of little old lady school that taught them how to act when they hit a certain age: keep an eye on your neighbors, offer everyone tea and cookies, and collect an absurd number of worthless nick knacks.

George's phone rang. That annoying submarine dive alarm. And for the billionth time Ocean pleaded with George to *get a new ringtone dude.* The caller ID said Dr. Phil.

"I've got to take this. Knock on the door and ask the old lady if she's seeing anything."

"How do you know it's an old lady?"

George inclined his head towards the shelf of statues like *duh* and walked down the steps, answering his phone on the way. Ocean stepped up to the door. He knocked, and the door swung open on the first impact.

"Hello." Ocean called from the doorway. "Hello." Maybe it was an old lady. Ocean raised his voice. Maybe the old timer had misplaced her hearing aids. "Hello! Hello! Anyone home!" There was no answer. Maybe she was asleep. Or maybe she was in the bath. Or -and his mind hated to admit this- maybe she needed help. He remembered the time his grandmother -god rest her soul- had fallen down the stairs and broke her hip. She had laid on the floor for a day and a half, before Ocean's mother, over for a lunch date, found her. Ocean decided to go in. Make sure the old lady was alright. He heard George's voice fading away as he walked deeper into the house.

"Hello! Anyone home!" He repeated over and over again throughout the first floor. Loud swing music filled the living room, emanating from a radio sitting noisily on top of a frilly end table. Guess George was right. That all-knowing, all-seeing shit again. The house was immaculate. Everything had a place. Photos of a man in a uniform, a woman in a white dress, a wedding picture of the man and the woman looking overjoyed and an abundance of pictures of smiling kids in various stages of development. They were all old pictures, in old frames, their edges yellowing and beginning to crinkle. And the refrigerator! Holy hockey sticks. The refrigerator looked like the bumper of a hippy-mobile. Countless magnets advertising different companies; postcards of faraway destinations; newer pictures of the same smiling kids, now older, with their own raucous broods; and calendars -yes multiple calendars- each from a different company or charitable organization.

The first floor was empty. Ocean began to worry. If the old lady was upstairs sleeping and she woke up to find Ocean in her house, she might have a heart attack. Even worse, she might wake up to find herself in the body of Tony Montana, say hello to my little friend and blast Ocean back to the stone age with an antique gun that hadn't seen action since the OK corral. But then again if he didn't check, and the old lady was in some sort of physical distress, he would never be able to live with himself. A nightmare, an image of a newspaper, its headline big, bold, and crisp popped into his head. *Old Woman Falls in Tub and Dies.* He peered up at the dark staircase and in a flash of bravado, decided to risk it.

"They're not natural." Dr. Phil said into the phone.

"Beg your pardon?" George asked.

"They're man-made. Manufactured in a lab."

"How can you manufacture bugs?" This sounded like another one of the doctor's wild theories. *I'm telling you George; some underground aliens control the world. No joke. Yes, I'm sane. Watch the videos yourself. They're out there George. They live underground. Hillary Clinton's one of them. Trust me.* And as funny and ridiculous as that sounded, Phil had actually told George that theory last June at a seminar. Word for word. Underground aliens, Hillary Clinton. The whole nine yards. And Phil believed it. Believed it with every ounce of faith in his body.

"Manufactured is the wrong word. These bed bugs have been genetically modified. It's not hocus-pocus. It's proven science that's been around for over a decade. Bugs modified to aide civilization. If you've got an invasive species that are damaging crops, scientists can genetically modify an insect to eat the invasive species. Several different processes can do it. Basically, in laymen's terms, they analyze the gene sequence of the insect and tune it to their specifications. You want a bug to be stronger, more agile, adverse to certain conditions, they find the gene and alter it to that effect."

"Come on Phil. Is this another one of your conspiracy theories? How do you know these bugs had their genes cooked up in a lab?"

Dr. Phil spoke, his voice laced with impatience. "Jesus George. Let's start with the fact that their rostrum tip is sharp enough to cut through hard plastic. Or that their body mass has been increased so they can take in more blood during feedings. Or that since they've been in my lab, two of the females have already gotten pregnant and are beginning to lay eggs. And the adolescents you sent me have gone through about two of the five nymph stages in less than eight hours. It's not natural George. There is no evolution at work here. No Darwinism. This is man-made."

"Okay. Okay. Say you're right. Who created them?" George asked.

"Who? I don't know who. It would have to be someone with unlimited resources or nearly unlimited resources. It would cost millions, tens of millions for labs, geneticists, entomologists, the works. The real question is why. Why would anyone want to create a bug like this and unleash onto the population?"

"I'm blown away." George said, and he was blown as if he were out on his boat in the middle of a hurricane.

"And that's not even the worst of it *pal Joey.*"

"What's the worst of it?"

Ocean moved carefully down the dark, narrow second-floor hallway. The wooden floorboards creaked with each step. "Hello. Anyone home?" He called out, his voice quieter than before. The *Tony Montana* possibility flashed in his mind. He kept visualizing the old lady standing before him, holding an assault rifle, hip level, grenade in the tube. He reached the bathroom at the end of the hall and found it empty. That was good. Ocean knew - thanks to TV and the constant bombardment of infomercials- that most accidents that occur in a home happen in the bathroom. The vacant hallway had striped wallpaper creeping down from the ceiling; flamboyant pink and white; looking very much like a zebra that Elton John would have as a pet. The strong smell of fermenting moth balls stung his nostrils. The townhouse's interior was laid out exactly like Tracy's next door -two bedrooms, a bathroom, and a closet. Thanks to that, Ocean knocked on the door of the first bedroom.

"Hello. Anyone home?" He said. The room was empty. A large collection of stuffed fluff lay in an intricate pattern on the bed. Raggedy Ann joined by a zoo of animals; their cloth bodies pristine, untouched, unmolested by the destructive little hands of children. The room looked like an exhibit in a museum. Ocean could almost hear the dull drone of a tour guide as his eyes took in the small space. He shut the door and continued down the hall.

He paused outside the second bedroom, his ear centimeters away from the wood, straining to hear a sound. Maybe the rustle of a large quilt, the deep snores of an ancient nose or the tell-tale cock of a pistol. There was nothing. Just silence. The silence of death. Ocean shook his head to clear his mind of premonitions. He knew the old woman was in there. It was a matter of simple deduction, that is unless she had pulled a Harry Houdini and had vanished into thin air.

Maybe she wasn't home? Maybe she went out of town? Yeah right, you idiot. Who the hell leaves their door open when they leave town?

He knocked. The thuds sounded like rifle shots echoing off the walls. No answer. The handle turned with ease. He pushed the door into the inky blackness. Again, he stopped to listen. *Please let there be some sign, some glimmer of light at the end of the tunnel.* The silence was overwhelming as if it were ready to swallow Ocean like a giant wave during a severe storm.

Ocean produced his flashlight and thumbed the button. The light cut through the blackness like a sword through a paper. The beam started in one corner and then worked its way over to the bed like a spotlight inspecting a prison yard. Ocean shuddered as his beam landed on her, his flashlight illuminating her body, scanning slowly from her feet to her head. She appeared to be sleeping, eyes shut tight, bundled under her warm blankets. *Maybe she's sleeping. I think I can hear her snoring. Yeah. There it is. She's breathing. I can hear it. Right?* He crept closer. His ears reaching out like long roots in search of water. But as he got within a foot of her, the reality of the situation crashed over him.

The old lady was dead. Ocean knew it like he knew his own name. Her chest wasn't moving. Her mouth stood agape and her eyes weren't shut tight but were half open with that dark, shallowness common in eyes that can no longer see. He unconsciously placed two fingers on the woman's throat feeling for a pulse. There was none. She was gone. Her body felt like meat in a freezer. It was so cold and stiff. How many more dead bodies would he come across on this job? A mouse, a rat, that was one thing but four dead people in two days, that was beyond acceptable. He reached for his cell. *Call George. Get George.* His mind commanded.

His thoughts ceased as he caught a glimpse of something crawling from under the sheets. Something small like a dot but the dot was moving. Ocean, his eyes trained, polished, over the last two years, identified the dot as a bug instantaneously. The bug climbed the Everest of the woman's head, pausing once it reached the top as if to relax after such a strenuous journey. Ocean aimed his flashlight beam on the bug. It was so small, he had to squint to see it. Ocean's mind hoped it was a figment of his imagination. *Is it looking at me?* He thought and indeed the bug seemed to be staring at him, challenging him like a bully on the playground. *Come on muthafucker. Make my day.* He was imaging it. There was no way. No fucking way. Yet the bug remained still. Ocean thought he could see the bug's eyes, the multilayered vision apparatuses, dissecting him as he had done countless times with members of the opposite sex, hungrily undressing them with his mind. Suddenly, another bed bug appeared on the elderly woman's forehead, standing next to the first. The bugs appeared to communicate with one another before both lifted their heads to look at Ocean.

Ocean stared at the little tick like bugs, studying them with a curious eye. He couldn't believe that these tiny bugs, these little shits could kill. Come on. The old lady died of a heart attack. There was no way. No freakin' way they did it. It was too unbelievable. Too remote. Too ridiculous to fathom. Then he felt a sharp pain coming from his leg. Then another and another, like little knives piercing his skin. He screamed in agony. They were under his pants. They were on his skin. More sharp pains. Damn those little bastards! Damn them! He slapped his legs vigorously. More pain. More sharp needles. Countless sharp needles being plunged into his ankles, his calves, his thighs. He smacked and punched his legs trying to kill them. Smash the sons of bitches. Crush them. It was fruitless. He had to get out of there, had to run, had to reach George. He leapt away from the bed. He was moving, but the pain was so intense. He reached down to smack his legs again and fell head first, mid-stride, into the door jam.

"The worst... oh brother... the worst is the bugs are totally immune to everything." Dr. Phil said.

George stared out into space. His mind heard what the doctor said but didn't accept it. "What about MOAC?" George was shocked.

"What?"

"Temprid. Did you try Temprid?"

"Yes, I tried Temprid." The doctor's answer was indignant. "No effect what so ever. Same with heat. Hell, same with everything. We even mixed up our own shit. Nothing. Not a damn thing. I've never seen anything like this."

"What about PI?" George asked, trying to come to grips with the impossible. Then he saw something, and his jaw dropped. She walked down from the front porch of the old woman's house. Her small afghan outfit, torn and tattered. Her face dark with inherited complexion and the dirt of third world poverty. Large holes were present in the rags she wore. Holes big enough that George saw the light of the old woman's porch coming through. *Not again. No more. Please God. No more.*

Ocean's vision faded. His body was weak. It shook violently. He slapped his legs. The sharp pains were becoming unbearable. He had to get out. Had to get to the stairs, to the door, to George. George could save him. George would know what to do. He mustered the last of his remaining strength and got up on all fours. He began to crawl. He made it to the first bedroom with the stuffed animals and raggedy Anne, then he collapsed again. He couldn't make it. His life flashed before his eyes. His mom. His dad. Ashley. The baby. He needed to live. Needed to be there for his baby. His unborn child. *I'm a dad!* The thought forced his last bit of strength into his muscles. He struggled up. He would make it. Then the pain. The fucking pain. Sharp knives. Torture. Incessant torture. It hurt so bad. All he could do was crawl. Crawl. Crawl. The stairs. The door. George. *George.*

"PI does nothing. It just runs them. I would not recommend using PI. This is no longer a pest control matter. This is terrorism. This is a matter for the…"

George hung up. PI would run them. *PI would run them!* They had used PI in Tracy's. Holy shit! George sprinted to the old woman's house. He ran right through the apparition of the little girl. The ghost that appeared more and more often these days. Ocean was in there. That thought superseded everything. *PI would run them!* He had to get to Ocean. Had to get the old woman. Had to get them both out. Evacuate the entire block. He ran through the open door.

"Ocean! Get out! Get out now!" He yelled. No one around. *Where are they?* He looked in the living room, dining room, kitchen. No Ocean. No old lady. He bounded up the stairs, taking them two at a time.

"Ocean! Get the hell out! Ocean …" He stopped dead in his tracks as if he had run smack into an invisible barrier. Ocean's body was at the top of the stairs. Bed bugs crawling all over him, like bees on a hive.

"Jesus Christ." George said. He dropped to his knees. He swiped the bugs away, flinging them off. He grabbed the boy up in his arms and carried him outside. Ocean wasn't breathing. His heart wasn't pounding the drumbeat of life. He laid Ocean on the sidewalk. He checked his pulse. There was none. He began doing CPR. It was hopeless. Ocean was dead.

George kept at the CPR. He compressed Ocean's lifeless chest. He breathed into the boy's deflated lungs. Tears rolled down George's cheeks. *Come on kid. Come on. Don't go.* It was George's fault. George and George alone. He had left Ocean. He had used PI in Tracy's house, forcing the bugs next door. He had been the careless one. And now Ocean was dead because of it. *Come on kid!* He pushed on the boy's chest, over and over again, trying to get his heart pumping... pumping... *pumping what?!* There was nothing left to pump. Ocean had no blood in his body. The realization hit George hard.

He sat back and pulled out his phone. He gave his location to the operator and hung up. George looked down at the small lifeless body. Too young to die. Too young to end the journey. He had grown to love the kid. A kid that had become like a son.

I hate bugs. I hate this fucking business. He hated it from the moment he sprayed his first house. Hated it for an eternity... except for the last two years. They had been... fun. Fun because of Ocean. He hadn't really thought about it until now. What was the reason for it? The reason lay lifeless in front of him. It was Ocean, the boy George had spent every day with for the last two years. George did something he hadn't done in a very long time. Something his mind had tried to forget, to abolish from his soul. Something he had abandoned. He made the sign of the cross and begged God for forgiveness. Pleaded with the Almighty to welcome Ocean with open arms. And he prayed for the child Ocean would leave behind. A child that would never know how great of a man his father had really been.

Chapter 43

Gleaming polished mahogany. Polished to the point that the lights had to be dimmed to see with some semblance of coherence. Dark brown was the color that infected the space like a disease that had reached its culmination. A dark brown table with dark brown chairs. All gleamed, coated with tanker trucks of lacquer. The table, massive in size, oval in shape, sat in the exact center of the room. Chairs, ten in all, encircled it. The chairs denoted rank. One chair was placed at each head, while four sat unimportant on each side.

The only thing in the room not cut from the heart of the forest were the ceiling tiles. They were white, not standard, not your run-of-the-mill-find-them-in-every-man-cave tiles. These were elegant tiles. Forged to spec and chiseled by hand. Placed by the fingers of men who would never again find themselves in this wooden Olympus. The tiles sat partly out of their frames like fat men attempting to escape if it weren't for their gargantuan waists, too large to fit through the openings.

Besides the wood; the elegant tiles; the green carpet -no other color would suffice- there was also tech. Tony Stark tech. *Ironman meets Batman meets Bruce Banner when he's not the Hulk* tech. Machines that would make the nerdiest of the nerds pee their pants with excitement. Flat, touch-screen monitors were embedded into the table in front of each chair. A sleek, modern projector, worlds away from the projectors of yore -six months ago- hung from the ceiling. And of course, all of the tech could summon anyone from around the globe, their faces appearing large and imperial on the projector screen.

The room had no pictures. No signs. No identifying characteristics at all, as if such displays denoted mediocrity. After all, this room is where the elites convened. Where the men -and the occasional woman, if she could break through the impenetrable barrier of misogynistic chivalry- made decisions that greased the world of finance and commerce. The men who caused the waves that made markets move. The men who could snap their blue-blooded fingers and cause worldwide depressions. The men who had not one Lear jet at their command but fleets of them. Men who commanded armies of accountants, lawyers and secretaries capable of conquering whole countries with a single stroke of their ballpoint pens. And this cold, calculating room fit them like a glove -well unless you're OJ. This room was their home. A room without feelings. A room where emotions were checked, like their tailored jackets, at the door.

Today the room had been rented to the lords of the bug world. Today the head of the table was reserved for the king roach himself, the big cheese, the bug man who battled bugs with a billion-dollar spear -his majesty Mr. Gordon Reynolds, who had yet to arrive. This didn't enrage the majority of the other nine people in the room. They wouldn't dare utter a whisper of discontent. Despite the fact that most of them had been waiting in the room for the better part of an hour. The lateness of the king's arrival didn't surprise them one bit. His Majesty was always late to meetings, sometimes very late, sometimes ungodly, unimaginably late. His majesty enjoyed being late. Enjoyed wasting the time of people inferior to him. It was his style.

The other head, closest to the projector screen, ensuring the occupant would have to turn his chair around to see -a constant reminder of his true place in life- was reserved for Carter Ritler. He, unlike Reynolds, was present, arriving ten minutes before the meeting. Carter was seated, his hands upon the table twiddling with the various pens, papers, and legal pads laid out before him. His tailored navy-blue sports coat looked like it had been pressed in the hallway just before entering. It was so neat, so crisp. He, unlike the other lackeys, looked pissed. His suave, hard face showed the obvious signs of irritation. His body language signaled he had better things to do than wait for the old pompous prick to arrive. *Be on time Gordon. For Christ sakes, be on time!* His thoughts thundered.

The other men at the table had all taken their seats, anxiously awaiting the king's arrival. The men comprised the upper echelon of Sentrix. The Chief Operations Officer, Mel Thomas, a man brimming with military precision, who's shaved head gleamed in the light like the wood surrounding him. The Chief Financial Officer, a squirrely man in his late fifties, with what looked like, no it definitely was, a piece on top of his head, a good piece but a piece none the less. The CFO sat to Mel's right and cowered in the COO's presence. Also present were the countless ass kissing VPs, looking like a collection of billionaire groupies. Some young, some old, some black, some white, mostly male and one female. The female was the most terrifying member of this group. She was young, had a body that would have tempted Zeus, and a mind that would have conquered Jeopardy. She was a true combatant. She had gotten her job via brute force and not via looks or sex. Her name was Sarah Ryan, and she also looked irritated at the absence of the chairman which was evident by her continual glances at a skinny gold Rolex perched on her wrist.

Finally, the trumpets sounded, the seas parted, the ornate doorknob turned and the king made his entrance. The men and one woman seated around the table stood to greet him. Each moved closer in a pathetic line to shake Gordon's antique, squishy hand. Everyone took their seats, reorganized the papers in front of them and waited for the king to speak. It wasn't noticed by anyone, except for Gordon, that Carter hadn't stood. Carter had remained seated, his face stern with steadied composure, his eyes dangerously narrow. Gordon noticed it immediately, of course, he did. Carter obviously didn't know his place. How dare he not show the proper respect! He, Gordon, was the goddamn chairman! Gordon's face became visibly red at the affront, but he remained silent. He would speak to Carter about his insolence later. Right now, it was time for business.

The old man in his beautiful black suit and red tie spoke. His voice like gravel covered with a coat of oil. "Let's begin. I want to hear how the IPO is coming along."

"The IPO is progressing as planned. We are ready to go public in three days. We have already sold a large block of preferred shares to Morgan Stanley and Goldman Sachs. The price of $50 has been widely excepted without hesitation." Sarah Ryan piped up. She was met with smiles from all those present in the room. All of them had been issued stock by the company and once the company began trading on the open market, would be able to sell those shares. The fact that the big investment houses like Morgan Stanley and Goldman had gladly paid $50 a share meant that they expected to fetch much more when the company went public. The men seated around Sarah had all become instant millionaires, all except Gordon and Carter who had both passed the big M milestone decades ago.

"Excellent. What's the target price?" Gordon asked.

"Our analysts predict the stock will open on Monday at $50 then soar to $80 by the end of the week. If the stock hits $80, the market capitalization will top $10 billion." The squirrel of a CFO said, his voice like that of a mouse standing before a hungry feline.

Gordon couldn't help himself. He grinned broadly, displaying his luminous white teeth. He already had a net worth of $2 billion, but now his fortune would rocket to $7 billion with the sale of his entire ownership share in Sentrix. $7 billion! He'd be one of the richest and most powerful men in the world. Well, he was already one of the richest, but after the sale, he'd be closer to the top. The four hundred list, the ranking of the world's billionaires, was the social ladder that every top business executive wished to climb. To be near the top, to leave all the multi-hundred millionaires and the one-billion billionaires far behind would eclipse Gordon's already successful career.

"That's fantastic." Gordon said, still grinning.

"What about the storm?" The shiny bald COO Mel asked in his tough, sharp voice.

Storms, especially winter storms, often affect the stock market negatively. Companies can't function in inclement weather. Cities become desolate ghost towns. Shops are closed. People stay home. The economy stagnates. Plus, if the damage is severe, which this storm was sure to cause catastrophic calamity, then the markets would move considerably lower across the board. That would affect the share price of every company, including Sentrix.

"I do not believe the storm will adversely affect the stock in the long term. We may see some short-term loss in the upward mobility, but long-term gains seem solid. We have a great company with assets that outnumber liabilities ten to one." Sarah reassured. There was an audible sigh from the men in the room.

"What about this mess in Havre de Grace?" It was Ritler that said it. Ritler that brought the mood in the room straight down, like an egg being dropped down eighty floors and splatting on the sidewalk.

Gordon looked at Ritler. He was pissed. *How dare that smug son of a bitch bring that up!* That was classified. Need to know. Now they all would wonder what was going on in Havre de Grace. Now, these insulant little pests would start to ask questions. Questions Gordon Reynolds didn't want to answer.

All the eyes in the room moved from Carter to Gordon as if they were watching a tennis match.

"I don't think we need to bring that up right now." Gordon replied in a harsh tone.

"We need to get a handle on the situation now." Carter said. He wasn't going to give it up. "I advised you to wait. I wanted to wait. I wanted to delay. No one wanted to listen, and now ten people are dead. Ten!" Carter yelled in the silent room. "The situation is very serious. It could significantly affect the share price if news…"

"Enough!" Gordon barked and smacked the table. The old man looked furious. His face as red as lava. His antique veins throbbed with the little blood that remained in his ancient body.

Carter sat back. He'd made his point. He'd succeeded in bursting the old fart's balloon.

Sarah Ryan turned to Carter. The rest of the eyes followed her. Her face asking the question before it left her lips. "What's happening in Havre de Grace?"

Chapter 44

"Jesus Christ Carter?! What the fuck is wrong with you?!" Gordon Reynolds screamed. The two men were still seated at opposite ends of the long conference table, engaged in a fierce discussion that had passed the ugly stage thirty seconds after it had commenced.

Carter, his pointer fingers touching in an arch directly below his lips, stared at Gordon with loathing. The other board members had been quickly dismissed after Carter had made his untimely Havre de Grace remarks. The majority of the ten-person board had no idea what Carter - the President of the company- had been talking about, but all were now very keen on finding out.

"What was the meaning of that? What?!" Gordon slammed his fist on the table. Hard enough that Carter thought the old man would turn to dust from the impact.

"I advised you to wait. I want that on record." Carter's reply was soft, showing a measure of keen calculation.

"On record with who?! Who the fuck did you put it on the record with?!" Gordon screamed, but he already knew the answer.

"The rest of the board."

"The rest of the fucking board!" Gordon exclaimed and suddenly, a sickening smile creased his lips. "They work for me asshole! They would lick the sweat off my balls before they came to your defense."

Carter ignored the vulgar insult. It was just like this insolent, ancient prick to say something like that. This old leprechaun can't see anything beyond his pot of gold. Carter continued to be maddingly calm. "I still wanted it on record that I advised you to wait. But you couldn't, could you?" Carter wagged his finger. "No, no, no. Haste makes waste Gordon. You wanted to play god."

"It was your fucking idea to begin with!" Gordon hurled at him.

Carter conceded the point. "Yes, it was. But it wasn't my idea to kill people. It was my idea to create bugs that were invincible to pesticides. We would have been able to control every aspect of the industry. We could mark up Dio Insecticide and sell it for god only knows how much. It would have been perfect." Carter placed his hands on the table. "The science wasn't right. Someone in the lab either unwittingly or deliberately screwed up and instead of waiting until the science was right. Instead of making sure everything was tip top. You pulled the trigger. I think they have a word for that. It's called premature ejaculation. Two pumps and squirt. But instead of a pissed off, unsatisfied hooker lying next to you, you've got ten people lying in the morgue."

Gordon was finished. He sat back and breathed. Freaking puffing like a freight train carrying an enormous load up a steep incline. He looked at Carter and his eyes were like little laser pointers cutting holes into rock.

Carter continued, he'd been dying to tell this fleabag how he really felt. He did it in the most gentleman-like manner possible. "And it doesn't matter if the board will defend me or not. Thanks to your greed, we are now going through an IPO and it's mandatory that we keep minutes of every board meeting, which means my words are indeed official record, whether you like it or not."

Gordon took a deep breath. His heart rate began beating normal once more. He could see a path in the snow. A light at the end of the tunnel. A chance, even if it was a slim one. He spoke calmly with deliberation. "You're fired." He said with abrupt finality. "Get the hell out of my office."

Chapter 45

Lenny felt depressed, like ready to skydive out of a 747 at forty thousand feet. Carter, his friend, his mentor, his boss, had been fired. Carter was his meal ticket. His backstage pass. His VIP wristband for life. Carter had seen his prospects five years ago and had promoted him, taking Lenny under his wing and moving him up the corporate ladder faster than the elevators at the Taipei building -101 floors in thirty-nine seconds.

Carter's firing had sent shock waves through the executive floor. Earlier that day, Carter had gone *on the record* at the board meeting denying any responsibility for the fiasco in Havre de Grace. Now the board wanted answers and they were seeking them like 1940s film detectives, skulking around corners, sifting through papers in trash bins and dogging suspects in the shadows. They'd be calling Lenny in soon. That's if Gordon didn't fire him as well. That would be the smart move. Fire Carter then fire his pit bull -Lenny. If Lenny were in Gordon's shoes, that's exactly what he would do. Shoot old yeller in the backyard. Put him out of his misery so he can't bite anyone ever again. Put him out to pasture before he turns into *Cujo* and tears your face off.

The best and wisest course of action Lenny could take, hell, the only path Lenny could take, was the path he had been trudging along for the last couple of days. The path which would lead him to his destination. A path that would make him indispensable to Gordon. The path of discovery. He had only one choice. Expose the man behind the curtain. Prove that the green wizard was really smoke and mirrors and not the sinister face that breathed jets of fire. Lenny was sure by now that the bed bugs had been created on purpose, with absolute, undiluted, criminal intent. The only piece of the puzzle that was missing was the *why*. He already knew the *how* and the *when*. It was the why that was so freaking troubling. Why create a bug that can kill? Beyond the obvious fear factor that would contribute to higher profits, Lenny believed there was more to the story. He had a theory. A vague theory, unproven, total speculation. The theory was: Rudd had conspired with Sangmore to create a lethal bed bug, unleash it on the population and let the chips fall where they may. Insane, sure, but what criminal nut-bag isn't? There was some precedent -well, not really, but still a little, a tiny bit, a morsel. Some men just like to watch the world burn as long as they're holding the matches. It was the same ideal that motivated Osama. He was blowing things up because of Islam but, in reality, the rich Saudi prince just liked to throw gasoline on a group of innocent people and light a match. Osama got a thrill out of it. A tingle up his leg.

The dilemma in proving his theory was the missing $10 million. Where did that fit in? People who like watching the world burn aren't typically motivated by financial gain. Money doesn't drive them. Terror does. So where does the money fit in? Could it be an escape plan? Maybe Rudd and Sangmore had envisioned this deal going south, and consequently, they had planned on making a clean and very funded off, get away. The key to this whole mess was the money. It was the Rosetta Stone. *Show me the money baby.*

Lenny called Gary Hendley, head of security for Sentrix. He ordered Gary to monitor all calls to and from Rudd's and Sangmore's labs. Record everything. He also told Gary to monitor any computer transmissions, i.e.

email, Twitter, Facebook, WhatsApp, everything. Gary said he would. Next, he called a buddy with the IRS.

"I need to know who owns Beautiful Horizons in the Grand Cayman."

"Holy shit Lenny. You want anything else like the author of the Dead Sea Scrolls or the truth behind the JFK assassination?" Special Agent Charlie Hesh sniggered. "I mean come on Len. We're talking about the Grand Cayman here."

"I know what we are talking about Charlie. They have assets in the US. There's got be some sort of paper trail."

"I'll see what I can dig up for you but don't hold your breath."

"I bet if they owed taxes, you'd be able to find them. Real fucking quick too. You're the *I R fucking S* Charlie."

"Very funny. Truth is Len. And this never leaves this conversation." Charlie dropped his voice to a mock whisper. "A lot of people in Grand Cayman owe us taxes." Charlie let out a laugh. "I'll see what I can turn up."

Chapter 46

George sat on the sidewalk forever. Sat while the ambulance came. Sat while the paramedics -crosses emblazoned on their backs- tried to revive, tried to save but eventually, officially, pronounced their verdict -death. He sat while the coroner came. Patty, tired, worn, depressed, wrapped Ocean in a body bag. George watched Patty load the skinny body into the back of the van. He sat while the police asked him questions. He answered them like a zombie, mindless, body here, soul missing. When he stood his legs ached. He ignored them as if they weren't a part of him.

He had to call Ocean's parents. He dreaded it. But he had no choice. He was Ocean's employer, and Ocean had been killed on the job. Ocean's mother screamed. Her wails pierced the night air, blasting from the cell phone speaker. Ocean's father, no longer the emotionless, stoic man Ocean had described, shouted with anger. He threatened to sue George. Sue his company. Shut him down. Have him arrested. Lock him up and throw the keys into the pits of hell. George took all of it, sitting in the cab of his truck listening to the shouts of shock and outrage over the speaker of his cell phone. He tried to explain. Tried to make sense of the senseless, to no avail. They wouldn't have understood anyway. How can you make sense of a situation like this? How can you justify losing someone you love to something you can't understand? Even if it was something normal -*Ocean had been hit by a car; Ocean had fallen from a ladder; Ocean hit his head in a crawlspace*- his parents still wouldn't except it. Still wouldn't be able to fathom the loss. Even if it were natural

-heart attack, blood clot, stroke- it wouldn't matter. That was death in a nutshell.

It felt too much like watching his father die. The crumpled old body, frail as a page from an ancient text, lying there in tortured agony. The screams. Those gut-wrenching screams. Watching the cancer eat him, mind, body and soul. George could still remember as if it were yesterday. He could still see everything. His sisters, his brothers, his stepmother, all milling about the house like ghosts. Their souls absent. Their motions choreographed, rehearsed as if they were in a play. Not real. All observing the man they called dad, dissolve before their eyes. That strong, courageous individual that had been bigger than life. A legend. A man that had raised nine kids by himself. A man that had built a business. A man that had changed an industry.

George drove, doing fifteen, slow as molasses. He ignored everything. The scurrying of the storm-scared townsfolk; the yellow street lights shining down on the late-night party goers in their scandalous clothing hopping from bar to bar; the bright red and green decorations draped from the row houses on Main Street; the buildings that looked so old, so ancient, so immortal. The water that looked so dark, endless and uninviting in the moonlight. He drove for what seemed like ages. He stopped the truck on the street outside of the police headquarters. He sat there, not wanting to go in, unwilling to be consoled. He wanted to feel the hurt. Wanted to feel the anguish, the loss. It was his penance. His punishment for allowing the kid to go in by himself. He should have been with him. Should have told Ocean to wait by the truck. Should have known better. *Known better!?* How could he have predicted this? Who would expect bed bugs to kill? The pest that had saved the industry. His industry. Who would expect them to be killers? No one. Not him. Never. Not in a million years. He wasn't guilty. He had sent Ocean in a townhouse. A townhouse occupied by an old lady. Not occupied by the Son of Sam or Jack the fucking Ripper. He wasn't to blame. Or was he? After several minutes he popped open the door and fell out onto the curb.

"Can I help you?" The desk sergeant asked, leaning down like a giant bird perched atop its nest.

"I've got it Ray." A familiar gruff voice answered. Patterson appeared and took George silently and gently by the arm, leading him to a small cafeteria. He sat George at a table and placed a bottle of water in front of him.

"Thanks." George muttered.

"I heard about the kid. Jesus Christ. I'm sorry buddy." Patterson said, his voice hard but surprisingly warm. "Anything I can..."

"No." George replied, cutting the detective off.

"I couldn't believe it. I heard the call come in and I just couldn't believe it. I wanted to be there, should've been, but things have been a little hectic here. You doing alright?"

George didn't reply. He just stared at the water bottle in front of him, as if he expected it to come to life.

"I shot a guy earlier today. He's dead." Patterson said matter-of-factly as if he were discussing the ball game. "I've got his girlfriend in custody whose name matches a woman killed in an automobile accident ten years ago and a couple of young-ins who happened across a double homicide."

George looked up. "That's a crazy day." He said and cracked what was intended on being a smile but came out as a half-hearted attempt at one.

Patterson smiled. "Yeah, it is. First time I used my gun. First time in twenty-five fucking years. The guy almost got the drop on me."

"What happened?"

"Well, it's fucking crazy. I get a call. Another body. This time at the train station in Aberdeen. I'm thinking that these fucking bugs are spreading. I mean we haven't had any deaths in Aberdeen. But when I get there, I find this dead hobo on a bench. It wasn't the bugs. It was exposure. Thank God. And I only say that because I hate these damn bugs. I'm standing over the dead guy when I see this couple I kind of recognize but I'm not really sure. Before my memory came back, they took off like the road runner. I chased 'em. They were about to get into a car when I caught up. I had my gun out, locked, cocked and ready to rock. Well, damn it to hell if the asshole didn't pull his own piece and try putting one between my eyes. So, I shot him."

"Damn."

"Tell me about." Patterson leaned back in his chair, interlocking his hands behind his back.

"I talked to Dr. Phil."

"From the university? Or the guy on TV? The way you look, I'd say it should be the guy on TV."

George gave another half-hearted smile at the joke. "He said these bugs were made in a lab. Genetically modified. They're *not* natural."

"What-the-fuck?" Patterson's face had darkened. "You're telling me some assholes made these fuckers?"

"Yeah."

"Who the hell would do that?" Patterson asked.

"Terrorists. The government. Maybe a corporation. Wasn't an individual. It would take millions of dollars. This isn't your run-of-the-mill science experience in a high school biology lab."

"Terrorism?" Patterson asked. His tone skeptic, disbelieving. "I don't think its terrorism."

"Why not?"

"Why target Havre de Grace? Why not New York? Chicago? DC?"

"Think about it." George said. "Havre de Grace is strategic. One, it's an hour's drive to the nation's capital. Two, it has access to a railroad, a major railroad that stops in DC and three, it's near a military base. A military base where weapons are developed and tested. Face it, Havre de Grace could be a target."

Patterson had to concede the point. George was right. Aberdeen proving grounds, a military weapons development and testing facility, was literally right down the road. The train station in Aberdeen, minutes from Havre de Grace, carried travelers up and down the eastern seaboard to cities like Washington DC and New York. And DC was an hour away by car.

George continued his analysis. "The places where the bugs were found -the motel, the hotel and the bed and breakfast- all board travelers. Travelers who could potentially spread these bugs throughout the country."

"What about Tracy's townhouse and Patty's house? No travelers there."

"That's true, but Patty's house was an unintended consequence of the work she does. Bed bugs travel with people. Patty, by being exposed to these crime scenes, to the bodies killed by these bugs, unintentionally brought the bugs home with her."

Patterson looked sick. His face had turned white, ashen. It took him a minute to gather himself. "If that's true, then I could've taken them home. I was at those crime scenes too."

"True. But you had limited contact with the deceased. Patty picked them up, stored them in her van and performed an autopsy on them."

This seemed to relieve Patterson of his nightmares, at least temporarily. "And the townhouse?" He asked.

George sat back. He couldn't come up with a reasonable explanation for the townhouse. If the intention was to spread the lethal little blood suckers, why plant them at the townhouse? What purpose would that serve? Tracy was a junky. She wasn't a high-value target. She wouldn't spread the bugs, well, maybe to her hoard of late-night-junkie sex partners. But what was the point of that?

"The link could be the bed and breakfast. The owner of the Blue House, Judge Julius, also owned the townhouse and rented it to Tracy. So, Julius might have accidentally spread the bugs to the house."

"I doubt it." Patterson said.

"Why?"

"You saw the conditions of that place. Do you really think the landlord set foot in there on a regular basis? He probably hadn't been there in years."

That's true. George thought. He had been called out on several occasions to treat the house while Tracy lived there. On each of those occasions, the judge had said the tenants were complaining not that he, the judge, had seen anything himself. Presumably, Tracy would call the judge and the judge would call George.

"Forget the townhouse for now. How did the bugs get here? Who brought them? It's not like they could have been shipped via UPS?"

"You said you were investigating a double homicide?"

"Yeah. Two guys in the Half Moon hotel. Each shot twice in the head. Real pro shit."

"Don't get a lot of double homicides around here, do you?" George asked.

Patterson shook his head.

"Don't get a lot of professional hit men either?" George asked.

Patterson shook his head.

"Any IDs on the bodies?"

"No IDs. No wallets. A few hundred bucks tucked in a dresser drawer and some clothing. That's it."

"How'd you find them?" George asked, his curiosity perked.

"Two reporters from Channel Nine. Said they got an anonymous tip to go to the motel room. They finagled a key from the manager and entered the room." Patterson answered.

"Did they find anything?"

"They say they didn't." Patterson answered in a tone dripping with disbelief.

"You don't believe them?" George asked.

Patterson shook his head.

"Are the dead guys locals?" George asked.

"I've never seen them before. I sent their pictures to the FBI. Maybe they've got something on them."

"Two reporters found them?"

"Kelly Halle with Channel 9 news…" Patterson answered but stopped short when George's eyes widened with recognition. "Know her?" Patterson asked, even though it was pretty damn obvious George did.

"She's my niece."

Chapter 47

Things were looking bleak. Especially since James was looking at them from a cold, metal bench sitting inside of a cage. He couldn't remember the last time he'd been so scared. It hadn't happened since... since that time... he'd broken his mother's antique vase playing ball in the house. The king of no-nos. *Look both ways when you cross the street. Don't talk back to adults. Don't trust strangers and for God's sake, don't play ball in the house!* But he had played ball in the house. He bounced that rubber tennis ball off of every possible surface. Literally everything. It was cool. Much cooler than playing with it outside. The taboo. The chance. The gamble. If it hadn't been for that wicked curve... He watched with horror -Dracula's hand slowly emerging from the crypt- as the vase teetered on the edge - for what seemed like an eternity.-before it toppled headlong on to the floor. He still remembered seeing the multiple hand-painted Italian scenes in pieces staring back at him. And he sure as hell could still feel the sting on his butt cheeks after his father had gotten home. He couldn't sit for a week. The recollection of this made James shift uncomfortably on the metal bench.

Kelly didn't seem so distraught. In fact, she seemed invigorated. She paced with renewed energy up and down the cell floor. She was thinking. Mentally she had left the cell, her mind exploring far away things. She was trying to work it all out. Trying to make sense of the situation. Trying to write her story. The scoop of a lifetime.

"My sister's daughter." George told Patterson.

The detective led George to the holding cells. There she was, still looking like the little girl George had bounced on his knee so long ago. Kelly, suddenly ripped from her thoughts, catapulted back to earth, traveling light years in a second, stared back at her uncle with shock, and relief. It took several seconds for her brain to make sense of what her eyes were seeing.

"Uncle George!" She shouted, gripping the metal bars.

"I had a funny feeling you'd end up here." George said smiling. A young black man dripping with melancholy looked up from the bench. Kelly implored the young man to join her. He did so with reluctance in every one of his sluggish steps.

"Nice to meet you. You're the only meteorologist I trust." George said, putting his hand through the bars. James shook it as if he were shaking the hand of the executioner before taking his seat in the lightning chair.

"You're the bug man?" James asked.

George nodded.

"Kelly's got something to show you." James said.

Patterson glared at Kelly who looked down at the floor.

"What do you have to show me?" George asked.

"It's in his car." She motioned towards James. His car happened to be in the police impound lot. James gave George his keys and within fifteen minutes George was back having retrieved the small wooden box from James' trunk. He sat the box down on the table inside the interrogation room. James and Kelly were already seated in their now familiar chairs opposite Patterson.

"Where'd you find it?" George asked.

"Hidden in the old AC shaft at the motel."

Patterson glowered at her. "I should lock you up and throw away the damn key! Throw it right into the Susquehanna! Withholding evidence in a murder investigation." He spat.

"You should've turned this over to the police." George scolded, a fatherly tone in his voice.

"I thought about it. I really did." She stammered, her eyes catching Patterson's look of rage. "But Uncle George, there's something in there that you need to see." James rolled his eyes.

"She get you into this?" George asked. James nodded.

George lifted the lid of the box and peered down at the six transparent plastic containers. Four of the containers were clearly empty and two contained small tick shaped bugs. George and Patterson stared at the bugs with a mixture of interest and revulsion. George pulled out one of the empty containers and put it up to the light. Tiny holes were clearly visible on the sides of the container, obviously drilled for oxygen. There was a strange symbol on the bottom. George couldn't make it out. He pulled out his phone and snapped a picture. The symbol had two small serpentine lines that formed into an H, connected in the middle by an arrow.

"UPS for bugs." George stated, turning to Patterson. The detective just stared at the tiny light brown bugs scurrying around in the container.

"What's going on?" James asked, anxiety gripping his mind.

George told them everything.

"Intentional?" Kelly asked.

George nodded.

"I don't understand." James said. "You say these bugs kill people? You say they chased you and murdered your partner?" George nodded. "Then why didn't they attack the cops when they arrived at any of the crime scenes?"

George thought about that for several minutes. His personal encounters with the bugs had varied. At Tracy's, the bugs had chased Ocean, Patterson and himself down the stairs but then at Patty's, they had remained still, docile even.

"They weren't hungry." George answered finally. He explained further. "Tracy and her two kids were discovered a day after they were killed. The bugs had just fed on them. They didn't need to feed again. Insects behave differently than humans. They eat because they must, not because they want to. It's survival as opposed to enjoyment."

"Then why did they go after Patty? They had already fed on her husband."

"Maybe they hadn't drained him completely. Once Patty had gotten away they returned to finish the job." George answered. The other three shuddered in terror. The thought of being eaten. That was uncommon for humans, after all, we're used to being on top of the food chain.

"The bugs have to feed every couple of days?" Kelly asked. "I thought bed bugs could go like six months or something crazy like that without eating."

"That's only in the lab. In actuality, bed bugs must feed after they transition between life stages. They go through five. According to Phil, the bugs are maturing at a rapid rate. My guess is that they need a blood meal every 36 to 48 hours." George deduced.

"Okay. Okay." Patterson grumbled. "Enough of the insect shit. My concern is what to do about them. It's going on ten o'clock and I'd like to get this situation under control before the storm hits tomorrow."

"Are we free to go?" Kelly asked. Her nerves tingled with anticipation.

The detective stared at her with an expression that was both tired and irritated. His eyes saggy but stern like an angry, sad dog.

"I think you both should spend a night in…"

"Bill, I think my niece -and I'm *not* defending her actions- wanted the contents of this box to fall in the right hands. "I sincerely doubt…" George looked over at Kelly, who in turn looked down at the table. "that she was intentionally trying to tamper with evidence."

"Fine." Patterson grumbled.

James looked like he had just won the lottery. *Thank God, I'm out baby.* He smiled. Last time he was ever going to a crime scene *especially* with Kelly. *She's lucky she's so damn beautiful.* James thought. He pranced out of the interrogation room followed by Kelly, who seemed reluctant to leave. She kept looking back at her Uncle and the detective.

"We need to evacuate the townhouse development before anyone else dies." George said. "And I think we need to evacuate the Best Eastern and the Goodnight Sleep Motel too. The bugs at those two locations haven't eaten in days. They will be actively hunting for food sources."

The police headquarters building was alive with action. The storm was on its way. Cops were everywhere gearing up, checking and rechecking their emergency equipment. This one was going to be bad. James nudged past on his way to the front desk where unlike the rest of the station there was absolutely nothing going on. The three heavy-set officers sitting behind the high desk were immersed in a rerun of Threes Company. James looked up. He felt like he was on trial, peering up at the judge.

"Excuse me." James said. The cop on the end, an older man, looked down at him in annoyance. "They told me to see you about getting my personal possessions back."

The cop pointed to a small office on the right side of the front door. "In there." He barked.

Five minutes later James hurried back to the interrogation room. Checking his phone had been a *real* pleasure. There were thirty-nine missed calls from his father and about three hundred unread text messages. The texts, which he barely skimmed through, because they all said basically the same thing, just with a little more vulgarity added in each subsequent one. They were from dear old dad and in a *very* unpleasant way, reminded James that the storm of the century was almost here and *where the fuck was he!* After getting his evening dose of anxiety and depression -as if he hadn't had his fill already- James checked the weather and… *Holy shit!* For the first time in his life, he had been wrong. Dead wrong. How had this happened? He'd predicted everything. Every storm, every front, every miniscule smidge of a change and now this. The storm wouldn't hit tomorrow. It would hit today, two hours from now.

"I screwed up." James said as he reentered the interrogation room.

"I know." Patterson growled. Pissed off at being interrupted. "That's why I locked…"

"No. No. I screwed up the forecast. The storm will be here in two hours." James said. He spoke quickly, more to himself, trying to make sense of his error. "It must have sped up, gathered speed over the ocean. That's the only explanation I can think of."

George looked at James then over at Patterson. "We have to get those buildings evacuated *now*."

"Why can't you just blast them? Kill 'em all. Hell, give me a spray tank and I'll do it." Patterson said.

"I guess I forgot to mention it." George said getting to his feet. Patterson looked up blankly. "They can't be killed."

Chapter 48

The phone rang and rang until finally, a cold voice answered. The voice was irritated which was just plain idiotic. After all, the man had given him the fucking number in the first place. *Come on, dude.* If you give someone a number, don't be pissed off when they *call.* And for fuck's sake, answer the phone. He had been calling all *freaking* night. A thousand *damn* times. And each time he had to listen to that drone of a ringtone that was driving him absolutely nuts. Ring, ring, ring, ring, ring, ring …. *Answer the phone asshole!*

"Yeah." And that's what the prick said when Carlos *finally* got through to him. *Yeah? What are you? Some high school quarterback taking calls from a cheerleader's snatch?*

"How many fucking times I gotta call you before you pick up?" Carlos yelled. He was pissed off. And right now, he didn't care who this prick was. He didn't care what this prick had on him. *Oh, so you gotta murder weapon with my prints on it. So what? Fuck you and the train you rode in on.*

The attitude didn't faze Tony. In fact, he kind of liked it. It kind of turned him on. He enjoyed making people mad. He liked having that power over them. It was fun screwing with their heads. It was entertainment, and he didn't get much entertainment.

"You got something?" Tony asked. His voice maddeningly calm.

Screw you! "Hell yes, I got something. That prick cop you had me follow, he went to a motel room. Cops found two guys in there. Two *dead* guys." Carlos said in a clipped monologue. "From what I heard, the cops arrested a couple out front before the detective arrived."

"Who'd they arrest?"

"I dunno. Two yuppies. A black dude and a white girl."

Tony was startled by that revelation. Startled and delighted. Two yuppies taking the fall for a homicide he had committed. What was this? Christmas? Had he just won the lottery? It couldn't be true. He got up from the coach chair and stretched. He had been drinking. Not too much. Vodka on the rocks. A light drink. Nothing that would fool with his senses. Hell, he could've had ten vodkas before he'd have to worry and even then, he could still shoot the head off a match at a hundred yards. He walked across the dark, warm motel room. He grabbed the thick red curtains with his right hand and parted them slightly, just enough to peer into the parking lot.

"You see 'em get arrested?" Tony asked.

"No. They were already in the car."

"Did the detective arrest them?"

"No. It was that cop you know."

Tony knew the cop. Officer Mike. His inside man.

"I followed the detective to the train station." Carlos said.

"Why'd he go to the train station?"

"You gonna let me talk? I mean, what the fuck? You got me standing out here in the freaking cold. Freezing my fucking sack off..."

"Shut the fuck up." Tony commanded. "Talk."

"There was a body. Some dead bum. At least he *looked* like a bum. I didn't get too close. Then you wouldn't believe what happened next."

What is this? A game show? Twenty questions? Pick a briefcase, any briefcase and see what's inside? Tony never played games and he wasn't about to start.

Carlos waited for several seconds before realizing Tony wasn't going to answer him.

"I thought for a second he spotted me man. I mean he looked right at me and his face had that stare. Like I know what you freakin' did last summer."

Tony rolled his eyes.

"But then I get the impression he's looking right through me like I was a freakin' ghost or something. I looked back to see what he was looking at and I see these two people. A white guy and a white girl. Probably thirty, thirty-five. They looked harmless. But that didn't stop the detective. He started toward 'em. They took one look at him and then they were off, running like a bunch of wild assholes. He chased 'em all the way to their ride before the dude pulled his gun. And then *POW!* Fucking cop blasted his ass. Put one in his head. Sprayed his brains all over his fucking ride."

"Where's he now?"

"At the station. Been there for a while. That other guy's here too."

"The bug guy?"

"Yeah."

"Stay there. Let me know if they leave…"

"Wait a minute!" Carlos exclaimed. He paused for several seconds. "The two yuppies just walked out."

"From the double homicide? Who are they?"

"I think. I don't know who the fuck they are. What, you think I got superhero eyes? Give me a sec. Let 'em get closer."

Guess he hadn't won the lottery after all.

"I know those two." Carlos' voice trailed off. He squinted, his eyes as cold as ice cubes in Alaska, trying to see the faces of the two people crossing the parking lot. "It's the weatherman!" He exclaimed as if Tony would know who that was.

"Who?" Tony asked.

"From Channel freakin' nine." Carlos replied. "I know him. He…" But Carlos didn't finish the rest. *He's got a video. A video of Officer freaking Mike molesting my girl and shakin' my ass down.*

Tony had to think. His mind was swirling with possibilities. Local reporters arrested at the double homicide he committed. And then released. Why? What the hell was going on in this shitty little town? He strolled back over to the coach chair and sat down. The drink, now half gone, sat dripping condensation on the surface of the small table next to him. He picked it up with his free hand and drained the last bit into his mouth. The vodka warmed his throat and cleared his mind.

"Can I go home now?" Carlos asked. He was tired and fucking cold like *never going to be warm again* cold. Standing outside of the police station freezing his balls off wasn't his idea of a bangin' occasion. Hell no! Shit man, if he didn't get warm soon, he could sell his freakin' junk as a snow man's face. Like use these for the eyes and nose.

"No. Stay there and tell me what happens."

Carlos pleaded. Hobbling from foot to foot. "Look, man, I'm freezing my ass off. I mean what the fuck am I *doing* here? What's this got to do with…"

Tony hung up. Carlos looked at the phone and almost screamed. He felt like throwing it into the air and letting it shatter into a million pieces on the sidewalk. If it wasn't for that fuckin' gun. If it wasn't for fuckin' Eddie. If it wasn't for the possibility that he might spend the rest of his days inside the bing playing the unit pin cushion. He wouldn't be here right now, cold as ice at the north freakin' pole, watchin' a bunch of cops play grab ass.

He decided to stay for five more minutes. Just five then he was gone. He'd tell the boys to arm the fuck up. Hit the streets. Find that unknown asshole and bring his head back on a pike. *What's a pike?* He could hear T-Bone saying. *Fuck the pike. Just bring his freakin' head.* But then again no one knew what the prick looked like. Carlos never saw his face. Didn't even know his name. Just a number. That was it. Just a phone number and one the prick barely answered. Plus, it was probably a throwaway but who really cared. They'd find him. It was a small town.

Couldn't be that many places to go underground. Not here. Not in Havre de Grace.

Five minutes went by at a grueling pace. The sky was becoming increasingly gray. Clouds were on the move. The wind was picking up. The storm was coming. And it was going to be a real shit show. Carlos decided the time was freakin' up. He'd rather go away for the murder. He'd plead out, get ten years, serve them with the big dogs and come out with more street cred than 50 freakin' Cent. Fucking major street cred. His mind made up he turned to leave and froze. Not from the weather. He froze because the most terrifying dude he had ever seen in his life was standing right behind him. *Fuck!* And he didn't even hear the bastard coming.

"Going somewhere?" Tony asked, sneering with mirth.

Carlos' face looked terrified. His eyes resembled a fly trapped in a web that had just caught sight of the giant spider that was going to eat him for dinner.

"Are you sure the yuppies that walked out of here were the same two arrested at the homicide?"

Carlos nodded. Suddenly, he got a feeling this dude knew a lot about those bodies in that motel room.

"They left?" Tony took up position next to Carlos on the street across from the police station.

"Yeah."

"Drove away?"

"Yeah. Crazy."

"What's crazy?" Tony analyzed Carlos' soul with his piercing eyes. The look would've made a great white shark rethink its present course.

Carlos melted before those eyes. He started to shake, again not from the frigid temperature outside. "They drove off in a car. The same car the bug man grabbed a box from."

"What box? What the hell are talking about?"

"The bug man came out about an hour ago. He went over to the car, opened the trunk and pulled a box out. A little box." Carlos made the dimensions come to life with his hands. "Then he took the box back inside. I thought at first it was his sled. The bug man's. But then the weather guy came out and drove away in it." Carlos' voice was nervous. He was scared to death with this asshole staring through him. The guy just looked like the angel of death. Like he could look at you and you'd just drop dead.

"A wooden box?"

"Maybe. I wasn't close enough."

Tony didn't blink. He just stared at the police station. He realized too late that he had screwed up - royally. He had checked everywhere. He had searched through everything. The closets, the dressers, the beds. No box. Sentrix had said there would be a box -a small wooden box. Tony was supposed to find it and send it to New York, but he had failed. He fucked up.

Suddenly the station came alive. Cops poured out. It was like a scene from a movie. Every damn cop in the whole place must have been dispatched at the same time. Motors roared. Lights flashed. Tires screeched. Blue and red strobes entered the street and zoomed past Tony and Carlos. The cops never even looked in their direction. Their faces sternly set forward, concentrating on the task at hand.

"What the fuck!" Carlos exclaimed as he watched one car after another pull out of the parking lot. "Hey, there's the detective!" He pointed to an older man in a long overcoat who was hurrying out of the station accompanied by another man.

"Who's that with him?"

"That's the bug guy." Carlos answered.

Tony watched as Patterson and the other man got into a Ford Crown Victoria and followed the rest of the cops in their mad dash to flee the station. The Crown Vic turned left out of the parking lot so that the passenger side of the vehicle was visible to Tony. He looked in, and for the first time in a long time, his heart skipped a beat. The passenger inside was looking right at him, a cold, heartless stare of recognition. Their eyes locked and Tony considered a face he hadn't seen in twenty years. A face that momentarily sent shivers down his spine. A split second later and the face had vanished, retreating into Tony's memories, leaving only the bright red of brake lights disappearing into the dark night.

Tony turned to Carlos. "Plans have changed."

Chapter 50

"What are you doing?" James asked.

Kelly had been typing like a madman on her phone for the last twenty minutes. Hell, she had been punching away like Floyd Mayweather since they left police headquarters. James had ignored her the entire time. His mind was laser-focused on the task of putting his neck under the blade of the axe. His father would decapitate him. No question. The text messages had made that crystal clear. He pondered whether disappearing might be a worthy act. Get his cash, a few books- well maybe more than a few books- pack some clothes, grab Kelly and stow away on a freighter to Zimbabwe.

"Writing." Kelly answered, her mind somewhere out in the abyss.

"Writing what?"

Kelly didn't answer.

"Okay." James gave up. No use in talking to a brick wall. He stared at the road. The wind had picked up. The temperature had dropped like a penny off the top of the Empire State building. The sky was dark. Not nighttime dark -dark as in Jesus dying on the cross dark. *You killed the Son of God* dark. And indeed, the heavens were about to open. Unleashing hell on mankind. And James loved every minute of it. He loved the weather. Loved the storms. Loved watching them swell up over the Susquehanna, churning the air like a deadly milkshake, then crashing onto shore like two eighteen wheelers in a head-on collision.

When he pulled in, he noticed every spot in the large parking lot had a vehicle in it. And most of them were

4 by 4s as if that would help in an ice storm. Jeeps, Explorers, Tahoes, F150s, F250s and even F350s lined the rows, parked with their grills facing out. It looked like a used car lot in redneck country, and for a split second, he thought the guy in suspenders approaching them would try to talk them into unnecessary expenditures like spray liners or anti-rust coatings. But it wasn't an oily salesman approaching, it was dear old dad with a face straight out of the Bride of Frankenstein. He looked pissed. His face was red, and his veins were popping.

"Where in the hell have you been?!" Harry Roseland bellowed, his nostrils flailing like a bull ready to charge. "I had to call that damn idiot from channel 11 because my own son, my own flesh and blood was out playing private fucking eye!" The big vein on Harry's bald forehead throbbed dangerously.

James stepped out of the vehicle. "Dad." He began. "It was a misunderstanding." He pleaded, hands in the air.

"Misunderstanding my ass…" Harry began but James cut him off. The tirade was coming. Fuck the storm. This was the real hurricane. "Do you know what I've had to do? Do you have a clue?!"

"Dad!" James yelled. "I'm here now!"

Harry Roseland stopped. He looked at his son, then without another word, turned around and marched back inside. James leaned against the side of the car and sighed. He had won this one. Not a flawless victory but a victory none the less. He knew his father had been worried about him and that's why Harry was pissed. His father had never done well with the emotional side of life. Sadness, anxiety, grief, they all got jumbled up and thrust out as rage. James didn't blame his old man. That's just the way he was but *damn. Chill out a minute dude. I'm safe. I'm cool. Let's worry about all the people out there. The people who aren't going to be able to leave their homes for the next forty-eight hours. Let's worry about them.* James looked out at the water. It was visible from the parking lot in between the dozens of condo buildings that had been thrown up during the coastal revival Havre de Grace had experienced a decade before. The water looked dark, uninviting, teeming with the unknown. After a few minutes of daydreaming, or was it daydreaming, because technically it was nighttime, he realized Kelly hadn't said a word. He looked in. She was still typing as if the outburst hadn't occurred.

"Hey!" James rapped on the glass. Kelly looked up startled. She opened the door. "Okay now tell me what in the hell you're doing." He barked, not in anger. He was genuinely intrigued.

"I told you. I'm writing." She said. Her voice distant, cold, like the dark, unknown water beyond the condos.

A thought hit James like a spitball in 8th grade. He whipped out his phone and began moving his finger around the icons. He clicked on the gallery. *It wasn't there! The video!* The evidence of Officer Mike abusing Sabrina was gone. Erased. That big dumb cop. James thought and smiled. No worries. He had a copy.

Chapter 51

Sangmore's office was a mess like *Who fired the maid and outlawed filing cabinets?* Documents, reams of them, lay scattered on top of every surface. It was as if Sangmore had a serious beef with the go green, paperless crowd.

The sheer chaos pissed Lenny off. How could someone live like this? He couldn't imagine what Sangmore's house looked like. Lenny would have canned the man just for his haphazard sloppiness. *Screw the killer bed bugs. You're fired because you're a worthless slob.*

Sangmore was still MIA. The geneticist hadn't returned any calls and hadn't, according to security, been in his office all day. That wasn't strange. Lenny had that effect on people. The *holy shit, I'm going to lose my job* effect. Sangmore was probably sitting at home basting in his sorrow like a fat bird in the oven on Thanksgiving. Lenny felt very confident that Sangmore would be back Monday, rested, refreshed, ready for more of Lenny's questions. And Lenny had plenty. Mainly about the $10 million paid to HydroLine.

There must be a method to the madness. Lenny thought as he perused the documents. Sangmore's office looked identical to Rudd's. It was small with glass windows on three sides that peered out into the now darkened laboratory. There was a metal utility desk in the middle and three filing cabinets that judging by the mess of papers hadn't served their purpose. Lenny considered them anyway and to no one's surprise found them to be almost entirely empty. *Why use filing cabinets when you have the*

floor, the desk, and the tops of the freaking filing cabinets!?
He thought sarcastically.

Document after document: lab tests, gene compositions, columns of random numbers, feeding charts -the list went on and on. The desk drawers squealed as they exited their sleeves. The sound jarred Lenny's nerves. Lenny skimmed, discarded, skimmed, and discarded thousands of papers before he gave up. Dead end. No purchase orders. No receipt. No record of the payment at all. Sangmore had the answers. He picked up the phone on the desk and dialed the number for a line out. Maybe the good doc would answer a call from his own lab.

And lo and behold he did. Sangmore sounded sleepy. The lazy bastard had probably just woken up.

"Dr. Sangmore. Leonard Schultz." He could here Sangmore leap to his feet as if a drill sergeant had just called him to attention. Lenny loved it. He salivated, his taste buds sensing the kill and the taste of the fresh meat. "I'm trying to locate a purchase order." Lenny picked up a blank piece of paper and acted as if he were reading numbers from a page. "$10 million worth of equipment from HydroLine."

Instant alertness. "HydroLine. HydroLine." Sangmore repeated, his neurological circuitry attempting to shine high beams into the fog. "I've never heard of them."

This shocked Lenny. He was certain the doctor would have some well-rehearsed bull shit to serve up on a silver platter.

"Your department authorized the transfer." It was a statement, not a question.

"Not me." Sangmore answered, a little too quickly in Lenny's book. "That would have been cleared by me, and I never saw it." Sangmore added.

"That's a pretty big expenditure doctor. Are you sure you didn't authorize it?"

"I'm sure."

Lenny let silence do his talking for half a minute.

"Thank you, doctor. Will you be in on Monday?"

"I will."

"One more thing." The thought had just occurred to him. "How did you pick the test sites in Havre de Grace?"

"I didn't pick them." Sangmore answered.

"Who did?"

"It was authorized by the board. By the chairman and the president."

"So, you had no input at all?"

"Dr. Rudd and I made our recommendations, but ultimately the decision rested with the chairman. If I am not mistaken."

"Thank you, doctor." Lenny hung up.

Another dead end. Another roadblock. Someone had to know about the ten million. If Sangmore hadn't authorized the transaction, then who had? Lenny picked his figurative shovel off the ground and once again began digging.

Chapter 52

"What do you mean I have to evacuate? This ain't no hurricane *hon!*" Hazel Rhodes bellowed. "You know how many folks I got staying here?" She didn't wait for a reply. "Fifty. That's how many. And I'm supposed to kick 'em all out?"

"It's for their own safety." Patterson said. He was standing alone in the office of the Goodnight Sleep Motel. Hazel Rhodes was behind her desk with a half-eaten container of Buffalo Wings sitting in front of her. The reddish-brown sauce dripped off her ample fingers and bloated face in slow disgusting dribbles. She looked like an angry gorilla -if gorillas were fat, little old rednecks who ran motels on Route 40.

"Safety from what?" She demanded.

Patterson wanted to hand her a napkin. *Here, wipe your face. You look terrible.* "There has been an outbreak of bed bugs."

Hazel rolled her fat, ugly eyes.

"Bed bugs that kill people." Patterson felt ridiculous saying it out loud. Despite seeing firsthand the carnage reaped by the little blood suckers, his skeptical side still gnawed at his mind. The words just sounded wrong like *aliens built the pyramids* or *the crash at Roswell really was a weather balloon.*

"Say *what*?! Bed bugs that kill? What is this? Some kind of joke? Where're the cameras? Am I on Youboob?" She asked sarcastically.

"Yes, bed bugs that kill people and no this isn't a joke and no, you are not on YouTube." Patterson said. *All though if you were, I'd probably be a millionaire.*

Hazel looked like she was about to scream. Literally, lose it. Call the men with the white coats and straitjackets and maybe the ones with the hazmat suits because baby, we're about to see this big momma go wild. Oh, and the straight jacket -better make it a wide one.

"Is anyone in room 16?"

"No. Why? You wanna rent it?" She asked, with a sly grin.

"Do you remember those two young kids that died there?"

"They was doped up. They didn't die of no bed bugs. The only bugs were the bugs in their damn heads."

Patterson stared at Hazel. He was tired of arguing with this hag. Why hadn't he gone to the Best Eastern?

"And we don't even have bed bugs! Never have!" She shouted.

Yeah right. Patterson thought. This place is probably crawling with bed bugs. They come free with the room. *Fresh towels, fresh linens, free bed bugs.*

"Look Mrs. Hazel. I am not going to argue with you. I don't have time. You either evacuate, or I'll shut you down. Understand?"

Hazel wanted to be defiant. She was about to argue, but one look at the detective told her that he was very, very serious. She reluctantly conceded defeat.

"Fine. I'll need help."

"No problem. I've got nine able-bodied officers outside." Patterson said, relieved. He walked out and dispersed his men like the leader of a search party. They fanned out, knocking on doors.

George sat in the crown vic. He looked disturbed. His eyes stared out the windshield but saw nothing. They were looking inward, into his mind, his past, his memories. The retinas watching something that couldn't be seen by anyone else. *I haven't seen him in what -twenty years? Now he's here, and that's not good.* He remembered the face. Pulled it up out of his subconscious brain. A nightmare of a bygone age, a forgotten time, a past that George never wanted to relive. Yet here was his past coming back to haunt him. *Tony.* He'd never forget the name. Tony had been standing there staring right at him. Tony with that drug dealing punk who drove the Mustang. Tony that cold, callous prick who had taken so many lives and laughed about it later. And he was with the punk in the Mustang. *Why?* The punk that had been following George and Patterson all morning. How had drug dealing Carlos come to be associated with a psychopath like Tony? Questions for the ages.

Patterson had remained oblivious to the situation. He hadn't even spotted Carlos, a character the detective knew. That was for the best. George couldn't imagine confronting Tony on the street, especially since George wasn't armed and Tony would most definitely be strapped to the max. *Have gun, will travel.* That wouldn't have ended well.

Tony was bad news. Very bad news like a worldwide pandemic; a plague set on humanity. George had lost track of Tony after the army. They had been in Iraq together. Fought side by side in numerous shitholes. Tony had George's back and George had Tony's. Brothers in arms. Brothers till death. But that had all ended. Ended the day they went into that village. After that George left the army and Tony sort of just vanished. He heard rumors from time to time that Tony was involved with some real serious shit. Rumors that his former comrade had taken his skills and applied them to the civilian market. Not the *private security, Blackwater* civilian market, more like the *Pablo Escobar needs a guy in the States* civilian market. *Have gun, will travel.*

Patterson walked up to the car window. "They're getting everybody out." He said to George who continued to stare into space. "You alright?"

"Yeah." George said, snapping back to reality.

"Thinking about Ocean?" Patterson asked, looking at George with concern.

"Something like that."

Patterson shook his head. "He was a good kid."

"Yeah."

"You know what shocked me about that woman?" The detective said, motioning towards Hazel, visible through the glass of the motel office.

George shook his head.

Patterson pulled a cigar out of his pocket and stuck it in his mouth. "She's going to tell her guests the truth.

Seems like that would be bad for business. Doesn't it? At least tell them it's a damn gas leak or something. Hell, anything."

George looked around at the concrete squalor. "I don't think it will hurt her business in the slightest." He said with a smile.

Patterson nodded, his lips curling around the cigar into a wide grin. He produced a lighter and cupping his hands together, lit the cigar, puffing large clouds of smoke into the air which George attempted to swat away.

"Damn man. Ever think of smoking cigarettes?" George coughed.

"I used to. They're really bad for you." Patterson replied.

"So are cigars."

"You don't inhale cigars. It's not the same thing."

"Ever try quitting?"

"Hell no. I need something. You know how bored I get on this job? Well, at least how bored I used to get on this job? I'm a homicide detective in a town with no homicides. These past three days have been the craziest I've ever experienced in my life. Now we have what? Thirteen homicides? Two committed by a man, unless those damn bugs have learned how to use a gun and eleven committed by *bugs!* Which still blows my mind."

Hazel came shuffling out of her office. Her ample rear end waddled across the parking. She went up to the first of fifty doors, rapping on it with her sledgehammer of a fist. The thuds echoed up and down the parking lot. A black man in his mid-thirties came out. He looked pissed by the intrusion. A pretty black woman -her dark, shapely body adorned in lingerie- lay on the bed as if posing for a Playboy spread. Hazel spent several seconds talking with the man before shouts could be heard across the parking lot. The man, obviously unwilling to quarrel with the likes of Hazel Rhodes, went back into the room and slammed the door. He came back out carrying a duffel bag and dragging the scandalously-clad woman by her arm. The woman was trying to dress herself as she stumbled along. Her shirt was half on, her pants were unbuckled, and her mouth was agape at this sudden change in her evening. Hazel shook her head at the couple then moved on to the next room.

George and Patterson paused their conversation to watch the theatrical production of Hazel and the Half Moon Motel. Patterson leaned on the car, puffing madly on his cigar, pausing every couple of seconds to spit out the remnants of the leaf paper in great globs of saliva onto the pavement.

"Any mysterious deaths anywhere else in the US?"

"Nope. Well, of course, you have your suspicious deaths, that happens every day but nothing like this."

"Who were the kids that died here?" George asked.

"Timmy and Amanda. Nice kids from good families up in Boston. Traveling to see grandma if I recall. Made a pit-stop for a little romp in the sheets and that was all she wrote. The maid found them in room fifteen." Patterson pointed to the room.

"What did their parents do for a living?" George asked.

"The file's right there." Patterson answered, indicating a manila folder on the back seat. George grabbed it. The file contained two neat stacks. The driver's license photo of each teen identified the corresponding stack. He read Amanda's first. She was eighteen. Just turned eighteen three days before she died. She had two younger brothers. Her father, Todd Meltzer, worked construction for a road crew. Her mother, Olivia, stayed at home and cared for the children. If Amanda's background was normal, then Timmy's was out and out boring. His father was a truck driver, his mother a school secretary. Timmy had two sisters, both of which were older and married with kids of their own. Timmy's parents were ultraorthodox Catholics, who followed the teachings of the church as stringently as an early morning golfer follows the rules of the game. Which would explain the reason Timmy found it necessary to sneak off with his chick and explore her body at one of the sleaziest motels this side of the Mississippi. George thought back to his strict Catholic upbringing. He felt a twinge in his groan reminiscing about the many clandestine rendezvouses with creatures of the opposite sex. In Cars, in the woods, in bathrooms, just about anywhere. Life was simpler back then. Now it was wine and dine, five-star restaurants and forty-dollar bottles. Then the caressing and the underdressing before finally falling into the sack and by then you're so tired, so frustrated, your balls so blue, that you'd rather just jerk off and pass out. Back in the day, the girls were anxious to get their skirts hiked up and their panties pulled to the side. George sat the folder back down. Nothing there.

"What was the name of the victim found at the Best Eastern?" George asked.

"Hank Anderson." Patterson pointed to the stack.

George opened the file. Hank's file read like a list of reasons to *off* yourself. Hank was a divorced traveling salesman, who spent his time in cheap hotel rooms and probably hadn't had a home-cooked meal in thirty years. He sold paper goods. Again, nothing in the folder peaked George's interest.

George knew the other three victims. Well, he knew Tracy, Judge Julius and Eleanor. Josh Kelly, the reporter for CNN, was a mystery. So were Tracy's kids. Josh Kelly's file was *SOP*. Young spoiled rich kid. Well-liked by his parents and *despised* by virtually everyone else. There was plenty of motive to cancel Josh Kelly's reservation, but George figured Josh was more than likely in the wrong place at the wrong time. Judge Julius, on the other hand, was a judge. A judge who had probably accumulated a very long list of people who would like to see the scrawny old man take his last breath. The judge was a prime target.

"I think you need to look at Judge Julius' old cases." George said.

"I didn't figure you for a homicide detective. I thought you liked killing things." Patterson said.

"There has to be some rhyme or reason for these bugs. I can't bend my brain around the fact that these people died randomly. If Dr. Phil's right and these bugs are genetic hybrids that were intentionally made and thanks to my niece-" Patterson shot him the stink eye. "we know they were brought here then..."

"Terrorism is random." Patterson shot back.

George nodded in agreement. "Yes, it is. But in most cases, some asshole group comes out and takes credit for it. Not this time. No one is taking credit for this."

Back to the judge. "Do you have any idea how many people that old bastard might have pissed off? Thousands. Maybe millions. The guy was a true-blue quack. A dictator in a black robe."

George couldn't argue with the logic of that. Julius was one hell of a quack.

Hazel Rhodes sucked in the air around her. Her chest filled to maximum capacity before a scream issued from her innards that would have put Norad on high alert.

George exited the car. He and Patterson surveyed the row of rooms. The scream had been so loud and so shrill, it seemed to be coming from everywhere all at once. They spotted the plump woman bent double in front of an open door.

"Jesus Hazel." Patterson said when he arrived at her side. "Was that really…" He broke off when his eyes caught sight of the scene inside the room.

The dim light from the bathroom illuminated the two people. The two dead people. Correction three dead people. One was a woman with a newborn child clutched against her bosom. She lay sprawled on the floor. Her eyes dead-locked, wide-eyed, staring at the ceiling. The dead woman's lips were parted in a silent scream.

The third body, a skinny ghastly creature that had at one time been a man, lay on the floor as if in mid-crawl, his arm reaching out attempting to grab the door. It must have been his last-ditch effort to escape. The last movement his muscles managed to make before they were drained of their blood. The eyes told the tale. One of terror and failure. The cold stare was fixed on the door, fixed on freedom, fixed on life.

"Holy shit." Patterson mumbled. "What the fuck are you doing?" He said startled as George elbowed passed. "What if they're still here?" Patterson whispered as if the bugs might hear him.

George ignored the detective. He walked into the room. He was afraid. Sure, who wouldn't be? Bugs lurking in every crack. Bugs that had murdered a father, mother and their newborn child. Left them lying dead on the floor like discarded, shriveled juice boxes. George could almost feel the bugs. Feel their presence. Feel their compound eyes boring into him. Seeing him multiple times as if he were on display at the local Best Buy's TV aisle. It gave him the creeps. He wasn't Superman. He was scared. Hell, he was terrified. But he kept going. The scene around him drove him forward. He had to check. He knelt next to the woman. She was plain in looks and wardrobe. *Plain Jane.* George was overcome with a sense of grief. A sense of loss. It brought him back to the curb, sitting over top of Ocean's lifeless corpse. That sense of looking down at innocence lost, never to be resurrected.

The baby really sent George over the edge like diving off the face of the moon and freefalling to earth. The baby looked so helpless. His little blue eyes looking longingly at his mother as if she were his world -the only thing he could see. His entirety. She was supposed to be. She should have been. The baby's hand was locked firmly on the thumb of its mother. The knuckles of the little fist were pasty white. George reached his fingers down and pressed them lightly on the neck of the newborn for several seconds. He felt nothing.

George got up and walked out. He made it ten feet onto the parking lot before he puked his bile filled stomach up onto the asphalt. He wretched for several minutes, hands on knees, head between his legs, his body outlined in the flashing of red and blue lights. His pile of hot vomit emitting steam as it sat on the frozen ground. George had never in his life felt so much hate. So much anger. So much revulsion. He could taste it. It drowned out the acidic sick in his mouth. The fact that someone was responsible for this. Someone had created these bugs. Someone had envisioned these dreadful things. Dreamt them into being. Someone so evil. So diabolical.

Patterson walked over and placed his hand on George's back. "You okay?" He asked soothingly.

George nodded and straightened up. Patterson reached into his jacket and produced a folded napkin. He handed it to George, who immediately took it and began wiping his face.

"We'll get 'em." Patterson stated.

"I want 'em dead. Fuck locking them up. They don't deserve to live. I want the worms of hell to eat their flesh. Did you see…"

Patterson cut him off. "Yeah, I did. Never saw anything like it in my…" Patterson's voice trailed off.

George bent down as if he were about to hurl once more. "What room?" He gurgled through clenched teeth.

Patterson squinted. "14." He said.

Hazel, whose stony callous demeanor, had been irrevocably cracked by the scene in room 14 sat down on the curb. Her face looked pale which contrasted obscenely with the red wing sauce giving her a crazy clown appearance -*It meets Goodnight Sleep Motel.* Patterson walked over to her and peeled the keys from her hands without any resistance.

Most of the uniformed officers had finished their sweeps and mandatory evictions. They joined the stunned and startled trio by room 14. Their curious eyes investigated the scene in the room, regretting doing so immediately. Some of the officers joined George and added to his pile of puke with their own steaming puddles. Even for hardened officers, the sight of a dead mother and her dead infant was far more than they could bear.

There were three more rooms to go. Three more potential surprises like wrapped packages under the tree on Christmas morning in the home of a psychopath. Could be empty. Could be a toy you always wanted. But more than likely containing a hand grenade with the pin missing. The thought of this made Patterson squeeze the keys in his hand. He glanced at rooms 15, 17 and 18. If the bugs had killed in room 14, two rooms away from the room Timmy and Amanda had died in then it was a good bet that he would find similar scenes of grotesque horror in the other three. He gathered up what remained of his dwindling strength and pushed onward like a traveler on the last leg of a tormenting journey, staring up the slope of the last mountain to cross or the last river to wade.

He wasn't alone. George, who had recovered some of his stamina, although his stomach still tightened as if it were in the stranglehold of a giant snake, joined the detective. They approached room 15. Patterson wrapped hard with his fist. No answer. He beat the door again. Still nothing. Patterson pressed his ear against the door. He could hear a television set blasting the laughter of a late-night talk show. He knew what he would find. It was obvious. *Three days of this shit.* He reluctantly put the key into the lock and turned. The door swung open, slamming hard against the wall. And lo and behold…

The room was dark except for the faint light of the TV. Patterson stepped in. He didn't yell. No need to announce himself. Not now. No one alive to hear it. He saw what he expected -two bodies, an African American couple in their late forties under the sheets. Two more to add to the ever-growing list of people who wouldn't be celebrating Christmas this year -or ever again. Patterson walked up to the TV and pushed the power button. The old set hissed like a cowed snake before going black. That's when all hell broke loose.

Then as if on cue the deceased male jumped up out of bed in a frenzy that belonged in a Three Stooges skit. The man moved so fast and so clumsily, that he smacked his head on the table lamp and fell headlong onto the floor. The deceased female, startled awake by her lover's mishap, began shrieking with terror.

"What the hell!?" The man exclaimed getting to his feet and rubbing his head.

Patterson, stunned speechless, stared at the man with blank eyes. George grinned, then burst into laughter.

"Who the fuck are you!? What the hell you doin' in my room!?" Veins began to pulsate in anger throughout the man's face. "Something funny!?" He advanced on George, his fists raised menacingly.

"Whoa! Whoa! Whoa!" Patterson said, cutting the man's advance off. Patterson thrust his badge into the man's bulging eyes. "Didn't you hear us knocking?"

"Hell no!" The man exclaimed. He turned to his woman, who was still shrieking sitting up in bed. The man waved his hand, silencing the woman as if he were a wizard. "You want to tell me what in the hell's going on?"

George continued to laugh. He tried to stop but he couldn't. Deep belly rumbles erupted from him. And they felt so damn good like taking a hot shower after a day of sweaty, filthy work. That feeling of being refreshed, of wiping it all away. Watching it swirl at the bottom of the tub and disappear down the drain. The feeling of absolution.

"You have to evacuate." Patterson said, trying to speak over George's hoots.

George held up his hand when he saw Patterson eyeing him indignantly. He exited the room, still roaring.

"What da fuck is his problem?" The man said.

"We thought you two…were dead."

"Dead! Why? Why would we be dead?" The woman shrieked in a high, agitated voice.

Patterson looked up at the ceiling. It was still hard for him to say. Despite witnessing the reality of the situation, the very words seemed difficult to verbalize.

"There have been several unexplained deaths in this motel recently." *Yeah, that's good Bill, give 'em the old unexplained deaths mantra, that should smooth it over.*

"What the hell ya talking bout? Who died?" The man asked.

"Yeah. Who died?" The woman chimed in.

Patterson thought. Should he tell them about the bed bugs? Doubtful that they would be able to comprehend the situation unless he took them over to room 14, but he couldn't do that. He decided on the best course of action. Stick to the script.

"We're just glad you're safe. Sorry for any inconvenience. I'll step out and let you gather your things." Patterson said.

"Gather what? Jesus man. You barge in here. You scare the livin' shit out of us and now ya throwin' us out? Hell nah. You need to explain yourself!" The man demanded.

"I'll be waiting outside." Patterson said ignoring the man altogether. He walked quickly out of the room to cut off any rebuttal. The man's voice still boomed in anger as Patterson closed the door behind him.

The Crown Vic idled, exhaust fumes billowing into the frigid night air. George stood with his back against the car trapped in a never-ending chuckle.

"Thanks a lot." Patterson said when he approached.

George shrugged his shoulders. "Honest to God. No idea what came over me."

Patterson sneered. He walked over to the driver's door, reached into the open window and picked up the radio. The cops at the townhouse development picked up right away.

"Four more 10-54s." Officer Walt, a fifteen-year veteran of the force, answered morosely.

The gargling voice sobered George up like a college punk pulled over by the sheriff.

"10-54s?" George asked.

Patterson spoke without depressing the transmit button. "Dead bodies."

George lowered his head. "It's spreading."

"Any IDs?"

"A mother and three kids. Ages six, seven…" Walt sounded like he was reading off a paper. "And 10. Same *MO*."

"How far away from Tracy's townhouse?" Patterson asked.

"Four houses."

Patterson looked over at George who shook his head.

"Everyone else out?" Patterson asked.

"Yes sir."

"10-4."

"Thoughts?" Patterson looked at George.

"Get the Best Eastern on the radio." George commanded. "If they've found the same thing…" George's words were swallowed by the night air.

Patterson depressed the call button. "Come in Al."

The static on the other end was tone deafening. No answer came through the radio. Patterson gave them a few more seconds before he called again. Still no response.

"Better head over." Patterson grumbled. "Probably found more 10-54s. That's why they ain't coming to the radio." He lowered his frame into the car. George did the same and they were off.

Chapter 53

Lenny watched the freezing rain run down the windows of his office on the seventy-second floor. He was staying. His office had a bathroom. The company gym in the basement had a shower. There was plenty of food -not that Lenny the health nut would be needing it- and plenty of emergency power. The only thing the gigantic office building lacked was people. There was no one. Every floor with the rows and rows of cubicles looking like a large farm straight out of the Matrix was quiet and still. The computers were off. Papers sat idle in their tills. Half empty coffee mugs and water bottles littered the room. Pictures of families tacked on the cloth walls were barely visible in the dim lights. The only thing this ghost town was missing was the tumbleweeds lumbering past in the sandy wind.

Lenny was alone which is the way he liked it. Why go home? Who would he weather the storm with? He'd rather be here. Rather be with some real company -his laptop, his ledgers, his contracts, his figures, his *real* friends.

He rode the elevator down to the basement. He got off and was met with complete silence. The motion lights flicked on as they picked up the thermal signature of the young work-acholic as he walked through the shabby hallway. The appearance of the basement was at odds with the lobby and the floors above. The lobby with its marble floors, marble walls and ornate fountain looked like it was airlifted from the palace at Versailles. And the other seventy-nine floors, although nowhere near as highly polished as the lobby, did give the distinct impression of class, wealth and power. The basement was different. The walls were painted decades ago and in desperate need of a recoat. The floor was linoleum. And not nice linoleum, old peeling cracking linoleum, whose tiles screamed with the abuse of a million soles. The decrepit drop ceiling was dotted with missing tiles and dark rings of countless leaks. And to top off the decay, there were the fluorescent lights, half of which had outlived their lifespans and the other half were flickering on and off like a gravely ill person begging to be unplugged.

Most people would have cut and run if they saw the state of the basement, but for those who made it past the battered façade, wonderful things waited just around the bend. Because Sentrix *did* spend cash on amenities. That was one benefit of working for old man Reynolds. A major benefit. Several years before the company had constructed an Olympic size swimming pool and a gym in the ruins of the basement that would have made the meatiest of meatheads drool.

Lenny stripped off his suit, tie, dress shirt, socks and underwear and dove in. His body slipped into the warm, chlorine embedded water. Nothing like swimming stark naked with no one around. *Absolute pleasure.* He back-stroked across the pool looking up at the ceiling enjoying his alone time, his break, his only vacation. He swam for what seemed like hours; cleansing his body, mind and -although many people would say he didn't have one- his soul. Relieving the tensions that had built up because of the case. He thought of nothing, concentrating on his strokes. Back and forth. Back and forth. Breathing, paddling, cleansing. After he was finished, he slowly rose out of the water pulling himself up on one of the many ladders.

"I wager that *HR* would probably consider this to be sexual harassment." A voice called to him.

Lenny wheeled around. His eyes registered a slim female form that was instantly recognizable. Sarah Ryan sat poolside in a chair. *Sarah Ryan* the Vice President of Sentrix; the meanest bitch around; the *cream* of the feminist's crop; the Me Too's *Me.* And she had just watched him swim -*naked!* Witnessed him break about three hundred company rules. Lenny did the only thing he could do. He groaned. He didn't bother to cover himself up. One, he didn't have a towel and two, what did it matter anyway? She had seen *everything* now.

"I thought I was alone." Lenny stammered. His body dripped pitifully onto the concrete. He looked down at his -*oh man, cold water, damn!*

"Shrinkage." She said, voicing his concerns out loud. "No worries Lenny. I know all about shrinkage. What cold water does to a man. For the record…" She smiled sheepishly. "I am still quite impressed."

Did Sarah Ryan just make a sexual advance at me? Lenny thought. Sarah Ryan, with her, *never missed a minute in the gym* body, and her *should be on the cover of a magazine* face. *Did this knock out make a pass at me? Me, skinny, Jewish, super-nerdy, super-self-centered Lenny?* Lenny from accounting? Lenny the guy with the office on the seventy-second floor? He was pretty damn sure she did. He tried in utter desperation to think of something else, anything else. His mind swirling with the remote possibilities that this *fifteen* on a scale of one to ten would want to make love to *him*, had started to arouse his man downstairs, waking him up from his cold snooze and making his shrinkage a thing of the past.

"Why don't you take a shower and put your knickers back on. When you're finished, meet me upstairs. Know where my office is?" She said.

Lenny nodded.

"Good." She stood, turned and switched her beautiful ass across the concrete floor.

Twenty minutes later the two were seated inside of Sarah Ryan's large well-appointed office on the eightieth floor. Lenny looked around and marveled at the modern furnishings, which included a desk that appeared to be floating in midair. He liked modern. The past is the past. He couldn't understand why people spent fortunes on antiques. It perplexed him. After all, it was second-hand stuff. Used and discarded. Modern was far better. New, clean and crisp.

Lenny had fixed Sarah and himself a drink from the small bar in the corner. She, a gin and tonic and Lenny, a straight bourbon. At first, Lenny didn't even glance at the bar. He was nervous being around such a hard woman - *well, bitch, is a better word.* Sarah had the reputation of a Black Widow. Black Widows are known to devour their male companions after mating with them. Use them for everything they're worth to advance their own cause then eat them alive. Lenny had no intention of becoming the male Black Widow. He had something Sarah Ryan wanted -not mating of course- but information, mating of the minds. Information that would advance her cause -*herself.* So, he stayed away from the bar until Sarah offered. She encouraged the drinking and readily agreed to it. She realized that maybe the only way to get the *great* Lenny to loosen his lips was to get him tipsy.

"You're very lucky security doesn't have surveillance cameras in the pool room." She smiled.

Lenny nodded and sipped his bourbon. His esophagus burned as the golden liquid made its way down. Great night for booze. He got cozy. *Real cozy.* Lounged his frame back into the chair and placed one leg up on Sarah's desk. She looked at him like *who the hell does this prick think he is?* But she needed this smug little bastard. Needed what was in his skinny, little head. So, she let him be an asshole. Let him feel smug. Encouraged him to feel at ease, cocky, sure of himself. She sat down behind the desk nursing her own drink.

"What happened in Havre de Grace?" She asked. Better to come right out with it.

"I don't know what you're talking about." Lenny answered. Sarah was his only chance and if he had to be someone's lackey -*why not Sarah's?* She was ambitious, driven, a rising star. She would be one of the top executives after Sentrix went public. If he told her the truth, placed himself in her good graces, then he would be safe. The *momma* bear would protect her cub. She would go to bat for him even if Gordon Reynolds wanted him gone. Her protection would help him whether the last remaining week of Gordon's reign and help him rise in the new publicly-traded company. After all, Carter was no longer here. But Lenny wouldn't give up the goose that easily. It was better to play hard to get. Don't want to become the black widow's next meal. Give it up too quickly and get eaten. Let Sarah Ryan savor the flavor. Tweak her taste buds. A pinch at a time. Too much information too quickly would equal Lenny's demise.

Sarah looked into his eyes. She knew he had something big he was hiding, and it wasn't his manhood - although the skinny little kid did have a surprisingly large bratwurst down there. No, he was hiding something that would either make or break this billion-dollar empire. Something that would bring Sentrix down. Something that she needed to use as leverage to climb to the top of the mountain -and slay anyone who got in her way. Leverage - the ability to stomp on the heads of the pompous, sexist men she had to endure every day.

"Carter's gone." She said, as if he didn't know. *Master of the freaking obvious.* "He can't protect you anymore. Gordon knows what you know and *Gordon,* that old bastard will destroy you to keep it secret."

Here comes the million dollars. Lenny thought.

"I can protect you. Gordon's time is almost up. He's selling his stake and hitting the road. You've put in a lot of time here Len. You really want to throw it all away?"

Lenny shrugged.

"Tell me what happened in Havre de Grace. It's serious isn't it?" She asked. "It has to be. Carter sacrificed his job for it. Put himself on record. That means whatever happened is very serious. Serious enough to follow everyone involved even after they depart these shores. Maybe even criminal."

Again, Lenny shrugged. *Hold out. Just a little longer.* The offer was on the table. The cards had been revealed and Lenny was holding a royal flush.

"Does it have anything to do with the deaths down there?" She asked, and Lenny's eyebrows lifted.

"How do you know about…"

"It's all over the news Len. What do you know about it? What does that have to do with us? Is it pesticide related?" That would be big. Pesticide related deaths would cost the company millions of dollars in lawsuits. The news said there had been nine deaths. All under mysterious circumstances. The media had speculated that the deaths may be linked to opium abuse, but Sarah doubted that. Some of the victims couldn't have been drug users. No way. Two of them had been children.

"Look, Sarah, I really can't say. Carter swore me to secrecy. I am supposed to report directly to him. If you called him. If you got him…"

She interrupted. "I'm not calling Carter. The IPO is in two days. If this information gets out. If this company is responsible for killing nine people, we're toast. The markets will crush us. They'll wipe out our stock and we'll be bought out by one of our competitors or worse, a corporate raider. And you know what they'll do? They'll cut the company up into little pieces and sell them off one by one. We'll all lose our jobs." She was getting frustrated with him. She needed the info. *Needed it bad.* The IPO was her baby. She stood to make millions from it. She had worked too hard, too damn long to be put in the poor house by some stupid mistake Gordon Reynolds had made. It was Gordon who had ordered it. Carter had said as much at the board meeting. Gordon was behind this tragedy, whatever it was.

Lenny sat up in his chair. He gulped down the last of his bourbon. "I can't help you." He said. He wanted her to *beg*. Wanted to bring her down to size. Make her pay for it. Make her indebted to him forever. Keep the marlin on the hook for as long as possible. She was worried about the IPO, but Lenny was worried about his very existence. Sarah *would* find another job. She *would* still be well off. Lenny *wouldn't* be anything. He would just *be*. *Be* out in the cold. *Be* out in the rain. *Be* in the unemployment line.

Desperate times call for desperate measures. Sarah stood up and walked around the desk. She elegantly undid the bun holding up her golden blond hair and let the gold strands fall slowly, landing gracefully around her neck. She put her hands through it, her fingers separating it like a comb. It was long and curly and looked like strands of silk. She made each step count. Giving Lenny a view of her salacious body with its curves. She was wearing a black skirt that ended just below the knee. It was tight -painted on tight- highlighting her delicate features. Her ass looked like the spitting image of the Valentine's Day heart as if the artist had used Sarah Ryan bending over as the model for it. Her high heels clicked on the tile floor.

Lenny looked scared. Frightened like a schoolboy who had just been sent to the principal's office. His eyes were wide. His breath came in gasps -deep, sucking gasps. Sarah sat down on the chair next to him. She placed a hand on his leg and caressed it.

"Lenny, I *really* need to know what happened in Havre de Grace." She said, pausing at "really" in a very sensual way. Her voice warm, inviting, dripping with sex.

He gulped. He could feel himself hardening. Feel his manhood come alive. He tried to swallow another sip of his bourbon before he realized the cup was empty. Sarah moved her hand further up his leg. She grabbed him in her hands. Stroked him. Unzipped his fly, unbuttoned his pants and pulled his phallus out. She looked deep into his eyes as she moved her hand up and down.

"Are you going to tell me?" She asked, her gaze intense as her hand expertly worked him.

He gulped again. Sweat began to bead on his forehead. Large beads that rolled down his cheeks. "I-really-can't!" He blurted out.

Sarah stood up. She unzipped the side of her skirt and let it fall off her hips. She wore a pair of white thong panties, the back of which delicately disappeared between her sumptuous cheeks. She undid her blouse and her bra and pulled her panties down. Naked she climbed on top of Lenny straddling him, her knees on either side of his thighs. The tip of his penis brushed against her. She was ready for him. She grabbed him with her hand and put him inside her. Again, she asked the question, while at the same time moving up and down, rolling her hips with each pass, feeling him throb.

"Are you going to tell me?"

Lenny didn't want it to stop. If he told her now, maybe she would climb off and this amazing moment would end. This was like a porno -in fact, it only happened in pornos. This shit wasn't real. Couldn't be real. It was a dream. A crazy dream. He felt like pinching himself. Felt like making sure this was really happening.

She asked the question again. Her hips rolling slowly up and down. "Are you going to tell me?"

He shook his head.

She turned it up a notch. She rode him harder; rolling her hips and popping her ass like a professional. She was good. She was *damn* good, and she knew it. He grabbed her ass, squeezed it, slapped it playfully. Kissed her breasts. She moaned as she pulled his head into her chest and faked her orgasm with unbelievable believability. She could feel him rounding third and the coach waving him in. He shook, his legs tingling with pleasure. She didn't get off, she pulled him closer, grasped him inside of her as he finished. And she still held on. Still played with him. Tweaked him. Rolling her hips on his sensitive post-orgasm manhood.

"How about now?" She asked in a whisper.

"I'll tell you!" He gasped in her ear.

Chapter 54

The doctor sat motionless in his easy chair. His living room was pitch black. He sat there in the darkness pondering, mulling things over in his head like a child with a hunk of play dough. Squishing, kneading, rolling, and squishing all over again. The look of worry creased his brow. Worry about what? Fear of what? Fear of who? He couldn't answer, well, he could answer, but he didn't want to. Was he really a part of this? He knew too much to turn back. But he wasn't dispensable. Not really. He wasn't just some piece of trash to be discarded. No. He was still useful. But now because of this mess, he was a target with a giant bullseye painted on his back. And the people that were hunting him? *Oh, my word.* Well, let's just say you wouldn't want them hunting you. *No sir.* These people were serious assholes. *Professional* assholes. Trained to kill. Trained to show no mercy. People who had spent their lives killing to protect their own hides.

The storm was coming, hell the storm was already here. And it was one hell of a fucking storm.

The small one-bedroom apartment he occupied was sparse, Spartan, boasting only what one would need with zero frills. He had one television, a small thirty-two-inch LED with a single easy chair sitting in front of it. The easy chair his nervous ass currently occupied. The room had no ability to entertain guests which is exactly the way Rudd preferred it. He didn't entertain guests. He had no friends, no family and no women. Sex was a luxury he never indulged in. Ditto with friendship. He was a career-oriented, driven son of a bitch. He was a ship that could only sail on one course with no deviations. No stopovers for pleasure at any port.

He was the only one who could stop the bloodshed. The only one. Audi Murphy on the Abrams tank, Sergeant Baker propped up against the tree, Lieutenant Frank Luke in the cockpit of his biplane. He had something in common with these men, although Rudd's enemies were not advancing Germans or Japanese. Rudd's enemies were bugs, genetically modified lethal insects that had already sharpened their teeth killing a dozen people.

There was a knock at the door. A quiet knock. *Thud, thud.* Like the final footsteps before the condemned rides old sparky into the sky *-or better yet into the ground.* Rudd looked up and stared at the door. Just stared. He didn't rise. He didn't grab a gun because he didn't own one. Nor a knife, nor a stick, nor anything at all. He had never needed one. Protection had always been the furthest thing from his mind.

So, he just sat there and stared. The knock came again. *Thud, thud.* The doorknob jiggled, almost imperceptibly as if it hadn't moved at all. But it had. It had rotated right to left. And it was locked. But that wouldn't matter. Whoever was on the other side of that door, would stop at nothing. No locked door would bar their entrance for long.

Rudd finally stood. He listened for another second and debated whether to let them in. Let this end. Let them put one between his eyes. End the torment. End the guilt. End it all. Let him sleep. Be at peace.

The doorknob jiggled again, this time the movement was louder, not chary at all. The sound of metallic instruments met Rudd's ears. *Lock picks.* He thought morosely. If these were professionals, they would unlock the handle and the deadbolt in the time it took Frank Sinatra to pick up a groupie -like no time at all.

Rudd hesitated no longer. He walked into the bedroom and grabbed the already packed duffel sitting on the bed. The deadbolt clicked open. Now all that was left barring their passage was the handle. The small, cheesy handle that wouldn't even stop a five-year-old. Rudd went into the small kitchen. The window above the sink led to the building's fire escape. It was the only way.

For his age, Rudd could move. He climbed up onto the counter and opened the window fast like *Night before Christmas* fast, but he wasn't about to see any fat man with twelve reindeer flying overhead. The only fat man was himself, and he was climbing out instead of in. And the twelve reindeer? Well, they were on the other side of the door in the hall ready to send Santa to the land of the elves once and for all.

The handle clicked, and the door flew open. But it didn't make a sound. No bang. They caught it before it hit the wall. Two men clad entirely in black and holding suppressed handguns cleared the living room and moved into the kitchen with the precision expected in men of this caliber. Quick, deliberate, trained precision. Their weapons aimed at the open window. *Hey Santa, time to die you fat bastard!*

One of the men held a small walkie-talkie in his hand. He lifted the device to his lips and blurted out a hurried message to his companions down below. They would be ready when fat old Mr. Claus made it to the ground. *Payback was a bitch.*

Rudd clambered up the fire escape. He hadn't gone down. And it was raining. Which was just *freaking marvelous!* Not just any rain but freezing rain. Ice from heaven above. Which was turning the big metal fire escape into the world's biggest ice luge.

His apartment building was twenty-two floors, and to Rudd's dismay, his apartment was located on the fourteenth. Eight floors to a man in his sixties is like running a triathlon. He was winded after four. He paused to catch his breath and promised himself that if he made it to the top, he would give up sweets and red meat *forever.* He'd go running or walk or bike *-yeah biking sounded good.* Rudd peered down through the slats in the grated iron. The two men were climbing out onto the escape from Rudd's apartment. These men appeared young, and that was unwelcome news for Dr. Rudd. He took off again climbing higher. The duffel slung over his shoulder felt like it had rocks in it. The weight was unbearable.

He was about to give up. About to raise his hands and surrender but the loud clang of metal behind him forced his forward momentum like the shot of the firing pistol at the start of the Olympics. A bullet, fired from one of the suppressed pistols had missed him by inches, probably by millimeters. It ricocheted off the iron escape like a drumstick hitting a cymbal. Two more loud clangs echoed into the darkness, one in front of him and one behind. *So, this was the end game. No prisoners. No surrender.*

The black-clad men were shouting. The language was foreign to Rudd's ears, although he thought he understood what the men were saying. *He's up there. He's up there. Get him.* No Rosetta Stone needed for translation. Common sense was the world's universal language.

He reached the roof. It was square with a three-foot wall ringing it on all sides. Two small structures jutted up as if they had been born from the surface like islands are born from volcanoes in the middle of the ocean. The structures looked like sheds, and each had a door. A door that would lead to the stairwell and to freedom but more likely to death.

Rudd ran to one of the doors and with a strong pull opened it but didn't descend. Instead, he left the door open and ran to the opposite side of the roof where he knew there was a second fire escape. Without looking down, because if he did *oh shit!* He climbed over the wall and shimmied down the ladder to the first landing.

The black-clad men reached the roof. Their eyes appeared like small white orbs in a sea of blackness. They scanned the gravel-covered roof. Nothing moved. No fat old scientist anywhere. Their eyes locked on the open door with the yellow glow from ancient bulb spilling out. One of the men pointed his pistol into the open door and walked through. The other man made his way around the roof, checking behind the numerous exhaust vents with their oversized fans gusting. After thirty seconds, they determined their target wasn't on the roof and hadn't descended the stairs. The black-clad men checked the other door. It was locked, they moved on looking for another means of escape. They found it and saw the doctor struggling with his wide girth five floors below. The men raised their pistols and aimed carefully.

Rudd saw it. The open window looked like a cold drink on a sweltering day. Like a mirage in the middle of the desert. Like McDonalds to a fat old scientist.

The first bullet ripped through Rudd's right arm near his shoulder. Blood and flesh landed like spilled soup on the grates of the metal escape around his feet. It stung like putting your hand in a hornet's nest. Rudd shrieked a loud, harrowing scream. He grabbed the wounded arm. The second and third bullet missed hitting the metal railing next to his head. He ignored the bullets falling around him as if they were merely a light drizzle. He ignored the pain too, although that was extremely difficult. His fight or flight instinct had kicked into overdrive. Rudd grabbed the window frame and pulled himself in as more bullets ricocheted off the metal in a shower of sparks.

The man on the roof yelled into his walkie-talkie. Static responses erupted from the device signaling compliance from the rest of his four-man team.

Rudd ran through the vacant apartment. It was being painted which explained the open window. He reached the hall door and peered out. *No one.* He had to get to the fifteenth floor. The building had an elevator bank in the center and two stairwells on either side. Rudd ran for the stairs, swung open the door and listened. He heard running footsteps several floors below. Rudd had to descend. He had to get to floor fifteen. He took a chance, rolled the dice and sprinted down which in his physical condition was more like gracefully falling down the two flights, taking the steps two and sometimes three at a time. He made it gasping for air, his chest heaving. Shouts met his ears from the floors below, the sound of his demise. And they were close. Much too close for comfort. Two maybe three floors below. Rudd didn't wait for them. *No party today fellas.*

Floor fifteen held something that was a throwback to the golden age of buildings in NYC. The architect that had designed the building in the 1940s had also designed the one next-door. They were identical twins down to the nuts, bolts and doorknobs. The architect had been obsessed with footbridges and had built one between the two buildings. The bridge was small, extending over an alleyway. It was closed in the 1990s for safety reasons but Rudd being the curious scientist that he was, had explored it several times. He was glad that he had.

Rudd made it to the door. He carefully opened it, sliding his wide body through without disturbing the yellow caution tape that crisscrossed the opening. The assassins were right behind him. But they were too late.

Rudd made it to the other building. He entered one of the four elevators and descended to the lobby. He walked out of the entrance as if he belonged there. *Just out for a stroll.* He nursed his wounded arm while trying to hide it from passing pedestrians which proved to be impossible thanks to the trail of blood he left in his wake. Thankfully no one seemed to notice. *Typical New Yorkers. They wouldn't notice big foot strolling down Park Avenue.* Rudd crossed the busy street and vanished into the night.

Chapter 55

Freezing rain fell on the town like demons from hell, droplets of fury. It had started a mere twenty minutes ago but was already covering the sidewalks and was even working its way onto the roads. Frosting them steadily, beginning in the gutters and swarming towards the center line like two advancing armies destined to meet in the middle bringing death and destruction to the battlefield.

George felt the Crown Vic slide. The tires slipping like a well-oiled drunk as the Vic rounded the corner and pulled into the parking lot of the Best Eastern hotel. Several police cars -red and blue lights going a mile a minute- sat in the lot. George stared at the bright flashes, momentarily transfixed by the beauty of them.

Patterson continued to try the radio. It was fruitless. The silence on the other end was eerie. He attempted the call a final time with the same disheartening response before stepping out onto the ice-covered pavement. His shoes gave way. He gripped the door of the Vic in a desperate maneuver to steady himself.

George, who was more accustomed to foul weather, thanks to his never-ending special ops training -the icy cold of Alaska proved to be the worst of it- balanced himself on the ice with ease. The two men walked, taking care with each step, across the lot. The freezing rain covered their clothes. Their jackets and pants froze, form-fitting around their bodies like poured cement on a corpse.

The Best Eastern towered before them, large and rectangular with four floors. It was the nicest hotel in Havre de Grace which was like being the smartest guy in the stupid class. But still, the Best Eastern's client list was almost exclusively comprised of white-collar businessmen visiting the town to peddle their wares. And why the hell not? The rooms were spacious. The amenities decent and the hotel was clean. Plus, there's *really* nothing else. Well, besides the Goodnight Sleep Motel and who the hell would be caught *dead* there?

Patterson and George entered the lobby and found not a soul in sight. Multiple sofas formed two giant squares in front of the reception desk. Over to one side was a dining room with tables, chairs and a countertop. Dispensers holding a smorgasbord of cereal sat in neat rows anxiously awaiting the arrival of the early bird crowd. The receptionist's desk was located near the front doors. Two computer monitors sat on the desk. But the receptionist was missing. No one was manning the phone. No snotty mediocre man present to punch his little fingers on the keyboard and inform you that *yes sir you do have to pay for the tiny liquor bottles you drank last night. And that goes for the adult film as well.*

"Where do you think they are?" George asked. He was talking about the team of HDG police officers who had been dispatched to the hotel.

"Upstairs." Patterson seemed unenthusiastic about finding out. It was the strain. The distress of finding so many corpses over the last few days. He assumed that the team of officers at the hotel were probably cataloging yet another body. That must be the reason why they weren't answering their radios. Patterson didn't think he could take the sight of one more. He was tired of death. Tired of bodies. Maybe he should have been a mechanic. Dead cars would be so much easier to deal with.

"Never seen a hotel lobby this quiet. Especially around the holidays."

"Yeah. Neither have I. But I guess that means my guys did their job."

George nodded. He agreed with the assessment, but it still bothered him. That sensation was back. That heightened sense of impending doom. He glanced around. Nothing. Empty. Desolate. Then his eyes fell on something behind the desk. He tried to make it out from where he stood. The object was small and u-shaped. It peeked out from the base of the desk like a tiny gnome trying not to be seen. George moved closer. He was walking as if the soles of his shoes were glued to the tiled floor. Each step was painstaking. Twenty feet, fifteen feet, ten feet, then he knew what he was staring at: the tip of a shoe, a highly polished, black dress shoe, turned on its side. He stopped and began walking to the right. Slowly things started to appear. First the shoe, then a leg, then a body. *Fucking brilliant.*

Patterson watched George with interest. What was the man looking at? His eyes and then his mind answered his own question, registering the presence of the body. Patterson groaned.

"Shit." He said, walking over.

George crouched. His fingers located where the man's pulse would normally be. Nothing. Deader than a rat with his neck snapped in a trap. The man was in his late twenties. He had a neatly trimmed beard and was wearing a suit and tie. His skin was ghostly pale like bright white paper.

"The receptionist?" Patterson asked.

George nodded, still crouching over the body.

"But this is the lobby." Patterson stated. His eyes roved the room. His skin crawling with goosebumps.

"Yeah." George muttered.

"But this is the lobby." Patterson repeated. He couldn't believe it. Couldn't fathom the ramifications. This guy had been killed in the lobby. Not in a room. Not in a bed. But here, in the middle of the lobby, which meant... Patterson dashed towards a doorway in the corner. A sign above the door said "Exit" in big, bold neon green. Patterson's feet pounded the tile floor. His heart raced in his chest. He flew up the stairs, taking them two at a time. He was sixty. Sixty and getting older by the second but his body overcame it. His mind forced him forward, pushed his system to the brink. Go, go, go.

"Hey! what..." George shouted after the detective. His words couldn't keep up with the fleeing man. George stood and gave chase.

Patterson reached the second floor. He grabbed the handle and pulled. The flow of sweat from his palm turned the metal surface into a frying pan with loads of butter. His hand slipped off.

"Muthafucker!" He cursed into the empty stairwell. He grabbed the handle again and this time hit pay dirt. It turned. Nothing. Nobody. A vacant hallway with closed doors. Patterson looked up and down. He reentered the stairs and almost ran headlong into George.

"Upstairs." Patterson blurted, and the two men ascended with the speed of the Roadrunner. *Beep, beep.*

The third floor was empty. Patterson walked a few feet in each direction. He saw no one. No bodies. No cops. He dashed up the last flight. Now his heart was lodged in his throat, obstructing his airway. They were up there. No question about it. There would be bodies. Probably two, maybe three, hell, maybe even four. Hotel guests. Businessmen in their sweater vests. Glasses of half-drunk scotch by their bedsides. Their laptops and Ipads left on. Copies of Think and Grow Rich lying open on their lifeless chests. Patterson's imagination swam. It stopped swimming when he saw the bullet holes. Or the exit wounds to be precise: three large holes punched jaggedly, disemboweling the white painted drywall. Patterson slowed his pace. He grabbed the railing. The gun was in its holster under his left shoulder. He reached for it, struggling against its restraints. He pulled back the slide and chambered a round. He looked at George. The exterminator wore an expression of unease on his face. Not fear. Not anxiety. Just unpleasantness.

George signaled with his hands. I'll go forward. I'll open the door. Patterson nodded his compliance. George grabbed the handle. Patterson pointed the gun. The door swung open. Patterson eased the gun into the hallway. He checked right, then left. His knees felt weak. His chest heaved. He lowered the gun, pointing it at the ground. He held onto the door jam with his free hand. He felt like vomiting. His stomach flipped like a washing machine with a pair of tennis shoes in it. *Da dump, da dump, da dump.*

George pushed Patterson aside. The detective gave way without a fight. George walked into a scene of absolute devastation. The three bullet holes in the stairwell were only the beginning. More holes stitched their way from one side of the hall to the other. They were even on the ceiling, in a neat pattern, one following the other. It was as if the gunfight at the OK Corral had been waged on the top floor of the Best Eastern Hotel. Wyatt and Doc Holiday shooting it out with the Clantons in an epic showdown.

The cops hadn't answered their radios because the cops were lying dead on the floor. Six of them in total, the whole team, positioned haphazardly throughout the hallway. A large, red-haired cop lay near the stairwell door, his gun empty, the slide locked back, his eyes wide with terror. His face showing the same signs George had seen so many times in the last three days. That ghost pale skin. The veins absent of the red liquid of life.

Gunfire didn't kill these men. It wasn't a super criminal like Lex Luther or a vicious gang of drug lords with AK47s that had claimed the lives of these keepers of the peace. Their lives were sucked out of them by a small, six-legged pest, a parasite, a plague. The gunfight had been one-sided. The cops versus the bugs. A failed attempt at defense. The last-ditch effort in a hopeless cause. It was obvious the team had been caught off guard. Ambushed by a deadly killer that hid in the dark, deep places of the world.

Patterson couldn't believe what he was seeing. How could this have happened? Maybe they hadn't seen the receptionist. Maybe they didn't know he was dead. If they did, they would have radioed. They would have called in a 10-54. That was the procedure. SOP like *stop, drop and roll.* No, they hadn't seen him. They came up here. Start at the top. Evacuate floor by floor. Move the guests down to the lobby. The guests. Jesus, what about the guests. Surely, the hotel had guests. They couldn't all be dead. Could they?

"This isn't a local matter anymore." George said. He turned to face Patterson. "We've got to call in everybody. FBI, ATF, CIA, hell even the KGB. This is crazy."

Patterson didn't answer him. The guests. That's where his mind was. He didn't want to see anymore. He hadn't signed up for this shit. Hell no. This definitely hadn't been in his contract. He was a small-town guy with small town problems. Not big city shit. This wasn't supposed to happen here. Not here. Not in Havre de Grace. Not in this small town on the shores of the Susquehanna, with its quaint shops, romantic bed and breakfasts and scenic views. This was Baltimore stuff. DC stuff. Places you go with an armored vest and a MG42 with a thousand rounds. Not here. *Get it together! You're a cop, god damn it!* There are people here. People who might still be alive. They need your help. That's what this is all about. That's why you signed up. Help people in need. Be their life preserver. Be their bright, shining beacon in the darkest of times.

"You hear me?" George said.

Patterson snapped out of it. "We've got to check the rest of the hotel."

"Check the rest of the hotel!" George exclaimed. "What are you nuts? You go batshit on me? Look around. This ain't a local yocal kind of situation. We need the guys in space suits. ET shit. We need to get the hell out of here. Call the big boys."

"And what? Wait outside. They ain't coming, George. There's a fucking ice storm out there. Ain't nobody coming. It's just us. We're it. We're the cavalry. What if there are people still here? You're saying we should leave them?" His voice clicked up a notch. "Leave them to get sucked dry?!" Patterson shook his head. "No way. No fucking way. If you don't want to come, wait by the car."

"If you haven't noticed there was a firefight up here. I'm pretty sure people heard that. Plus, how do you know these guys…" George nodded towards the dead cops. "Didn't already evacuate the guests?"

"They didn't. They started up here. They started at the top. It's SOP. Standard operating procedure. They didn't have a chance to check the other floors. We've got to. So, are you coming with me? Or are you going to tuck your tail between your legs?"

George glowered. "Listen to me." He said, and his voice was so dark, so cold, his eyes so intense that Patterson actually took a step back. "I've done things and seen things that would make this scene look like Christmas presents under a tree."

"So, you're coming with?"

George didn't answer. He just walked down to the end of the hallway. He stopped at 401, reared back and crashed his shoulder into the door with the force of a Panzer tank in the forest of Ardennes.

Chapter 56

Betsy Richardson came to life in the same boring, mundane manner as every other human on this giant rock we call earth: squeezed out between two fattened thighs, covered in blood and white powdery vernix; padded, toweled off and placed in the arms of the first and only person she would ever love -her mother. That had been fifty-two years ago.

Now Betsy was alone in the world. Her mother, Ruth, had died four years prior. She had been Betsy's world. The sun to her galaxy. She missed her terribly. Thought of her day and night and just couldn't seem to adjust to life without her. After all, Betsy had never lived anywhere else but in her mother's presence.

Ruth Richardson had been single. Never a good-looking gal, as far as her face was concerned, she nevertheless became popular in her hometown of Gnat Hill, Tennessee because Ruth had something no other girl had, a set of the nicest, perkiest knockers anyone had ever seen. And most people, or boys that is, in Gnat Hill had seen them. In fact, Ruth showed them off quite a bit. She started showing them off behind the swing set on her high school playground. She was fifteen at the time. A mature fifteen. She took Bobby behind those swings, lifted her shirt and changed Bobby's life forever. A year later, she showed them off to Eddie in the boy's bathroom. Unlike Bobby who was just a *looker*, Eddie was a *toucher*. Eddie spent the next fifteen minutes groping every square inch of Ruth's bosom. Squeezing, caressing, kneading, mashing and even sucking, twirling his tongue on her nipples as if they were a freeze pop on a hot August day.

Ruth didn't care. She liked it. And she liked Eddie - *a lot*. Eddie was what you would call *cool*. He strutted around town wearing a leather bomber jacket with a white tee shirt underneath. His jeans were always skin tight, *and he smoked!* Cigarettes. Reefer really wasn't *in* in the fifties. Eddie got Ruth's motor running. She felt hot all over every time he went to town on her chest which was becoming more and more frequent. It had started in the men's room but had gradually shifted to the alley behind the school, then finally to Eddie's car, and that's where Ruth's life changed forever.

Instead of just being satisfied with the old breast fondling bit, Eddie wanted to try something else. Something *cool*, something *far out*, he told her. They were out at Point Lookout -every town's got one. Eddie had just finished a long, slobbery session when he started to move his hands further south eventually crossing the equator. Ruth let him. His hands found what they had been searching for. Ruth felt great. *That's the ticket, Ed.* She thought as her eyes rolled back in her head. Eddie tried to maneuver, but Ruth's dress was in the way. It didn't take much convincing. Her dress went over her head, and that was all she wrote. Ruth gave birth to Betsy nine months later. And of course, Eddie, upon hearing the godforsaken news, had pulled a Harry Houdini faster than you could sing *Go, Johnny, Go*. All this instilled a sense of anger, resentment, and mistrust in Ruth Richardson. Sentiments she passed on to her daughter.

Ruth couldn't stay in Gnat Hill. Hell no. A single mother in the 1950s? In Gnat Hill? Hell, that was like being a devout atheist in a Roman Catholic congregation. It was almost as bad as being black, which in Tennessee in the 50s was saying something. She had been shunned. Her parents had thrown her out. Her grandmother was always conveniently playing bridge when she stopped by, and even her own sister wanted nothing to do with her. So, she left. She packed up what little belongings she had which included a three-month-old baby girl and hopped the bus for a one-way trip to a small town on the shores of the Susquehanna in Maryland. A town she had heard about in history class. A town that had missed becoming the capital of the United States by one vote. That town was Havre de Grace.

Thankfully she had found a nice apartment above a garage which she paid a pittance a month for, to a fine family -the Peterson's. And they became *her* family. Mrs. Peterson, who was cursed with a barren wasteland for a uterus, delighted in caring for Ruth's sweet little girl. Mr. Peterson gave Ruth a job. He owned a prosperous flower shop in town. He hired Ruth and taught her the ins and outs of a business that would eventually be passed onto Ruth and therefore eventually would be passed on to her daughter.

Betsy never married. She took pride in the family trade. She worked day in and day out, fielding orders, chopping stems, building arrangements and running deliveries. But that wasn't all she worked so hard at. Betsy, like many spinsterish old maids, ran the local gossip column. Many a town rumor had gotten started among the arranging tables in Peterson's Florist. Rumors that had far-reaching ramifications. Rumors that could make and break reputations, sink marriages, collapse political campaigns and in this case, cause a major panic of epic proportions.

The newest rumor, the hottest thing off the Peterson presses was *killer* bed bugs.

"You know Johnny?" Betsy said into the phone. This was the beginning of every Pulitzer Prize-winning piece of gossip.

"Yeah sure. The coffee shop guy." Evelin replied in the croaky voice of a chain-smoking frog.

"No, not that Johnny. Chief John."

"The fireman?"

"No, not the fireman. The police chief. Chief John." Betsy barked. Her lumpy rear end sagged over both sides of the wicker chair positioned directly under the corded phone that she just wasn't ready to part with. The yellow linoleum under her feet was spit-shined to a mirror-like finish reflecting the light of her ridiculous chandelier.

"What about 'em?"

"I was talking to his wife down at the Center Street Market. My word, did she have a story to tell. You won't believe it. I sure as hell didn't."

"Well, what is it?" Evelin blurted, impatience ringing in her voice. It was like a heroin addict seeing a fully loaded needle lying unattended in the gutter. *Give me more baby. Give me more.*

"Have you heard about all the deaths lately?"

"All the deaths!" Evelien croaked. "Who the hell hasn't? ODs, that's what I say. Some new crack these kids are shoving up their noses. And that Tracy. Local bar whore. Would have bet a thousand dollars she'd end up like that. Trailer trash."

"Yes. Yes. But you don't know the half of it."

"And I won't if you damn well won't spill it. Come on Betsy. I ain't got all night. Gotta call my son. Make sure he's got plenty of water and toilet paper. One hell of a storm out there."

"She says Johns been out twenty-four-seven working on these cases."

"Sure. Twenty-four-seven." Evelin scoffed. "More like Johnny boy's been hanging up there at Pierce's twenty-four-seven, taking licks off the old bottle. Working." Sarcasm saturated every word. "Chief John ain't worked a real job in his whole life. Probably wouldn't know how."

Betsy couldn't argue with that logic. Evelin, of course, was right on the money.

"She says John and the whole entire police department think bed bugs are killing those people. Can you believe it? Bed bugs?"

Evelin erupted in wheezing laughter which sounded like a bullfrog being bashed against a brick wall.

"Bed bugs?" Evelin cried. "Bed bugs? Come on Betsy. You of all people should know better than that. How ridiculous! Bed bugs don't kill people. They've been around for decades. Centuries! I remember, we use to burn our beds in the backyard when we were kids. Dump kerosene…"

Betsy felt anger well up in her. Evelin, that old hag.

"Well, that's what she said." Betsy stammered. "What do you think is killing all those people?... Huh?"

Evelin stopped laughing. She tried to catch her breath, taking several long rasps before speaking.

"I dunno. But I know it ain't bed bugs. I mean come on Betsy. Bed bugs. Sounds like a bunch of codswallop you ask me."

"Well, I hope you're right. I've got to go, that's my other line." She hung up without another word. Her other line wasn't ringing. She just couldn't stand to listen to another minute of that hag's breathing. Smokers. She couldn't stand them. They stink. They get the big C. And they rasp like a bunch of damn fools.

Who would believe her? It sounded like a bunch of bull. Bed bugs killing people. She hated to think that perhaps Evelin was right. But she had talked to Chief John's wife. And Betsy believed her. Yes, she did. Believed every word. Bought the whole song and dance. Hook, line and sinker.

Betsy peered out of her kitchen window. The Christmas lights of her neighbors blinked in her face. *Could they have any more decorations? My god.* She thought. Probably costs them an entire month's check to pay the damn electric bill. All those lights. And blow up dolls. Gigantic blow-up dolls swaying back and forth in the wind like bobbleheads. Their cloth hides covered in a shimmering layer of ice. What if the power went out? And those fools using all that electricity. *How dare they.* If the power does pop, it'll be their fault. Well, if that's the case, she would march right over there and give them a piece of her mind. Tell them that she was glad the lights were finally off. That she hoped they stayed off for the rest of the damn month. She, herself, decorated modestly. A wreath, a classy strand of white lights wrapped around her porch railing and that was it. None of this multicolored frivolity. It was uncivilized, to say the least. She thrust the curtains back in place in a fit of rage and sat back in her telephone chair.

Matilda! Her mind boomed. *Matilda!* She would telephone Matilda or Till as she was called by her friends. Till would believe her story. Till trusted her judgment. She picked up the phone from its cradle and dialed the number. It rang three times before the familiar voice of Till's husband Bernard answered.

"Hello, Bern. It's Betsy. Is Till home?"

Bernard scoffed. "Is Till home?" He mocked in his gruff voice. "Oh, course she's home. Haven't you looked outside Betsy? There's a damn ice storm out there raping and pillaging. Think I'd let Till go out on a night like this?" He said goading.

"No, I didn't think so Bernard. Can I…"

"Till, you got a phone call!" Bernard hollered across the room. "It's that flower woman!" He said, replying to Till's inaudible query. "I don't know. Why don't you just pick up."

Till's voice came over the line. "Betsy is that you?" She asked in her sweet voice.

"Meddling females." Bernard mumbled as he hung up.

"Hello, Till. Seems Bernard's in a pleasant mood." Betsy greeted her friend.

"Oh, just ignore him." Till said, dismissing her husband with an unseen wave of the hand. "Satellites out. So, of course, I'm to blame. It's okay. A couple more beers and he'll be dead to the world in his easy chair."

"You won't believe who I ran into today." Betsy began and didn't stop until she had Till convinced that Chief John's wife was indeed telling the truth, *the whole truth, so help her God.*

The chain of events that would transpire, thanks to that single phone, would alter the history of Betsy's small town in such an unprecedented manner, that it would make the burning of the town by the British in the War of 1812, seem amicable by comparison. But Betsy would never live to see it. Like a fuse that leads to a mountain of TNT, Betsy's days, in all actuality, minutes, were numbered. The match that would light the fuse came in the form of small bugs, their fangs sharp, their senses smelling the succulent aroma of carbon dioxide. The bugs had made their way to Betsy's, starting two houses down at the former home of one Ted Kilgore, the late husband of Patty the coroner. The bugs migrated house to house like jolly old St. Nick but instead of squeezing their fat asses down chimneys and bringing loads of joy, they scurried beneath door jams and the only present they brought was a one-way ticket to destiny. The true ghoulish ghost of Christmas future. *Bye, bye Betsy.*

Chapter 57

"Pull everybody out!" Patterson barked into the cell phone from the fourth floor of the Best Eastern Hotel.

"What the hell happened?" Officer Walt asked with panic in his voice.

"I'll explain later. Just get everybody out. All the cops and all the civilians."

"Jesus Bill."

"It's just Bill. Trust me, we're gonna need Jesus by the end of tonight."

Patterson clicked the end button. He was standing in the center of the hallway, surrounded by death. He should have been scared, but he wasn't. Adrenaline coursed through his body. He saw George crashing through another door, the man's tenth, if Patterson's count was accurate. So far, no additional bodies had been found. Thank the Man upstairs. Still, there were a hundred and some odd rooms to go. The odds were stacked heavily against them.

The door bristled with the first blow. It was tough work. George, who was in tremendous physical shape, was making it look easy. Patterson's shoulder ached already. The throb began near his bicep and slowly made its way north. He pushed on. The door gave, the frame splintered, a loud explosion of wood pounded in his ear. He stepped in. The room was empty. This process was repeated nine more times. By the end of the fourth floor, Patterson felt as if someone had been using his shoulder to hammer in railroad spikes. He ignored the pain. Pushed it out of his mind like an unpleasant thought.

"No one, living or dead." George said when he had regrouped with Patterson near the stairwell. He looked down again at the dead cops. They had died in vain. There had been no reason for them to come up to the fourth floor. If the receptionist had been alive when they arrived, he would have told them that which may have saved their lives. The key word being *may*. *May* have saved, but probably not.

They descended the stairs at a slow drag like a boat moving through shallow water. The third floor was also empty. Patterson could no longer hide the pain in his shoulder. He grabbed it, squeezing it with all his might, trying desperately to extract the diseased tissue that hurt so bad.

"You gonna make it?" George asked while the two men descended the stairs.

"Yeah." Patterson grimaced.

"You sure?"

"Do I have a choice?"

"I'll take the second floor. Wait in the lobby."

"Why? So I can get sucked dry and left on the floor like a raisin? Hell no. We're sticking together."

"I don't think it matters. Look what happened up there." George said.

"Yeah, but you know what you're doing."

George scoffed. "Really? I don't know shit. I've never encountered any insects like this in my entire life. I'm about as clueless as you are."

"I'll stick it out." Patterson said firmly.

"Okay."

"Does it bother you that three and four were empty? It's almost Christmas. This is a decent hotel. Those floors should be packed."

"Maybe the cops evacuated them before they…" George couldn't finish the last part. Maybe they evacuated them before they kicked the bucket. Before their reservations were canceled. Before they checked out early. Any way you put it, the reality of the situation was terrible. It was a nightmare. What would they tell the family? Killed in the line of fire? What fire? Killed by bed bugs? How would the families handle that? What could you possibly tell your kids when they got a little older, a little wiser? Sorry honey, Daddy died like a hero, he was drained like a coconut on Gilligan's Island.

The second floor was also empty. Now things were becoming *skunk ape* hairy. The feeling of impending doom had begun again in George's abdomen. It was strong. The sense that they were being watched. George's hair was *electric eel* on end. He felt a tingling sensation crawling up his back. His eyes were on high alert.

"Absolutely insane." Patterson said when the two men found themselves back in the lobby.

"Tell me about it."

"I just did. Where are all the guests?"

"Maybe we should ask him." George said sarcastically, pointing over to the sprawled body of the receptionist.

"Haha. Seriously though. I've got a bad feeling about this. No way my guys evacuated this place that quickly and even if they had, why return to the fourth floor?"

George shook his head. "I don't know." He leaned against the large reception desk. It wasn't safe to be in the lobby. The bugs had already devoured one person in here. They might still be hungry. The safest place was outside even if there was an ice storm underway.

"This is just a theory. Let's say they did get everyone out. Let's say they were able to accomplish that in record time." George said. "Then let's say, just for shits and giggles, they thought they missed a room on the fourth floor. So, they all went up and…"

It was Patterson's turn to shake his large noggin. "That would make sense. But let me show you the holes in your theory." Patterson walked over to the full-sized windows overlooking the vast parking lot. The blue and red lights from the police cruisers danced ominously in dark night.

"Parking lot's full." He said. "If the guests had gotten out where did they go? I doubt the MTA is running this time of night and I highly doubt it would be running in this kind of weather." The detective was spot on. The parking lot was indeed full. Rows upon rows of ice covered vehicles, their engines as cold as the frigid temperature outside. "Then there's the luggage." Patterson walked away from the window. "I saw at least fifty rooms with luggage in them. And that's just the rooms I checked."

"Same." George said.

"So where did all the people go?"

"Maybe they walked."

"Yeah right. In an ice storm?"

"Okay. Okay." George pondered the thought. The cars were there. The luggage was there. The people were not. Then it hit him. "Hall!" George exclaimed. He began to look frantically, opening several doors off the main lobby.

"Hall?" Patterson said dumbfounded. "What hall?"

George kept opening doors. "The nicer hotels have halls. You know, party rooms. Halls you can rent for events."

Patterson started opening doors as well. For a small lobby, the place sure had a lot of doors. There were closets, pantries, offices and even a small kitchen. The last set of doors were in the rear of the lobby. George took one worried look at Patterson then proceeded inside. He knew what he would find. Deep down in the pit of his gut he knew it.

All the special operations shit, all the combat, all the violence, the death, even that fateful tragic night so long ago that haunted his sleep could have never prepared him for this. This was a scene out of a nightmare. Something so vicious, so obscene, so filthy and rotten. The end result of a plague, or a nuclear explosion. The conclusion of something the army had unleashed. One of their war monsters they kept hidden away in their deepest caverns.

The room was indeed a hall. A massive hall, with an elevated stage equipped with a translucent glass podium.

The lights were on full blast as they would be at the end of a special night or during a boring conference. It looked like a nice place. A place where you could almost imagine the frivolity of a great night. But this wasn't one of those nights. This nice place had been transformed into a mass grave.

The shiny tile floor where tens of thousand had *cut a rug* was covered in bodies. They lay toppled onto each other as if they had fallen in mid-dance. The last song of the party had been a real heart stopper. There must have been sixty or seventy in there. All races, all genders, all ages, equal in death, a politically correct burial ground. All of them clumped in the middle of the room. Stuck together like sardines.

The kids lay with their parents. Small kids, who looked no older than three or four, teddy bears and Barbie dolls still clutched in their tiny hands. They wore pajamas with Hello Kitty, Batman, Spiderman, Princess Jasmine, Mickey Mouse, Donald Duck and Sponge Bob SquarePants. Their little eyes peered at George and Patterson as if to say: *You're too late. We needed you, but you're too late. Look at us. We're dead. You failed us. You couldn't save us. We didn't have a chance.*

Patterson felt his gut writhe. He was about to lose it. About to give up. Pull out his service pistol and end it all. Join the ranks of the people on the floor. They could have him. They could accept him in their midst. Pull him into Hades with their cold dead fingers. He never signed up for this. Never wanted to see this kind of devastation. Life's ugly underbelly like the stomach of a rat, dragged upon the disgusting paths of its existence. Tarnished and soiled by the numerous diseases of this miserable planet. He had always wanted to be the hero. To save people. To rescue them from destruction, from peril, from death. But he had failed. He had let them all down. The cops upstairs. The pompous looking greaseball behind the reception desk. The children in here. He had let them down. It was as if his life had lost all its meaning. The bottle from the illustrious vine had gone stale, tasted sour like vinegar left in the sun. He fingered the butt of his gun. Stroked it like an old loyal dog. A dog that could bite, tear into your jugular and rip it out. Leave you bleeding on the floor. Bleeding, dying, but at peace.

"Why didn't they run?" George asked. The question was directed at space, answerable only by cosmic beings who it was believed held such solutions. "Jesus, why didn't they run?" He repeated.

Patterson sure as hell couldn't answer. In fact, he didn't even hear the question. His mind was mush. Deep fried mashed potatoes smothered in shit sauce. He couldn't fathom this. He was tripping. LSD. Sure, why not? He could have scored it from the evidence locker. Yeah, that's it. He was definitely tripping. This wasn't real. It was a fraud. An illusion. A game his mind was playing. A nightmare come to life.

Patterson couldn't answer George's question. The cosmic beings couldn't answer either. But the bugs could and did. Neither man had noticed them, their minds so focused on the spectacle of death before them. The bugs had multiplied, bred like rabbits on Viagra. They were so numerous now that some of them hadn't eaten in days. Shocking though that was. Shocking because their brethren had consumed sixty-three people in the hall, one in the lobby and six upstairs, yet their numbers were so vast and rapidly growing that almost thirty percent had been unable to partake in the feast. Thirty percent seems like such a trivial amount. Not in this case. The thirty percent in this room amounted to thousands of starving bugs with one food source locked in their minds. They stared with their complex eyes at their prey from their lofty perch in the crack at the top of the crown molding that accented the walls of the great hall. Their skin piercers poised to strike. They couldn't wait any longer. They could taste the kill in the air, that sweet, salty taste of blood. *Time to feed.*

Chapter 58

George knew right away why the people in this room hadn't fled. He knew the minute his eyes fell on the sea of reddish brown moving quickly down the walls. The people whose bodies he and Patterson were looking upon couldn't flee. Fleeing was not an option. They had been trapped. Swarmed like a dying whale surrounded by sharks.

"Bill." George muttered grabbing the detective's arm. George was unable to find his voice. It just wouldn't come. He looked at the sea of bugs and tried to speak. "Bill."

The detective ignored him. He shrugged off George's hand. He paid no attention at all. He didn't care. His eyes fixed on the children. Their innocent little faces. Their big bold, terrified eyes. How could this have happened? It wasn't fair. God wasn't fair. Right before Christmas. *Why? Fucking why?!*

"Bill!" George had found his voice. "For Pete's sake!"

There was no response. The detective ignored him.

The bugs made it to the floor with incredible speed. They were moving in a massive ring encircling the two men. It was time. Time to feed. Time to survive. To further their existence. Their senses were alive with the smells of CO_2. The very thing that humans exhale. A natural habit of life. A pheromone map leading to their destruction.

"Bill!" George turned away from the bugs and grabbed the detective with both of his massive hands. He shook Patterson. Patterson was gone. His mind was in outer space, far away no longer a part of this universe. Patterson's eyes were unfocused and vague.

"Bill! Bill!" George shouted, shaking the man with all his might. Finally, Patterson's gaze began to become clear like foggy glasses brought back to room temperature.

"What the hell!?" Patterson shot back, pushing George's hands away. He glared at the exterminator. *How dare you touch me.* His look said with total clarity.

George turned back to the advancing hoard. That's when Patterson saw *what the hell* and his heart skipped a beat, actually, a whole series of beats.

"Holy shit!" He exclaimed. Terror engulfed him, penetrating his body and mind like a virus overtaking a daycare center.

"What are we going to do? They'll kill us!" Patterson was losing it. Panic had officially reared its ugly head. "They'll kill us!" He repeated. "We gotta get outta here!"

"Shut up!" George commanded sharply. "Stay put!"

Patterson shut up. The staying put part he was already in the process of doing. He didn't need George to tell him that.

They couldn't run. The bugs would surely cover their fleeing legs, wrestling them down to the tiled floor. George looked around the room. There were tables with white clothes draped over them. Sparkling silverware, neatly folded napkins and candles. Not wax candles -oil candles! Transparent plastic bottles with little wicks protruding from their metallic tops. That gave him an idea.

The bugs were closing rapidly. Their tiny legs moving as if they were powered by the warp drive of the starship Enterprise.

George hurried over to the nearest table. He had seconds to act. He snatched the candle off the table. His hands felt weak as he tried to peel off the lid. The bugs were only feet away. The lid popped. Oil spilled down his hand in shiny rivulets. In one fluid motion, he showered the floor around himself and Patterson, forming a circle of refined crude. He grabbed another candle and another and another, making the circle thicker. Oil streaked the floor. The smell of the flammable liquid coated the inside of his nostrils.

"Lighter." George said.

Patterson stared speechlessly.

"Give me your lighter damn it!"

Patterson snapped to attention. He rummaged through his pockets. Nothing in this one. Nothing in that one.

"Come on! Come on!" George exclaimed.

The bugs reached the circle of oil and began crawling through it. They slipped trying to gain traction. Still, they kept coming. Nothing would stop them. Nothing would impede their progress, their survival. They were close. They could taste it.

"Here!" Patterson yelled, handing George his silver Zippo from inside his jacket.

George lit the Zippo with a twirl of the flint wheel. The lighter sparked, flame shooting up from the wick. He held it for a brief second, staring at the oncoming hoard, half of which were trapped in the oil. George's eyes mirrored the flames. That sweet taste of revenge, of getting even, of justice permeated his mind. He smiled and then tossed the silver instrument of death.

It didn't catch. The Zippo, still lit, lay helplessly in the center of the oil. The bugs around the lighter began crawling onto it as if it were a life preserver in heavy seas. The flame flickered then went out. Most of the bugs had made it into the oil, and a few had even made it to the other side.

It was the end. No way around it. Patterson and George would join the bodies piled in the room. Two more victims to be chalked on a blackboard in some high school history class years down the road. "These are the last two victims of the great bed bug outbreak." George could hear the mundane voice of the teacher recite.

He shut his eyes and for the first time in decades, he prayed. He said the act of contrition, at least as much of it as his mind was capable of scraping together. He apologized for his sins. Recounted the horrors he had committed. That night in Iraq. The reason he left the army. The night that had sent him on a one-way course back to a family he couldn't stand and to a company he never wanted to be a part of. He had regrets. *Big ones.* After all, he wasn't Frank Sinatra. *Hell no!* He wished he would have lived his life the way he wanted to live it. Forged his own path. He wasn't ready to die. He wanted to fight. He wanted to survive. But he couldn't. It was fitting really. Going out like this. A bug man killed by bugs. Ironic. The bugs would have their revenge. He smiled to himself and accepted his destiny. He opened his eyes.

There before him was a shining image of God Himself or one of his angels or was it the devil, wreathed in fire because there was fire. A sea of fire like an excerpt from the Old Testament being acted out before him. The fire formed a scolding ring and in the center was George's savior -Detective motherfreakin' Patterson with an open book of matches clutched in his hand and a broad grin on his face.

Chapter 59

The sounds of tiny snaps, little miniature kernels being roasted in a popper, filled the air. George wanted to hug Patterson. He wanted to jump up and down in jubilation. He wanted to scream. He had thought the detective had lost his marbles. That the man had succumbed to the demons in his head. And yet there he was, matches in hand, to save the day.

The bugs were dead. Their corpses engulfed in bright red flames. George thought he could hear them screaming. He had to be mistaken. They didn't have the ability to scream. No way. It was his imagination. Still, though, he was almost certain that a tiny shriek was emanating from inside the roaring flames.

"Let's go!" George shouted. He took two steps and jumped. He could feel the heat from the flames lick at his shoes and legs as he passed through hell's kitchen.

Patterson, older and with a busted shoulder, fell as he hit the other side. George ran over and knelt beside him. The detective looked battered, bruised and exhausted like an old worn out soldier fresh from the field of battle.

"You alright?" George asked.

Patterson shook his pounding head to clear it. "I'm good." He muttered. He tried to get to his feet, struggling with all his might, his muscles on the verge of giving up. Physically he had had it. Mentally he had had it. He wasn't cut out for this. He had been going for almost thirty-six hours without sleep and with little food. His mouth was dry and haggard. His tongue felt like new sandpaper.

George lifted the worn detective with a great heave. The two limped out of the hall of death without a second glance.

The fire didn't spread. It survived nimbly for several more minutes, feeding off the remainder of the oil and the dried-out carcasses of the bed bugs. Then it died as suddenly as it had begun. Then as if it were the end of a play, the hall fell into complete darkness. The lights in the ceiling died then resurrected then died again as the power in the area struggled then failed completely. A tree was to blame. A lonely elm weighted down with heavy ice that had fallen unceremoniously into a transformer, causing an explosion of sparks. The hotel was left in an eerie black silence like a cemetery on a cold winter's night.

Chapter 60

It started with Matilda. Well, in all actuality, it started with Betsy, but since Betsy was down for the count, her role in the affair was over. So, it was Matilda that everybody, those who would survive the last leg of the journey, would remember as the one who lit the fuse.

The fuse that had sparkled to life, burned. One house at a time. One phone line at a time. One nosey busybody at a time. And on and on it went moving quickly towards its inevitable conclusion: *the big bang!*

Matilda called Alice McCabe as soon as she concluded her call with Betsy. Alice answered on the first ring as if the old woman and town council member, had been sitting stoically by the phone, stroking her fat cat Peter with a wrinkled hand. Alice couldn't believe what she was hearing. *Killer bed bugs!* It was too fantastic. No way. Not in her town. But after five minutes and very little convincing on Matilda's part, Alice became the third devout convert. A very powerful and influential convert indeed.

Alice called Frank Duisenberg. Old Frank was also a board member and the most vocal board member, with his loud, reverberant voice that filled hall meetings like a loudspeaker at a hostage standoff. Frank, his booming voice audible for miles, called Joanne Bright, who called Phyllis Tannon, who called old Marv Fletcher, who called Joyce Brunner, who called Ernie Platt, who called Sally Wayneright, who called Jamie Hatner, who called Carla Short, who, being the unofficial town columnist, called the world.

Panic had set in. The kind of fear that causes riots, lootings, and every other form of mass confusion. Word of the newly discovered corpses at the Goodnight Sleep Motel, the man and the woman and worst of all their infant child, passed from lip to ear of every townsfolk within a five-mile radius. To make matters worse, the word also spread about the townhouse community's deadly discoveries. How many more could this town handle? How many more people would die? Those were the questions on everybody's mind. It was like binge-watching the ID channel with those catchy shows, Wives with Knives, Deadly Dentists and now Killer Bed Bugs, or Sleeping Death or What Lies Beneath the Sheets. But unlike TV this was real life shit and it was real life shit going down feet from where most of these old townies stood.

Where were the bugs now? People began taking an inventory. Who had they not talked to in the past day or two? Friends, girlfriends, boyfriends, acquaintances, colleagues, and even mortal enemies. Each made a list and began one by one to contact the loved, to make sure they were okay, the lost, to see if they were found and the hated, with their fingers crossed snidely behind their backs. After all, none of the townies had anything better to do. They were stuck in their houses, iced in like Eskimos in an igloo.

The loneliness and the isolation made them fear the unknown even more. The sense of impending doom embodied the town. It was the feeling one gets when something really bad is about to go down. You can just perceive it in your gut: that electricity that sets your hair on end and sends a tingle up your spine.

The bugs were everywhere and in everything. If someone saw a cockroach, it was immediately identified as a killer bed bug. Fruit flies buzzing around a dozen bananas: killer bed bugs. A ground beetle running across the floor: a killer bed bug. A spider spinning a shiny web: a killer bed bug. The sightings were increasing at an alarming rate.

Where were the cops? The army? The navy? The Marines? Where were the heroes? The men and women who run towards trouble. Surely, they could save them. Surely, they knew how. But where were they? Even if there were a cop on every corner and a contingent of heavily armed soldiers hanging off the back of an Abrams tank making house calls, the townsfolk would feel the same: neglected, alone, forgotten, vulnerable.

Order was needed. And who better to instill calm and reintroduce some semblance of sanity than the town council. A town meeting was needed. Storm or no storm. Ice or no ice. A meeting was a must. The town was on the verge of mass suicide, everyone waiting with their glass of chilled Kool-Aid for the comet.

Alice called Frank Duisenberg again.

"We need to hold a meeting. It's a must." Alice said in her sing-song voice.

"I agree. What about the storm? Driving is out of the question." Frank boomed into the phone.

"They can walk."

"You can walk. I can walk. What about the others? Old Marv couldn't make it across the street on a Spring day."

"Most of them are young."

Frank laughed. Big guffaws. "Hell Alice. Most of the council have been around since the founding of the republic, some of them may have even signed the damn Declaration."

Alice stayed silent for several seconds, allowing Frank to finish his laughing spell.

"Not just the council. I'm talking about the town. A true town hall."

Frank swallowed, his Adam's apple moving up and down like a bobber on the end of a cartoon fishing line. "The whole town! What are you nuts? Lost your marbles. Checked your sanity at the door." Frank bellowed. "It's an ice storm out there. How do expect people to get there?"

As if she didn't know. "Yes Frank, the whole town. They need it. I talked to chief John. He said he'd come. He'll tell everyone to remain calm. Everything'll be okay. No need to panic."

"Chief John said to come? Chief John told you it was a wise idea to hold a town hall in an ice storm?" Frank asked rhetorically. "Come on Alice. I wasn't born yesterday."

"Yes. Yes!" She yelled into the phone. "He said…"

Frank interrupted her. "That's a big risk. A hundred, maybe two, out in this storm. Even if they walk, it's still dangerous. It's like a giant ice rink out there! Rockefeller center without the tree!"

"How else can we reassure everyone all at once? Burn up the phone lines all night long. Even if we could do that, which I'm not sure we can, it's not as good as a face to face. If these rumors are true, if these bugs can kill, we're in deep doggy do."

"Not the whole town Alice. I won't stand for it. Just the council. We'll discuss what to do next." Frank said with a tone of finality in his words.

Alice gave in. "Okay. Just the council. But I don't see what good that'll do."

"We'll figure that out when we're together. The council all live within four blocks of the VFW. That's a safe distance to travel. Well, hell, that's not even safe, but it'll have to do."

Chapter 61

Water poured from the heavens and was transformed into ice by the freezing air, landing indiscriminately on the earth below. The frosty layer began to form on the cars. The cold metallic bodies ideally suited for the transformation of liquid into solid. The trees followed quickly behind. The sidewalks and the roads were the last to fall, putting up a good fight but inevitably succumbing. Emergency vehicles, lights flashing a brilliant yellow, waged a hopeless uphill battle. They sprayed salt onto the streets, trying desperately to unfreeze the frozen.

The streets were empty except for a few remaining vehicles that braved the winter onslaught. The occasional passing motorist skidded and slid like a five-year-old out for his first skate at the local rink. It was very dangerous, almost suicidal, to be out on the roads.

Carlos stood out front of his apartment, shielding his body from the prevailing winds and the freezing rain. Tony, totally unaffected by the deteriorating conditions, stood opposite Carlos, his face half hidden in the glow of the streetlight.

"Let me get this straight." Carlos said through chattering teeth. "You want me to walk into police headquarters without anyone noticing and then walk out again with a box under my arm? You're fucking nuts."

But Tony wasn't nuts. He glared at Carlos. He hated this punk ass piece of shit with his Baltimore Orioles ball cap pulled low and cocked to one side as if he was the Latino version of Jay-Z. Who the fuck dresses like that? Carlos wore jeans that sagged so low, his ass was in danger of frostbite and a puffy jacket that looked like *Charlie*

Brown's the Great Pumpkin and Timberland boots that were worn for looks and not their utilitarian purpose. Tony, of course, had come prepared. He was sporting a jacket lined with Canadian goose feathers, a pair of long johns under his jeans and a black skull cap.

"I am very serious." Tony replied coldly. "You have a guy inside the department. Use him."

Carlos shook his head, blowing into his cold hands, trying unsuccessfully to warm them. "The guy has me. I don't have him. Remember?"

"I have the gun. The entire arrangement you had with him is now off. He cannot link you to any homicide, so the three grand you were paying him is now a bribe and not blackmail."

"Fuck you man! No fucking way I'm walking into that station." Carlos said shaking his head vigorously.

Tony just stared at him. He was seconds from pulling his gun out and putting two into the Oriole bird. He would love to do just that, but he knew he couldn't. He needed this punk. Needed his connections. If not, then it would be *bye bye birdie*.

"You have one choice, go into the station and get that box or you can spend the rest of your life in the can. I hear the boys in there love little Latin wannabe punks like you. I wonder how they would feel if they knew that you grew up like a white boy? A preppy white boy? You'd probably end up as the community pin cushion." Tony's eyes narrowed dangerously. The look sent shivers down Carlos' spine. Death was in the air and it clung to Carlos like a terminal illness. The grim reaper was seconds away from making his appearance stage left.

"Even if I could get in there. How do you suppose I get over there? Have you seen the shit falling from the sky?"

"Walk." Tony said.

Walk, in this? You have got to be joking. Freakin' an inch of ice out there and growing by the second. He'd have a better chance skating there. Fuck walking.

"Who's the bug guy?" Carlos asked, and he was surprised that Tony looked anxious.

"I don't know him." Tony lied.

"Yeah fucking right." Carlos said. "You knew him. I could read it in your expression. You got real intense. Real fucking intense. So, who is he?"

Tony sighed. No sense lying to this punk. He was planning on killing him eventually anyway.

"His name is George. I was in the army with him. We fought in the First Gulf War together."

"Friend of yours?" Carlos asked.

"No."

"You said you served together."

"George and I belonged to the same unit. He specialized in reconnaissance and intelligence. He also did a lot of sniping."

"Like with a rifle." Carlos said, holding up his hands as if aiming a rifle.

Again, Tony glared. He didn't laugh. It wasn't a movement his mouth was designed to make. "Yes, with a rifle." He said, now very annoyed.

"That's badass. What did you do for the army? Bet you was a really heavy fuckin' dude. Kick in the door and spray…"

"Shut the fuck up." Tony growled, cutting Carlos short. "Just get the box." Tony walked away, disappearing into the shadowy sheets of ice.

The glass entrance door to the hallway of the apartment building opened and closed with a swish. Carlos walked down the hall to his apartment, rubbing his extremities, trying to transfer warmth to them. It was cold as shit out there. He couldn't remember ever being colder. He fumbled with the key, his icy fingers trying to fish it into the tumbler. Finally, he hit pay dirt and stumbled inside.

How did Tony know about the gun? How did he know the gun was at Mike's? He was an out of towner. It didn't make sense. He, Carlos, had an arrangement with Mike, only Mike. So, was Mike playing him? Mike, the crooked cop, the guy who, for the right price, would look the other way even if his own mother was being robbed? Maybe Mike had sold out to a higher bidder. It was possible. And where did Tony fit into this? Where had he come from? He was an ex-soldier. A serious asshole with an axe to grind. A man with no past who had, at least in Carlos' mind, already committed two homicides in town.

Carlos grabbed a beer out the fridge. Then he thought better of it. He sat the cold beer down in favor of a warm one off the counter. He popped the top of the can, hearing that familiar snap, before guzzling half of it with one mouthful. It tasted like piss, like warm piss. He kept drinking it anyway. Beer in tow, he went over to a small heater and switched it on, aiming the glowing red coils towards his frozen legs. He allowed his body to collapse into his big soft armchair. The heat against his legs felt great, warm and inviting, like climbing into bed with a sexy woman on a cold night. Curling up next to her, skin to skin, not for sex, strictly for warmth, for heat. Feeling her hot thighs. Her thermal buttocks against his groan. Putting his arms around her, spooning. Their feet touching each other, caressing, caressing. He drifted off into dreamland. His mind imagining Sabrina between the sheets. The warm beer tipped gradually, slowly in his hand, until it spilled onto the floor, fizzing like a child's baking soda and vinegar volcano.

Chapter 62

Tony felt anxious. Nightmarish scenarios played out over and over again in his mind. Nervous, anxious, whatever you want to call it, they were all emotions Tony wasn't accustomed to experiencing. It was new territory. A new path that was unchartered on his maps.

Ice formed on his skull cap and jacket. His feet slid on the sidewalk with every step. He ignored the ice as if it didn't exist. He was oblivious to his current surroundings. Totally lost in his conscious mind. His thoughts playing cruel tricks on him. Twenty years making a living without a snag, with barely a hiccup. Now there was a goddamn roadblock, a brick wall in his path.

He was good. He could make a murder look like a suicide. A jealous husband look like a grieving widow. A greedy businessman look like a generous coffin side mourner. Killing was his talent, his life's work and he made a *killing* doing it. Millions upon millions of dollars. A very good run with the dice. Now the crowd had gathered. The women in their glamorous sparkling gowns. The men in their tuxes. All with their breath held. All watching as Tony took his next shot, his hand rolling towards the felt with momentum, his fist clutching the numbered cubes. *Seven or eleven. Seven or eleven. Go big or go home.*

This job would have been his largest payday to date. Sentrix was willing to fork over $2 million to clean up their mess. He planned to take the money and run. Planned to live out the last half of his existence in the lap of luxury, on some Caribbean island, before, undoubtedly, he spent eternity in damnation, if he really believed in such things, which he constantly told himself he didn't. Now, it was all in jeopardy. George was here. George could ruin it all. George, the only man in twenty years that knew his past, knew his identity.

Sentrix's orders were precise. Eliminate the two assholes in the motel. They had to be the first to go and for good reason. They could bring the whole ship down. Tony had accomplished the task with ease. Next, retrieve the box. The box held clues to the company's identity. This he failed to do. Failed for the first time in his life. Failed miserably. Now, the box was in police custody.

The box hadn't been in the motel room. He had checked while the two morons bled out. Slipping on his trusty gloves, he had inspected every square inch of the room. The dressers, the closet, the beds -that hadn't been easy, thanks to the underwear-clad, dead fat ass on top- and the bathroom. He even checked their car. The box was gone. *So long. Adios amigos.*

He had sat on the edge of the bed, his nose pinched to avoid smelling the foul odor emanating from the pants of the guy on the floor. He looked down at the brown stain that had spread there. That was the thing about death that always bothered him. The evacuation of the bowels. It was disgusting, inhumane and just plain foul. It was like the song said, the one about the Grinch, "stink, stank, stunk." And this asshole on the floor stunk, royally. He couldn't even remember his name or either of their names. They were like flies to him. Nothing more than common flies, whose destiny in life was to end up smeared on the polished wood of a dining room table. He sat there thinking. The box was a fundamental problem. Sentrix was adamant about recovering the box. Kill the flies but definitely recover the box. Well, the flies were dead, but the box was MIA. Where could these two have stashed it? They were outsiders, strangers in this town. No chance of them having an accomplice.

And what the hell was in the damn box? If they were trying to hide something, why would they leave clues behind? That was black ops 101. Leave no trace. No evidence. You send a team out in the field to do something they aren't supposed, in a place, they aren't supposed to be, you strip the dog tags and disavow any knowledge of them. That's the problem with civilians. They never think. They always assume everything will go according to plan.

Havre de Grace had one detective. One flat footer whose sole job was investigating homicides in a town that seldom had a homicide, until now. So, he made up his mind. Put surveillance on the detective. If the detective discovers the box, he, Tony, would know. If the detective didn't discover the box then it had most likely gone the way of the Titanic, straight down to the bottom of the sea.

The problem, or the newest problem, was that Tony was also an outsider. If he attempted to follow the detective himself, he would certainly be spotted, picked out of a crowd like a black guy at a KKK rally or a white guy at a Black Panther meeting. Havre de Grace is a small town, with small-town folks, who are used to their small-town lives and everyone *really* does know everyone else's name and where you grew up, met your wife, conceived your first child, adopted your first dog. So, Tony would stick out. He had to find someone who would do the deed for him.

Tony had only one friend in life and he didn't even know the guy's name or if really was a guy, he could be a woman, but he did sound a hell of a lot like a man. It was his handler. His partner. The man on the other end of the line. That cold voice that set-up the jobs and forwarded the instructions. The handler, or Bobby Sue, as Tony secretly called him, had a Rolodex of corruption on tap: crooked cops, crooked lawyers, crooked judges and to top it off, although Tony's was pretty sure all of them were -crooked politicians. Bobby Sue had consulted his Rolodex and had come up with a name: Officer Mike Rossi.

Officer Mike was so crooked that if he were a building, he'd probably resemble half of the *M* in the famous golden arches. Just a giant upside-down U. Mike gave Tony everything, over the phone of course, crooked or not, Tony didn't meet with anyone, unless they were expendable. Officer Mike told Tony that the local drug dealer and wannabe-*wiseguy* Carlos would be Tony's best bet. Carlos knew the town, knew the cops and best of all the little Latino punk was expendable.

"He hit a guy a few years back." Had been Mike's answer to Tony's question on how to win Carlos over. "Guy's name was Eddie. I've got the gun." Mike said laughing. "Dumb *spick* punk. Should have stuck to drug dealing and stayed away from murder. Now he pays me three g's a month."

Tony could picture the asshole cop smiling as he said this. "Give me some background on Eddie." He had commanded.

Now, he was relying on Carlos -*Mr. Expendable*- to walk into a packed police station and steal a piece of valuable evidence. And Tony was pretty sure it wouldn't go down well. Tony was grasping at straws. Last ditch effort.

Or was it? He was better than that. He was smarter than that. He just needed a plan.

Tony kept walking down the street or better yet, skating down the street, the ice was so thick. He was so entrenched in his thoughts that he nearly ran into a family. Tony stopped short, or tried to when he saw the man, the woman and the two little tots, bundled up before him. Their bodies were highlighted in blue Christmas lights that rung their home.

"Sorry fella." The man said in a jovial voice.

Tony fingered the suppressed pistol in his pocket. He probably should just shoot this *fella* right here. No witnesses, no identifications. And what the hell were these happy assholes doing out on a night like this? Shouldn't they be snugged in their warm beds, dreams of elves and candies dancing in their virtuous heads?

"Bad night to be out." Tony remarked. He tried to put on his nice mask, but it didn't work. The man took a startled step back as Tony's cold, dark eyes fell upon him.

"Yeah, y-y-you're right about that." The man stuttered. "We're heading off to a town meeting."

Town meeting?! Town fucking meeting?! What kind of backward, shit eating town is this? These assholes called a town meeting in the middle of an ice storm?!

"Where you headed?" The man asked. "Something big's happening. All these deaths. Crazy stuff fella."

Tony almost shot him. He gripped the gun handle even tighter. In his mind, he could see the man's brains flying out the back of his wool knitted skull. He could visualize the shocked, anguished look on the stupid face of the man's ugly, bland wife before her brains exited as well. Pleasant thoughts. Tony kept his cool.

"I'm here on business. Picked a bad day to come to town." Tony smiled. "Secretary never checks the weather. Too busy doing her nails, know what I mean?"

The man smiled back. "Sure thing fella. My name's Henry." He said, sticking out his hand.

Tony stared at it with disgust. "Forgive me, I don't shake hands." He said with ice in his voice.

The man pulled his hand back, a little hurt by the stranger's coolness. His family looked anxious. Tony could almost hear the man's sniveling wife's voice, "come on Henry. Let's go. We're gonna be late."

"Gotta be off. You have a safe night fella." Henry said in parting.

Tony didn't say anything. He just nodded. He watched the family slip and slide down the street until they were out of sight. And a delicious, malicious idea sprang into his mind.

Chapter 63

Kelly's fingers punched the keys faster than Manny Pacquiao doing a seven-slug combo. She ignored the chaos of the news station. People ran from one end of the station to the other as if they were participating in a relay race, but instead of a baton, they passed copyright from hand to hand. The storm outside was *big* news which meant *big* ratings, which translated into *big* money. Kelly hadn't even looked outside. Hadn't even gotten up since sitting down an hour, or maybe two hours ago. Time stood still. The only thing she concentrated on was the clicking of her mouse, the letters on her keyboard, and the words that were appearing on her screen. It was music to her ears.

Her story was taking shape. The plot was good. Actually, it was stellar. The headlines were writing themselves: *Genetically Modified Bed Bugs Slaughter Innocent People; Big bad bugs; Six legs of death; Frankenbug.*

But who was behind it? She was missing that part. And that was a big problem. No culprit. No evil villain for readers to gasp with shock, clench with anger and seethe with hate. Every story needed one: the antagonist. The man behind the curtain. The powerful entity who pulled the levers controlling the frightening face equipped with the gusts of fire. She had to connect the dots. Solve the case. Become Nancy Drew. That was her favorite book series when she was growing up. That's what made her want to become an investigative journalist. Those harrowing tales of intrigue. She looked up to Nancy, her hero, her role model. She still read them. One of her closely guarded secrets. She enjoyed the mystery. Loved the quick, comforting read. It was like watching your favorite comedy sitcom, even if you've seen it a thousand times. It's a security blanket. Kelly had looked up to the author, Nancy Drew's creator Carolyn Keene and she had been thoroughly shocked to find out that her hero, Carolyn, who had transformed her life and made her aspire to be a writer, was, in fact, a fraud. Carolyn wasn't real. She was a pseudonym for countless ghostwriters. But that was okay. The ghost writers had been pretty damn good.

Kelly sat back and examined her work. Without the antagonist, the story was junk. Trashcan material. She needed to solve the case. Mentally she went over what she knew. Her trusty legal pad sat in front of her, a blank yellow lined page staring up at her like the eyes of an appealing dog. *Pet me. Stroke me. Write something on me baby.* The pad cooed in her ear.

George had said the bugs were an intentional act and not a random natural occurrence. It was an attack. He thought whoever unleashed the six-legged assassins, had meant for the bugs to spread, like poison in a well, into other major cities: Baltimore, New York and of course Washington DC. What if the attack had gotten that far? What if the bugs were in New York or Baltimore or DC, right now? It would be terrible, awful, catastrophic. A plague, Egyptian style, set upon mankind. It would cripple the country, destroy the economy, bring the nation crawling on all fours and there would be no one to blame. No one to drop bombs on. No one to chase through the caves. No one to waterboard. No one to hold accountable.

Then it hit her like a sledge hammer dropped from the top of the tallest building. *Kapow!* The chink in the armor. The soft spot. The townhouse. Why the townhouse? Why murder an alcoholic and her two children? Tracy was a nobody, a member of the forgotten. She served no political, ideological or economic purpose in this master scheme. She just existed, drenched in her own sorrow, trapped in a downward spiral that would have inevitably ended in her demise anyway. So why end it early? There was no gain in it. Tracy wouldn't have triggered a spread. She was a loner. Was it a test? An observable exhibition for the guilty party? Something they could point to and say *yes, it works*. Maybe. It sounded more personal. More like a targeted assassination. Something that fulfilled one's own agenda. Revenge, very, very cold revenge.

Tracy's background was the standard who's who of the dramatic rendition of the *forgotten*. A drunken father who abused her and her mother. A drug-addicted mother, who cared more for her needle than for her own daughter. No siblings. A trail of tears of self-loathing and societal rejection. Was there a connection? Some minuscule past glitch in the programming of Tracy's existence? Maybe she owed money to someone? A drug debt? Perhaps she was a mule. Perhaps she had lost or better yet, injected a large portion of someone's product, that she was meant to deliver to someone else. Someone could have made an example out of her. But what about the kids. That was truly bizarre. Kelly had heard of children being killed as part of the drug trade, but that kind of shit happens in Mexico, or Brazil, or Chicago, not in civilized communities. Not in small towns like Havre de Grace. Right? Why murder the little kids? Children were born innocent despite their parents' indiscretions. Could it be wrong place, wrong time? The children were merely unintended targets? That was possible. But then that's assuming drug dealers were behind this plot. What benefit would drug dealers reap killing thousands, maybe millions, of innocent people?

None. Let's face it, drug dealers are businessmen. They kill to further their trade and protect their territory from rivals. They're maggot-ridden, scum bag pieces of shit, but they wouldn't have done this. So, it had to be revenge.

Kelly began to dig like a bulldozer on steroids. She started with the courts. She had acquired copies of the kids' birth certificates from her ex, Officer Mike, along with the coroner's report. Mike that ass. No sense in dwelling on him. She had James now. The certificates listed the boy, Shaun, age six, and the little girl, Allison, age four. Six and four, what a shame. The father's slot was blank. It had never been filled out. Okay, not totally abnormal. Not when you're dealing with someone like Tracy. Hell, she may not have known who the father really was.

The internet is a miracle. Countless amounts of research available at the click of a mouse. Most private and/or public information could be downloaded easily from the right site and for the right price. Kelly went to a familiar site online, one that she had used countless times before and in an instant, after the proverbial credit card information was entered, she had every document pertaining to Tracy and Tracy's children downloaded onto her computer. Nice and easy. Scary what you can accomplish with a computer nowadays.

Kelly opened each PDF. Tracy had been married. That was shocking. Her former husband's name was Raymond T. Hastings. Apparently, the marriage lasted for six years. The couple was separated for a year before officially divorcing. Six years and how old was Tracy's son? Six. Born on October 4th, which means he was conceived, barring any unfortunate premature calamities, on January 4th, exactly two months before the white-trash groom-to-be was dragged unceremoniously down to the courthouse in Bel Air. So, Raymond T. Hastings, whoever the hell he was, was the father of Shaun and Allison. So, why hadn't Tracy listed Raymond's name on the birth certificates? Maybe Tracy, who had a reputation of opening her legs for anything that dangled, hadn't known who the father was. Maybe it was Raymond, or maybe it was some surly character she had run into down at the local dive. From what Kelly had gathered from people who knew Tracy, with the right amount of body ink and cheap beer, you could easily see what was under her skirt.

The divorce may hold the answers. Kelly opened the file, a very long file, comprising the divorce settlement and the custody arrangements. She began to read. The divorce was contentious. Raymond had sued for full custody of both children siting alcohol abuse, physical abuse and adultery. The judge had denied the request and granted full custody to Tracy, leaving Raymond with only supervised visitation.

Raymond was a great guy, as far as the online history had dredged up. He wasn't a white trash loser as Kelly had originally surmised. He had a bachelor's degree from the University of Maryland and a doctorate from Johns Hopkins. Both great schools. Difficult schools to gain admittance to and even more difficult to graduate from. Raymond was a smart guy with his head on his shoulders. There was a deed in the folder for a house purchased in the exclusive Bulle Rock neighborhood and his credit rating was out of this world as in the bank would literally give you, well, the bank. Raymond had worked for MelWeb Labs, a pharmaceutical company in Baltimore. Everything Kelly read spelled *CATCH* in big bold letters.

So, why had the judge awarded the sleazy, alcoholic Tracy with custody of their two children, as opposed to the doctor, scientist, financially adept Raymond? Was this another case of judicial abuse in Maryland? Overlook the sins of the mother because, well, she is mother? Sounds ridiculous but not that far fetched in this backwards state.

Kelly kept reading the divorce settlement. Raymond was ordered to pay Tracy a sum of $1,000 a month for child support. She read on. Supervised visitation for two years after which he would receive overnights at his home. The order was signed by both parties and the judge. She read the judge's signature. She recognized the name: *Julius Smith*. She let out a little gasp. Judge Julius Smith and his wife, Eleanor, were the owners of the renowned Blue House Bed and Breakfast and both had been victims of the attacks. The judge and Tracy, both involved in the same contentious divorce, had been killed by genetically altered insects. Coincidence? Probably not, at least not in the mind of a journalist like Kelly.

Raymond Hastings' trail ended abruptly and mysteriously, mirroring the late Jimmy Hoffa, although unlike Hoffa, as far as Kelly could tell, Raymond hadn't had any run-ins with the mob. After the divorce, Raymond had stopped using credit. It's hard to trace someone if they use cash. His house in Bulle Rock was foreclosed on and sold at auction. There were no records of Raymond Hastings after this point. No run-ins with the police. No newsworthy articles were written about him. No trace of employment. It was as if he had decided that his life was so terrible that he had better just end it. Perform the coup de grâce in some desolate place where no one would ever find him. It was a sad case. Raymond seemed like a good guy that had made one hell of a mistake by marrying the girl from the trailer park. A mistake that had cost him dearly. He had lost his wife, which wasn't a huge loss, his financial future, thanks to the high child support payments and most of all, he had lost his children.

"Hello." A woman's voice answered.

"Is this Mrs. Shirley?" Kelly said into the phone. Mrs. Shirley had been one of Raymond's next-door neighbors in the exclusive Bulle Rock community.

"Yes." The woman said hesitantly.

"This is Kelly Halle with Channel 9 news."

"Okay."

"Did you know a Raymond Hastings?" Kelly asked.

There was a small pause on the other end. "Yes. I did. He lived next door."

"When did he move out?"

Another pause. "Years ago. Why?"

"I am doing an article about Raymond's ex-wife Tracy. She was murdered."

The woman gasped. "Murdered?"

"Yes."

"Well, I can't say I am too sad to hear that. What happened to the children?"

Kelly spoke slowly. "They were also murdered."

The woman gasped again, this time much more audible. "Oh my God." She said. Her voice sounded upset. "They were the cutest little kids."

"You remember them?"

"How could I not? I helped Raymond and Tracy with them when they were born. I loved those kids." She started to get choked up. "You know it wasn't right what that judge did to Raymond. He was a good man. A good father. He loved his children."

"How about Tracy?" Kelly asked, already guessing the reply.

"She was terrible. When she first moved in, I liked her. She was nice, but then she went downhill. Started disappearing at night. Drinking. Doing drugs. She would come out in the yard and start fighting with Raymond, screaming at the top of her lungs. Right in the back of the yard in the middle of the night. Raymond would stand there and take it, just take it! She would hurl insults at him. Throw things. Cops came a few times, but they couldn't do anything because Raymond would never press charges." Mrs. Shirley paused to catch her breath. "Sometimes she'd stay away for days. Leave her kids and who knows what she was doing. I'd go over and help Raymond out. He was a mess. Knew he made a big mistake but would never admit it. He kept it hidden as if it wasn't happening at all. Tracy actually brought a guy home one day. They pulled up on a motorcycle and went inside. I had the kids. I had been watching them while Raymond was at work. Tracy was inside screwing that man, that stranger, for hours. In Raymond's house! She never even tried to see her kids. Never came over to make sure they were okay. Just went and screwed that man until Raymond came home. He found them. Threw her out. She screamed. She threatened him. The motorcycle guy threatened him. It was very bad."

"Wow." Kelly said, shocked at Tracy's nerve. "Why did the judge award her custody?"

"That's Maryland. If you're a woman, no matter what kind of woman, you have a five hundred to one advantage over a man. That's just how things work here."

"Did you testify?"

"No. Raymond didn't want me to. He just shook his head when I asked him and told me it was better if I didn't get involved. He was a very private man."

"How did he react to the verdict?"

Mrs. Shirley broke down. She sobbed into the phone. "He was devastated. Couldn't believe it. It was the only time I ever saw him angry. He cursed the judge. Cursed Tracy. Cried into my shoulder. He loved his children. Said he wouldn't let them grow up like that, with her. Wouldn't let them be neglected."

Kelly let her sob. She didn't want to cut in. Finally, Mrs. Shirley stopped crying. Kelly had one more question. "Do you know what happened to Raymond? Where he is? What he's doing?"

"The divorce broke him. Emotionally, mentally and financially. The bank foreclosed, and he moved." Mrs. Shirley replied.

"Any idea where he went?" Kelly asked.

"The day before he left, he told me he had gotten a job in New York City."

Chapter 64

"Who chose the test sites?" Sarah Ryan asked Lenny as the two sat post-coitus in her spacious office.

Lenny had told her everything. Of course he had. He would have given up his own family members to Stalin's secret police after Sarah Ryan's sexual interrogation session.

Sarah knew how to get what she wanted. She had figured out life's big secret: sex was the easiest and quickest way to a man's heart. Not through his stomach, which is something everyone proclaims. It's through a man's groin. Through his testicles. That's the key. You want something bad enough, have sex and you'll get it. Sarah had learned that lesson from an early age, much too early in fact. She remembered it verbatim, although she wished she could forget.

Friday night lights. The bright flashes that engulfed her inner thoughts when she remembered the scene. The lighting. Those big, bright, overpowering miniature suns, blanketing the high school football field. She had been young, fourteen, or *yeah,* fifteen at the time. Fifteen but with a body pushing twenty-one. Stacked and packed. That was one way of putting it. Young Sarah Ryan was stacked and packed. She had big, come-do-me lips and golden blond hair that sashayed down her back.

Sarah remembered seeing him in the bleachers. That smug, stunningly handsome asshole of a teacher, Mr. York. Mister *give me some of that after-school detention, so I can sit and stare at you all day* York. And there he was. Sitting with his squeeze of the week, making her laugh, making her giggle, like a stupid fool. *Oh, she's eating it up, that two-bit hooker, straight out of the Bronx. Give me a break Mr. York. You can do better than that.*

"He's so dreamy." Sandy drooled into Sarah's ear.

Oh, would you please shut the fuck up, you bubble gum chewing freak, with your hair puffed up looking like someone tossed your head into a cotton candy machine. But Sandy was her friend, so for the time being all Sarah said was "Yeah."

Sarah needed Mr. York. Sarah's parents were draconian like dungeon masters, who would hang her over a pot of boiling oil if she came home one more time with a D on her report card. One more D and it was off with her head. Which translated in the modern times of the 1990s as grounded to your room and no TV for two weeks. The TV part didn't bother her. She didn't watch the damn thing anyway. It was the grounding part that bothered her. Stuck in the house with that little shit of a brother, who at twelve, played army in the house every single day with his stupid little friends, running up and down the hall issuing loud bangs from their mouths as if it *really* sounded like a gun, which it didn't. It just sounded like three morons making make-believe with their pie holes. Plus, she'd rather be out. *Like Duh! Umm, she had a life*, unlike her mother. The most exciting part of her day was when one of the soap opera stars died on the silver screen Or her father, who was always pissed off unless he had one too many or her stupid little half-witted brother.

See Sarah wasn't only extremely good looking. She was also extraordinarily smart. So smart in fact, that her grades didn't suffer from lack of intelligence, they suffered because Sarah Ryan was so damn bored. Well, that was except for French class. French class was one of those things she just didn't get. Who the hell needs French anyway? Math, science, history, art, all no-brainers but French. *Yuck!* And guess who the French teacher was? *Million-dollar question.* That's right, it was Mr. picture perfect York. So, not only was Sarah having problems speaking French, she couldn't even pay attention long enough -thanks to Mr. hunk- to even pass with a C., But she had a plan.

Her plan was what she was thinking about as she stood there next to puffed-up Sandy under the lights of the football field, watching Mr. York as he made his weekly screw pee her pants with mock hilarity. Very freaking funny. It took her a week. But after her first time with Mr. York, he couldn't have remembered *Mrs. Giggles*, if she was standing in front of him with a belly that said *Daddy why didn't you pull out*. And ever since she screwed the brains out of Mr. York for that very impressive A on her report card, Sarah Ryan knew she could get anything she ever wanted from a man.

Their sex was strictly professional. Both received pleasure out of the arrangement, Lenny a little bit more than Sarah but it was very much a consensual contract on favorable terms. It ended passionately, in fact, Lenny could still feel himself inside her when he closed his eyes. He could have let it go on forever. Laid with her for days, caressing her body, kissing her lips, pulling her tightly against him and making love to her every twenty minutes for an eternity but Sarah wasn't having it. When it ended, she had gotten up, pecked him on the lips as if to say *thank you* and switched her perfect ass into the bathroom. She returned a moment later, got dressed and sat down, ready for work. *Strictly professional.*

"Sangmore said he and Rudd put forward recommendations but Gordon Reynolds and the board…"

"What board?" I'm on the board, and I've never heard anything about this until yesterday." Sarah blurted out with indignation. "The board doesn't know shit."

"Then Sangmore is lying?" Lenny said. He had another drink in his hands, ice cold cola as opposed to alcohol. He didn't need any more stimulation tonight. The storm was raging outside. Ice coated the windows with an impenetrable shield making visibility impossible.

"I don't think Sangmore is lying. I think Reynolds chose them alone. He never sought approval from the board. His hands are bloody. The real question is, did Reynolds know the bugs were lethal? If so, then he's not only a lying piece of shit, he's a murderer."

"Carter said that when he told Reynolds, the old bastard wasn't alarmed at all. Jubilant, I believe is the way he described Reynold's reaction." Sarah's eyes narrowed dangerously. Lenny continued. "It meant more money. More fear equals more profit, at least in Reynold's mind."

"Why?" Sarah waved her hand at Lenny, stopping him from answering. "I understand about the fear and money aspect but to take the chance. I mean, he's Gordon fucking Reynolds, one of the richest men in the world. Why take the risk of losing your company, your fortune and very likely, your freedom? It doesn't make sense." Sarah tried to reason it out. Carter Ritler had had a great idea: *genetically alter bed bugs, so only Sentrix had the solution.* Create a monopoly over the entire industry. An industry that last year had grossed nearly $25 billion. Sentrix's revenue was an astounding $2.25 billion but to increase that to $10 billion or even $15 billion would be unimaginable. Carter had the right plan, but apparently, it went wrong and then was permitted to fester like cancer until it was now threatening the life of the company as a whole.

"You have to wonder whether or not it was for entertainment." Lenny replied, and Sarah raised an eyebrow.

"Entertainment?"

Lenny stood up from the chair and walked to the window, cola in hand. He couldn't see through the ice but he stared out as if it were a beautiful sunny day in Manhattan. He needed to clear his head. To think. To reason with his own mind. His emotions. Finally, he turned to face Sarah.

"Rich men tend to become bored. Bored with life. Nothing entertains them. The cars, the houses, the yachts, the jets, it all becomes so very dull. So mundane. They begin to look for entertainment that their wealth may not be able to afford them. Surely you've heard of the S&M clubs for the wealthy? Or the private islands with the underage girls? Or the crashing of priceless sports cars just to watch them burn? These things are very real. Rich people trying to spice things up. To get their jollies off."

"Killing people?" Sarah asked incredulously.

Lenny nodded. "You've heard of Truman Fry the third?" He asked, and Sarah shook her beautiful head. "Wealthy, lived alone in his castle, became a serial killer.

Murdered twenty-one people before they finally caught him. Told the police he just wanted to have some fun. He had inherited fifty million dollars. He could have bought almost anything, yet he chose to kill because money can't buy that kind of pleasure."

"Okay. I get the point." She said in an exasperated tone. "What if this was accidental? What if the consequences were unintended?"

Lenny shook his head. "No. They weren't."

"How do you know that?"

"This is a hundred-million-dollar project. Not a run of the mill middle school science experiment. Those bugs had their genetic code modified. A very specific code. Sangmore told me everything. Told me the insects he chose. Each picked because they had a specific trait. These bed bugs were modified to be faster, stronger and lethal. The original idea that Carter had championed was lost in the shuffle. Someone manipulated the code. The bugs began to kill in the lab. They killed the mice they fed on. And yet still they were released. Someone at the top gave that order. Someone who knew the consequences. Someone who either didn't care or willed it to be." Lenny finished and returned to his seat. He had made his point.

"A hundred million?"

Lenny nodded. "Well, ninety to be exact. Ten went to a company in the Grand Cayman."

Sarah stared at him wide-eyed. "Ten what?" She asked.

"I went through the budget line by line. The biggest expense was labor. The second was a purchase for ten million made to a company called HydroLine which, as far as I can tell, doesn't exist. The trail I followed led to a company in the Grand Cayman with ties to the Russian government or Russian organized crime, which as I've been told, is pretty much one and the same."

It was Sarah's turn to stand up. She paced around behind her desk, cutting perfect lines, turning on her heels with military precision. She was deep in thought.

"Where did this expense originate from?"

"Sangmore's lab." Lenny answered. "I talked to Sangmore about it. He didn't have a clue where the money had gone. He said he never even heard of HydroLine and had never authorized a purchase from them."

Sarah turned a skeptic eye on Lenny. "I find that very hard to believe."

"I know. So do I. But I did go through his records. There was nothing to indicate he was lying. No receipts. No purchase orders. Nothing. Maybe he's lying. Maybe he hid the money as a rainy-day fund. I think he and Rudd are into this up to their eyeballs, so I wouldn't put it past them."

"You believe Sangmore and Rudd both are culpable?"

"It's a theory. I tend to always see negativity in people. It's my gift or more like my curse. Plus, I truly believe that most conspiracies are true. I think aliens really did crash at Roswell and now reside under our oceans. I believe in the Illuminati. I think JFK was killed by the mob working in conjunction with the CIA. And I wouldn't be surprised if it comes out that George W. Bush staged 911 to go to war so he could clean up the mess his dad started."

"So, you're a nut?"

"No, let's just say that I'm a guy that doesn't trust people very often. And I always verify."

Sarah said she wanted to check Sangmore's records again. Lenny was reluctant. First, he was kind of pissed off that she felt he hadn't done a thorough job to begin with. And second, he really didn't want to set foot into that slob's office one more time. If he did, he would undoubtedly succumb to his demons and start cleaning. But Sarah wouldn't take no for an answer and well, Lenny's groin was still pulsating, so they went.

They searched Sangmore's chaotic office for the second time and as Lenny predicted, they found nothing. Sarah suggested they read through the lab reports to rule out once and for all whether the lethality of the bugs had been an unintended consequence. The lab reports were long and arduous, totaling eight two-inch binders with pages numbering into the thousands. They described the genetic makeup of each of a dozen different insect species used in the experiment. The Horned Dung Beetle and the Sahara Ant stood out. The beetle for strength and the ant for resilience to extreme temperatures. The Sydney Funnel Web spider also stood out, but in a very cringe-worthy way.

"Did Sangmore tell you this?" Sarah asked, pointing to the entry in the binder.

"Yes, most of it. He didn't mention the spider. I would have remembered that. I hate spiders." Lenny replied, looking around and scratching his arms like a paranoid schizophrenic.

Sarah stared at him with disdain. Another rich little college educated puke afraid of a tiny eight-legged arachnid. She wasn't afraid of bugs. Hell, that's what she did for a living. She ran a company that killed bugs. How can you work for a bug company if you're terrified of bugs?

Sarah typed in Sydney Funnel Web into the search bar of Google and waited for the results. The spider was a nasty one. She read the bio out loud. Lenny seemed to cringe with every word. The Funnel Web spider was fast and agile and known to have one the sharpest set of fangs in the world capable of biting through something as thick as a human toenail.

"Bite through a toenail." Lenny stated, his face pale with horror.

Chapter 65

The ancient fireplace roared. Yellow and orange flames danced about inside its blackened rock walls, casting a brilliant glow in the semi-dark manor house. The smell of burning wood and the crackle of protesting logs filled the air. It was toasty, comfortable and serene. The perfect place to be on a night like this with a winter storm roaring outside.

The house was old, a century to be exact. Built in 1890, it had been the home of an affluent shipping magnate and his family. The large rooms and tall ceilings were adorned with ornate molding, hand-carved molding. Totally unlike the trim of the modern area, which was machined in massive quantities and looked the same everywhere. Old molding, like that which was found in this manor, was unique, a work of art, special. It hadn't been precisely replicated anywhere. It was fine craftsmanship, a masterpiece, a Monet or a Michelangelo.

Sabrina Holden sat on the deep cushions of the sofa. Her legs were crossed in utter relaxation. She read quietly, her eyes straining to see the pages in the low firelight. She loved to read this way. To hell with the bright overhead lights. The cozy atmosphere of the room was what she desired. The feeling of being trapped in a large house, warmed by the glow of a fire, captivated her soul. It reminded her of cold nights at the family cabin. That feeling of being snug and content in a remote wilderness setting.

Sabrina was a beautiful girl. Her blond hair was shiny and long. Her body was perfect. Her legs were long and magnificently toned. She came from good stock. Well breed wealth. The bluest of blue blood. Money and stunning beauty ran in her family for generations. Something that her parents prided themselves in. The typical country club crowd. The I know somebody that is important. The I had lunch with Senator *what's his face* or judge *who's it*. Sabrina wanted nothing to do with any of it. Sabrina was different. She was a person out of her class. A person who had betrayed her class, betrayed her birthright, burned the country club to the ground. Fanned the fire of class rebellion.

Since she was a little girl, she found it fascinating to delve into the murky waters of the impoverished peasants that tended her manor and its lavish gardens. She joined them for lunch and dinner and often played with their children instead of the children of her parents' wealthy friends. She hated wealthy kids, who stunk with the stench of entitlement and nepotism. She absolutely loathed her predestined place in life. No, she wasn't Jasmine, and no she wouldn't marry prince *Ali-no-body*. She would choose her own path. Forge her own destiny in the furnaces of life's smelter. That's why she had chosen Carlos.

Sure, she had heard the rumors. Who hadn't? This was Havre de Grace after all. Where everyone really did know everyone's name, and more importantly, everyone's dirty laundry. She knew Carlos was a drug dealer. A criminal. A snake who slivered in the underworld. Instead of repulsing her, this only made Sabrina more attracted to him. Not because she was some white, rich rebel but because she saw something in Carlos that he couldn't see. She saw a real gentleman. An entrepreneur who was just in the wrong business. The same qualities of hard work, ingenuity and perseverance that made her father so successful were evident in Carlos. Both men were natural born leaders. Hustlers. Salesmen. Just in two very different fields. And she believed she could change Carlos, make him a legitimate businessman and pillar of society. How great would that be. It was like a movie. A plot for a Disney love story. Rich girl meets gangster. But maybe she was just naïve. That's what her mother liked to say.

"Oh darling, you're so naïve."

She missed her gangster. Missed his smile, his hopeless romanticism, his debonair demeanor. She had talked with him a few times since that dreadful night. She couldn't get that night out of her head. It had scarred her. She had teetered on the edge of a knife and it had cut her. She had walked the tightrope, the fence between the sinful underbelly and the private country club and she had fallen. She could still feel that scoundrel of a cop molesting her. Touching her in her special places. Bringing her down. Humiliating her. Kicking her and spitting in her face like some kind of filthy gutter rat. It was terrible. She had nightmares that she couldn't wake up from. The thoughts imprisoned her. And when she finally broke free she was sweating and screaming with terror.

Her parents would have eaten that cop for breakfast like a bowl of the favorite family cereal. Hell, the courts in Maryland would probably bring back hanging to appease her father's and mother's wrath. That's if she had told them, which she hadn't. She couldn't bring herself to. Not because she wanted to be a rogue hero independent but because she wanted to protect Carlos, who inevitably would be strung up right alongside the corrupt cop. Her parents would see to that. So she kept the molestation quiet. Bad people get what's coming to them and in that cop's case, Sabrina hoped it would be horrendous. She only wished she could be there personally to witness it. That would be truly satisfying.

She closed the book in her hands. Her mind had gotten the better of her again. She couldn't concentrate on the text. She thought about calling Carlos. Hearing his voice. Laughing at his jokes. He was a funny guy. But she decided against it. Her parents, though they were upstairs, might still be up and she didn't want to disturb them. Her father had been on another one of his rants about politics, and she didn't want to get that ball rolling again.

Suddenly, there was a tap at the living room window. It was barely audible over the crackling of the fire. It could have been the fire, she thought, or it could have been her imagination. The book she had been reading was a horror novel by that sultan of Satanism, Steven King. She heard the tap again. This time louder. She got up slowly. Was there someone outside? Was it Carlos? But then what about the storm. Surely, no one would be out braving this hellish weather.

The tap grew louder. Tap, tap, tap. The glass in the window actually shook. She moved over to it. She reached out and gripped the heavy curtains. She pulled them open exposing, nothing. No one was at the window. She looked out at the ice forming on the street and the sidewalk in front of her house. She shut the curtains again and began walking back to the couch and the comfort of her book. The tapping sounded again. This time she froze in her tracks. This time was different, the tap had a distinctive pattern only a human being would be able to make. She ran back over and threw open the curtains. Nothing. Okay who the hell is messing with me?! She thought angrily. Local punks out in this weather?

Sabrina walked to the front door. She opened it and stepped out into the freezing air. Damn it was cold. She shivered. She was wearing sweats and a hoodie, not enough to combat the chill. She walked over to the side of the large porch and peered into the yard below. No one was there. No trees or bushes either. Just bare, slick ice over frozen grass.

She never heard him coming. Never heard a sound. Just felt the cold metal in the back of her head.

Chapter 66

It was a suicide mission. *Kamikaze shit.* Going out with the intent to die. Something Carlos wasn't about to do. *Hell no.* Waltz into a police station and steal a piece of evidence. *Yeah freakin' right.* There was no way and no how. He was a drug dealer -a *known* drug dealer. Reputation is key in his industry. The fear that the rep gives you makes for a very smooth business but doesn't score any brownie points with the local pig farm. They know who you are, and their job is to see that you get three hots and a cot. Lock you up and throw away the freaking key. He wasn't about to give them that chance. He wasn't about to walk calmly into the den of wolves covered in chicken blood.

Even if he used Officer Mike -which was a freaking joke. Officer Mike, the guy who's got him on a homicide? Call Mike up and give him orders? Not happening. He'd rather stick his head in a urinal while a bunch of drunk bikers pissed on him. Mike was a wolf dude. Out for his own benefit. Screw the pack. Mike wouldn't help him commit a felony, especially a felony right in Mike's backyard. Tony was a nut. *Fuck Tony.*

Carlos had slept for an hour. He was tired, pissed, scared and in need of a strong drink. Hell, he could use a whole bar of strong drinks. He sat there in his lazy boy mulling his options, which didn't take long because there weren't many. He had two as far as he could tell: do what Tony said, storm the station, get locked up and spend the remainder of his worthless life behind bars or grab what cash he had stockpiled and take off. Head somewhere south. He had family in Mexico. He could hide there. No one would find him in that little village where his ancestors lived. It was remote and clandestine. The people of El Bollilo in Sinaloa knew how to protect their own. They would form a wall of concrete, a wall of absolute silence. They wouldn't sell him to the authorities or to Tony. Sure, El Bollilo, that's where he would go.

The more his mind kneaded the idea of this course of action, he began to believe it was his only chance of survival. He had never seen Tony kill anyone. He had only seen, or better yet felt, Tony pull a gun once, but he knew the man was capable of murder. Carlos could read it in Tony's eyes. Those cold, dead eyes. The eyes of an animal, a predator. He had to get out of dodge. Had to fly like a bird or more like a jet.

Carlos cracked open and drained a beer in a single gulp. He burped louder than a bull elephant. The alcohol took hold almost immediately. It dulled his anxiety. Right now, he could use a mentor. Someone he could consult with. His homeboys were shit. They couldn't digest a piece of good advice, let alone give it. Their solutions were always the same. *Let's tool 'em.* That was it. Violence was the answer to all of their small, pitiful dilemmas.

He set about the task of leaving. Saying goodbye to this small town. *Adios.* He was out. He thought about Sabrina. Pondered whether to take her with him. Driving up to her manor house, snatching her up in his arms, ordering her to pack a bag. But he couldn't do it. She wouldn't be safe where he was going. Sinaloa was no place for a white girl. She would stick out like a sore thumb in the midst of the poppy fields. No. He would have to say goodbye to his love.

There was a small safe in his closet. The steel box held all his worldly possessions: a semiautomatic nine-millimeter pistol with an extra magazine, a diamond engagement ring that had been worn by his grandmother and a gold coin that had been carried by his grandfather when he came to America so many moons ago. The gold coin was rumored to be a piece of the treasure of Hernan Cortez, dating back to the late fifteenth century. Also, in the safe was cash: fourteen grand in stacks of fifties, twenties and tens. Carlos emptied the safe's contents into a backpack. He pulled back the slide of the nine, checking to make sure it was chambered before stuffing into his waistband.

He would have to take the bus. That was his best hope. The bus would ensure his anonymity. If he took a plane, his cash would be confiscated by the TSA and he, himself, would be questioned as to where a young Latino would have acquired such vast paper wealth. He would also have to change buses several times. The first would take him as far as North Carolina. The second would take him to Florida. The third to Texas, where he could safely cross the border at an inconspicuous spot.

The storm would hinder his escape, at least for now. That was okay. He could hide out for the remainder of the storm. He would walk up to a sleazy motel, check in under a false name and *weather* the weather. Once it cleared, he'd be on his way.

He sat the packed bag next to the front door. He went into the kitchen and guzzled another brew. The alcohol would help with the cold outside. He adorned his puffy jacket, zipping the zipper up to his neck. He walked to the door and hefted the backpack over his shoulder. He turned and surveyed his apartment one final time. It was his life. His whole world. He could see the ghostly images of T-Bone and Juan Green, laughing, pouring liquor, smoking joints, playing Xbox, *just straight chillin'*. He'd miss 'em. The whole crew.

The knock at the door sent chills up his bones. He stared at the handle, waiting for it to turn. The knock came again. Carlos was rooted to the spot. His arms crawled with unpleasant goosebumps. The color of his face drained out onto the carpet.

"Wh-wh-who is it?" He managed to say.

There was no answer. The doorknob jiggled. It was Tony. It had to be. Tony with a suppressed pistol in his hands and fury in his eyes -those dead eyes. Tony, intent on killing the man he had sent to do a job, the man who had refused, the man who was about to run.

"Who is…" But Carlos never finished. The door came crashing in hitting Carlos square in the face. He tumbled backward landing on the floor.

Mike, bringing his kicking leg back down, stood in the doorway. He was dressed in his police uniform, pistol gripped tightly in his hand. He looked down at Carlos with his yellow teeth sparkling in the light.

"Going somewhere asshole?" He asked.

Carlos shook his head.

"Looks like you are." Mike said. "Got your bag packed. Your jacket on. Running out, eh?"

Carlos repeated his noggin shake.

"What the hell are you doing here?" He asked, getting some of his nerve back. At least it wasn't Tony.

Mike walked further into the apartment, glancing around with distaste as if he were looking around the inside of a dumpster.

"I'm here on business." Mike replied grinning.

"You got your shit. So, fuck off." Carlos retorted.

Mike wagged his finger. "That's no way to talk to a cop Big C." He kicked Carlos hard in the groin.

Carlos yelled with pain and writhed on the floor, grabbing his *precious* in his hands.

"Plans have changed Big C." Mike said. He crouched down, staring directly into Carlos' agonized face. "Did you know that the old buzzards called a town meeting tonight?" Mike didn't wait for Carlos to answer. "Yeah, they did. Those freaking fruit loops. So, you're going to go. Be a productive member of the town and all that shit."

Carlos was pissed. Angrier than a rattlesnake that had just been run over by a wagon wheel. Ready to bite and kill anyone in his path. "Fuck you, Mike. I ain't doing shit for you. I work for someone else now."

Mike, in an exaggerated manner, glanced back down the hall. He shrugged mockingly. "Don't see nobody. And judging by the packed bag you were carrying, I'd say you were planning on retiring anyway. Am I right Big C?" Mike stood up. "Funny thing isn't it? Random dude comes to town and knows every damn thing about you. Knows about the gun. Knows about Eddie. Knows where you live.

Knows your routine. And you don't even think anything of it."

Carlos' face turned cold. "It was you." He whispered.

Mike nodded triumphantly. "What can I say? He pays better."

Carlos attempted to swing a kick from the floor in Mike's direction. Mike easily avoided it, aiming his own kick at Carlos' thigh. The gangster howled with pain.

"You were always a dumb brown punk." Mike jeered. He crouched again. "Stupid fucking wet back." He said in a low tone. "Here's the deal dickhead. We gotta get that box."

"You get it! You're the fucking cop! You got the access!" Carlos shouted.

Mike shook his head slowly from side to side. "No. I don't. Patterson doesn't trust me anymore. Thanks to that bitch whore, nigga fucker I was dating." Mike spat on the floor inches from Carlos' head. "But no worries, no worries. Tony's got a plan."

Carlos grimaced. No plan of Tony's was ever going to be good for him.

"See, I'm gonna blow this joint just like you. But I'm going to do it with a hell of a lot more loot. Tony's people upped the money. So, he turned around and offered the increase to me." Mike could hardly contain his enthusiasm. "Seven figures. Seven fucking figures!" He slapped Carlos on the leg. "I can hang up this uniform and hit the islands. No more cop shit. No more locking up drunks, giving out speeding tickets or busting whores. I'm out baby, I'm out."

Carlos smiled which momentarily shocked Mike.

"What's so funny dick head?"

"You really think Tony's gonna pay you?" Carlos asked. "And you call me stupid. You're expendable Mike, just like me. He's gonna kill both of us."

Mike smacked Carlos in the face. Smacked him hard. Spittle flew from Carlos' mouth and red blood vessels burst in his flesh, revealing an instant imprint of Mike's hand.

"You need to learn some manners." Mike growled.

Carlos put his hands up to shield his face.

Mike calmed perceptively. "Here's the deal amigo. You're gonna go down to that meeting. You're gonna bring your friend there." Mike pointed to the nine stuffed in Carlos' waistband. "And you're gonna start shooting. Doesn't matter who. Just shoot the first person you see. And keep shooting until the cops get there. Understand amigo?"

Carlos was startled beyond comprehension. "You're fucking out of your mind." He said and immediately covered his face for another blow, but Mike kept his cool.

"No, I'm not." Mike said.

"Ain't no way I'm gonna do that." Carlos stated affirmatively. "You think I'm crazy. I'll end up dead or in the bing. And what the hell would that accomplish?"

"It's called a diversion, you dumb punk. Every cop in the station will slip and slide their fat donut-eating asses down to that meeting. The whole station will empty out. Then Tony and I will casually walk ourselves in, take that box and be on our merry rich way."

Carlos shook his head. "No way. No fucking way! Not doing it! I'm out. I've done enough for both of you assholes."

Mike smiled his evil grin. "But you're not gonna do it for Tony or for me." He said, and his voice was chilling like the freezing rain outside. Mike pulled a small, paper-wrapped package from his jacket pocket and tossed it onto Carlos' chest. It landed with a muffled thud against Carlos' puffy coat.

Carlos picked it up. His hands shook. His fingers tried to untie the knotted bows. Finally, he managed to remove the small rope. He folded the paper back and screamed -a terrifying howl that sounded like a pack of wolves in the deep forest. Inside the paper was a severed finger. The blood from the knife wound had stained the paper a deep, dark brown. The fingernail was pink and manicured professionally. Carlos knew who it belonged to even before he saw the ring, a silver band with a pink stone set in the middle of it.

"Do it for her amigo. Do it for poor Sabrina."

Chapter 67

The first reported fatality of the ice storm occurred on I-95 in Cecile County. The eighteen-wheeler had left the safety or what used to be the safety of the asphalt and sailed headlong into a group of trees at the edge of a dense forest. The driver of the big rig died instantly, which was a blessing because seconds after the truck hit the trees the fuel tanks caught fire. The burning inferno could be seen for miles.

Channel nine reported the accident with an air of sorrow even though the state of emergency declared by the governor made it illegal to operate any motor vehicles other than emergency vehicles on the roads. Still, it was the job of the news to report on such matters, and it would be cold-hearted to say the least, to reiterate the big rig driver's negligence while reporting the fatality.

The ratings kept climbing with every hour. Everyone was watching. The storm kept people inside and kept them superglued to their television sets. James was on twenty-four seven. The weathermen were now the gods of the airways. They were the gatekeepers to the vast wilderness of the unknown. The only people who understood this type of force. The full force and fury of mother nature.

James didn't get a break. He had to eat vending machine candy instead of a meal He had to pee faster than the Guinness book world record holder and he had to chug more coffee than an army of lawyers waiting for their turn in the docket. He loved it. This was his chance. His shot at greatness. Storms like this come once in a century, once in a generation. They're the storms old men sit their grandkids on their knee to reminisce about. Their old eyes becoming glassy. Their hoarse voices recreating the events. *I remember the ice was so thick you could skate to your neighbor's house.*

While James was busy sucking up the glory, Kelly was typing. Court stenographer typing. Fingers to the keyboard, eyes to the screen. Armageddon outside and she'd still be typing. Funny thing was it really *was* Armageddon outside, and she *was* still typing. She could care less about the storm, the ice, the danger, the insanity unfolding at the station. All Kelly cared about was her story. It was steadily evolving, yet she was still missing that one key piece to the puzzle. The culprit. Sure, she had probable cause to indict Raymond Hastings, but the problem was Hastings was nowhere to be found. She had called the police in New York City to no avail. Hastings had no criminal record and no traffic violations. So, either he had lied to Mrs. Shirley, or he had simply vanished. To make matters worse Hastings had no family, at least he had no family left. His parents were both deceased. And he had no siblings.

What really nagged at her was the child support payments. A background check of Hastings didn't list him as being delinquent in his child support. So, he had been paying Tracy for his two children. Obviously, Hastings hadn't disappeared entirely. Kelly made a mental note to check with Detective Patterson about any financial records that may have been discovered at Tracy's townhouse. If Hastings had been sending her checks, then there would be some record of it. Not that she thought Tracy would have kept such things. After all, alcoholic, drug addict losers who can barely care for their own children aren't the best record keepers. Still, it *was* worth a shot.

She was rudely interrupted by the phone ringing. It was her office phone. She snagged it, and in a halfhearted manner said hello.

"Did you find the bodies?" The cold voice asked.

Kelly sat bolt upright in her chair. "Who is this?"

"Did you find the box?" The voice asked.

"Yes." She paused, looking around the station. "How did you know it would be there?"

There was silence at the other end. Kelly thought for a minute that the caller must have hung up.

"Hello." She said.

"I'm here." The voice answered.

"How did you know the box would be there?"

"You need to write this story." The voice commanded.

"I am going to write it. I'm writing it as we speak. Look, you have to answer some questions. Who are you?"

"Sentrix."

"That's your name? Sentrix?" Kelly asked.

"Are you sitting down?" The caller asked.

"Yes. Why?" Kelly answered.

"Check your email." The line went dead.

She looked at the caller ID. The number had been blocked. Damn. Kelly thought as she replaced the receiver. Who the hell was Sentrix? She looked around the room. She saw James, quickly devouring a bowl of Ramen noodles and guzzling a bottle of water. He smiled at her. She returned the smile.

Google. That was the answer. Google would know. Google always knows. She typed it in. Was Sentrix a foreign name? Some bad actor in the Mideast? She had never met anyone called Sentrix. But for some reason, the name jogged her memory. In an instant, she knew why. The search results for Sentrix popped big time. Ads for pest control. How to kill spiders. How to get rid of stink bugs, ants, roaches, bed bugs and a home page. Of course, she had heard the name. Sentrix was the largest exterminating company on earth. *Holy shit.*

Then she checked her email. There it was. The email was from a generic address and it had an attachment. She thought for a second that perhaps it was a hoax. Open the PDF and some nerd in a basement has access to all your files, passwords, bank accounts, basically your life. She clicked download on the attachment. It was worth the risk. Hell, what was she protecting anyway? Last time she checked, she had what? A couple of hundred dollars in the bank. The file took several minutes. It was big, a massive amount of data. It finished downloading and Kelly took a deep breath before clicking it. She gasped. She had to talk to George. She tried his cell. No answer. She tried police headquarters. Patterson wasn't there. The desk sergeant who answered informed her that Patterson was out wrapping up the evacuations and yes, her uncle George was with him.

"Can you give me Detective Patterson's cell number?" Kelly asked.

"I can't give out that kind of information. I'm sorry. He should be back anytime now."

"Thanks anyway." Kelly said and hung up.

She stood up from her desk, stretched and gulped the last bit at the bottom of her water bottle. The best place for her to be was police headquarters. George would be returning soon, and she would be able to talk to him and Patterson together. Kill two birds with one stone. She hefted her coat and headed for the door. James grabbed her arm, stopping her dead in her tracks.

"Where the hell do you think you're going?" James said. He had become somewhat cocky. A little fame had turned up his arrogant chip to full power. Kelly kind of liked it. She liked the confidant James as opposed to the shy, bookish James. That had always been her problem. That's why she ended up dating pricks like Officer Mike.

"I have to talk to my uncle." She said, trying to pull her arm away. She was determined. No one, not even the newly crowned king of the weather was going to stop her. Not when she was so close.

"Have you seen the weather outside? It's kind of an ice storm." He said sarcastically.

Well, maybe she liked the old James better after all. "Yes. I'll be fine. I'm going to walk."

"You're crazy. You can't walk in this shit. Skate maybe but walking is suicide."

Kelly thought about this for a moment. James was right. The conditions outside were really bad. More like horrendous and getting worse by the second.

"I can't let you go Kell." James said. He was worried.

"Come with me." She stated. She knew he wouldn't. He could never give up his moment of glory. Plus, his father would fire his ass in a heartbeat. She felt guilty for even asking. They had pushed Harry Roseland's buttons a little too far. And son or no son, Harry was no one's idea of a wimp.

James looked around at the station, his throne room, his Mount Olympus. "Why do you have to go? What's so important?"

"I got another call. Same person as before." She said, and James' eyes popped. She knew why. The last time she had gotten a call from the anonymous tipster, James and her had landed in a metal cell. "He said the name Sentrix and sent me a file."

"Sentrix. Sentrix." James repeated to himself. "What kind of name is that? I've heard…"

"It's the biggest pest control company on earth. They're the ones, James. They did it. It's in the file. The whole damn thing."

James leaned back against the wall. "Why?" He said.

"They wanted to create a monopoly. Control the entire industry."

"Jesus Christ." James muttered.

Kelly shook her head. "We might need him right now. I've got to go see George."

James realized he didn't have a fighting chance. He looked around the room again. This was his big shot. This was his means for a future. The game changer. The career launcher. A couple of hundred thousand people tuning in to view this broadcast. He couldn't leave this behind. Not for anyone. He turned to face Kelly, the love of his life, the only girl he had ever wanted.

"I don't want you to miss your big shot." She said, motioning towards the bustling station.

James looked at her. "I'm not." He said and hurried to get his coat.

Chapter 68

There were scrubs as far as the eye could see. A sea of blues, pinks, yellows and even a few oranges. Obviously, there were no uniform restrictions here. The policy seemed to be as long as it was scrubs, it was any color, any time.

The man who approached the desk attracted the eyes of every female nurse on the floor. He was a big man, with muscles so enormous it appeared as if he spent the majority of his days building the pyramids by hand. His large, square, handsome face was tilted down as if he were in deep thought or devout prayer. His shift had ended an hour ago, but on a night like this, with an ice storm raging outside, no one was really off the clock, so he kept his police blues on, the legs of which were covered in white, powdery salt dust.

"Hi." Officer Walt said in his deep crooning voice to the nurse seated behind the round, cream-colored desk. It was a male nurse, an older male nurse, who peered intently at his computer monitor, his face lit up by the artificial LED glow.

"What can I do for you officer?" The nurse said without glancing up.

"I am here to see Samuel Gellar."

"Visiting hours are over." The nurse replied.

"I understand. I just got off. Any chance I can still see him? It would mean a lot." Walt pleaded.

The nurse looked up and something about Walt's face, maybe it was the concern in the man's eyes, changed the nurse's hard demeanor.

"He's in room 402."

"Thanks a lot." Walt said, overjoyed. "Merry Christmas."

"Happy holidays."

Walt hurried away as quickly as his oversized legs could carry him as if he expected the nurse to change his mind. He knew Sam was in room 402 and he knew precisely where room 402 was located. He was a regular at the hospital although he had never been here this late. Thus the after-midnight staff had no idea who he was. If they had, they would have let him pass with a smiling nod. He came up to the closed door of the room and knocked. His heart skipped a beat, his stomach fluttered with uneasy butterflies and his mouth felt dry. He didn't wait for a reply. He wasn't expecting one. He pushed the door open and stepped inside.

The sounds and scenes of the Terminator flashed about the dark room. Curtains blocked Walt's view. He walked forward and parted the sea of thick fabric. The young boy sat upright in bed. He had no hair on his seven-year-old head. His eyes followed the action on the TV screen until they caught the real-life image of his father standing nearby.

"Don't tell mom." Sam said, grabbing the remote and shutting the TV off.

"No worries champ. It's our secret. How you feeling today?" Walt said. He walked further into the room and took a seat in one of the two chairs by the window.

"I'm good dad. Is it really icing outside?" Sam asked. His voice a tad playful, which brought an instant smile to Walt's face.

"It really is."

"Man, that's something. Wish I could see it." Sam said with sad eyes.

Walt smiled broadly. "Trust me champ, you're not missing anything."

"Hey Dad, when I get out of here, can we go to Universal Studios? I heard another kid talking about it. I think it's in a place called Forida."

"Absolutely. And it's in Florida. That's a state down south."

"Do you think the ice storm hit there?"

Walt laughed heartily. "No champ. It's really hot in Florida. Like summertime here but down there its summer all year round."

"Summer all the time? That's awesome."

"Yes, it is." Walt said. They sure as hell could use some summer up here right about now.

Walt was a man who played everything close to his chest. No one would ever have guessed that the big, burly, tough cop had a son, his only son, in the hospital, diagnosed with acute leukemia. Walt wanted it that way. He preferred it. He didn't need the sympathy, his son did.

It all started six months ago. His son, Sam, usually a ball of energy who spent the majority of his days, running, jumping and somersaulting, began complaining about pain in his joints. At first, Walt and his wife dismissed it as adolescent growth spurts. But then the fevers started. Burning 104-degree scorchers that erupted on a daily basis. Sam's complexion also changed. Walt's wife was pure Italian, a dark, olive Italian and Sam inherited her skin tone. But his usual tan complexion became milky pale. Walt and his wife began to feel very uneasy. There was this feeling, this pit developing in the bottom of their stomachs. So, they brought Sam to the doctors.

"Just kids. Probably a virus. Might take a couple of weeks. Nothing to worry about." Was the doctor's nonchalant reply to their inquiries.

That wasn't good enough for Walt's wife. She had always preached about being an advocate for one's own health. She begged and pleaded with the doctor for a blood test. The know it all doc argued with her. It literally almost came to blows before *Dr. Smartass* relented and ordered the test. That simple test, if Sam lived through this, would prove to be Sam's saving grace. The test showed Sam's white blood cell count was through the roof.

Oncology is a dreaded word, no matter what age, but especially for parents. But it is the miracle-working oncologists of Greater Hearts of Maryland Hospital in Havre de Grace that were currently working to rid Sam's seven-year-old body of the aggressive cancer. It was an uphill battle. A fight to the finish. And the amazing people in this hospital shed their own blood and tears right alongside parents like Walt and his wife. Walt thanked the Lord every day for doctors and nurses. He had a powerful respect for their profession. To hell with the common complaint everyone mutters. *Doctors just rip you off. They only order tests to take your money.* In Walt's mind and in every parent's mind that has ever been dealt such a fateful hand, the argument of frivolous tests is in and of itself, frivolous. Parents of cancer patients would sacrifice everything and anything, to see their children get better. To observe their little ones riding bikes again, running, playing catch and chasing fireflies. They would gladly pay anything. Any amount of money, any amount of sweat, blood, tears and even their very own lives. Parents aren't supposed to outlive their children.

"What did you have to eat today champ?" Walt asked. His son's appetite had been returning as of late.

"I had pancakes this morning. Grilled cheese for lunch then they tried to give me broccoli." As if this was some sort of mortal sin. "Yuck!" His son uttered, holding his nose.

"Did you eat it all?"

"As much as possible." Sam answered. "Hey dad?"

"Yeah champ."

"Am I going to get out of here soon?"

Walt stared down at his son with the eyes of a man who has lived a thousand years in the last four months. "Absolutely. Very soon."

Of course, this was a lie. The fact of the matter was, the doctors were unsure if Sam would ever leave. His condition was stable, but the cancer hadn't gone into remission and wasn't responding to the high doses of chemo.

"I can't wait. You know what I'm going to do first?" Sam said, his eyes lighting up with unbridled pleasure. "I'm going to ride my bike faster than a racecar. So fast, it'll be like a blur. Like Donald Duck running when the witch put a spell on his feet. Remember that one Dad?"

"Witch Hazel."

"Yeah. Witch Hazel. I liked her. She turned Donald Duck's legs blue and made him run really fast. I wanna run like that. Really fast."

"You will champ. I promise. Maybe I'll have Witch Hazel come over and trick your legs."

Sam shook his head. "That's silly dad. I don't want Witch Hazel to trick my legs. She made Donald Duck crash. Remember Dad? Donald Duck crashed. I don't want to crash."

Walt smiled. "That's true champ."

Sam yawned, and in an instant, his eyes went from light and cheery to tired and droopy.

"Are you sleepy?"

"Y-e-a-h." Sam said through another long yawn. He settled back onto his pillow. "Dad?"

"Yeah champ."

"Will you hold my hand?"

Walt's heart clenched. His throat swelled, and he fought back tears.

"Absolutely champ." Walt managed to say. He grabbed his son's hand with his big, bear paw. Sam's hand felt so tiny, so pitiful, so miniscule in his own. He squeezed it, not hard but enough so he could feel the sensation of his son's life force.

God, please save my son. Please God. He prayed in his mind.

"I love you dad." Sam said.

Tears slid down Walt's cheeks. He held that little hand in his and wished he could take his son's place. Take Sam's suffering. Take his pain. Let him live. Let him be free of this terrible, monstrous disease.

"I love you Sam. Goodnight champ."

Chapter 69

A bell sounded. It was loud and shrill and was accompanied by a blinking red light at the station. The nurses hated hearing that bell. It was the last sound a person made before checking out. The flat-line siren. That was their nickname for it. And it was a bell that often sounded on the first floor.

The first floor of Greater Hearts of Maryland Hospital in Havre de Grace, or hospital point, as it was known by the locals, was populated by long-term patients. The elderly and the physically and mentally impaired. Most of the first-floor patients would never see the light of another day. They would leave the facility via the cold holding room. A small, rectangular, cinder block box in the basement of hospital point. The room was designed to hold six bodies in all, lined side by side on their rolling gurneys. The room had only one light, a small bulb that had probably been installed by Thomas Edison, judging by its size and ancient characteristics. The light lasted all these years because it was only switched on when a body was placed inside or when a body was taken out and no one in their right mind, spent much time in the holding room.

Tonight would be no different. Everett Thomas had lived a charmed life. He had been a Marine and had stormed the beaches of Iwo Jima and Okinawa to rid the world of the tyrannical Japanese menace. Everett had almost died on Okinawa, and he had left a piece of himself behind. A big piece. His right leg, which had taken the mortar express, sailing twenty feet, landing unnoticed on the blood-soaked sand. At the time, Everett was twenty-one.

Since then, Everett had spawned a large and robust family: six kids, fourteen grandkids, two great grandkids and a multitude of dogs, cats and even a couple of chickens. His wife Cecilia had kicked the old tin can down the road four years prior and now Everett, a ripe old ninety-six, took his turn on the fifteenth-yard line, connecting squarely with the can and sending it through the uprises in perfect form. *It's good.*

"It's Everett! Ol' Jesus, it's Everett!" One of the nurses shouted as she ran. "I need an R U to room 141 stat!"

The call fell on deaf ears.

"What the hell's wrong with you people? I need an R U to …"

"He's a D N R." The on-call doctor said nonchalantly.

The nurse stopped in her tracks. Sweat ran down her face. She swiped it away with her shoulder.

"Not Everett." She said, knowing full well that indeed it *was* Everett. "When did he become D N R?" She asked.

"Last month. The old man wanted it that way." The doctor responded.

"Well, I guess he's up there with his sugar. God bless you Everett." The nurse said.

DNR was code for Do Not Resuscitate. It was a patient's right, at least in the state of Maryland, to choose this course of action. Basically, if the patient, in this case, Everett Thomas, goes into cardiac arrest or stops breathing, the hospital is ordered not to perform any life-saving measures. No CPR. No defibrillator jump start. The staff has no choice but to sit back and watch as the patient dies. It's not pretty and it's not pleasant but it's the patient's wish.

The doctor walked into room 141 a few minutes later. He didn't run, didn't hurry, he simply walked as if he were strolling through a meadow on a beautiful spring day and he wanted to suck up as much of the atmosphere as possible. The doctor chose to wait. He hated seeing people die and hated the DNR code. He joined the medical profession to save lives, not to watch them expire before his eyes.

The room was cold and smelled of death. Not of decay. That was physically impossible but of death, which was probably more of an imaginative odor as opposed to reality. The body of the frail old man, crinkled and arched, lay crumpled on the bed. The thousand-yard death stare peered heavenward. The mouth was open, gaped in an eternal scream. A scream that could and would never be heard.

The doctor strolled over to the bed. He placed his fingers on Everett's lukewarm throat, as expected there was no pulse. No heart thumping the rhythmic beat of life. The doctor lifted his fingers. His eyes flitted up to the monitor. The flatline, illuminated in bright green against a black screen, seemed to go on forever. The doctor unplugged the monitor. The sound of the everlasting beep faded and died. He checked his watch. 12:11 a.m. He jotted down the relevant information in the chart. Next came the hard part: he would have to call the family and inform them of their loved one's earthly departure. Well, that was his job, even though he dreaded it. That's why they paid him the big bucks. Or so he told himself every time he made that blasted call.

Hadn't he met Everett's daughter not two days ago? Or was that yesterday? His memory was really going. It was the long hours. Those twelve-hour shifts. The *all work, no play* lifestyle he had been leading for the last twenty years. Surely, it wasn't Alzheimers, not yet at least. Not for another ten, maybe twenty, hopefully, thirty years. He was only fifty-one. Then his mind began working again. He *had* met Everett's daughter, Jane, yesterday. It was coming back to him. She was sixty. She was in town for the holidays to see her dad. She was staying at a hotel nearby. He couldn't remember the name of the damn place for the life of him. She had two sons, both of whom were staying with her. Her husband had died of...*damn*...lung cancer! That was it. Her husband had died of lung cancer at sixty-three. The doctor remembered telling her sixty-three was young and the guy wasn't a smoker, never had even taken a single drag.

He left the room in the same manner he had entered it, slow and steady. The nurse was gone, out on her rounds tending to the other patients. The station was desolate, not a soul in sight, well, maybe a soul or two but no one else.

The doctor sat down and leaned back in his swivel chair. He felt something tickle his neck. It reminded him of a strand of stray hair or a fabric pull. He scratched the spot with his hand. The sensation disappeared.

He picked up the chart and glanced at the emergency contact information on the cover page. The person listed was Michael Thomas, Everett's son. A local man. The doctor made to reach for the phone on the desk. Better get it over with. But his hand barely touched the receiver when he felt a piercing prick on his neck. He smacked it hard. What the hell was that?! It felt like something bit him. Like a large mosquito or a spider. Was it a spider? Those eight-legged bastards were as common as muck in this fly infested town. But its winter and icing. No way a spider could have survived the wicked weather outside. The doctor flinched again. Another bite. Painful as hell. Like a sewing needle being driven up to its eye in the flesh of his neck. Again, he slapped it with his open hand.

He was positive he had killed the damn thing that time. Certainly, he would see some sort of crushed exoskeleton remnants in the palm of his hand. But there was none. There was only blood and lots of it. Spiders didn't bleed. At least he didn't think so. He wiped the blood off on his pants' leg and rubbed the spot again. More blood. His blood. He had to find a mirror. Maybe it really was a sewing needle, left in his scrubs by his wife. She was always doing her own tailoring. It was possible. He stood up. The station bathroom had a mirror and it was only feet away. That was a blessing because he was starting to panic. There was a lot of blood on his hand. Maybe he had pierced an artery with his ferocious smacking.

He grabbed the handle of the bathroom door and yanked it with all his might. The light came on instantly thanks to the small panel on the wall that detected his motion. He stood before the mirror. Blood soaked the shoulder of his blue work scrubs. The two colors mixed forming a deep purple. He turned to look at his back, where the pain had originated from. What he saw made his knees go weak.

A hoard of small insects, tiny and tan, gathered near his left shoulder blade. They weren't moving as insects do when they're startled and at first glance, none of them seemed to be injured. The doctor had no time to ponder what this bug was because a split second later the pain that shot through his body made him lose consciousness. He passed out and fell backward, his body wedging itself between the toilet and the white tile wall. He died there three minutes later from total blood loss.

Chapter 70

"I've got something for you." Special Agent Charlie Hesh of the Internal Revenue Service sounded extremely tired on the phone.

"Jesus Charlie, do you know what time it is?" Lenny replied.

"It's just Charlie. Although after I tell you what I've got, you might be worshipping me. And it's twelve a.m."

Sarah had passed out; her body was lying comfortably on the large sofa in the corner of the lounge. This lounge was reserved for Sentrix's administration and even Lenny, the former president's pit bull, hadn't been allowed to kick up his feet in this holiest of holies. Boasting three Alcantara sofas, each with a modern glass coffee table and four Alcantara coach chairs, it was galaxies ahead of the other employee lounges in the building. The regular lounges, designated for the peons, resembled high school cafeterias. This holy lair was heaven if heaven was made of rich, microfiber material with a state-of-the-art coffee bar.

Lenny sat in one of the coach chairs, his Allen Edmonds perched on the glass coffee table, his cell phone gripped in his hand.

"What do you have?" Lenny asked in anticipation.

"The Russian government bought $500 million worth of bitcoin."

"Yeah, so? What's so impressive about that? Everyone is buying bitcoin."

"Not the Russians. They don't believe in bitcoin. They buy gold." Charlie answered.

"Okay." Lenny said, still not getting it.

"And they got rid of it fast. Faster than a hand grenade in a foxhole. The bitcoin made its way over to a bank in Grand Cayman. There, the coins were exchanged for gold. The gold was later exchanged for silver. The silver became US dollars and eventually landed itself in the hands of Beautiful Horizons, deposited in their accountant at the French Rivera Bank."

"Holy crap." Lenny muttered. "You are good. How the hell did you trace all that?"

"That's classified. If I told you…"

"You'd have to kill me." Lenny broke in.

"No. No. If I told you, then I wouldn't be able to catch you cheating on your taxes."

"$500 million?" Lenny was still shocked.

"Yep. I still haven't been able to find out who owns Beautiful Horizons, but, whoever does, is now half a billion dollars richer."

"Do they own any other companies in the States?"

"Nope. Other than their acquisition of KS Oil."

"What were the Russians buying?" Lenny asked.

"Weapons. That's the word from Langley and Len I'll cut your balls off if you ever mention this conversation to anyone. I have a friend in CIA who owes me a few favors. Let's say he used several very questionable write-offs."

"What kind of weapons?"

"No clue. CIA doesn't know either. All they know is that their contacts within the Kremlin told them the money was slated for the purchase of weapons. Some kind of new technology, developed by a company in the States. I can't begin to tell you how concerned CIA is about this." Charlie answered, yawning loudly into the phone.

"What about HydroLine?"

"It's a shell company."

"Yes, I know. Why would Sentrix purchase 10 million dollars' worth of equipment from them? Do you think we were attempting to purchase the same technology?"

"Why? Sentrix is a pest control company, not a foreign state. It's probably safe to say that you fellas were ripped off by Beautiful Horizons through a myriad of shell companies. A high-stakes heist. That sounds more like it. It happens all the time. Large corporations are being plundered by Russian controlled companies on a daily basis."

"Doesn't that boggle your mind?"

"What?"

"I spoke to the FBI. They say Beautiful Horizons is owned by the Russian mob or the Russian government. So why would the Russians transfer money to themselves? And if they did, why all the rigmarole? Buying Bitcoin, then gold, then silver."

"That's easy."

"Really? Take your best shot." Lenny said.

"If the Russians are really purchasing weapons from the US, then they would want to conceal their identity. Remember, the Russians are still technically our enemies."

"But the wall fell."

"Fuck the wall. So, they were a civilized country for a few years, until the damn thieves-in-law turned Moscow into Chicago of the 1930s. The Russian mob took over the economy. Then they bought the Presidency, now they own the country. The president does anything those fat, gold wearing bastards with their super yachts say. They say jump, he says how high."

"So, it's a shadow game?"

"Pretty much. At least I'd put my money on it."

"What the hell are you talking about Charlie? You don't have any freaking money." Lenny joked.

"That's what you think pal. Remember, the tax collector man has *all* the money. It's even in the Bible."

"No, it's not." Lenny said, laughing.

"Hell, I didn't read it anyway. You know how long that damn book is?" Charlie replied.

"Thanks a lot Charlie. One more thing, how long has Beautiful Horizons been in business?"

"At least a decade, maybe fifteen years." Charlie said. "Stay out of the storm Lenny."

"Thanks." Lenny hung up the phone.

He watched Sarah Ryan sleep. She looked stunning, her soft lips, her angelic features, captured in that perpetual beauty that was sleep. He debated whether to join her. Kick back on one of the sofas and just let it take him. Man, that would be nice. But he was Lenny and Lenny never stopped. He had work to do. Silently, he crept out of the lounge and made his way back to his office. He fired up his computer and punched in the password.

The first thing Lenny checked was the company ledger. This was no small matter. There were millions of entries. He was looking for anything that might stand out. If Charlie Hesh was right and HydroLine had defrauded Sentrix of the $10 million, then perhaps they had done it in the past. He typed in HydroLine. Two entries popped up. The $10 million expenditure and a $2 million debit from three years prior. The $2 million was debited from research and development. Interesting, very interesting. He clicked on the entry.

The purchase had been authorized by Donald Kinney and listed hose equipment in the description. Hose equipment for $2 million? What are they trying to put out the California wildfire? Lenny had never heard of Donald Kinney but at a company the size and scope of Sentrix, that was not uncommon. He cross-checked Donald Kinney's name throughout the ledger. Kinney had overseen hundreds of purchases, totaling millions of dollars. Most them at first glance seemed to be on the up and up. Okay, so, Beautiful Horizons had profited $12 million ripping off Sentrix. Not unheard of. Not when you're managing $2.25 billion a year in revenue. It was easy to lose a few million. That's the way it is. *Yeah freaking right.* Who are we kidding? Maybe losing $10 is justifiable but $12 million? Absolutely not. There is no way Gordon Reynolds would ever allow $12 million to slip through his greedy grasp. Not that old miser.

Lenny decided to focus on Donald Kinney. Sangmore and Rudd had both denied approving the $10 million purchase. Was it possible Kinney had? Kinney had been a small-time purchasing agent employed by Sentrix for eight years. For being small time, Kinney handled big time transactions. The purchase orders he authorized totaled well over $350 million to firms all over the world. Companies with names like HydroLine, FDT, and Detrin, with headquarters in the United States, China, Russia, Japan, South Korea, Europe and South America. The list was long. Lenny printed it and began researching the firms one by one. It took over two hours. Except for the $2 million, every other purchase was legit.

According to company records, Kinney was hired to oversee purchases for the Pioneer Initiative which was a focus group made up of researchers employed by Sentrix to boost company growth and innovation. The group had originally been chartered by Carter Ritler and Gordon Reynolds, when Ritler had first come on board with the company. The work of the Pioneer Initiative enabled Sentrix to boost their yearly revenue by over a billion dollars. Other than that brief summary, records of the Pioneer Initiative didn't exist. There was no list of accomplishments or new innovations. There was also no list of members. How did they achieve such success? How did they increase revenue by that much?

Donald Kinney had resigned from Sentrix a year ago. Lenny cross-checked the date of the 10 million dollar transaction. The transaction had been made six months before Kinney resigned. Maybe the mysterious purchasing agent had authorized that as well. His parting gift. A little fuck you to the board.

Kinney's phone number was listed in the records. Lenny looked at the clock on the wall next to the portrait of Rockefeller. *Well, why the hell not?* Lenny grabbed the phone and dialed. No answer and no answering machine picked up either with the familiar, *hi you've reached whoever and whoever is not available*. The phone just kept ringing until finally, Lenny hung up.

He was almost as sure as shit certain that he had just stumbled on a criminal conspiracy to rip off his company. And he had discovered it accidentally, via his investigation into the bed bug fiasco. Not bad Lenny. Pat yourself on the back why don't cha. Maybe later. He had bigger fish to fry, specifically one mammoth whale named Donald Kinney.

He had to find Donald Kinney. Find him and get to the bottom of this. He executed a background check on Kinney. It came back with a shocking revelation. Lenny had to make sure what he was reading was true. He cross-referenced the information on the New York Times website, and sure enough, a headline popped up confirming Donald Kinney's death. He had died in a car accident. Lenny read the article from the Times. Kinney had been walking his dog along a country road near his home in upstate New York when a passing motorist struck and killed him. It was a hit and run. The motorist was never caught. Police suspected alcohol and high speeds were contributing factors.

The article said Kinney was survived by his daughter, Catherine Kinney. Lenny wrote down her name. A quick internet search yielded Catherine's address and home telephone number.

The phone rang a thousand times. Lenny was on the verge of giving up when a tired, dreary voice answered.

"Tell me no one died."

"Mrs. Catherine Kinney?" Lenny asked.

"Is this the state police?" She asked in a terrified tone.

"Yes." For some reason, the lie just popped out of Lenny's mouth.

"Is it my son? Is he…"

"It's not your son." Lenny said quickly. His palms were beginning to sweat. Why had he lied? This woman was about to have a heart attack.

"Then why the hell are you calling at this ungodly hour?" Now the woman sounded ticked off like her team had made it all the way to the Superbowl and had lost by one point.

"My name is Leonard. My apologies. It's about your father. About his accident."

"What accident?!" Catherine exclaimed. "It wasn't an accident! It was murder! You cops are all the same. Accident, accident, accident! That's all I hear from your holes."

"Okay. Okay." Lenny said, trying desperately to stop the ball from rolling too far down the hill. "Something came up in the case."

"Oh, this should be good." Catherine said sarcastically.

"Why do you think your father was murdered?"

Catherine laughed derisively. "Who are you? Some little man in the basement filing room? Has his case reached that level of insignificance?"

"Can you just tell me what you think?" Lenny tried to keep his cool. He was the one lying, but this woman was a real piece of work.

"Absolutely." Again, the sarcasm was at a fever pitch. "Let me see. My father worked for a company in New York. Big pest control firm called Sentrix."

Lenny swallowed.

Catherine continued. "He was a purchaser. Flew all over the world buying shit. Sounds boring as hell, doesn't it? Well, apparently it wasn't. My father told me that he didn't agree with some of the things his company was involved in. Never gave me details but it must have been something really bad because my father resigned over it."

"Why didn't he opt out of the bad stuff?"

"He tried. He told me he went to see his boss. But his boss wasn't hearing it. So, my father quit. They gave him a real nice *shut the hell up* package. Nice enough that my father didn't have to worry about money anymore. I already told this to you guys. I guess you didn't get the memo. Probably didn't make it to the basement."

Lenny ignored the jibe. "Go on please."

"A month after my father quit, he was diagnosed with terminal cancer. Then the guys in the suits started showing up."

"The guys in the suits?"

"You know the type. Dark suit, dark sunglasses, dark attitudes. Feds. I guess my father reached out to them. He met with them several times. Coffee shops, restaurants, even in the pool hall. Donnie loved to play pool."

"How do you know about these meetings?"

"He told me. He said it was the right thing to do. He wanted to die with a clear conscience. But he never got the chance."

"What happened?"

"Two days before his accident, he started to act really strange. He showed up one day at my front door. He was a mess. Shirt untucked, his eyes darting nervously up and down the street. He hustled inside. They're going to kill me. They're going to kill me. He said over and over again. He kept moving from window to window, cracking the shades with his finger to look outside. I asked him who was going to kill him. He didn't answer. Then he left as quickly as he came and that was the last time I ever saw my father alive."

"Did he ever mention a company called Beautiful Horizons?"

"No."

"Did he have any Russian friends?"

"No. What the hell is this about? You're supposed to give me answers, not the other way around. Sounds like you don't know shit."

"Look, I believe your father was murdered, and I'll do my best to bring the people who did it to justice."

"I'm sure." Again, the sarcasm. "Sounds like you're the right man for the job. Let me know if they ever let you out of the filing room." She hung up without another snide word.

Chapter 71

Donald Kinney had been murdered. *Murdered!* But by whom? The Russians? It was possible. Beautiful Horizons was, according to the FBI, a shadowy Russian corporation and Kinney had transferred $2 million to them. The Russians may have assumed Kinney had become a snitch and decided to put him on ice. But then why had his daughter said Kinney was unhappy with his job at Sentrix? That *was* the reason the late purchaser had resigned. Maybe he had been working for someone farther up the food chain. Maybe a Sentrix VP.

The more sinister theory was that Kinney had been killed as a direct result of something he was doing at Sentrix, the very company that Lenny was working for right now and in whose offices, Lenny found himself presently trapped. His daughter said Kinney had been given a hush package upon his resignation. She said it was enough money to keep Kinney out of the unemployment line for the rest of his life. That had to be a lot of money. Millions of dollars. Why would Sentrix pay millions to a small-time purchasing agent to keep his mouth shut? What kind of information could Kinney have had to warrant such a payoff? Was it about his work for the Pioneer Initiative? Is that what the feds were interested in?

Lenny leaned back in his chair and rubbed his temples. Circular motion. Two fingers moving on each side of his head. The massage soothed him. He felt tired and worn out like a pair of overly treaded soles. These boots will keep on walking but not when it's one o'clock in the morning. Lenny stood up. Time for joe, not the person, but the black, bitter, jolting liquid of morning gold. Except it wasn't morning. Screw it. He needed it.

The coffee pot steamed to life, gurgling like a monster lurking in the shadows. The smell penetrated Lenny's nostrils, bringing his mind back to reality, restarting his sludge filled motor. The fog cleared, and Lenny began to see the outline of terra firma on the horizon. The land of knowledge was dead ahead. When the pot stopped its guttural moans, Lenny poured a generous amount into his personal mug with the catchy slogan *The early bird catches the worm.* tattooed on the side. Well, it sure as hell was early or late, depending on how you looked at it. Glass half full or half empty.

He formulated a plan. He would put the bed bug shit on the sidelines for now. He was a finance guru and was better suited investigating the missing millions. To hell with those little blood suckers. After all, Carter had given him that task and Carter was no longer here. For Lenny to keep his job, he would have to suck up to Gordon Reynolds and Reynolds was obsessed with money. If Lenny could crack the case, and either retrieve the missing money or at least point the authorities in the right direction, he would score some serious brownie points with the old man. The bed bugs could wait. Sure, the IPO was in two days, but there was nothing to trace those miserable little creatures back to Sentrix, therefore, the IPO wouldn't be affected in the slightest.

Lenny set about the task of digging up Donald Kinney's corpse and questioning his spiritual embodiment, in a manner of speaking. Kinney had worked for the same corporation, ChemShield Inc., for thirty years before being hired by Sentrix. At ChemShield Kinney was a Vice President in charge of logistics. *A Vice President?* So, he was no small fry. He was a great big potato. And

ChemSheild was a decently sized corporation, about half the size of Sentrix.

ChemShield, a company that manufactured concrete floor coatings, had ten thousand employees, offices in twenty states, four factories and about $600 million a year in revenue. Why would Donald Kinney leave such a plush job with a big corporation to become a small-time purchaser at Sentrix? Lenny doubted the money was better, in fact he would have bet his savings on it, and he would have cleaned up in Vegas. He knew old man Reynolds didn't pay shit. So, why leave? Or had Kinney been fired? Forced out? Kicked to the curb?

The records said hell no with capital letters. ChemShield's president, senior vice president and even the chairman of the holy board, had submitted letters of recommendation to Carter on Kinney's behalf. Lenny read the letters all the way through and envied their contents. Man, he wished someone would speak so highly about him. These people worshipped Kinney as if he were a god, which he was, a god of logistics. Kinney could organize massive shipments of raw materials and labor from one state to the next without breaking a sweat. He excelled at his job both at ChemShield and at Sentrix.

Kinney's unblemished reputation seemed to rule out theft. He had been an honest guy. Abraham Lincoln of logistics. So, where had the two million gone? It just didn't add up. Incredible logistical genius spends three decades building his reputation then decides to steal for the Russian mob? *No way.* Not in Lenny's mind anyway.

So, what *had* Kinney been doing at Sentrix? He was a purchaser. That's what the official file stated. But his daughter said he traveled a lot. That seemed odd for a purchaser to be frequently traveling. Lenny figured purchasers, or logistics specialists, sat behind desks moving large pieces on imaginary boards. Buying a product from point A and moving it to point B. But they themselves seldom moved. Hell, Lenny knew several people in the logistics department at Sentrix. He couldn't recall any of them having to travel. So, where had Donald Kinney been going?

If Kinney traveled, Sentrix either reimbursed him for the expenses or paid for the trips outright. That was information Lenny would be able to find, and he did it in record time. He accessed the company ledger. Travel expenses were listed under general expenditures. He typed in Donald Kinney's name and came up with an extensive list of flights, hotel stays and food bills. Lenny wrote down each of the destinations on a pad. Most were in the states, Florida was number one, trailed closely by Boston. Some of the destinations had been abroad, St. Lucia and Mexico, two countries Sentrix didn't have a presence in. Mexico was deemed not profitable enough and the pest control market of St. Lucia was dominated primarily by local inhabitants, who had such a stranglehold on the island's bug killing business, it would have been impossible for a giant multinational corporation to gain a foothold. What in the name of Black Beard's dark and curly was Donald Kinney doing traveling to these two countries and why in the name of Dire Straits' guitar strings had Sentrix paid for these trips?

Lenny typed in St. Lucia into the company database. Nothing materialized. He did the same with Mexico, specifically the towns of Palo Solo and Santa Rita, identified in Kinney's hotel stays. Again nothing. Dead end. Maybe there were factories in these two towns that produced something Sentrix used that Lenny was unaware of. Some kind of roach bait or glue board. Lenny clicked open his internet icon and typed the town names into google followed by the word bug. Google must have mistaken the word bug as an illness instead of an insect because it produced search results of news articles, most of which were written in Spanish, about a mysterious illness that had taken the lives of hundreds. *Health problems were rampant in third world countries.* Lenny thought as he perused the articles. He opened one written by the Dallas Herald, the only English one he could find and read it purely out of curiosity.

Palo Solo, a small town located in the Mexican state of Tamaulipas, has been afflicted with an illness that has claimed hundreds of lives in less than six days. Authorities and medical personnel are baffled as to the exact cause of the illness but said that symptoms are nonexistent up until the time of death. No unusual fevers, rashes, vomiting, or diarrhea have been reported. Dr. Garcia Vargas, a physician with the department of health in the region, described the crisis as baffling. "The department of health was alerted after the second day when the death toll had reached forty people. When we arrived, we discovered twenty more people had died the night before. They simply went to sleep and never woke up. The next night twenty more and thirty on the night after that. Then it just stopped. We have not experienced any deaths in the last two days." The department of health will be conducting autopsies on the deceased. They advise local residents to practice good hygiene and report any...

Lenny felt sick. His guts flipped and flopped like a newly hooked fish on the deck of a boat. He sat back in his chair. Sweat began to bead on his forehead. Droplets of fear, nervousness and desperation. *It couldn't be. It wasn't the same thing. No way. No how.* But deep down he knew it was. He didn't want to check. Didn't want to know. His brain told himself as much as he stared unseeing at the computer screen. Then his hand moved of its own accord. It reached for the mouse. It moved the arrow on the screen and double-clicked. He tried to shut his eyes. Tried to blind himself to the horrible reality of the situation. *No, no, no.* But they flung themselves open. They moved down the screen, his pupils scanning. The dates. It was there. Right there. Exposed like a naked, senile old man in the middle of a playground.

The mysterious illness in Palo Solo lasted for six days, it ended the day after Donald Kinney arrived in the small town.

Chapter 72

"Have you ever seen anything like that?" Detective Patterson asked.

"No." George answered. His voice quiet, detached, distant.

The two of them sat wide-eyed and open-mouthed in Patterson's Ford Crown Victoria. The engine purred softly like a cat being gently stroked. The car was warm. Hot air blew out of the vents like a giant hairdryer. The radio played soft tunes in the background that neither of the two men paid any attention to.

Patterson had recovered slightly from his initial shock. The pain of losing fellow officers and that scene straight out of a war zone in the hotel's ballroom, still affected his sense of reality, bringing about an incalculable dread he couldn't shake.

"I lied. I have seen something like that before." George said, his gaze fixed on the windshield wipers as they made their way back and forth over the ice-covered glass.

"What?" Patterson muttered.

"Yeah. A long time ago."

"Where?"

George shifted his weight uneasily in the wide seat.

"It was different though."

"What do you mean? How was it different?"

"I've never told anyone. Not a soul. I tried telling Ocean…" The thought of his late friend gripped his heart in an iron squeeze. "But I couldn't."

"I don't have a clue what you're talking about."

"I remember not being able to see. We were blind. I remember the bullets, hearing them wiz over my head. And the explosions. One after another. They shook the earth. I can still feel the heat from the blasts. It felt like Satan was throwing fireballs at us."

Patterson looked over, his eyes wide. He could feel the terror in George's words and could almost picture the scene playing out in the man's mind.

"I remember seeing or better yet, hearing, the lieutenant taking one to the head. Half his face came off. I knew I had to take charge. Get us the hell out there, but I couldn't move. I was frozen. All the training. The hours of live fire drills. None of it prepares you for the real thing. You've got to live it. Try to live through it. And we weren't going to live. We were going to die right there in the middle of that shithole village, next to some asshole Iraqi general who got his jollies off molesting little kids."

Patterson stayed quiet, listening.

"Finally, I got up. It took everything in my body. All my energy. All my strength. I stood, lifted my rifle and fired. Just let it rip. Pulled the trigger and sprayed everything in front of me. I couldn't even hear the fire. I just remember hearing the shell casings hitting the sand, which is bullshit because there's no way I could hear that, but I remember hearing it all the same. I dumped my mag, loaded another and fired. Then the storm ended. The wind just stopped, and the sand fell, and I could see." George's voice cracked. "I could see, and what I saw…"

"Unit 111!" The loud squawk of the radio made Patterson jump. "Unit 111. Detective Patterson, are you there?" At first Patterson didn't move. He sat there and stared at the receiver as if he could use the force to will it to his hand. "Bill. You there?" The messages were becoming less formal with each transmission.

Finally, Patterson reached over and picked up the damn thing. He depressed the button. "Go ahead."

"Bill, its John. The shit has hit the fan. I repeat the shit has hit the fan."

Patterson looked over at George, who continued to stare at the moving windshield wiper blades as if he were expecting them to detach themselves from the car and fly away.

"What happened?" Patterson said into the mic.

"Ten more. We've got ten more. Betsy Richardson and…"

"The flower lady?" Patterson asked into the mic, not realizing that the transmission couldn't go through while Chief John was speaking. He depressed the button again and repeated his question. "The flower lady?"

"Yeah and nine others. Almost every person on her damn block. All of them, except one."

"Jesus. How'd you find them?"

"Abigail Hugh's house caught on fire. It took us forty-five minutes to get over there. She left her stove on.

The house is gone and Abigail with it. We rapped on the neighbors' doors to evacuate them. You know how close those houses are? Practically, right on top of each other. No answer, so we kicked in the damn doors."

Patterson hadn't noticed it before, but now he could see a faint orange glow in the distance coming from the direction of where Abigail's house would be or had been. He had met Abigail a few times. Nice old gal.

"They were all dead. Betsy Richardson, Pauline Swanson, George Holder, Mark Grant and five more. Then the whole block went up in smoke."

"I'm heading over there."

"Don't. The fire department has the whole block locked down. I need you at the station. I'm heading to a town meeting."

Patterson was blown away. "A town what?!"

"A town meeting. The council, those morons, called a town meeting. Everyone knows what's going on. They're freaking out Bill. Melvin Keyes…"

"The butcher?"

"Yeah. He killed himself and his whole family. Lost his mind. We figure it was because of the bugs. Guess he didn't want to become the next fly in the spider web."

"Jesus Christ."

"Yep. Better say some prayers Bill."

"I'll head to the station."

"Ten-four."

Patterson put the car in drive and crept out of the lot. Despite the slow crawl, the tires slid on the ice like a giant sled down a hill. Patterson pumped the brakes, it did nothing. The car slid into the street fishtailing as Patterson turned the wheel hard and hit the gas. The car began to squeal wheels like a drag racer on a slick track. The tires tried desperately to gain traction. The smell of burning rubber made its way through the air vents and into the car. *This is what it must be like driving a 1,000-horsepower Corvette with its unnerving rear wheel drive. All torque and no traction.* The car's rear end swayed back and forth like the shake of an oversized ass in a disco.

"Stop the car." George said, but Patterson wasn't listening. "Stop the damn car!" George shouted over the noise of the burning tires.

Patterson eased up on the gas. The shrieking stopped.

"You just got to give it some gas. It'll get there."

"No, it won't." George replied. "Let's walk."

"Walk? It's a mile and a half to the station. How the hell are we going walk in this? We barely made through the damn parking lot."

"The car's shot. It ain't going nowhere. So, we either sit here and freeze to death, or we walk." George said. He opened the door and got out. "Come on. The faster we get started, the faster we'll get there."

"Fuck you." Patterson said, but he did get out, reaching in to shut off the ignition and yank the parking brake up.

"What about the car?"

George looked around the deserted street comically. "Yeah, I think all the traffic might be a problem."

Patterson slammed the door shut.

Five minutes later, the radio in Patterson's empty car squawked a frantic call, the most important call that the thirty-year veteran would ever receive. The call went unheard and unanswered.

Chapter 73

Since the founding of Havre de Grace in 1785, the town has been run by a council consisting of twenty-one of the most influential town inhabitants. They're the town gods with an omnipotent aura that would have made Napoleon wrinkle with envy.

The number twenty-one was chosen to avoid stalemates, not that a tie would ever materialize. All twenty-one members always vote either yay or nay with zero detractors.

The council makes the laws. The members are conservative, old school, sticklers. They don't adhere to progressive thought and shun any and all change. The rules they set forth mimic what one might read outside of a senior living community. *No skateboarding. No biking. No smoking. No profanity. No spaghetti strap tops in public areas. No belly shirts. No "yo" pants.* And on and on.

They also don't allow giant corporate entities to set up shop in their town. *No siree bob.* Mom and Pas all the way. You won't find a Starbucks, a Walmart, a Panera Bread, a Chilis, an Applebees, a Target, a Dick's, a Chipotle, or a Home Depot anywhere within the town limits. You *will* find a Cozy Corner Coffee Shop, a Tom's Hardware and Tackle, a Suzy-Q's Deli and even an Old Ma's grocery store. The closest corporate America has ever gotten to setting a slimy toe in Havre de Grace is the Royal Farms, because everyone needs gas and the McDonald's, because, well, the old folks on the council ain't gonna miss their morning grease and coffee.

And the crazy part is the people who live in town really like it. They like the slow-paced, old-fashioned way of life decreed by the council. They like the little shops where you can meet the owner. They like the fact that everyone has a seat in Suzy-Qs and almost everyone has a damn sandwich named after them. They like Old Ma's, even though Old Momma's prices have edged up a notch ever since she bit the dust and her spoiled kids took over. They like Tom's, where you can get the kind of stuff Depot doesn't really have, even though you're gonna pay twice as much for it. But the people of the town especially like the rules that keep the burgeoning riff-raff out.

This ain't Baltimore hon. You'd often hear them say while they ate their *Gail on Rye* in Suzy's. And they're right. This sure as hell ain't Baltimore, although they do still say *hon.* Try to figure that one out.

"Thank you all for coming." Frank Duisenberg boomed from the head of the table. "I know it was a treacherous journey."

"Here. Here." *Old Man Marv* barked, his sallow body leaning heavily on his cane.

The council was in their customary meeting spot, the VFW hall on the corner of St. John and Union Avenue. The Hall, as it was called by the locals, was an enormous dark blue house, with two 75 mm antitank guns posted threateningly at each end of the vast front porch.

Old Man Marv once joked in his gruff voice, "If they don't listen, we'll point one of dem there artillery pieces at 'em." Lucky for most, the old guns hadn't seen battle since V.E. day and had, in the meantime, been rendered inert, kind of like *Old Marv.*

Frank looked around the table at the twenty-one faces seated before him. What a group. Ninety percent of them had reached that stage in life described eloquently as over the hill, except for Marv, who had gone over the hill twenty years prior and was on his way down the hill like a boulder pushed over a cliff. The other ten percent of the council were handpicked proteges. Younger men and women, schooled in the art of preservation, who would continue the council's civic duties long after their predecessors had gone up to stand before St. Peter.

Alice McCabe sat stoically with her perfect gray hair looking like the million bucks her late husband had supposedly left her. She wore a gold brooch with tiny diamonds sparkling like a thousand stars in a night sky.

Joanne Bright and Phyllis Tannon eyed each other nervously and eyed Alice enviously. Both wondered wordlessly whether the rumors of Alice's excessive windfall were true. The two ladies, identical in dress and demeanor, were known around town as the *Twin Dictators*, although *only* behind their backs. No one would ever dream of uttering it to their faces for fear that an untold number of laws would be decreed, and the perpetrator would literally be excommunicated out of town. *No more Havre de Grace for you, thank you very much hon.*

Jamie Hatner was hands down the hottest gal in the room, which in this room wasn't saying much. She sported sleek brown hair that glistened in the light, leaving many of the old hatters wondering what exactly she used to get that shine. Jamie had curves in all the right places, perfect curves, curves that nearly killed *Old Man Marv* every time the nice young lady walked in the room. Jamie was the leader of the young guns, the protégé wing of the council crime family. She was rarely opposed by anyone, except of course Alice, Joanne and Phyliss, purely because of the insatiable jealousy the three ancient shrews exhibited towards this young, pretty *chippy*.

Henry Bennett, another of the young guns, had made the unfathomable and unfavorable decision to bring his two small children and plump little wife to the meeting where, as indicated by the judgmental eyes of the eldest members of the council, they weren't welcome. The kids roved noisily around the room, hooting and hollering their juvenile delinquency, while circling the empty tables in a bad imitation of an epic scene from a spaghetti western.

Old Man Marv was the most irritated by the presence of Bennett's young whippersnappers. Marv kept one of his greying eyes on Jamie -he couldn't stop mentally undressing her- and the other one on *those damn kids!* Marv wondered if he stuck those *damn kids!* inside the two barrels of those elephant guns out front how far they would fly over the Susquehanna. *Bet they'd make it eight freakin' miles.*

Frank's mind tried and failed to come up with the words to say, which was new for the ancient orator. And in reality, what could he say? *Sorry folks we're here to discuss killer bed bugs.* It sounded so absurd. *Bed bugs killing people!* It was crazy, ludicrous, loco. He could almost hear the orderlies over there at the psych ward. *Hey pops, come sit on this couch here. Are you hungry? Thirsty? These are your new friends. Everybody say hi to Frank. He's going to be staying with us UNTIL HE DIES!*

"I don't know how to say this…"

"Well, then just spit it out!" Marv roared as one of the kids came dangerously close to knocking over his walker.

"Thank you, Marv. Well, I'm just going to come out with it. Apparently, we have killer bed bugs on the loose." Frank said.

There was a collective gasp from the group, as if they hadn't heard all ready. Hell, gossip traveled faster in this town than a naked preacher through a raided whore house.

"I know. I wouldn't believe it myself if I didn't hear it from Chief John." Frank said.

"And where the hell is he?!" Marv shouted. "Later than Toby going to service." Which is something only people in Havre de Grace would understand. Toby Hayes, the local idiot, was notorious for arriving after the homily every single Sunday. The saying later than *Toby going to service* had become so popular in town that it had even spread to outlying communities, although those outsiders had no idea what it meant.

"Thanks for the introduction, Marv. Glad to see you were able to get that walker of yours skating." Chief John said. His red face redder than ever. It almost looked like the side of a fire truck. He took a seat in between Phyliss and Joanne.

Marv grumbled an inaudible reply that began with a *C* and ended with an *UCKER* and was followed by several huffs from the ladies in the room and a mad scramble from plump Mrs. Bennett towards her little tots to cover their ears.

"Can we get back to business, please?" Frank said, irritated by Marv's outbursts. The room became silent again. "Thank you. Anyway, as I was saying. We are faced with a very serious problem here ladies and gentlemen. People *are* dying. These bugs have killed dozens."

"Where'd they come from? I've never heard of bed bugs killing people. It's insane." Jamie Hatner chimed in.

Chief John answered. "We don't know where they came from. I agree with you Jamie, it is insane. I've never heard of this before either. We've been on the phone with the department of health, the department of agriculture and also the CDC. And they're blown away. I think they believe the whole town has gone completely nuts."

"Why the health department and the CDC? It's not a disease." Jamie said.

"That's true, but at this point we could use all the help we can get. We're doing everything we can." Chief John replied, a little defensively as if he were on trial, which in reality he was. The twenty-one people in this room decided his fate. If he failed to reasonably assuage their unease, he would be stood up against a brick wall and listen to Old Man Marv yell *FIRE!*

"How many people have died?" Alice asked.

"Our estimate is thirty-two." Chief John answered as another gasp rose throughout the room.

"Thirty-two!" Marv exclaimed. "And what the hell have you guys done to stop it? Have you thought about calling a damn exterminator? Jesus Lord!"

John shot Marv an ungrateful stare. "Yes, we have. Apparently, these bugs cannot be killed."

Old Tom, of Tom's Hardware fame, laughed heartily. "Not if I had my way. I'd let 'em see what I have in my cellar."

"So, they're invincible?" Frank asked, ignoring the rantings and ravings of both Marv and Tom. He too was shocked. How in the hell had this happened? A new breed of bed bug that kills people and survives anything an exterminator can throw at it? How is that possible?

"Sounds like you need a new bug guy." Marv said.

John waved his hand towards the windows. "Guess you haven't noticed the weather outside Marv. It's a damn ice storm. The exterminator we've been working with is trapped here just like the rest of us. If this storm continues, we can kiss any additional help goodbye."

"What about the national guard?" Phyliss asked.

John shook his head. "The governor offered. The national guard can't even get to us. This ice storm is the worst we've seen in ages. The whole state, hell, the whole northeast is on lockdown. We're on our own. Plus, what help would the national guard be? These are bugs we're talking about not rioters or terrorists. Guns and tanks won't do a damn thing."

"So?" Alice asked.

"We have to control the panic. Panic is the worst thing. We have already lost Melvin Keyes and Sam Bly."

"Melvin, the butcher?" Frank asked, his eyes wide with shock.

"Yes."

"How?"

"He panicked. Shot his family then himself." John answered.

Another collective gasp.

"Sam Bly packed his wife and four kids into his minivan and tried to flee. He didn't make it very far. He lost control down by the marina. Slid down the slope and went into the water. Everyone drowned before we even got the call." John said, his face downcast and sullen. He knew Sam Bly. Knew him well. He had coffee with him regularly at the Cozy Corner. He knew Sam's wife and all of Sam's kids, and it killed him to have to think of their tiny little hands beating against the glass as the frigid water poured in.

"We need to evacuate! Get everybody the hell outta here!" Marv bellowed, and several people around the table nodded in agreement.

"Did any of you hear what I just said? We can't evacuate. Driving out there is suicide. Walking is suicide. Hell, I don't even know how you all are going to make it home."

"Then what? What do we do?" Frank asked.

John never got the chance to answer. Before he could, the door to the hall opened, and hell opened with it.

Chapter 74

He trudged along with his destination in the furthest corner of his mind. He focused on the ice-covered ground. His steps were uneasy, unmeasured and reckless. He fell several times. Each bone-crunching impact on the concrete caused tremendous pain. He didn't care. He was oblivious to the pain.

The rain didn't stop. It was endless, like a dark tunnel with no light at the finish line. It covered his head, dripped down his face, formed icicles under his nose, turning his nostrils into miniature cave openings. Everything was coated with a protective sheen. It was pretty if one stopped to admire the beauty. Carlos didn't stop to admire anything. He was a man on a mission. A Satanic mission. A dark, disgusting, hellish task.

Man, my life has really taken a shit. A great, big, steaming pile. He thought. He was more depressed than the suicide hotline. He had gone from the top to the bottom faster than a bullet being shot from the observation deck at the summit of the Empire State building straight into the ground.

He thought about just letting her die. Truth be told, Sabrina was probably dead already. No way Tony would let her go. No way in hell. She was a liability. A living witness. A living witness whose finger had been severed in a testament of absolute resolve. They would definitely kill her, if they hadn't already. So, why couldn't he bring himself to just take off? Why couldn't he go back to his apartment, grab his backpack and beat it? Could they be watching his place? Observing his every move like Will Smith in Enemy of the State? Most likely. And what if they hadn't killed Sabrina yet? What if they were actually planning on letting her go? If he ran, he would guarantee her death.

A drink. That's what he needed. A drink. A smoke. Something to calm him. Something to make him carry on. He fumbled in his pockets. It had to be there. Rolled by the maestro of blunts himself, Juan Green. He found it a second later. The blunt looked like salvation. He lit it, his hands shaking, not with cold, but with fear, with nerves. The end of the cigar paper flared red. He inhaled deeply, giving the fire oxygen. He puffed. Big clouds of smoke poured from his mouth. *You da man Juan. Don't let anybody ever tell you different.* He coughed, long rasping coughs, coughs that felt so freaking good. He held the smoke in his lungs, absorbing every ounce of its potency. The familiar feeling of enlightened euphoria entered his mind. He could do it. He could survive. He *would* survive.

He had another four blocks to go. *Only four short blocks, in an ice storm. An ice storm!* He thought to himself, laughing like a madman on his way to the gas chamber.

Pierce's was alight with the excitement of late-night revelry. Men and women were partying till the cows come home, even on a night like this with a storm the likes of which most of the millennials in the bar have never seen. The sounds seeped out of the cracks and crevices around the windows and doors. Sounds of laughter, clinking glasses, dancing feet and loud music. The sounds of life being lived to the fullest.

Carlos crept up to the window and peered in like a voyeur. Inside was warm and inviting. It called his name in soft, soothing tones. *Come on in. Enjoy yourself. Make love, not war. Everything's okay.* But it wasn't. Carlos could never go back there. Never laugh and clink glasses with his homeboys. Never feel the music pulse through his veins. Never hear the whisper of forbidden love in his ear. Never feel the hips of a sexy body jive against his own. Never again. His life had changed.

He turned from the window and saw to his dismay, the cold steel cannons of a forgotten war aiming in his direction. There it was, his destiny, directly ahead. He sat there looking at the cannons across the street, hoping they would fire, hoping they would send twin 75 mm projectiles right into his chest, end his life in a flash of orange smoke. He wasn't that lucky. The guns remained steadfast. Instead of freeing Carlos from his fate, they were merely guarding the path for him to meet it full on.

Well, better get this over with. He walked forward, leaving the sounds and sights of his past behind.

Chapter 75

Carlos weaved his way through the cars in the lot without realizing what he was doing. It was as if he was being steered by an unknown force. His feet were on autopilot. He reached the spot where one of the antitank guns sat. There he paused for several seconds, gathering his courage. His heart pounded uncontrollably like a concert drum solo.

The river looked so calm, so peaceful. A shimmering black lake cut in two by the dark silhouette of the famous railway bridge. Carlos looked out at the water, watching the rain hit the surface like a thousand small pebbles chucked from a child's hand. He pondered wading in and letting the current take him, allowing the freezing depths to wash his soul, take away his worries, his failures, his past. Drown him and birth him into a new beginning. A new life beyond the grave. Salvation from his torment.

He grabbed the railing of the Victorian porch and lifted himself up the steps, taking them one by one. The clocks stopped. Time stood still. He grasped the cold metal in his waistband. It felt unnatural, surreal. His hand tightened over the ruff grip and yanked. The gun came up. He pulled the slide back as he moved forward along the porch. The door was now within reach. The gun felt heavy, weighing down his conscience.

Innocent people. That's what they are. Don't lie to yourself. They are innocent people. They never did anything to you. Nothing at all. They are simply a tool in the devil's game. A tool. A distraction.

The voice inside his head was that of his brother, the priest. It was a tranquil voice, that spoke with unquestionable logic, yet he chose to ignore it.

Carlos grabbed the doorknob. He stopped again and leaned forward on the door, his head laying against the hardwood. His brother's voice came to him again, from somewhere deep inside.

Last chance. You may have done a lot of bad things in your life, but you don't have to do this. Think about it. Think about the consequences. Don't listen to them. Listen to yourself, the little voice in your head. Think about your life. You really want it to end it like this, because that's what's going to happen. You're going to die. You know it. No prison, just death and an eternity in hell.

"What about Sabrina? What about her? What's your answer to that father? Huh?!" He exclaimed to himself.

There was no reply.

"Damn you!" He whispered angrily. "Damn you! I thought you had all the answers. I thought you knew. But you don't. They'll kill her. I have no choice."

There was only one reply. Three simple words.

Yes, you do.

Carlos turned the handle. The wind from the storm blew the door open with incredible force.

The twenty-one faces stared at him from across the wide expanse of the room. They looked at him with frustration as if he had simply come to interrupt their very important discussion. Two children played around the table closest to him under the watchful eye of their mother. They kept playing, ringing the table, their little feet pounding the linoleum floor, their tiny sing-song voices filling the room with glee.

Carlos stared at the kids, transfixed for what seemed like an eternity. He never expected children to be here. And in that instant, his brother's words came back to him with the force of ten bears. *Eternal damnation.*

He made up his mind, and before a single shout could arise from the gathered crowd, he aimed the gun and fired. Loud explosions bounced off the walls. Then the screams came. Screams of fear and anguish that joined the concussion, forming a symphony of gloom. Carlos fired twice more. The shell casings ejected out of the gun and hit the ground, spinning like toy tops, the shiny brass reflecting the light like pieces of gold lying in the sun.

"No one fucking move!" Carlos commanded. He lowered the gun from the ceiling and leveled it once again in the direction of the councilors, sitting around the table. "You." He said pointing at the chief of police. "Take out your fucking phone!"

Chief John stared at him with uncomprehending eyes.

"Get your phone out!" Carlos shouted. "Now!"

The chief snapped back to reality and scrambled inside his jacket, his hands plunging into pocket after pocket in a mad dash. Finally, he produced his cell phone. He didn't go for his gun, because he didn't have one. He had left it at home in its customary resting place -*My goddamn dresser drawer!* He hadn't carried it in years, after all, this was Havre de Grace. He cursed himself for his grievous error in judgment.

"Call it in." Carlos commanded.

"Beg your…" The chief began. He was truly perplexed. What was this punk's problem? Call it in? Call what in?

"Call it in!" Carlos exclaimed. "Active shooter. VFW hall. Call it in now."

The chief just stared at him in amazement. His facial expression looked like a billboard with the words *WHAT THE FUCK* written in big, bold capitals. The chief came out of his daze when the next burst of gunfire sent pieces of the ceiling showering down onto his head.

"This is chief John. I'm at the VFW hall. I need back up. Active shooter. I repeat active shooter. This is not a drill."

Just for good measure, Carlos fired again. Two more rounds hit the ceiling. The sound of gunfire was picked up perfectly by the chief's phone.

Chapter 76

"I must be crazy." James said. He was shivering. Chilled to the bone. He felt like an ice cube that had been returned to the freezer after a short reprieve in someone's glass.

The streets were desolate. It was like looking into a snow globe. A scene frozen in a glass ball. The houses glowed with bright, twinkling Christmas cheer. They were sheened with a coat of ice as if God had chosen this precise moment in time to freeze the world, shellacking it and placing it in His gallery for His future enjoyment.

"I told you to stay. You wanted to come." Kelly answered.

The two of them slogged along in the frigid tundra. They clung to anything they could get their hands on, including each other, to maintain some semblance of balance in a world that had gone to hell, if hell were a giant frozen lake. The sidewalk offered them very little. A few fence posts here and there, and maybe a mailbox or two, but most of the journey they were on their own, forging their own slick path.

"What kind of man do you think I am? Letting a woman go out in this alone." James said, putting on his chivalrous armor.

Kelly turned one of her frozen eyes on him. "I would love to debate sexism in extreme weather with you, but I highly doubt this is the time or place. Let's just say I can paddle my own canoe, or better yet, I can skate in my own pond."

Coming from the girl that dragged me to the scene of a double homicide. James thought, angrily.

"I'm glad you're here." She said.

James' anger melted away. He loved her. The realization hit him hard. He loved her! That was it. He loved spending as much time as possible in her company. Sure, they had only made love once, but it had been one of those things. Kind of like the Cole Porter song, *Night and Day. You are the one, only you beneath the moon, under the sun.* James had longed to hold her in his arms since the day they met. His love had been years in the making, like a fine bottle of Dom Perignon. Sewn, cultivated, harvested, extracted, aged, all to perfection and now sipped with complete adoration. He wanted her forever. He wanted to share his home, bask in the warm glow of the fire and her beauty, share the moments of life together. Grow ancient together, till their hair turned winter white and their love was as timeless as the world. That is why he had come. Not for chivalry but for love.

"If what you're saying is true, do you have any idea how enormous it is?"

"Huge." Kelly said.

Suddenly she lost her footing. Her shoes slipped, and she began to go down, James reached out his hands and caught her before she hit the ground.

"Bigger than Enron. Bigger than Madoff." She said.

"And you're the one that uncovered it. You'd be like Julius Chambers or Bill Dedman."

"I don't know if I'd go that far. Someone gave me the evidence. I didn't discover it."

"You pursued it. You thought there was something fishy about the deaths from the get-go." James said.

"Yeah but Julius Chambers?" She said, scoffing at the idea. Chambers was one of her heroes, a journalist who faked his own insanity to expose the corrupt inner workings of an asylum.

The station loomed in the distance. Both of them looked at the building as deliverance. A warm place in this ceaseless cold. Two more blocks. Two more grueling blocks but they could do it. They'd come this far. Turning back wasn't even a remote possibility. It was all or nothing.

"I'll race you." James said. He took off and fell flat on his face.

Kelly laughed uncontrollably. James sat up and stared at her indignantly. She continued to laugh. She had to clench her legs to stop herself from peeing. James smiled. It reminded him of that day so long ago.

"Are you okay?" She asked.

"Fine." He said.

"I guess you won."

"Very funny."

She reached her hand down and grasped his. He pulled, and she fell headlong into him. Now it was his turn to laugh. They both did. Giggling like school girls. Then they kissed long and hard, their cold faces pressed against each other in a never-ending embrace. They knew little of the gravity of events taking shape in their small town, if they had, they wouldn't be laughing at all.

The station was fervently alive, buzzing like a nest of pissed off bees. There was so much commotion that the cops didn't even notice James or Kelly at all, ignoring them as if they were phantoms floating in another dimension. The same heavy-set desk sergeant sat behind his raised throne. The big man was busy. He fielded phone call after phone call, shouting commands in every direction, like a short order cook with a long order.

"Excuse me." James said.

The sergeant ignored him, picking up the phone for the tenth time in the last sixty seconds.

"Havre de Grace police, Sergeant O'Hara speaking. Yeah. Yeah. Okay. We'll try to get someone there right away. Thank you."

"Excuse me!" James shouted, trying to cut in before the next call.

The sergeant peered down at him, pissed at the interruption.

"Is Detective Patterson here?" James asked, his voice still slightly raised, as he attempted to be heard over the loud hubbub.

"Aren't you that meteorologist?" The sergeant asked. "I thought we let you go. Hey Chuck!" The sergeant shouted to a uniformed officer nearby. "Didn't we let this guy out?"

Chuck, who seemed more interested in getting to his patrol car, gave James a perplexed look before shrugging his shoulders at the sergeant.

"I need to see Detective Patterson." James said.

"He ain't here." The sergeant said. "And he ain't answering his radio."

The phone rang again. The sergeant grabbed it faster than Doc Holiday could draw a six-shooter.

James turned to face Kelly. "Now what?"

Kelly, ever the investigative reporter, grabbed the nearest uniformed officer.

"What's going on here?" She asked.

"I don't have time." Officer Walt began to say.

"It's Walt isn't it?" Kelly asked.

Walt appeared anxious, desperately trying to free himself. He was decked out in his winter garb, hat, gloves and heavy blue coat. He looked haggard and worn out. A man in need of a good night sleep. His batteries were almost completely dead.

"Yes. Who are you?" He said quickly, eyeing the doors in his peripheral vision.

"Kelly Halle, Channel Nine." She answered.

Officer Walt rolled his eyes. His face went from anxious to pissed off in a split second.

"I really don't have time." He said. He started for the door. His stride quickening with each step.

"Can you tell me what's going on? Please." Kelly said running after him.

"Give it a rest Kell." James said, pretty much to himself, before he started after her.

Officer Walt made it outside. The majority of the cops at the station were jumping into their cruisers. Engines were turned over. Lights were switched on, strobing their familiar blue and red. They pulled out one by one, slipping and sliding onto the ice-covered street, almost as if they were participating in a choreographed show at the Winter Olympics or better yet, as if they were extras in a Three Stooges short.

Walt hurried to join them. He was ranking officer now. Patterson was MIA. Chief John was at the town meeting which apparently had turned into the OK Corral at high noon, so the chief may very well be KIA. That left himself, Officer Walt, in charge. A ton of responsibility and duty sat on his head like a lion sitting on an ant. He had to lead his men into battle as if he were a general facing a large force on the field. His chief's life, as well as the other members of the council's lives, depended on it. His car was feet away when he lost his footing and slipped.

Kelly watched the event happen in slow motion. Officer Walt's boots slid forward leaving his body behind. The officer fell back. She reached out to him, tried to break his fall, but she was too far away. He landed hard, the back of his head hitting the asphalt with a thud. She could almost hear his skull cracking. He laid there, sprawled out like a frat boy after his first party bender. It didn't look good. She ran over to him and knelt.

"Holy shit!" She exclaimed. "Are you okay?"

Walt stared at her as if he were looking up from the bottom of a pool, completely submerged in water, barely able to comprehend the words coming from Kelly's mouth. His head was swimming or better yet, drowning.

"What the hell happened?" James said, even though he witnessed the whole thing.

"I think he hit his head." Kelly replied.

"He's bleeding." James said pointing to a dark puddle that had begun to form underneath Walt's skull. "Hey, buddy can you hear me?"

Walt nodded painfully. His head pounded. He tried to sit up of his own volition and failed. The pain in his head was far too great.

"Stay put." James said. "I'm going to go get help." But as he said it, he watched as the last police car left the lot. James looked back into the large glass window panes of the station and saw the desk sergeant still at his post answering calls as if he were manning the PBS telethon by himself. James hurried inside.

"Hey! There's a cop outside who needs help!" James hollered up at the sergeant.

The plump man ignored him. James rapped his knuckles on the side of the desk. That got the man's attention. The sergeant gave James a *great it's you again* look.

"A cop fell outside. I think he may have cracked his skull. He needs help."

The sergeant looked up through the glass entrance in front of his high perch. It almost seemed like he wasn't going to do anything at all. Finally, as if it took every ounce of strength he had, the sergeant rose as slow as sap from a newly tapped maple tree in the middle of winter.

It was infuriating to watch. James stood there for what seemed like a thousand years. His fists clenched and unclenched. Frustration coursed through his body.

"Come on man." James spat.

"All right. All right." The cop said. "Who'd you say it was?"

"I don't know his name." James said, leading the big man outside.

"Oh my God. It's Walt." A female voice exclaimed.

James whirled around. A tall, athletic woman in her late forties stood there, gaping at the scene. He only got a quick glance at her because a second later the woman had taken off, ignoring the ice on the ground, moving like Superman racing a locomotive. She arrived at Kelly's side a good minute before James did, and at least two minutes before the puffing, heavy-set desk sergeant.

"Walt. Walt. Can you hear me? It's Patty." The woman said, holding Walt's hand in a comforting embrace.

Walt nodded. Again, he tried to rise.

"No, no, no honey. Stay there. Let me check a few things before you move." Patty said, gently pushing Walt's head back down. She reached her hand below Walt's head, feeling for a wound. Walt grimaced at her touch. She pulled her hand back which was covered in blood. Then she removed her keychain from her pocket. She pushed the power button on a little black flashlight that hung alongside her keys. She played the light back and forth into Walt's eyes.

"He's got a laceration on the back of his head. It's not severe. Head wounds tend to bleed a lot. He's definitely got a concussion." Patty said, mainly to herself as if she were speaking into a voice recorder.

"What can we do?" Kelly asked.

"Funny thing is the best thing we can do for a concussion is ice." She said, smiling as she waved her hand to indicate the copious amounts of ice lying around. "We're going to have to get him inside. You there." She said, nodding James' way. "Run inside and grab me some paper towels from the restroom."

James did so, returning a split second later with a handful.

"Great. Now, we're going to lift him up. I'm going to hold is head, putting pressure on the wound while you three walk him inside. Let's get him to the lounge. There's a sofa in there. We'll lay him down, get him some ice and I can clean the wound and try to stop the bleeding."

It worked like a charm. A few minutes later, Officer Walt was on the couch with an ice pack, several bandages and one hell of a headache. Patty checked his oxygen level with a pulse oximeter. Concussion victims tend to lose oxygen in their blood. Walt's was a very respectable 98 and his pulse, considering everything that had happened to him in the last fifteen minutes, was an even more respectable 62, but that didn't last long. A few minutes later and Walt's pulse had reached heights no mortal man should ever have to endure.

Chapter 77

Steve Powers had spent his whole life, at least the last thirty years of it, as a security guard at hospital point; Greater Hearts of Maryland to out-of-towners. He loved his job, as any man loves their job when they've been doing it for three decades. You either love it or hate it and if you spend thirty years doing it, hating it is kinda pointless unless you've got bats in the belfry. That's how Steve felt. The job was fun. Sure, it had its ups and downs, as every job does, but the ups outweighed the downs ten to one.

And there was a degree of excitement to it. That's why he worked the night shift. He *had* tried the day shift before, which was about as boring as watching a worm cut its way across a patch of concrete. But the night… that was a whole different story. Things just tend to happen at night.

Bewitching hour, midnight crazies, moon madness, whatever you want to call it, was one hell of a time. Havre de Grace was thirty seconds from heroin highway, a.k.a. I-95 north. The shit, and it was shit, lower than maggots infesting the gut of a pig, made its way north from the poppy fields in Sinaloa. Then it came across the poorly guarded border, into Texas, where the cowboys were more *real* high than ye high. After that it came up 95 where it passed through *B-more* -or *Bal-more* depending on what neighborhood you're from- then on to its final destination, the big apple. The problem was that some of the maggot shit fell off the big rig wagons truckin' up the freeway. And in the last five years, Havre de Grace saw a serious uptick in the amount of drug use and with that, like happy meals come with toys, an uptick in nonviolent, violent, and just about every other kind of crime imaginable. Therefore, Steve Powers witnessed a hell of a lot of crazy shit come midnight. A hell of a lot of addicts, scratching themselves as if they had a bad case of poison ivy, so doped up they didn't know their own names, made their befuddled way into the E.R. Mainly for common ailments, things they could've cured at home, if they'd a listened to their *mommas* when they was *youngins*. Probably wouldn't be shootin' that shit either though if momma knew best.

Steve Powers listened to his momma. *Yes sir. Listened to 'er real well. She was da one that kept me off of dem drugs. Kept me outta da gangs too. Kept my nose clean. Nobody messed wit momma. No sir. Nobody dat had any brains about 'em. Momma could see outta da back of her head. No shit. She had dem eyes, dat only mommas have. Peeking from underneath her hair. And she had dat sense when you're about to cross dat line. Take dat ciggy from da ol' devil's hand. She knew. She always knew. And if she found out… you'd better just take da tannin' ya had comin', cause if ya split and she caught ya, she'd tan ya till ya couldn't sit down for a week.*

He wondered what momma would say now. There was some real crazy shit going down, like Steve had to check his coffee two or three times to make sure his old lady hadn't spiked his mug. Maybe a little E&J, or better yet, some LSD. That stuff they use to feed to the soldiers. Stuff that made them see shit. Because Steve *was* seeing shit. He had to be. This couldn't be real. No sir. He had never in his wildest -and he's had some wild ones- dreams seen anything like this kind of shit.

The hospital had three entrances: the emergency, the main and the employee. Steve worked the emergency entrance. That was his post. He was the best, although the big humble man would never admit it. And the best in the world of hospital security guarded the hospital's version of San Juan Hill.

Steve was at his post, sitting behind the circular desk doing his crossword puzzle, on what had been a quiet night, despite the storm, when the call came through. It was Nelson, who worked security over at the employee entrance, definitely the quietest post in the hospital.

"Hello." Steve said in his big, burly voice.

"You won't believe this. I'm telling you, Steve, this shit is off the chain." Nelson said, speaking so fast the transmission hadn't caught up with the words leaving the young man's mouth.

"What happened? Code blue?" A code blue was hospital lingo for crazy on the loose. Sometimes, and it didn't happen often, one of the loonies from up on the third floor, got loose and ran ripping and roaring through the hospital.

"Man, I'm telling you, you won't believe this shit. Ain't no code blue. It's a code red. There something over here. Something bad and big Steve... we need you down here."

"Code red? Ain't been a code red around here for years? You sure Nelson? You ain't pulling my chain is you?" Steve said. He listened for a reply. "Nelson? You there?" The line was dead.

Steve looked around the waiting room. Two people sat in chairs waiting to be seen. One had her head in a bucket, puking profusely. The other, a man in his late fifties, with a large laceration on his face, held a bloody towel to his wound and peered with one nervous eye over at the woman whose head was in the bucket. Steve figured he could leave his post for a minute. If Nelson really had a code red on his hand, that was bad, that was *real* bad. Code red meant Armageddon, catastrophic collapse, worlds colliding.

The big man grabbed his walkie-talkie and walked towards the doors that read: *Authorized Personnel Only* in big red letters. He pushed the double doors open. The brightly lit hallway was deserted. No nurses. No doctors. The only sounds present were the never-ending beeping and whirring of countless lifesaving machines. He looked up and noticed the emergency lights weren't lit. There were three of them: a yellow, a blue and a red. They signaled disaster and based on their colors, which degree of disaster was afoot.

That boy better not be foolin'. I'll ring his scrawny neck if he is. Steve thought as he left the emergency wing and entered the main lobby. It was deathly silent. That wasn't odd for this time of night but Lavern not being at her desk was odd. The front desk, which eclipsed Steve's in size and majesty, was empty. Steve walked over to it. He lifted his walkie-talkie to his mouth, depressing the transmit button, but before he spoke, he noticed to his utter dismay, Lavern's unit, sitting on her desk. Now, that was totally against the rules. You never leave your desk without your radio. Even if you went to take a leak, you take it with you. That was protocol. They drilled that in you at every meeting. You walk, you bring the talk. Well, Lavern had walked, but her talk was sitting on the desk. Steve picked it up. He'd have a word with her for this. Yes sir. No foolin' about it. That was bad shit.

He continued on. The employee entrance was in the back of the building by the kitchen and the loading dock. He would have to pass through the old folks' ward on his way. Steve loved that ward. He'd stop by there two, three, maybe four times a shift to visit with the old folks. *Learn a lot from dem ol' folks. They've been there and done dat.* Plus, they didn't get as many visitors as they should. Funny thing about it. *Their families would just drop 'em off, lock 'em up and throw away da key. Never see 'em, cept on holidays, and maybe not even then.* Steve was allotted three breaks a shift. Two for leisure and one for lunch. Lunch, who could call a 3 a.m. meal lunch? Well, he packed his own lunch, and unlike Nelson and Lavern who sucked down cancer sticks on their breaks, Steve spent his breaks visiting. He'd go over and sit with the old folks for a spell, or he'd make his way up to the fourth floor where the kids with cancer were. The young kids loved big Steve, who always packed a broad smile and a pocket full of sweets.

When he turned the corner to go through the double doors to the old folk's wing, he stopped dead in his tracks. The double doors were propped open by a body, that lay sprawled between them. Steve hurried forward, his natural guardian instincts taking hold and giving his legs the oomph, they needed. It was Lavern and she was dead. He knew it without even touching her. He just saw it in her eyes. They were open with a horrified look in them, as if the last thing she saw was T-Rex coming down the corridor. He checked her pulse just to make sure. *Yep, she was a goner but how?* Steve thought. *Where were her wounds? Where's all da blood? No blood. No wounds. No nothing. Maybe her heart exploded like ol' Mr. Gunther? No way. Not at her age. She was a youngin. I'd have a heart attack before she would.*

"You there Nelson?" Steve said into his walkie-talkie. There was no reply. Just the dull static of open air.

"Hey Nelson. Come in Nelson."

Still the static.

Now where in Sam Hill is he?

Steve looked up and past the body of Lavern into the old folk's corridor. His eyes sprung open. Terror gripped his massive frame. Goosebumps shot up his arms and down his spine. He had never seen anything so terrible, so godawful in his entire life. That's when he decided to call. Nelson was right. This was a code red. The biggest code red in history. Steve grabbed the phone and dialed 911. That would be the last phone call the gentle giant would ever make.

Chapter 78

"Active shooter. This town's really gone to hell in a handbasket." James said, shaking his head in disgust.

"Tell me about it." Patty answered.

"Do they know who it is?" Kelly asked.

"Nope. All they know is that the entire town council is there and the chief of police."

James and Kelly both stared at Patty with wide eyes.

"Well, I hope they shoot the son of a bitch before he kills any of those old farts."

"So, do I. More work for my department." Patty said with a sigh.

"What do you mean?" Kelly asked.

"Assistant county coroner." Patty said raising her hand.

"Geez, you've had a rough job recently." James said.

Patty filled James and Kelly in on what she did for a living, or had done for a living, because she was pretty sure that she would be taking early retirement after the last few days. Having to deal with so much death, as well as coping with the death of her husband, was something she never wanted to go through again.

The three of them were seated around one of the folding tables in the officer's lounge, sipping coffee and trying to get warm. The desk sergeant had waddled his rear end back to his perch, seconds after laying Walt down on the couch.

"I don't know if I could ever do what you do." James said, frowning at the thought of dissecting a human corpse.

"You get used to it. Hell, I could never do what you do. Predicting the impossible and having everyone either hate you or love you for it. No thank you. I'll stick with the dead, at least they don't complain if I'm wrong.

"I'll drink to that." James said clinking his coffee mug with Patty's.

"How did your husband die?" Kelly said. She always had a way of bringing the mood of the room straight down to negative three hundred. Just the reporter in her. Always interested in the scoop, no matter how many feelings she hurt in the process.

Patty looked downcast. The smile that had creased her face seconds before had vanished like Jimmy Hoffa at a diner. Her eyes suddenly found something very interesting on the surface of the table.

"I'm sorry." Kelly said, and there was actual, genuine empathy in her voice, this got Patty talking. Kelly was a damn good reporter.

"Those fucking bugs killed him." Patty said in a cold voice. Anger pulsed up her throat like a high striker being hit by Arnold Schwarzenegger, blasting the bell on the top to the moon.

Kelly and James remained silent. Neither one of them knew what to say. Finally, Kelly spoke up.

"I know who made them." Kelly said.

Patty just looked at her with eyes that held the fury of the entire planet. "What?" Patty said through clenched teeth.

Kelly cleared her throat. "Those bugs were no accident. They were created, and I know who created them."

"Who?" Patty snarled.

Kelly began to answer but was abruptly cut off by the reappearance of the desk sergeant, who looked like he had just seen Casper and Scooby Doo eating his lunch.

"That was Greater Hearts Hospital." The desk sergeant said, panting. Walt instantly perked up, jolted out of semi-consciousness. "They said people are dropping like flies all over the place."

Everyone stood in unison. Patty, the only one in the room who had any experience with those bastard little blood suckers, looked scared. Walt tried to sit up. He swung his legs to the floor and grasped the seat cushion till his knuckles turned a ghastly white. Then he crumpled to the floor. Patty, James, and Kelly rushed over and lifted Walt back onto the sofa.

"My son! My son! I gotta go." Walt yelled, raving like a madman. Sweat was pouring from his face. His body trembled.

"Lay down." Patty said in her calm, soothing voice. "You can't go Walt. What about your son?"

Walt swallowed hard. "My son's there, at the hospital."

Silence descended onto the occupants of the room. It was so quiet, the sound of the clock ticking and the compressor inside the vending machine boomed like cannon fire and hummed like a diesel engine. The phone rang, startling everyone. The desk sergeant hurried back to his post, his keys on his belt jingling in concert with the phone.

"We have to get to the hospital." Walt said. "They've got to get out. Get him out."

"How old is your son?" Kelly asked, always the reporter.

"Seven." Walt replied.

"Why is he in the hospital?" Kelly asked, not entirely sure she wanted to know the answer.

"He's got…" Walt swallowed again. His throat was dry, scratchy. "He's got cancer."

Patty recoiled, shocked by the revelation. She had known Walt for years. And not just professionally. She considered him a friend. Not a close friend. Not an *invite him over for a cookout* friend, but a *hey we're all going out to lunch, want to join us?* friend. Still, she assumed he would have told her about his son, hell, he talked about him enough. How the kid loved baseball. How he had met Cal Ripken and got him to sign the newspaper from Ripken's historic 2131 game. How the kid was a great ball player himself. But she had no clue the boy had been diagnosed with cancer. Seemed like something you'd want as many of your friends to know, just for the support. Suddenly, she was struck by how tough and stoic Walt was. Enduring such a gut-wrenching experience all by himself.

"I'm so sorry." Patty managed to say. Her throat was rather dry as well. "We'll get them out. Don't worry. We'll get them out." She repeated with fortitude, still holding Walt's hand.

"What can we do?" James asked. He needed to do something. He couldn't just sit by and watch from the sidelines.

"I'm sure the sergeant has already put it out over the radio. We've got to get a hold of Bill. Let him know what's going on, wherever the hell he is. I've got his cell number." Patty pulled out her phone with her free hand and handed it to James.

James scrolled through the contacts. "You've got two Bill's in your phone."

"Patterson. Bill Patterson."

"Got it." James said, hitting the call icon. He held the phone up to his ear. It rang several times before a rough voice said "Hello" followed by heavy breathing, almost as if the guy were running a marathon.

"Bill Patterson?"

"Who is this? And why are you calling me from Patty's phone?" Detective Patterson asked.

"My name is James Roseland. You locked me up earlier today. I'm here with Patty and Officer Walt. Where are you?"

More heavy breathing. "What the hell's going on?"

Two loud cracks filled the station in quick succession. The desk sergeant began to shout, a terrible animalistic sound, like that produced by a wounded beast. Two more cracks rang out and the sergeant's screams stopped. The phone slipped from James' fingers and crashed to the floor, shattering into a thousand pieces. Patty dropped Walt's hand. Everyone stared at the open lounge door.

Chapter 79

"What the shit was that?" Detective Bill Patterson said, pulling the phone away from his face and staring at the screen. Rain began to soak the phone's surface, first a few droplets, then steadily becoming a puddle. Patterson pushed the redial button, smearing the water with his fingertip. It went right to voicemail. Goosebumps crawled up his back like an army of invading ants.

"Who was that? What happened?" George asked.

The two men were slogging along on the frozen pavement. They hadn't gotten far. Farther than they would have in the car but still nowhere near the mile and a half distance to the police station. It reminded George of his childhood, the famous *Mount Everest* of his neighborhood. He'd fly down that hill, doing what seemed like a hundred miles an hour, snow dust and cold wind pelting his face in the most sensational way possible. Once he'd gotten to the bottom, it was a whole different story. Getting up Everest was the toughest struggle known to children. He'd get a quarter way, halfway, three-quarters of the way up, his boots digging in the frozen, packed, ice-coated snow like a mountain climber, then he'd slip and slide all the way back down. That's what this journey felt like now, just without the main ingredient- fun.

"It was that black kid, James. The one I arrested with your niece. He said he was with Patty, then I heard what sounded like firecrackers in the background and the phone just cut off."

"Firecrackers?" George asked, perplexed.

"Or gunfire. But why would there be gunfire?"

George thought about that for a moment.

"Where was Patty?"

"Last time I saw her, she was at the station." Patterson answered.

"You sure it was gunfire?"

"No, I'm not sure." Patterson said. His feet began to slide uncontrollably. George reached out and steadied the man while at the same time steadying himself by gripping a *For Sale* sign, hanging over the sidewalk.

Tony. That was the thought that crossed George's mind. He had seen Tony at the station, out front of the station.

"We've got to get back there."

"No shit Sherlock. What the hell do you think we're doing?" Patterson replied.

"I mean as fast as possible."

"Listen, James Bond, I ain't got a…"

"Look, I saw someone out front of the station when we left earlier. A guy I knew in the army. A bad fucking dude."

"And you didn't tell me?"

"I forgot. A lot of stuff happened since then. His name's Tony. I haven't seen him in years. Last I heard he was a gun for hire. And with all the other weird shit going on, I wouldn't put it past whoever created those bugs to bring in Tony to keep things quiet. I saw him standing out front of the station with that drug dealer who's been following us."

"Carlos? He's harmless."

"Out front of the station Bill." George reiterated.

Patterson stopped talking.

"He's after that box." A light bulb went off in George's head. "He killed those two guys in the motel, but he missed the box. They sent him here to clean things up." It was all making sense to him now. Tony had come to mop up the mess. Tie up loose ends, but he had failed. Maybe James and Kelly had startled him when they found the bodies. Tony hadn't had time to retrieve the box with the bed bugs in it.

"So, what are you saying? This Tony character is going to storm a police station? I seriously doubt it."

"He was part of a special unit. Highly trained. The best of the best. No offense, but your cops are no match for him. They'd be outgunned in a heartbeat."

"He'd be dumber than a guy trying to rob Fort Knox."

"I hope you're right. But you heard what you thought was gunfire. If Patty's at the station, then the gunfire can only mean one thing. We've got to get back there fast. Move your ass." George commanded.

Chapter 80

Carlos paced the room, the gun gripped in his hand. The eyes of everyone following him as if he were the main act of an enthralling show. Everyone wondering what the man of the hour would do next. Would he shoot them? Turn around and let loose? Turn them into a bloody mass on the floor? Or would he flee? Run out the door like the coward he was? They hoped and prayed for the latter.

Frank worried about Marv. The old man was gripping the handle of his walker a little too hard. Either old Marv was feeling the onset of a cardiac disaster, or he was feeling frisky, maybe thinking about reverting back to his WW2 days, charge the enemy at point blank range. Marv had nothing to lose, but the rest of them did. Frank wished Marv could hear his thoughts. *Stay calm Marv. Don't do anything stupid. You might have seen the best of your days, but the rest of us haven't.*

"So, what's your plan?" Marv asked.

Great! Talk to the psychopath. Good plan Marv. Frank thought, looking down at the table.

Carlos stopped pacing. He turned to face the old man. Marv was old. Ancient, like something that would be dredged up from the ocean floor. Marv's fingers were twisted and gnarled like a tree that had grown obstructed at every turn. Patches of what were probably once skin, hung, wrinkled and rotten on his pale face. But it was the old geezer's eyes that really turned Carlos white with fright. The old man had the eyes of a warrior. Eyes so intense they burned like fire.

"Shut the hell up, if you know what's good for you." Carlos blurted out. He really had no clue what to say.

Marv rolled his fiery eyes. "You ain't gonna kill nobody." He said.

Frank gulped. So, did everybody else. Big gulps and not the ones you get from the local 711.

"Maybe I'll start with you pops. You want that?" Carlos said, but he didn't move. He was frozen to the spot as if someone had driven railroad spikes through each of his feet.

Old Marv shook his head. "You ain't got it in you."

"Oh yeah? Try me pops."

Marv smiled a grin of false teeth, bad false teeth from the looks of them.

"Something funny old man?" Carlos asked. But he still didn't move. The gun remained quiet at his side like a tamed wolf, calm, steadfast and deadly.

"I'm curious." Marv began. Everyone looked at him like he had sprouted several heads. The old bastard had finally gone completely crazy. Totally insane. There's an unhinged lunatic with a gun and Marv is curious?

Carlos stared at him. He tried to talk, but words escaped him.

"I've been sitting here wondering why."

"Just shut the fuck up." Carlos said.

"Why?"

"Why what?"

"Why come in here blasting away like Wild Bill, then tell the chief to call the cops? I mean, you missing some screws upstairs or what?"

Frank clutched at his chest. There it was. The big one. It was coming. One more word from Marv and his heart would explode into a million tiny fragments.

"It doesn't make sense. If you really were an active shooter, then you'd have shot all of us by now. But you ain't kid. You ain't no shooter. So why put yourself through this? You know how this is going to end."

Carlos stayed quiet, the gun still at his side.

"I know you. You're Jose's kid. Aren't you?"

Carlos almost peed himself. He felt the familiar sensation of urine being released from his bladder and had to stop it with all his might.

"Your father and I go way back. Your brother's a priest, right? And your other brother's a lawyer? And you're a punk!"

The silence in the room was earthshattering. Carlos dropped his eyes to the floor.

"Your father told me about you. You like the high life, but you never wanted to work for it. You took the easy way out. The pussy way." Marv said. His gaze cutting holes into Carlos as if the old man were the reincarnation of Superman equipped with heat vision. "Now I can understand drug dealing. I don't like it, but I can understand it. But this?" Marv waved his hand towards Carlos. "I don't understand this. What the hell's wrong with you? Seriously? You got a death wish? Cause that's what's coming, kid. You hear it?" The sound of sirens wailing in the distance grew louder with each passing second. "Know what that is? That's the sound of you dying. That's the sound of your life ending in a hail of gunfire and for what?"

"You don't understand." Carlos said, his voice low and feeble. His eyes still studying the floor, wishing he could dive into the linoleum and escape.

"You're right. I don't. I'm totally fucking shocked. Pardon my French ladies." Marv said to the women in the room, who could have cared less by the use of the mother of all curse words. "So, what's your plan kid? Because the cavalry is coming and you're out of time."

Chapter 81

The station was deserted, as he had planned it to be. *Good job Carlos. Too bad you couldn't save the girl.* Tony thought. *Rule numero uno in crime, never under any circumstance leave a living witness.* He glanced down towards the body lying in the gutter. He touched her face with the point of his boot, nudging her chin, rotating her head. *Pretty girl.* He thought. But she made one crucial error in judgment -befriending a drug dealer. That never ends well.

There was only one squad car in the lot. Tony assumed it belonged to the sergeant stationed at the desk. It was a good guess. He had arrived across the street from the station only minutes ago. As soon as he had arrived and observed the stillness of the place, he had snapped Sabrina's neck like the stick of a popsicle. She was no longer of any use to him.

He hadn't witnessed the long caravan of blue and red lights leave. His goal was invisibility. He had taken a risk earlier and had paid for it. Paid dearly, principal plus interest. Of all the places and all the times, he, Tony, had to be right across the street from police HQ when his erstwhile comrade from Delta, a man he hadn't seen in twenty years, recognized him as he drove by. *Georgie Porgie.* He'd deal with him later.

Officer Mike stepped out of the shadows to Tony's right. Tony, the cold, dark man, never flinched. He had felt the cop coming as if he could actually hear the vibrations of Mike's shoes meeting the ice-covered pavement. Mike looked down at the girl and a sinister smile grew from the corners of his mouth.

"Awe. Poor thing. Glad I got to play around with her before she checked out."

Tony wanted to kill this punk so bad. He pictured pulling his gun and putting one between the crooked cop's eyes. It aroused him, nearly giving him a hard-on. *Later.* He told himself. Right now, he needed this asshole in blue to get him into the police station. Tony still had a job to do, but he had no intention of giving Mike any of the loot. The rule. Always follow the rule. Never leave a living witness and Mike was a living witness. By following the rule, Tony had become one of the most prolific hitmen in history, probably the most and he was so damn successful at it, that most of his killings went unnoticed, like random acts of violence or freak accidents. The key to his success was simple. *Trust no one. Stay invisible.* And the most crucial one of all -*No witnesses.*

"Guess that little brown piece of shit did what he was told." Mike observed that the station lot was empty. "You gonna leave her here." Mike pointed at the body of Sabrina. *Kind of stupid, leaving a dead body a hundred feet from police HQ.* He thought but didn't say.

Tony didn't answer. He just looked into Mike's face with those terrifying eyes. Black eyes, dead eyes. Tony pulled a black ski mask over his head and started to walk, casual like, across the street as if he had not a worry in the world. In front of him was salvation and the biggest payday he'd ever received. $3 million! Enough to set his life anew. Mike followed. He didn't wear a ski mask. He wasn't planning to return. Not after this. He would take his millions Tony had promised him and jet off. So, screw anonymity. Hell, he wanted these bastards he had had to endure on a daily basis to know who it was.

Tony stopped midstride, causing Mike to look around nervously.

"What is it? What'd you hear?" Mike asked, his voice shrill.

The freezing rain coated both of them, glazing them like succulent confections. Tony reached into his pocket and produced his cell phone. It vibrated in his hand.

"Fuck man!" Mike exclaimed. "Almost gave me a coronary."

Again, Tony's terrifying, haunted eyes stared at Mike with such loathing, such disdain, Mike turned away immediately.

Tony flipped the phone open.

"Yeah." He said in his cold tone.

The person on the other end muttered something. Tony stared straight ahead, listening intently, ignoring the ice falling from the sky. When the person was finished speaking, Tony pushed the end button.

"The plan has changed." He said. He started walking again.

"What changed? Who was that?"

"Take me to the holding cells." Tony commanded.

The glass entrance to police headquarters was dead ahead. Mike could see the obese desk sergeant busily answering the phone. The sergeant didn't look up when the doors opened.

"Havre de Grace police, Sergeant O'Hara speaking. Hello. Hello. What a night for pranksters." The sergeant said with disgust. Finally, he looked up. "Hey Mike what's going…" Tony shot him mid-sentence. Two rounds hit the sergeant's oil tanker of a chest millimeters apart. The sergeant gasped. A horrible noise exploded from deep in his gut. It was the sound of a dog that had been hit by a car, or a deer plugged with an archer's arrow, or an elephant brought down by a shotgun blast. Tony fired twice more. The sergeant's head ruptured, sending brain matter, bone fragments and gallons of dark red blood onto the floor.

Mike laughed, actually roared with deep, guttural guffaws. He always hated Sergeant O'Hara. *Big, fat Sergeant O'Hara. The chief's golden boy. Everybody bring a donut for sarge. Or better yet, bring Dunkin Donuts, the whole fucking store for this fat fuck.*

Tony wasn't amused. He caressed the trigger of the gun with his finger. He was in the zone. The killing zone. Anyone who crossed his path would be long gone before you could count the number of pure souls in church, which by the way is none, zero, but they'd be dead before they even got that far.

Mike saw the look. He noticed that finger on the trigger and his laughter died quicker than a set of batteries in a children's toy on Christmas morning. Mike started to conceive the feeling that maybe, just maybe, Carlos was right. Maybe Tony wasn't planning on cutting him in after all. Maybe the satanic man with the bad attitude was planning on double tapping him on his way out the door.

"Cellblock." Tony said, his voice as cold and dangerous as the weather.

Chapter 82

Walt sat up, and no one tried to stop him. Not this time. They were all too busy being terrified. There was no mistaking what they had just heard. Gunfire, plain and simple. Followed by howls of death and then more gunfire. Walt's head swirled like a twirled soft served ice cream. He felt sick to his stomach from the overwhelming fear for his boy and the traumatic head injury. He doubled over, sticking his head between his knees, but no vomit came up.

James, Kelly and Patty had their faces glued to the open door. They were scared. Frightened beyond belief. It was the silence that did it. The gunshots were bad, but the deathly quiet that followed was like the calm before the storm, and a storm *was* coming. The dark clouds were building on the horizon and the cracks of lightning and earth moving rumble of thunder could be heard clearly in the distance.

"Everybody stay calm." Walt managed to say in a low tone. His voice sounded groggy, like a man who had way too much to drink the night before.

Kelly was losing it. She trembled from head to foot. Her body shaking with a case of serious nerves. Tears were forming at the corners of her eyes, beginning their long descent down.

"Stay calm." Walt whispered. He held up his hand to make his point.

No sounds came from inside the station. No footsteps on the tile floor. No voices bouncing off the walls. No explosions of detonated gunpowder. Nothing. Just silence. Eerie silence.

Walt tried to stand up. He made it to his feet using the couch's arm to lift himself. It was no good. His legs wobbled like a rag doll, or jelly in an earthquake. *Jesus, my head feels like it's going to explode.* He thought, or better yet, tried to think. The words in his mind came out just as muddled as the words from his mouth. But he had to get up. He's a cop god-damn-it! He had to get to the hospital. Had to save his son. *Please God, save my boy. Get him out safely. Please. Jesus, please.* He pleaded, lifting his head up as much as he could to peer heavenward. He hoped God hadn't taken a vacation, sure as shit seemed like He had, especially considering the last three days in this town.

"You got to sit down Walt." Patty said. She had just noticed that her patient was standing.

"No. No!" Walt shouted in a loud whisper. The rest of them peered at the open door as if someone would walk in any minute. "I've got to."

Patty stopped resisting and returned to staring out into the quiet station.

"Who do you think is out there?" James whispered.

"I don't know." Patty replied, her eyes never leaving their post.

James moved with cat-like agility, tiptoeing over to the hallway and risking a look see. The hallway leading to the lounge was empty. There was no sound either. Just dead silence.

"I'm going to go peek." James whispered.

"No!" Kelly, Patty and Walt exclaimed in hushed tones.

James waved them off with his hand. His body was halfway through the door frame and into the desolate hall, when Walt grabbed his sleeve.

"I'll be fine." James whispered, but Walt didn't let go.

"You know how to use this?" Walt asked, placing a loaded Glock 19, handle first, into James' hand. Walt wanted to keep the gun on him but knew he couldn't hit the broadside of a battleship in his condition.

James squeezed the gun's handle and nodded. "I used to go to the range a lot." Kelly and Patty shook their heads in disagreement. The tears that had begun only moments before on Kelly's beautiful face had converged to form a steady stream which threatened to become a gushing river.

"Good. Don't get killed." Walt commanded weakly, sitting back down.

James entered the hallway. He tiptoed, taking care with each step, the gun pointed forward in a stellar impression of the classic law enforcement shooting stance. He hoped the hours of leisure he had spent, plucking the controls of his Xbox 360 playing Call of Duty, would come to his aid in a time like this. But then again it was a game. No game, TV show, movie or even book could prepare one for something like this. Not in a million years. James discovered that dreadful truth as he approached the end of the corridor. It was different in a game. There if you die, you come back, you might lose points, but you'd come back; here you just died.

The station was still like the morning after a heavy snowfall. His ears listened for anything, something, to give him an indication of exactly what he might be up against. Maybe whoever had fired the shots had left. That was a possibility. Pretty good one in fact, now that James pondered it. *The guy probably got cold feet. Fired a couple of rounds then high tailed it out of here.* It was a comforting thought.

He reached the corner, leaning his back against the wall, trying to make himself blend in. What he would give right now to have a little of Griffin's invisible serum. Just a little. Short term invisibility.

It was the *looking* that paralyzed him. James could have remained against the wall forever, letting the voices in his head duke it out. *Let it all pass. It's nothing. Just stay here and don't get shot. Come on! You're better than this. The people in that room need you. Kelly needs you. Come off it coward!*

James gathered every ounce of his courage, took a gigantic breath, and peered around the corner. Nothing. Empty. He could see the countless desks and computer terminals. He could see the glass enclosure that housed the conference room. He could see the doors of the two interrogation rooms along the opposite wall. That brought back an uncomfortable feeling in the pit of his stomach. He had found himself in one of the rooms earlier that day, on the side of the table no law-abiding citizen would ever want to be. Things had really changed and in such a short amount of time. He went from being a suspected criminal being questioned about a double homicide to a savior whose bravery was being tested in a pit of fire.

He took one more look around the room. The coast was most certainly clear. He moved, swinging the gun back and forth in wide arches. If anything stirred, he'd shoot. No questions, no greetings, he'd just pull the trigger until the slide locked back. But nothing moved.

Suddenly an ear-piercing squawk came from the radio on the sergeant's desk. James jumped, almost coming out of his boots. The hair on his arms, back and head stood up like soldiers being called to attention. He froze there, in an imitation of a wax museum dummy. Only his eyes moved, back and forth, back and forth, scanning the room. The radio screamed again, gargled words spewing forth, being answered by more gargled words. *Damn that thing!* James thought. He kept going, the sergeant's desk was now a few feet away. The desk was separated from the rest of the station by a large half wall, that stretched from one side of the station to the other. This acted as a partition, shielding the going-ons of the station from visitors, until, and James had recently had that experience, you were unceremoniously invited back, usually in handcuffs.

James approached the half wall. His heart was pounding hard and fast. He could feel it leaving his rib cage and climbing into his throat. He swallowed, trying to push it back down. If it were going to happen, it would happen as soon as he jutted his head around the corner of the wall. He knew it. He could feel it. Sense impending disaster. If someone had killed the sergeant, then they were probably right on the other side, crouching over the body. He didn't want to look. Decided life was a little too precious, but again his conscience won out and he looked. Hair, forehead, then eyes and then he saw. The front entrance was empty, however behind the desk, to James' horror, was the blood-soaked body of the sergeant.

James tiptoed over. The scene was grotesque like a Quinton Tarantino movie, all blood and no dialogue. The heavy-set sergeant bled from his head, mouth and chest. James had never in his life witnessed anything so evil. And he'd *seen* some things. He remembered seeing that kid get hit by a truck when he was eleven. He remembered watching a car accident where the driver's head was decapitated by the sunroof when the guy's car flipped. He remembered watching a football game, where one of the players was hit so bad, he ruptured his spleen and died right there on the field, but this, this sickening scene of murder turned his stomach full tilt. He looked down and watched as a glob of brain matter drooled out of the sergeant's torn open skull, hitting the ground with a splatter. James covered his mouth with his hand holding the gun. He felt sick, as if his stomach would empty its contents all over the tiled floor. A second later he forgot all about the sergeant, the blood, the guts and everything else for that matter.

Two more gunshots pierced the air, emanating from the back of the station and causing James to do something that would significantly alter his chances for survival. He lifted his gun -pure amateur hour reaction- and fired, sending the entire clip into the half wall.

Chapter 83

Tony sauntered through the empty station as if he owned the joint, which in essence he did. The fat guy at the front desk was now working the fryers in hell's kitchen, serving up salacious snacks for Satan and his hoard of demons. Tony was alone, well, except that idiot cop that led the way. Man, what he wouldn't give to get rid of that asshole. The way he had laughed at the sergeant's demise. Very sick behavior. Psychotic behavior. *Throw on a straight jacket and into the padded room* behavior. Tony wasn't a sicko. He was a murderer, that was true but sicko, he wasn't. He killed purely for profit, selling death as a stockbroker sells shares. The guys like that idiot cop Mike, made him want to spit his guts up. Guys like Mike weren't out for profit, they were out for pleasure. The kind of assholes you read about strangling little kids or dragging blacks behind their lifted pickup trucks. Guys like Mike were impossible to comprehend, like a hunter that kills but doesn't eat. There's no logic to it. It's a perverse practice.

Mike had no clue why Tony wanted to see the holding cells and he didn't ask. As far as he knew there was no one in the damn cells. Not unless someone had gotten locked up while he was off duty. Maybe a drunk or two but that was it. Mike led him there anyway. He just followed orders like the SS commanders after they were caught with their pants down; their pale faces and blonde heads, sitting in front of the Nuremberg judges swearing up and down that they didn't believe in what their Führer spewed, that they were just following orders.

The Havre de Grace police station had four concrete holding cells studded with steel bars. Four was a small number compared to the overly crowded big city booking centers, but this was good old Havre de Grace, and four had always been enough. The prisoners that were housed here weren't housed for very long. The longest a prisoner ever spent here was a week, before being transferred out to the Harford County Corrections Center in Forest Hill.

To Mike's amazement, there was a prisoner in one of the cells. He could see her as they approached. She was middle-aged and somewhat pretty in a dominatrix kind of way. The woman sat like a block of stone on the bench in the last cell. She glanced up. Her look conveyed a quiet intelligence, not something that would be visualized often in the riff-raff usually arrested in Havre de Grace.

"Friend of yours?" Mike asked.

Tony didn't answer.

"You want me to let her out?"

Again, Tony didn't answer. It was really starting to piss Mike off. He hated the quiet, sinister types. Hated them because he feared them, and he was deathly afraid of the quiet man that he had personally witnessed kill two people so far. Well, kill one, the girl was already dead, but still, you didn't need to have a degree in molecular physics to figure Tony had cancelled her reservation as well.

The woman took in the two men as a person takes in a moth that has landed on a window screen. Not interested, only slightly aroused. That expression changed to one of abstract terror when the woman looked into the hard, satanic eyes of Tony. She jumped from the bench and dove into the corner, cowering like a wounded child. She said something, but the words were inaudible. It sounded to

Mike's uneducated ears like a different language. Not English. Something foreign, something eastern.

"You want me to let her out?" Mike repeated.

Tony answered him, not in words, but in gunshots, two gunshots, aimed into the cell. The bullets ripped through the woman's chest and forehead, decorating the wall with blood and brains.

"What the fu-" Mike began, but his words were drowned out by a cacophony of gunfire that erupted from the direction of the front doors, and just like that, both men realized they were not alone.

Chapter 84

What was his plan? He didn't have a clue. No idea. He had floated here, as if he were in a dream, or more like a nightmare. The winds of disaster had carried him to this very spot. The rest had come as a result of pure instinct and maybe a degree of conscience thrown in for good measure. His future… that was a laugh. He had always lived for the here and now. Get drunk now. Get high now. Get laid now. Make money now. Fuck the future. Live like there's no tomorrow and now this old geezer with the smart mouth wanted to know what he was planning to do.

Carlos took a deep breath and glanced up from the floor. A second later, he wished he hadn't. The power in that old man's eyes. Holy crap. It was like peering into a deep pool with no discernable bottom, just a sea of blackness.

"So, whatcha gonna do, punk?" Old Man Marv said as if he were attempting an impression of Clint Eastwood.

The sirens had stopped. Car doors opened and then slammed shut. Carlos could picture the boys in blue with their choppers set to full auto, waiting for his brown ass to emerge from the structure. Then they would flick him from the shelf of existence onto the floor of forever. Where he would go from there was anyone's guess, but if Carlos were a betting man, he'd put a hundred to one on himself, that he would end up feeding wood to the everlasting flame of eternal damnation. *Drug dealers don't go to heaven.* The voice of his brother the priest said in his head. head. A statement that he had heard the clergyman utter to his own face from time to time. What would his brother say now? *I told you, mom and dad, Carlos is a bad seed. A terrible seed. One of the worst seeds I've ever had the misfortune of seeing, let alone being siblings with.*

"This is the Havre de Grace police department!" Someone shouted into a bullhorn. "Drop your weapon and come out with your hands up!"

Time was up. It was now or never. If the cops came in, he was a goner. The only thing he had going for him was a room full of hostages, and these were 24-carat gold hostages. The town council and the chief of police. Surely, the cops wouldn't risk the lives of the council let alone their own chief. Carlos didn't think so, or at least he prayed that wasn't the case.

Either way he looked at it, he was a dead man. If the cops came through the door, they'd shoot him down like a ravenous dog. And if by some miracle -like winning the Mega millions, the Powerball and getting struck by lightning ten times in the same place- he made it out of here alive and free, then Tony would kill him. No question about that. He knew that like he knew it was icing outside. It was just a fact. He had one chance. One last toss of the dice and he took it.

"So?" Old Man Marv said.

Carlos told him everything. He started by admitting his life of crime: the drugs, the cash, the guns and the murder of Eddie. The people around the table listened intently. They hung on every word. To them, it was probably like watching a really juicy episode of Jerry Springer. *So, you were a drug dealer, who killed a guy because he was threatening to snitch on you. Interesting. Interesting. Tell me, Carlos, do you feel any remorse for what you've done?* Carlos could feel the eyes of the council on him, a sensation of being burned, slowly cooked over a fire, rotated on a spit. His face never left Marv's. There was a bond there as there is between an Uncle and a nephew or a teacher and a student. Familiarity and trust.

Carlos told Marv about Tony. How Tony had shown up out of nowhere, appearing like the ghost of Christmas future. How Tony had him running errands for him like following Detective Patterson. How Tony had flipped out over some box that had been recovered from the scene of a double homicide. He told Marv about Officer Mike, which seemed of particular interest to Chief John. The Chief's face became so red he could have played the role of a hot pepper in the next Chipotle's TV ad. And last but not least, he told Marv about Sabrina, about her severed finger and the ultimatum that had landed him in this very room. He told them about Tony's plan to assault the police station and retrieve the box.

"He's there right now?" The chief asked.

"Yes." Carlos responded, looking at his shoes.

"Shit!" The chief exclaimed. "And I bet you every damn cop in the station is standing outside."

Marv, his eyes still menacing and tough, turned to face the chief. "Call off your dogs." Marv commanded.

"Wait a freaking minute." Frank Duisenberg said. "You mean to tell me, you believe this guy? What the hell Marv! He's full of shit! First, he comes in here and starts shooting. Threatens our lives." Frank motioned to the council. "Then tells us some bullshit tale when the police arrive, and he knows he's fucked. My apologies ladies. But you do. You do know you're fucked."

Carlos' shoulders drooped. He was finished. He'd said his piece. He had gone all in on a really shitty hand. A two, a four, a six, a jack and a queen and only two of them were the same suit. But he wasn't bluffing. Everything he had said was true. Everything.

"I do." The two words left Old Man Marv's wrinkled lips without a second's hesitation.

"You believe him?" Frank sounded bewildered, shocked into incoherence. "I…I…mean… you really fucking believe this punk? Jesus Marv."

"Yes. I do." Marv answered again. Absolute surety in his voice. "You know why I believe him?" He waited for Frank to answer but Frank looked too flummoxed to speak. "Because he didn't kill any of us."

"He shot at us Marv." Alice said, putting in her two cents.

"No, he shot at the ceiling. Then he told the chief here to call in the cops."

"I can't call them off Marv." Chief John spoke up. "It doesn't work like that." The chief held up his hand. "Don't get me wrong. I do believe him, for the same reasons you do. I get it. I understand your back is against the wall. You were trying to save your girl. I get that. But I still can't just call it off." He said looking up at Carlos. "What am I supposed to tell them? That it was all a misunderstanding? It was a prank pulled off by some Youtuber? There are twenty cops out there. Twenty cops who risked their lives driving here in this beautiful weather we're having. Plus, I'm a man of law and order and I took an oath. This kid is an admitted murderer. An admitted drug dealer. I can't just let that slide." The chief swallowed a great big gulp of saliva, praying Carlos wouldn't kill him for uttering those last words.

Marv gripped his walker and nodded his head up and down solemnly.

"He's got a point." The old man said, turning back to face Carlos.

Carlos looked at Marv, then at the chief. He couldn't go to prison. That would mean twenty years of being porked relentlessly in the shower rooms. Demeaned, humiliated, beat-up, raped. He couldn't do it. He wouldn't do it. On the other hand, he had already accepted the other route, his destiny. The quicker this situation was resolved, the faster the cops could return to the station, kill Tony and Mike and save Sabrina.

"Do me a favor." Carlos pleaded. "Save Sabrina. She's probably already dead. But…" He let his words trail off. "Please save her and Mr. Marv…" He said, choking on his words.

"Yeah, kid."

"Tell my brother… tell my brother I turned it around at the end. Tell him that. He'll understand."

"Wait a minute kid." Marv said. He began to rise from his chair, his hands holding tight to the walker for support.

Carlos didn't wait. He took one last deep breath then took off running towards the door.

"Kid! Kid! Stop kid!" Marv shouted, his old voice stranded with overuse.

Carlos heard the old man's pleas die away as he ran through the door, using his shoulder as a battering ram. He emerged outside, and a thousand lights hit him full in the face. *Damn, they were bright.* He could barely make out the blurry images of police cars with their blue and red flashing strobes parked haphazardly before him. He couldn't see the cops at all. But he knew they were there. Knew they had their semiautomatic pistols aimed at him, coiled like snakes, ready to strike. He thought of something just then. A line. A line from a movie. A line he had used a thousand times with the ladies. Probably the best line ever uttered in any movie since movies were invented, whenever the fuck that was. He imagined saying it to Sabrina. Tipping his top hat, looking into her beautiful blue eyes and saying *Here's looking at you kid.* Carlos smiled his last smile before he lifted the hand holding the gun and got off one shot into the cloudy night sky.

Chapter 85

James ran back into the lounge. His heart was racing like a Ferrari F50 rounding the final lap, gunning its engine down the straightaway, heading for the finish line. The shade of Walt's face was pale green. He stood, trembling. Patty and Kelly looked terrified. Their faces weren't green. They were white as if all the blood had left their bodies.

"What... the... hell was that?!" Walt blurted out under immense strain.

"We've got to hide!" James roared. No more whispering. It didn't matter. The people who had killed the detective, they were coming. James was sure of it. If they hadn't known the station wasn't as empty as it seemed, they sure as hell knew now. Thanks to him. He cursed himself. Actually, cussed himself out. *You stupid fucking fool! You idiot! You moron! Mine as well have hung a fucking flag on the door! Hey, come get the assholes in the employee lounge! We're over here! Come kill us!*

"What happened?" Kelly shrieked. "What's going on?" She was in full-blown panic mode. She had completely surpassed reasonableness. Not that James could blame her. Her hands pulled at her hair like a raving madman.

"Look, no time to explain!" James shouted. "Just hide. Please just hide."

Walt vomited. A putrid jet of hot acid shot from his mouth onto the floor showering James' boots. Normally, that was something that would have garnered instant revulsion from the other people in the room, but under the present circumstances… well let's just say a steaming puddle of puke was the least of their worries. In fact, James and Kelly didn't notice it all as if people shooting jets of sick out of their mouths was a common occurrence, as common as someone scratching their brow. Patty noticed and she quickly ran over and helped Walt sit down.

"He's not going anywhere." Patty stated.

"Then he's dead. We're all dead. They killed the sergeant. Shot him in the head. I saw it with my own eyes. His brains were on the floor." James grabbed the top of his skull as if to tell the veteran coroner just where the brain should be.

"Oh my God! Oh my God!" Kelly shrieked.

"You take her." James said to Patty. "Take her and hide. Please. I'll stay with Walt."

"But…" Patty began.

"No buts. Just go. Go now. They're coming." James said urgently. "Walt, do you have any extra magazines?" He asked. Walt was incapable of answering. James didn't wait. He checked the man's utility belt, searching until he found two extra magazines strapped in a holder on the side. James removed one. He ejected the Glock's spent clip and inserted the fresh mag. Then he punched the slide release, chambering a fresh round. He handed the gun to Patty.

"You need…" She began.

James shook his head. "They already know I'm here. If I'm armed... Stay hidden. Stay safe. Go!"

Patty went. She grabbed crazy Kelly by the shoulder and led her into the hall. Patty glanced around.

The coast was clear, for now. She dragged Kelly down the hall away from the station's main room. There were bathrooms down there and a janitor's closet. The janitor's closet would be too small for them. She pushed opened the door to the women's restroom and shoved the weeping Kelly inside.

Tony walked with determination. He didn't know what he would find. He knew someone else was here but who and how many? The front lobby was empty except for the body of the desk sergeant. Tony looked at the partition wall. It was riddled with holes. *Amateur hour.* He thought. *Good. That makes things much less complicated.* A police veteran might be able to put up a good fight, maybe even win, although Tony seriously doubted it. But a cop that unloads his weapon into a wall, that would be a piece of cake, a walk in the park, not even a workout for the ex-Delta commando. He only had to find him.

The station had an open floor plan. The conference room was made of glass. The desks were open at the bottom. Not many places to hide there.

"Where are the bathrooms?" Tony asked.

Officer Mike pointed. "Two there and two by the lounge."

Tony took off at a trot. This was a serious complication. He had already been there for three minutes which was two minutes and thirty seconds longer than he had anticipated. And he still had his original task to accomplish. Find the box. That's why he was here to begin with. Not this bullshit. He would have to find the amateur cop fast, dispose of him then find the damn box before every cop in Havre de Grace returned, transforming the place into an active war zone.

The set of bathrooms off from the station's main room were empty. Tony kicked open every stall. Nothing but white porcelain. He had posted Mike outside to make sure that nothing moved while he searched. It would be just his luck tonight to search one set of bathrooms, only to have the amateur-hour cop sneak up behind him and this time put a bullet in his head instead of the damn wall.

"Where are the others?" Tony asked. Mike pointed to the opposite end of the station where a long hallway disappeared into the distance.

"Lounge, bathrooms, locker rooms and a mop closet." Mike said but Tony wasn't listening, he had already started in that direction.

The hallway was empty. Tony paused for a second to listen. No sounds could be heard. Complete silence. He walked cautiously, waving his gun back and forth, covering every inch. He could see the bathrooms and the mop sink at the end of the hall. The lounge was to his right a few feet away. The door to the lounge stood open, held back by a small kickstand that looked strained from overuse. He stopped just shy of the open door. Mike was behind him. The crooked cop had his gun out. Tony hoped Mike wouldn't shoot him in a moment of confused panic. If it were another team member like George, well, that would be a different story. No worries at all with Georgie covering your ass. Complete trust in your fellow teammate. It was the training. Minutes, hours, days, weeks, years of constantly rehearsing the same drills over and over again until they became second nature like riding a bike or tying a shoe. Engrained within your core. Tony didn't trust Mike at all. Cops don't train like team members. Sure, they have a crash course on assaulting hostile locations but it's just not the same. Tony remembered an incident from his time in the army. A young recruit named Victor Gillibrand, true blue dumbass. Arrogant son of a bitch. Victor was a cop or had been a cop before he joined. Victor thought he knew everything. How to do assaults. How to fight. How to shoot. Well, the shooting wasn't an issue. Every cop in the world is a better shot than most of the newly minted army soldiers. It was the assaulting element that was the problem. Victor just didn't know how to stack up. He always managed to shoot the guy in front of him in the stack which most of the time was Tony. It had only been a paintball gun, but still, the lesson was crystal clear -cops just don't have the same professional expertise as team members.

Tony signaled Mike to follow him. Then Tony pointed at Mike's gun and made a gesture with his hands that said: *Don't fuck up. Keep that hole puncher pointed skyward.* Mike nodded in agreement. He hadn't really understood what Tony was saying with his hands, but the stealthy assassin's eyes were loud and clear. Mike understood full well that if he made a mistake and shot Tony, he, Mike, was as good as dead.

Tony went in. He checked left, nothing. It took a little under two seconds. He checked straight, nothing, then he checked right, and he saw them. His finger gripped the trigger but he didn't fire. The training had set in. His eyes fell on the two men, one who looked totally messed up with a bandage on his head and the other, a suave black man who looked like a plainclothes detective. Both men weren't armed. Their hands, which were placed on their knees as they sat, were bare. They looked scared. Tony didn't lower his weapon. Armed or not the two men seated on the couch were threats.

"We're unarmed!" James shouted. He had never in his life seen anyone like the man standing before him. This man was the absolute epitome of death. The man was dressed head to toe in black. He wore a black ski mask that added to his fearsome appearance. But it was the man's eyes, those cold, black, dead eyes, that sent chills up James' spine. Mike walked in. James cringed.

"Ho ho ho. Look what we have here." Mike said joyfully. "Officer Walt and the nigger. Where's your girl nigger?" Mike taunted, throwing around the racial slur like a redneck straight out of the 1950s.

James remained silent and still. He desperately wanted to diffuse the situation. Not add to it, but that was already a moot point. His very presence was throwing gasoline on Mike's ready-made fire.

Mike walked over. He bent down so his face was on the same level as James'. Mike put the barrel of the gun up to James' chin. The ski mask hid the crooked cops smile, but James knew Mike was grinning from ear to ear. A big, shit eating grin, as if he had just scratched the last number on the card and realized he had won a million bucks.

"Got your videotape nigger? Gonna tape me? Why don't you tape me blowing your fucking head off? How 'bout that?" Mike pushed the gun deeper into James' chin. "How 'bout that?" He repeated. Mike turned to Walt. "What happened to you officer?" Mike said with the maximum amount of sarcasm he could muster. "Patterson ain't here to save you. Not this time. That's too bad. Too damn bad."

"Knock it off." Tony commanded. Mike reluctantly complied, stepping back. "Who shot the gun?" His cold stare looked from James to Walt waiting for an answer.

"I did." James answered.

"Where is it?"

"I threw it down after I shot it." James lied. He hoped the eyes of this terrifying evil man hadn't detected his lie.

"I didn't see it." Tony said. He thought back. He hadn't really checked though. Maybe the gun had been there. It could have slid to some hidden corner after it was tossed. It was possible.

James shrugged his shoulders. "I threw it." He said looking directly into the ski-masked face, trying to convey sincerity.

"He's lying!" Mike exclaimed.

Tony ignored him. "Who are you?"

"The weatherman."

This took Tony aback. "The weatherman? What the hell is a weatherman doing in the middle of a police station at this time of night with an ice storm raging outside?"

"Visiting me." Walt said.

Mike shrieked with laughter. "I could have guessed that. Friends with a nigger. Now that's fucking funny."

Mike continued to laugh, a sick cackle. The sound of witches brewing cauldrons of children's bones.

Tony knew what he had to do. No witnesses. Ski mask or not. It was his rule. Living witnesses were a problem. He raised the gun and took aim. Then he stopped. Just stopped. He had heard something. A name, spoken, not shouted, from inside the station. A name he hadn't heard in years, vocalized by a voice from his past. The voice only said it once, because once was enough. Tony lowered his aim and walked out of the room.

Chapter 86

"Anthony." George said. He stood alone in the main room of the station amidst an army of desks. Patterson had remained outside, which took a great deal of convincing on George's part.

"This is something I have to do alone." George had told Patterson when the detective had insisted on accompanying George into the station.

"It's my house." Patterson had said in rebuttal.

"That's true, but this guy is beyond anything you've ever experienced. This guy can out shoot and out fight every cop on the force combined. It's got to be me."

"What the hell did you do in the army?"

"It's a long story. Maybe I'll tell you sometime."

Patterson handed George his gun. George slid back the slide, ejected the magazine, and checked the firearm as if it were a part of his anatomy like one of his appendages. He held up the gun and checked the sights then he nodded at Patterson, turned on his heels and walked inside.

"Good luck. Try not to get killed." Patterson's words died, swallowed whole by the wind and the rain.

The last great warriors. Two men who had been honed until they were razor sharp, until their abilities could slice a hair from top to bottom. Experts in their craft. How many of them were left? They had been a part of the team. Not originals. They weren't old enough for that. They weren't there when that guy named Charlie had convinced the high command that the US needed some of those crazy boys, boys like those SAS guys over there in the UK. Kind of like the SEALs, but not really, hell those Navy boys love the water way too much. The team would be born from the Army. Breed from the howling wolves of the 82nd, 101st and the baddest muthas of them all, the Rangers. That's where they had come from. The two of them. Straight out of the Rangers, thrown into a pit amongst the biggest and meanest wolves the Rangers could produce, slashed, tormented and mauled, and the ones that had survived, the last two out of a hundred, made it to the team. That had been them. The last two. Tony and George. Brothers from boot camp who climbed mount *Eat you alive* and made it all the way to the top.

The two men faced each other, their guns aimed with expert hands. Triggers squeezed with only an ounce to spare. They stared into each other's eyes, like two wild beasts in a standoff.

"How long has it been?" Tony asked.

"Twenty-two years." George replied.

"Good to see you again brother." Tony said. Neither of them relinquished their grip on their respective firearms. Neither willing to give an inch. An inch in this game was your life.

"Likewise." George replied. "What are you doing here Anthony?"

"Working. You?"

"Same. I've heard things." George said.

"Gossip. You always liked a good story, George."

"So, what now?" George asked, his eye peering down the handgun's sight. "What happened to you brother?"

Tony smiled. The ski mask covered it, but George could tell. When you fought alongside someone for ten years, you pick up on his eccentricities.

"Just trying to make a living."

"Protecting mass murderers."

"They pay very well." Tony was sure what the inevitable conclusion would be to this conversation. Two alpha male wolves don't just walk away from each other. That's not how life is. They fight to the death. Rip out each other's jugular veins. Leave each other bleeding in the snow. The first to bleed out loses. He was confident. Nervous, which was a sensation he wasn't accustomed to, but confident. George had been better. No bullshit. George was always the better operator. But that was twenty years ago. Since then, Tony had continued to hone his craft in the private sector, while George had quit being a wolf. Still, Tony was nervous. What if a wolf never forgot how to bite? What if a wolf remembered what blood tasted like? The salty sweet taste. Does it ever leave? Can a wolf ever forget?

"Mass murderers." George said again. Hoping he could bring Tony around. Knowing he could not.

"That shit over there fucked with your head. You never walked away, did you? It still haunts you. That's bad brother. Real bad. You got to let it go."

The conversation ceased for a time. A few seconds that felt like years.

"What now?" George asked.

"You walk away. Leave me to finish my job, my mission."

George started to shake his head before Tony finished his sentence. "No more missions Tony. The war's over. Time to go home."

"Not for me."

That was it. Three words. Three final words before the bullets started flying.

Chapter 87

"Funny how life works out. Ain't it?" Mike said.

James didn't answer. He was confused. *Why had the other guy left?* James had known he was going to die. He had read it in the guy's eyes. It was like looking into a grave and seeing your face on the corpse in the coffin. A premonition. James had cringed, waiting for the shot to hit him. Wondering if he would feel it. *Would it hurt? Would he die immediately? Would his soul rise to touch the face of God or would he remain on this planet to walk amongst the ashes of a world gone by?* But the guy had just stopped. The bullet had never come. The puff of smoke, the copper warhead, the end, had never come. He remained tethered to his body like the moors of a ship destined to survive the hurricane.

"Hey asshole, I'm talking to you!" Mike exclaimed. He walked over to James and backhanded him. James didn't flinch. *Maybe this guy was fucked up. Maybe he hadn't slept with Kelly. Maybe it was an act.* Mike thought, looking down at the black face that hadn't moved when he slapped it.

"Where is she?" Mike asked.

James remained silent, as still as stone.

"Where?!" Mike slapped him again but again James didn't flinch, staring straight ahead as if in a trance, a place within his own mind, not here, not anywhere.

Mike decided it was pointless to continue with this asshole. He moved on to Walt.

"What happened to you poncho? This nigger fuck you up?" Mike asked letting out a snort of laughter at his own joke.

Walt, his head still woozy, his mind at sea like a ship on a giant swell, tried to give his best angry glare. It didn't come out well. "Fuck you asshole." Walt uttered, which warranted him a backhanded slap from the crooked cop. Walt flinched. Despite him being twice the size of James, Walt's condition intensified the slap, transforming it into a punch from the likes of Muhammad Ali. Walt's head broke sideways into whiplash territory, hard and fast. Mike cocked back for another one, enjoying his momentary triumph over his much larger opponent. Mike's arm came down again, swishing through the air like a whip, before the back of Mike's hand could make contact with Walt's wounded head, James held up his arm and took the brunt of the blow. Mike's forearm pounded hard against James, causing the crooked cop to recoil with the pain. Mike grasped the forearm with his gun hand. Now, he was pissed, angry beyond belief. His eyes appearing like tiny balls of hellfire.

"You're gonna pay for that." He said through gritted teeth. He straightened up, lifted his gun and pointed it directly at James' head.

"Say goodbye nigger." Mike spat. His finger tightened on the trigger. Then there was a blast.

James flinched. He didn't feel the bullet. *Maybe that was better.* He thought. He looked down at his body and saw that it was covered in blood. His head began to feel heavy. His heart pounded with the last beats of life like a drummer sounding out the last stand of a tired army before it's defeat at the hands of the victor. He knew this was it. He didn't feel the pain. *No pain. Thank God for that.* He took a deep breath, probably his last. He sucked in the air like a man in the desert drinks his last gulp of water, savoring every ounce of it. Feeling it enter his mouth, how it blew through his teeth. How it tasted on his tongue. How it felt going down his throat. How his muscles in his chest expanded. Then he looked up and was instantly relieved by what he saw. A little confused but unbelievably relieved.

What he saw was as unexpected and unbelievable as seeing a unicorn rearing its haunches at him. The face with the hellfire eyes was replaced by a face with a ghastly wound. Smoke and blood poured from the wound before the body of the crooked cop collapsed, folding in on itself like a suit of clothes held up by air. Behind the body stood Patty, the Glock in her hand still smoking from the recently fired shell. Her look was as hard as Superman's chest. Her hands shook uncontrollably, but there was a smile on those thin lips. A smile that said, *So long asshole.*

Chapter 88

George heard him laughing. He saw him laughing. That was the video that played in George's mind. Tony laughing. At first, George had the thought the man must have lost his mind. It wasn't funny. The whole goddamn situation wasn't comical at all. And yet Tony had laughed. And that laugh. That sickening, evil laugh would stick in George's head for the next two decades. And that's what came to George's mind as he squared off against his old teammate.

Each one waited for the other to move. Waiting for the other to let his guard down for the briefest of seconds. They were matched, equal in skill, shooting abilities and hand to hand combat, although Tony always thought George was the better of the two. Tony focused on George's eyes. If the man blinked, the game would be Tony's and Tony's alone.

This had to end soon. Tony had to complete his mission. That's the way his life worked. One mission after another. He had gone from the team to the private sector, his life a series of missions. He had no wife, no kids, no relatives at all. His mother had been a drunk. She died when he was nine. He never knew his dad. The sperm donor had flown the coop when Tony was one. He never wrote. Never sent money and never tried to seek out his son. That was fine with Tony. He wasn't quite sure what he would do anyway if his father decided to make a sudden reappearance in his life. Probably kill him, as he had done with countless others. When his mother died, Tony became a ward of the state. He bounced around from one foster home to another. He had no interests. No hobbies. He did fairly well in school but lacked the discipline to excel.

Maybe if I had gone to college… No, no, no. No maybes anymore. No regrets. His first taste of solid discipline was in the army, and he surpassed all expectations. He rose quickly like a teenager's dick when he sees anything with shapely curves pass by. The army was his home, and he loved it. The missions became his life's barometer, dictating how he should wear his clothes and what he could eat and where he could go. If the mission failed, he failed. And in the last forty plus years, he had never failed. He wasn't about to start now.

The shot rang out. Loud, ear deafening shot. The echo bounced from wall to wall. That's when the man whose life was a series of successful missions made his costliest mistake. It was subtle but unmistakable. Tony flinched. His eye left the sights of his handgun for a tenth of a second, but in a game like this, that was like an eternity. George didn't hesitate. He depressed the trigger. The bullet flew out of the barrel and crossed the twenty feet of computer terminals and cubicles. It entered Tony's skull, crushing the bridge of his nose, tearing a wide gaping tunnel through his brain and exited out the rear in a pink cloud of blood. Tony stood there momentarily in total shock. His eyes wide. His mouth agape. Then he crumpled to the floor. Game over.

Patty, Kelly and James ran into the room. George held up his hand for them to stop. He walked up to Tony's body, taking his time, the gun in his hand aimed precisely at Tony's chest, just in case. George looked down at the body. Tony was dead. He kicked Tony's gun out of his hand. It clattered across the floor. Then George lowered his own weapon and looked up into the faces before him. The first thing he noticed was James. The young man was covered in blood and tissue that looked remarkably similar to brain matter.

"Where's the other one?" George said. His gut told him there was one more.

"Dead." Patty said matter-of-factly.

"You?"

Patty nodded. She too still had a gun in her hand. George looked down at it. Patty recoiled and dropped it as if she had forgotten the damn thing was there.

"You okay?" George asked, looking into the face of the coroner.

"Yeah."

"You tough lady." George said. "Been through the ringer these last couple of days."

Patty nodded.

"And what the hell happened to you?" George asked looking at James.

Patterson burst into the station with about twenty heavily armed police officers. The big detective led the group around the partition wall. Their guns were up and out. Locked, cocked and ready to rock.

George dropped the gun in his hand. "Put your hands up!" He shouted at Patty, James and Kelly. All four raised their hands to the roof.

Patterson and the cops saw them. He lowered his gun.

"Lower your guns!" He shouted at the cops around, some of whom looked like the lions in the Colosseum with their teeth bared, waiting for the Christians to be marched in. "God damn it! I said lower your guns!" They listened. "Everybody okay?" Patterson asked.

George's hands returned to his side and as if on cue, James', Kelly's and Patty's did the same.

"We're good. This is Tony." George said as if the man lying on the ground in a puddle of blood would stand up and shake Patterson's hand.

"Nice to meet you Tony. What happened to your face?" Patterson joked.

No one laughed.

"Geez. Lighten up people. The bad guys are dead. Everyone's alive. It's a good day."

George smiled.

"And what the hell happened to you?" Patterson asked James.

James piped up to answer, clearing his throat.

"Hey detective, you might want to take a look at this." A uniformed cop called from the rear of the station near the holding cells.

"Tell me later kid." Patterson said to James before taking off at a trout with George following close behind.

"Holy shit." Patterson muttered. He was looking down at the corpse of the woman he had arrested earlier that day.

"So, that's what those shots were." James commented. "They must have done the sarge at the front desk before coming back here. Who is she?"

"Good question." Patterson answered woefully. "Jane freaking doe. The name was bogus. Belonged to a woman who was killed in a car accident years ago. She was with the guy I shot. She pulled a gun on me too."

"She obviously meant something to Tony." George commented.

Explain."

"Tony was never one to do anything outside of mission parameters. If she's dead, then he had a very good reason."

"Holy shit!" James exclaimed. "I forgot. The commotion, the shooting…"

"Spit it out!" Patterson spat. Angry that his conversation had been interrupted.

"The hospital. Right before Tony and Mike walked in, the hospital had called. They said people were dropping like flies."

"The hospital? Greater Hearts?" George asked.

"I guess. Walt said his kid was there."

"That's Greater Hearts." Patterson said glumly.

"We got to go. Right away." George started for the front.

Several members of the council, led by Frank Duisenberg, entered the doors of the station. They appeared awed at the violence that had transpired in their police station, *in their beloved town!* Joanne Bright and Phyllis Tannon stared at the body of Sergeant O'Hara. Hands holding white handkerchiefs covered their mouths. Old Man Marv had managed to maneuver his walker over to the partition wall and had stuck his gnarled old finger into the drill hole left by James' appalling marksmanship. Hardware Tom, his head as bald as the day he was born -just with a few more wrinkles- looked around like a kid in Toyland, his eyes wide, his mouth a gaping chasm. Frank noticed Patterson and walked over, blocking the detective from exiting.

"What the hell happened here Bill?" Frank asked.

Patterson pushed the ancient council member out of his way in a gentle, forceful manner.

"No time Frank. My apologies but no time." Patterson said. A group of officers had just walked through the door. Patterson hurried forward, intent on turning the group around.

"Head to the hospital. They need help evacuating." Patterson told the young men donned in ice-covered coats and salt covered pants. They looked tired, their eyes droopy but they stood straight, eager to serve.

"My son! My son! Bill, my son is over there." Officer Walt emerged from behind the partition wall. He could barely walk straight and was quickly grabbed by two uniforms standing nearby. They attempted to steady the big cop.

"It's okay Walt. We're heading there now." Patterson said, approaching the man he considered his protégé.

"The hospital?! What about the hospital?" Frank bellowed.

"They called. Said people were dying. Not sure why. Just a precaution." George said, holding up his hand. He didn't want to reveal what he really thought was happening over there. *Really bad time to have the council up in arms.*

"The bugs?" Frank gasped. "It's the bugs isn't it?" Joanne and Phyliss recoiled at Frank's words. A sudden silence had befallen over the nearby crowd. It seemed that everyone was holding their collective breaths.

"Not sure." George answered. He was almost a hundred percent sure that that was exactly the case but again he wanted to err on the side of caution.

"I'd take care of dem bugs. You mark my words sonny. They ain't seen what I got." Hardware Tom said. "No sir. Ain't seen it. No one has. I kept it, all these years. Not sure if it's even good anymore…" Tom droned on ignored by the others except for George, whose interest was piqued.

"Look we're going over there and we're going to get everyone out." Patterson said, mainly to Walt.

"I'm coming." Walt said, he struggled to free himself from the comforting, supporting hands of his fellow officers.

"Jesus Walt. You can barely move. You ain't coming. You're staying here. Everything will be fine."

"What about Sam?" Walt said.

Patterson walked over. He hugged Walt, his arms barely making it around the frame of the titan. "It'll be okay. I promise. I won't let you down. I love Sam. He'll be fine." Patterson whispered into Walt's ear.

Walt seemed to shrink a little. He slumped back into the arms of other officers. They guided him back behind the wall without another word. He was scared and Patterson was scared for him. Patterson had been so damn depressed the day Walt told him about Sam and his diagnosis. Walt didn't tell anyone, but he told Bill Paterson. Bill had always been a role model for Walt, taking him under his wing as a rookie and guiding him for the last fifteen years. And when your son gets diagnosed with cancer, you tell your role model, your confidant, about it. You've got to because if you keep it all to yourself, tucked inside, buried in a chest in the great desert of your heart, you're bound to explode at some point from the grief.

"Let's go." Patterson said. He hurried through the door before he could be stopped. Time was of the essence.

"What do you have in your basement?" George asked, turning to Hardware Tom.

"I got the good stuff." Tom said, with a toothless grin. "You wanna see?"

"I do." George replied.

Chapter 89

The first floor of Greater Hearts looked like something one would see in a horror film or on the Twilight Zone but what Patterson was seeing was real. It was happening. It wasn't something he could have picked up his trusty clicker and shut off if the images became too terrible, too disgusting. Bodies were strewn throughout the brightly lit halls. They laid exactly where they had fallen almost as if a poisonous gas had been silently released. It reminded Patterson of those old photographs of the village Pompeii. People frozen in time as if God had pressed the pause button on His remote.

Patterson had a terrible feeling. The group of officers with him seemed paralyzed, unable to comprehend devastation of this magnitude. They had all entered the hospital through the Emergency Entrance which was empty other than the bodies of two patients -one with a nasty gash on his head and the other lying next to a bucket of spilled vomit. The same pale complexion was visible on their faces. That ghostly look that Patterson had seen far too many times. The security guard, big Steve Powers, wasn't at his station. *Probably helping in the evacuation.* Patterson thought as he passed by the vacant desk. He knew Steve well. Patterson had visited the ER on numerous occasions, usually holding the manacled hands of some drunk or drug user in need of medical attention. The kind of menial task most detectives, or Chief of Detectives, would never soil their hands with. Patterson did. It came with the territory. *A homicide detective in a town with no homicides.*

The party made its way through the Emergency corridor. The sounds of flatlining machines were the only noises that could be heard. It was an eerie sound. That long, never-ending beep as if someone had fallen asleep while punching in Morse code with their hand depressing the straight key. Nurses, orderlies and doctors lay dead in the hallway. Their skin the same pale color as the two bodies in the waiting room. The scene was too much to bear for the uniforms. Two of the eight stopped in the middle of the hallway to empty their stomach contents onto the white tiled floor.

"Let's go. We've got to get upstairs." Patterson said. He didn't want to stop. Didn't want to slow down. He felt sick as well. His stomach lurched back and forth, sloshing the acid inside like a can of soda on the verge of bursting. Patterson managed to control himself. He had been desensitized so to speak, thanks to his recent run-ins with so many dead bodies. So many victims of these terrible pests that were plaguing the town. The hotel alone would have scared any sane man loony.

Where the hell was George? Patterson pondered. He assumed George had tagged along, but when they had arrived at Greater Hearts, George didn't emerge from any of the squad cars. That was unsettling.

They entered the main lobby. Nothing moved. The place was still. Patterson walked around the desk, his eyes fixed on the corridor, the nursing home wing. What he saw there almost did it. The vomit that had been welling up, momentarily contained by his stomach walls, and now it had worked its way aggressively up his esophagus. He would have puked if he hadn't tripped over the corpse of Steve Powers. The giant man lay sprawled on the floor, his massive hand still clutching the telephone.

"Oh shit." One of the officers said.

Oh, shit was right. The other security guard, a young woman, lay in-between the double doors to the nursing home unit, blocking them from closing. If two of the three security guards were dead, then it was a good bet that the patients on the floors above hadn't been evacuated. Patterson felt that sense of dread sweep him off his feet like a young lover on her wedding night. Patterson glanced around. He felt exposed, scared to death. Images of the hotel flashed in his mind. The way those damn bugs had moved down the walls, crowding himself and George into the center. He pictured that exact same thing happening here. And what could they do? Run? They wouldn't be able to. Shoot? That was a joke. Even a Navy Seal sniper -like those guys that shot those pirates and saved Captain Phillips- would have a hell of a time hitting something smaller than a dime while it moved on the floor. So, in other words, if the bugs came, the uniforms and himself were toast. Patterson gathered what was left of his courage, which wasn't much, and pushed on into the oblivion where he would certainly meet his doom.

One of the officers had knelt down to check Steve Power's pulse.

"He's gone." Patterson replied. "Let's go. We've got to get upstairs."

The cop kneeling on the ground looked up. He looked terrified. "What the hell is going on in this town?" He asked, his voice was choking and trembling under strain.

"Listen to me." Patterson commanded. "I know this sounds crazy, but those of you who have seen the bodies before know what I'm saying is true. Bugs did this. Bugs!

And they're here. All around us. Watching us as we walk. Licking their chops." The cops looked around with panicked expressions as if a thousand eyes were peering at them from the walls, which was probably true. "They feed on us, on people. They are tiny, about the size of a dime and brown in color. They move fast, much faster than any bug I've ever seen."

"What's the point?" A young uniform officer piped up. He was busily scratching his neck. His eyes were roving the corridor. He was petrified.

If these were normal circumstances, Patterson would have torched the younger officer for his sheer belligerence. However, these weren't normal circumstances and Patterson could tell the young man was scared. He wished George was there. He'd be able to give this speech a lot better. *Where the hell was George anyway?*

"The point is that if these bugs come after us, there's no standing your ground." Patterson replied calmly. "You run. Nothing kills them. Nothing. So, just run."

"Hey detective. What about this?"

Patterson turned to see another uniform holding a fire extinguisher. Now that was something. It probably wouldn't kill them but smothering them might slow them down. He walked over and inspected the extinguisher. It wasn't Halon, which had been banned years before. It wasn't CO_2 either, which would have been nice. CO_2 may have choked the life out of the bugs. Even bugs need oxygen to survive. But CO_2 wasn't being used in modern day fire extinguishers either. Patterson wasn't sure what was in the damn thing. The side of the container listed three main components. All mumbo jumbo to him. Hell, it was worth a shot though. He looked around the main lobby and spotted three more extinguishers in their glass coffins affixed to the walls.

"Grab those three." Patterson said pointing to the extinguishers. "Let's head up."

He decided to take the stairs. He hadn't even pondered taking the elevators. He wasn't going to make it that easy for those little blood suckers. Packing an elevator full of warm-blooded humans with those bugs around was like being locked in a 4 X 4 cage with a tiger. They took the stairs at a slow pace, watching for any movement. The uniforms that held the four fire extinguishers trained their foam filled weapons back and forth in wide semi-circles. It reminded Patterson of Ghostbusters Bill Murray and Dan Ackroyd armed with their proton packs.

They reached the second-floor landing and paused by the door. They all leaned their ears close to the door, trying to hear sounds of life, if there was any left. Nothing came from beyond the big metal door. It was as quiet as a graveyard at night.

Jesus, were they too late? Were they all dead? The whole hospital?! What about Sam? Is he dead? Patterson thought to himself. He didn't dare share his suspicions with the rest. That would be a huge killjoy. *We risked our lives for nothing! We're probably all going to die and for what? Nothing. We didn't save a single soul. Not a man, woman or child. Hundreds of people and we couldn't save a single one.*

Patterson grasped the handle of the door, he pulled, but the door didn't budge. He tried again. It didn't move. *What the hell?* A uniform reached his hand forward and pushed a big green button marked *Push to Exit* on the wall next to the door. The uniform smiled at Patterson. *Smartass.* Patterson thought. He pulled the door, and this time, the heavy metal door opened with ease. They moved out into the hallway, Patterson flanked on four sides by uniformed cops holding fire extinguishers. The hallway was empty. Not a living or deceased soul present. That was a blessing but what kind of a blessing. The same sound of flatlining machines reached their ears. Patterson was sure he would find scenes of grotesque horror awaiting him in every room he passed, but that didn't come to fruition. Instead, the rooms were empty. The monitoring machines, screaming their incessant distress calls, were unplugged from the humans they were supposed to be watching over. Some of the rooms were missing beds. Others had IV stands with bags of fluids still draped over their metallic arms, standing idle in the corners.

"Where are all the people?" One of the uniforms asked in a hoarse whisper.

"The bugs can see us, smell us, so it doesn't matter if they hear us." Patterson replied. "I bet the staff moved the patients upstairs."

They made their way up to the third floor and found it to be as vacant as the second which was a very good sign indeed. Patterson didn't mention the hotel which weighed heavily on his mind. The hotel rooms had been empty. Every one of the rooms George and himself had checked had been empty but instead of finding a troop of living human beings huddled up in a corner, safe and sound, what they had found was a group of humans huddled in the banquet hall, that had been consumed down to the smallest child. He prayed that wasn't the case here. He knew his heart wouldn't survive another hellish experience like that.

The fourth and last floor relieved their fears at least for now. When they opened the door leading to the corridor, they found a jumbled mess of hospital beds, wheelchairs and rolling stretchers as far as the eye could see. It was like a traffic jam in LA. No one getting in or out, at least not in a timely fashion, but at least they were all alive. Patterson smiled from ear to ear. His heart skipped a beat. He cut his way through the crowd of gowned patients to the group of scrubs nearby.

"Who's in charge around here?" He asked, holding up his badge.

"Depends." A nurse answered him. She looked old, tired, worn out.

"On what?"

"How much money you've got." The nurse answered. She cracked a good-natured grin.

"This is a serious situation." Patterson replied flummoxed.

"Just trying to lighten up the mood. Name's Carla. I'm the director of nursing around here."

Patterson wasn't sure what that meant, but it sounded important.

"We've got to get these people evacuated."

"Not happening." Carla replied. She had a no-nonsense attitude about here and an air of mental superiority and unprecedented fortitude. She reminded Patterson of Patty the coroner.

"I don't think you understand. There are these bugs that kill people. They killed everyone on the first floor."

Carla put her hand up to stop the detective. "I think we're well aware of what's going on." She indicated the mass of patients in front of her. "You think this is part of hospital procedure?" She asked sarcastically. "The problem is officer, some of these patients are bedridden. They cannot be moved even if we tried. Where would we take them? We can't take them down the elevator. And there's no alternative exit."

Patterson was mind boggled. "What do you mean no other exit? Don't you people plan for this kind of thing? What happens when there's a fire? People just wait in their rooms to be roasted alive?"

Carla gave him a hard stare. "Of course, we plan for things like this. But our plans never involve millions of tiny blood sucking insects."

Patterson looked around hopelessly. He needed an idea. He needed a lightbulb to spark to life in his mind. There were hundreds of patients. Twenty-five percent of them were laying in hospital beds. The rest were either sitting against the wall or in wheelchairs. And where was Sam? Where was Walt's boy?

"We can at least move the people that can walk and wheel."

"And what about the bugs? What if we get half of these patients down the stairs and those bugs attack?" Carla replied. She had her hands on her hips and was rearing for a fight.

"You don't get it! The bugs are coming!" Patterson shouted. Suddenly the hallway went so quiet that an ant crawling across the floor would be heard like an elephant walking on hardwood. Patterson didn't look around. He could feel every eye on him. His eyes fixed on Carla who looked shocked by his outburst. Patterson's voice lowered but remained stern, *drill sergeant on the first day of boot camp* stern. "The bugs will find these people. They need their blood to survive. Their entire lives revolve around feeding on humans. That's it. This isn't a debate. There is no other option. We cannot fight nature. And that's what you're suggesting, fighting nature. Trust me, we'll lose."

Carla stared at him. She was thinking. "Okay. I see your point." She conceded. "Can you guys give us a hand?"

"That's why we're here." Patterson turned to face his men. "Get the fire extinguishers on this floor. Four of you will lead the patients downstairs in groups of ten. The other four will stay up here and take posts guarding the hallway. Where are we taking them?" He directed his question to Carla.

She thought about it for several seconds. "There's the parking garage or…"

"Parking garage is great. Let's get with it men. Time is of the essence." He turned to one of the officers nearby. "Call John."

"Chief John?"

"Fire chief John." Patterson answered. If he made it out of here alive, he would have one those two idiots change their names. *A town with two chief Johns. Kill me now.* "Tell him to get two ambulances over to the parking garage. Tell him to start taking the patients over to the police station. Call over to the station and let them know they're coming. And kid…"

"Yes sir." The uniform replied.

"I need more men."

Chapter 90

The first group of patients accompanied by police escorts armed with fire extinguishers made it to the parking garage in under fifteen minutes. When the police escort returned, there was another group ready to go. Patterson decided it was better to get the wheelchair-bound patients out first. It was a tough job navigating the wheelchairs down the stairs, but with the help of the nurses and physicians, it became much easier. The decision was a simple one. Wheelchair-bound and bedridden patients would be the slowest, if they could move at all, in the event the group had to flee post haste. He'd rather escort the walking patients out last.

Twenty more officers had arrived after the third group had returned. Patterson was extremely relieved to see them. He instructed the group to scour the hospital in search of more fire extinguishers. They all returned, each carrying an extinguisher. Patterson instructed six of them to join the four officers on guard on the fourth floor. The other fourteen would aid in escorting patients out. This sped up the process, and the hallway was quickly emptying.

The bedridden patients proved to be the hardest to move. A group of police officers raided the emergency ward on the first floor and found a multitude of rolling stretchers. They moved the stretchers to the stairwell entrance and waited. Each of the bedridden patients was carted down the stairs on crudely made stretchers that had been assembled from bed sheets and IV stands. Once they arrived on the first floor, they were placed gently on the rolling stretchers from the emergency ward and were rolled to their final destination -the parking garage.

The bugs remained on everyone's mind. The police officers guarding the fourth floor were jolted every time a shadow passed in their peripheral vision. So far, the bugs hadn't been spotted. *So far.*

Patterson was busy shouting orders. He cut an impressive figure like Patton in his Jeep Wrangler. Sometimes he dashed about aiding his men, gathering patients, lifting them out of beds and onto makeshift stretchers and holding the door when the groups departed. He was constantly aware of the goings-on. Reports from the first floor were delivered to his ears upon each safe return. Reports from the guards on the fourth floor were relayed to him every minute, or so it seemed, usually via shouting.

"Left side good." One of the uniforms shouted, his fire extinguisher gripped tightly in his hands.

"Right side good." Another shouted from the opposite end of the hall.

"Center good." And so on and so on.

Patterson didn't see the young man approach him. In the chaos, he had forgotten entirely about Walt's son Sam.

"Uncle Bill." Sam said.

Patterson looked down, and his heart was filled with sadness. He had seen the boy many times since he had been diagnosed. Patterson made it a point to visit young Sam in the hospital at least once a week. Still, he was taken aback by the boy's feeble appearance. Sam's head was bald. His arms and legs looked like toothpicks in his hospital gown. The young man reminded Patterson of the pictures at the

Holocaust museum in Baltimore. That sickly gaunt look. That look that signaled death. And Patterson had a sinking suspicion the boy wouldn't triumph in his battle with human kind's deadliest of adversaries -the big C.

"Hey kid. How you doing?" Patterson said. He genuflected and took the frail boy in his arms. Maybe it was the boy's appearance, or the heart-wrenching pain Patterson felt in his chest, or the whole damn situation, that brought him to tears. But whatever it was, small droplets of water pooled in Patterson's eyes and slid down his cheeks.

"I'm doing good." Sam answered. "Why you crying Uncle Bill?" A question only a small child can reasonably ask.

"I'm not crying, kid." Patterson said. He wiped tears from his face with his shoulders.

"What's going on Uncle Bill? Where's my Dad?"

"Nothing to worry about champ. We just gotta get everybody out. Your Dad's back at the station. He's got important stuff to do back there. He's helping out the chief. Your Dad's a smart guy. You know that don't you?"

Sam nodded his head.

"Listen Sam, I want you to go with the next group." Patterson ushered over a nearby officer.

"I'm scared. I want to stay with you Uncle Bill." Sam hugged Patterson hard.

Patterson's heart cracked in two. "I know you do buddy." Patterson said, patting the boy's back. "I know. But listen, you listening?" Sam nodded. "I've got to stay here buddy and make sure everybody else gets out." Sam started to cry. "Hey, hey, hey. None of that." Patterson said soothingly. "I thought you were a big baseball player like Cal Ripken. Isn't that right?" Sam nodded. "What would Cal Ripken do if he were here?"

"He'd go." Sam replied.

"He would. He'd go. So that's what you've gotta do champ." Patterson's voice was soft. "I want you to get up and walk down those stairs with these nice officers. Okay?"

"Okay." Sam replied.

"Good job champ. Uncle Bill loves you buddy."

"Thanks Uncle Bill."

Patterson looked up and down the hallway. Twenty patients to go. All of them, like Sam, could walk. *Good.* He thought. He stood up. "I want you to take care of my buddy here." Patterson said to the officer standing next to him. The cop nodded sternly. "Real good care. He's a really good baseball player."

"Hey Sam, my name's Pete. Can I have your autograph?" Officer Pete said, kneeling down in front of the boy.

Sam's smile could hardly be contained. "Sure." He replied.

"Here's a pen." Pete handed Sam a pen from his shirt pocket.

"Here's a piece of paper." Patterson said, removing a piece from his trusty notebook.

Sam scribbled his name in the best elegant cursive his penmanship could muster.

"Wow." Officer Pete said, studying the autograph as if he were looking at a rookie Babe Ruth card in mint condition. "Thanks a lot, Sam. I'm going to keep this safe so that when you do become a famous baseball player, I'm going to tell everybody that I was the first one to get your autograph." Pete put it into his back pocket. "Now as soon as my friends come back, I'm going to hold your hand and lead you down the stairs. Is that okay with you?" Sam nodded.

Officer Nick Hayden watched the exchange between Pete and the young boy from his post at the right end of the hallway. He wiped a tear away from his eye. Nick was a sap for sentimentality. He'd admit it. He cried at the end of those freaking love-sick chick flicks his wife made him watch.

"You crying?" Officer Phil asked, standing next to Nick.

"No." Nick said, trying to hide the emotion in his voice.

Something moved. It was a small movement, maybe even a jerk in the wrong direction, a pull in the fabric of time. So miniscule, so insignificant that it might have been missed but Phil didn't miss it. His eyes narrowed on an area ten feet away. It was a crack cut into the drywall, probably chiseled by an out of control wheelchair. Phil leveled his fire extinguisher and stepped closer. He had to see. Had to know.

"What are you doing?" Nick asked, more puzzled than alarmed.

"I don't know." Phil replied. He walked with the gate of a man attempting to peer over the edge of a great chasm. The crack became bigger with each footfall.

The crack shuddered. That was what it looked like - a shudder, as if the crack was alive, as if it were still forming, cutting its way deeper into the wall. *What the* ... Phil thought. Then they poured from the crack like water from a penetrated dam. Thousands of bugs moving in mass like a sea of brown, across the floor.

"Bugs!" Phil screamed. He turned his fire extinguisher on the hoard and cut loose. White chemical shot from the hose. The sheer force blasted the bugs back several feet. They seemed stunned. Wriggling in place like beetles on their backs. The short-lived victory buoyed Phil's spirits, propelling him further down the hall in a mad dash. *Damn those bastards!* Became his brain's war cry as he charged, spraying his extinguisher as if it were a flamethrower.

Nick kept his hand on the trigger of his own extinguisher, ready to blast if it was necessary. Phil had them on the run. *The extinguishers really do work.* This pleasant thought repeated itself in his mind, giving Nick false hope. Nick watched Phil as the latter pushed the bugs further and further down the hall. Soon Phil would have them cornered, trapped like rats. Something caught Nick's eye. Something much closer to home. He turned his head sideways, momentarily ignoring Phil's heroic stand. Nick's face went pale. His mouth dried like a grape on a sweltering summer day. His body trembled. He saw a mass of brown moving down on the wall. They had emerged from the drop ceiling.

There's millions. Nick thought. His legs went weak, unable to support the weight of his body. Then he remembered the extinguisher in his hand. He lifted the nozzle and squeezed. Nothing happened. The mass reached the floor. It was like a story from the bible. The plagues in Egypt. *God will unleash a plague of bed bugs that will devour every man, woman and child that opposes Him.* The bugs scurried picking up speed. Nick squeezed the trigger. Nothing. That's when Phil screamed. It was an agonizing scream like a man being burned alive. A startled Nick turned to look down the hall in the direction Phil had gone. Nick couldn't see Phil. *He must have dashed into one of the rooms.* Phil screamed again and then there was silence. Nick focused on the mass of bed bugs coming towards him. He squeezed the trigger. Nothing. He moved back. *What the hell was wrong with this thing!* Again he squeezed. Nothing! He looked down the hose nozzle to see if the damn thing was jammed. He kept moving backward. The bugs covered the entire floor and moved like a magic carpet floating noiselessly along. Nick looked at the trigger. He examined it. Then he saw the reason the damn thing wouldn't work -the safety pin was still inside. He grabbed the ring and pulled. The pin flew out. Now it was ready. Now he could fight. He looked up, aimed the extinguisher and was instantly covered by the brown mass. He screamed in terror. The feeling of those little legs crawling on his skin was mortifying. The bites were even worse. Needles piercing his skin everywhere. He rolled and writhed. He could feel his heartbeat quicken. A hundred. A hundred fifty. Two hundred beats per minute. His vision began to fade. He screamed louder than ever. It was the last thing he could do. The last-ditch effort. The Hail Mary pass. His heartbeat shot up to two-fifty before it stopped and Nick's scream died in his chest.

Chapter 91

"Run!" That was it. The final command. The shout heard over the tortured screams of the dying officers. "Run!" Patterson screamed again. He tossed young Sam over his shoulder and made for the stairwell. When he reached the open door, he turned. His job was to make sure everyone made it out. Three patients jogged past him in a blur of hospital gowns. More screams came from the mass of bugs that had swallowed up Officer Nick only seconds before. *They were eating him alive! Jesus Christ, they were eating him alive!* Patterson's mind exclaimed. The screams were horrible like listening to a loved one being maimed at the hands of the Taliban. Sam gripped Patterson's back hard, his fingers digging in. No one else ran past him. *Why weren't they moving?! Life or death people! Move your asses!* But they didn't move. They stood there paralyzed, their eyes full of fear but they weren't staring at Officer's Nick's plight. They were staring into the stairwell. Patterson didn't want to. His body stayed rigid, rooted to the spot, unable to move. More screams came, but this time they came from the stairs. His mind took control of his torso and rotated it sideways, his fight or flight reflexes engaging like a steam engine pulling a monstrous load. Patterson's jaw dropped, dropped and fell onto the floor like a piece of discarded food. The three patients that had run through the door were covered in brown bugs from head to toe.

"It hurts! It hurts!" One of them screamed, trying to fling the bugs off with both of his hands.

The patients fell to the floor writhing in agony. Their screams mingled with Officer Nick's forming a tremendous, continuous shriek that could wake the dead.

More bugs covered the floor, greedily fighting their way onto the infected humans. *Let me have a bite! I want a bite! You're hogging him!* He could almost hear them saying. Patterson moved back. *There must be more stairs.* Patterson thought, glancing down the hallway in the opposite direction of the incoming hoard. What he saw froze his blood solid -the officers at that end of the hallway were firing away with their extinguishers at full blast. They were surrounded! *No, no, NO! The elevators!* That was their only chance. The bank of four elevators was ten feet away. But that wouldn't work. It was a dead end. There wasn't enough time. No time to call the elevators up, wait for the doors to open, pack everyone inside, then wait for the doors to close. The bugs would be on them by then. Covering them, biting them, drinking their blood. It was over. This was the end. He had to try. Had to. It was their last hope. He glanced back down the hall, the cops had disappeared, their bodies lying underneath a vibrating mass of brown. He rushed over to the elevators.

"Over here!" He shouted. He punched each of the call buttons with all his might. *Come on. Come on.* The indicator light at the top counted the floors one by one. First, second… More screams sounded. Patterson saw two more of his cops go down, their extinguishers clanking to the floor in dramatic finality. Too late. The mass of insects had reached the group. Patients and cops alike, scrambled towards the elevators, pushing the rest back towards the closed metallic doors. There was nothing left. It was over. Patterson knew it. He couldn't change the outcome. Couldn't wriggle free from the clutches of destiny. He lifted Sam off his shoulder and hugged the boy in a comforting embrace. Then he prayed.

The outward ring of people began to shriek in terror. Patterson waited for it. He had resigned himself to the fact that he would indeed inhale his final breath. He knew it was upon them. He squeezed his eyes shut. It was coming, coming, coming... BEEP! The sound startled him. The next thing he knew he was bathed in white fluorescent light. The elevator was here. The doors were open, but it wasn't empty. Darth Vader was inside. *Darth Vader! What the fuck!* Two men in masks began to push their way through the gathered crowd. One of the men pulled his mask down. It was George. *George! Hell yes!* Patterson's mind shouted.

"Get everybody on!" George yelled.

"There's no time!" Patterson shouted back over the terrified shrieks of the crowd.

George smiled which seemed so incredibly out of place Patterson almost wanted to belt the man.

"Yes, there is." George replied and lifted his metal spray tank up for Patterson to see.

"You said nothing will work."

"This will." George stated. He pulled his mask back down and pushed the rest of the way through the crowd.

"Get into the elevators!" Patterson shouted. "Everybody inside!" The group began to race inside, and within seconds all the survivors had filled two of the four cars. The bugs began to move forwards. Patterson punched the button with the letter L inscribed on it. It lit up with the dull shimmer of salvation. Patterson could see George and his unknown partner standing like sentinels, engaged in a last stand to the death with the mass of brown that had encircled them. The last thing Patterson visualized before the doors closed was the wand in George's hand unleashing a torrent of spray upon the charging hoard.

"Ready?" George asked through his mask.

James nodded.

"Let's get some." George squeezed the trigger. The chemical shot out, drenching the bugs. The bugs tried to scatter. They knew something was wrong. Something was amiss. They could sense the danger. But they were invincible. They couldn't be killed. Not by shoes. Not by heat. Not by cold. Not by chemical. This was different. This smelled different. This was old, ancient, a deadly warrior from the past, their most powerful foe. The realization came too late.

Chapter 92

"I's told youse I had da good stuff." Hardware Tom said. The old man was standing in the lobby of Greater Hearts amongst the survivors.

All twenty of the remaining patients, three nurses and five police officers including Patterson had made it down, safe, sound but severely rattled. James and George had joined the group, their respirators dangling from their necks, their empty metal tanks sitting idle on the floor.

"I thought you said nothing would work on them." Patterson said. He wiped a generous amount of perspiration from his brow with a clump of paper towels.

"They were using the wrong stuff." Tom remarked.

"What do you mean?" Patterson asked.

"Bed bugs died off in this country almost sixty years ago, thanks to a chemical known as DDT." George replied. "In the 1970s DDT was banned by the EPA. Ol' Tom here had some in his basement that he had kept. *Illegally.*" George smiled towards the old man.

"Don't lock me up." Tom said, smiling his toothless grin.

Patterson glanced at him. *Lock him up!* Patterson wanted to give him a metal. *Thanks for breaking the law ol' boy and saving our skins.*

"Whoever created these bugs obviously didn't think it was necessary to inoculate them to a pesticide that had been banned for fifty years. At least I hoped as much. Turns out I was right."

Patterson sat back against the imposing security desk in the main lobby. "So, they're dead?" He asked.

George nodded. "Died instantly."

"How many?"

"Millions. The way I figure, and I'm no scientist, so this is pure speculation. The first wave of the bugs was released in four sites: Tracy's townhouse, the Goodnight Sleep Motel, the Best Eastern Hotel and the Blue House Bed and Breakfast. According to Dr. Phil, and not…"

"The guy on TV." Patterson finished the familiar sentence.

"Right." George said smiling. "According to Phil, these bugs bred faster than anything he's ever seen. I believe they multiplied exponentially, and each time they bred, they spread. Going from house to house to feed." George took out his cell phone and opened up the *Maps* application. A satellite image of Havre de Grace popped onto the screen with a blinking blue light indicating George's current location. George slid his fingers together on the screen, zooming out on the map. "The three original locations in town are here, here and here." He said pointing to the map. "Subsequent victims were found in homes located up and down each of these blocks. Bed bugs are attracted to the CO_2 we breathe, they have an incredible sense of smell and can detect a human thirty feet away, and we're talking normal bed bugs, not *super* bed bugs. Who knows how far away these particular bed bugs can sniff out a fresh host. I think they moved along these streets, the whole time whiffing a strong scent of humans coming from this place." George waved his hands, indicating the hospital. "It was the largest concentration of people in town. And it drew all the bugs, every last one of them, right to this spot. In essence, this hospital was like a giant pheromone trap."

"What about the hotel and motel? They're not in town." James asked, taking the question right out of Patterson's mouth.

"The motel is in town." George pointed to the map. "The hotel, on the other hand, is not. But its isolated, on a section of Route 40 that is almost all industrial. I think the bugs are still there. But not for long." George nudged the metal spray tank with his foot.

"Then its finished?" Patterson asked.

George nodded. "I think so."

"Now it's time to bring down the bastards that did this." Patterson said, and his eyes narrowed with ferocity.

"I think I can help out with that." James interjected. Patterson, George and Hardware Tom looked at him.

"Explain." Patterson commanded.

"I know who's behind it, well, your niece knows." James said.

"Who's behind it?" George asked.

"Sentrix." James answered.

George's look became so terrifying that James looked away as if trying to shield himself from some its destructive force.

"How do you know that?" George asked through gritted teeth.

"Kelly received another phone call from her source. He identified them. Sent her a file via email. Looks legit, at least as far as I can tell. The source said Sentrix created the bugs to take over the industry. If they had a bug that no one could kill except for themselves, they could literally control the market."

"A monopoly." George said.

"Precisely." James replied.

"So, this was all just a corporate powerplay?" Patterson asked. The sheer ramification of what James was saying hit him like a gust of strong wind, taking his breath away. The situation would have been different, somewhat understandable, if this had been terrorism or a criminal act by some nefarious organization but an American company trying to create a monopoly? To quote General McAuliffe, that was just *Nuts*!

George couldn't believe what he was hearing. He wriggled his finger inside of his ear as if to remove an obstruction. He always hated the corporate pest control goliaths with their *cheaper than dirt* prices and their shoddy work ethics. He hated the way they moved into an area and crushed out the little guys like himself, who worked long grueling hours to eke out a living, feeding off the rotting bones left behind by the mammoths. Competition was already a lost cause when it came to the big guys. *How could you match their prices?* $50 a month for a restaurant. $250 a month for a nursing home, when George was charging two maybe three times that. And it always came down to the bottom line. When it was said and done, most people would prefer a healthy profit as opposed to quality pest control. A couple of roaches in your mashed potatoes -*who cares!* A mouse who visits your great aunt in her nursing home room -*it's only a mouse, plus they're kind of cute.* And apparently, Sentrix wasn't satisfied with their $2 billion in annual revenue; Gordon Reynolds wasn't satisfied with his platinum plus lifestyle; so, they had to annihilate what meager competition they did have by taking the lives of hundreds of innocent people. *Assholes!*

George picked up his tank and began to walk away.

"Where are you going?" Patterson asked, perking up.

"The hotel." George shot back. "I'm tired."

"I hope your freaking pulling my chain."

"No. I'm not."

James picked up the second tank and hurried to catch up with George.

"Mind if I tag along?"

"Up to you."

"I kind of like this job. Sure, as hell beats the weather." James remarked.

A bandaged and semi-delirious Officer Walt passed George and James on their way out. His brain was still in recovery mode. Still cracked and confused. He should have but he wouldn't have sat in that station for a second longer, not while his son's life was in danger. They wouldn't have been able to locate straps strong enough to tie Walt down.

Patterson spotted his wounded comrade coming towards him. "I thought Patty had you locked up?"

"I couldn't wait any longer." Walt answered. "Is he… did Sam…"

"He's right here." Patterson answered. "Safe and sound."

Sam, looking feebler than ever but smiling walked around Patterson's leg where he'd been hiding. The corners of Sam's mouth shot up towards the sky, and his face brightened with the light of a thousand suns when his eyes fell upon his hero -his dad. He ran forward, his hospital gown billowing in the wind of his stride and nearly tackled Walt who had knelt down. The embrace reminded Patterson of two bears locked in a struggle of immense power. Walt and his son were both crying, tears of joy, tears of relief. Patterson turned his head. He felt like crying as well. Just letting it all flow down. Letting the tears wash away the last three days. Allowing his body to cleanse itself of this tragedy once and for all.

"I missed you…I was so worried…I love you." The words came out of Walt in a flood of emotion.

"I'm okay dad. I was with uncle Bill."

Walt smiled, the tears outlining his mouth. "Uncle Bill's a good man."

"Yeah he's okay." Sam answered.

Walt laughed.

"Officer Pete asked for my autograph, just like the real ballplayers."

"Did you sign it for him?" Walt asked, glancing over at Pete who grinned broadly.

"Of course, I did. I didn't want to be rude."

Walt let out another laugh. His head throbbed, but he ignored it. He was too happy to be bothered by something so insignificant. Walt kissed his son. Sam wiped the kiss off with a playful grin.

"Come on dad." He said. "I'll just keep wiping them off."

"Can you give me one?" Walt asked. Sam did. Walt pinched the skin of his cheek where the kiss landed.

"What are you doing?" Sam asked.

"I'm saving it." Walt placed the kiss in his pocket. "I'm going to keep it forever."

Chapter 93

"You gonna pay!" Seth screamed. "You gonna pay!" Seth punched him. The other teens, his gang, the six of them, watched with amusement. The boy on the ground squirmed in Seth's monstrous grip, his hands trying desperately to grab hold of something, anything, to fight back. Blood poured from the young boy's face, mixing with his Irish red hair. Seth hit him again -a solid punch that sounded like a piece of wood beating a rug. Seth gripped the boy's shirt tighter. The shirt was ripping, buttons sailed through the air like tiny projectiles.

Lenny watched from a distance. He was at the bakery with his mother's bread order under his arm. The smell of freshly baked flour and the sour, pungent odor of yeast tickled his nostrils. He watched Seth pummel the younger boy. Lenny knew him. Irish kid from the neighborhood. *What was his name? O something.* It was always O something. *O'Reilly, O'Malley, O'Connor, that was it! Bryan O'Connor.* They called him Reds, for obvious reasons. Reds was getting the shit kicked out of him, and that too was probably for obvious reasons. Reds wasn't the sharpest tool in the shed. Hell, he wasn't the sharpest tool anywhere, he was just a tool. A kid who always wanted to be someone's friend and who always chose the wrong friends to cozy up to.

"You gonna pay!" Seth screamed. *Was he actually expecting an answer?* Reds couldn't even open his mouth, it was swollen shut, glued together like someone who had chewed a whole pack of gum. The punches were coming fast, one after another.

Lenny moved closer to the group. It was broad daylight, but no one seemed to care. No one stepped forward to help. Shopkeepers and pedestrians glanced over nonchalantly, going about their daily routine as if the sight of someone getting the shit kicked out of them was as common as a bird landing in a tree. Cars zoomed past in an endless stream. The sounds of the city bounced from one building to the next. Sounds of conversation, loud music, horns honking, sirens wailing and of course, the sound of a classic beat down.

Seth paused. He looked up, and his cold, black eyes hidden beneath wisps of long black hair, x-rayed Lenny. "You gonna do something?" Seth asked Lenny menacingly, still holding Reds' shirt, so the younger boy's upper body dangled in the air like some kind of morbid magic trick.

Lenny stood stark still. He held the bread closer to his chest. He didn't dare protest. Didn't dare answer. He just looked into Seth's cold eyes.

"Hey! You want a cup of coffee?" Seth yelled into Lenny's face.

Lenny started. *You want a cup of coffee? What the fu-?*

Seth's lips moved again, but his voice was different. Soft, angelic, feminine. "Hey! You want a cup of coffee?" Seth asked again, and then the whole picture swirled before Lenny's eyes, and he came back to consciousness inside his small office. His head was lying in a pool of drool on his desk. He could see the mountains of paperwork and the cup holding his pens sitting sideways in his vision. He lifted his head upright and rubbed his sockets.

"You okay?" Sarah Ryan asked from the doorway.

Lenny nodded. "I'm fine."

Sarah walked, hands outstretched with a cup of coffee in each. She placed one on Lenny's desk.

"Thanks. What time is it?" He asked, stretching in his chair, yawning, his mouth open wide.

Sarah walked back to the doorway where she leaned against the frame, sipping her coffee.

"Seven thirty." She answered.

Lenny looked at her with wide, startled eyes. Bug eyes. Just saw bigfoot getting out of a flying saucer eyes.

"Holy shit." He exclaimed, frustrated with himself. He didn't need sleep. He was Superman, Dracula, Batman, in one package.

"What are you worried about?" Sarah asked. "What time did you pass out?"

Lenny didn't know. He remembered working. Remembered talking to Charlie Hesh. Remembered looking at the clock at two-thirty in the morning. He recalled calling Donald Kinney's number, reading about Kinney's demise in the news, then talking to Kinney's daughter. He remembered those small towns in Mexico. Palo something. And that was about it.

"I don't remember." He said.

"You left this upstairs in the lounge." She handed Lenny his cell phone.

"Thanks. I don't even remember dropping it."
Maybe the long hours were catching up to him. If he ever made it out of this one, he'd take a vacation, first in his life. Maybe somewhere warm, palm trees and margaritas, g-strings and oiled skin -*yeah right! who was he kidding?*

"No problem. Did you discover anything?"

He told her everything. It took a while. Her expressions changed from intrigued to shocked, to pissed and back again to intrigued.

"Kinney's daughter thought he had been murdered?"

"Yes." Lenny replied. "She was certain."

"Do you think he was working with the Russians?"

"I don't know."

"What about the towns in Mexico?"

"I found articles about a mysterious flu that killed off hundreds of people in both towns."

"People are always dying in third world countries."

"That's true. I thought about that. This time was different."

"Why?" Sarah Ryan replied.

"Because Donald Kinney showed up in both towns and when he arrived the deaths stopped."

"Holy shit."

"Tell me about it."

"I've got to go to my office. Storms still raging. Looks like we're stuck for the day." She said. She gave Lenny a wink, and he felt an instant warmness in his crotch.

Lenny had an idea. One of his brainstorms. The night before, which was beginning to reconstruct itself in his foggy mind, like the memory of a wild college night of drunken debauchery, he had quickly inspected Kinney's purchasing records. He wanted to do a more thorough search, now that his brain had awoken and the coffee in his hand had begun to jump-start his motor. He pulled up the file and began checking each and every one of Kinney's purchases. He had no clue what he was looking for. Something that stood out. Something that didn't fit like a zit on the prom queen's angelic face. The purchases were very normal -tons of equipment, office supplies, consulting fees, and marketing services. Lenny scanned the entries, as he did one popped. It had come right after the $2 million purchase from HydroLine. It stood out because the amount was so small. A $250 from a company in New Freedom, Pennsylvania. The description read *general supplies*. This was hands down the smallest amount spent by Kinney ever. Lenny checked. And double checked. It was so small that it was $24,750 less than the next smallest purchase. *What the hell were you buying for $250 Donald?*

The company in New Freedom made handmade wooden furniture. Lenny pulled up the company website. The stuff was expensive. Ornately carved desks, large lacquered bookshelves, glossy tables and chairs. Everything was priced well over a thousand. Lenny narrowed the search. He set the maximum price at $250. The website displayed one item -a small dark brown sofa table.

Donald Kinney was sending a message beyond the grave. That's what Lenny thought the minute he saw the table. It was no coincidence. The two sequential purchases -the $2 million that went to HydroLine and the $250 for a sofa table. Donald Kinney was hoping someone would discover it. He knew his life was at stake. Knew whoever he had been working for would silence him, so he left clues behind. The $2 million led right to Beautiful Horizons and the sofa table -*what did the sofa table lead to? It had to be here. But where?* More memory suddenly flooded back. *Microfiber sofas and chairs. Glass coffee tables. His Allen Edmonds. Sarah Ryan sleeping. Charlie Hesh. The executive lounge!* He had seen a dark sofa table in the executive lounge. He remembered thinking it was out of place, that it didn't belong. Lenny stood up and ran to the bank of elevators. He was in the lounge in two minutes flat. There it was. He walked over. The table was beautiful. He ran his hand over the smooth surface. Examined the hand carved legs. It was a work of art, a masterpiece, something that belonged amongst the upper echelon of society like the men and women who frequented this room, but it didn't fit with the room's ultra-modern décor. He wondered how it had been overlooked for so long.

The table was three feet in height and stood against the wall under one of the large LED television sets. It had four legs and one long drawer in the center. Lenny opened the drawer. The remotes for the TV and projector were inside. He pulled the drawer all the way out. He turned it over in his hand. Nothing. No folded sheet of paper. No secret inscription carved into the bare underbelly. Lenny replaced the drawer. Next, he laid down on his back, turned on the flashlight app on his phone and began to examine every square inch of the hardwood. There was no inscription, but there was a key. It was a small key, one that might unlock a strong box or file cabinet. The key was taped under the table in the far-right corner. Lenny got back on his feet. He held the key up to the light. The numbers *541* appeared on the key's head. *What the hell does 541 mean?* Lenny pondered. It could be anything. A rogue master lock. A lockbox. A drawer to a file cabinet. Lenny bet that if Kenny meant for the key to be found, then the numbers probably referenced a drawer of one of the millions of filing cabinets in the building.

Lenny returned to his office. The key was pressed tightly in his palm. So, tight that when he dropped it onto his desk, the numbers *541* were imprinted deep in his skin. He looked up the location of Donald Kinney's former office and was blown away to learn that it had been right next to his. *Holy shit on a shingle!* Lenny remembered him. *Yes!* He remembered the sulky old man with his wrinkled shirt and frizzled hair. Hell, he probably hadn't said two words to the old guy the whole time he was next door. Lenny had always been too busy. And he had hated the way the old man had always peered at him as if the old fellow felt sorry for Lenny. The old guy always seemed to frown when Lenny appeared. Not a frown of distaste. A frown of sympathy as if he thought Lenny was being worked to the bone. Then one day the old guy was gone. Lenny didn't pay it any mind. In fact, it had only crossed his overworked mind once. He had looked into the old geezer's office and noticed his trademark picture of Ronald Reagan was missing from the wall. Well, good riddance, as far as Lenny had been concerned *and take your sympathetic frown with you.*

The office next door was empty. No one had ever moved in once Kinney had vacated it. The door was locked until the ever-enterprising Lenny slipped a credit card in and popped the lock with ease. Sometimes growing up on the wrong side of the law has its advantages. The air inside was stale, foul, ancient like the air in a tomb. Lenny combed the office top to bottom, opening every drawer and flipping every piece of furniture. First, there were no filing cabinets, and second, there was nothing in the office with the numbers *541*. Lenny felt a sense of sadness wash over him as he looked around. He had spent years next to a man he had never known. A man that had been used, corrupted and then murdered. Lenny had to change. Enough of doing business for the sake of accumulating power and making money. Sure, that's what drove him, but what about the people around him. The compassion for your fellow man. That's what he was missing. He was missing company and not the stuffed shirts he frequently met with on a daily basis. Normal people. Good people. People like Donald Kinney who may have needed a friend. Someone to talk to. Someone to listen, to lend an ear, to nod and smile sympathetically. He closed the office door and in a gesture of the curtain descending, flicked the light switch, plunging the office back into darkness. *Goodbye Donald.*

There was one filing room in the whole building. Skyscraper in Manhattan and yet, thanks to the age of computers and digital copies, the company dedicated a small twenty by twenty room to the archaic tradition of paper. The room was staffed by one man. A grouchy old type that could have played the identical twin of Dennis Farina. Lenny didn't know the man's name. Around the building, he was only known as the Godfather. *Don Paperpano*. The Godfather, of course, wasn't in, and the kingdom he ruled over was locked -handle and deadbolt. No chance Lenny's street smarts would help this time. It was a good bet that Sarah Ryan had a key. *What could he tell her though? Hey, by the way, I found a key taped under a sofa table that a dead guy purchased. Could he trust her?* Well, they had made love last night. That surely was something. Maybe she had a thing for him, or maybe she was using him as she had undoubtedly used so many others. *Make something up.* The little voice in his head commanded. *Good idea.*

"Anything new?" She asked when Lenny entered her office. His eyes drifted to the coach chair they had so salaciously defamed.

"I need to get into the file room." He said. His eyes left the chair and looked at her.

"What's up?"

"Just a hunch. I need to check something."

"Most of the files are digital." She responded. She looked deep into his eyes. *Was he hiding something from her?*

"I know. Like I said it's just a hunch."

"I'm really not supposed to. How about you fill me in and I decide whether the hunch is credible or not." Her gaze was breathtaking. Her face. The way she smiled. "You can trust me Lenny. I'm trying to do the right thing here. My career, everything I worked so hard for, is at stake."

There it was. *Trust me Lenny. Trying to make things right.* She was a cut-throat businesswoman. A real shark. *But that face. That body. My God.* And she was right.

Everything she had worked so hard for was at stake. Hell, the whole company was at stake. Billion dollar enterprise or not, if they didn't figure out what the hell happened, things could go south real fast, and might already be heading in that direction. Lenny dreaded what was happening in that small seaside town hundreds of miles away. He had decided not to focus on the bed bugs. *Focus on the money.* But what about the bugs. The IPO was tomorrow. What if the authorities were able to link the deaths to Sentrix? It would mean disaster. He had to get in touch with Tony. Check in with that scary asshole and find out what he had discovered. First things first, Kinney was connected with this mess somehow. Kinney's travels had led him to villages in Mexico plagued with death that sounded ominously similar to what was occurring in Havre de Grace. The clues Kinney had left may very well lead Sarah and himself in the right direction.

"Okay. I found this." He handed over the key.

She examined it. "It's a key. So, what? I thought…"

"It's a key I found taped under a sofa table in the executive lounge. I think Kinney taped it there."

"Why?"

"Your guess is as good as mine. I think it unlocks a drawer in the file room."

"Let's go." She said. "Lead the way."

The filing room was a bland place. Metal cabinets with four large drawers lined every wall illuminated by the ghostly glow of fluorescent lights that filled the gloom with their never-ending hum. One desk stood in the center. An island in an ocean of paper. The desk was metal as if the

Godfather refused any other material so as not to disrupt the coldness of the room. There was no paper on the desk. It was blank, vacant, chilly. The room was spotless as if it were cleaned on a regular basis, polished with care.

"You take that side. I'll be over here." Lenny said. He checked each drawer, looking for the number *541. 541, 541, 541*. It was becoming an obsession, taking over his mind, consuming his thoughts. But he knew right away his search would turn up nothing. The drawers started with number one and judging by the size of the room and the number of filing cabinets present, there was no way the number would even reach two hundred, let alone five hundred.

"You seeing what I'm seeing?" Sarah Ryan asked from her side.

"Yeah." Lenny mumbled, disheartened.

"Worth a shot." She replied, walking towards the door.

No, it wasn't. Lenny thought but didn't say. He joined her by the door.

"Any ideas?" She asked.

His mind was blank except for the number which danced there, spinning and twirling like a Cole Porter musical. *541, 541, 541.* He could think of nothing else, so he merely shook his head at her.

"I'll be upstairs. I've got some prep to do for tomorrow. Let me know if anything comes up." She left.

Lenny plodded back to his office. When he reached the door, he stopped and glanced over to Kinney's former salt mine. *What are you trying to tell me, Donald? I never gave you the time of day before, but now I'm listening. You hear that Donald? I'm listening.* He paused for an answer from beyond the grave. Nothing but eerie silence. After several minutes he retreated into his own office and sat down behind the desk. He needed to think. Needed to clear his mind, wipe away the fog of ignorance, flip to a new blank page. He rubbed his temples, trying to relax, trying to concentrate. *541, 541, 541.*

Food. He needed to eat. His body and mind were out of gas. That was it. His tank was bone dry, running on fumes, in need of a serious recharge. The bottom drawer of his desk had always been his dirty little secret. He worked out like a fiend -running up and down the blocks of his neighborhood in his trendy Under Armor attire. He spent countless hours at the gym, blasting self-help books or biographies of billionaires in his ears while he counted down the minutes spent on the stationary bike. He ate well - an apple or grapefruit for breakfast, a light salad for lunch, a fish or white meat for dinner. But the bottom drawer of his desk contained something that canceled out all of that. Inside was a box of powdered donuts, fresh powdered donuts, their white surfaces looked like miniature snowcapped volcanos. He pulled out the box and began to eat greedily. The taste was amazing. The coffee Sarah Ryan had brought him earlier was cold, but it still did the trick, wetting his whistle after a bite of sugary confection. He could feel the energy pumping through his veins after the very first bite. His stomach stopped growling. His mind began to clear. He ate fifteen of the little fat filled monsters before shoving the box back into the drawer and cleaning up his powder-covered desk, which looked like it belonged to Al Pacino playing Scarface.

The idea hit him hard, almost knocking him down. *Where was the one place in this building that Donald Kinney would have hidden something that no one else would find, or even think to look?* The answer was staring him full in the face -*Gordon Reynold's office*. The holiest of holies, the inner sanctum of the kingdom nestled on the highest peak of the most unassailable mountain. The king's lair. It had to be there. *But how to get in?* He doubted Sarah Ryan would be willing to offer a helping hand. *The chairman's office!? Have you lost your mind!?* He could hear her saying. And she would be right of course. He had lost his mind. It had jumped out of the top of his skull and was running pell-mell down the corridor on its way to the window where it would leap, splatting hard on the concrete below. What made him believe he was on the right track was the fact that he had looked everywhere else. The eighty-story building had many offices, many cubicles, many desks, but few of them had locked drawers. In fact, nearly all of them had no locks at all, except for the doors, which every maintenance technician, security guard and senior administrator had a key to anyway.

He dialed the number on his desk phone. She picked up. "Yes, Leonard." She said, a little irritation in her voice.

"Do you have a moment?"

"Need to get back into the file room?" She asked. She sounded distracted.

"Not exactly. I'm coming up."

"I can meet you."

"That would be the purest definition of a frivolous action."

"Why?"

"Because what I need is at the top."

She groaned.

Chapter 94

Sarah Ryan met Lenny outside of Gordon Reynold's office. She appeared flustered and nervous and for good reason. They were getting ready to break into the chairman's office. The boss of all bosses, the sole owner of Sentrix, one of the richest and most powerful men in the world *and they were going to break into his office!*

"I don't think this is a good idea." Sarah said.

"Do you want to go down for this? You want to lose everything because this old bozo decided he wasn't satisfied with being a billionaire and wanted to be a trillionaire? Cause that's what we're talking about. If those bugs were created by our company, released by our company and then killed people, then we're sunk. The whole ship."

Sarah didn't look convinced. She stood in front of the door leading into the *King's* chambers with her arms crossed in defiance.

"Do you think he'll take the fall?" Lenny asked pointing to the closed door. "He won't. He'll survive. That's what happens. The little people like you and I..." Lenny thought about that. *Well, the little people like me. Sarah hasn't been a member of that club in a long time.* "...we'll take the fall. We'll lose our jobs. Guys like Sangmore and Rudd and maybe even Carter will go to jail. Reynolds won't. But if we go in there and find something, we can use it."

"We'll still lose our jobs if this story gets out."

"Yes. You're right, but at least we'll have a clear conscience. At least we can point the cops in Gordon's direction. Finally, see someone of his ilk pay for their crimes."

"There's cameras."

"Not inside. Gordon would never allow anyone to observe him in his sanctuary. No way. Not at his company."

"I don't have the key."

"I figured as much." Lenny said, pulling a small leather pouch from his pants' pocket.

"You've got to be kidding." Sarah Ryan muttered.

The door to Gordon's office had two locks. One on the handle and a deadbolt. Lenny was confident he could *handle* the handle, but he wasn't sure about the deadbolt. Evidently, he misjudged his own prodigious skill. Both locks were open in less time than it took him to ride the elevator up. He grabbed the knob, winking at Sarah before he turned it and pushed the door open. They stepped in. Even though both had been in the office numerous times for meetings with the *King,* the place was still breathtaking, the way it conveyed refined wealth, blue-blood wealth, the kind of money that went with manor houses, servants, fox hunts and horse stables.

Lenny surveyed the room, his eyes roving in every direction, looking for surveillance cameras. There were none, just as he had surmised, unless they were very cleverly hidden and what could he do if they were. He had accepted the reality that he would most likely lose his job no matter what and he'd much rather go out with a bang so to speak. He'd rather stand in the chilly air of the unemployment line with a clear conscience than without one.

They searched quickly but thoroughly. The goal was some sort of locked drawer or strong box. Lenny had imagined a secret bookshelf, that slid sideways revealing a locked steel door with clandestine documents inside, pointing to cloak and dagger operations and maybe even some real juicy shit, like the alien landings at Roswell or the identity of the gunman on the grassy knoll. *Hey, I can dream, can't I?* There was nothing. No secret doors. No lockboxes and the only locked drawer present in the office was at the bottom of the desk, which when Lenny tried the key, didn't open at all. He guessed the suspicious Gordon Reynolds, kept his secrets under lock and key inside his palatial home and not in his office. Sarah shrugged her shoulders then hurried to exit the office as if the floor were on fire. Lenny reluctantly followed. It took him a great deal longer to lock the door than it did to open it. But eventually, he managed to turn the deadbolt.

"I don't know what to tell you." She began. "Maybe the key doesn't unlock anything. Maybe it's just a mistake or a red herring. You said it yourself that you believed Donald Kinney had been stealing from Sentrix, maybe he figured he'd set up this elaborate hoax to cover his tracks. Keep people guessing. Wondering if maybe he really was a decent guy."

"He was."

"What?"

"A decent guy."

Sarah sighed. "Even still, whatever the key had unlocked may have been removed since Donald's departure. It's a possibility. Maybe it was a key to his locker. You know that might…." Lenny took off, running down the hallway to the elevator. "What? Was it something I said?" She called after him. *Did this guy ever slow down? Geez-o-wiz!* She thought, speed walking to keep up.

"What the hell?" Sarah asked as she stepped into the elevator car. Lenny pushed the button labeled *B* for the basement. The doors remained opened. Lenny punched the button several more times until the doors closed so slow it was as if the elevator was protesting the rude, mishandling of its equipment. *Kindly keep your fingers to yourself why don't cha.* Lenny ignored Sarah, his eyes fixed on the stainless-steel walls of the car as it plunged downward at breakneck speed.

"Hello." She stammered. "Earth to Lenny. Anyone home."

He looked up distractedly. "You were right Sarah."

"Right about what?"

"The lockers. The key."

"Okay." She drawled.

Finally, the car reached the basement. They both could feel the brakes of the car being forcefully applied as if it were a mountain bike on a hazardous descent. Again, the doors opened at a leisurely pace as if the car were really trying to rub it in at this point or as if the entire building as a whole were attempting to stop Lenny from completing his task. Stop him from digging up the bodies and throwing the skeletons out of the closets in full view of the public's scrutiny. Lenny hurried down the helter-skelter corridor leading to the gym and the pool.

The locker room smelled like sweat and chlorine, giving the impression to one's sniffer that room was both clean and dirty simultaneously. The lockers themselves were old, rusty, and rundown, like a trusty old automobile. It always reminded Lenny of high school. The routine wardrobe swap before physical education. In his mind's eye, he could see one locker that stood out in this swamp. A locker that he had passed on numerous occasions, each time wondering whose it was. It was the lock that did it. A massive padlock that had cost the owner a fortune. A lock that belonged in a museum or on a vault at Fort Knox or on a cabinet in the West Wing, but not here. He found the locker, which seemed to glow with the light of an eternal flame. The lock was still there. Still imperious looking. A thick hunk of steel forged in a molten pot ages ago. Forged to last the trial of time. Lenny pulled at it, lifting the heavy bastard up and down. He knew the key would work and he wasn't disappointed in the slightest. The lock gave a snap as if signaling its compliance with the powerful key master. Lenny removed it and laid it on the floor. He grabbed the handle and lifted it up, the locker clanged to life, and the door fell open. This was it. This was the good stuff. The Roswell file, the JFK assassination, the identity of DB Cooper. Bloated accordion folders were stacked, nice and neat, within the small metal interior. Lenny heaved the top one out. He twisted the small tie, flipped it up and removed its contents. He read each page, taking his time, not wanting to miss anything. His eyes grew wider with each word. His heart rate ticked up perceptively. The files were very detailed and mutinously organized. Lenny flipped page after page, each one uglier than the last.

"Listen to this." He began, reading from the document. "There were eight scientists employed by the Pioneer group initially. Eight. And check it out." Lenny showed Sarah the page. Every scientist's name was listed and next to each name was a small hand-written note. Each note listed a date and cause of *DEATH!*

"Oh my God!" Sarah Ryan gasped. "They're all dead."

Lenny nodded. "Dr. Roger Hayfield, killed September 6 of last year, hit by a bus. Dr. Sonya Zapatero, suicide by hanging. Dr. Nikola Horvat, suicide, jumped off the roof of an apartment complex. Dr. Marshall Thomas, died in a fire. Dr…"

"Enough, please." Sarah wiped perspiration off her brow. She tried in vain to catch her breath. "Who wrote the notes?"

"I don't know, but if I had to take a guess, I'd say Donald Kinney."

"Kinney was keeping records of his own. Why?"

"Isn't it obvious?" Lenny answered, still scrutinizing the documents. "Look at this." Lenny said, again showing Sarah the page with the scientist's names. "They're all dead. Everyone one of them. Kinney knew that. He watched it happen. He knew his time was running short. That's what his daughter said. That's what she told me. He was acting weird. Acting scared."

Sarah Ryan felt woozy, dizzy, ready to pass out. She stumbled. "Do you have any idea how big this is?" She asked. "We're not just accusing the company of creating a bad bug, we're accusing them of knowingly creating a lethal bug then systematically trying to cover it up."

Lenny nodded. "I know." He replied. "I made a mistake. There's one scientist on that list who hasn't died."

"Who?"

"Dr. Richard Sangmore." Lenny answered, looking at Sarah Ryan full in the face.

Sarah Ryan's face said it all, like a giant billboard sign the read *WOW*, in bold letters.

"Tell me about it." Lenny said. "He never mentioned that at all, and you'd think that would be a valid topic of conversation." Lenny held his nose, mimicking the nerdy scientist's voice. "By the way, I used to work with a group of scientists that mysteriously all bit the dust."

Lenny read through the rest of the personnel files with the scientists' lives spelled out in neat manila folders. Lenny felt creepy, like a voyeur peering through a window pane at a young lady stripping to her panties. It was the fact that all these men were dead that did it. He read their names, the names of their kids, their spouses, their parents, the addresses of their homes, their high schools, colleges, favorite football teams and their favorite foods. It made them seem all too real in his mind, like ghosts prowling the halls until they're set free, until they're avenged.

Lenny sat on the floor, his legs bent at the knee forming a natural desk to lay documents on. He read like a man whose life depended on it, digesting each word, trying to come to conclusions that were anything but horrific. He failed miserably. Each new accordion folder he pulled from the locker revealed new sinister machinations. There was a folder dedicated to lab tests which proved that the bed bugs now plaguing the town of Havre de Grace were anything but a new innovation, in fact, according to the contents of the most recent folder, the bugs in question were eight years in the making. And they had killed before. Several test sites were listed including the Mexican villages of Palo Solo and Santa Rita and the island of St. Lucia. The results of the tests conducted in these three sites were evaluated as promising and listed the death toll in each town. The number of dead matched the number listed in the newspaper article Lenny had read on the net the night before. These bugs weren't designed to eliminate competition in the industry as he and Carter were led to believe. No, no, no. These bugs had been designed from the get-go to be weapons, weapons of mass destruction that breed strikingly fast and killed when people were most vulnerable -when they were asleep. *This was unbelievable!* Lenny exclaimed silently. *They were lying! Rudd, Sangmore and Gordon! All lying!* He took his eyes off the page for a brief moment to glance at Sarah, her blond hair up in a stylish take no prisoners bun, sitting on the floor next to him with her nose to the papers in front of her.

What was Kinney's role? The question landed on Lenny like a brick thrown from the roof of a tall building. Kinney's name had been noticeably absent from the documents. He had probably purged himself from the files before having that blind, fatal date with the car. Lenny knew Donald Kinney had traveled to the towns in Mexico and St. Lucia, so his role was an important one. Donald always came after the bugs began to get out of control and what he used to cleanse the area of insects wasn't available in the records unless it was in the last accordion folder, which lay dusty and forgotten on the floor of the locker.

According to the documents there were two separate sides to the Pioneer Initiative, both existing apart from one another, neither knowing what the other was doing. The first was brilliant. It focused on the introduction of the once extinct species onto American shores. Bringing bed bugs back to a public that had nearly forgotten about the little blood-sucking pests that had plagued their ancestors. Sentrix had cultivated live bed bugs from countries in South America and had released them in cities like New York, Boston and Los Angeles, ensuring a spread on both coasts and culminating into a nationwide epidemic. This part of the initiative worked seamlessly and undoubtedly explained Sentrix's boost in revenue over the past decade. It was still unbelievable and extraordinarily unethical, but it wasn't illegal, at least not technically. This part of the plan was obviously what Carter Ritler had championed and endorsed. It was classic Carter and Lenny couldn't help admiring it. The second part, well, the second part was just evil, sick, demented and smelled of a sour old man, the smell Lenny had often inhaled when Gordon Reynolds walked past.

Time stood still as if the clock had stopped, frozen in place, unable to move. Lenny had no clue how long he had been sitting on the floor. The revelations revealed in page after page of type were startling, powerful, like waves hitting a beach, eroding reality. He kept glancing at the last folder. He knew it was important. He knew it would hold the clues to who was responsible for this project, this diabolical scheme. It would reveal the names. It would be the final nail in the coffin, the last bar of the cell. Before he grabbed it, he thought about the consequences. He pondered what to do with the information. Sentrix would protect their name at all costs. That was obvious. The eight scientists who worked on the project had been murdered. That was the conclusion he had reached. No way all those deaths, so close together, were mere coincidences. It had been murder. Murder to protect secrets. And whoever did it would kill again. The proof was in the pudding so to speak. Really the proof was Donald Kinney, who had been killed a year after the eight scientists. Kinney had threatened to expose the project. Sentrix had tried to throw money at him. It didn't work. Kinney wasn't a man who could be bought. So, they had to kill him and how many others? How many people had known about this and had died as a result? Ten, twenty, thirty? And they would certainly kill Lenny if on Monday, after the successful IPO, Lenny waltzed into Gordon Reynolds' office and presented him with this information. Reynolds would have him killed before he left the building. Probably before he left the office. Lenny wondered what method they would use. Would it be hanging? Plunging? Drowning? Shooting? It was like a game show, but instead of the check for a hundred grand and a brand-new car, all you get is a bullet, a dull piece of metal, fired into your brain, ending your existence, forcing you to join the hoard of translucent witnesses wandering the afterlife.

Sarah had stopped reading. She looked pale, haggard, worn out. Gone was the pretty face and in tune body. In their place were expressions of bewilderment, rage, anxiety and dread. She wore these feelings like a tattoo. She scrolled on the screen of her phone aimlessly, with little or no direction what so ever. She checked the weather, tracking the storm. Then she checked the news, which proved to be a costly mistake. Her phone slipped from her grasp and landed on the floor with a plastic thud. Sarah scooped it up.

"Look at this!" She exclaimed, handing her phone to Lenny.

Lenny took it and read the screen.

Hundreds of deaths reported in historic Maryland town.

"Hundreds. Hundreds!" Lenny shouted. He looked like a man on the verge of a breakdown. "Hundreds!" He couldn't believe it. It couldn't be. "Hundreds!" He shouted again. He stood up. Sarah Ryan stared at him. She had no clue what to say. Hundreds of deaths caused by her company. It was incredible. Lenny yanked at his hair as if he were trying to remove a wig. "Hundreds." He muttered. "We're through." He said. "This is the end." He walked up and down. His throat was dry, his voice hoarse. He couldn't believe this was happening. Maybe in a shit hole village in Mexico, maybe there, where the cartels killed hundreds of people a week, but not here, not in the United States of white-gloved America. Here, hundreds of dead people meant gas chambers, electric chairs, drone strikes, MOAB bombs. Americans don't tolerate such atrocities.

"The article didn't mention how they died. The deaths are being investigated." Sarah said timidly.

Lenny slumped back down, his back sliding against the wall. He remained silent for quite some time. Kinney's documents littered the floor around him, forming a collage of paper and ink. After a few minutes, he looked over at the last unopened accordion folder. It was now or never. He needed to know what was inside. He needed that final satisfaction of seeing Gordon Reynolds name etched on the documents authorizing this terrible tragedy. *Would it make it all worth it? No, but at least it would give me the satisfaction knowing that old bastard would pay for his crimes, knowing that Gordon would spend the rest of his life playing hide the zucchini in Sing Sing.*

Lenny reached over and lifted the folder from its dusty, metal grave. He placed it on his lap and stared at it for quite some time. He had known from the beginning -the day Carter had assigned him this task- that the creation of these bugs was no accident. No screw-up, no mistake. They were intentional, at least in his mind. Call it a hunch or just his personality, but he had been right the whole time. His theory, or presumption of guilt, had been vindicated. Now, he would see just how far up the buck would ascend. Silently, in his mind, he placed a wager that the buck would stop at the ornate, hand-carved desk of the *King*. And this time, there wasn't enough money, corrupt politicians, or homicidal hitmen in the world that would save the *King* from losing his crown and quite possibly losing his head. *OFF WITH HIS HEAD!* Lenny untwisted the cord that held the lid of the folder shut and removed its damning contents. He sat the papers in his lap and began to methodically analyze each page. He went slowly at first, scanning the documents line by line, then he sped up as if he couldn't believe what he was reading. The documents were indeed authorization forms and leadership flow charts, but there was something terribly wrong. Something that forced Lenny up from the floor. He couldn't believe what his eyes were seeing. Page after page fell to the floor in a flurry. Purchase orders, lab rentals, meeting minutes, letters to the board, letters to Gordon, letters to scientists, travel logs, all cascaded to the floor as Lenny slid one after another off the stack in his hands. He moved faster and faster, no longer reading the documents in their entirety but simply glancing at the bottom of the page, at the signature there, a signature that couldn't be there, that must be a mirage, a hallucination, a trip on LSD. It was his name, Leonard Schultz, at the bottom of each page. His signature, an elegant display of his vanity, a display he had practiced over and over again to make sure it was perfect, inked at the bottom, inked on the dotted line.

"This is bullshit!" He screamed. He had never heard of the Pioneer Initiative until yesterday. He had certainly never signed any of these documents, had never even read them until right now, *right fucking now!* He paced the room, throwing papers like a tornado ripping through an office building. He was deranged like a wild animal whose blood was infected with rabies. Shell-shocked like a survivor of a nuclear blast. *How could this have happened? How?!* Then with a tremendous pang, a cataclysmic punch to the solar plexus, he realized why Donald Kinney had stared at him with sympathy and maybe even a little remorse. Kinney had known all along that Gordon Reynolds would pin this on the little Jew boy in accounting, the little Pitbull whose loyalty belonged solely to Carter Ritler, a man Gordon both admired and feared. This had been planned from the beginning. Lenny had always been the scapegoat. That's why Donald Kinney, a man who belonged in the logistical section of the building, had his office next to Lenny's in accounting.

Reynolds had picked both of them -Carter and himself- to take the fall. It was a simple solution to a burgeoning problem. *What had Carter said?* Gordon Reynolds had recruited him, pulled him right out of a list of names, some of those names much more capable and more experienced than Carter, yet Reynolds had pulled his name. Carter had always been flummoxed by that, proud but confused. And Reynolds had suggested Carter recruit the promising young man in accounting. The lonely Leonard Schultz who had zero friends and very little family. *Train him, take him under your wing.* The voice of Carter quoting Reynolds flooded back to him. And now it all made sense. Instant fall guys. That's what they were, instant scapegoats. Just add water, or better yet, just add blood. But Carter had beaten Reynolds to the punch. Carter had his own sources out there, he had found out about the bugs. He had uncovered their true anatomy. He had confronted Reynolds, confronted him in front of the entire board. Had gone on record stating his innocence. He had protected himself. *Or had he?*

Lenny wasn't protected. He could never prove his innocence. He had been at Sentrix since the start of these experiments. He had met with both Rudd and Sangmore on numerous occasions. *Bet Reynolds had surveillance tapes of those meetings. Oh yes. No doubt about it. He probably has tapes, photos, logs. He planned it perfectly.*

Lenny felt sick. He wavered, his legs wobbling in place as if they were made of string cheese. He fell back, crashing against the lockers like a high school nerd in an epic showdown with a colossal bully. His body hit the ground hard. He didn't pass out. He was totally awake, just shaken, brutally shaken. He sat there for what seemed like forever, as if the earth matured another ten thousand years, as if humans no longer populated the world and the great metropolises lay empty and eternally eerie.

Sarah Ryan stared at him wide-eyed. She hadn't fully grasped the situation unfolding in front of her. She was too shocked by the news article. One of the papers Lenny had dropped lay inches away from her foot, she reached out, grabbed it and began to read. Then she gasped, her hand covering her mouth, her expression that of surprised horror. She stood up.

"I don't understand. This has to be a mistake." She said. Lenny didn't answer her. He couldn't, even if he wanted to. He just sat there, a man whose mind had left his body, a vacant, absent look in his eyes. "But you weren't…you couldn't…I don't get it. Why is your name…" She dropped the paper, it fluttered the short distance to the floor.

Sarah walked over to him. She knelt down. "Len, we can destroy them. Burn the whole lot. They'll never know. Gordon didn't know Kinney kept records."

Lenny looked up at her and for the first time and marveled at her ignorance. "Burn them!" He chuckled. "Burn them! That's good. That's rich. No, no, no Sarah. These are copies." He waved his hand at the documents scattered on the floor. "Reynolds has the originals."

She shook her head. "This isn't true. It's bullshit. Total bullshit. You know it. I know it. We can prove it."

Lenny laughed harshly. "Prove it. Prove it! How? He planned it perfectly. The whole damn thing. Reynolds knew the experiment might go south so he picked a fall guy, someone he could point the finger at. Someone he could say I didn't authorize that. It was that young guy. That young guy who's an asshole that everyone hates. It was him and his crooked boss. It was Lenny and Carter. That's who did it. Lenny and Carter. Not me. Not big, powerful, rich, Gordon Reynolds. No sir. Those two clowns did it. Lock them up. Here are the documents. Take a look, they did it." Lenny lowered his eyes. His mind ached. His body was out of gas. "Face it, Sarah. It's over."

"What about Kinney? He obviously left these behind for someone to find. He wanted someone to know."

Lenny laughed again. It sounded painful. "Someone to know." He drawled. "Maybe Kinney did, but he didn't dispel any of the fraud. All he proved was that the conspiracy existed, not that the players were being framed."

"There has to be a way." She pleaded. "Call Carter. Tell him what happened. His name wasn't on any of the papers. Just yours. Yours and Sangmore's."

Lenny's eyes lit up. "Mine and Sangmore's?" He asked, jumping to his knees and beginning to rifle through the pile of papers. He flipped through each one until he found what he was looking for. "Sangmore." Lenny said, holding one of the documents. The doctor's ugly scrawl was etched on the bottom of an authorization form. Lenny looked around at the rest. His name was everywhere, just like Lenny's. "Sangmore's name is on everything."

"I know. I just said that."

"That means he's being framed as well. First, he's alive and well, despite the demise of his other colleagues. Second, if he was part of the conspiracy why would he leave his name everywhere? It doesn't make sense."

Sarah nodded.

"Still what does it matter?" Lenny asked. His new-found pep left his system as quickly as it had arrived. He reverted back to his morose, defeated attitude. "Nothing. It doesn't mean shit. All it means is that the hangman will have two nooses, instead of one."

Sarah didn't reply. She had nothing. No comforting words. No defensive battle cries. Nothing.

Lenny leaned up against the lockers. This was it. His life was effectively finished. The war was over, and his troops had surrendered, facing the inevitable execution that awaited them. There was no coming back. Reynolds had the documents which meant by tomorrow Lenny's name would be on every mouth of every talking head from sea to shining sea. They would label him a corporate villain, a mass murderer, a person who put greed above the lives of hundreds of innocent people and Gordon would be hailed a hero. A man that had exposed the monsters within his own organization. Sure, Sentrix's stock would plunge. That was inevitable. It was too late to call off the IPO. It would plunge. The company's shares would suffer but only briefly. After the initial blow, the shares would rise steadily and thanks to the news of killer bed bugs on the loose, pest control stocks, namely Sentrix, would see an enormous boost in their prices. Gordon would be able to unload his shares for even more money than he had originally anticipated. Or had he anticipated it? Lenny was pretty sure he had. The timing was too perfect. A week before the IPO the bed bugs wreak havoc, Carter gets canned, Lenny gets the axe -on his neck- and Gordon's net worth soars. The perfect crime.

He went to see his boss. The voice of Catherine Kinney rang in his head. *But his boss wasn't having it.*

"I've got to…" Lenny walked away before he finished his statement.

Sarah stood up and followed. "What? You've got to what?" She called after him. They left the documents and the dusty accordion folders strewn on the floor.

Lenny arrived back at his office in a daze. His brain fired synapses like a fleet of waring pirate ships. He sat at his desk. He ignored the figure of Sarah Ryan leaning against the door frame.

"Can I get you something to drink?" She asked in a soothing voice, not wanting to disturb him, but at the same time wanting to help.

Lenny didn't answer. He was busy typing away. His eyes stared at the computer screen intent on its contents. After several minutes Sarah walked into the office and sat down on one of the two uncomfortable chairs in front of Lenny's desk. She remained quiet watching Lenny work which eventually became boring. She pulled out her phone. The time on the screen read three o'clock. The whole day had drifted away, and she had so much to do. The bed bug story would certainly sink their stock on its opening day, but that didn't really register with her. She had a duty. A duty to this company and her own financial wellbeing to see this messy business through. She debated whether she should stand up and excuse herself, then she nixed the idea. She had to see what, if anything, he uncovered.

"Storm's over." She said, as if that mattered at this point. Lenny remained sucked into his machine.

Finally, he stood up from his desk. He looked pale again. Much paler than before. His eyes were still fixed on his computer screen. She thought he would be sick and began to look around for a trash can to hand him.

"What?" She asked.

His voice was calm, steady, composed. "I remembered something Kinney's daughter had told me."

"What?" She had butterflies in her stomach.

"She told me that Kinney had met with his boss to voice his disagreement. He had had misgivings about what he was doing here. What his job entailed, and he had voiced that to his boss. It hit me that whoever he had voiced it to had complete knowledge of the conspiracy. Remember Donald Kinney was up to his eyeballs in this. He was the man on the ground. The man that had the unpleasant task of traveling to the towns and villages where hundreds of people had died, murdered by bugs Sentrix had designed."

"So?"

"So, whoever Kinney had met with was the person behind the curtain so to speak. The man pulling the levers." Lenny looked hurt, wounded, heartbroken.

"Who did he meet with?" Sarah asked, her hands gripping the sides of her chair so hard, her knuckles had turned a stark white.

Lenny looked at her for a long time before answering. "I think it's time I pay my respects to an old friend."

Chapter 95

This is what it's like to live like a king. Lenny thought as he stared at the towering luxury residential high rise in midtown Manhattan. The building was a white glove affair which is exactly what the red vest clad valets would wear as they opened the doors of the multitude of fancy automobiles that pulled to the curb, their occupants dressed to the nines in suits and furs. The storm and the thick sheets of ice covering the city had forced the valets and their suited, furred tenants to hunker down inside.

If he weren't so damn depressed and quite a bit determined, Lenny would have marveled at the city with its new frozen sheen. The streets were empty, deserted as if New York were a ghost town in the wild west. He could picture tumbleweeds rolling lazily along 5th Avenue. Everything was enclosed in ice. The buildings towering as high as the clearing sky looked like vertical ice luges. The trees -despite what one might think, Manhattan did have some trees- looked dipped, preserved, as if they were in a gallery. The cars sat in hibernation lining the streets, unoccupied and forgotten. It was a moment in time, a point in eternity, that should be remembered, snapped with the camera of one's mind. And Lenny could have cared less.

The trek, and it was a trek like being stranded in the frozen tundra of Siberia with little or no food and a thousand miles to go, sapped Lenny's strength and very nearly collapsed his body and mind. Determination and sheer force of will drove him forward, gave his feet traction and steadied his legs as he walked or skated down the sidewalks that had become frozen paths in this urban wilderness. He had forgotten Sarah Ryan, even though the pretty lady skated right beside him, sticking with him like glue. They both fell several times, some of the falls were pretty severe, but they kept going, counting down the blocks, intent on arriving at their destination.

"Think they'll let us in?" Sarah asked as the two of them stood outside the luxury high rise.

Lenny looked at her as if he were seeing her for the first time. "One way or another, we'll get in." He said. They crossed the street and stepped in front of the gold lined glass doors. The door opened with the sound of an electric motor humming steadily. They walked into a gilded marble world of impeccable decadence. A world that was inhabited by the elites. A world that reminded Lenny of his low station. A world that even Sarah Ryan, with her $300,000 a year salary, couldn't afford. It was as if they had traveled through space and had landed on a different planet.

"Can I help you?" A white-gloved, red-vested man said in a polished, ivory tone.

"Carter Ritler." Lenny commanded, dropping the formalities entirely. He noticed two men sitting in the corner of the lobby. The men had hard faces and even harder eyes. They looked at Lenny suspiciously, their right hands tucked under their jackets.

The doorman took Lenny and Sarah in with one glance, knowing immediately that neither of the two belonged here. He looked over at the two men across the lobby. One of the men nodded. Lenny saw the nod and with a pang, knew he and Sarah may not make it out of there alive.

"Is he expecting you?" The doorman asked.

"Not unless he's psychic." Lenny answered, continuing to stare at the two men in the corner.

"May I have your names?"

"Leonard Schultz and Sarah Ryan." Lenny answered.

"One moment." The doorman walked over to a marble desk. He picked up a golden telephone that must have been one of the first ever invented. "A Mr. Schultz and a Miss Ryan here to see you sir." The man said on the phone. "Very well." He hung up. "This way please." The man led them to a bank of elevators. He pushed one of the call buttons. The elevator door slid open. The man leaned in and punched several numbers into a keypad. Then he stepped back and ushered Lenny and Sarah inside. "Have a nice day." The man said in his polished tone.

The elevator sped upwards like a drag racer. It stopped on the forty-second floor, the very top of the building. They stepped out and were met by a smiling Carter Ritler, decked out in a green cardigan over creased Khakis, holding a snifter of golden liquid and wearing a pair of reading glasses perched smartly on his nose.

"Len!" Carter said. He reached out a hand to shake.

"Fuck you, Carter."

"Well, skip the pleasantries why don't you." Carter pulled his hand back. "What's gotten into you?"

Lenny walked in without answering. Despite his anger and feelings of betrayal, he couldn't help marveling at the platinum lifestyle of his former boss. The sheer elegance of the condo was breathtaking. Everything from the marble floors, to the columns -*who the hell has columns in a condo?*- to the canvas and oil depictions on the walls. Simply breathtaking. The main entrance, or better yet the main lobby, was vast and Herculean. It felt like a museum rather than a home. Lenny saw a living room, or what was undoubtedly one of several living rooms, and entered. There was no couch here, as if that would have diminished the class of the room. Instead, there were four coach chairs, set in a semicircle, in front of what should have been a TV but instead was a portrait of an oddly shaped woman done in the impressionist style that, judging by its gilded frame, could only be real and not a copy. Lenny took his seat in one of the uncomfortable chairs and readied himself for a fight.

"Again, I ask what's gotten into you?" Carter said upon entering the room. Sarah Ryan followed close behind and sat down next to Lenny. Carter stood as if he wished not to soil himself with such plebeians. He nursed his drink, taking small sips, the ice barely moving in the glass. "You come to my home, in the middle of an ice storm, waltz in a tell me to go fuck myself?"

"I have to say Carter, I'm surprised."

"By what?"

"A man of your talents. A man of your intelligence. Making the mistakes you made." Lenny shook his head. "It blows my mind."

"I don't know what you're talking…"

"Cut the shit!" Lenny shouted. "You know damn well what I'm talking about. Your master plan." Carter's face was impassive. "You almost got away with it, didn't you? But not this time. Oh no, not this time. Biggest mistake Carter was hiring me. You thought you'd get away with it." Lenny let out a laugh of derision. "Both of us…" He indicated Sarah and himself. "Know what you did. I've got the evidence. All of it. And Kinney, I mean seriously? Did you think that maybe he'd have a failsafe in place? Just in case? You did kill all of his colleagues. Every single one of them. Don't you think he realized his time was running out?"

Carter remained clam. He didn't utter a word. He walked over and sat down in the chair opposite Lenny. Sarah did likewise, taking her seat next to Lenny, signaling her support, her allegiance.

"Nothing to say?" Lenny taunted. "Huh?"

Carter crossed his legs. "Why don't you tell me why you're so upset?" Again that calm tone, that calm demeanor. It really pissed Lenny off.

Lenny laughed. "Asshole." He said. "You know that Carter. You're a real asshole. Like an actual hole that shit slides out. See, being a piece of shit is one thing but being the hole that continually produces the shit, now that's a whole different ball game. Get it? A *whole* different ball game?" Lenny's tone was sardonic. Carter ignored the jibe. "Let me start from the beginning. You correct me when I'm wrong. Can you do that Carter? Can you correct me when I'm wrong? Please. For fuck's sake." Carter didn't answer.

"The way I see it, you came to work for Sentrix. Now you said Gordon Reynold's hired you. I do believe that. I believe Gordon Reynolds was either that naïve or you were that convincing, either way, I believe Reynolds did seek you out. You, being the slick dick that you are, conceived the Pioneer Initiative. Know that one?" Lenny asked. "Come on Carter, give me something here. The Pioneer Initiative? You know grow Sentrix's revenue? Release beg bugs on an unsuspecting, ill-prepared, defenseless public? No?" Carter stayed quiet. "Aww, couldn't even give me that. Okay. No biggy. Anyway, you convinced Gordon to go along with the plan, and he does because he's not perfect. Hell, no, absolutely not. He's a greedy, self-centered bastard that would jump at the idea of adding another comma to his name. He endorses the plan. Gives you access to his resources. Then you discover KS Oil and Gas. See…" Lenny hit his head hard with his finger. "I did my research asshole. I know KS Oil and Gas, Dr. Rudd's old firm, had the technology to genetically modify insects. They'd been doing it for years. It was one of their biggest sources of revenue, aside from the oil. They developed the technology and sold their genetically altered bugs to farmers all over the world whose crops were plagued by beetles. KS' modified wasps, killed the beetles, ridding the farms of the invasive pests. You figured that out. You collapsed KS' stock. I read about it. Insider information. KS tried to cover up an oil spill in the Gulf of Mexico, and they would have gotten away with it if one of their employees hadn't leaked it to the press. And I'm betting their inside man was none other than Dr. Rudd. The same Dr. Rudd who developed Dio Insecticide, the only chemical capable of killing the genetically modified bed bugs. Come on out Dr. Rudd!" Lenny shouted. Sarah looked at him in utter disbelief. "Come on out! I know you're here." There was no response and Carter's face remained impassive. Suddenly a low shuffle could be heard in the hallway and a second later Dr. Rudd, his pot marked face looking uglier than ever, appeared. He was holding an impotent right arm which was bandaged at the shoulder. Rudd shuffled over and a took a seat next to Ritler. He stared at Lenny with killer eyes.

"I knew you would be." Lenny said triumphantly. "Wouldn't want to miss the show. After all, you played a pretty big part.

"I always hated you, you little prick." Rudd growled.

"How's the shoulder? Heard you had a run in yesterday with some very pissed off Russians." Sarah looked from Rudd to Lenny. She couldn't believe anything she was hearing. She hadn't realized that Lenny had recovered so much information and had left her in the dark. It was impossible. She had been with him the whole time, well, not the whole time but a large majority of it.

"Well, now that we're all reacquainted, let's get back to the program." Lenny said. Carter remained quiet. He had taken off his reading glasses and was busy chewing one of the rubberized ends so that the glasses stood upright and only one of his eyes peered through as if he were analyzing Lenny. The look was terrifying, and Lenny had to shuffle in his chair to regain his composure. He thought momentarily about the men in the lobby. About their hands that had done a Houdini under their jackets. Lenny was pretty sure he knew what was under there. Something cold. Something metallic. Something with a big hole in the middle and a bunch of friends stacked inside impatiently waiting to get out. He shuddered.

"That's where the ten million went. You had Donald Kinney transfer the ten million through your myriad of shell companies so you could purchase KS Oil.

That was brilliant Carter. You kneecapped a $200 million company and picked it off for a measly ten million. Incredible." Lenny stated. His praise was genuine. "But that was your first mistake. I always wondered how you snuck $10 million right out from under Gordon Reynold's nose, but then I thought about it and realized that Gordon was well aware of what you were up to, at least to some degree and had even given you his blessing. Am I right?"

Carter didn't answer. He studied Lenny with that one eye, magnified by the glasses' lens. He was cool and collected. Relaxed as if he were sitting watching a movie and not hearing his high crimes and misdemeanors read aloud.

"I think I am." Lenny answered. "KS had the technology. KS had the scientists, you know, the dead ones, the ones you killed? Did Tony do them too, just like he did your sisters last three lovers?" Lenny waited for an answer he didn't expect to receive. "Yes. That's what I thought. The scientists including Sangmore gave you genetically modified bed bugs, but you didn't know at the time that they were lethal. You thought they were only immune to every known pesticide. And I do believe that. I believe at first your plan was simply to overthrow the industry by releasing a hoard of bed bugs that only Sentrix had the technology to eliminate. That's where Dr. Rudd came in. Rudd developed Dio Insecticide." Lenny looked at Rudd for some acknowledgment, but the pot marked man took a page out of his boss' playbook and remained impassive. "You released them in South America and low and behold..." Lenny said dramatically. "You nearly wiped out an entire village. Holy shit!" He clapped his hands making Sarah Ryan jump. "And you realized your little creation was a dime sized killing machine. It must have made you sick at first. All the money. All the resources. The planning. The developing. And for what? For failure. But by this time Gordon is pressing you for results. He's really pounding on you, and you begin to hate the man. Despise him. Fantasize about putting these bed bugs in his giant mattress and watching them suck the greedy old miser dry. That's when I think, you hatched your plan. Lightbulbs exploding in your brain. Boom! Presto!" Lenny exclaimed. "You approach Rudd. You approach Kinney, and you hatch the scheme. You're not satisfied with being president. You're not satisfied sitting on Gordon Reynolds' lap. Diamond encrusted collar or not. You're no lap dog. You're a warrior. You're a pit bull. A wolf. A lion. But you know you have to be a fox. You deserve it all, so you convince Gordon to sell his stake in the company on the open market. Cash out. You throw him a bone by releasing a batch of regular bed bugs into the US, triggering a pandemic bigger, I think, than even you realized. The industry changes overnight. Gordon makes another billion. He agrees to take the company public and you murder another village in South America this time with the world watching. Well, not the world, just the Russians. That was your second mistake. I stumbled upon it. A little article in a Latin American newspaper about a Russian diplomat that was killed two miles from the town of San Palo. The same town where hundreds of people died mysteriously from an unknown illness. The same town Donald Kinney traveled to. At first, I overlooked the story, I was so focused on the hundreds of deaths and the similarities to what was happening in Havre de Grace. Then I went back and read that the Russian diplomat had wandered very far off the beaten path, so far off in fact that the journalist who had written the story had mentioned that the DFS, Mexico's FBI, was worried that the Russian diplomat may have been cultivating ties with one of the left-wing militias active in the area. But the Russian wasn't there for that, was he? No, he was there to observe the effectiveness of a weapon his country was getting ready to purchase. A weapon designed to covertly kill thousands, maybe even tens of thousands of people with little or no recourse. A silent and deadly weapon developed by a pest control company in the United States. A weapon that would cost his country $500 million." Lenny looked deep into Carter's eyes. Carter slowly chewed the rubber end of his glasses. He was still relaxed. Lenny was really starting to get pissed off. He was passed the point of being scared. He wanted to kill Carter. Kill both he and Rudd. Strangle the two right here in Carter's living room. Watch as Carter's face turned blue. Watch as Carter's chest heaved his final breath. Feel as Carter's heart gave its final thud. *Man, what he wouldn't give...*

"But Kinney got cold feet. Came down with a serious case of them, so serious that if he had held his feet over the mouth of a volcano, it still would have felt to him like a bucket of ice water. Maybe it was the sight of all those dead bodies. Kinney had been the man on the scene. He was the one who brought the Dio Insecticide in. He was responsible for mopping up the mess, killing the bugs, bribing the officials, sweeping the mess under the carpet. But Kinney didn't want to do it anymore and just when you were so close. It might have been the innocent dead people in those small towns or the dead scientists he had grown so fond of, but a part of me believes it was the fact that you were planning on pinning the whole mess on me. After all, I was the perfect fit. I'm a loner. No friends. No family.

Obsessed with money and power. I believe in monopolies hell I even have a picture of John D. freaking Rockefeller hanging on my wall. I was the perfect scapegoat. And at first Kinney went along with it but then he got to know me. He felt sorry for me. He sat in his office next to mine day after day watching me diligently fetch you coffees. Get your mail. Schedule your appointments. Deal with your problems. Listen to your whining. Basically, be your bitch, and Kinney felt for me. Maybe he was me at some point in his life. Maybe he had to crawl in the trenches. Maybe he had to fetch the coffees. Whatever it was, he decided enough was enough. He went to you. You quilled him. You told him everything was going to be okay. He didn't buy it. He began to leave clues behind. Clues he knew I would pick up on. You tried throwing money at him. It didn't work. He quit. Walked out. You flipped. I remember the day. You were flying off the handle at everybody, me, your secretary, the guy in the bathroom, Gordon, everybody, even your stapler. Until recently I just figured it was because your brother had blown another hundred grand in Vegas or your sister had fled to Europe with another one of her monthly flings. I know now that that was the day Kinney resigned. You assumed he was going to snitch. So, you gave him more money. And that didn't work. You threatened him. He got scared. He called the feds. Then you killed him." Lenny stopped talking, leaving the room in total silence. So quiet that the sound of the radiator creaking its warming flow echoed from wall to wall. No one spoke. No one refuted the claims. Just the radiator, creaking its disproval as if to say *tis tis*.

"Thanks to Kinney, I know and so does Sarah." Lenny looked over at Sarah. She nodded. "And we're going to the FBI. Both of us." Lenny's face turned red with rage.

He was shaking. "You're not going to stick me with this. You hear me Carter? You're not. I beat you to the punch. I figured out the puzzle. By this time tomorrow, you'll be in a federal lockup. That's bad news for you. I hear they've got some pretty big Russians in there that would die to get a crack at you. I figure you might be able to last two days before they find you hanging in your cell. The Russians don't like getting fucked over. Not at all. You didn't deliver their weapon. They paid you, and you fucked them over. That's why they were after Rudd. You took their $500 million and placed a put option on Sentrix's stock."

This made Carter lift his eyebrow. It was a subtle gesture. Nothing crazy. But it was there, and Lenny saw it and, in that instant, he knew he was right.

"And Tony. Third mistake buddy. Tony that fucking asshole. How many of your sister's exes did he off for you? Four, five maybe six. A whole shit load. Even if Sarah and I hadn't figured it out. Even if you somehow escape the Russians. Your connection with Tony would bring you down to Chinatown. You tried to set me up for that too, but you failed. I never contacted Tony. There's only one path that leads to that psycho's door and its through you." Lenny waited for Carter to respond. He didn't. He just sat there, voicing no rebuttal and showing no remorse. Rudd glanced up at the mention of Tony's name. First, he looked at Lenny with a killer fucking gaze, then he turned to Carter. Again, a long, impenetrable silence fell on the room. Carter didn't break it, neither did Rudd and for the first time tonight, Lenny, the man of so many words, finally had nothing to say. It was Sarah Ryan that broke the silence.

"I need a drink." She said. The statement was so bizarre. So out there that the three other men looked at her as if she had just appeared out of thin air. *Beam me up Scotty.* Sarah ignored the surprised faces. "Do you mind?" She asked. Carter remained stoic. She didn't wait for his reply. She stood and walked to the bar. For the first time in her life, no eyes undressed her as she glided by. She fixed two scotches, handing one to Lenny before she sat back down.

Lenny looked at the amber liquid. He sloshed it around the glass. Then he looked up at Carter.

"Do you know what bothers me the most?" Lenny asked. "I trusted you. I looked up to you. You were my best friend, my closest confidant, my role model. I loved you Carter. I would have followed you to the end. That's what bothers me. I don't have anyone Carter. I'm alone and the only person in my life I trusted betrayed me, stabbed me in the back with a motherfucking chainsaw." Lenny took a swig of the scotch. It was good, burning its way down his throat. He took another long pull. Sarah was right, he needed the drink. Needed the cleansing. Needed to be numbed. He went to take another pull, but his arm was suddenly too heavy. He looked at the glass. There was something wrong with his arm. His mind told it to move, to lift the meager weight of the glass towards his mouth but his muscles failed to respond. The glass fell from his hand and shattered on the marble floor. His heart was pounding, thumping madly against his rib cage. He tried to inhale. Tried to fill his lungs with oxygen. It felt as if a pro wrestler was squeezing his chest. He looked up and to his surprise, to his utter dismay, Sarah Ryan stared back at him with a smile that would have sent the devil cowering back to his hole. It was a look of pure evil.

"I had to know what you knew." Carter said softly. He stood and walked over to Lenny. He knelt down, putting his mouth right next to Lenny's ear. "I had to find out. That's why I sent her. She's good, isn't she?" Carter asked. "Real good." Carter's face was impassive, emotionless, logical. His voice was even and cold. "You're smart Len. I can't take that away from you. But your greatest weakness. Your greatest flaw is that you trust people too easily. You're so lonely." He mocked. "That you fell right into my trap. And yes, everything you said is true. Just wanted to clarify that."

Lenny's breathing became shallow. His heart rate had to be at least three hundred beats per minute. His vision was fading, going from dull and dark to bright and white then back to clear in quick succession.

"Congratulations on a job well done. Oh, and by the way…" Carter leaned even closer. His lips were now almost touching Lenny's face. "Those documents you found were copies. The originals are in the hands of a nice, young, ambitious reporter in Havre de Grace and yes Len you did contact Tony. There was a call made from your cell phone last night to his. Remember? No? That's because you didn't make it. She did." Lenny's eyes moved to Sarah. His vision blurred. "You see Len, I thought of everything. I'm perfect. I'm a winner and you're, well, you're a fucking loser. Say hi to the devil for me." Carter stood up.

Lenny's lungs tried to take one more breath. His heart attempted to thump a final beat. They both failed miserably. The last thing Lenny saw before his vision darkened forever, was the smiling face of his friend, his boss, his mentor, shining its hideous light down upon him.

Chapter 96

The only light in the small room was a laptop, opened, in the center of the table. The article on the screen was from CNN. The headline which shot through the dark like a .50 cal through a piece of drywall, was *Death toll in Maryland Town Reaches 200.* That made him physically ill. And why not? Hadn't he been the one who produced the vile creatures that had so coldly taken hundreds of lives? Yes, he had. But it wasn't the headline that made him puke four times in the last two minutes. It wasn't the news of the hundreds of deaths or the likelihood that he would be spending the rest of his days inside of a metal cell. It was the beginning that really did it to him. *The start of the terror.* That's what CNN had called it, but for Dr. Richard Sangmore aka Raymond Hastings, it was the beginning and the end of his life.

He had read the article twice. Had concentrated his will power on the lines surrounding the first deaths. *A woman and her two children.* And it listed the address, 1215 Morrison, an address he knew very well. So well in fact that the address had haunted his mind, invaded his nightmares for years. It was his past. Those miserable yet memorable years spent with the two loves of his life, his children, Shaun and Allison. He could still smell their scent. That adorable fragrance of infancy. That was one of the things he had carried with him all these long years. Their smell. It was stuck in his nose, forever lodged in his brain in a comfortable place. So were their hugs and the feeling of intensity that erupted inside him every time he held them in his arms. That feeling of undying and unconditional love. He could still feel it if he closed his eyes. And now that was all he had. Just the feelings and nothing more. They were dead. Gone from this world. His chances of seeing them, smelling their aroma and holding them in his arms was gone forever.

He had always harbored hope. It was buried deep, but it was there. A hope that one day he would be able to see them again. That's what kept him going. He didn't know how it would happen, maybe Tracy would decide they were too much for her, or maybe, hopefully, she would inject herself with a little too much and meet Satan face to face. Either way would be fine by him as long as he was able to see his children again. And now that hope had vanished quicker than a lit match in a wind storm.

Tears drooled steadily down his face. Droplets of sadness that formed a river of guilt. He held their pictures in his hand and sobbed uncontrollably, his finger touching their little innocent polaroid faces. *How had things gone so sick and wrong? How had he not known the address of the test site? He was the head scientist, wasn't he?* The top of the nerd food chain. And yet he had never inquired as to exactly where the damn bugs had been planted. All he knew was Havre de Grace. That had been his fault too. He had chosen the town simply because that's where he was from. At the time he thought it would be the perfect place. Small, remote, a controlled setting, a lab setting. He didn't know the bugs would kill. He would have never guessed it, not in a million years. If he had, he would have destroyed them, burned them, torched those sinister little assholes in their cages. He would have never unleashed them. Not in Havre de Grace. Not anywhere. He should have known better. He couldn't live like this, not with this tremendous sadness and guilt.

The pen lay nearby on top of the heap of papers strewn on the table. It was blue, he hated blue, but it would do just the same. He took the pen in his right hand, still holding the picture in his left, placed the tip of the pen on a blank piece of paper and began to write. The words came out jumbled, incoherent, splotched with tears. When he finished, he laid the pen beside the paper and sobbed harder than ever, reading what he wrote.

To my angels Shaun and Allison,

I have loved you from the first moment I held you in my arms. You are my life and now you are gone. I have failed you. I am truly sorry. I hope that we will meet again somewhere beyond the stars.

I love you.

Dad

The tears were unstoppable. The sobs shuddered his entire body. He read the note one last time. Then he picked up something else sitting on his table. Something he had stowed away. An heirloom handed from his grandfather, to his father and finally to him. The last piece of his past. The only thing, beyond the picture of his two children, that he had saved from his life, his real life. He hefted it in his hand. It was heavy, much heavier than he had ever realized. The weight was more spiritual than physical, existing primarily in his mind. He cocked back the hammer with the last tiny bit of strength he could muster. He placed the gun to his temple. His eyes never left the picture as the bullet passed through his brain.

And it had all been for not. Dr. Richard Sangmore, aka Raymond Hastings, hadn't birthed the bugs that had taken the lives of his two children. The bugs he had genetical modified had never left his lab and were totally benign. Sangmore wasn't a member of the Pioneer Initiative nor had he ever been. He was simply a pawn, like Lenny Schultz, in one's man's quest for wealth and power. Sangmore had been used. He was a puppet, and Carter Ritler was his master. Ritler had discovered Sangmore's true identity, and in his quest for a viable scapegoat, Sangmore's name was the first on his list. It was too easy. Ritler targeted Sangmore's ex-wife and his two children. The cops would, of course, see it as revenge and some sick manifestation of protection -saving his children from a life of poverty and misery at the hands of such an ungodly addict. Then Ritler targeted the judge, the very man who had taken Sangmore's children away in an unfair and ridiculous decision. It was picture perfect. A setup worthy of an Oscar. Beauty to the eye of a very demented beholder. And by killing himself, Sangmore had sealed the deal, preventing any of the truth from ever surfacing, burying himself in a pit of guilt and sorrow.

Chapter 97

The old man stood elevated before the masses of men and women clad in blue jackets. Banks of computer terminals and giant monitors stretched into the horizon as far as the eye could see. The confraternity of financial power was awaiting the signal. The signal that would ignite the furious conflagration of money moving fluidly from one account to another over a vast network of electronic transmissions. This room -if it could be called a room, it was more like a stadium- represented the summit of economic supremacy in the world. The shining castle on the hill, a shrine to power and finance and it was anxiously awaiting to crown their new king.

The king wore his finest suit, a black Kiton with a startling red tie. The $50,000 ensemble was lavish yet tasteful. No Giorgi Armani or Ralph Lauren for him. He was a man of class. A man bred for this moment. This would be the crown jewel of his kingdom. The heart of his mountain. This moment was what he had slaved so tremendously hard for. It was his and his alone. He didn't owe anyone anything.

Gordon Reynolds wasn't alone on the throne. He was flanked by several of his ardent loyalists. His minions, like COO Mel Thomas, his CFO and several vice presidents including the lovely Sarah Ryan. All looking elegant. All responsible for making this moment possible. Well, at least they all thought they had. In reality, the only person who had been equally responsible for the success was his number two-man, Carter Ritler, who thanks to his recent dismissal, wasn't able to attend. Reynolds scoffed at the thought as he smiled and waved at the crowd. *Carter almost blew it all. All the work, all the planning and he nearly threw us to the wolves.* Well, it had been Carter who had been thrown to the wolves, their snarling teeth now ripping and tearing his flesh to the bone. Reynolds would never again allow one of his underlings to become so powerful. That would be a colossal mistake, and he wasn't one to repeat an error.

It was almost time. Sarah Ryan, her blonde hair appearing as if it had been wrought of pure gold, her black pantsuit conservative and loose, hiding her astounding curves from the cameras, stood there with a smile etched on her rose red lips. It was a genuine smile, a winning smile. She had to look the part. After all, she was an Oscar winner and today would be her greatest performance.

The silver metallic bell clanged to raucous applause as Gordon Reynolds tapped its shiny surface. The trading had begun. The moment everyone was waiting for. The moment Gordon Reynolds could taste in his spit like swirling a fine red wine around in your mouth, touching every inch of your tongue, savoring the flavor. Sentrix was now a publicly traded company, and Gordon Reynolds could now take his seat at a much more exclusive table. A table with the likes of Bill Gates, Warren Buffett and Jeff Bezos. A table where Reynolds had longed to reserve a chair.

Sarah Ryan saw it first. She had been watching for it, and the sight of it turned her smile even more delicious. The corner of her beautiful eyes picked it up on one of the giant monitors. A pretty young woman was talking on the news. Her name was Kelly Halle. The network identification in the corner read ABC in big bold letters. Some of the traders on the floor turned to face the monitor.

The headline of the story read *Corporation Kills 298 in Maryland Town.*

It had worked even better than we had planned. Sarah Ryan thought as she watched the screen. Slowly, one by one, every face in the room began to turn. Sarah watched them turn, their eyes and ears attracted to the screen. It was like watching a voluptuous beauty walk past a construction site filled with gawking, horny men, their hard hats on a swivel, their eyes fixed, hungry, ready to strike.

They struck in unison, their fangs sinking into the neck of their victim, draining its precious blood. Gordon Reynolds looked on in horror. It was pandemonium. Traders began taking calls and punching keyboards in a wild feeding frenzy. Sentrix began at $50 a share. It fell to $35 in mere seconds. Beads of sweat rolled down Reynolds' face. *How? Why? What the hell was going on?* He looked around desperately. Checking faces. Checking expressions. Checking body language. Sentrix was now at $20 and falling like a barrel going over Niagara Falls. This couldn't be happening. Traders rushed from one terminal to another like children in a toy aisle. Sentrix at $15. Sentrix at $10. Gordon's eyes looked like they were bulging out of his cranium. His veins throbbed uncontrollably. His heart thudded in his chest. Sentrix at five. *FIVE! FIVE!* His company had collapsed. His life's work. His family's legacy. Gone. Ruined. He stumbled, his body crumbling, his hands gripping the railing before him as if he were on the deck of a sinking ship which in essence he was. Sentrix at $4. $3.

The traders ignored the old man that had only moments before been the center of their universe. They ripped apart the old man's bones like a carcass in the desert sun, devouring any meat they found. Transforming a $10 billion goliath into a $200 million pile of rotting dog shit. The bleeding went on and on and on. Blood ran out in zeros and commas, spilling out onto the white floor. The men and women in blue jackets trampled the carcass of the once powerful giant then in utter finality they set the bones on fire, leaving ash, black dust to scatter in the wind.

Gordon Reynolds fell. His hands could no longer hold his weight. He landed on the floor of the elevated platform. The people around him, his loyal minions, never noticed their master's descent. They were too busy worrying about their own hides, their fortunes, their own futures, which had unexpectedly taken a turn for the worse. Reynolds lay for several minutes on the floor. His body writhed with agony. Tears streaked down his face. His left arm felt numb. His chest felt like it was going to explode.

Suddenly the bleeding stopped. Ceased as if by some miracle, as if an armistice had been agreed upon and signed. The price actually ticked up, not much but it went from $2 a share to around $5 and then settled. It never moved again. Some of the traders looked up, shocked with bewildered looks in their eyes. Something had happened. Someone had come along with an extra-large gauze bandage and a bucket of quick clot. Someone had rescued the survivors. Sent in a coast guard cutter with plenty of life jackets on board. It wouldn't be known until the closing bell that TR Pest Management, Sentrix's main competitor, had decided the time was ripe to swoop in and carry off what was left of the carcass before the hyenas could arrive. After all, despite the feeding frenzy, Sentrix still had some marrowy bones to suck on.

Sarah Ryan looked over at Mel Thomas. It was time for her to deliver her rehearsed lines. "What happened?" She asked.

Mel didn't immediately reply. His face was still affixed on the monitors. "Someone bought us out." He managed to say in a low, uninterested voice.

"Who?" Sarah asked.

"I don't know." Mel replied, his voice distant, eyes still transfixed. Finally, he averted his gaze and saw Gordon Reynolds sprawled out on the floor. He didn't rush forward. He took his time, as he wished death upon the man that had ruined him. *Let him rot.* He thought staring down at Reynolds as if he were gazing upon a sickening but satisfying scene. Then as if Mel's body had a will of its own, he walked forward to check on his former employer.

Chapter 98

He went from being worth $2 billion to nothing. His company was in ruins. His wealth, fame and fortune had been flushed straight down the old u bend, swirling in a never-ending spiral and deposited into the black abyss. It wasn't a heart attack according to his doctors. It had been stress that had brought him to the floor of the exchange hours before. Shock brought on by a tremendous force. What did they know? As far as he was concerned it had been a heart attack. The reality of losing your company, your wealth, your class, your existence was enough to blow any man's heart sky high.

Gordon Reynolds stood in his office staring out of the window eighty floors in the sky. His legs felt like jelly, wobbly mush that could barely hold his own weight. He was propped on a cane, relying on the thin wooden stick like a man relies on his arm or his leg. He would have to vacate this office. It wasn't his anymore. It belonged to someone else. The very idea of that was depressing beyond belief. He felt like crying. He felt like flinging himself out of the window and splatting on the sidewalk like an egg. Going out in style. Ending it all. He couldn't go on. Couldn't face the elitist snobs at the country club, his fellow billionaires as merely a millionaire. The thought of it made him sick, violently ill. Vomit swelled in his stomach like a monster trying to escape from a little boy's closet. The monster's hands gripped the door, hairy fingers protruding out, visible on the frame, coming, coming. He turned from the window and threw up. The bile landed on the floor in a puddle of yellowish liquid. He stared at it before dismissing it. *A parting gift.* He thought. *Let the new guy clean it up.* He was finished.

It was obvious he had been played, screwed like a slut on prom night. Lenny Schultz, the wizard accountant, and Carter Ritler's bulldog was being propped up in front of the television cameras as the mastermind behind the whole operation. Lenny was dead. He had committed suicide by drinking poison and plunging off the Brooklyn Bridge. Dr. Richard Sangmore, another mainstay in the television broadcasts, had also taken his own life by shooting himself in the head with a picture of his dead children clutched in his hands. Apparently, the same children who had become the first victims of the attacks. Although these two men were being blamed, they were pawns in one man's disturbing game to monopolize the industry. That man, according to the news, especially Channel Nine of Havre de Grace, was Gordon Reynolds. Channel Nine showed copies of authorizations signed by himself, Lenny Schultz and Dr. Richard Sangmore that spelled out a conspiracy the likes of which hadn't been seen since Watergate. However, unlike the 1970s eavesdropping scandal, people had died. Hundreds of people.

The whole thing was a farce. He had never signed any of those documents, and he was sure that Lenny Schultz and Dr. Richard Sangmore hadn't either. That's what really pissed him off. He knew he had been duped. And he was pretty sure who had done it. *Carter!* That double-dealing asshole had orchestrated the whole thing. Gordon may have blue blood in his veins. He may have grown up with the silver spoon. He may have inherited a vast empire, but he was far from idle rich. He wasn't stupid or ignorant by any stretch of the imagination.

There was a loud rapping on the door that sent shockwaves through Gordon's chest. A chest that had already received enough distress to last a lifetime. He didn't answer. He walked calmly over to his desk. *What an incredible desk.* Hand carved, immense, powerful, a true display of his stature in the world. He would have to give that up as well. The desk went with the office. Purchased by Sentrix as a business expense. It was part of the company's assets. A very expensive part to say the least.

The booms on the door echoed again. Gordon heard shouts from the hall.

"FBI! Gordon Reynolds, we have a warrant for your arrest! Come out with your hands up!" The voice shouted.

A warrant for my arrest! Funny. Very fucking funny. He thought.

The knocks became louder if that was at all possible. Soon the door would break, slammed by a ram, shattered into pieces, and the feds would spill in like water through a breached dam. They would cuff him, drag him out in chains, a saint, a king, disposed from his throne. His subordinates would point their fingers and laugh. *Look at the king. Look at him. Look at how far the king has fallen.* He couldn't let that happen. He wouldn't be humiliated anymore. No way. He was Gordon Reynolds. *Gordon fucking Reynolds!* And he was still a king. *Still a king god damn it!* A general who may have lost the battle but who would go out with honor. He remembered reading about the great leaders of ancient times. How they protected their honor, went out with decency, refused to be held publicly accountable. He fumbled with the drawer of his desk, the long drawer in the middle. It opened reluctantly as if it knew what its master was planning, as if by refusing to open it would delay the final task.

The door smashed in, splinters flew from the frame littering the office floor. The agents rushed in, guns drawn, circling the old man at his desk. Reynolds held a revolver to his temple. The lead agent shouted words that Gordon couldn't hear. *Drop the gun! Drop it!* Gordon scrunched up his face, flashed the agents his most arrogant, pompous sneer before he pulled the trigger.

Chapter 99

The town would never be the same. The horrific events of the last several days could never be undone. Sure, things would go on. People would fall in love, get married, have children, work, play and sacrifice just like always but deep down they would never forget. Never. The stain of death, unprecedented death, would blotch the white tee-shirt, unable to be removed by even the strongest mental detergents. The inhabitants of this small, historic town had gone through hell. They had lived history, not the great *I love to talk about it* history, as it had been before, but the *do you remember where you were when shit it the fan* history. The same history that encompassed events like 911, Pearl Harbor and the battle of Britain.

The fear remained. The bed bugs that had claimed so many lives had been eradicated, but no one really knew for sure. The legend of the bed bugs would go on for years. No one really believed they were truly gone. People were still terrified to go to sleep at night. They stayed up playing games, talking, watching TV, reading books, even doing chores to avoid the basic necessity of life -sleep.

Detective William Patterson would never forget. He had seen more bloodshed, death and destruction in three days than he had seen in his thirty some odd years serving the people of this little town. Hell, he had seen more death and destruction than he had seen in thirty years watching television and that included all of the Arnold Schwarzenegger movies. He had been working with the FBI since the conclusion of the tragic events, trying to put the last few pieces of the puzzle together. Kelly Halle of Channel Nine had turned over all the documents she had received. What they spelled out was horrific. A big corporation attempting to monopolize an industry through any means necessary. The documents said it all. They would have to be verified of course, which was in the works but all and all they seemed genuine. The most compelling piece of concrete evidence was found on Tony's person in the form of a throwaway cell phone. There had been one number on it, an incoming call. The FBI traced the number back to the personal cell phone of Leonard Schultz. The call had come in just seconds before Tony had entered the station on his bloody rampage. The box that housed the bed bugs had contained no evidence after all. It was thoroughly checked and rechecked by the FBI crime lab. The prints of the two delivery boys, Detective Patterson, George, Kelly Halle and James Roseland were all found on the box, but no other prints were discernable.

The men responsible were dead. All of them. Peter and Eric, Sentrix's delivery boys, had been murdered. Their assassin, Tony, had also dramatically lost his life -gunned down in the middle of the Havre de Grace police station. Dr. Richard Sangmore aka Raymond Hastings, a former town resident, ex-husband of townhouse Tracy and father of townhouse Tracy's two children, Shaun and Allison, had shot himself. Leonard Schultz, the junior executive who had led the project from day one, had guzzled poison before throwing himself off a bridge and finally, the ringleader, the head of the asshole brigade, Gordon Reynolds, had put a bullet in his head in front of FBI agents before they could arrest him on murder charges. It was a sad day in the annals of justice. None of the culprits would serve a day in jail. That depressed Patterson and it depressed the public, who wanted more than ever to watch a public trial and witness a fiendish villain get their just reward.

There were funerals planned, lots of funerals. Weeks' worth of funerals. Months' worth of funerals. Patterson sighed just thinking of it. He would have to attend some. He hated funerals. Hated going knowing that the person you were going for would never know you came. He'd suck it up. He was glad that none of the funerals were for members of his family. They had all come out unscathed. He would go and mourn with the bereaved especially his friends, like Patty and George, who had all lost someone special in their lives.

Christmas was almost here. Festivity and all that jazz. It just didn't seem the same. Of course, he would go shopping, buy everyone what he thought they wanted, dress in his best suit, attend the midnight mass because who really wanted to get up and go to church Christmas morning. He'd smile, shake hands, wish peace, toast merrily but his heart wouldn't be in it. Not this year. Not after so much death and destruction. How many people had lost loved ones who wouldn't be joining their families at this year's celebration? Probably most of the families in town.

"Detective Bill Patterson?" The man asked approaching the detective's disheveled desk. The station was still in shambles. The priority of the last few days was the dead. Removing the hundreds of dead bodies all over town including the bodies in the station -Jane Doe, Tony, and the disgraced Officer Mike. Patterson still had no idea who Jane Doe was or why she had been killed. The FBI was checking it out.

Patterson looked up to see a soft man, that was his first thought, the guy looked soft as in his voice was soft, his outstretched hand felt soft, his demeanor was soft. Patterson nodded and shook the man's hand.

"Agent Jack Wolfe, FBI." The man said.

Patterson motioned towards the one wooden chair opposite his desk. The man took off his charcoal overcoat, folded it, sat down and placed the folded coat on his lap.

"Man, you guys really come out of the woodwork. What can I do for you?" Patterson said, smiling.

"I know you're busy." Jack said, indicating the crumbling station. Patterson waved it off like an irksome fly. "If you have a second, I've got a story to tell you about a friend of mine."

Chapter 100

"What do you mean you want out?" Patrick asked. His older brother George stood leaning his muscular bulk against the door frame of their office in White Marsh. George had just told him *-could it really be true?-* that he wanted out of the business. That was bad news. Sure, Patrick had always dreamed about owning their million-dollar pest control business solely on his own, but now that he thought about it, now that it was quickly becoming a reality he was kind of scared and reluctant. George had always been the bug man. He was the face of the company. The brother that the customers trusted. George, and not Patrick, had taken the mantle from their father. George *was* the business.

And Patrick wasn't. Sure, he'd work the jobs and occasionally make an appearance at the office where he'd act like the boss but that was the thing *-he'd act like the boss.* Acting was different than living. He really didn't desire the crown. *No sir.* Fishing was his thing. Fishing, and hunting and watching his kids play sports and hosting cookouts and, well, everything else except for running the company. *No, no, no.* George was the one. He loved having George around to manage the business and take the burden off his own back.

"I never wanted to… you know… I never wanted to get involved in the first place." George said dryly.

"But you're so good at it. I mean, come on man, you're the face, you're the future. The guy people want to talk to when they call this office. It's in your blood. You're like dad. You even talk like him." Patrick implored. *Please don't leave. I don't want this responsibility. Hell no, absolutely not.* He thought.

George smiled and shook his head. "Pat, my entire life has been spent doing things I didn't want to do. I was forced into them…"

"No one forced you into the army. You made that choice." Patrick blurted out. George leaving for the army in the midst of a family feud hadn't sat well with their father or Patrick. George Sr. was very much the old school family man. *You tended to your family before you tended to your country.* That was George Sr.'s motto, and he stuck to it. He was very much like the fictional character Don Corleone. In fact, George Jr. could almost hear his father quoting Santino Corleone -*Your country ain't your blood.* George had never felt that way. He was tired of blood in all its forms.

"You're right. I did. But that was more of a temporary hiatus. An escape from this existence. That's the problem with family businesses. It's bondage. Generational servitude. The family expects you to serve. The customers expect the same level of service. It really is generational servitude." Patrick began to interrupt again, but George held up a hand and gave him a look that silenced his younger brother immediately. "I know we were blessed to have this company. Blessed to be so fortunate. But I never wanted it. I wanted something for myself. Up until dad died, I worked to give him a paycheck, to ensure he would get a premium on his shares. Now I work to ensure that you get the premium. I work Patrick while you've skated along. Don't argue with me." He said, his voice angry. Years of pent-up rage bursting at the seams. "I have put in the time, the energy, the sweat, the blood. I never had kids. Never got married. You did, and I am not holding you responsible for it, but you know as well as I do that I took up the mantle. I carried on the family name, worked fifteen-hour days, six, seven days a week. I went out on weekends and holidays to ensure that dad's legacy, that this company." He waved his hand around the room. "Would survive. Would thrive. Now I want something for myself."

It took Patrick several seconds to recover. George had never talked to him like this. Sure, they had argued. What brothers in business together hadn't? But George had never been so serious with him before. He had never spelled out Patrick's faults and shortcomings so clearly. Patrick didn't know how to take it, so as people do in situations where they're faced with reality -he got mad.

Patrick's face went red. He was pissed. Okay, sure everything George had said was true, but he, Patrick, didn't want the gravy train to stop. He didn't want to go to work at seven in the morning and come home at ten o'clock at night. He didn't want to run out on Christmas day because one of the nursing homes spotted a bed bug in a patient room. He didn't want to sacrifice his weekends because one of his restaurants saw a bird flying through their dining room. Hell no. He wanted his brother to do it. Not that he was lazy or inept. He'd gladly work his eight hours, sometimes even ten, five days a week. Gladly would -on those very rare occasions- take the crazy midnight phone calls. He just didn't want to do it all the time. In essence, he didn't want to wear George's shoes, even for two steps, even just to put them on to keep his feet warm. He wanted things to be exactly as they were before. He was against change.

"What are you going to do? Sell snowballs?" Patrick asked, his tone rising, his eyes narrowing at this unprecedented turn of the tide.

"I don't know. I might. In all honesty, I might sell umbrellas someplace warm and sandy. I don't really care what I do, as long as I do it for myself." George replied.

Patrick shook his head, depressed, morbid thoughts invading his mind. "I don't have the cash to buy you out. We're talking half a million at least. I don't have that kind of money." His voice rose even higher. "And if you think that I'm going to get a loan to pay for your…"

"A hundred thousand." George said, cutting his brother off. "That's all I want. One hundred thousand. I know you've got that much."

He did, and he knew it. Patrick had always been a saver. In fact, he was probably the wealthiest sibling of the lot. Wealthy even though he had three kids in private schools, two mortgages -his house and his vacation home- and an RV. *Penny Pincher Patrick.* That was his nickname, ever since childhood. Give Patrick a penny and he'd squeeze every last ounce of value out of it. *A hundred grand.* He definitely had it. A hundred grand and the business, worth nearly a million two, would be his and his alone. The sweet, tantalizing thought staved off his anger.

"Have you lost your mind? Is this about Ocean? It wasn't your fault. They can't sue us. You know that? His parents, they've got no leg to stand on. He signed papers when he started. We told him the job was danger…"

George held up his hand again, his eyes closed, almost as if he were deep in thought or spiritually connected with the Almighty. "I just want out. A hundred cash and the business is yours. You want it or not?"

"Okay. I'll have the check in the morning." Patrick answered a little too enthusiastically.

"Make it certified."

Relief. Blessed relief. That was his first thought as he walked down the strip mall in White Marsh known as the Avenue. Despite the number of shops, coffee houses and restaurants, George hadn't gone there to indulge his cravings. He was there to think. He was there to reinsure himself that he had indeed made the right decision. His first attempt at setting his life's GPS for a destiny of his own choice. He thought he would have some doubt for his chosen course, but surprisingly he didn't. He was free, to live, to paddle his own canoe, to set his own sail and toss the map into the blue expanse of the sea. He watched, in his mind, the map go, floating in the wind like leaves in a fall breeze until it landed ceremoniously into the water, slowly being swallowed by the waves.

George returned home with renewed vigor in his step. He stared up at the house he had worked so hard to acquire. He could still feel the anxiety that gripped his stomach when he submitted the bid, waiting reprehensively for the call from the agent and jumping for joy when the seller accepted his meager offer. He remembered putting on the deck, the roof, the siding, the shed, the near-miss accident when the garage door spring snapped, and he was only a few feet away. All the memories flooded back to him as he stared at his castle. He would have to sell the house. That was it. No looking back. Sell the house, take the money, move to somewhere hot, sunny, sandy. A place loaded with the scent of suntan lotion and the sensual display of tight bodies in tiny fabric. A place where no one knew his name. A place where he could start over, sit under a palm tree with a good book. Inhale the salt and the fresh air. Clear his mind.

He was startled awake from his daydream by the sound of a car pulling in behind him. He turned, always in tune with his surroundings, always aware. He had seen the car often over the last few days. It had survived its abandonment on route 40. Patterson must have picked it up after the thaw. The black crown vic with its flashing blue and red lights embedded in its windshield. The lights were still and hollow.

"Haven't left yet?" Patterson asked as he stepped out, a signature cigar stuck between his grinning lips.

George shook his head.

"Can't believe you're giving up the business. I mean, come on, you're the bug man. How can the bug man sell umbrellas on the beach?"

"I take it you talked to my brother." George said.

"Yep. I know he's your brother and all but the guy's kind of an ass."

George smiled in silent agreement. "Take him with a grain of salt. He's a bit antisocial. So, what can I do for the HDG police today?" He said, taking a seat on his front steps.

Patterson strolled over puffing nonchalantly on his cigar. "Funny thing. Here I am, thinking this thing is done. The bugs are dead, the criminals are dead, case closed."

"But?"

"Then this fed comes in. Jack Wolfe. Nice guy. He's with the FBI's New Orleans office. Flew all the way up here to talk to me. Told me about a buddy of his, Lenny Schultz."

"The mastermind?"

Patterson nodded. "That's what I said. Jack disagreed. Said he knew Lenny for years. Went to college with him. Said Lenny was working on the case from inside Sentrix. Apparently, Lenny was assigned the job by his boss, the former president of the company, Carter Ritler." Patterson looked longingly upon the open spot next to George on the steps. George put out his hand palm up in invitation. Patterson sat then continued. "Jack said Lenny had contacted him a few times to ask for help in determining the ownership structure of a company in the Grand Cayman's called Beautiful Horizons."

George looked around him. He had never realized just how beautiful his street was. The way the houses were loved and nurtured by the people who occupied them -his neighbors. Neighbors he had never really taken the time to get to know. He was always so busy. Now, as he looked out, he noticed things. Small ornaments that had been carefully placed in pine trees, ornaments made by the hands of children. Children he had seen a thousand times but had never met. Maybe he should have settled down, had children of his own. Helped them forge their own ornaments to hang in the pines.

"You listening to me?" Patterson asked.

"Yes." George replied.

"I was telling you something important."

"Tell me again." George said, pulling his focus away from the ornaments.

"Lenny sent Jack Wolfe everything the night of his death. He emailed Jack a file. Pretty crazy shit if you ask me. But it's meticulously researched, and I'll be honest, I believe him."

"Lenny Schultz was innocent?" George stated.

"Yep."

George shook his head in disbelief.

"Lenny was framed. Agent Jack did his own checking, and he was able to verify most of what was in the file. The kicker for me was the phone call and my dead broad."

George raised an eyebrow. "Your dead broad?"

"The Russian chick. The one whose boyfriend I personally introduced to Satan."

George nodded. "She's Russian?"

"Alena Dobinin. Jack Wolfe checked with the boys in Langley. They positively IDed her as a Russian diplomat with known ties to the SVR."

George knew all about the SVR, Russia's intelligence agency for external affairs. During George's time with the Unit, he had been involved with the missions that brought him in contact with the Russian First Chief Directorate of the KGB, the predecessors to the SVR.

"Why were two SVR agents impersonating bums in a run-down motel in Havre de Grace?"

"That's the best part. Jack Wolfe found out via his contacts in CIA that the Russians had recently purchased a weapon from a firm in the United States. Our friends in Moscow paid half a billion dollars for it. The only problem was they never received it. Jack is positive that the SVR agents were in town to retrieve the weapon."

"What weapon?"

"The bed bugs." Patterson answered and George looked at him with one hell of a bewildered stare.

"What?"

"Lenny uncovered it in his research. He passed that information along to Jack Wolfe before he died. Jack concurs and so does CIA. Think about it. The perfect mass killing machine. Untraceable. Unstoppable."

"Wow." That was the only thing George managed to utter.

"You can say that again."

"So why kill Alena?"

"Jack figures that served three purposes. The first was to link Lenny indefinitely to the crime. Lenny's cell phone made a call to Tony's exactly three minutes before Alena was gunned down in her cell. The second was to silence her for good. If we were able to get her to talk and that's a big if, then we would have discovered the plot to sell the bugs to the Russians which would have added another element to the investigation. And the third was to send a message to Moscow to call off their dogs which I guarantee won't work."

"But we only recovered Tony's cell phone after he was killed. There was no way to predict that outcome. If I hadn't been there... and I'm not tooting my own horn here...but if I hadn't been there, Tony would have survived."

"It wouldn't have mattered. Once we locked onto to Lenny Schultz as our main subject, we would have traced the call from his phone and triangulated the coordinates of the phone that received the call." Patterson replied. "The phone call is what made me a believer."

"Why?"

"Because Lenny didn't make it." Patterson sucked deeply on his cigar and blew an enormous cloud into the air. "Sentrix has one of the most state-of-the-art surveillance systems in the world. Seems the old man who owned the company didn't trust anyone. Jack was able to subpoena those files. He was also able to triangulate the location of Lenny's phone inside the building at the time the call was placed. Lenny's phone was in the executive lounge while Lenny was forty floors below, passed out at his desk. It's all on tape."

"Then who made the call?"

"Sarah Ryan." Patterson replied. "She was the VP that swore she witnessed Lenny ingest poison when he learned of the extent of the tragedy he supposedly set in motion."

"What happened to the $500 million?" George asked, momentarily changing the subject.

"That's the best part. Someone used the money to buy put options on the share price of Sentrix's stock. That same somebody pocketed a cool $5 billion when the price of the stock plummeted on news of the disaster in Havre de Grace."

"Who was that?"

"Carter Ritler, Sarah Ryan and Dr. Paul Rudd." Patterson filled George in on the details and by the end he had not only convinced George, but had him red with rage. That death stare once again took over George's eyes. The look terrified Patterson who sat there puffing on his cigar uneasily.

"All this for money?" George asked rhetorically. "All the lives that were taken. All the suffering. For money." He spat. "Where are they now?"

"Grand Cayman. Out of reach by everyone. Enjoying the sunshine."

"Are the feds going after them?"

"They're certainly going to try, but Jack said they don't have enough evidence." Patterson answered glumly. "It takes time to build one of these financial cases."

"Financial?" George blurted out. "How about mass murder? How long does that take?"

"That will be even harder to prove. We're talking about bugs here. Not people. You know how hard it would be to convict on the far-fetched notion that some overzealous asshole created a super insect to collapse a stock and make a few billion?"

George shook his head. "So, it's over? The bad guys got away with it."

"Looks like that."

"Why tell me? Did you want to give me my daily dose of depress-loft?"

Patterson stood up from the step. He turned and shook George's hand. "Just thought you'd want to know." Patterson released George's hand. "Remember that thing you told me? The thing you did when you were in the army?"

"I never finished telling…"

"Don't beat yourself up about it. You've spent your life running away from it. Don't run anymore. See you around." Patterson said, knowing he would never see George again.

The detective walked over and slid behind the wheel of his car. He backed out of the driveway and sped away, leaving George alone, sitting on his steps, gazing into space.

Chapter 101

The scariest journey one could ever embark on is the journey of giving birth for an unmarried, single woman, straight out of adolescence. Most women -and all of men- will never experience the harsh critics, the shameful looks, the anxious waiting, the fear and the pain of the delivery. And as insane and harrowing as that sounds, it is merely the beginning. What follows is a torturous journey up a steep slope filled with rocks and deep chasms where one slip will lead to certain failure. It is daily and nightly torture. And it's the little moments. Those tiny, precious moments when time seems to stand still that make it all worthwhile.

Ashley Johnson was on such a journey. She was scared. She was timid, nervous, frustrated, angry, resentful, wishful, happy and all the above, all at once. She had already been on the receiving end of the stare of shame, not from the public, she wasn't showing yet, but from her own parents. They hadn't been happy to receive the news that their daughter and their hopes and aspirations for her, had been flushed down the white porcelain bowl of life like a pile of shit. Gone, finished, destroyed. A thousand questions flew like a barrage of arrows as if the elves of Tolkien's adventures were standing in their living room. *Do you have any idea how bad this is? Why didn't you use protection? How do expect to raise it? How can you afford it?* And her favorite one of all: *What were you thinking?* Not much actually, stuck in the moment, hot, sweaty, orgasmic indulgence of one's sexual desires. Thinking was something she hadn't thought about the entire time she and Ocean were doing the dirty. If she had been thinking, she would have demanded he wear protection. Would have thought it ludicrous that he would have time to pull out.

Would have done a lot of things differently. But she hadn't, and she was sick and tired of beating up on herself. It was time to move on. The baby was growing inside her. *So, get a freaking grip, shut up mom and dad, and let's get this thing done.* Plus, as if she needed even more disaster in her life, the icing on her rotting cake, Ocean, the love of her life, the father of her child, was dead.

Tears poured from the corners of her eyes, tracing paths down her beautiful face, that should have glowed with the pleasantness of pregnancy. The droplets of water fell like a drizzle onto the surface of the white coffin covered with blossoms. She looked around at the mass of mourners clad in black. If only Ocean knew. If only he could see who and how many had turned out for his funeral. That was the problem though, he would never know. He was dead. *Dead. Dead!* She shouted inside her own head. Her hand brushed the baby bump that she could almost feel as she pulled another tissue from the pack in her handbag.

What would she do without him? How would she go on? How could she possibly raise this baby on her own? She did have her parents, which was a blessing. Plus, Ocean's mom and dad, although devastated by the loss of their only son, pledged their undying loyalty and commitment to his unborn child. This gave her some calm, some peace, but she still didn't have Ocean, and that made her sob uncontrollably.

Ocean's sendoff couldn't have been more beautiful. It started with the traditional Catholic mass coupled with a powerful, tear-soaked eulogy delivered by Ocean's father. The burial was the best part of it all if there was a best part. The grave overlooked a misty valley from the top of a large crest that rose up behind the parish of St. John's in Hydes, Maryland.

Ashley took a minute, inhaling the fresh chilly air as she gazed out over the landscape. It was truly breathtaking. She rubbed her stomach in a gentle swirl, caressing the baby. Sadness threatened to engulf her. Ocean would never know. Never hold, rock, comfort his daughter or his son. Never play the games, teach the skills, kiss the booboos, rub the backs and hug the hurts. She began to cry again.

Patterson wore a black suit with matching black tie. He wasn't smoking his cigar, having wisely left it behind for such an occasion. He watched the young girl, tears streaming down her face. He fought the urge to walk over and give her a hug. Try to absorb some of her pain. Try to bestow upon her some of his strength, toughness and resolve. She looked so helpless to his eyes. Finally, with great effort, he pulled his eyes from her and peered around the group. He didn't see George. The bug man hadn't come. That was unusual, but it didn't shock Patterson in the slightest. George had been close to Ocean and he had blamed himself for the kid's death. The pain and anger in Ocean's mother and father hadn't subsided. They would have undoubtedly pounced on George the minute the man showed up. Totally unfair and one-sided but who isn't in a time like this. No one should outlive their children. Ocean's parents would and so would Ocean's unborn child. Patterson had known the last time he saw George would be *the last time*. He knew then, and he certainly knew it now.

Ashley turned back to face the casket. The service had ended. The priest had pronounced the final blessing and the mourners had begun to stream forward in an endless line to lay their fingers on the cold surface, saying their last goodbyes to the lifeless body inside. Ashley watched them one by one. The young, the old, the sick, the weak, the healthy, the strong, the rich and the poor, all equal in death. They each placed their hands on the casket, taking their turns, murmuring sweet nothings, then moving on down the hill to return to their normal lives.

She waited until they had all walked down the asphalt path leading to the parking lot before she slowly approached the coffin. The tears flowed like a river. She tried to breathe. Tried to catch her breath. Tried to find her voice. She placed her small delicate palm on the head of the casket. She thought for a moment that she could feel the warmth of Ocean's grip. The feeling she got when they had first held hands. That time after the movie. Their first date.

"I miss you so much." She sobbed. "I promise, I'll make sure the baby will always know who you are. I'll never forget you Ocean." She couldn't talk. Her words were broken and scattered. "I love you." She nearly fell. Her knees buckled. Suddenly a strength came over her as if Ocean's hands were under her arms, lifting her up, pushing her on. *I'm here beautiful. I'll never leave you.* She could hear him whispering in her ear.

The envelope was sticking out from the floral display atop the casket. It was a square card with her name on it, written in eloquent cursive. She looked around expecting to see someone, anyone watching her. *Where had the card come from?* She grabbed it. Her hands trembled as she slipped the flap open.

Dear Ashley,

I knew Ocean very well. He was the son I never had. I loved him. I know he would be very proud of you.

Proud of the fact that you are so strong. The baby you are carrying is a gift. The last remnants of a young boy whose heart was made of pure gold.

There was no signature. No return address but there was a check. Ashley's knees really did buckle this time. It was a certified check made out to Mrs. Ashley Johnson for $100,000.

Epilogue

What does $5 billion buy you? A ten-bedroom, twelve-bathroom mansion on the shores of the Grand Cayman in an exclusive area that is frequented by the richest of the rich. A $2 million Lamborghini Reventon, chassis number twelve of twenty ever produced. A Patek Phillipe watch that is one of three in the world. A view of one of the most delicately beautiful white sandy shores. That and much, much more.

Carter Ritler pondered this as he sat soaking up the radioactive rays of the hot sunshine on his beach chair. His feet were buried several inches beneath the sand. Dr. Rudd was reading. Of course, Dr. Rudd was reading. The scientist had done nothing but read since the moment they had arrived. He must have read a truckload of books in a month.

The view was everything the brochure had advertised and much more. The ocean with its majestic beauty done in shades of light aqua blue and green. Calm, serene, placid. There was something that was even more amazing then this little slice of heaven and that something had just emerged from the water. Her hair a golden blonde. Her body curved with perfection barely hidden beneath the strings of bikini that left nothing to the imagination. Water dripped off her as if she were modeling for the Sports Illustrated swimsuit edition. Sarah Ryan made the whole world stop and gaze. Men, women, rich, poor, she made them all stare. Her beauty, her unbridled sex, was like a giant magnet for every eye that laid its pupil upon her. Not that there were many eyes here. Another blessing of having this house on the shore, with not a neighbor or a curious tourist in sight. Only mere mortals shared beaches with the mindless masses of the rabble, the sea of umbrellas, the babies screaming, the fat men oiled up like chicken in a fryer and the women who were the total opposite of hot and sexy. Not here. Not on Carter's beach. This place was for the gods -the rich, the famous, the world's playboys with the money to afford such luxury.

Sarah walked from the waves and joined the men. Carter's tanned, toned physique was shirtless sporting khaki shorts and Louis Vuitton sunglasses. He looked like he belonged alongside the beautiful woman. The paparazzi would eat them alive. Rudd, on the other hand, appeared totally out of place. He wore a green boonie hat, the strap hanging loosely around his chin. His pockmarked face was pale, hot and sweaty as if he were deliberately trying to scare his other two companions away.

"Are you *ever* going to get with the program?" Sarah asked Rudd, who briefly glanced up from his collection of Edgar Allen Poe short stories to sneer in her direction.

"I'm not the beachy kind of guy." He replied, annoyed at having been bothered by this brainless floozy. His eyes went back to scanning the text.

"Okay, but you're dressed like you're going into the jungle or on an African safari. No lions, tigers or bears around here Rudd." Sarah said, rolling her eyes. She finished toweling off and took her seat at Carter's side.

"So, what's next?" Rudd asked, shutting his book.

"Evergreen Pharmaceuticals." Carter answered, swatting away an irksome fly. "They've got this drug

Halantra. It was designed to help people with diabetes. Very popular drug and it works."

"But?" Sarah Ryan asked.

Carter smiled. "It's got this little glitch. Halantra filters through the liver as opposed to the kidneys. Seems that a large percentage of patients taking the drug experience liver problems and eventually die. Scientists haven't attributed these problems to Halantra but it's only a matter of time before they do. I've been in contact with the chairman of Evergreen. He's the son of the founder. It's a family affair. Evergreen plans to go public in about a year. The chairman just fired his president, seems the man had an affair with the chairman's daughter. Someone…" Carter winked. "obviously caught the affair on camera."

Rudd and Sarah looked at Carter knowingly.

"He wants me to start in a month." Carter finished.

"How much is Evergreen worth?" Rudd asked.

"$20 billion." Carter answered calmly as if the number was small potatoes.

"Nice. Very nice. I take it you want both of us to apply for jobs as well?" Rudd asked.

Carter nodded. The trio fell silent, their minds filled with the eagerness of the thought of another kill, another payday in the near future.

After several minutes, Rudd returned to his book. Sarah Ryan reclined in her chair, laying it back, allowing her body to absorb the full benefit of the tropical sun. Carter picked up the newspaper that had been lying in the sand. He flipped it open and stared with blank, uncomprehending eyes at its contents. Inside the paper was a message, typed onto plain white computer paper, taped over the headline. It was a brief message. A sentence that made zero sense. Carter read it several times. His mind whirled with the possibilities of what it could mean.

The message read: *Look out. What do you see?*

What the hell does that mean? He thought. Carter wheeled around in his chair. *Some kind fucking joke? Who delivered my paper? The cabana boy? One of the other countless servants?* He wasn't sure. *Look out. What do you see? The sun? The horizon?* He was facing the water. *The ocean?* That's pretty much it. He saw nothing but sand and water. Then as if by magic a neat hole appeared in the paper. It had come out of nowhere as if an invisible cigar had burned its way through the thin cellulose.

Carter looked at it then he looked over at Sarah. She was lying perfectly still, her body frozen in a tranquil sleep, her mouth carved into a wordless scream. A neat hole, the same hole that had appeared in his paper, was visible over one of her perfect breasts. His mind was trying to make sense of it. Trying to come to terms when he noticed the blood. It poured from Sarah's back, dripping through the mesh chair and onto the sand below, already forming a small pool. Carter shifted his gaze to Rudd, or what was left of Rudd. Rudd's pockmarked face had been torn in two. Half of it lay on the beach yards from where they sat. Rudd's body was slumped sideways as if he were being strung up by some invisible teether.

Carter knew something terrible had happened. He knew his life had ended. His mind knew, even if his body still hadn't received the message. He turned his eyes from

Rudd to his own chest. Blood spurted from a hole that corresponded with the hole in the newspaper. His body caught up with his mind quickly, and Carter toppled sideways landing dead in the sand.

The authorities never discovered the identity of the person responsible for murdering the three wealthy Americans on their exclusive patch of sand. The only thing the local police were able to determine was that the shots were taken at an extreme distance, with a high powered .308 rifle. The thing that really baffled them was that the shots originated not from the land but from the rolling surface of the sea and were by all accounts impossible. Legend has it that there are only a handful of men in the world capable of such precision marksmanship and those men officially don't exist.

CPSIA information can be obtained
at www.ICGtesting.com
Printed in the USA
LVHW081711120419
613992LV00015B/269/P

9 781727 612295